table of contents

acknowledgements

This book is dedicated to my wife Melenie Stevenson for ongoing support relating to my passion for obscure underground music.

Gratitude to family and friends for interest and encouragement with my publishing endeavours.

Thanks and respect to all of the artists/projects/labels featured in pages of *Noise Receptor Journal*. Special thanks to all artists featured in this Volume 1 book edition.

Thank you to Cyril Adam for being interested enough in my writing activities to undertake the exclusive long-form interview with myself featured herein.

Thank you to Jennifer Wallis for her invaluable input with proofreading and editing suggestions.

Thank you to David Kerekes/Headpress for his support and enthusiasm in making this book a reality.

Thanks is extended to all labels, mail-orders and individuals who have assisted in getting *Noise Receptor Journal* out to a global audience and providing support with booking advertisements.

A final thanks to everyone who has supported *Noise Receptor Journal*, purchasing copies and offering words of support.

Greetings also to all those I have met along the way (either online or in person), but as there are too many to mention — by naming none, no-one is forgotten.

Note: refer to liner notes of each archive issue for further credits and contributor details.

Richard Stevenson

noise receptor
journal : archive volume 1

edited by Richard Stevenson

introduction

Influence & Inspiration: The Noise Receptor Journal Story
by Richard Stevenson

The story of *Noise Receptor Journal* is inextricably linked to my first book *Spectrum Compendium*, published February 2019. Its release was very much a major milestone for me personally, as it documented the totality of my earlier coverage of the late 1990s/early 2000s post-industrial underground. Coming off the back of extensive work in collating all content for publication in a single volume, it was fantastic to finally have the finished product in my hands. As I write this, *Spectrum Compendium* has not yet been out for a full year, but it appears to have been well received. Thankfully this confirms there is ample interest in the most obscure corners of the post-industrial underground to justify a dedicated publication. *Spectrum Compendium* has paved the way for this first collated archive volume of back issues of *Noise Receptor Journal.*

To take a step back, it is important to highlight the motivations for the creation of *Noise Receptor Journal*. In mid-2012 I embarked on the setting-up and launch of the *Spectrum Magazine Archive* blog, with the intention of providing an online portal for PDF versions of *Spectrum Magazine* to be downloaded. Given how much I enjoyed the process of revisiting my first zine publication, it led me to consider launching a review blog. At the time I was also inspired by a close friend, Scott Van Dort, who had started a music review weblog of his own. I figured I could perhaps do the same and return to writing about underground music via an easily manageable online forum, without the headaches of producing a printed publication (in my introduction to *Spectrum Compendium* I highlight Scott's role in the originally inspiration to create *Spectrum Magazine*).

After launching the *Noise Receptor* weblog in September, 2012, I was happy enough to write sporadic online reviews of material I was inspired by, and any thought of turning the weblog into a printed journal was simply not contemplated. But in early 2013 I read an online forum comment of Mikko Aspa (Freak Animal Records), in which he said something along the lines of: *'things which are not important remain unfinished, but what is truly important gets done.'*

I was inspired by its simplicity in describing motivation, and it set in motion the chain of thoughts that led to the eventual launch of *Noise Receptor Journal.* Around the time that I read Aspa's comment, I had been publishing online reviews for around six months and had begun to feel that something was missing in terms of physical tangibility. Initially I resisted the thought of launching another magazine as I knew the amount of work it would entail, and I had no idea how a new print endeavour would be received within the underground. Despite my reservations, the desire to create another print publication remained. I devised a 'journal' concept based around a single long-form interview, associated artwork and various reviews previously published online. I reasoned that this streamlined format would allow the print version of *Noise Receptor Journal* to be a shorter and focused document, without the headaches associated with the larger scale preparation of multiple interviews, organizing advertisers etc. An A5 booklet format was chosen to keep printing and international postage costs down.

In hindsight, the first issue of *Noise Receptor Journal* was more of a case of 'testing the water', as anyone who has followed the publication will note that it has substantially evolved in terms of overall length and content of each subsequent issue. I also wanted to differentiate it from the preceding *Spectrum Magazine,* where with *Noise Receptor Journal* I opted for simplified but stricter design 'rules', with a view to having a consistent and uniform presentation between issues, and in clean and timeless style. So, on one hand although *Noise Receptor Journal* is clearly a continuation of what started with *Spectrum Magazine*, equally the chosen design ensured it would look and feel like a completely different publication.

I remember asking Thomas Ekelund of Trepaneringsritualen for a long-form interview and artwork, and deciding that if he said 'yes' I would proceed with publishing *Noise Receptor Journal* No.1. I duly sent Thomas an email on a Friday night and, when I woke the next morning, was pleased that he had already replied with a positive response.

Around the same time I was made redundant from my day job, so with the resulting increase in available time I set to learning the intricacies of the layout software InDesign, and around four to five weeks later the first issue was released. In reflection, it was a very easy and organic way in which Issue No.1 came together.

In the years since, *Noise Receptor Journal* has grown in both content and page count, to the now established length of around 100 pages (give or take). With the expanded number of interviews and articles, advertising has also been an integral part of offsetting the ever-increasing print and postage costs, not to mention a targeted platform for relevant underground labels and artists to promote their releases. Since 2013 an issue has been released each year.

Some may have noted that the same tag-line of *'archival documentation of the post-industrial underground'* has been used for both *Spectrum Compendium* as well as this current publication. I personally see the role of *Noise Receptor Journal* and this *Noise Receptor Archive Volume* 1 to be slightly different. Essentially each issue of the *Journal* functions to document current/recent activities of the underground post-industrial scene and seeks to balance interviews with new projects and long-term established artists. From this perspective each issue functions as a snapshot of the period in which it was created, and the audience are the fanatics actively engaged with the underground. But I see the role of this book to be subtly different; as implied by the title tag-line, I see it as a documentation archive. The fact that it has been released by a major independent publisher gives it a far greater global reach and longevity than that of the original sequential print issues, effectively a self-published underground magazine, in a limited print run and with limited distribution.

Having *Noise Receptor Journal* move into book format is in no way an ego stroking exercise. Rather, I see its content as important countercultural information, which deserves to be more widely available to anyone who is potentially interested, either now, or in years to come. This is much as the same role that the *RE/Search Industrial Culture Handbook* plays, first published in 1983. That book remains relevant as a document of the initial wave of the underground industrial movement, and is still in print and available today, some 37 years later.

Finally, it is also important to highlight how *Noise Receptor Journal* should in no way be viewed as singular mouthpiece or spokesperson for the post-industrial underground. I make no attempt to cover all of its varied aspects. Rather, my writing should simply be viewed as a window onto what I personally find most engaging. Clearly not everything within the underground appeals to my artistic preferences, and nor should it: there is a vast array of projects to appeal to all manner of fringe sensibilities and personal fetishes. Also, I am only one person with one perspective on post-industrial related music. If anyone feels my coverage is too narrow (or too wide for that matter), I would implore people to start their own underground focused publications to cover exactly what they want to read about and use it to document their own opinions and perspectives. I for one would certainly want to read such publications; the post-industrial underground needs more detailed coverage than it currently receives.

But enough of all that. I hope you enjoy and appreciated the detailed material contained herein. I also hope *Noise Receptor Journal : Archive Volume 1* will be revisited in later years as an archival resource of the post-industrial underground.

Richard Stevenson/*Noise Receptor Journal*

www.noisereceptor.wordpress.com

noise receptor journal : chronology

Noise Receptor Journal Issue No.1

Released April, 2013. A5 format. 56 pages. 500 copies (three editions). Featured interviews: Trepaneringsritualen. Artwork by Thomas Martin Ekelund. 45 in depth music reviews.

Noise Receptor Journal Issue No.2

Released April, 2014. A5 format. 66 pages. 450 copies. Featured interviews: Aural Hypnox, Blitzkrieg Baby, Grunt and Halo Manash. Artwork by Kim Solve. 58 in depth music reviews.

Noise Receptor Journal Issue No.3

Released May, 2015. A5 format. 114 pages. 500 copies. Featured interviews: Aischrolatreia, Alfarmania, Fieldwork, Puce Mary, Survival Unit, Wertham. Genocide Organ profile. Artwork by Kristian Olsson. 100 in depth music reviews.

Noise Receptor Journal Issue No.4

Released July, 2016. A5 format. 116 pages. 500 copies. Featured interviews: Concrete Mascara, Damien Dubrovnik, John Murphy (2002 archival interview), Posh Isolation, Ulex Xane (Streicher). Tower Transmissions V live report. Artwork by Ulex Xane. 70 in depth music reviews.

Noise Receptor Journal Issue No.5

Released October, 2017. A5 format. 100 pages. Featured interviews: Anemone Tube, Armour Group, Human Larvae, Inade, Trapdoor Tapes, Young Hustlers. Tower Transmissions VI live report. 'Visual essays' by Anemone Tube. 70 in depth music reviews. 500 copies published.

Noise Receptor Journal Issue No.6

Released December, 2018. A5 format. 114 pages. 600 copies. Featured interviews: Death In June, Detrimental Effect, Kevlar & Prurient/ Hospital Productions. Detailed article on Genocide Organ's :CIVILIZATION: with archival live images. Tesco Organisation 30th Anniversary festival report. Cold Meat Industry 30th Anniversary festival report. Artwork by Dominick Fernow. 70 in depth music reviews.

Noise Receptor Journal Issue No.7

Released August, 2019. A5 format. 94 pages. 600 copies. Featured interviews with: Am Not, Cloister Recordings Himukalt, Ochu, Pterygium, & Tone Generator (of SPK & Last Dominion Lost). A series of six previously unpublished SPK group photos, taken at The Brickworks, Sydney, March 1982. Artwork by Richard Stevenson. 50 in depth music reviews.

Noise Receptor Journal Issue No.8

Released April, 2020. A5 format. 90 pages. 600 copies. Featured interviews with: Moral Order, Nordvargr, Post Scriptvm, Total Black, Cloister Recordings 5th Anniversary festival report. Artwork by Nordvargr. 50 in depth music reviews.

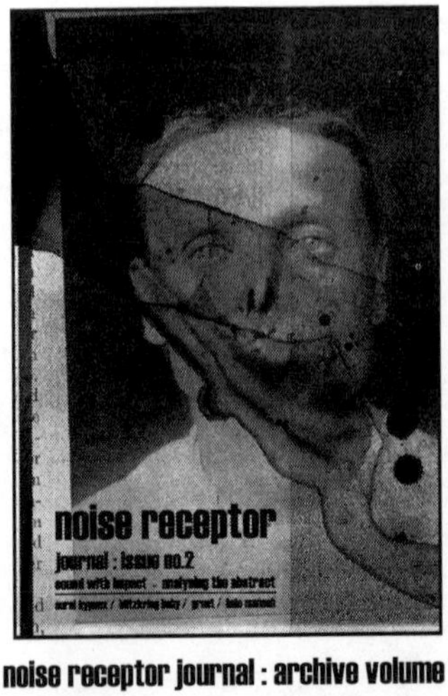

noise receptor

journal : issue no.1

sound with impact - analysing the abstract

noise receptor

journal : issue no.1

sound with impact - analysing the abstract

editorial

Welcome to the first issue of *Noise Receptor Journal*. Effectively this constitutes the physical manifestation of the *Noise Receptor* web-blog, but also contains new interview and art content to differentiate it from the already published web-based reviews.

Regarding reasons of '*why?*' I have primarily embarked on this venture to document the online reviews in physical printed form. Whilst the *Noise Receptor* web-blog has been receiving a steady amount of hits since its inception in September, 2012, after six months of writing web-reviews I felt there was something missing, given the words existed only in the digital world. It was this perception along with my previous background in publishing *Spectrum Magazine* which ultimately spurred me on to create this print version.

Whilst *Noise Receptor Journal* is not intended to replace the web-blog, it is however targeted at an audience who values the permanence of print media over the transience of web-content. In this context other print publications such as *Special Interests, Terror, As Load As Possible, Night Science* etc should be commended for their own dedication to producing and publishing printed magazines.

With *Noise Receptor Journal* I have attempted to avoid this being a typical 'zine venture (i.e. inclusion of multiple interviews etc), by instead focusing on being a more streamlined music and art type journal, hence the 'journal' title. At this stage the plan is to release future issues infrequently as is warranted, and within each issue include a long-form and in-depth feature interview with a single artist as well some visual material / artworks.

The A5 format of this publication has primarily been chosen for ease of publication and to reduce postal costs insofar as possible, which I note have become far more crippling than when *Spectrum Magazine* existed. Also given that I have no idea of how a venture such as this will be received, Issue No.1 has been printed in a limited and hand numbered edition of 200. Should the demand warrant, further editions will be printed as necessary, with the edition number and limitation indicated on the back page. In future I may also decide to publish a digital PDF version online - time will tell on this front though.

Regarding the long form interview with Trepaneringsritualen (T × R × P) featured herein, this has certainly exceeded all expectations and is exactly the type of in depth interview I am hoping to continue with for future issues. I also feel there is also a nice degree of synergy between my review of *T* × R × P 's 10"EP being the first ever to be published on the *Noise Receptor* web-blog and featuring T × R × P's interview in Issue No.1.

april 2013

Ultimately this project warrants a huge 'thank you' to Thomas Martin Ekelund, who has been a key contributor to the project through the completion of the long-form interview and the submission of artwork for publication. Thomas, my absolute gratitude is extended to you for your interest and dedication to this project! Thanks also to Paul Carland for technical assistance.

Lastly thank you to you the reader for picking up a copy of this issue. I hope you enjoy *Noise Receptor Journal* and I look forward to seeing where this new micro-publishing endeavour leads.

Richard Stevenson / *Noise Receptor Journal*

access

noisereceptor.wordpress.com
spectrummagarchive.wordpress.com
noisereceptor@hotmail.com
follow *Noise Receptor* on facebook

credits

editor, interviewer, reviewer and layout: Richard Stevenson
cover image: Warren Mead, from his Dark Poland series 2000
all artwork contributions: Thomas Martin Ekelund
trepaneringsritualen live photos: Richard K. Szabó

contents

T R E P A N E R I N G S R I T U A L E N

...an industry of ritual and death...

Trepaneringsritualen (aka T × R × P) are a relatively new project but with an approach and sound delivered with intelligence and conviction, T × R × P have garnered high praise in a short space of time. Utilising occult / heretical religious themes and melding a heavy ritualistic aura with hallmark aspects of Scandinavian death industrial, T × R × P produce a sound that acknowledges its heritage and at the same time achieves a trademark of its own. In response to my detailed interrogation, sole project member Thomas Martin Ekelund provided an insightful analysis of his work.

Welcome Thomas. To kick off the interview it is worthwhile noting that T × R × P is not your first musical project, as your earlier now defunct project Dead Letters Spell out Dead Words (Dead Letter) existed between 2000-2010. Given that Dead Letters is vastly differing to T × R × P (noting it contains a more musical and song based focus with an overarching abstract and fragile melancholic atmosphere - 'drone pop' as you have coined it), what was the motivation for the significant change in focus and evolution of sound and approach from one to the other and what led you to form a project in such an obscure underground genre such as ritual / death industrial? Please also discuss your initial aims, concept and agenda for T × R × P and how these may have evolved over time.

The last few years of doing Dead Letters I felt that I was simply going through the motions both thematically and aesthetically. It simply wasn't rewarding anymore. At that point I had already started working as Trepaneringsritualen — originally intended as a one shot diversion — and those kinds of themes just seemed much more interesting. Dead Letters was always a very solipsistic endeavour, an attempt to exorcise my demons and the search for redemption. From my viewpoint Dead Letters was a lot heavier than T × R × P is, but obviously not musically. Both Dead Letters and T × R × P investigates suffering, redemption and death, but the latter in a far wider perspective. I've always been drawn towards dark themes in art in general, and ritual / death industrial has always resonated deeply with me, and has been an integral part in my artistic development since my late teens. The impetus to start making that kind of music was a spur of the moment thing, just working in the studio and coming up with a sound that was very different from what I was normally doing at that point, and feeling good about it. Like I said, I never intended T × R × P to be a ongoing project.

The first recordings are substantially less focused than what I am doing now, both thematically and musically, but the feel was there from the beginning. That oozing, obscure and archaic sensibility that I believe is the core of the T × R × P sound. The only thing that has really changed since the start is that it's now my main focus so I naturally put more time and effort into both research and production, and perhaps my pallet has been slightly extended to include more rhythmical and tribal influences. The themes and concepts are ever-evolving and basically reflects what ever interests me at any given moment. Lately I've delved more into what is often dismissively labeled pseudo-history, something that has already resulted in the *Konung Dómaldr Vid Upsala Hängd* cassette.

'Trepanning' as a process involves drilling a hole in a human skull, which has been utilised throughout history for medical / quasi-medial reasons, including: pressure relief due to a head injury, preventing migraines and seizures, curing metal illness, purging demons etc, and has also has been used as part of ritual means of achieving enlightenment. Noting your moniker's reference to ritual, what meaning do you personally ascribe to the context of its use to define the project?

Trepanning is the oldest form of surgery known to man. There are archeological finds from 9000 years ago of trepanned skulls and evidence suggests people actually survived these procedures. Some say it was a means of releasing demons from the possessed, while other's think it was an attempt to re-open the third eye and once more allow for direct communication with planes of existence we are no longer able to perceive easily.

It is believed that the third eye was connected to the pineal gland, that's still a part of our brain today even though we've long since lost the third eye. This has led to speculation that the gland — the only part of our brain not present in a pair — to be the dwelling place of the soul.

So, basically, the trepanning ritual is a ritualised attempt at achieving enlightenment and direct communication with the gods.

T × R × P appears to focus on a range of topics including the darkness and brutality of religion (stigmata, flagellation, crucifixion etc), the occult, magick, alchemy, the ouroboros and cyclic change. How do you see these thematic elements (and others which are present) are interrelated / interlinked within the context of T × R × P?

Ever since my teens I have considered myself an atheist, which naturally extended to all metaphysical things. Around 2005 I started experimenting with ritualised performances in a very rational and thought-out way, first under the Dead Letters banner, and later as Teeth. These rituals led to some absolutely terrifying experiences. I tapped into forces that I still can not explain rationally. It's obviously a painful exercise to shift ones entire world view, but ultimately that's what I was forced to do.

Even though I can no longer call myself an atheist, I have a strong dislike of religion in general, and the three desert religions in particular (judaism / christianity / islam). But at the same time as I detest them, I am endlessly fascinated by them, by their brutality, by their feeble obsessions, by the suffering they've caused and continue to cause. They profess spirituality, but in reality these sects have degenerated into something very profane. Their fixation on flesh and gold and ultimately power over others just seem very tawdry and ugly to me. And even disregarding the actions of the adherents, Jehovah / Jahveh / Allah is a pitiful god. His constant need for reassurance and adulation, his spitefulness and pointless destructiveness makes it self-apparent that he is ultimately a powerless weakling.

I've had a long time obsession with themes of suffering and blood atonement. The impetus was probably a perceived personal suffering on my part, wanting to find the meaning of that pain, assign it a purpose. In Dead Letters the focus was very much on that personal experience, but with T × R × P I try to approach it in a more detached way. Christian mythology has always had the same obsessive focus on blood atonement.

You are urged to consume the actual blood of god, blood spilled to atone for a sin you've supposedly inherited through blood.

The crucified or hanged god-man — be it Odin, Jesus, Mithras, Osiris, et al — is a very powerful image. Literalists might interpret this as an actual, physical act of having your self killed or mutilated (in itself a very powerful concept, be it utterly deluded), but to me it represents the initiation into mystical wisdom. Only through great sacrifice can we hope to achieve understanding.

Similarly, the circle motif is something that have been with me for a very long time. Again this obsession started on a very personal level, with me finding myself trapped in endless circles of destructive behavior. When my focus shifted from the micro-cosmical to the macro-cosmical, I started investigating mystical implications of the circle; Ouroboros, cosmic renovation, birth / death / birth, and so on. The cyclicality of time seems so apparent to me, it's all around us all the time. The passing seasons, matter turned to energy that fuels the creation of new matter. This is something that our ancestors took for granted. Basically all so-called 'primitive' mythologies feature some sort of cyclical concept of time, and that's something that science have since confirmed. This universe started from nothing, is expanding, and will at some point start to contract again, to ultimately be destroyed and then start over.

Ouroboros is an interesting image. It can symbolise the above-mentioned renovation of the world, a perfect being that subsists on what it defecates, existing in a perfect state in the formless disorder outside of creation. In an alchemical setting also appears as a ying-yang symbol of sorts, half black and half white representing the dichotomy of darkness / light, understanding / ignorance, good / evil, matter / spirit. I also like to draw parallels between Ouroboros and Jörmungandr from the norse mythos, where he serves an important role in the destruction of the world, and in this enables a new world to emerge.

I believe that art is in itself a form of alchemy. You use base materials in the form of text, sound, texture, et cetera, attempting to transmute them into something possessing great power. A great piece of art is always much more than the sum of its parts. It invokes an ethereal godliness, as close as we can get to perfection in this world.

With reference to terrifying experiences mentioned above, would you be willing to divulge any further information and specific details and your revaluation of your worldview as a result?

I don't like going in to too much detail, partially because it's very personal and partially because it's quite difficult to put into words, as most of these contacts are quite elusive.

I have on multiple occasions been visited and even possessed by various unseen forces and entities, the most prominent one, that haunted my for a number of years in the second half of the 00's identified itself as Teeth. I believe this is a reference either to the fangs of a wild beast, or to the dream archetype of crumbling teeth as a symbol for powerlessness. This period was an especially trying time in my life, and it's all together possible that it's just a part of my subconsciousness manifesting, the self-loathing, powerless part of me, but since I often experienced inexplicable physical injuries during these encounters I have come to believe that it is an actual demonic force, perhaps attracted to my mental frailty at the time.

Noting there have been countless lines of psychological investigation which have sought to study the power of the subconscious mind to manifest physical impacts on the individual, is this something you have contemplated in your attempted rationalism of your experiences?

I did explore such avenues to begin with, but the more I've read about how science views the subconscious the more convinced I get that they don't know anything at all about it. At some point the scientific method may have developed far enough to be able to explain more things, but for the time being the exploration of the subconscious will remain a purely mystical endeavour.

With your critical commentary of organised religion what are your views on the fact that Christianity has effectively co-opted elements of early pagan and solar worship cults, including visual motifs, religious days / dates, themes of resurrection, sacrifice, blood worship etc?

I suppose my main irk isn't so much that Christianity is based on its antecedents, but their unwillingness to acknowledge it. It's inevitable that any system of thought takes influences from earlier sources, but since the Roman church's main instrument of oppression and terror is that it's the one true word of god, they can't very well own up to that. Christ was not unique in anyway, and his bride isn't either. It's a sad testament to their success at brainwashing that most Christians aren't even aware of the pagan roots of all their festivals.

How in depth is your interest and study in matters relating to your chosen thematic content? Have you undertaken serious studies, or is it a case of being suitable thematic fodder for a project like T × R × P where you follow your intuition and subconscious regarding such matters, leaving you to intrinsically self analyse your output later?

My interest and my research is certainly sincere and serious but I am not much of an intellectual, and I am far too easily distracted to undertake any scholastic studies. My mind has a tendency to be a blur of disconnected thoughts. At the best of times this leads to unexpected and intriguing results, making connections on a subconscious level that would never be made consciously, and at the worst it leaves me feeling like an absolute dilettante.

I think intuition is a very important part when it comes to both art and esoteric matters, if you go purely by reason and logic you're bound to end up treading water. It's important to relinquish control, and let the hidden forces guide you. Only after that can you begin to process what you experience.

T × R × P's visual presentation is also heavily embedded with symbolism relating to its broad thematic content. What is your understanding and appreciation of the power of symbolism both within the context of T × R × P and a broader cultural and historic context?

My fascination for symbols stem from the fact that my mind works visually. I am a graphic designer by trade for this very reason. Naturally the visual representation is an integral part of T × R × P.

I see two distinct groups of symbols. There are the archetypal symbols that have been part of man's collective subconscious since before the dawn of history. I firmly believe that these symbols where handed to us by the gods when they walked the earth. All early cultures describe similar stories of god-men (Bene Elohim, the germanic pantheon, the Annunaki, Quetzalcoatl and so on) bringing civilisation, culture, language, so it's only natural to assume they were part of the original, pre-tower of babel language. These kinds of symbols obviously have a great allure for men, the speak directly with our subconscious.

The other kinds of symbols are more personal, and sometimes just as powerful, only that they have to be loaded with meaning and purpose. Sigilisation is something I am intrigued by, and experiment quite a bit with, and naturally these are an integral part of the T × R × P presentation. I also enjoy hiding symbolism in artwork, track lengths, number of copies, et cetera. Symbols doesn't have to be apparent to possess power and purpose.

With regard to your comments relating to 'gods' and 'god-men', these statements are made in their literal context. Can you further elaborate on what you mean? Likewise although recently presented to the masses via Ridley Scott's movie *Prometheus*, how familiar are you with the 'engineers' theory as an explanation for the evolution of human civilisation (i.e that the 'gods' of prehistory were in fact advanced humanoid races aka 'aliens', who either 'seeded' human life on earth or otherwise imparted their advanced knowledge which spurred on early civilisations). What are your thoughts on these theories?

The term god-men can easily be substituted for alien engineers, the basic premise is the same. A race of supreme beings that bestowed enlightenment on humanity, causing the sudden jump in civilisation that occurred around the globe. So I do believe in this as a literal occurrence, not a metaphor. The myths of entirely disparate cultures just have too much in common to be coincidental.

To date your releases have been issued exclusively on analogue formats (a couple of vinyls but the clear majority on cassette). What drives your connection and appreciation for analogue formats and particularly cassettes?

I enjoy the ritual of listening to a tape or a vinyl, and when I go for convenience I prefer files to CDs, so I haven't actively pursued having material available on CD. I want to make sure that all my work is available on an analog medium because those are what resonate with me emotionally, but I don't mind if they are also available digitally, be it on a hard drive or on a compact disc. There's two collections of out-of-print material in the works, to be simultaneously released by Silken Tofu and Malignant, for that small minority who prefer CD, or simply didn't have a chance to get all the limited stuff.

Thus far you have issued a large quantity of limited releases on multiple labels, which in turn has fostered a degree of 'cult' obscurity around the project. What is your impression of how the interest in and knowledge of T × R × P has developed since its formation in 2008?

I am certain the early releases being quite mystic and in small editions have helped build up the aura around T × R × P. Making things scarce and unobtainable has never really been part of a conscious agenda on my behalf. It's usually more about financial constraints and perhaps under-appreciating the demand. I am trying to get as much of the hard-to-find material reissued at the moment, because I want people to hear it.

Brighter Death Now, and the general sound from the early days Cold Meat Industry, Loki Foundation, Tesco Organisation etc seem to be mentioned with reasonable frequency when placing T × R × P within a genre context. How close are these to the mark are these perceived influences and what are the broader influences for T × R × P, either musically or aesthetically you would acknowledge? Likewise what was your path to being introduced into the underground music scene you work within?

Year Zero for me musically is really when I finally managed to wrap my head around Crass. It was hard to grasp as a teenage punk, but ultimately they led me to realise that 'music' can be what ever you want it to be, and down a path of discovery that has been such an integral part of my life ever since.

The influence of Brighter Death Now really can not be under-estimated. Together with early Lustmord, Mr. Karmanik represents my earliest contacts with industrial music, and as such has left an everlasting mark on my aesthetic senses. I would also site Current 93, Korpses Katatonik / Zero Kama and Psychic TV to name but a few as influences in various ways.

So, being placed in a CMI / Tesco context is something I am quite comfortable with, thought I hope I bring something new to the table too, not just clone what others have already done.

Is there a typical approach you have to music production and is it centrally important to have the thematic context and lyrics established early in the composition process? Likewise how much is your music specifically composed compared to potentially being the result of studio experimentation?

I find it less and less rewarding just mucking around in the studio, so I usually have a pretty clear idea of what I want to create. Naturally, some exploration and experimentation always goes on, and sometimes that leads me off in an entirely different direction than I had planned, but I try more and more to write songs, in a sort of traditional sense of the word.

Sometimes the theme is already set when I start working, and I use those parameters to guide the creative process. At other times it's the other way around, a musical idea suggests a thematic direction.

Many ritual industrial / death industrial type acts shun live performance, yet this is something you have taken to quite strongly. What are your motivations to perform live and have these been met in execution? How many live performances have you delivered to date, what is the process of performing (backing tapes etc) and what have the locations, audiences and responses been like?

I only started performing as T × R × P in 2010, so there hasn't been that many rituals yet. My notes are a bit sketchy but I would say less than 20 times all in all, with more than half being done in 2012. And 2013 seems to be even more busy on the live front.

With T × R × P, it's actually the first time I'm enjoying performing. My previous projects have been very much introspective, so performing live have been similarly introspective and frankly quite boring. I can count the number of Dead Letters shows I actually enjoyed doing on one hand.

While introspection is very much part of T × R × P, most rituals so far have focused on the more aggressive material, and trying to forge a connection with the audience.

It's a very rewarding experience when you manage to get a frenzied reaction out of the crowd, something akin to a political rally or an ecstatic ceremony.
I fully intend to explore more explicitly ritualised performances too, but so far I haven't found the proper venues for it. I am working on an invocation that will be performed in an abandoned mine called Mimerlaven in Norberg in mid-Sweden this summer. It's a simply awesome venue, with a beautiful natural reverb and an inherent majesty that should prove to be quite helpful in my endeavour to reawaken the head of Mímir from his deathless sleep.

Whilst I would not say that you have cultivated a specific image for yourself within the context of T × R × P (given that no release contains any images of yourself), nevertheless from the photos of your live performances you seem to present an imposing visual presence which suitably reflects the scope of the project. What is your impression of such an assertion and how important is 'image' to you in context of either your releases or live shows?
Image has a tendency to sound very vapid, but yes how my work is presented is of utmost importance to me. T × R × P is a *gesamtkunstwerk*, and all aspects are of equal importance, from the way the artefacts look, to how I look, to how the venue's look, feel and smell when I perform. It all has bearing on how the work is perceived. With unlimited resources I could achieve a lot more in this sense, but I try to work with what I have at my disposal to achieve as much of an emotional impact as possible.

I would like to put forward a view that there is degree of thematic crossover between your musical works and those within the black metal scene which have been labelled 'orthodox', although admittedly your approach differs significantly from that of the 'orthodox' bands which seek to focus on the worship and adoration of the devil / satan / shaitan. I was interested to hear whether you have knowledge of and an opinion of such bands? More particularly are you aware of the Swedish group Reverorum Ib Malacht which started very much as an 'orthodox' black metal band, but later converted to Catholicism resulting from a key band members study of the bible during the conceptual formulation of the project? Impressions / thoughts?
I've never been much attracted to what might be called orthodox satanism. If you want to wallow beneath a deity, that's your choice, but there's no great difference between submission to Satan and submission to Jahve. So converting from orthodox devil worship to Catholicism doesn't seem all that weird to me. If you are looking for TRUE evil, you can't do better than the 'Holy' Papal See.
Since I grew up with one foot in the 90's death metal scene, I pretty much had a front row seat to the development of second-wave Black Metal, and my perception of it then was that it was pretty childish. Most of the time it was more about saying outrageous things and throwing the devil's sign, than anything approaching spirituality. It seemed to attracted mostly half-wits and sociopaths. It just wasn't a rewarding scene to hang around at all, even though I enjoyed some of the music.
These days the term can mean so many things that it's hard to say anything generalising at all. I still enjoy a lot of orthodox bands, and I also enjoy a lot of the artists that strive to expand the horizon of the formula, and both forms at times offer something more spiritual besides simply being good music. Other than some apparent vocal technique influences, I don't think much of my sonic signature is influenced by Black Metal though.

Although your releases have been issued in limited numbers on various labels, the profile of the project has been raised through multi-platform promotion (blogs, forums, websites etc) and use of promo clips etc. How important are these aspects of promotion to you, or can these methods be viewed as an extension of your professional work as a graphic designer?
I apply the same basic principles to promoting my artistic endeavours as I use when doing my day job. The only real difference is that I am emotionally attached to the former. For a long time I totally refused to do that, but I came to the decision that what I am doing is important to me, and I want as many people as possible to hear what I have to offer, and hopefully take something with them from the experience.
I am very fond of the idea of releasing more or less exclusively on one label, and at some point I'd like to be in that position too. I have begun to slowly say no to labels, with my sight set on settling down on one or at least a handful of labels that I feel at home with in the future.

Apart from T × R × P you are active with various side projects, some solo and some collaborative. Can you briefly introduce these other projects and the styles they inhabit?
It's getting hard to keep track of all of them, but here goes: I am working on a 7" as Th. Tot, but I am still not certain of what direction to take, so it's pretty much still up in the air. I've tried to find the time to work on more material for Swollen SS with Lina Baby Doll, En Kropp with Joachim Nordwall, Ogham with Kevin Gan Yuen, and two new, unnamed projects with Ex Luminiaire and Michael Idehall respectively.
There's also a sort of avant-black metal project that's been on the drawing board for several years, but never seems to get off the ground.
And I also have a synth pop project called Soma Sema, which is slowly working on a follow up to our debut 7".
All this on top of a full-time day job, a label and Trepaneringsritualen, so it's understandably hard to find the time and energy.

In addition to the your musical endeavours, you also operate the micro cassette label Beläten which issues beautifully presented, pro-pressed cassettes. What are the central aims of this label?
I've run labels in the past, but I took a three year break since I wasn't excited about any of it at the time. The urge eventually returned, and what was intended as a fairly low-key thing have sort of snowballed with 13 releases in a year, a steadily growing mailorder and a healthy amount of interest from the public.
There are no fixed notion of what Beläten is or what it will and will not do. I view Beläten as an experiment with the cultish tendencies of music and art, seeing if I can build up something coherent while still being all over the place.

Seeing as though you embrace the digital medium for Beläten releases (either through direct downloads or the inclusion of download cards with physical items), what are your views on the future of physical format for releases?
I don't think physical formats will go away, simply because the tactility is such an important aspect of the experience of listening to music, reading, viewing art. But I think the numbers will continue to dwindle, and the prices for the artefacts will continue to rise, but there will always be people who appreciate the medium as well as the art itself. I don't really sell a lot digitally, and the last time I checked less than 20% of the download codes from the releases have been claimed, so obviously the people I cater too don't care much about listening digitally.

As mentioned earlier T × R × P have two upcoming compilations of out of print material, which is in addition to new material featured on the recently issued *Judas Goat* 7"EP and the *Konung Dómaldr Vid Upsala Hängd* cassette. What other new / upcoming material is in the pipeline for T × R × P?
Since both of these titles are already sold out, part of that material will be on the collections as well. Other than that I am working on an album for Lust Vessel in Japan, a 7" on Triangulum Ignis, split LPs with Deathstench and Body Cargo. I also hope that 2013 will see a vinyl reissue of the *Septentrional* cassette.
In the new year I want to slow things down considerably. It's a bit stressful to constantly have a backlog of releases to get done, and I want to be able to give myself more breathing room.

Thomas, thank you for the lengthy and elaborate interview - do you have any final comments to impart?
Thank you for taking the time to ask me some interesting questions, Richard!
People interested in keeping up with the activities of T × R × P may do so via:
de-za-kh-a-da-sh-ba-a-ha-v.se

Photos: Richard K. Szabó

reviews

by Richard Stevenson

Abre Ojos – *Häxan* DVDr not on label (self released) 2012

Abre Ojos are a project that I have only been made aware of recently, but from their self-described tag line of *'improvised sound and vision for dystopian meditation'* it provides a strong indication that the project is concerned with more than just its audial aspects. Further investigation reveals that Abre Ojos functions as a staunchly multi-media project where the visuals as a counterpoint to the music are considered an integral part of the overall whole. Evidently *Häxan* is their fifth release since 2009. Conceptually the album has utilised a 1922 silent film titled *Häxan - Witchcraft Through the Ages* as an initial inspiration source (...albeit with a intention of inverting the message of the film). Likewise visual elements from the film have been sampled and in turn manipulated and processed beyond recognition. The end result is a multi-media album containing specific visuals for six tracks (which incidentally span 66.6 minutes to obviously align with the conceptual content).

Given the multi-media nature of the project it would be remiss not to mention the visual aspects first which are certainly a visual feast of kaleidoscopic effects. Here the viewers' retinas are treated to multi-coloured miasma of computer generated geometric shapes which are constantly shifting and morphing into new patterns and sequenced formations. During some sections the visuals are limited to a swirling mass at the centre of a black screen, whilst during others they extend across the entire visual frame. Although it is somewhat difficult to describe the visuals in words*, they are most definitely hypnotic to watch and constitute the perfect visual backdrop for this type of music in a live setting - of which Abre Ojos do exactly that when playing live.

(*Hint: the album covers gives a good indication of what to expect).

Coupled with the visuals the audio elements consist of some excellent archaic drones and cosmic dark ambience, where each of the six tracks follow a similar sound palate and sonic structure. Effectively this is droning dark ambience done with a heavy dose of pulsing cosmic radiance, bass heavy rumblings and sections of jagged tonality that avoid becoming all out noise. Likewise there is a heavily processed aspect to the sustained synth textures and cyclic drones, which are also occasionally underscored by slightly more animated pulsing rhythms and crystalline metallic elements. Yet this is not to say that *Häxan* is a totally alien soundscape bereft of human aspects, as ritual chimes and processed vocals (ranging from whispers to chanted choir like textures) are sporadically utilised, thus providing some earthly grounding to the material. To give some more focused and comparative markers, *Häxan* has a certain linage with the dark ambient material coming from the likes of Malignant Records or Loki Foundation - think Phelios, Phaenon, Sphäre Sechs, Blood Box etc and possibly the abstract elements of Inade for suitable reference.

From the liner notes evidently both the music and visuals are interactive and were performed and recorded live in the studio, which is surprising as both the music and visuals come across as far more considered and composed than a live studio recording might suggest. However due to the similarity of the sound across the six tracks *Häxan* is best approached as a singular metamorphosing and meditative composition. Likewise despite being a multi-media project when approached from a meditative listening perspective the music is such that it can actually stand on its own as a pure audio piece.

Noting this is a self released production the overall packaging and presentation is slick and professional and although the physical release was limited to a mere 50 hand numbered copies, the full release is available for viewing or download via their website and bandcamp pages. At this point Abre Ojos may be an obscure project to many, but based on *Häxan* further attention is warranted.

KOLLI 1:1

Aderlating – *The Golden Mass* MC Fall of Nature 2012

For those not aware, Aderlating are a side project of the more famous (…or is that infamous?) Gnaw Their Tongues, with Mories of that particular nasty audio terror unit teaming up as a duo for Aderlating. So in the first instance there is no getting away from a passing compassion to Gnaw Their Tongues, and on a superficial level Aderlating does comes across as the more placid (…but still disturbed) brother of the OTT ambient / noise / industrial / orchestral chaos of Gnaw Their Tounges. But that is not to say that *The Golden Mass* is easy listening by any stretch, as this contains some damn unsettling and abrasive atmospheres.

Consisting of an amalgam of ambient, industrial noise and orchestral elements, this however is not the bombast of a militant orchestral style. Rather the orchestral aspects here are of a horror driven discordant violin strings type, as a counter point to the industrial noise, which leans towards harsher end of the sonic spectrum. On the first side, the title track commences with a bass driven ambient drone, scraping industrial elements and some great Asiatic tuned ritual chimes, which gradually builds with windswept intensity. *Rapture* on the other hand contains a mass of disharmonic orchestral strings, echoed drones and field type recordings of what sounds to be a creaking rope on wood (…swinging corpse perhaps?!), to create a suitably tense aura. On the flip side *Song For Mahapadma* opens with heavy doom riddled death industrial cacophony, sampled Tibetan throat chanting vocals and ritual chimes, before shifting off into a echoed mass of what sounds to be scrap metal abuse, overlaid with male choir chants and rapid bowing of discordant orchestral strings.

Although not a lengthy release, some reasonably diverse and intense soundscapes are created here, from noise industrial, dark orchestral and ritual ambient to name a few. Pro printed crystal clear red tape and full cover J card round out this tasty morsel of a release.

Alfarmania – *Skräcken* CD Autarkeia 2012

With Alfarmania's staunchly analogue focus (evidenced by four vinyls and 21 cassettes released since 2004), *Skräcken* breaks the mould as Alfarmania's first digital CD release. Noting also that Alfarmania have been described as '*post-mortem / power electronic depravity*', this release is comparatively subdued, leaning toward the post-mortem (aka death industrial) aspects of their sound, yet still maintaining their characteristic oppressive elements.

With regard to conceptual themes at play on *Skräcken*, the opening segment includes spoken vocals (Swedish?), which I assume relates to the source inspiration. From what can be established from the promo blurb (coupled with some additional investigations), *Skräcken* explores a fictional future apocalyptic scenario, based on the current and factual global initiatives of George Soros' Open Society Institute - such global initiatives which seek to implement drug harm minimisation programs, including specific campaigns to encourage drug addicts to use Methadone and Buprenorphine to combat heroin and other opioid drug withdrawals (…whilst still on the factual side, quite bizarrely the Open Society Institute partly promoted these initiatives were via a ludicrously titled comic book *Methadone Man and Buprenorphine Babe*). Noting that drug themes have played a central focus for Alfarmaina in the past, *Skräcken* represents yet another interesting angle on this theme.

But what of the audio aspects? Apart from the cover indicating four tracks, in actuality these have been consolidated into a singular and continuous 30 minute composition. Again noting this is relatively subdued compared to other Alfarmania works, the agenda here seems to be to evoke tense and slowly building atmospheres, in order to achieve an increasing sense of suffocation, claustrophobia and paranoia as the album progresses. With a general lack of the chaotic, and noisy junk metal clatter which Alfarmania are known, here multi-layered queasy ascending / descending wavering analogue sounds and catatonic pounding pulse provide the platform

for Alfarmania's trademark vocals – distant, slightly distorted and barking in delivery, akin to the ravings and ranting of a lone lunatic from the depths of a cavernous warehouse. Whilst there are certainly 'phases' which this album moves through, it could be said to replicate some sort of drug haze, where the segments shift so slowly that you don't actually notice the change has occurred. Yet the concluding album fragment is individually notable, more so due to its differing sparse experimental sound, which offers momentary respite from the claustrophobia which has preceded it.
As with all Autarkeia releases, the package is top notch – pressed on heavy weight cardboard stock for the six panel digi-pack, completed with excellent full colour scrap collage artwork courtesy of Kristian Olsson aka Alfarmania.

Anemone Tube - *Death Over China* CD
Topheth Prophet / Silken Tofu 2011

Although a 2011 release *Death Over China* is the latest from Anemone Tube and an album I had read a number of very positive reviews about before checking this out myself. This also constitutes the second release in a trilogy which commenced with the *Dream Landscape* album from 2010. Conceptually the album is focused on China and from an analysis of the track titles and various cover photos (included within the beautifully designed DVD sized ten panel cardboard fold out cover), it appears to be making conceptual commentary on the negative cultural and environmental impacts of rampant industrial development and progress experienced in China over recent decades.
At its most simplistic level the sound of *Death over China* is very much one rooted in a sphere of dark ambient and heavy industrial, which edges towards power electronics territories during a couple of segments. However such a statement effectively ignores the means of how this album was constructed and composed. Interestingly the album's liner notes states that all music was solely created by field recordings made by the artist during a trip to China in 2007 (specifically Nanjing and Shanghai), with additional synthesiser elements added to only two of the six album compositions. This sort of dedicated concept for the construction of the music makes the overall sound and atmosphere of this album all the more remarkable.
Of the six varied album tracks they each take a multi-layered approach to composition, where recognisable field recording elements (car horns, passing traffic, police whistles, loudspeaker / radio announcements and general urban chatter etc.) are looped in combination with other less recognisable distortion and static driven sounds to achieve vague soundtrack like movements. Likewise with new looped elements being continually introduced, the atmosphere is one that morphs and builds in tone and intensity as the tracks progress.
With the sound source predominantly consisting of field recordings it engenders the album with a varied and interesting tonal quality, which is rich and unique when compared to dark ambient and industrial material that is reliant on synthesised and computer generated sounds. Effectively Anemone Tube achieves a sound that spans the divide between 'academic' experimental material and 'underground' industrial territory. Likewise within this context Anemone Tube have achieved a particularly unique sound, which these days can be a challenge to say the least within ambient / industrial spheres.
With is central reliance on field recordings *Death Over China* avoids the pitfalls of the field recordings which can come across as unnecessarily abstract or academic. Anemone Tube has also successfully realised the concept of utilising field recordings as a instrument and in the process has executed an album which is intricate and tonally varied, yet highly listenable. With its complexities and nuances this warrants and demands multiple rotations and detailed attention.

Anemone Tube / Dissecting Table – *This Dismal World* LP Peripheral Records 2013

This Dismal World is a split recording from the German Anemone Tube and the Japanese Dissecting Table which is conceptually inspired by Buddhist related themes. To quote from the promo blurb it is: *'a dark concept album about the Four Nobel Truths: suffering, it's origin, cessation and the path leading away from suffering'*. This concept is also expanded upon with a printed insert which includes the lengthy written piece: *The Lotus Sutra Chapter Twenty Five: The Universal Gate of Bodhisattiva Kanzeon* (which specifically ties in with Dissecting Table's contribution). Additionally the cover depicts Guanyin Bodhisattva aka the *Goddess of Compassion* in the form of a 21-metre high bronze statue located in Longxing Monastery, Shijiazhuang.
Anemone Tube lead off and based on the sheer quality of their recent output (specifically referring to the *Death Over China* album), it is great to see the new material is as equally stunningly here. Effectively Anemone Tube's style of taking various field recording elements and welding them into abstract industrial / dark ambient soundscapes is fully on display here (the field recordings utilised here were evidently made in a Mausoleum and other locations in China). Of the two presented Anemone Tube tracks they are slightly on the noisier side - and great for it. *In The Mausoleum* is digitally crisp, bass heavy and sweepingly evocative in its cyclic tone and perhaps reminiscent of earlier Inade. Alternately the second track *From Anthropocentrism To Demonocentrism* aligns more towards a power electronics structure, its sharp tonal squall and looped sampled elements is clearly recognisable as that of Anemone Tube.
Dissecting Table's contribution *1000 tones* is presented on the second side of the vinyl which forms a singular monolithic 20 minute composition. Here the loose and chaotic track infuses stoic ritual percussion, clanging metallic elements, an abundance of noisy outbursts, chanting Buddhist monks (...presumably reciting the written tract from the Lotus Sutra), screamed quasi extreme metal vocals etc. Here these disparate elements are loosely melded together to generate a heady dose of chaotic industrial madness - Dissecting Table style of course. Although I may not be a massive Dissecting Table fan, objectively I can say the track is a heavy hitter and based on the above description you should know if it is suited to your listening preferences.
As a whole *This Dismal World* delivers solid material from both projects, but from my perspective Anemone Tube's tracks hit the high mark of the two.

Body Cargo / Pogrom – *Resistance* CD Terror / Cipher Productions 2012

As a split / collaborative release, this thematically focuses on the album's title, albeit in markedly different contexts as indicated within the promo blub: *'This album has united two Lithuanian projects under a theme of resistance. Papua New Guinea cannibals' resistance against outsider effects is different from resistance of interwar period Lithuanian guerrillas, but you can find these associations on a musical plane, and Body Cargo and Pogrom each present their own interpretations'*. Regarding the format, both acts are well suited to this pairing as they travel very similar sonic terrains. Here each act provides four tracks in addition to two collaborative tracks for good measure (each provides vocals for a track of the other).
Body Cargo is up first and although billed as 'post-mortem', they effectively deliver death industrial at its most lo-fi and dirty, where echoed, muddied and morbid analogue sonics are the order of the day. *Black Smoke Obelisks* provides an extended nightmare of muffled factory drones and croaked deathly vocals over what may or may not be sonically buried orchestral / radio samples. *Gutpath* presents a more forceful framework, consisting of a malfunctioning conveyor belt type rhythmic element, various distortions layers and a sampled / looped tribal chanted vocal for good measure. Alternately *Sacred is all Red* presents a more meditative, muffled and windswept industrial / drone piece. For Body Cargo's final track (and the first collaborative track with

Pogrom on vocals), is *Resistance (Survival Method)*, which delivers a great multi-textured death industrial piece of swelling / driving layers, vague pounding rhythms and waiving distorted vocal lurking within the sonic mass.

Moving on to Pogrom's half, they approach their sound with a little more vigour, pushing their tracks towards a power electronics tone, but still sheathed in a heavy dose of muffled lo-fi production. *Resistance (Guerrilla Method)* is Pogrom's first track (and last of the collaborative tracks), featuring muffled, idling factory machine sounds and morbid, catatonically spoken vocals of Body Cargo, which functions as a great introduction for Pogrom. Next track *Dar negimes (Igarka)* amps things up along a power electronics line with crude / nasty / scuzzy / no frills distortion and distorted vocal abuse. Likewise *Toks melsvas vakaras…* balances the line between death industrial and power electronics, with morbid spoken vocals, grinding industrial undercurrent and forceful squalls of distortion. Final track *Girioj gules* takes a slightly different tangent, where it commences with a maudlin solo folk type vocal sample, before succumbing to a muffled mass of grinding death industrial sounds, which also includes a sampled piano accompaniment to play the track though to its conclusion.

Taken in totality this is certainly a grim and harrowing release from these two aligned projects (which is a compliment for this style of music), rounded out with cover artwork which is also suitably old school and lo-fi with its black and white, cut and paste aesthetic.

Brighter Death Now – *Very Little Fun* 4xLP Cold Meat Industry 2011

Although initially very excited at the pre-release announcement, as the days counted down to actual release I had a nagging worry that this set might lack a degree of cohesion, given tracks were billed as having been recorded variously between 1998 and 2005. As it transpires this concern was unfounded, as V*ery Little Fun* is a totally cohesive release. Of the 28 tracks, it consists of unreleased material as well as various tracks previously issued on a range of limited vinyls (including the tracks from the *Proceeded in Death* 12"LP limited to a ridiculous 20 copies). Also, whilst billed as 'box set' the sleeve constitutes more of a deluxe gatefold cover housed within an outer slip sleeve. So to be pedantic, this 'aint a box set in the typical sense, but the packaging is totally worthy of the material – de-bossed, block foil stamped outer cover, with an the visuals and layout reflecting Roger Karmanik's recognisable design aesthetic.

As for the 'music' what you get herein is the well established trademark sound of BDN, but leaning towards the suffocating death industrial atmospheres of earlier material. Particularly much of the material here channels the slow stalking nightmare of their classic *Great Death* era and *Necrose Evangelicum* album - with *Shall I Die?* being a particularly good example. Although it is not entirely all lo-fi death industrial doom and gloom - some tracks ramp up aggression towards BDN's later power electronics type material, including the lurching mid paced bass heavy noise loops of *Getaway* and late album track *Never Again.*

As per usual there is a degree of 'blink and you miss it' bleak black humour at the core of BDN's work. This is evidenced through the cover of Michael Jackson's *Bad* (recognisable only for the vocals yelled over a slab of pulsing bass noise), and on *Next Train* where Roger's rambling vocals advises us that *"he will get the next train"* as the sound of passing train horn pans through the speakers.

Whilst there sheer extent of material on here could potentially lead to exhaustion, I found this was not the case at all, and one to quite easily get immersed in from start to finish. With BDN being in existence for some 20+ years now, you should know by now what to expect, which is exactly what you here – nothing more, nothing less – without evolution, without progression – and still totally worth your investigation. Still available on 4xLP, or 3xCD if that format is more to taste.

Caul – *The Long Dust* CD Malignant Records 2013

Caul's gradual ascent from murky dark ambient depths to more serene musical fields has been a slow process over some sixteen years and multiple albums, which has certainly been a positive evolution to bear witness to. Yet during this metamorphosis rather than leaving behind core aspects of their sound, it has been more a case of augmenting the haunting dark ambient drones with more musical aspects. As such the maudlin atmospheric layers remain, acting as the base for the instrumental elements (including: percussion, bass, guitars, piano, orchestral strings & brass, sparse vocal textures etc), which are seamlessly woven into the musical tapestry.

Whilst acknowledging the continued presence of a dark ambient undercurrent, it is the addition of the more musical elements that have had a profound effect on the overall mood. Accordingly the word 'ethereal' comes prominently to mind when reflecting on the tonal characteristics and overall atmosphere of current Caul material. As a result the definitive mood presented can be described as being in a '4AD' atmospheric style, reminiscent of number of acts coming from that legendary label. In fact some compositions with their orchestral and semi-tribal percussive elements play out very much like an instrumental Dead Can Dance song, which is a compliment to the quality of the song writing. For those who have not followed Caul since their last album released on Malignant Records way back in 1998, you will be in for quite a surprise as to how far Caul's musicality has been pushed over the intervening years. However for those who have keenly followed Caul's progression, this is another welcomed step in their evolutionary process.

Deathstench – *Massed in Black Shadow* CD Black Plagve 2012

Deathstench are a new signing to Black Plagve (Malignant Record's 'bastard child' side label), and being my first introduction to the group it appears this Californian duo has been active since 2009 and already have a couple of extremely limited releases under their belt (a split, an EP and a full length). *Massed in Black Shadow* is their sophomore album and their first more widely available release.

Before we get to the music, based on the artwork and visual presentation it very much screams underground black / death metal, yet this initial perception belies the actual 'music' to be found herein. This in fact is not a death / black metal release, rather it aims at a black industrial sound which heavily borrows aesthetically and sonically from the black / death metal spheres. From this perspective Deathstench can be viewed as a crossover act which straddles genres and merges aspects of death / black metal and black industrial / ritual noise styles. This 'crossover' perception is further solidified by the fact that the group are listed on the Encyclopaedia Metallum: Metal Archives web resource (...typically only metal or metal related bands are listed).

The inky sonic blackness and distorted echoed roar of *Extract Ex Infernis* introduces proceedings and sets the scene. Here bass heavy and cavernous death industrial loops provide a semblance of structure, whilst vocals evocations are recited amongst the backdrop of brooding menace - but rather than resembling anything remotely human, here the vocals are relegated to almost outbursts of distortion. *Corpse Upon a Throne of Worms* opts for a more sinister death ambient vibe, which provides the backbone for slow strummed distorted guitars and course black metal vocals, thus demonstrating the knack of the project to merge the tonal elements of differing genres. The sound of Sunn O)))'s Black One album (aka black metal inspired doom drone) is a suitable reference point here, although the guitar playing is slightly more animated (...which is hardly a difficult task based on the catatonic pace of Sunn 0)))). On the gritty and windswept

Symbols In Warm Flesh an overloaded bass guitar appears to sit prominently within the mix, but rather than being riff based the playing is abstract and forms a nasty distortion / feedback layer. Moving on to the pair of back to back tracks *Circle of Black Blood* and *Shrine of Viscera*, a more structured 'metal' sound is present but each differing in style and presentation. The first delivers slow strummed distorted guitars and rasped vocals of doom cast over a rumbling death industrial base, whilst the later with its blast beats and murky black / death metal riffs is reminiscent of the aura of underground legends Blasphemy or similar ilk. The final album track *Bastards of the Black Flame* arrives as a multi-layered black ambient slab of dread evoking sonics and murky abstract hellish noise, all whilst grimly screeched vocals and riffed guitars (slow to tremolo style) complete the wretched sonic picture.
Whether or not you will find some to your liking on this album will depend greatly on your penchant for lo-fi underground death / black metal, but at the same time this is clearly not a metal release. However to consider wider genre implications it is worthwhile highlighting that throughout the early 90's there was some significant dislike to the increased interest of 'metal heads' in the dark ambient / industrial scenes. Yet with the rise in the total dominance of the internet, as a result genre boundaries and scene politics has been greatly diminished which has encouraged the cross pollination of musical genres. Within this context Deathstench are a flag-bearer for genre splicing which has achieved prosperous results.

Desiderii Marginis – *Procession* CD Cyclic Law 2012

Constituting the seventh album for Desiderii Marginis, I have to admit that for no particular reason I have not kept up with the group since their third release. Upon reflection this is somewhat odd, given I was huge devotee of the group from the debut album *Songs Over Ruins*, and additionally featured an interview with sole member Johan Levin in Spectrum Magazine Issue 4 way back in 2000. Nevertheless the seventh album this is and the first to be released on the respected Cyclic Law label (with the majority of earlier albums being released on Cold Meat Industry).
So, whilst not being able to compare *Procession* to more recent albums, to this ear Desiderii Marginis continue to deliver their particular version of sacral infused dark ambient hymns. Yet what is also clearly evident is the overall tone is slightly more composed, flowing, mature and confident in presentation. Whilst I would also say that in the past there was inevitable comparison to fellow Swede raison d'etre, given the more sparse and abstract directions that raison d'etre have headed on recent albums, such a comparison today is greatly diminished and further assisted by the honed compositional slant which gives this a recognisable Desiderii Marginis sound.
Although articulating a broad cavernous and echoed dark ambient aesthetic, the album is impeccably produced to allow the varying tonal layers, and individual instruments (piano, violin, moody orchestral synth melodies, sparse choral vocals), to breath and float within the mix. Notably there is also the occasional interjection of slightly jagged tonal elements (metallic scrapings, clanging sounds etc.) to keep the listener on their toes.
When closely listening to early album track *Her Name is Poverty* I was struck by the parallel which could be drawn to the feel and atmosphere of their debut album (which I mean as a clear compliment), with a similar atmosphere flowing through the following track *Silent Messenger*. Yet this is not to suggest a mere re-tread of the aura of earlier material. Here the track excels with its morose tone (lone

le·pape
blason·de·la·mort

wind instrument floating over a slow shifting moody orchestral base), ultimately representing an artist who has nailed down their sound with self-assured clarity. Interestingly *In Brightness* manages to achieve an atmosphere that is the polar opposite of what the title might suggest – a distant and bleak sounding composition of shifting droning semi-orchestral layers that are partially grounded with scrapping metallic industrial elements. Excellent to say the least. Alternately *Adrift* seeks a slow build structure, here relying on cavernous reverb and swelling, bleak piano / orchestral melodies which rise and build in intensity throughout. The final of the eight album tracks presents the title piece, representing a great finale due to its distinctive dual intertwining bittersweet violin lines, and slow, echoed dark ambient undercurrent.
To conclude I am glad to say that *Procession* confidentially represents the aural space I expected (…or hoped) Desiderii Marginis to still inhabit, and for me at least amounts to the welcomed return of a familiar yet matured sound. Definitively worthy of investigation if you have had any sort of appreciation for Desiderii Marginis in the past.

En Nihil – *The Approaching Dark* CD Eibon Records 2012

The long standing project En Nihil returns with a new album, which on face value stylistically fits with the current crop of American acts cultivating the grey areas between dark ambient, death industrial and power electronics genres.
Album opener *The Tomb of Empire* acts as a relatively short intro piece, which has a tonal range spanning a low humming drone at the bottom end, coupled with blasting static at the forefront and upper ranges. This piece then bleeds seamlessly into *Frozen Posture*, which with its rumbling mass and subtle textural elements shifts towards an isolationist ambient frame. Alternately *The Hearts Relent* is a total surprise (given the tracks which precede it), containing a melancholic fragility evoked though through a sparse orchestral melody and distant hummed vocals. Although unexpected, it works exceptionally well in a restrained and cinematic dark ambient style. *Futile Man – The Weight of Absolution* is another stand out, with tonality quite akin to the fractured and digital filtered laptop sound of Fennesz – although this piece does move away from the 'summery' electronica atmospheres of the aforementioned project to heavier distorted death industrial realms.
In covering yet more sonic territory *Souls to Cease* delivers some buried factory ambience which builds in static intensity as the piece progresses. Likewise *Vulture Reign* pushes a heavier and more forceful power electronics sound with its rough loops and cascading noise and squalled distortion – excellent stuff. Final album track *Darkfall* provides another moment of listening respite, being a bleak and desolate slab of dark ambience built on a cyclic melody and muffled distant storm rumblings – a musical statement of relative calm and great concluding piece.
Although largely sitting at the heavier end of death industrial and power electronics genres, this is a varied and considered release with some excellent forays into dark ambient territory. With the sound production En Nihil illustrates clear attention to detail with the separation of tonal elements, which only enhances the listening experience. Gatefold digi-card sleeve with suitably dark imagery rounds out this tasty release.

Funerary Call - *Nightside Emanations* CD Malignant Records 2012

When approaching the review of this album, it dawned upon me that I have known about Funerary Call since around 1998 when I read their interview in Heresy Magazine, but for no particular reason have never got around to investigating their works in depth (of which six albums have been released in that time span). I must admit that the folly of this was evident from the moment I listened to the recently issued *Nightside Emanations*.
Incidentally what first provoked my interest in this album was the artwork – a wonderfully archaic and occult infused painting by Russian artist Denis Forkas, which calls to mind the works of Austin Osman Spare, but at the same time has a clear stylistic slant of its own.

Likewise given that the album has been pressed as a DVD sized case the artwork is far more stunning in actual form than as an on screen thumbnail, and based on the quality of the artworks and presentation, it is releases like this which REQUIRES and DEMANDS a proper physical release.

Darkened gloom illuminated by flickering candle light - bone, ash, feather and claw strewn alter - tendrils of incense smoke slowing rising from burnt offerings - shadow shapes lurking at the periphery of ones vision - these are just some of the images emerging in the mind's eye when immersing oneself in this album's spectral aura. With the use of an array of instruments (chimes, wood blocks, singing bowls etc) the album it inhabits a ritualistic / organic aura not too far from the fields ploughed by a number of the Aural Hypnox label collective (Halo Manash, Arktau Eos etc), yet this does have a darker and more occult streak to its archaic ambience. As with most ritualistic ambient material space and depth play an important role in creating a cavernous aura, where echoes tones ring out, build and fade. *Thee I Invoke* is a particularly focused track which brings to mind early era Archon Satani, with its slow, heavy, pounding, echoed beat, background drones and whispered vocal invocations. Alternately *The Calling* is more sparse and distant with the call / response of wailing horns, and sparse disharmonic string scraping sounds. Final album track *Upon the Heath* again reveals a ritualised aura, containing sustained droning layers, slow tribal bass pounding beat, and garbled / chanted vocals. Ominous and heavy in tone, it is a great album conclusion. Noting this is my first proper introduction to Funerary Call, based on the strength of this album I will be definitely tracking down other Funerary Call offerings.

Funerary Call – *Beckoning at the Black* CD Fall of Nature 2012

This new release from Funerary Call does not contain new material per se, but constitutes the resurrection of earlier material previously released on a limited CDr via the Fossil Dungeon in 2004 – with an extra track added for good measure. So, when *Beckoning at the Black* is contemplated in context the organic / ritualistic direction of recent Funerary Call, this older material clearly has more direct linage with 90's sounds coming from Cold Meat Industry, i.e. the orchestral / industrial / ambient material of In Slaughter Natives, or the more composed and percussive material of early raison d'etre etc. Yet not coming off as a bland copy, Funerary Call evokes a certain dark classic horror soundtrack type vibe that sets it apart. In broad terms the seven tracks are built around a framework of doom evoking orchestral elements, which (dependant on the track) includes: wailing horns, pounding ritual drums, shrill strings, operatic wails, sparse piano / flute melodies, a heavy dose of echo and reverb and whispered / treated vocals which arise out of the sparse aural muck. Also to provide another comparative marker, the mix of ambient washes of sound and sparse ritualistic persuasion of *Hel's Hymn* and the moody orchestral strings, horns and piano of *Of Death's Breath* brings to mind early Desiderii Marginis, which is certainly a compliment from my perspective.

Whilst *Beckoning at the Black* constitutes a deviation in sound from the current direction of Funerary Call, this is a worthy release, including a great cover image (taken the 1970's motion picture *Wicker Man*), to provide a suitable visual counterpart.

Funerary Call – *Fragments From The Aethyr* CD Crucial Blast 2012

Fragments From The Aethyr is the third album I have heard from Funerary Call, and while this is a relatively recent recording (recorded 2010 and mixed in 2012), is quite stylistically different to the ritual dark ambience of *Nightside Emanations,* both in terms of sound and length of tracks. Here the album consists of three lengthy tracks, the shortest nearly 10 minutes and the longest pushing 18 minutes.

Libation commences proceedings with a tense semi-orchestral tone of echoed drums and heavy echoed ambience, with the track propelled forwards but a prominent violin. The sound however quickly amasses to a forceful sphere of grinding noise, sparse guitars and multi-tracked shrill violin strings, before falling away to the calmer concluding section of the track. At this point I feel it necessary to highlight that the violin presented on *Fragments From The Aethyr* has not been sampled nor synthesised, rather has been specifically recorded for this album, which certainly gives a unique edge. Second piece *Fragments* again utilises a wavering solo violin, yet overall has a contemporary composition / modern classical edge to its sound, albeit of a pretty dark and bleak variety. As the track progresses and builds the instrumentation is accentuated by droning orchestral horns, backing electric guitar and booming kettle drums. Third and final track *Transference from the Void* pushes more towards the ritualised tone of *Nightside Emanations*: a sparse catacomb ambient soundscape with semi-chanted / semi-whispered disembodied and echoed voices which fill out a large part of the sound spectrum, with further scattered ritual percussive elements for good measure. Excellent to say the least. Noting the more ritualised tone of the final track, I feel it is reasonable to view this album as sort of a logical precursor to what would follow on the subsequent *Nightside Emanations* album. Suitably aesthetic artwork from Australian artists Orryelle Defenestrate-Bascule rounds out another interesting and worthy release from Funerary Call.

Genocide Organ – *Under-Kontrakt* LP Tesco Organisation 2011

This new album for German power electronic legends was highly anticipated, being seven years on since *In Konflikt*, and thankfully does not disappoint. Thematically G/O have always worked with interesting subject matter and this time round is not exception, being based on mercenary soldiers throughout the ages, including the current trend of private military contractors used in various conflict zones around the world.

Given that G/O have matured in both sound and conceptual content, *Under-Kontrakt* sees a further honing of their aesthetic. Clearly less brute force than early material, here the tracks are more considered and 'composed' for what of a better term. Tracks are primarily driven by multiple synth lines, noise layers and looped sounds to create loosely constructed and abrasive elements that weave, interlink and overlap. Yes, this is a noisy album, but noisy in a way that the layers have clarity and most importantly - volume.

Noting that a number of compositions incorporate vocals, interestingly rather than an standard power electronics vocal attack, they are delivered here in a spoken, reserved tone and almost apathetic in places – sort of akin to a nihilistic resignation of circumstance which can descend with age and the passing of years. However early album track *It's Over* with its queasy wavering noise layers and radio static include a more animated vocal delivery with a mantra like delivery of the song tittle towards the end.

The track *Denard* seems to be concerned with Colonel Bob Denard, who was a French mercenary operating in Africa from the 1960's to the 1990's. However the vocal sample used throughout appears more akin to a Black Panther Organisation speech (*"white man can't fight a guerrilla warfare"*) which is placed over repetitive and drilling / burrowing noise elements. The aforementioned apathetic vocals are most evident on the relatively ambient noise of *Armour Group*, allowing the lyrical message to be clearly articulated. Arriving at the final piece *We're Here To Have a Good Time*, this

rounds out the album with its composed pulse, droning noise and restrained and spoken lyrics delivered with a mix of spite and cynicism. At this stage in the game G/O may be a stalwart of the scene, but with the strength of this album it is clear why they are so well regarded. Obviously the LP is long sold out, but still available on unlimited CD. Without a doubt highly recommended.

Genocide Organ - *Genocide Organ* 2xLP Tesco Organisation 2012

When I first reviewed the original 2003 version of this album, I had a bit of whinge about the packaging due to the flimsy card stock of the cover. Thankfully such complaints have been duly addressed with this re-release, where the tracks have been re-mastered for maximum sonic punch, pressed on pristine black vinyl, housed in a de-bossed and spot varnished gatefold cover, and treated to added bonus tracks and extra poster inserts* (*only if you have a G/O re:con unit number).

As the story goes this is G/O's 'lost' album that was meant to be the bridging release between the first *Leichenlinie* LP and the *Save Our Slaves* LP. Slated for release in 1990 on a Japanese label, this never eventuated, but was later released by Tesco to commemorate the group's two live performances in Japan during March 2003.

Regarding the music contained herein, the main self titled portion of the album consists of 10 tracks including some classic tracks that were previously released on other formats (such as *Death to China* parts *I & IV* and *White Power Forces*), that have now been released in the rightful place alongside the remaining album tracks. Overall the album isn't as brute force as some of the *Leichenlinie* material, rather presenting tracks of more subdued and seething anger (such is the case with the slow throbbing mass of distorted noise of vocals that comprises opener *Death to China I*). *White Power Forces* ups the anti, with quicker and higher pitched modulated distortion, whilst the monotone vocals spit forth a barely decipherable sermon. Punishing indeed..... Alternately *Swamp* contains a sickening and lurching atmosphere derived from its mid ranged noise and disfigured loops, with spoken vocals barely puncturing sonic mass. *Sturmfieber* chooses a more straight forward construction, using layers of mid ranged frequencies and a what sound like an archival type nationalistic song. *Death to China IV* continues a seething atmosphere of loose rhythms and fluctuating noise, made all the more poignant by the sampled music lifted from a traditional Chinese opera. *In the Ghetto* is more atmospheric then other tracks, using a distant and echoed noise effects and throbbing elements that almost represents the sound of a helicopter's rotor blades swooping low overhead. As for the slow and caustic death industrial vibe of *Born to be Slaughtered*, it could easily have been lifted from any of Brighter Death Now's CD's from the *Great Death* trilogy (yes that is a complement to both!). Alternately *Und morgen die ganze Welt* is noisy, chaotic and most importantly foreboding, with its doom laden loops, splintered noise and urgent shouts & wails of the vocals, with the aural torture dragged out over 11 minutes.

Regarding bonus tracks these include three tracks lifted from the 1991 / 1992 Japanese acetate 7"EP's *A Case Of Orthopaedic Fetishism* and *A Functional Chapter of Sexual Process*. Given these bonus tracks were recorded from the same era, they nicely bookend the main album tracks, which were nigh on impossible to obtain due to their original limitation. Overall this new version of the 'lost' album of archival material does clear justice to the legacy of G/O.

Gnawed – *Terminal Epoch* CD Phage Tapes 2012

Following a myriad of cassettes, split releases and CDr's over the last three years, *Terminal Epoch* arrives as the debut album proper from Gnawed (featuring 12 tracks over 51 minutes). So for those not familiar with Gnawed, they are amongst the current crop of US power electronics / death industrial artists who have been receiving a fair amount of positive interest in recent years, which includes the likes of Nyodene D, The Vomit Arsonist, Steel Hook Prosthesis etc. Thus taken from this perspective

Terminal Epoch presents yet another solid and pulverising release from the US power electronics / death industrial scene.
Generally speaking I would say that Gnawed are slightly less polished and refined when considered alongside the aforementioned acts, but nevertheless they represent a project which appreciates the means to deliver a forceful album. Each of the tracks follow a fairly straight forward structure and tend to quickly establish their core elements – distortion, feedback, synth drones, vocals etc – and then loop the formed structures for the length of the track (which range from the shortest at 1.36 minutes to the longest at 7.07 minutes). Yet as the average length of tracks is in the order of four minutes, it seems the modus operandi of Gnawed is to quickly establish the tone of each piece, but not extend it to a length which becomes tedious or otherwise loses impact. In effect this is somewhat similar to the short, sharp and to the point approach of Ex.Order.
Overall one of the clearest impressions I get from this album is that it achieves an atmosphere which welds the aggressive with the ominous, which is certainly a positive combination. The multilayered aspect of sound helps achieve this via an array of elements including: sustained / fluctuating noise; tense and atmospheric synth layers; scrap metal abuse; drilling distortion etc. The vocals are also an absolute highlight, presented with a raw, harsh and searing treatment of the power electronics variety. Ultimately *Terminal Epoch* is a heavy, no frills, and straight to the point power electronics / death industrial album - and a commendable one at that. Recommended.

Grunt - *World Draped In A Camouflage* LP
Freak Animal 2012
The last proper album from Grunt was *Petturien Rooli* in 2009 and although it received significant praise from various quarters, for me at least it was not an album which grabbed my full attention. Although I can acknowledge it is a solid album (if not somewhat sprawling in scope), on the other hand it does not have that certain 'something' to keep me returning for frequent listens (…let's put it down to personal taste).
So when approaching *World Draped In A Camouflage* I immediately found it to be much stronger and focused but also diverse album, which still inhabits the particular sound which can be ascribed to Grunt. Likewise despite the brute force sound for which Grunt are known, this comes across a clearly sophisticated power electronics album – and by 'sophisticated' I mean it is an album of a diverse range of sonic elements utilised by someone highly skilled in the composition of harsh sound structures. Thus with regard to the range of sonic elements, the album has been composed with an assemblage of: static riddled tape loops, textural noise, decaying feedback, harsh blasts of distortion and general overloaded noise manipulations, in addition to other more diverse elements such as sampled operatic vocals, orchestral strings and tonal aspects more akin to pure experimental material. Apart from the constructed sound elements, there is also fantastic diversity with the vocals, spanning the trademark gruff yelled style, through to more urgent and higher pitched screeched variety – some sections being clearly audible, with other highly modified through echoed and distorted treatments.
From the outset the first two tracks illustrate the scope and diversity of the album. The title track is up first and is quite experimental in tone, with a soundscape of deep echoed drones, layered queasy electronics and sampled operatic vocals, whilst the second track *Kansanmurhan Infarastrukktuuri* is a straight down the line avalanche of searing brutal noise and aggressive vocals. With *Maailmanlopun Mekanismi* despite the loud, rough and cyclic 'steel in a cement mixer' type clatter, it manages

to display a meditative quality within its noisy framework, which is also one of the longer tracks of the album at around six minutes. Following track *Dance for the Genocide* delivers an absolute album highlight, and although its core is a power electronics track, it is also driven by instrumentation you would not typically expect. Built on a base of controlled distortion and acerbic flanged vocals, what makes this track so distinct are the modern classical elements, including urgent angular orchestral strings and sparse tympani percussion (sounding to be real rather than synth derived). *Ritual of Mortality* provides a tense almost death industrial base, with later introduced looped flaying noise and trademark heavy gruff vocals to provide a power electronics slant. *Like Dead Dogs* is yet another album highlight, with its squelching and decaying noise loops, wavering noise and some seriously heavy and unhinged vocals – tremendous stuff. Late album *March of the Titans* displays a suitable amount of echoed and jagged metallic crunch (built of multi-layered loops), with the later segment having a more ominous tone built on pulsing static, sampled choirs and vocals of shrieking intensity. Noting that the 10 tracks are between two and six minutes, each piece illustrates individual character yet collectively embodies a fully coherent album and highlights the degree of focus and skill encapsulated within. As such the complexity, depth and multi-layering of this collection of tracks is exceptional, with all elements having clear purpose and place within the mix. Although it is far too early to be proclaiming this as a 'classic', it is definitely an essential release of 2012. For either old or new listeners, surely *World Draped In A Camouflage* cannot disappoint.

Grunt – *Someone Is Watching* CD Force Majeure 2011
Grunt – *Europe After Storm* CD Force Majeure / Industrial Recollections 2012

These two albums are not new, instead are re-releases from the lengthy Grunt back catalogue. Incidentally the combined material was recorded in 1998 with *Europe After Storm* also containing some live tracks from 1999. Whilst both albums clearly sit within the European power electronics genre, here there seems to be a general reliance on oscillating synth textures for a basis of the sound. This aspect effectively highlights a clear difference between older and newer material, as recent Grunt albums appear to focus on self produced and specifically recorded sounds (sheet metal, effects units, homemade noise apparatus etc.).

In its original version *Someone Is Watching* was first issued on tape in 1998 and given its limitation of 128 copies it clearly warrants this less limited CD repress of 500 copies. Likewise as is suggested by the title, the album's concept focuses on CCTV / video surveillance and the associated control that a faceless authority seeks to impose by such technological means. Album opener *Watch Your Back* feature a prominent synth drone, a crumbling mass of distortion and high pitched processed vocals which sweep and pan trough the mix over the extended nine minute length. Definitely a great start and with the track being heavy and noisy but at the same time structured and loosely composed, it establishes the prevailing theme throughout the album. Interestingly *You Can't Hide* is quite reminiscent of Propergol's *Cleanshaven* album, due to the prominent use of movie dialogue samples and subdued ominous atmosphere, yet as *Cleanshaven* was also released in 1998, the question is who might have influenced who, or are the similarities a mere coincidence? Towards the middle of the album *Secrets Of Technology* takes a much looser approach and is particularly heavy with an overloaded noise productions and metallic clatter, with the distorted vocals barely being able to break though the sonic mass. Regarding the concluding arc of the album, the final three tracks each contain a notable controlled

sweeping noise aesthetic, which evokes a stalking and threatening type mood that certainly suits the album's concept.

Moving onto *Europe After Storm* it has a slightly more storied history as it was first issued as four track cassette in 1998, before being reissued on CD in 2001 with three additional studio tracks and four live tracks. This version contains the same material from the 2001 CD release but is packaged here is a standard jewel-case. Although from the same era, from the outset it is evident that *Europe After Storm* differs from *Someone Is Watching*, given it sonically it is more brutal and less atmospheric as a result. *Project Eden* opens *Europe After Storm* and descends with an assemblage of rough loops, drilling synth elements and heavily processed vocals and a building mass of distortion and random clatter. On the other hand *N-Force* uses a sustained synth drone to provide a somewhat filmic quality to a backdrop of modulated noise, which is soon crushed by the following track *Blood On Concrete* with squalled noise layers and prominent anger filled power electronics vocals. Alternately *Peacekeepers* stylistically shifts the sound towards a death industrial tone, due the heavy droning synth line and distant noise and sampled dialogue, although the later half of the track does morph into a proper power electronics blizzard. *Cleansweep* rounds out the collection of studio tracks, which loosely knits together layers of pulsing noise, dialogue loops and chaotic vocals. Of the four live tracks, these conceptually fit the studio tracks (two studio tracks from *Europe After Storm* feature in live version), but within the live context there is a looser and heavier presentation, including the vocals that come across as more prominent and forceful. Sonically it seems the live tracks may involve the use of a backing track (...I could be wrong on this point), which are augmented with live noise and vocals. Yet either way the live tracks are a solid live representation of studio material.

Clearly both of these older Grunt albums contain strong and focused material, which differ slightly in sound and style consistent with their differing themes. Likewise both albums have stood the test of time positively and can hold their own within the context the current crop of newer power electronics releases. Yet when these earlier albums are compared to the current Grunt album *World Draped In A Camouflage*, it only emphasises how far Mikko Aspa has pushed his project and the levels of sophistication he has achieved within his chosen power electronics framework.

Hall of Mirrors – *Altered Nights* 2xCD
Malignant Records 2012

Hall of Mirrors constitutes a collaborative duo, consisting of Amon member Andrea Marutti and Giuseppe Verticchio of Nimh. Although having not heard any of Nimh's releases, I am well versed is the sweeping cavernous dark ambient works of Amon, which was clearly enough to garner my interest in this.

Regarding the material presented on *Altered Nights* (Hall of Mirrors' third album), it is expansive to say the least, spanning two discs and around 100 minutes of desolate, brooding dark ambience. *Night 1: The Meeting* kicks off the first disc, and quite quickly builds in to a multi-faceted dark ambient / drone-scape which teeters on the edge of abrasiveness. *Night 2: Invocation* arrives next, sprawling over 20 minutes, and is calmer and more organic and in tone than the first, with a watery ebb and flow to the multi-faceted drones. Although *Night 3: Magmatic Resonance* may commence in murky cavernous depths, it slow ascends into a quite animated and forceful frame, which seems to multiple in intensity through the introduction of a stratum of flowing / sweeping layers and disharmonic wailing tones. Mining a slightly different sound, *Night 4: Immaterial Bodies* flirts within an ethno ambient tone, with it shimmering sound textures, and the vague rhythmic effect created by the various sound loops.

On the second CD, it reveals a single 45 minute track *Last Night: Late Summer Ceremony,* which gradually builds into a stormy crescendo of jagged droning frequencies, before reaching a calmer plateau with a sparse melancholic melody. This calm section however is relatively short lived, as through the mid section the track builds back up to a serrated, swirling tonal range. Towards the conclusion of the album,

the lead out section of this track is excellent (and dare a say it) beautiful and serene in sound, with a calm sweeping undercurrent and sustained harmonic tones.
Within a broad drone / dark ambient framework, the five tracks across 2xCD's reaches both spiralling heights and cavernous depths, and spans a sonic spectrum from stormy to calm, resulting in a meticulously constructed and nuanced album.

Inade – *Audio Mythology One* LP / CD Loki Foundation 2012

As is the case with the publication of any new release from Inade this is usually reason enough to celebrate, however with reference to the album's title it is indicative of being the first in a series of archival material. So given that subsequent releases are slated in the *Audio Mythology* series, clearly this is additional reason to celebrate. Regarding *Audio Mythology One*, the album consists of eight tracks derived from 2001-2012, with the liner notes revealing that four tracks were released on various compilations, whilst the remaining four were previously unreleased until now. It also seems that tracks have been further mixed, edited and in some cases reworked in bringing these tracks to fruition for this release.
Noting the span of years in which these tracks are derived it is appropriate to reflect on Inade's modus operandi over their 21 year history. Upon such refection an evident characteristic has been Inade's inclusion on a significant number of compilations, where submitted tracks have formed important parts of their sonic puzzle and vital stepping stones in the evolution of their music. Ultimately this tells volumes of the commitment of Inade to their craft and is a far cry the attitude of many acts that seem comfortable with using compilations to off load second rate tracks. Thus based on the above circumstances *Audio Mythology One* contains fantastic material and through the further editing, mixing and mastering comes across as a release that is as strong as any of their main 'official' albums.
Referencing its scope and style, the collection of tracks which makes up *Audio Mythology One* are very much rooted in the later era of the group and the sound of what Inade do best. That is esoteric mysticism set to sound – emanations from the void which intertwine deep space cosmic tones with otherworldly and occasional orchestral elements. Yet on a more bland descriptive level this can be defined as experimental music which combines aspects of abstract modern classical music with more traditional dark ambient material. Variously the tracks are meticulously composed with sonic elements including: slow wailing of ceremonial horns, deep ritualistic percussive beats, melancholic orchestral elements (strings / brass), multi-layered and interweaving drones, echoed and abstract metallic / crystalline / shimmering sonic textures, disembodied vocals and well-placed dialogue samples to flesh out thematic context.
Across the span of their career Inade have managed to reach spiralling heights through the refinement of the compositional skills and in the process have created a multidimensional aural world. Their status is clearly evidenced by their ability to effortlessly evoke archaic and universal vistas of a monolithic scale, which effectively elevates the listener out of a limited human scale perspective. As an overall experience *Audio Mythology One* is exceedingly masterful – transcendent even – and in many ways trying to describe the album merely in context of the sum it its parts does not do it adequate justice. Ultimately Inade's 'sonic sculptures' need to be experienced via full audio immersion (…noting that *Audio Mythology One* has been released in limited edition of 300 vinyl LP / CD set and unlimited CD for such purposes). Without a doubt *Audio Mythology One* is far more than a mere stop gap release and is another welcome addition to Inade's discography.

IRM - *Anthology* 2xCD Autarkeia 2012

Is it really thirteen years since the then young upstarts IRM burst onto the power electronics scene with their debut *Red* album? I guess the answer is 'yes' as here we are with an 'anthology' released to celebrate the fifteen year anniversary of the formation of the group (... time certainly seems to pass quickly). Starting in 1997 as a two piece and consisting of Erik Jarl on music and Martin Bladh on vocals, IRM issued a single demo *The Green Tape* in 1998, before the debut vinyl only *Red* album the following year. In the intervening years they have since evolved into a trio, with Mikael Oretoft joining on bass on 2007 to further flesh out their powerful and oppressive industrial / experimental / power electronics soundscapes. Although very much driven by a standard power electronics framework in their formative years, IRM's sound was still varied and forceful, and by demonstrating an intelligent if not obsessive streak with their inspiration and conceptually varied themes they quickly garnered a loyal following. Likewise over the subsequent passage of years IRM have further honed and refined their sound into something particularly unique and individual, consequentially elevating themselves into a league all their own (... refer to the last album *Order4* as evidence in chief). Referencing their style IRM evoke sound structures ranging from meticulous experimental / industrial soundscapes (shimmering metallic drones, subterranean bass, echoed percussive elements and an array of other tonal textures), through to harder and harsher power electronics aspects. One constant however has been the yelled and slightly treated vocals which have remained a trademark throughout.

Anthology itself is split into two halves, consisting of a collection of studio tracks (CD1), and another collection of live tracks recorded at various 'live actions' (CD2). The studio material includes an unreleased piece in addition to a collation of tracks from various sources, including: *Sweetness Will Overcome* comp, *split* 10"EP with Skin Area, *Four Studies For Crucifixion* 10"EP, *Nihil* 2xLP comp and two tracks from the *The Green Tape*. With the studio tracks presented here in reverse chronological order, it provides the listener with a clear perspective of the evolutionary arc of the group: from the hard and clinical earlier programmed sound, to the later more free-form framework with a greater reliance on organic sound textures and elements of real instrumentation (free-form bass, disharmonic strings, stilted piano notes, sparse percussion etc).

The first studio track on CD1 is the unreleased 2008 track *Order* and appears it may have been recorded during the same recording sessions for the *Order4* album. Here the track is intense and domineering in its musical delivery, consisting of slow throbbing bass, seething industrial tones, experimental sound textures and dual tracked spoken and yelled vocals found on more recent IRM material. Regarding the balance of the studio tracks, it is the *Four Studies For Crucifixion* compositions which stand out as particularly focused, being constructed around pulsating industrial soundscapes, urgent, emotive vocals and disharmonic trombone wails. These four tracks are also probably most representative of the transitional point between the earlier forceful sound approach of the group, and the burgeoning looser and more experimental focus of later material. However when referencing earlier IRM material, the five tracks from the *Nihil* vinyl only compilation certainly hit hard (...clinical, throbbing, heavy and harsh power electronics on display here), and represent a clear document of why IRM garnered such high praise early in their career.

Moving onto the second disc the 13 live tracks are derived from seven 'live actions' recorded between 2002 and 2011. The live tracks however are not presented in any sort of chronological order, rather the listening experience has been enhanced by the re-ordering and further mixing of tracks to present a singular flowing set. Although slightly looser in presentation, the sound is faithful and recognisable as live renditions of their studio counterparts, and in many instances the vocals appear more urgent and unhinged in their delivery. Referencing a specific live track (and final album track at that) *Sebastian* is a stunning example of live experimental minimalism,

INRI

constructed with a nonstandard power electronics element of repetitive and sustained disharmonic piano notes, coupled with agonised flanged vocals – an exceptional end to an exceptional release.

Beyond the music, the packaging is stunning and has been given the special Autarkeia 2xCD box set treatment, with distinctive embossed digi-pack / box cover, including colour booklet with lyrics and artwork courtesy of vocalist Martin Bladh. Ultimately *Anthology* is not a mere collection of scattered tracks, rather represents a strong document of the group's history and as with all IRM's outputs this is mandatory listening, made all the more essential by the stunning packaging.

Isomer - *Nil by Mouth* MCD Cipher Productions 2011

Here we have the new mini release from Isomer, which takes the nosier aspects of the last album *Face Towards the Sun* and consolidates it into a slightly more focused and forceful sound (...which I might add also deviates quite heavily from the dark ambient style of earlier albums). Essentially *Nil by Mouth* seeks out heavy electronics / power electronics avenues - a la the sound of early Tesco Organisation and Loki Foundation labels, such as Dagda Mor, very early Inade, Genocide Organ, Ex.Order etc.

With six tracks featured over 30 minutes, the sound bridges the clinical (computer generated perhaps?), and a tone with a bit more grit and punch (analogue synth and distortion pedal derived perhaps?). Yet regardless of how sounds were generated, opener *Slave Ritual* more than positive sets the tone – wavering noise layers, semi-militant looped percussion sample and an excellent vocals which are heavily distorted / echoed in treatment. Within a similar focused frame *Regaining Our Faith* presents a multi-faceted heavy electronics piece, built on multiple, downwardly spiralling noise layers, sustained drones and static crunch, complimented with echoed vocal sample. Wearing its influence on its sleeve and coming across as a solid homage to Genocide Organ, *When We Burn* takes a layered approach to its wavering distorted core with occasional interjections of heavily processed vocals which suits the sound and approach perfectly. Final track *Infant Promise* has some great random factory type clattered (recorded with some serious cavernous depth), heavy grinding bass textures and again with the heavily processed vocals, which all ramp up through the track's duration before abruptly cutting out.

Although released in a short pressing for availability at a live action Isomer played with Genocide Organ in Mannheim Germany in May, 2011, this should not be passed over as some sort of minor stop gap release. *Nil By Mouth* illustrates a strong sound and focused direction for Isomer, and as such I am greatly looking forward to what comes next.

Linekraft – *Bouryoku Kikai* CD Black Plagve 2012

Not having come across Linekraft before, my inquiries revealed this Japanese project has been active since 2008, with three albums issued prior to this. It was also noted that Linekraft have been billed as 'japnoise', which based on this album does not really tell the complete story. Yes, there is a fair dose of chaotic noise, but also a large proportion of the sound is built around an old school industrial aesthetic of sheet / scrap metal and oil barrel percussion and / or abuse.

Delivering a commotion of junk metal noise punctured with static squalls and distortion drenched vocals, the title track opens the album, whilst static radio snippets (voices, vocals and music), bleed in and out of the mix. Next track up is *Jinkaku Syougai* which the longest of the five pieces (pushing nearly 20 minutes), and across its sprawling expanse shifts through a number of segments from doomy grinding industrial to passages of clanging metallic intensity.

Yugou again provides an old school percussive industrial type vibe, with its stilted, clanking mechanical pulse and wavering analogue noise. Alternately *Kenjyu Jisatsu* moves towards a more caustic and loosely composed power electronics / harsh noise piece, complete with segments of yelled / distorted vocals. Demonstrating yet further diversity to the sound, the final track *Kigurui* flirts more with a death industrial vibe,

with an ominous undercurrent and pounding metallic elements.
With its chaotic distortion based aesthetic *Bouryoko Kikai* has a partly composed, partly improvisation quality to its sound and production, which definitely sits within an old school industrial / experimental noise style. Noting that this Malignant Records side label seems to cater for less refined and noisier fare, Linekraft have certainly found a suitable home.

Maculatum – *The Nameless City* CD Malignant Records 2012
HP Lovecraft and his trademark unspeakable and unknowable horror styled writings have long struck a chord with travellers on dark paths of inspiration, and interestingly it seems that his writings, and particularly his Cthulhu Mythos, has been obtaining wider appreciation in recent years. For this new project Maculatum – a collaboration between two existing Malignant Records artists Collapsar and Rasalhauge – they have taken inspiration from a short story of Lovecraft's, and used the name for their album's title.
Whilst archaic sweeping dark ambience is certainly the over arching tone, *The Nameless City* is far more than just being cavernous droning fodder, particularly as the album contains considerable motion and dynamics throughout. Ranging from tense and brooding to calmer passages, there are various tonal aspects which liven up the sound palate, including: segments tribal percussive rhythms, garbled disembodied voices and chanted vocals (sampled?) which sporadically appear. Actually being quite heavily percussive in parts, such sections hold a deft tribal / otherworldly aura which very much suits the source material which inspired it. The production and mastering also adds a great deal to the atmosphere, as sound wise the whole album is impeccably produced, with both its sonic clarity and tonal depth.
People familiar with the artist's main projects, or more broadly the dark ambient aspects of Malignant Records roster, will find much to be pleased with on *The Nameless City.*

Maison Close – *Maison Close* CD Force Majeure 2012
Maison Close is not a new project / album, rather is a ten year anniversary repress which has been reissued in much the same presentation and content as the original release. Regarding its genre Maison Close could be described as something like noise infused dark ambience, which verges on a windswept power electronics sound. As such the sonic palette consists of sustained analogue drones, sweeping ominous textures and slow grinding loops which evokes a partial linage to the early Loki Foundation heavy electronics style - think Predominance, Dagda Mor, Ex.Order and early Inade. The overall atmosphere generated by the heavy use of dialogue samples is also reminiscent of what Propergol would later do with the same concept, yet Maison Close generates a more consistent soundtrack type atmosphere due to the singular source which the movie dialogue is sampled from.
Regarding its usage of sampled dialogue, thematically the album focuses on the 1971's motion picture *Johnny Got His Gun* which makes for great conceptual fodder. Although the movie is in effect an anti war tome told from the perspective of an severely wounded soldier, here Maison Close have focused on aspects which address the existential fear of being mentally cognisant, but trapped in a comatose and nonresponsive body with the following panic and terror which would ensue. Noting the albums visuals have also been lifted from the movie, the album very much plays out as an alternate experimental soundtrack to the source material.
Noting the calmer arc of the first half, things step up on mid album track *Tom-nihil-rec* that contains the first use of prominent vocals, presented in an agonised power electronics style that soar above the sonic undercurrent of grinding and crumbling noise. The track *Pain* also utilised prominent vocals, which achieves an agonizing climax with its combination of swelling distortion and deranged vocal delivery. *Interferences* mines a similar vein to Brighter Death Now's death ambient sound, which here combines a cavernous echo chamber ambience

with a prominent singular mid range piecing tone that burrows deep into your psyche and making this track anything but easy listening. A heavy noise squall and agonised vocals then reappear on *Eclats de vie* before one final section of sampled movie dialogue to conclude the album (*"SOS help me… SOS help me…"* repeated...).
Given where others have taken this sort of sound in the years following the original release, I would not necessarily call this classic or ground-breaking. Yet it is still a solid album all the same which had successfully merged its overall tone and atmosphere with its conceptual context.

Mind & Flesh – *Marytr Generation* CD Force Majeure 2012

Although Norway might not be a highly recognised country for death industrial and power electronics music, this has done little to hamper the enthusiasm of Anders B with his Mind & Flesh project. It also seems this is not Anders first release, as he has previously issued two albums under a separate moniker Babyflesh, before rebooting under the guise of this new project name.
Being the Mind & Flesh debut, *Martyr Generation* consists of nine tracks recorded between 2005-2008 and by way of indicative sonic markers, this is musically in the vicinity of early Genocide Organ, early Haus Arafna, Brighter Death Now etc, yet does manage to evoke a sound of its own. Overall the album follows a path of being loose and unpolished in delivery, being built on repeated looped structures to form the basis of each piece. Likewise the tracks are structured enough to not appear improvised, but chaotic enough to suit its death industrial / power electronics guise. The roughly stilted loops and acerbic distorted vocals of *Walking Target* introduce the album and include the dually consoling / menacing lyrics of: *"I will keep you safe. Nothing is going harm you. As long as you play my game"*. Yet things really kick in with full force on *From the Cradle to the Grave* with fast, pulsing metallic loops and flanged vocals that hint at the vocal style delivery of the Grey Wolves. This track is blunt and to the point and all the more effective for it, and continues in a similar stylistic slant on *Alone Against All* which also brings the mid era Brighter Death Now compassions to the fore. The elongated length of *Blodskam* evokes some great droning death industrial (complete with distant wailing chants), while *Destroyers* achieves a more loose rhythmic sound with its various loops and decent amount of crisp and sharp distortion. Noting that *Purgatorium* is credited to both Mind & Flesh and Atrax Morgue (aka the late Marco Corbelli who regrettably committed suicide in 2007), there is no further information regarding this collaboration, but obviously this was composed before Marco's untimely passing. Here *Purgatorium* presents a cavernous atmosphere built with a basic yet crushing beat and sermon like distortion treated vocals, being broadly characteristic of the minimalist approach of Atrax Morgue. Alternately the final track *Clashing Icons* bleeds out over an extended 10 minute length, evoking a cavernous death ambient soundscape of echoes, metallic textures and occasional vocal wails (…a commendable conclusion which is certainly a hell of a lot calmer than much of the material which precedes it).
With *Martyr Generation* Mind & Flesh delivers a solid and no frills death industrial / power electronics album. Whilst it may display its influences fairly prominently, when armed with such conviction and delivered with such passion as displayed here, it provides Mind & Flesh with requisite individualistic flair, thus worthy of full attention.

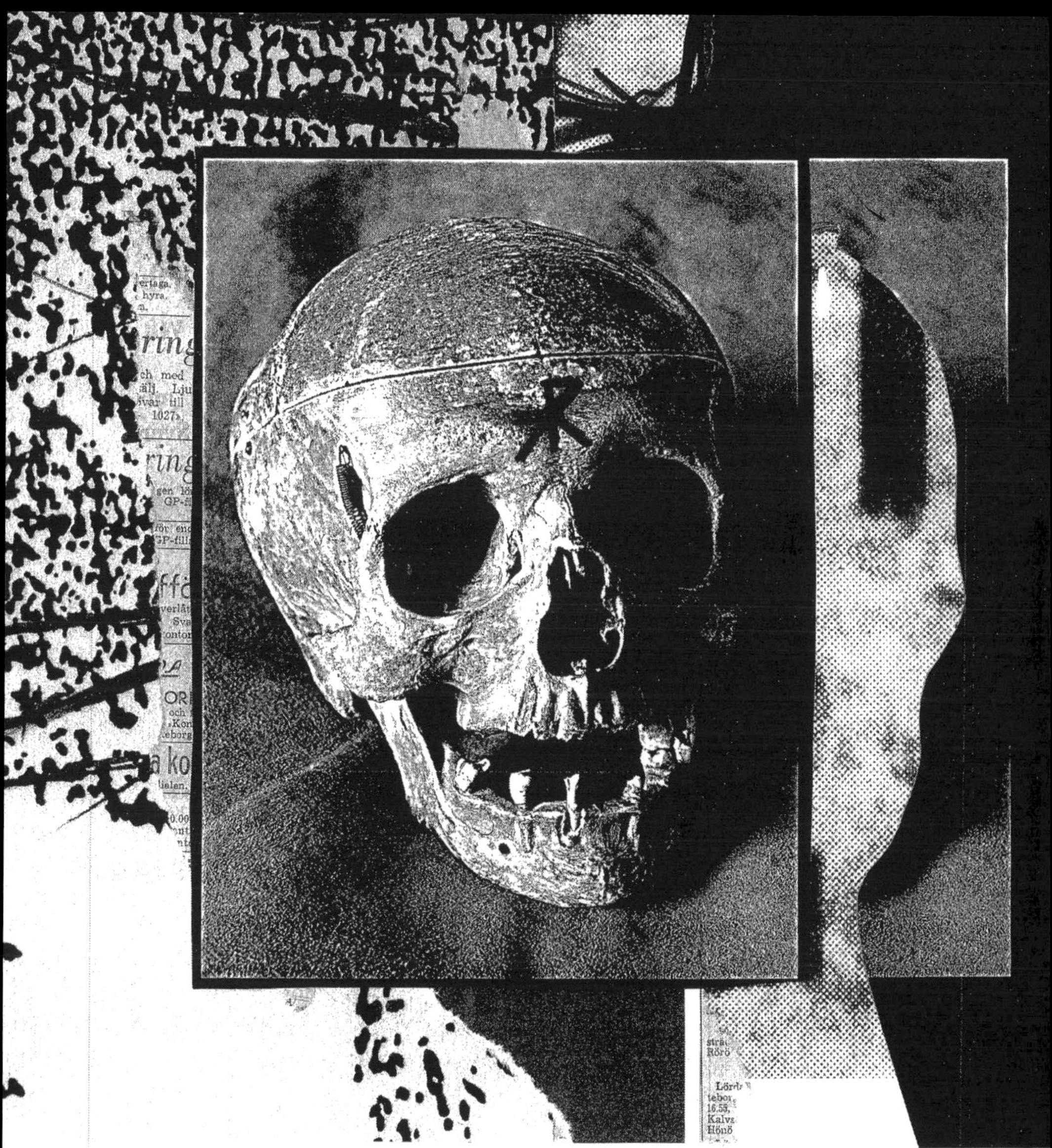

Navicon Torture Technologies – *Your Suffering Will Be Legendary* 2xCD Malignant Records 2013

Your Suffering Will Be Legendary does not herald the return of Navicon Torture Technologies (NTT), but resurrects a collection of bonus tracks that were originally packaged together with *The Gospel of the Gash* double album (...mind you in a super limited box set of 100 copies). Incidentally *The Gospel of the Gash* which was released in 2009 also constituted the final official release from NTT before Lee Bartow relaunched under the new guise of Theologian.

Regarding the eighteen tracks that make up *Your Suffering Will Be Legendary,* these are not merely left over studio material, but constitute collaboration tracks from eighteen different artists, both well known and obscure. For posterities sake the acts which feature alongside NTT include (in order of appearance): Aun, Black Sun, Cenotype, The [Law Rah] Collective, Inswarm, Covet, Autoclave I.I, Herbst9, Hecate, Jarboe, Deutsch Nepal, Fragment King, Kristoffer Nystroms Orkester, Prometheus Rising, Steve Moore, Eidulon, Troum and The Bird Cage Theatre.

Given the magnitude of material here (which spans 2xCD's and a total play time of a whopping 143 minutes), there is little to be gained by slogging through a track by track review. Yet to provide an overall impression, the music sits mostly within a droning / dark ambient style, with some pieces pushing towards heavier death industrial and power electronics spheres (being entirely consistent with the varied sound NTT is recognised for). Despite its collaborative nature all tracks are of a high quality standard that manage to hang together as a consistent and coherent album. Clearly this can be put down to NTT's base material providing a degree of tonal consistency, which has allowed contributors to weave their own varied elements into the compositions.

Although that there is nothing on here which could be deemed as a weak contribution, conversely some of the stand out moments to this ear includes:

- Covet - *I Won't Survive In A World Without You:* understated dark ambience with maudlin piano and orchestral melody which evokes a bleak cinematic atmosphere.
- Autoclave I.I - *An Exercise in Pain-Extended Version*: warm enveloping drones, wide screen choral vocals textures and thunderous percussive underbelly.
- Herbst9 - *Eclipsed By A Blue Star*: a tribal infused, cavernous dark ambient monster that stretches out over 20 minutes.
- Deutsch Nepal - *Victvm Vermis*: meditative drones with a fantastic tribal rhythm element and clean sung echoed vocals.
- Fragment King - *Gumrot (decaying face edit)*: upfront mid paced IDM programmed beats offset against a droning undercurrent.
- Eilulon - *Pillars of Flesh*: Dread filled catacomb ambience combined with deep orchestral elements, slow pounding beat and part yelled part sung vocals.

Beyond the musical sphere, the packaging is also exceptional and mirrors that of the DVD sized, multi-panel fold out cover of *The Gospel of the Gash*. Either as an essential bookend to *The Gospel of the Gash*, or otherwise as a stand-alone release, *Your Suffering Will Be Legendary* is a welcomed more formal addition to NTT's legacy.

Nyodene D - *Every Knee Shall Bow* CD Assembly of Hatred 2011

Despite numerous cassettes and CDr releases prior to this album, this seems to be considered as Nyodene D's 'proper' debut release – and what a release it is at that. The style of Nyodene D is an ominous one, constituting an assemblage of death industrial tones and power electronic elements for good measure. Vocals also feature on all tracks, and when they appear they take centre stage, being rough, forceful and clearly audible in delivery (additionally treated with an echoed effect).

Harbinger leads off the album an with a doom riddled death industrial style, before layers of blast furnace noise ushers in the aggressive and apocalyptic vocal sermon. *Against the Age of Kali* has a suitably appropriate sample repeated throughout the length of the track (*"Let us face, without panic, the reality of our time"*), and includes a great mid section of junk metal abuse and random clatter, which has been looped to create a vaguely rhythmic effect. Chaotic looped scrap metal abuse also constitutes a large chunk of the title track, before it shifts towards a more melancholic sound, stripped of the metallic noise, and bringing to the fore wavering synth drones and echoed vocals, with lyrical lines overlapping one another – clearly the album's highlight. Again the melding of the aggressive synth lines and scrap metal abuse feature prominently on *There Will Come Soft Rain*, which is the shortest of the four albums tracks (which still manages to span a total play time of 51 minutes).

Maybe I am somewhat late to the chase on this one, but Nyodene D for me at least are an act to keep a keen eye on – particularly as a new full-length *Edenfall* is slated for release on Malignant Records shortly.

Nyodene D – *Edenfall* CD Malignant Records 2012

The 2011 album *Every Knee Shall Bow* was my first introduction to Nyodene D, and based on the quality of that album, I had high expectations for what would be delivered with their Malignant Records debut. So, from the get go *Edenfall* does not disappoint and actually manages to build on every aspect which made *Every Knee Shall Bow* great. The major aspect of this is down to the production, which has been mastered with loudness and clarity. Effectively the multitude of noise elements / layers are clearly audible and individually discernible, allowing *Edenfall* to deliver a heavy sonic punch in the power electronics / death industrial arena.

The title track introduces the album and kicks in with full force: rough crunching noise, loose static riddled loops and overloaded feedback, later introducing distorted synth squalls to amp up the atmosphere. As the vocals arrive to drive home their message, their slight difference in presentation is immediately evident. Whilst similar in delivery and style, vocals here are drenched in distortion, meaning a greater degree of concentration is required to pick up what is being said (…or if that is too difficult, full lyrics are printed in the cover). Second track *Damnatio Memoriae* is up next and presents a straight down the line PE attack, reminding somewhat of Ex.Order, being built on looped wailing / drilling noise elements, and heavily treated harsh vocals - delivered courtesy of another PE project Shift. Alternately *Anasazai* is a little less bludgeoning, being melancholic in tone and consisting of a more sparse death industrial noise framework, with looped tribal / ritual type vocal sample and junk metal clatter to good effect. Partly reminiscent of early to mid era Brighter Death Now, *Nihilation* drives forward with its nauseous loops and roaring noise – although the vocals very much place a clear Nyodene D stamp on the piece. Rounding out the album *Borne on Vultures Beak, I Am Carried Into The Heavens* takes a tense droning approach to its PE sound, which may be due to the sound source credited to Sky Burial (…with the track title also seemingly paying homage to this contributing project). With a sustained background textures (…treated orchestral strings perhaps?!) and cavernous echoed loops, the immense flanged and distortion tinged vocals reign prominently up front within the mix. Fantastic.

Apart from the excellence of the music, the artwork is worthy of a mention, which is suitably slick in appearance, where the chosen images are cleverly utilized to imply the album's title theme. To conclude there is not much else to say other that *Edenfall* is easily a pinnacle release of 2012 and highlights the current supremacy of Nyodene D and more broadly the American PE scene.

Nyodene D / Sektor 304 – *split* CD Malignant Records 2012

Two of the heavy hitters of the current Malignant Records roster have teamed up on this release, which comes packaged in the limited box set of Nyodene D's monster of an album *Edenfall.* So what we have on this collaborative release is a total of five tracks spanning 34 minutes (three tracks from Sektor 304 and two from Nyodene D), where each artist has constructed their submitted tracks from source material provided by the other. In fact to thematically tie in with the parent release, Sektor 304's tracks have been constructed from sound sources specifically derived from *Edenfall.* So although containing the inputs of two projects, pleasingly the final result is a cohesive collection of tracks which sits somewhere in the middle of their respective sounds. Yet at the same time the tone does sit closer to Nyodene D's power electronics / death industrial sound due to the reduced focus of the trademark heavy industrial and driving percussive aspects of Sektor 304 (…although there are scant smatterings of such elements throughout).

*The Human Fractal** commences the CD, which has the feel of a slowly building intro track, consisting of sustained doomy synth layers, slabs of junk metal feedback and scattered percussive elements (both distorted and organic in tone). *All Over All*** steps in next, where Nyodene D puts the brakes on the driving forward motion of Sektor 304's rhythmic oil barrel percussive sound, morphing it into a mass of distorted noise, looped vocal samples and squalled power electronics vocal attack. Here the heavy, noise bloated atmosphere is unrelenting over an extended 10 minute duration (…great might I add!). Although *The Shaft** includes some metallic percussive elements, these tend to not function as a rhythmic driving force, rather are relegated to being one of the many sound layers utilised. Consequently the track achieves an ominous, staking atmosphere, created via synth drones (which resemble sustained orchestral horns), and spoken vocals partially buried in the mix (…again an excellent track). *Vulture – For Gill Scott-Heron*** is somewhat reminiscent of Ex.Order, built around looped noise elements and flanged vocals, but also achieves a death industrial aura through the militant and heavily echoed, bass pounding beat. Final track *Furnace** edges towards the percussive sound associated with Sektor 304, where a rhythmic percussive loop sits atop a bed of metallic scrapping textures, pensive drones, and vocals (courtesy of Sektor 304), which build in distortion and intensity over its short length. Based on the general respect garnered by the contributing artists, in combination with the sheer strength of collaborative material presented here, it seems an absolute shame for this to be limited to a mere 200 copies. To avoid seething disappointment, grab a copy of the *Edenfall* box set while you can…

* Sektor 304 track

** Nyodene D track

Poena – *Likboden* MC Beläten 2012

Given that Poena is a new project, after reading the promo blurb I was admittedly sold before I had heard a second of this release – and I quote: *'Poena – the spirit of punishment as channelled by Kristian Olsson (Survival Unit / Alfarmania) and Christian Godin – perfectly blends the rank atmosphere of early Brighter Death Now with the obscure ritualistic rattles of Zero Karma and Ain Soph. Likboden was recorded in the old morgue of the Sidsjön mental hospital in Sundsvall, a fact that permeates every death reeking, unsettling second of this 30 minute piece'.*

With its single abstract composition *Likboden* commence with assemblage of slow wavering bass drones, ritual chimes, loose percussion, rattling chains and distant groans emanating from the depths. Following on crude rhythmic beats are pounded out in the bowels of the asylum, whilst sustained vocal wails inject a tenseness to the dank atmosphere. At about the 10 minute mark the ritual percussive elements fall away into a cavernous death industrial territory, complete with bass loaded synth drones and the sporadic wailing of a horn that build to occasional tonal crescendos. For the final 10 minute stretch the track moves towards slightly noisier territory, with metallic scraping textures and animated vocal / horn wails, whilst some forceful percussive ritualistic elements are resurrected late in the piece.

Noting there is a general looseness to the way to the track plays out, this possibly alludes to a semi improvised live context during which this material might have been recorded. With that said *Likboden* is not without focus and structure, as clearly the duo of Poena know what they are doing given the degree of restraint displayed in the way abstract material such as this unfolds. Certainly the chosen recording location is also clearly reflected in the distant cavernous sound production which has been captured. With pro-printed tape and cover, everything from the sound to visual design, reeks of old school ritual industrial, done in the best way possible.

RJF – *Greater Success in Apprehension & Convictions* CD Segerhuva 2008
Blood Ov Thee Christ – *Master Control* CD Sergerhuva 2005

These two older releases were both issued by the now defunct Swedish Sergerhuva label, but given they are both representative of the mid 1980's Swedish industrial underground they are reviewed together to provide a quick history lesson.

First up is RJF (being the earlier of the two projects), with the album being a re-release of their only album from 1983 (issued in a run of 300 LP's). Lo-fi experimental electronic minimalism is what we have here, being built on somewhat simplistic elements - yet simplicity is used to utmost effect. *Maximum Pain* introduces the album with a singular burrowing mid-range analogue texture, overlaid with distant agonised vocal screams. However the next track *Jugend Dance* is totally different with its use of sparse squelching noise and a minimalist programmed beat which clearly holds an 'eighties' sound to the production. Alternately a drugged haze permeates the tone of *Minimal Brain Function*, which is composed with spare programmed beats, sustained distortion and monotone spoken vocals. Likewise late album track *No Room* does away with any programmed beat elements, instead opting for a more urgent noise pulse, oscillating noise and garbled vocals. The sound is clinical and morbid in the best way possible, with this atmosphere continuing into the final album cut *Zuweiderandlungen* which is built on a mechanical beat, noise and screamed vocals.

Noting the 'eighties' sound of the beat programming on various RJF tracks, it is interesting to note that it is exactly this is a type of approach that would be later honed by the German scene and in particular Haus Arafna. Yet closer to home the RJF's sound was also clearly an influence other early Swedish industrial acts such as Lille Roger. The A5 booklet cover also includes an article written by current Swedish scene stalwart Kristian Olsson to provide some very useful background context to the group.

The later of the two projects reviewed here is Blood Of Thee Christ, which although commenced only a few years later than RJF is all the more heavy and harsh for it. *Master Control* constitutes a re-release of their debut tape of the same name, issued originally in 1987 and containing material spanning 1984 to 1987. The full contents of the original tape are re-issued here, along with a bonus track dating from 1988.
The title track is up first and an absolute monster 45 minute piece - although given the track has a silent break in the middle this is perhaps indicative of the two side of the original cassette. Here we have a heavy slab of industrial noise with oscillating harsh frequencies, crumbling seething noise and occasional aggressive distorted vocals. With the length of the composition and its heavily free-form sound it projects a loose and potentially improvised aesthetic. Yet walking the line between controlled and unhinged this is scuzzy, harsh and filthy industrial noise at its most depraved. The second track *Pain and Pleasure* is a much shorter piece, being a minimalist piece of pulsating static, made all the more a difficult listen due to the use of sustained and repeated trash film dialogue (which narrate confessions being extracted by torture). At only four minutes and 44 seconds *Exzesse* is a focused yet chaotic maelstrom of harsh controlled distortion. As for the final of the four albums tracks, *Forced Entry* seems to focus and distil the most dynamic elements from the title track into a solid and brutal piece, which in a contemporary scene context could be compared to the most chaotic material produced by Deathkey – yet this was recorded in 1988!
Given that both projects and albums date from the mid 1980's, they each illustrate a clear difference and diversity of sound. This can obviously explained by the fact that at the time genre 'rules' had not yet been established, meaning both albums can be broadly filed under power electronics, industrial and noise, despite sounding nothing alike. In a final compassion between the two projects, today RJF sounds somewhat simplistic and 'old school' due to the production and programmed elements, while Blood Ov Thee Christ has aged a little more gracefully. Possibly benefiting from a loud and crunchy remastering treatment, *Master Control* is less easily pigeon-holed in a 1980's frame and can certainly stand up against current scene material.
With the slew of continual releases being issues year upon year, sometimes it is refreshing to look backwards and discover some hidden gems from the murky past. As such Sergerhuva should be commended for digging up these obscure items and furnishing them with a proper re-release.

Sphare Seches – *Tiefschlaf* CD Malignant Records 2012

Sphare Seches are a drone ambient duo, consisting of Martin Sturtzer of another Malignant Records project Phelios, who has teamed up with another individual Christian Stritzel. From the outset the back story of this particular album provides a pretty significant indication of what to expect herein, as *Tiefschlaf* is a live recording from a 'sleep-concert' held in Germany in September, 2011. So when taking such a concert format in mind, it is quite reasonably to expect calm uninterrupted ambient drones which seek to lull the listener into meditative or dreamlike states.
Although containing six untitled 'phases', these interlink into a singular 55 minute musical piece which reveals calm, slowly evolving abstract ambience, which skirts the edges of darker soundscapes and sonic terrains. Noting the sparseness of the compositions the overarching aesthetic is one which ebbs towards isolationist ambient spheres and maybe a reasonable comparison would be a slightly more animated and less cold and bleak version of Thomas Koner. Also whilst a lot dark ambient material seems to evoke a perception of vertical depth, here *Tiefschlaf* contains a similar tonal depth but instead sonically articulates a wide screen and infinite horizon type of ambience.
By now it should be pretty clear of whether this is material to your interest and if so this will provide a suitably engaging listen. Great stuff.

Theologian – *The Chasms Of My Heart* CD Crucial Blast 2012

The ever productive Lee M. Bartow (formerly of the defunct Navicon Torture Technologies aka NTT and now of Theologian), returns with his formal sophomore album – although numerous cassettes, CDr's and digital only releases have been issued in-between this and the 2010 debut *The Further I Get From Your Star, The Less Light I Feel On My Face* (also released on Crucial Blast).

Anyone familiar with Lee's work to date will be aware of a particular hallmark sound: one which has linage extending back to NTT and now further refined in a less harsh but more bleak and expansive guise as Theologian. That recognisable sound is obviously on display here, consisting of heavily layered distortion, cyclic drones and orchestral synth textures which are produced as a singular echoed mass of sound, further punctuated by heavy programmed percussion and smatterings of vocals (both choir sampled and semi sung / semi aggressive power electronics type). Armed with these elements Theologian ultimately delivers grim, pitch black, sweeping soundscapes which blur the boundaries between dark ambient, death industrial and heavy / power electronics genres. With slow pounding beat, wavering drone and maudlin synth melody, *Abandon All Hope* sets the scene, yet still managed to surprise with the introduction of vocals and clean sung vocals at that. The slightly echoed treated multi-tracked vocals are certainly unexpected, but also work amazingly well to provide a new aspect to Theologian's sound. However after the relative calm of the first two tracks *My Body Is Made Of Ash...I Live As Ash* steps up in intensity – here evoking a seething mass death industrial emanations, including slightly Asiatic toned percussion and scorching / distorted vocals. *We Can't All Be Victims* is similarly intense, with its forceful and urgent tribal industrial percussion, sweeping layered drones and quasi choral vocals.

Apart from the prominent droning and sweeping noise / ambient framework, a number of the tracks contain the faint ghosts of a more rhythmic electronica / IDM sound*, evidenced by subtle programmed elements and / or rhythmic beat sequencing. But don't let this throw you – the sound is still staunchly within the death industrial / heavily electronics genres.

In the most part the eight tracks bleed out over an extend length, generating a total album play time of a whopping 79 minutes. Although all tracks have slight variations on the core aspects of Theologian's sound, *The Chasms Of My Heart* is best taken as a singular harrowing listening experience, rather than 'enjoyed' as single tracks. Visually the six panel oversized digi-pack cover is splendidly designed, displaying the trademark graphic style of Lee, being is suitable visual counterpart to the sonic bleakness within.

* – Referencing such rhythmic electronica / IDM elements found here, these play a more centrally dominant role on another just issued Theologian album, *Finding Comfort In Overwhelming Negativity*, also released in 2012 by Handmade Birds.

Trepaneringsritualen – *Deathward, to the Womb* 10"EP Release the Bats 2012

Seemingly appearing out of nowhere Trepaneringsritualen, aka T × R × P, have certainly been turning heads of late. Armed with what appears to be a master's degree in the study of a Scandinavian death industrial and German heavy electronics, T × R × P produce a sound that acknowledges its heritage and at the same time stamps a trademark of its own.

With an echoed, distant and slow bass driven sound, *The Birth of Babalon* commences proceedings, complete with muffled rambling vocals (or sample perhaps?). Following the ritualistic tones and drugged miasma of the title track, it shifts into a queasy bass lurching rhythm on *Osiris, Slain and Risen*, which is complimented with chanted / yelled caustic vocals. On the flip side *She is Flame of Life* has slightly move movement in tone its pulsing / wavering layers – again with the garbled vocal effects. Final track *All Hail the Black Flame* pushes things up a notch to a rhythmic pounding death industrial beat and screeched vocal delivery – a fantastic ending to a far too short of a release.

BROTHER
BETRAYER

Apart from this vinyl T × R × P also have four cassette releases out, which is rather frustrating as I tend to be a vinyl and not cassette junkie (…despite growing up in the 'cassette age' I can't say that the format holds much aura for me). However based on the sheer quality of this item I think I will need to bite the bullet and track the cassettes down (…or heres for a suggestion – is there a label willing to see if T × R × P are interested in doing a compilation of the cassette tracks on vinyl?! Now that would be a grand idea!). Noting that Release the Bats have folded as a record label and that this is DEFINITELY worth owning, any remaining copies of this should be hunted down as a matter of priority. Totally worth the time, effort and dollars.

Trepaneringsritualen – *Roi Perdu* MC Black Horizons 2012

Not a new release from T × R × P, rather a repress of an earlier 2010 tape, with this new edition limited to 150. Here the packaging is beautifully presented, including gold print on iron black card stock for the inner J card and jet black casing with metallic printed stickers for the cassette.

Less harsh than the recent 10"EP, this MC focuses on more ritualised ambient fields for its atmospheric and archaic analogue sounds. This alternate sound approach is immediately evident on the first track *De La Mer* with its slow ritual percussion, wavering wood wind instrument and great croaked and slightly distortion treated vocals. Moving onto the second track *Le Seul Vrai Roi* seeks a more ominous path of sustained drones and vocals distorted to the point that they become yet another sound element within the soundscape. On side two *Champ Sacre*, toys with the similar sound elements of synth layers and ritualised chimes, but the percussive pounding elements engender a more classic death industrial tone, again with the screech / distorted vocals which are very much a trademark of T × R × P's sound. This track bleeds into the final of the four tracks *Decoupage De L'Orme* which strips away the percussive elements to reveal a sparse windswept soundscape with field recordings of a burning fire, distant agonised screams (…heretics being burnt at the stake perhaps?) and vocals of the deep 'demonic growling' variety. Although a short tape, a very strong occult vibe permeates all facets of this release and demonstrates a very strong a focused approach of the artist, where clearly T × R × P deserves all the accolades coming their way of late.

Trepaneringsritualen - *Ritualer, Blot & Botgöring* LP Strömkarlen / Verlautbarung 2012

Although not constituting a new album from T × R × P, this is a welcomed vinyl reissue of their debut cassette from 2008. As the tape was issued in an almost unobtainable run of 75 copies it is a positive to be given the opportunity to obtain an insight into the early works of this project via this re-release.

From the commencement of the first track it is clearly evident that the sound of *Ritualer, Blot & Botgöring* differs from the more composed and occult / ritualised sound of recent material. Rather the sound presented here is of the lo-fi murky death industrial type, which draws parallels and comparisons with the more ambient works of Brighter Death Now. As such the prevalent atmosphere could be hyperbolically described as *'the creeping dread of the unknown'*, or *'the rising horror of what might be lurking in the basement'*.

Bloodletting Ritual opens the album and delivers a cavernous echoed undercurrent offset with gritty, lo-fi grinding textures. *Black Heaven / White Hell* follows with a sporadic knocking percussive element coupled with mid to high pitched noise squeals, before settling into a grinding bass loaded furrow (...the track bleeding out over an extended 13+ minutes). *Knife Play* opens the second side and is slightly more animated with its bass percussive pulse again being partially buried by echoed lo-fi muck, before falling away into a muffled ambient segment with occasional rasping vocalisations. Alternately *Bestraffning & Beloning* is one of the more composed tracks of the album, with a slow pounding beat and oscillating noise frequencies providing the death industrial rhythm, and is one of the main contenders for the aforementioned Brighter Death Now compassion.

With the overall presentation, the design of the predominantly black LP sleeve is simple and classy, adorned with images of trephination (both medieval woodcuts and photographic examples). Noting that this was issued with a print run of a mere 250 it is anticipated that copies won't hang around for too long.

Trepaneringsritualen – *Judas Goat* 7"EP Fang Bomb 2013

With reference to the recent T × R × P re-releases, *Judas Goat* thankfully represents some bona fide new material. Here the two tracks are presented as a double A sided single, which both demonstrate a more streamlined ritual industrial and somewhat 'song' based approach.

Judas Goat leads of the first side of the vinyl and is a beast of a track, where its construction relies on cyclic intertwining rhythmic elements. Muffled drums and corrosive garbled vocals introduce the track, yet these elements remain fairly subdued and sit within the background. These base elements are then complimented by stilted and jittery rhythmic elements which burst forth at cyclic intervals throughout the track and are duly accompanied by seething vocals yelling the repeated lyrics of: *"My Brother. Betrayer. Your blood on my hands. I claim your death. I claim your death. I claim your death in my name"*. In a word: superb.

On the flip side *Didymus Christ* is less complex, built on fast paced tribal percussion, various fractured sonic elements and again the use of prominent vocals. Due to its central driving beat *Didymus Christ* evokes a trance-inducing aura and as a consequence is entirely different from the focused force of *Judas Goat*.

As with other T × R × P's output the productions is murky and ash black, which suits the material perfectly. White vinyl and a black and white, double sided fold out cover rounds out this collectable release, issued in and edition of a mere 141 copies (141 = I-4-I = eye for eye?). Regardless of any symbolic context of its edition *Judas Goat* delivers a powerful but all too short 7" worth of new material.

Triangular Ascension - *Leviathan Device* CD Cyclic Law 2011

The Canadian label Cyclic Law has over the course of the last ten years slowly raised their profile to that of a leading light within the broad fields of dark ambient music. During this process they have released established acts, built the profile of younger ones and launched the careers of others. Triangular Ascension, a Venezuelan dark ambient project, is one such act that Cyclic Law have recently launched but I have only just picked up on. However from a cursory listen it is absolutely clear as to why Cyclic Law signed Triangular Ascension to release *Leviathan Device* as their debut (which I understand was submitted to the label as a demo).

Having listened to a substantial number of dark ambient albums over the past 17 years, there are few albums which have an immediacy such as this, i.e: being able to launch themselves into your psyche from the first listen and also to reveal new sonic elements on subsequent listens. In general terms *Leviathan Device* inhabits sweeping dark ambient territory, but rather than being murky and shadowed in scope, this is multi-leveled in its sonic clarity. The tonal qualities include deep and stormy bass drones, galactic fog horns, melodic wailing textures, subtle rhythmic / percussive elements and detailed textural noise at the higher ends. In this regard the sound production is immaculate, achieving a crystalline sound where all elements are balanced and audible within the mix. Yet rather than being floating, abstract and passive like many dark ambient acts, *Leviathan Device* is an active and engaging listening experience. Here a subtle rhythm undercurrent and cinematic quasi-orchestral melodies constitutes the engine which drives the overarching atmosphere of the album and provides a central focus throughout. There is also a significant degree of variation between the nine album tracks which interlink over an hour playtime. Some tracks are subdued, others forceful, but always the flow between pieces is impeccable, again raising the cinematic scope of the material. Also whilst being clearly within a dark ambient style,

this is not all doom and gloom as the use of slow droning melodic elements evokes a contemplative tone than anything particularly depressive.
Even if dark ambient fare is only of passing interest to you, do not ignore this act. Triangular Ascension deliver meticulously detailed and animated dark ambience of the highest calibre, which highlights the pure folly on my part for not checking them out sooner.

Various Artists - *Epicurean Escapism* MC / DVDr 2012 The Epicurean / Silken Tofu
Not a typical compilation in the traditional sense, here we have a multi-media document that was issued as a companion release for a live festival of the same name (held in Berlin on 7th of July 2012). This release features all artists who performed live, including: IRM, Krank, Anemone Tube, Jarl, Human Larvae, as well as further contributions from Dissecting Table and Martin Bladh (who both presented video screenings at the festival). Although festival compilations can often be somewhat uninspired, *Epicurean Escapism* avoids this pitfall in term of both the artistic contributions and the packaging and presentation (silver bubble wrap pocket sleeve and pro-duplicated tape).
Krank (an old resurrected project of John Murphy) is first up, presenting a dose of ritual industrial sounds - multi-tracked vocals and myriad on tonal textures are the order the day here. Anemone Tube follow with a remixed track from the excellent *Dream Landscape* album, presenting a multi-dimensional dark ambient track constructed field recording and droning synth textures - great stuff as expected. The next track is a devastating live attack from IRM, here presenting the title track from their last album *Order4*. Built on a base of heavy droning distortion and crumbling static Martin Bladh's vocals suitably unhinged, sounding if he is pushing himself to an absolute point of collapse. Jarl rounds out the first side of the tape and present an animated yet meditative ambient track consisting of a multitude of clinical throbs and pulsing elements, and a looped bass line that is quite reminiscent of early Deutsch Nepal.
Flipping over to side two Human Larvae present two short tracks in quick succession. The first is a layered dark ambient / industrial track with an ominous droning atmosphere, whilst the second drives a more static riddled power electronics tone including obligatory yelled / distorted vocals. As my first introduction to Human Larvae both are solid and enjoyable tracks in their given styles. Dissecting Table follows whose track is the longest of the compilation, but from my perspective is the weakest (…but to qualify this view I have never been a huge fan). The track presented here is free-form noisy industrial, with cascading waves of distortion and heavy dose of digital clatter, rounded out with aggressive processed vocals in the dying minutes. Anemone Tube return to conclude the music part of the release with a calm and melancholic track, built on a dour synth line and 'composed' field recording elements – again an excellent contribution.
In addition to the music, a short art film by Martin Bladh is presented entitled *Pig and Tomboy*. Experimental filmmaking in its styling, the short video juxtaposes visual cuts ups of various disturbing scenes being acted out (...Martin Bladh and an accomplice in a pig mask). These images play out seemingly in response to an audio collage of interview dialogue which has been collated and contributed by Peter Sotos (...dealing with a girl's decent into drug use, prostitution and subsequent death by unknown means). Interestingly in some sections the footage is filmed via the reflection of a mirror, where the tripod camera that has captured the scene is clearly visible in frame, which raises questions of whether the audience is a mere passive viewer, or perhaps an active voyeur just out of frame. The video certainly warrants more analysis and dissection than can be provided here, but it is uncompromisingly executed by Martin Bladh, which should be no surprise at this point given his artistic endeavours to date.
From packing to the multiple formats of contributed material, it provides *Epicurean Escapism* with a clear point of difference from the more 'standard' approach to a festival oriented compilation. Yes this is ludicrously limited at 100 copies, but worthy of investigation all the same.

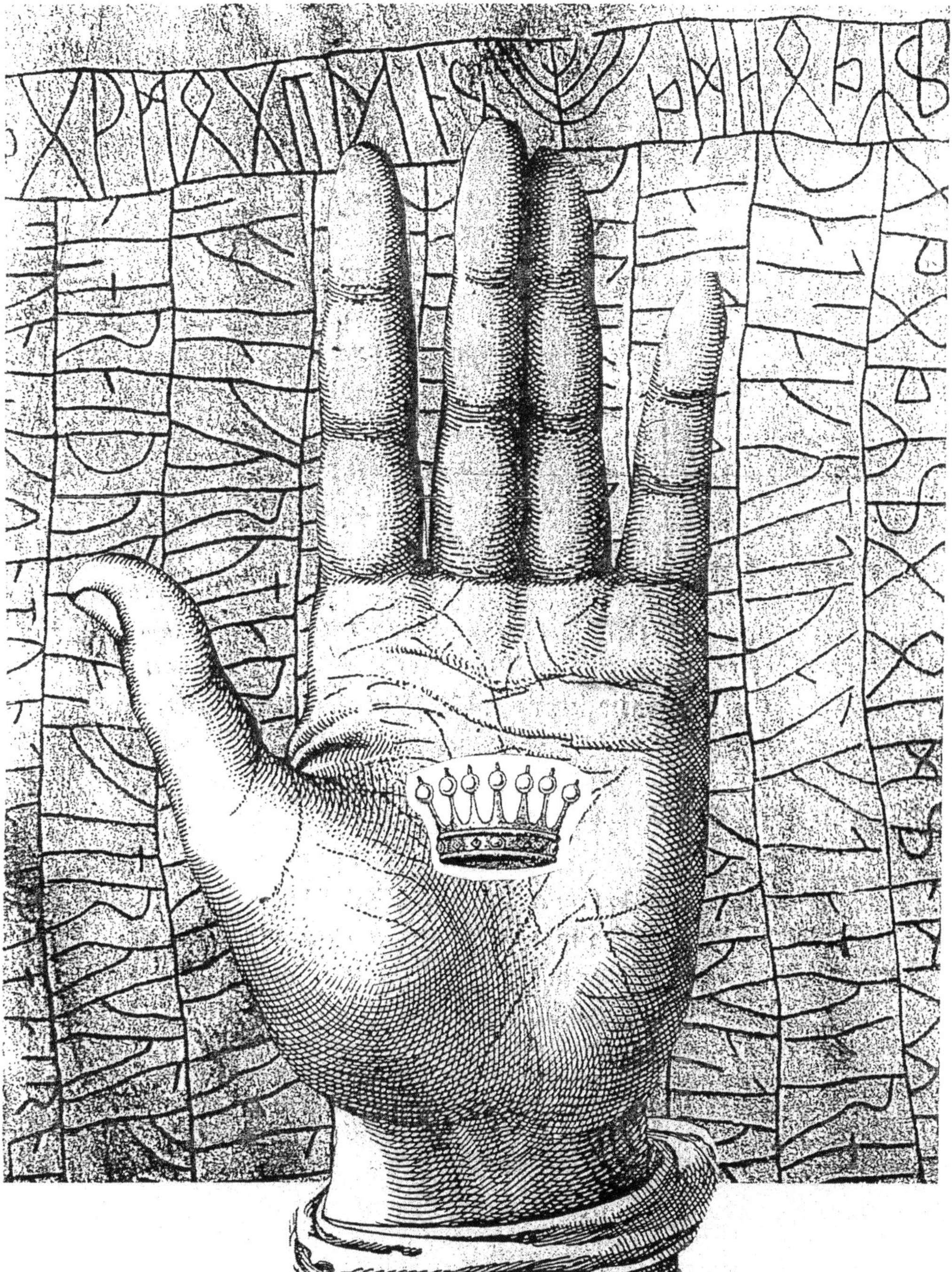

The Vomit Arsonist – *Go Without* CD
Assembly of Hatred CD 2012

Noting that The Vomit Arsonist labels their own sound with the descriptive tags of death industrial and power electronics, I must admit this is pretty much spot on the money. However, rather than having separate tracks in these two styles, their sound seeks to blur the line, constituting a careful blending of the two - i.e. merging the ominous factory rhythms, echoed warehouse atmospheres and bass pounding tone of death industrial, mixed with the harsher, distorted vocals and junk metal sound of power electronics. Likewise across the seven tracks and 45 minutes, a broad consistency to the sound is evident. Thus depending on the piece, the various tonal aspects include: stalking synth lines, metallic percussive / scraping sounds, mechanised factory conveyer belt type rhythms, which are further complimented by harsh distorted vocals. Finally these various sound elements have then been treated with a cavernous, rumbling, echoed and bass driven production. For sake of comparisons, The Vomit Arsonist shares a certain linage to the sound of other US based projects, with elements of Steel Hook Prothesis, Navicon Torture Technologies and Nyodene D all coming to mind. Thematically the cover art alludes to disturbed mental states and a dependency on prescription medication, and whilst the vocals are rendered indecipherable through the yelled / distortion treatment, the song titles only serve to emphasise themes of self loathing and negativity (i.e. titles like *where there is none one else to blame, I must blame myself*). These predominant themes of *Go Without* are further embedded through the use of vocals samples, where *Anhedonia* includes a vocal sample which seems to reference drug addiction / dependency, whilst *The Futility of Life* contains another great vocal sample focusing specifically on nihilism. So whilst *Go Without* does not break the mould, The Vomit Arsonist instead has focused on clearly understanding the core elements of the death industrial / power electronics to deliver a strong, focused and forceful album. With this agenda in mind, *Go Without* absolutely delivers the goods.

Xiphoid Dementia – *Secular Hymns* CD
Malignant Records 2012

Xiphoid Dementia have been around for quite a few years it seems (…since 1999 accordingly to the promo blurb), yet this is my first introduction to the solo project of Egan Budd. *Secular Hymns* is evidently his second official album, yet based on the myriad of tonal aspects covered herein I am finding it rather difficult to pin down some words to describe it. This comment however is not intended as a negative, as by ignoring genre 'rules' Xiphoid Dementia have effectively turned any preconceived expectations I might have had on their head and produced a complex and striking album in the process. Likewise with the varied and multi-faceted sound of each composition which runs the gamut of multiple genres, it is akin to having multiple tracks within the lager compositional structure. On the other hand to provide an overly clinical description, *Secular Hymns* blends aspects of noise, industrial, dark ambient and power electronics across four tracks of extended length (10-14 minutes each). Although the album commences calmly, the droning melodies and choir vocals of *Abortion Rites*, are soon enveloped by harsh, blasting, free-form noise (…let's call this a positive pairing of dark ambient and industrial noise). Yet the opening track does not remain solely in a noise guise, instead edges into a loose power electronics arrangement complete with heavily treated vocals. Within its roughly hewn industrial soundscape the second composition *My Time Will Never Come* presents a vague tribal / experimental character, which mid track falls away into a section of meditative synth melodies and further punctuated by metallic echoes and the tolling of a lone church bell. In a further display of the album's bipolar tendencies, *What We Believe* heads off on a totally different tangent, starting as a loosely structured experimental / ambient track, gradually building into a harder edged industrial noise and pulsing power electronics piece. Likewise based on its harsh overloaded bass / noise production and further use of sampled dialogue, this track is not too far from the lauded sound of Propergol. For the final of the four tracks *Breathe* commences as a slab of droning, viscous dark ambience that gradually morphs towards death industrial aura through the introduction of sporadic jagged tonal aspects catatonic bass heavy beat and distortion scarred vocals, making this track a focused and passionate ending to a solid album. With the variation in sound and strong disregard for established genre boundaries, this attitude (along with a few of the calmer dark ambient moments), brings to mind the early works of BJ Nilsen (aka the final Morthound album T*he Goddess Who Could Make The Ugly World Beautiful*, and to a lesser degree the first Hazard album *Lech*), which is high praise from my perspective. Likewise with its varied and complex scope and the finesse and confidence in which the material is delivered, Xiphoid Dementia is yet another excellent addition to the Malignant Records roster.

discretionary

terms for potential submission of material

Noise Receptor Journal is a personal endeavour where the majority of items reviewed have been sourced from my personal collection. Accordingly I don't have any sort of hidden agenda of using this as a means to getting as many free releases as possible. If nothing else, it constitutes a creative outlet where I can promote material I feel is worthy of support and added exposure. As such I am not interested in allowing unsolicited material to be submitted for review. I personally buy enough music to keep me very busy with music listening, and the last thing I need is to wade through bundles of material I don't have any passion or connection with. I am also not interested in fulfilling some sort of 'scene documenter' role, in trying to review every single new release which comes out. Quality over quantity I say!

Noting that I am not actively seeking submission of material to review, there may be circumstances where I accept some items, provided the following terms are agreeable:

- I will only review material that has been furnished with a physical release.
- The release must be current and have reasonable availability (i.e. not be limited to a stupidly low number).
- The genre of the music must be suitably aligned to the types of items reviewed herein.
- I will review CDs and vinyls (and perhaps tapes – depending on the release).
- If a release is produced on multiple formats, my preference is as follows: vinyls first, then CDs, followed lastly by tapes.
- I will generally not review CDr's (too often this is indicative of a hastily produced and/ or derivative type release) .
- I do not review digital releases or accept MP3's, download links / files etc as a substitute for a copy of the actual release.
- If I do accept the submission of a release for review, a full and complete copy of the physical release must be provided. Any promo versions, or versions stamped 'promo', 'sample', or with corners cut off, holes punched in covers or other markings to indicate its 'promo' status, will not be reviewed.
- To reduce postage cost, sending CD's (including front / back covers) without the jewel cases is acceptable.
- Any items submitted will not be returned.
- I am not interested in reviewing hastily thrown together releases, with little care of quality, aesthetic and design.
- I am not interested in reviewing second rate and / or derivative releases – again quality over quantity. Before you seek to have an item reviewed, undertake a detailed assessment of your own work and make an honest judgement of how it stacks up against other 'pinnacle' works. If in your heart of hearts you feel that your material is second rate, or pales in compassion to comparative material – it is probably true – in which case I am not interested in reviewing it.

If the above terms are not agreeable that is quite fine by me. I will happily continue buying releases and reviewing the ones I feel are worthy, thank you very much! Life is too short to be burdened with listening to and writing about boring, bad, uninspired or derivative music. This is a passion – not a job!

If you have got this far and are still interested in trying to submit an item for review, contact me with a proposal, including relevant details at: noisereceptor@hotmail.com

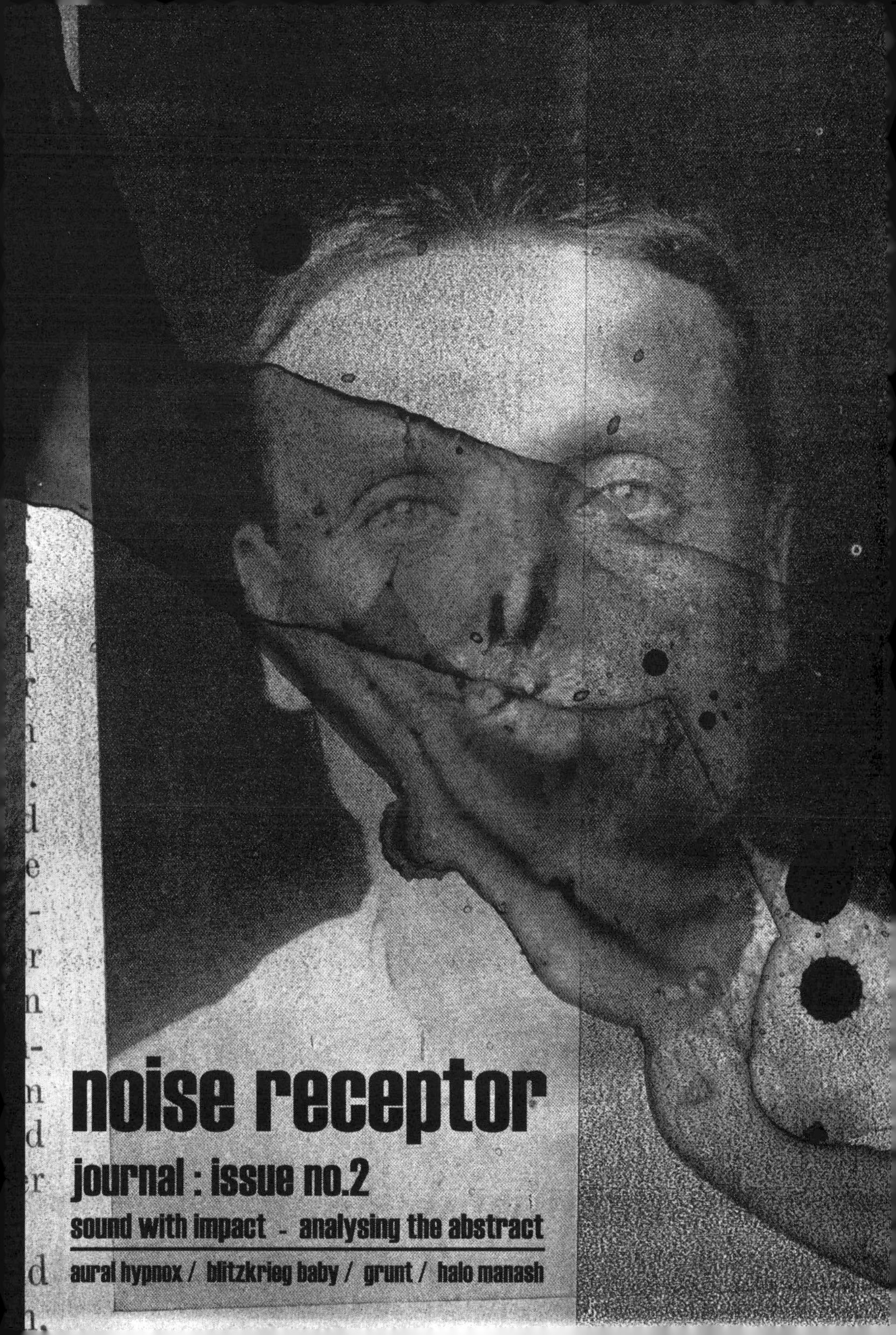
noise receptor
journal : issue no.2
sound with impact - analysing the abstract
aural hypnox / blitzkrieg baby / grunt / halo manash

coil / nine inch nails: recoiled
cd / lp / dl
throne
merzbow vs nordvargr
partikel III
PSYCHIC TV
THEE FABULOUS FEAST OV FLOWERING LIGHT
VA 'THRONE' 2CD SAMPLER
Nice price! 33 tracks
MERZBOW Vs NORDVARGR
Partikel III CD Noise / Electronica
BURIAL HEX
In Psychic Defense CD Horror Electronics
PSYCHIC TV
Thee Fabulous... CD Industrial
Z'EV
A HANDFUL OF ELEMENTS
IFOTS
PSYCHIC TV
HAÇIENDA
SLEEP RESEARCH FACILITY
Stealth 2CD Dark Ambient / Drone
Z'EV
A Handful Of Elements CD Ritual
IRON FIST OF THE SUN
Who Will Help Me... CD Industrial
PSYCHIC TV
Hacienda CD Industrial
SCHLOSS TEGAL
Oranur III "The Third and Final Report"
SCOTT MILLER/LEE CAMFIELD/MERZBOW
NO CLOSURE
TUNNELS OF ĀH
LOST CORRIDORS
PSYCHIC TV
LIVE AT THEE MARQUEE
SCHLOSS TEGAL
Oranur III CD Dark Ambient
S.MILLER / L.CAMFIELD / MERZBOW
No Closure CD Experimental
TUNNELS OF AH
Lost Corridors CD Industrial Esoterica
PSYCHIC TV
Live At Thee Marquee CD Industrial
Troum
syzygie
Mesektet
Wicked King Wicker
TROUM
Syzygie CD Drone / Dark Ambient
MESEKTET
Towards A Black Sun CD Dark Ambient
DEADWOOD
Sheolic CD Black Industrial / Ambient
WICKED KING WICKER
Evolving CD Black Noise / Doom
WWW.COLDSPRING.CO.UK
STORE.COLDSPRING.CO.UK (FREE UK P&P) | FACEBOOK/TWITTER: COLDSPRINGHQ

noise receptor

journal : issue no.2

sound with impact - analysing the abstract **april 2014**

editorial

Welcome to the second installment of *Noise Receptor Journal* which comes a year after the publication of the first issue. As with the first it effectively constitutes the physical manifestation of the *Noise Receptor* website, but also features new interview and art content to differentiate it from the already published web-based reviews.

At the time of its launch, the original intention was for *Noise Receptor Journal* to feature a single long form interview and exclusive art per issue, and whilst Issue No.1 was successful in this regard, I have opted this time around to move more towards a 'typical' 'zine format. By this I mean that Issue No.2 features multiple long form interviews to provide for additional content, rather than just a single interview, artwork and a bunch of reviews. Advertising space also provides a platform to promote relevant underground labels and to help offset printing costs, increase print run and reduce cover price. Hopefully a positive situation for all involved.

For this issue I have enlisted the formidable artistic talents of Kim Solve and even if you do not know that name, surely you will recognise his work from the covers of many underground albums. In fact Kim originally approached me with an offer to provide exclusive art - and for this I am grateful as I would not have thought him to be interested in such a small scale publication as this! Likewise, this initial approach led to me being introduced to Kim's musical project Blitzkrieg Baby and onward to the interview featured herein. There is probably not much else to say other than a huge 'thank you' to: Kim for his original artwork (as well as the Blitzkrieg Baby interview), and Mikko Aspa of Grunt; Antti Haapapuro & Jaakko Padatsu of Halo Manash/ Aural Hypnox for their detailed and long form interview contributions.

Lastly a 'thank you' to you the reader for picking up a copy and hopefully you enjoy the revised direction of *Noise Receptor Journal.*

Richard Stevenson / *Noise Receptor Journal*

access

noisereceptor.wordpress.com
noisereceptor.bigcartel.com
noisereceptor@hotmail.com
follow *Noise Receptor* on facebook
spectrummagarchive.wordpress.com

credits

editor, interviewer, reviewer and layout: Richard Stevenson
cover image and all artwork contributions: Kim Solve
image credits: Grunt live photos (in order): Karolina Urbaniak, Maija Lahtinen and Eric Byrne. Blitzkrieg Baby, Aural Hypnox, Halo Manash images courtesy of the artists.

contents

BLITZKRIEG BABY

Although Blitzkrieg Baby might appear to be a new project, in fact main member Kim Solve has been privately active under this moniker since 2001 and only recently deciding to unleash his twisted version of industrial music on an unsuspecting underground. Likewise, by taking a varied and creative approach to the broad 'industrial' genre, whilst paying scant regard for sub-genre boundaries and rules, Blitzkrieg Baby has garnered a high degree of positive praise in a short space of time. Following below Kim expands on many of his creative pursuits, both related to and outside of Blitzkrieg Baby.

Would you care to introduce the project, its origins, general focus and direction?
Blitzkrieg Baby was founded by me in 2001, and is defined by its outlook on life. Musical approach and process, mindset, and sources are more important to what constitutes a Blitzkrieg Baby track than more than purely musical references.
More superficially, the musical origins stem from me discovering Industrial music in the early nineties. That was a time in my life when I started seriously investigating everything that was experimental, dark, and seemingly (hopefully) dangerous. Deeper down, and more importantly, it stems from me being a frustrated part of human existence and needing to ventilate and filter my frustration through something.

Noting that Blitzkrieg Baby was established in 2001 as predominately a solo endeavour (with occasional collaborative assistance and input), the debut album was not released until 2013. What were the reasons for this large gap of time?
I made the music by and for myself. Instead of finishing and releasing it upon my fellow humans like most people do, I just went along with my inspirations and made more of it instead; keeping it all stored and shackled in the dark of my studio. But I came to realize that the music of Blitzkrieg Baby is like a tumor, it starts out all petite and cute, and might even seem benign until it grows into a screaming, rabid, caged disease I have to release to get rid of. So there you go. The first album was *Porcus Norvegicus* on Neuropa, and the second release was the recent *Kids' World EP* on Beläten in February.

I understand that you have taken you moniker from a 1940's song *Blitzkrieg Baby (You Can't Bomb Me)* by Una Mae Carlisle. Would you care to explain how you were originally introduced to this song, what attracted you to it and why this resonated with you to take this title for your project?
I am fond of music, style, and productions from that era. And it's a catchy tune. Unfortunately I don't remember where I heard it first, but it was some time during the nineties.
The war theme was appropriate at the time, and will be as long as humans exist. At the time of choosing the name, Blitzkrieg Baby was not much more than a pig-nosed embryo, but the name still fits to this day. I am of course aware that the meaning behind the original lyrics is different from how I use them in the name, but that is in Blitzkrieg Baby's nature: to twist, distort, steal, tear down, strip, ridicule, pervert, and inseminate.

You also seem to use the expanded project name of *Blitzkrieg Baby And The Squealing Piglet Ensemble*. Can you please explain its use and relevance?
I work on the music with different people, and giving the different constellations of people different names is something I do partly for the sake of my own entertainment, partly because the names are made according to the main concept or theme on each release, like a secondary band name. In the end it is still Blitzkrieg Baby.

***Porcus Norvegicus* is your debut album which was released in 2013, although I understand the production of the album was many years in the making. Would you care to explain the process of recording? What has the reception been like since its release?**
Porcus Norvegicus has been met with overwhelming response from pretty much everyone I have heard from. The reviews have mostly been great too, and beyond my expectations. Blitzkrieg Baby is the musical equivalent of a collage of tabloid newspaper clippings, psychiatric reports, bogus love letters, suicide notes, death threats, crossed out family photos, pornography, television commercials, slaughter tutorials, pop culture, eighties B-movies, BDSM, war propaganda, reality shows, cartoons and everything in between. All filtered through our minds and built into one body that is then properly fucked and let loose upon the world. I play, record, collaborate, steal, desecrate and slice apart whatever I feel like to put it together again in the name of Blitzkrieg Baby. If it puts a wicked smile on my face, it is done. As long as the result feels like Blitzkrieg Baby, it is Blitzkrieg Baby.

Clearly Blitzkrieg Baby's sound is driven by a varied approach which can be broadly categorised under the 'industrial' banner, which includes dark ambient / orchestral / martial elements. Can you discuss your approach to what makes up Blitzkrieg Baby's sound? What would your acknowledge as critical influences?
Early Laibach, NON/Boyd Rice, Coil, Swans, and Cold Meat Industries are early and formative influences that somehow still breathes within what I do. Honestly, I don't feel we are doing much that these artists or other early Industrial artists haven't done before in one way or another. The eighties and nineties had much to offer and much of Blitzkrieg Baby's roots are there. I feel that my attitude towards making music is old, I just do whatever feels right, taking no consideration to the sub genre mind slavery. That people consider the music of Blitzkrieg Baby original now is a compliment I appreciate and take to heart, and I am not saying they are wrong, but at the same time it says just as much about the current state of music as it does about Blitzkrieg Baby.
Nowadays the inspiration can be anything and come from anywhere. I am guided more by my own mental state, the creative musical process, gut feeling, and thematic continuity than specific directions in music.

Sonically there seems to be a heavily visual side to your music and almost filmic and soundtrack like, as if to be for scenes of an imaginary movie. As I gather this is an intentional trait to how you compose music, is there a specific approach you employ to writing?
Movies and their soundtracks are an undeniable part of Blitzkrieg Baby. Music stimulates my mind visually and visual art can inspire me to make music. It is all closely tied for me, aesthetics knows no boundaries - it doesn't matter if its visual, words, or sounds. I like albums to be built, and play out, like a movie. It has a narrative, it is an abstract one but still a narrative, it changes during the course of the playing time. A great album is often more than a mere collection of tracks.

To this ear you employ a sly sarcastic tone and aspects of black humour within Blitzkrieg Baby. Would you agree with this assessment and what is the role - if any - of such humour in an often humourless scene?
Sure, I can see where you're coming from. However, it is not something I have decided to do, it just comes naturally to me. When sticking ones head that far down in the stinkhole of human condition it would be pretty damn pathetic if we couldn't have some fun with it at the same time.
To me it doesn't detract from the message, quite the contrary. Blitzkrieg Baby is spitting and kicking in every direction, including inwards. We are no better that others, we are just as worthless as anyone else. Blitzkrieg Baby is stomping my own face into the pavement, which is what I get for giving birth to such a freak creation. Nothing is sacred, everything can be abused.

A lot of people have asked me about the humor, and I often reply with the same words: If someone is smiling while doing something atrocious, does that make him unserious, or his actions a joke? Would you fear him any less? That's how I view Blitzkrieg Baby: a volatile, smiling creature with no regard for anything living or dead.

Within the cover of *Porcus Norvegicus* it contains text which states: *'The need for atrocities is what makes us human'*. Would you care to expand on its meaning, context of use and whether this falls into the sarcastic tone you employ?
Blitzkrieg Baby dives into my nastier sides and resurfaces wearing my dirtiest secrets like a strap-on, ready to rip. Human history is riddled with atrocities. It seems obvious that we crave it. Violence and death is revered and feared. We are not, when everything is summed, sensible creatures. I am not an optimist. What is sarcasm and what is not is really not up to me to decide. It all comes from the same place, it is not that deliberate because I don't differentiate in that way, I simply follow my creative needs and ideas without hesitation.

Following your debut album the next release was the cassette only *Kids' World EP* recently issued on the Swedish label Beläten. Noting the wide variety of styles and sounds released on Beläten to date, how did this release come about?
I have been in contact with Thomas Ekelund of Beläten and Trepaneringsritualen for at least five or six years now. When he started his label, Blitzkrieg Baby was invited to partake on the *A Somatic Response* compilation tape, and from there we decided to do a tape together.

Given that the *Kids' World EP* features half previously unreleased tracks and half previously issued compilation tracks, I gather this is to be considered as an intermediate 'stop gap' release which brings together various Blitzkrieg Baby recordings? What timespan were these tracks recorded over and how did you approach bringing together these different recordings under a single theme, which based on song titles seems to revolve around children?
Childhood is a recurring theme in a lot of my work in general: the so-called innocence, the inherent sadism, the adults of the future. I work with certain themes over long periods of time and often come back to the same themes in everything I do. Blitzkrieg Baby has been in the works for over a decade. The material spans throughout the life of Blitzkrieg Baby. The earliest material dates back to the mid nineties and is made with Anders B. of Mind & Flesh (previously Babyflesh), whom appears on all tracks and is as such also an important factor in tying the tracks together. He has also been co-writing a lot of the upcoming material. I strongly suggest readers of *Noise Receptor* to search for his albums released by Slaughter Productions, Vendlus, and Nuit Et Brouillard.

Noting that much of the material featured on the *Kids' World EP* sits more within a structured 'song based' industrial sound, it therefore differs somewhat from the material of your debut album. Do you consider that the *Kids' World EP* is representative of the future sound and direction of Blitzkrieg Baby?
Both yes and no. Blitzkrieg Baby will continue to evolve in different directions. I have music in the making that differs from anything we have released so far if judged on a more superficial level. Some of it is song based, a lot of it is not. However, I see everything we have done and are about to do as a natural variation upon the same theme.

As song structured vocals also play a prominent part of the material presented on the *Kids' World' EP* (and to a lesser degree on *Porcus Norvegicus),* to my mind it is their use which sets Blitzkrieg Baby apart from the multitude of instrumental based industrial projects. What is your inspiration for making vocals a prominent part of your sound?
Lyrics are something that comes to me whether I like it or not. So making the lyrics a part of my music is a natural thing to do. To get the lyrics across they need to be delivered by someone. Although I still sometimes do the vocals myself a lot of the vocals are being done by Mr. B, who also shares the lyric writing with me. As 'Kids' World' is a testament to, his vocals merge very well with the music and overall attitude of Blitzkrieg Baby.

Noting what I understand was a relatively long gestation period of the debut album, do you have any expectation or self imposed timeline for upcoming releases? What might be on the horizon and what might be expected?
It is safe to say that the bubble has burst and people can expect frequent Blitzkrieg Baby releases from now on. We have pretty much finished recording the second album and time will tell if I manage to get it out in 2014 or not. We have also finished a collaborative album with Corrugator Supercillii, a Belgian project previously known as Camisole. Some other collaborations, singles, and a split is also being discussed. Too early to say what will become of it at this point though.

Your musical works seem to be have spread well beyond the confines of underground music, as I understand you have recently written music for a contemporary ballet. How did this eventuate, what was the collaborative process and have you seen the final production? Were you pleased with the final result and will the music see a formal release?
I have been composing music for modern ballet for over a decade now, mostly in connection with the group Swarms and my solo project K100. This time the choreographer had heard Blitzkrieg Baby material, and wanted that sound and expression. I composed several tracks and together with the choreographer chose the ones that were best. Then I worked them into a whole that would flow well as a continued piece on stage. The music will be spread over upcoming releases, but will not be collected and presented as a release with the original commission in mind.

Noting you are from Norway and given that one of the major 'cultural exports' is black metal, by default Norway is far less recognized for its ambient / industrial / etc output (say when compared to neighboring Sweden). What is the reality of underground Norwegian ambient / industrial scene?
It has been worse than it is now, as it has seemed almost non-existent at times. Grimtown Records is doing a good job of collecting some of the few outsiders on their download compilations from time to time. Trondheim has a small dark ambient scene, some of whom are, or have been, releasing albums through Cyclic Law. Then there is the impressive Where Frost Reign distro / label / press specializing in transgressive literature and music, and the label Records Of The Fleshgod, both of whom are affiliated with an event team whom arranged a show with Trepaneringsritualen, Bizarre Uproar, Shift, and Arkhe here in Oslo in November 2013.

With reference to the black metal scene, what was / is your own involvement - if any - and do you have a view of its current cultural acceptance?
Black Metal was neutered twenty years ago. Not because of cultural acceptance, but because of herd mentality from both

performers and audience.

I was disappointed at the time, but quickly learned that is how it works: everything that seems vital and exiting quickly gains attention, then soon loses momentum and gets watered down. The formative years of any genre are when it appeals the most, perhaps mostly because of naivety and a youthful inability to see the whole picture. To me, any subculture should be a springboard to self-expression and self-awareness, not a mold to further shape and facilitate people's tendency to become (or stay) dead-eyed sheep. That is what I took with me from Black Metal, but I would probably have taken the same attitude with me regardless which scene I had my teenage years in.

None of us can control when and where we are born and what we are able to be a part of. Black Metal in the early nineties was a brief flourish of youthful rebellion and creativity that, due to its dark nature, appealed to me and seemed to be something genuinely exiting. The public acceptance is nothing more than a fancy headstone to the part of the scene that first got me interested in it. What I find more annoying is the train jumpers who believe they are controversial because they use skin-deep imagery from the Black Metal scene for their brand or product or whatever. What a bunch of limp dicks. But I find the orthodox know-it-alls and dogmatic wannabes annoying too. What were we talking about again? Cultural acceptance, yes. It is sometimes annoying, but only because my feelings for the music go back such a long time and to an important part of my formative years.

It is in the hands of others now, and it is treated in the same manner as any former subculture, and is for the most part a laughing matter like most things in life.

However, Black Metal is in my blood, and I have no way of getting rid of it. If I pick up a guitar you can bet your ass I will be regurgitating Black Metal riffs for hours on end. So I will close this rant by saying that I still play in a Black Metal-oriented band called MANIMALISM, which I founded back in 1992 as a wide-eyed fourteen year old exited by what I saw going on around me at the time. Some things cannot be shed.

On a professional level you are a partner in the Trine + Kim Design Studio, which anyone with an eye for design should be well aware of your design work in both underground and overground music scenes. What do you see are the similarities and/ or difference in the creative process between your design and musical work?

To put it simply: the main difference is that with our professional work we use our skills and crafts to create a visual expression on behalf of clients. Even though we invest a lot of ourselves into the work, at the end of the day it is made to fit and represent the artistic expression of someone else, and in the end needs to be shaped to correspond with that. With my music it is all about me, myself and I: no holds barred, no limits, no compromise.

The design aesthetic you bring to many of your album commissions (be it within black metal, industrial and related genres), contain quite a refined graphic design look and feel. How do you approach the design process and what is you impression of presenting a more refined design style and aesthetic in context of genres which during their infancy cover design was predominately rudimentary and DIY in aesthetic?

The process is different every time, except for one thing: the importance of getting under the skin of the individual project. To get to know and feel it, become a part of it, and then combine that with our own input, research, experience and creative need to make something that represents whatever we are working on. It is about searching beneath the surface and making something from what we find and experience.

All art comes from somewhere and has some kind of intent, preferably something personal that transcends pure genre exercises or perhaps something conceptual, although it may be abstract and not easy to put into words. That is what I am interested in: diving into it to find what lies behind a project and giving that a visual representation.

To me, underground mentality is not firstly about being amateurish and thereby perhaps making something average or worse. It is about not compromising, about expressing something without any limitations or without being handicapped by actual limitations, and to do it the best you possibly can with what you have at hand both in terms of talent and equipment. Some people are technically apt and some are not, that is beside the point. Having a talent alone doesn't make you mainstream. One of our approaches was, and still is, to find some kind of essence in each project we work on, and base our design upon that. And honestly, most of the compromises made in Trine's and my design work up through the years comes from the clients and their goals and tastes, not input from Trine or me.

However, at some point it seemed like using us for artwork became the right thing to do, and that made us decide to pull back for a while. I am not interested in being a part of the underground establishment's mindlessness. It is just as media-led, trendy, and thoughtless as any of the mainstream cultures many believe they are opposed to. It left a foul taste in my mouth. Therefore we took a step back and have watched from a certain distance for a while. Anyway, since then we have branched out and most of our work now is for publishing houses, theaters, and other clients within art and culture. To a certain degree we do album covers of course, something we love and will continue to do, but we choose to accept the artwork assignments which are either from decent people, interesting artists, or simply allow us to make something worthwhile. For example, I had a nice time working on the images featured in this issue of your magazine.

Apart from Blitzkrieg Baby you are active with a number of other projects, including K100 (dark ambient), Swarms (dark ambient), Three Winters (experimental synth pop). Would you care to briefly address each of these and any other musical projects you may have?

Blitzkrieg Baby is what I see when my eyes are open. K100 is what I see when I close them. It is just as dark either way, but there is a huge difference between what I observe. When recording for K100 I visit places that have an unreal or dreamlike quality about them. I record the atmosphere, perform and record music or sounds there: abandoned factories, silos, burial grounds, shores, ancient forests, basements, tunnels, whatever catches my attention as a place of intriguing atmosphere. Then I work on the music in the studio by myself for a long time afterwards.
I have been doing this since the nineties, it is like a chemical process, distilling the essence into a place of sound where I can lose myself for a bit. It is an over-used term, but to me there is a ritualistic aspect to this. If I can be said to have a spiritual side, K100 is where it artistically comes to the fore. If I could move into K100 for the remaining days of my life, I would. The result is often but not always mediative, electronic, ambient music. Several tags have been placed on K100, and a lot of the material fits comfortably into what most people now define as Dark Ambient. The first album was released by Neuropa in 2010, and the next album will be out on Cyclic Law some time in 2014, if all goes as planned that is.
Swarms is a group I founded in 1999. We are a strangely weaved group of people with an inner logic and aesthetic that I have a hard time putting into words. Our music ranges from electronic ambient or electro-acoustic, percussion music, cinematic jazz to dissonant rock.
We have composed a lot of music for modern ballet and a few smaller television productions and are working on recording our second album now. Thematically Swarms is a close sibling to K100, whom it also shares a lot of sound sources and recording processes and state of mind. To put it bluntly: where K100 end, Swarms begin.
Since 1992 I have also played and composed in MANIMALISM, the Metal band mentioned earlier on. We will release our first and self-titled album via Adversum during the first half of 2014.
Three Winters make cinematic music inspired by John Carpenter, Fabio Frizzi, Goblin and the likes, performed on vintage synthesizers. Most if the music is initially made by Anders B., and developed and arranged as a trio with him, me, and the religiously gifted Lars Fredrik Frøislie of Tusmørke. Our debut album will be out on Termo Records in 2014.

Final concluding comments?
I trust my ranting to each and every question has covered it all. I am grateful for this opportunity to talk with you and to spread the gospel of Blitzkrieg Baby. Readers can drop by facebook/blitzkriegbabyofficial or trineogkim.no if more information is desired.

grunt

By now the Finland native Mikko Aspa has firmly established and clearly demonstrated his commitment to all forms of extreme underground art. Such activities extend to his many musical projects (ranging from noise, industrial, power electronics, experimental & black metal), as a label boss *(Freak Animal, Northern Heritage, Institute of Paraphilia Studies),* or even as scene commentator and chief editor of *Special Interests Magazine* and associated online forum. However noting that Grunt is one of his oldest musical projects (in operation for two decades already), following below is a detailed and in-depth interview where Mikko reflects on many topics relating to the noise/ industrial/ power electronics activities and focus of Grunt.

Noting Grunt has been in existence for 20 years now, what are your own impressions and appreciation of what Grunt represents and how it has changed and evolved over time?

I have been doing Grunt since I was kid. This means that project has been going basically my entire 'conscious life'. I have seen people come and go, labels come and go, bands come and go.... some eventually come back. Meanwhile I have kept working on this non-stop for 20+ years. There are merely couple years (like 2004 and 2008) when there have not been any physical releases published, but usually recordings and live gigs have taken place. Not to mention works of related side projects. As person who appreciates long term commitment towards things people feel strongly about, I consider this element to be proud of. I always remember old Bananafish magazine where Jojo Hiroshige of Hijokaidan concluded that if he would stop the band now, it wouldn't have been worth to start in first place. He didn't treat it as hobby or part of temporary fad, but integral part of his life.

20 years behind, I feel perhaps even more enthusiasm and inspiration to create. It only conflicts with constantly growing critical evaluation of my own works what sometimes becomes an obstacle. If feeling is a mixture of doing best works I have done, but it doesn't appear to be good enough, what to do next? Most cases I'm very satisfied with unfinished sessions, often captured in raw live-in-studio recording, yet feel it's not enough to constitute material for a 'release'. Yet refining material may result in it losing its edge.

Given that you have addressed a range of 'difficult' subject matter and material over the years, in your own mind is there any easy way to sum up the conceptual focus of Grunt?

Despite radical changes between the mind of teenager and, ehm, grown up man, I think things what sum up Grunt is merely: focus on strong, obsessive interests at the moment of creation. There has not been any strict image. Nor limits in aesthetics, what would limit the project into narrow and calculated form.

This lack of coherent form has most likely been something why especially early Grunt material has never been much of an interest beyond handful of people. Especially power electronics and industrial crowd is drawn towards strict and uniform visual presentation that hammers the impact time after another. While I appreciate such clear and refined forms in some bands and labels, I can't really adjust myself to follow such guidelines of design or direction.

Early years was about filling long length of tape with recordings that had emerged after previous release. Naturally some curating skill was put into selecting material, but one can barely talk about 'making albums'. Shorter tapes and vinyl are perhaps more focused. One can observe development quite easily. From '93 to '96 a lot of youthful teenage rebellion soon mixed with attempts to distance oneself from 'content'. That backfiring and bursting into going all the way into 'hands on' approach with all sorts of things. I recall talking in some interview or correspondence back then about avoiding clichés as pornography in visuals, but what can one do? How long should I avoid the personal interests? It's like attempts to remove 'politics' from music. '93-95 being very raw recordings with great variety of styles from harsh noise to acoustic metal junk, kind of old school power electronics sound to goofy Masonna & Gerogerigege influenced screaming and making racket. And a lot things between '95-97 continued 'noise for sake of noise' approach, overloaded with effects (most of all delay/echo!). Finally '97-98 starting to take move into darker, constructed, rhythmic. And perhaps this Grunt is what most people know. Since then plenty of development in all levels, though.

Grunt often operates on many levels of sound and approaches what are not clear for most, as very few have followed entire output. Most live shows have been dominated by sexual perversions. Most full length albums are political or social matters. Smaller releases something between as well as pure experiments of sound. I think, instead of 'focus', one could perhaps talk lack of it. While clearly most noise simply 'multiplies', sometimes best of it certainly grows and expands.

Even if it happens without a very clear plan. My plans remain semi-unconscious until specific project starts to take shape naturally. First things are just done, and when bigger form becomes visible for its creator, project can be attempted to be finalized into coherent form.

Although working in an 'underground' environment, it is clear that you have elevated your knowledge of sound creation / production / recording to an expert level where every element is treated as an (albeit unconventional) instrument within a compositional framework. This is most clearly evident on your most recent album *World Draped in a Camouflage* which balances noise and chaos with clear direction and within a defined compositional framework. Would you care to provide an overview of this process of building your knowledge and skill? Self-taught I assume?

Beyond regular school music class and couple years of piano lessons as kid, there is no education. I think there can be some advantage is formal education of music, but I feel art education can be also harmful. There is hardly use for know-how, if there is no burning spirit.

I work in different ways. Some work starts from 'sound fishing'. Simply making field recordings or improvised noise sessions, testing specific gear, situation, combinations of all these. If something worthy is captured on recording, it will be saved while worthless moments are rejected. While material that is interesting keeps cumulating, one starts to hear possibilities of combinations and necessities for additional sounds or mixing. Sometimes work has conceptual nature, where due lyrics, theme of album or atmosphere of already existing other tracks guide direction of sounds I need, including specific sound, how it's made or where such sound is found. I like to play with contrasts as well as things removed from their original context. Sonically this is very clear since early days, where ruggedness and noisiness is combined with subtle and calm 'ambient' layers or droning noises broken with screaming vocals. Raw feedback and field recordings combined with structured and composed works.

I feel that quite many, especially 'older artists' and 'real artists', appear very jaded and trapped. Wanting to isolate themselves from rest of creative world, especially if it's near what they are doing, or trying to avoid 'influences'. Or simply not being interested beyond making. I recall some guys conclude, 'I make, I don't listen'. No wonder that perspective can be utterly lost and some old timers churn out awful waste nowadays.

I consider myself first and foremost fanatic observer. Be it voyeurism, collecting things of interest and absorbing creative works of other people. I don't need to expect myself to create any sort of revolutionary innovations, nor sink into sheer plagiarism. I consider process being about living within what has happened and is happening and what will happen. Without need to isolate myself out of it. Not outside or ahead. There are endless amount of possibilities to be explored further.

Of course it may be healthy to remove yourself from unnecessary 'social scene', what can drain life-force from creative impulses.

But as said, isolation can lead into utterly lost perspective. Being self-taught could be the wrong word, as especially nowadays it's very common to discuss matters of body, soul and technology with other creators. Getting and sharing advices, ideas, experiences. It may not be formal education, but I feel many times one can gain plenty of advice from newbies as well as long time active sound creators - even if you have long history behind you already. I think it's crucial for me to go beyond mere sterile sound creation.

It involves physicality, body, action, specific situations and locations. These days, being trapped in a room with computer, shake-box and distortion pedals doesn't work for me. I will use it, just like all means, but there needs to be more. Each album is built over months or years of work. Most of all consisting of brain-work, not merely gear or recording devices.

The track *Dance for the Genocide* off *World Draped in a Camouflage* is intriguing as it utilizes some surprising modern classical elements to underpin the power electronics composition. As you have use such real instrumentation on another of your albums (Alchemy of the 21st Century - *Beauty of Aesthetic Imperfection)*, I was interested to know whether the classical strings and percussion on *Dance for the Genocide* were sampled or specifically composed? Noting this track's divergence from much of Grunt's material, is this at all representative of where you may take your sound in future?

Material is sampled, but method includes cutting parts and re-arranging them to become rhythm of what was wanted. Some may recognize where it is taken from, since it is very famous, well known and released in countless editions. There is intentional multi-layered theme, where references of Stravinsky's *The Rite of Spring* could become obvious from sound and lyrics, while taking the context from pagan Russia and dance to death by sacrificial victim into next level. Dance For The Genocide: "*Humans are taking geometric form, transforming from individual to part of bigger organism*". Besides the sound and lyrics, one could perhaps need to take a look in booklet with collage artwork and additional quotes related to lyrics/music/visual pieces. Of course one can listen it as mere musical piece, but it has more levels than that.

I have used some kind of musical elements since quite early days of Grunt. Not all classical, but guitar melodies, keyboards, piano, violin, cello, etc. Most often these blend together in mix quite smoothly are appear in smaller profile releases that have not gained much attention. Such musical elements are used when it suits the purpose. I don't have any detailed plan about going to specific direction. Only work in order what suits the project that emerges.

On the track *Psychosomatic STD* from your latest album *World Draped In A Camouflage* it raised the interesting concept of an 'idea' or 'thought' being akin to spreading disease or infection. Can you explain its meaning and application further?

Most tracks on the album work on many levels and connected themes and sound. Many fragments meet, 'under camouflage', so to say. While origin of Psychosomatic STD is more of dealing with irrationality, almost mental disturbance level of thinking of having STD - while there is no possibility for getting one. Track can also be expanded wider than Sexually Transmitted Disease. One could consider almost everything what man does, sexually transmitted disease, as for many sexuality remains the most basic urge that directs through life. And this certainly has more mental/emotional side than physical.

Noting the skill and control you display within your sound works, it to this ear at least is blurring the line between low art (meaning 'underground' music scenes) and more academically minded experimental music. Do you personally see Grunt as partially blurring of the line between such spheres? Alternately do you consider that your use and treatment of thematic material to be a barrier for acceptance outside of underground circles, where listeners to academic experimental music may be unaware with the 'difficult' thematic preoccupations of the underground industrial scene?

Perhaps back in the day, there was drastic difference. Times when electronic music equipment was mainly accessible in high class universities. Now people can program their computer music or use vast amount of free software and anyone can buy electronic music hardware easily. Difference of low art and academic appears to be most of all theory and can it be placed within lineage of art music or mere bastard offspring of sub/countercultures that exists outside of institutions. I feel that there is great amount of excellent sound art coming from so called academic circles, done by 'modern composers'. However, many of them appear to be trapped within conventions of 'art music'. Even more so than in so called low arts.

What are your personal opinion of the academic / Wire related experimental music scenes and any parallels displayed with underground music? Also do you feel that there is less respect shown for thematic driven underground music, than more pure academic sound art?

Grunt doesn't have any potential to blur lines in sense of being accepted in field of 'art music'. It does not bother me at all. Plenty of 'home made noise' lives in much more healthier environment. A lot of academic music operates solely within environment created of government grants. Our low arts exist based on its own energy. This energy is able to sustain itself, year after year, decade after decade.

Within so called high arts, legit concert venues, neat professional factory packaging with long artists CV's and liner notes printed on covers, sold in special high profile shop and placed in shelves of libraries, may give unrealistic illusion of higher level.

Still reality appears to be that many concerts and recordings happen solely because of funding. Recently even some higher profile labels have been sending CDR's instead of CD (as they advertised) since there hasn't been market big enough to cover actual CD represses of some of the biggest names in the game. Musical products of 'experimental high arts' collect dust in high priced classical music stores and darkest corner of bigger libraries. Not just my own prejudice, but my impressions after talking with people involved in this. If someone once in a while complains that 'noise is dying', at least it is not dead yet, like vast majority of high art that has needed large scale life-support mechanism already for decades!

This basically raises a question of what respect or attention one needs? If the respect can be only gained by joining the formal world of art institutions, as one of the many career artists, I say no thanks. I'd rather offer them possibility to join 'our thing'! There is very little to be gained in art world that exists in tidy auditoriums, annual process of sending applications, praying to be featured in next uninformed newspaper article, hah... When the spirit of underground finally becomes acceptable for places like this, it has been watered down and distanced enough from its raw virility. Safe enough to be capitalized and for journalists to get credit for 'finding' such obscurities.

Noting your response above, what are your thoughts on the Wire covering and promoting Whitehouse for many years, and during the mid 2000's embarking on a process to hype up 'avant-garde' black metal*, yet effectively ignoring much underground industrial and power electronics? (* - tellingly black metal has seemed to fall out of favor within the Wire in recent years). Do you think the Wire has an agenda or reason for this and do you understand or have an opinion on this type of 'journalism'?

There are two things that amused me quite a lot. One author of magazine had to issue an apology in the following issue of Wire due having one of my metal releases in his playlist, and some readers had been upset about it. Another person who was asked to contribute list of top 10 releases of year, was told he is not allowed to include one specific Freak Animal title in the top list. In such cases, I think it appears that integrity of music magazine is compromised. Wire is music magazine that is interested in new things and perhaps does that very well. I assume journalists do promote something that exists merely in deep underground. However, it is curious that writers are not allowed to speak about best albums they heard, because its content may offend readers or advertisers or staff political sensitivity?

If power electronics qualifies only when it's distanced as nostalgia of teenager years, and if black metal qualifies only when it's removed from black metal culture itself, then fine.

I don't have any issues of Wire magazine, nor I have much possibilities to read it anywhere (distribution in Finland is very small) so it's very rarely I see the magazine.

It has been claimed by commentators for years that 'shock tactics' is now an entirely redundant and played out technique, by virtue of being a well-established genre 'rule' and only used today as a plagiarised pastiche. What are your opinions of controversy and 'shock tactics' in context of underground music, be it in the past, currently and its role into the future?

If it only was this simple. First we should ask, what are 'shock tactics'? And is there other value beyond that? I realize that for some people, throwing swastika or bondage picture in tape cover has no other sense than attempt to shock. But who was shocked? And when was this? And if it was shock tactic - historically there has been a psychological reason for its usage. Second, we should ask, is the world linear in its development? If something has been done, does it become obsolete forever? Even in new era and new context? Thirdly, we could perhaps ask, if there is controversy and shock, was that all? Back to normal then. Are you sure it was enough to give small poke with finger or is there need for collectively generated flood of material and only after constant hammering for decades, we can observe the results?

If people treat 'shock tactics' as their personal novelty show, it might not work out for them. They can yell to artists that give me something new, I'm not amused anymore. Artists can reply, tell me something new Mr. Pavlov's Dog. As every bit you consume triggers expected results, it's a decent reminder, right there as it is.

It is curious to realize that in this day and age, it appears unbelievable that within burning flame of creation, is also born the most obscene, most fanatical as well as most vital results. It remains an extremely curious fact, that so many appear to think, content that bands are presenting could be only some sort of shock tactics to shake people awake, or be exposed to evils of world and sort of feel cathartic relief to return into safety of western liberal hegemony. To treat every so called 'offense' as display of evils and wrongdoings what 'should not be forgotten'. I personally do not believe that. There is some of that too, but there are great deal of artists who deal with their personal interests, personal beliefs, righteous - yet different world views. Alternative lifestyles, political & religious beliefs that are for reason or another considered 'shocking'. It's quite nonsense to expect such people to clean up their 'act' or deliver something fresh and new to you, when their purpose never was to entertain. And even more nonsense would be to claim such content would be blunt shock, when its doors open to a different world. Perhaps a wonderful world beyond programmed illusions.

I believe necessity of negative provocation is gone. I don't see much purpose these days to travel across Europe to make people 'pissed off'. I'm much more firm believe in positive provocation, where it fuels dialogue, research and alternative angles. You could simply call it inspiring energy, as opposed to provocation. Nothing is gained by simply aiming to be hated for simple and obvious reasons. More is to be gained by exposing the bluff of contemporary secular humanism, as one example. Or perhaps selfishly exploring your own sexual interests in form of art, regardless what 'audience' feels about it.

Speaking of potential provocation, in your many years of activity have you / Grunt generated any particular controversy, or been the subject of overt boycotting or censorship attempts?

Not much. I mean, there were concerts being cancelled back in the day. Not anymore, as I tend to know what kind of places do not favor stuff like this. There have been people online calling boycotts once in a while, but that's kind of expected and I believe it most likely works for my benefit, hah.

Some of my work is now blacklisted at discogs marketplace, so stuff like Nicole 12 or Clandestine Blaze can't be sold or purchased there anymore. Curiously, I think some people who know me, have had more problems than myself, because of small link towards me. There are a lot of bands who are ready to apologize for what they do or what kinds of friends they have. To issue statements in front of barking dogs leads nowhere.

Given you now established status as one of the 'elder statesmen' of underground industrial / power electronics, what is your opinion on the current state of the scene? Do you consider the enough 'young blood' being injected into the scene; is there enough clear direction, creativity and new ideas being displayed (rather than just rehashing the old; or is the scene at risk of degenerating into being a niche interest of middle age men into 'difficult' music? In your estimation what will be status of the scene in future be it 10 or 20 years or beyond?

'Elder statesman' status sounds quite amusing. Perhaps my constant presence for many years as publisher and magazine editor makes me different from plenty of other die hard noise fanatics who follow the global noise scene. Because the 'scene' is so fragmented into various sub-genres (based on style or location), it's impossible to fully understand what is happening now. History that is being written years after, might not acknowledge the important factors and what did not leave strong visible signs, but were crucial. For example I have been thanked for organizing live gigs of specific bands, but all I did was drive car a bit, and it was other people who were promoters, handling venue, bringing gear.

Also label as it is, could not exist without loyal co-workers who rarely (if ever) get credited for all sorts of shit work they have to do, while people like myself collect all the credit! For vitality of domestic scene, some of these live events were crucial to build a 'scene'. While smaller bands and various people involved don't get much credit, they have often still strong role in cumulating energy and getting things done.

Most of the new blood will prove their worth during next 5-10 years. In Finland there has been rising new blood, involved in projects, magazines, live gig organization, labels. Perhaps all have not found their own identity for sound or style and many are in shadow of more well established labels/bands. They have already presented material that captures attention and continue to improve their work. In Finland there are new projects, bands and labels that have appeared within the last couple of years. Not side projects of those who are already in, but new and younger people. I feel that this happens between certain years. One can see early 90's when emerged things like UND, Bizarre Uproar, Grunt, etc. Then late 90's when Cloama, Strom.ec. Pain Nail, Order and more. And as modern pace gets faster, in early to mid 2000's Gelsomina, Haare, Squamata, 'resurrection' of Bizarre Uproar, Halthan and so on. Now in 2010+ one can see wide range of artists more or less active, and often more or less clear continuum of what happened after mid 2000.

Despite there is something many people call 'Finnish sound', what is often loosely the rough side of Freak Animal and Filth & Violence, there is plenty of other stuff that co-exists in same scene. Finnish sound could be Bizarre Uproar, Grunt, Pain Nail or it could be Umpio, Keränen, Vanhala. Or Strom.ec & Cloama. Or Arktaus Eos, Halo Manash, Zoat Aon! Perhaps Verde and Grey Park! It could be many things. I think most of the 'elder statesmen' who complain of things going wrong, often see that the bands they and their contemporaries used to worship, are largely ignored when new guys have new influences and new targets of interests. That they buy stuff from other labels or other distros, or simply download. Crumbling empires of once huge labels or mailorders might not be a sign where the scene is dying. Simply momentum of specific energy has gone down and attention is elsewhere. After novelty goes away, there has always been very small number of devotees who stay interested.

Especially when pace is growing and growing, even pure mathematics can explain that everything can't be 'popular' or 'wanted'. It would be sheer insanity to think there would be market for such amounts of underground music that has been published in last 10 years. It's like belief in ever growing economy. Reality simply hits in. When this type of growth is not possible, perhaps instead of multiplying with constantly faster pace, growth would be focused in other things. Creativity, quality, timelessness and ability to build monuments instead of disposable junk.

In case the financial possibilities of publishing CD's and LP's in large print runs goes away, one can still trust that there is most likely the same amount of fanatics as in early days. That artist's were happy to put out 50 or 100 copies tape and correspond with people directly. I've been listening a lot of old Grunt tapes what back then were dubbed and sent out no more than perhaps 35 copies. I never considered that that was somehow too low number and it would prevent me from working hard with next release. Or play live without all-costs-paid festival surroundings. I think shift of focus into enthusiasm of creation & communication would be most welcomed. Not reduce all underground art forms to more or less commercial products aimed for niche market.

Playing live is something that seems to have always been a preoccupation of Grunt. How has your approach to live performance changed over the years? It also seems in recent years Grunt's performances have been a duo. How does this change the dynamics of your live performances and are you always assisted by the same individual or do your live collaborators change with each performance?

I played my first live gig in mid 90's. It was very far from what I intended. Utmost lack of technical know-how for live situation resulted it being more of noisecore performed with regular instruments. Curiously it included strong line-up featuring people who were or would later be known from projects like UND, Will Over Matter, etc. I had never seen a real noise show. I traveled abroad to see bands like Con-Dom and Stratum Terror. Seeing how its really done (just play the tape, haha!), 1998 was first live show close to similar standards like today. Video backdrop, live vocals, live noise, some backing tapes.

First it was roughly one gig per year. When first show abroad was coming, I had decided no more backing tapes, all must be live sound created on stage. It wasn't perfect, so after that there was constant evaluation how exactly and what kind of material to play. After playing in France in 2003, it was continued with shows in USA and UK in 2004 and exploded to 15 shows in Japan, UK, Germany, Finland in 2005. Since then total number of shows have reached c. 60.

During the years, despite most smaller gigs I have played as solo, some 'big stage' shows have been done with session members. Cloama, Strom.ec, Pain Nail, Anon+, When Grunt was going to play show in Broken Flag 30 years festival, I knew Jaakko Vanhala was going there as visitor and asked him would he be interested to join as session member. We know each other since 90's. I knew he has both talent to create sounds as well as vision that he can operate not only by strict guidelines, but follow the flow of material. This gig went very well and since then all shows have been played as duo. Basically he works under guidance what needs to be done, but I don't need someone to push sampler buttons or stand as decorative element, but actually create live material that contributes to overall atmosphere. Live situation, where nothing is 'just background tape' and even loop fragments that are played from sampler often are processed live, creates challenges that one simply needs to overcome by playing and rehearsing. Good vocal sound, good sound balance.
Right balance of 'nerdy' equipment tweaking vs. strong stage presence. Importance of physical action, yet not allow shows to be just reckless mess without control. Importance of the flow of the set when it reaches a relatively long 30 minute milestone. Some flaws can be ok, when wholeness works. Some flaws add the spontaneous and accidental element, making sure it is not just sit-through presentation of pre-recorded material. Duo changed dynamics greatly. One is not completely tied to table full of gear, but neither looks dull like karaoke set with music played from iPod. Even if rough frame is planned, it is very flexible to make changes according to feeling based on venue, PA system and atmosphere in general. My intent is to go further into actual live creation, where even bigger part of set is 100% created on stage and hopefully with such diversity of approaches as on releases. Most of the live sets have often focused on vocal dominated power electronics works of Grunt, but there is certainly more to be explored!

What is the role and function of the S&M mask you wear when performing live? Is this to keep your anonymity, to present a stage prop or to assist your focus of performance?
True anonymity is luxury one doesn't have these days, but yes. I think removing noise from mundane experience to something else can be good, although most Grunt live gigs have happened without mask. Like material that is played, also stage presence reflects atmosphere. One can approach mask from many angles. Sometimes it is directly related to songs performed and video material that is shown (where exact same mask appears). There it ties all threads together, being one element of the wholeness, not separated or isolated. Sometimes it doesn't need to be explained. Simply appeal of leather mask. Black solid, handmade, leather mask.
One can throw hints toward orthodox old school s/m code build in it, though. Mask of sadist. It is not just hiding personality, but making things visible.

Seemingly in recent years you have been performing at a wide variety of types of shows, be it underground private shows to more academically minded festivals. How do these performances eventuate and what are the similarities or differences in reaction of audiences depending on the performance setting?
In noise shows it is generally people who know what they're getting. In other type of shows people can be irritated by piercing feedback and lack of musicality. Occasionally also offended or repulsed by content of video material or even mere atmosphere that some individuals on stage creates. Shows themselves are not much different. There hardly is any conscious idea to play to different audiences. I have no need to avoid 'standard' noise shows. It's very normal way of getting offers and either accept or reject based on possibilities we have. Be it private event of 20 people or 300 people festival, it is quite irrelevant if it just seems something that can be done and should be done.

Beyond Grunt you have numerous other music projects (too many to mention), record companies (Freak Animal Records, Northern Heritage being the main two main), and other artistic/ publishing endeavours. How do you managed time / inputs and have you managed to combine all these pursuits to your full time job?
One can perhaps talk more about lifestyle. It is at the same time job, as it is something I do, regardless of financial gains. Most often major part of time goes on things what mean basically only loss of funds and 'loss' of time. But what needs to be done. As soon as one would treat this as job and start making calculations of what can be gained, motivations change and I'm confident it has a corrupting influence. Almost everything I do is connected to each other. I never had to make choice whether I'd be using my time with passivizing drugs, laying down doing nothing or playing video games. As such things have never been an option, there has been vast amounts of time to get other things done.
Merely daily amount of time people appear to watch something from TV they didn't want to see, would be enough to get plenty of things done. However, urge to do things, is perhaps not only blessing, but also a plague.

You are also involved with painting, drawing, and collage art, but as I understand it you have no formal training in any form of artistic technique. What is your view of what constitutes 'good' or 'bad' art? Likewise what is your view of today's contemporary art where often the idea is the art, with its execution being barely based in technical skill or practice?
It is endless debate that has been going on since dawn of man, I guess. One should obviously consider purpose of art. If it reached what it was aimed for, maybe it was good?
One could also consider different types of artists. I appreciate artists who are like artisans. They are talented craftsmen, who have possibility to work on commission.

If there was needed to make monumental statue, or portrait, they'd be one to go for. They don't necessarily need to have utmost burning vision to create something of their own, yet remain much more artists than 3rd rate art school graduates doodling nonsense in their sketchbooks. Anonymity of artist hardly matters, when they take part in much bigger picture than boosting their ego or trying to gain name for themselves. But in end remains question if they really created something? Is it more like musicians playing in cover band? In other type would be artists that simply do their things, regardless of income, popularity or demand. They have thing they need to express, instinct they follow and it has nothing to do with issues such as whether government grants are coming this year or whether they are accepted members in art community. What I personally dislike, is perhaps a group who do not really exists, but which I often think exists. Artists of a welfare state who feel entitled for a job as artists as they have education for it. They have no skill or potential to 'work as artisans', neither they have the burning spirit to create something without financial aid, hefty financial restitution or some sort of status within art world.
I see talented painters quite frequently. And when try to find out what they have done, they haven't done shit. Talent is there, but no true urge to make things happen. No ideas what to do, and if there is idea, no willpower to make it happen. Certainly magnitude of output is not in numbers, but... let's say, it can be part of it. I don't think art necessarily needs skill or perfected practice. At least not in a technological sense. However, I have quite little time for art or people who isolate art from life and meaning. Who have no answers nor questions. No experience or spirit. Critical comment being, that vast majority of modern artists, conceptualists etc carry the forms of past achievements but now devoid of ideas. One can always try to claim new era of 'deconceptualism', new era of postmodernism and whatever, yet very few buy into this. This argument certainly can be used for noise too, but some guy churning next harsh noise wall or throbbing Korg ms-20 tone most likely remain in different situation than guy decorating gallery with immigration applications pasted next to McDonalds hamburger wrappings (...anyone, feel free to use this 'idea').

Whilst Finland has always had musical acts/ projects working in the most obscure underground music genres, it would seem in recent years that overall Finnish acts have been received allot more attention. How do you see the Finland scene/s be it: industrial, noise, ritual, black metal etc?

Finnish underground music has always been exported to quite large extent. Country is small, so contacts are often made abroad. Be it punk/ hc, metal of all types, techno/ electronic music... even jazz or such 'normal' musical genres. Finnish industrial/ noise, in my opinion, has been gaining strength. New people with the right kind of motivations and more things happening than in the past. Older bands still producing new albums that are not just routine jobs, but search for new ways of expression. New bands doing things, with enough potential to catch attention of labels both in and out of Finland. And most of all, also energy to do self financed releases. Hardly any competition or too much of internal fights.
Black Metal is still going strong, yet bubble has exploded years ago. All sorts of rock'n'roll side effects, involving strong commercialization of entire genre, when gigs appear as supermarkets of merch. Too many releases, too many assuming it's some sort of birthright to gain popularity and financial restitution for making under par releases. Sometimes even blaming fans for lack of 'support', when income isn't easy and guaranteed. Global trends affect the integrity of genre where previously influences were absorbed, but regurgitated back with more or less personal touch. Looking at history of genre, very little was particularly 'well done' in sense what is big and popular in metal. But neither it was just useless and disposable nonsense put together in a couple hours. Material at its most vital form, always kind of rough and aesthetically unfinished, stubbornly standing against current trends. But not now, I'm afraid. Of course there is always a scene inside a scene. New good things keep coming when you have patience.

One attribute you display is a forthright willingness to provide detailed information on your activities and to discuss in depth topics, which clearly differs from many underground acts who choose to function in total anonymity by providing no information or interviews. Such an example is Deathspell Omega - a group which you have long been rumoured to be their singer - but a fact you have to my knowledge chosen to neither confirm or deny. What is your view on such underground acts (be it metal or industrial) and whether a strict code of silence is a cleaver tool to create an aura and mystique in an age of information saturation, or is it perhaps symptomatic of an act or project with little to stay or substance to back up their releases or image?

Despite there is hardly difference in my case what is 'private' and what 'public', there is always choices of what things are not meant for 'audience'. I don't see myself talking much of 'private life' beyond the ideas I deal with in music or art in general.
It is perhaps unfortunate reality in bigger metal scene, that it suffers the contemporary 'Reality TV' mentality. Too often focus could be merely to all the banal and all that is unnecessary. Where right questions are never asked, where right answers would never be really listened. All the deeper urges or messages can be forgotten if there is available some sort of gossip level chit-chat. Or at best, some sort of sensation/scandal.
To reduce individuals as part of group or anonymous 'entity' (band), where group speaks for itself (even exclusively through their work) can be good. It removes vast amount of possibilities to banalize work of art to be vehicle for personal fame or be reduced to less than it actually is.

When I started Clandestine Blaze back in 90's, it never mentioned line-up details or included member photos in releases. It wasn't a big secret, yet removing the typical rock'n'roll element from metal worked out well and all what one could focus was music, lyrics and interviews.
There certainly can be cases where it is all surface, and all cleverly calculated pose. Other times we can ask why we assume it's all surface? Let's say bands dealing with sexual themes, alternative world views, violence, politics, etc. what do we expect? Come clean about every detail of your daily thoughts and actions? Offer logical and credible sense to everything? This is what I mentioned before. Even in underground metal scene as small as it is, there's people spying on what 'celebrities' buy from ebay.
People lust for knowledge of next instagram update about singer's breakfast photos. Or is noise scene, people nosing around what noise tapes Henry Rollins buys.
I recall one Finnish ritual music group performing live, where fans later discuss about bottle of beer on stage, so can the live performance be 'credible' anymore. If audience is stuck with irrelevant nonsense, maybe cure is to offer absolute minimum to feed such habit.

In some cases, one may learn to find more from art than its creators consciously created. In some cases a bit more human interaction is necessary in form of communication of some sort (live shows/ interviews/ correspondence).

What would you say are your proudest moments with Grunt to date, be it in terms of releases and live performances?
I can't name such moment. Every proud moment is also shadowed with merciless criticism, hah!

What is currently on the horizon for Grunt?
New album recordings ongoing. Hard to say when things start to take proper shape. Maybe in a month. Maybe in a couple of years.

Any concluding comments?
Thanks for interview - it's kind of rare to get good interviews these days!

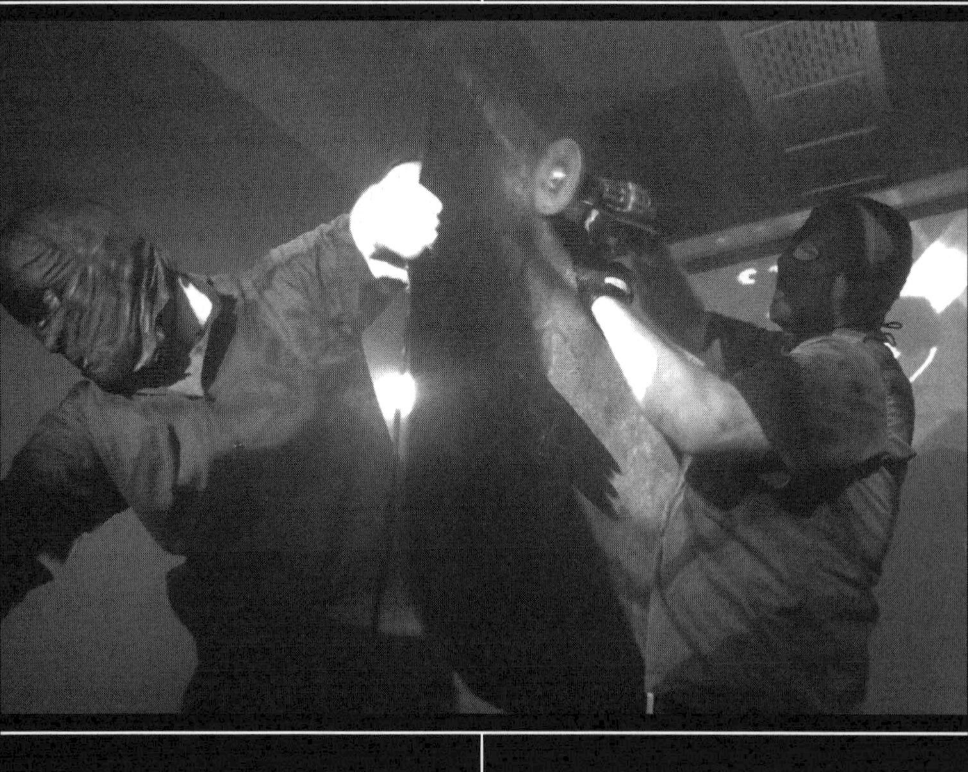

HALO MANASH

With a highly immersive and trancelike sound (created with field recordings, acoustic instrumentation and studio treatments), Finnish band Halo Manash have become a revered ritual ambient project. To better appreciate the group's inspiration and evocative musical approach Antti Haapapuro (aka AIH) and J. Padatsu (aka OAK) obliged by responding to a lengthy interrogation.

Halo Manash have existed for just over a decade now, starting as a solo project, and later expanding to a duo and then trio. Would your care to introduce yourself and the other members and provide an overview of the group from inception to now?

AIH: I'm not so good in introducing myself, nor do I have much interest for that either. Let just say that I am a person who enjoys working in the field of creative arts. In addition to my work in Halo Manash, I am the founder of Aural Hypnox record label and working currently in the following groups: Arktau Eos, Aeoga, Dolorian & I.corax.

You are partly right, Halo Manash started as a personal project of myself, but even from the first official release 'Se Its En' I was accompanied by a multi-talented musician and a good friend, IWO with whom I have worked in various groups together over 17 years. He is currently an integral part of both Halo Manash and Arktau Eos, writes music for Dolorian and plays in several bands that I am not even properly aware of. Throughout the years the live and studio line-up of Halo Manash has changed quite a bit. Couple of year back we returned back to the group's early formation where IWO and I are currently accompanied by a new member, an old friend of ours, OAK with whom this interview is given. OAK has released several albums as Lingua Fungi and with him I nowadays run the Aural Hypnox record label.

In addition to the persons above, the following artists have been an integral part of the group's history and releases: Juhana Partanen (in live line-up 2005), Aki Cederberg (in studio, film & live line-up during 2005-2009), Mikko Pöyhönen (in live line-up during 2009). There are also few people who are part of the Halo Manash continuum, but they have chosen to work only in the shadows.

I understand that prior to the formation of Halo Manash you were involved in other musical projects which aligned more with the 'standard' western expression of a band. Was this musical background in anyway an influenced to the formation of Halo Manash and how did you originally become aware of and interested in ritual oriented music?

AIH: Working with the standard band line-ups, with conventional musical instruments has surely opened new pathways and taught many important things. From there and from the personnel I have been playing with I have learned a great deal.

Actually, I would say that with Halo Manash we are currently following quite closely the form and even some working methods of a so called standard band. The main differences are in the musical dimensions, choices towards used instruments and in performative elements. I am rather sure that no one can deny the fact that a group playing tight together with a concentration on the same focus can deliver an overwhelming energy.

To be honest I do not really know the original reason why I became interested in, and started to work with the music we do. It seems to be something that is built deep within me. For the lack of a better word I guess I have been kind of a 'spiritual person' all my life. For the involved personnel, Halo Manash is most of all a concrete and powerful tool, through which we communicate, and bridge the worlds of being and non-being. It is a vehicle enabling a comprehensive communication with transpersonal reality and awakens the hidden passages to ones subconsciousness.

A brief 'equipment related review' might reveal another perspective to your question. Before I was part of any band or group, I had already made the first experiments in the field of 'experimental music'. These took place back in 1992/1993, when I was still a youngster fooling around with very simple computer based trackers and sequencers.

Mainly because of the computer's low memory capacity I had to play with very short samples and I guess this really pushed me onward on creating something very different from regular band music. These limited working methods pointed my interest towards editing single sounds by stretching, reversing and manipulating them with effects. So, all in all in my musical trajectory the early years were full of experiments that opened my eyes to a bunch of different methods on how to approach and carry out, through the limited equipment and musical skill, the vision you have inside.

My musical taste towards experimental, ambient, drone, electro-acoustic, ritual, death industrial et cetera 'strange music' grew more and more and it was in 1997 when I came across through my own research and a friend of mine the music of for example Coil, NON & Ain Soph. I was never really involved in the international tape trading scene myself, but my friend Jaakko Vanhala, with whom I became acquainted and formed I.corax at the end of 1998, was. During that time Jaakko introduced me to a bunch of great groups and projects; such as Maeror Tri, Schloss Tegal, Aphex Twin, Autechre, Endura, Allerseelen, Inade, Atrax Morgue et cetera.

But what is ritual music anyway? Since the 90's I have listened to a lot of music ranging from death, grind, doom, black metal to various electronic music genres, post-punk and to very traditional music et cetera. Many of these are not typically categorised as ritual music, but still are for many.

With your chosen band name there appears to be a multitude of interpretations depending on cultural / religious context. Noting that 'Manash' can be translated as meaning 'desire', the word can also be broken down into other words such as 'mana', with its own multiple meanings, including: the mind; spiritual understanding; a blessing; supernatural force etc. 'Manash' could also be interpreted as 'man-ash', which leads to connotations of death, cremation and 'rebirth' within the afterlife. Despite these various potential interpretations, what are your personal reasons which underpin the chosen moniker?

AIH: The name of the group derives its origin from simple, but effective combination of words and diversity of concepts associated with them. Also, I cannot deny the fact that anagrams and 'word play' both are closely related to our textual output; e.g. 'Manash' is an anagram of 'Shaman' et cetera. You are totally right in saying that there exists a multitude of interpretations of the name depending on the background of the people, and this is something intentionally done. From the very beginning the intention was to come up with a name that would carry multiple meanings and concepts, rather than a strict single idea. Moreover, we have always encouraged fellow travellers to go deep into themselves on approaching our material and to utilize their own instincts. Words that ignite or awaken are *Words of Power.*

The time when Halo Manash was chosen as the name of the group dates back to the period where I examined day and night various archaic ideologies and esoteric traditions. On a personal level, it was an interesting time; I started to test and practice different methods and techniques and to combine together the elements that worked out the best for me. It was a time when I went beyond the profane human condition, re-entered the womb of primordial life and contemplated before the very source. Thus, the name Halo Manash could be 'translated' to something like: a *radiant crown with thousand eyes, the pure Power, arising after the transient being/form is burned*. However, the meanings and/or concepts are changing from time to time.

From an outsiders perspective there seems to be an established tradition of Finish ritual music. Does this have any relationship to the context and approach of Halo Manash?

AIH & OAK: We are not sure if you are now referring to the very recent experimental ritual music scene or centuries old traditions and to their use of sound and music as a tool. Anyhow, we can say that Halo Manash does not follow any schools of thought or other traditions.

It is widely know that the early Finnish ritual music has always been, among other factors very situational and nature oriented. These are the only aspects that we can consider to be common with our work in Halo Manash.

The tradition exists and can sometimes even guide our approach, but in the end our working methods are guided by our own intuition, primal experiences and knowledge arising from such experiences.

For us Halo Manash is nothing but an exacting yet rewarding and continuous pilgrimage to the borderlands of dreams, pure consciousness, and primal being.

From my (albeit external) assessment of the intent of Halo Manash, there seems to be a ritual and trance driven agenda which appears to be guided mostly by intuition. Would this be a correct assessment? Noting that Halo Manash sonically and visually includes some markers which lean towards Buddhist and Asiatic spiritual expression, do you follow or has any particular religion/ school of thought/ spiritual teachings guided your approach?

AIH & OAK: Although we are aware and have been studying with deep interest diverse paths, practices and beliefs of for example shamanism, these have never been in any way pointing the direction to our work. There exists several spiritual revelations and subconscious triggers guiding our doings, but not a single one is drawn from any of the existing spiritual systems, symbols or traditions. They are results from the deliberate and accidental personal encounters received usually in the states of heightened awareness.

These encounters, findings or revelations are then approached in our work via self-made instruments, which strive to resonate with the primal experience or to communicate with the elements or elementals in question. On a group level, we are trying to reach state where rhythmical language re-opens the *half-hidden passage* and establishes a direct communion.

What do you consider as the critical role of Halo Manash within the context of a modern society which although underpinned by western religion is largely secular in practice? Do you even have a role or agenda in this context?

AIH & OAK: We cannot say that we have any kind of conscious role or agenda pointed towards the modern society or world in general. The role in the context implies some kind of agenda to teach, and that is not nor has ever been the aim of Halo Manash.

Of course, if you think our work with Halo Manash (or with our label Aural Hypnox) comprehensively, you could say that via our doings we are encouraging people worldwide for critical awareness and that we support something else than a society based on competitive routines.

Looking at the trajectory of your releases, there seems to be a clear shift in sound between your first three albums, with a new more organic sound and much greater degree of focus on real ritual instrumentation displayed on the *r.A.S.H.N.K.A-RA* LP/ DVD set, which was continued in variation on subsequent albums. Was this a clear and conscious decision?

AIH & OAK: Yes, it was a conscious decision. As all living things, we also aspire to develop and find new ways to carry out the vision of the current phase.
During the years we have used a wide selection of musical instruments, holding in various qualities, in different albums. Our work is based on resonation and communication with the elemental beings through sonic invocations, and in this process the instruments have central significance. In our past *Forest Music* era we used a variety of acoustic instrumentation that could have been categorized under traditional or archaic musical instruments or ritual tools. Back then, we put a lot of emphasis on the organic and animate materials that often had a definite aura. Depending on the intentions of sessions or a larger concept the instruments with suitable material, sound and spirit were chosen, acquired or handcrafted.
This in itself was and still is an integral part of the creation process; the instruments and the sound they produce have to correspond and resonate properly with the intentions.

Within your discography you have already presented two DVD releases, which in the most part of ritual / dark ambient music is a rarity. What are your aims with providing a visual representation of Halo Manash?
AIH & OAK: Much of what comes to the music also applies to the visual representation. The aspects of cinematic language, expression and of course the images in themselves carry deep and personal, experience related visions and are chosen and carefully produced every time. The visual aspects have been an integral part of Halo Manash from the beginning, but the lack of proper video recording and editing equipment has made many projects too complicated to carry through. This is something we are hoping to change in the near future. Anyway, everything in our films is meant to convey or symbolize something, be it the shifting of colours, things happening in background or foreground, fire burning or vapour arising et cetera.

On both the *r.A.S.H.N.K.A-RA* and *Taiwaskivi* DVD's it broadly show what appear to be various rituals in progress. In reality, are these visual representations of studio recordings or are the visual and sound more specifically intertwined?
AIH: *r.A.S.H.n.k.a-RA* is a result of very intense work and experience – a real and primal ritual. It has nothing to do with regular studio recording, where you have a possibility to replace the bad or unwanted parts. Everything was captured on tape and film during the rituals that lasted in all four days and nights.
The days were spent preparing, building and setting up things ready for the night when the rituals took place. However, in the end we found out that those days and nights both in themselves became important parts of the ritual as a whole, as we constantly experienced and sensed various presences. The audio and video were both finally processed in studio environment by following and respecting the original shape and form.

Taiwaskivi is a bit of a different work; everything was filmed in parts and in several places. Apart from some field-recordings most of the tracks were recorded in studio. The visual material on the video focuses on presenting the themes related to our *Forest Music* era trilogy. The trilogy can be viewed as a *treelogy* – a tripartite work in the shape of a tree, with roots, a trunk and branches. The first part, *Language of Red Goats* is the celestial lunar seed in the dark earthly womb that gives form to the roots that spread themselves in the underworld. *Am Kha Astrie*, the second part is the trunk, the pillar that breaks the surfaces and planes, crossing the thresholds, and emerges upward, rising into this world. *Taiwaskivi* is the branches of the tree, reaching toward sol, stars and beyond; it is the leaves and fruits of those branches and their skybound nectar. It is the crown at the peak, the bright, clear light – the fire above.

Can you describe the creative process for the filming of visual material and the how you go about determining what locations will be used for filming?
AIH: The creative processes have been different in each project so far, and it is usually the inmost vision that leads and dictates the method and form.
The locations or *the elemental landscapes* shown in our two previous films are situated near to our living places or are special places from where we have been drawing inspiration from. Needless to say, for us these are nothing but places *of Great Power.*
We have also a new film in the making and it is once again nice to notice it taking steps towards previously unexplored territories via special visual dynamics and production choices. During the past two years we have been capturing on film several encounters with manifold entities and a selection of these *liquid entrances* were already shown on screen in 2012 during our performance at the WGT festival in Leipzig, Germany. These were part of the new production, but the work is progressing slowly as most of the editing is done on VHS film by using analog video mixer.

One of your most recent releases is the *Wesieni Wainajat* mini CD which contains some of the most composed and focused tracks from the group to date. Is this representative of the direction of Halo Manash's in future? How do you collectively as a group approach the composition and recording process? How much is composed verses being improvised?
AIH & OAK: During the past three years we have been working mostly in shadows; the time was right to go deep into one's mercurial self to have conversations with the archaic instincts and to meet the *Unspeakable.*
Wesieni Wainajat starts the new Halo Manash cycle after a few years break in releasing material. The album is an evocative lunar-hymn, a call for the elements and elementals approaching and a leading for the forthcoming full length album. The personnel and times have changed since the *Forest Music* phase and the driving forces have evolved naturally into new directions.

The album should not be taken as the new direction of the group as we have already moved on. The composed form of the album origins from clear choice; plain and repetitive melodies accompanied with simple meditative rhythms are exceedingly trance inducing and when one has moved from the level of normal awareness to a deeper state, he is more receptive to the subconscious revelations – to hear and sense comprehensively the approaching of the *One who is moist*. Musically the album includes composed, solid backgrounds that have been afterwards enriched with textures coming far beyond human-oriented touch. The field-recordings have been captured on tape in various locations during invocation sessions.

Referring to the recent re-release of *Caickuwi Cauwas Walkeus*, and now that I have had an opportunity to hear this album, its original limitation seemed far too small for the quality of the material. Was there any particular reason behind its original limitation of a mere 29 copies?

AIH: The reason why the 1st edition of *Caickuwi Cauwas Walkeus* was extra limited and exclusively available during our mini-tour in France in 2009 is actually very simple and pragmatic. I prepared the layout and put together the album covers only couple of days before we left to France in 2009. 29 copies is not that many in numbers, but when you start to burn the cds, design the layout, print, cut and glue the inserts and finish some parts with fire you will soon notice that the project actually takes more time than you thought. Almost half of the performances during that tour took place in remote places far from regular club surroundings, so people had to make the effort to come and attend. Because of this we wanted to have something very special to offer for them. In addition, traveling by airplane is always a kind of struggle for us. The weight restrictions are something we all the time have to consider and more than often we are forced to make e.g. gear-wise compromises. We are glad to see the album now properly re-released; it should not be taken in any way as a separate or half finished album, as it reveals a crucial and necessary bridge to our past. It is *Forest Music*, recorded live in private sessions, in its purest form.

It seems relatively clear that Halo Manash is a celebration of life / life force / spirit which clearly differs from other aspects of underground music which are preoccupied with negative thematic material. Seeing as much of the interest in Halo Manash would appear to come from such underground music spheres, what is view on the contextual fit or seeming disparity in conceptual focus?

AIH & OAK: We prefer not to extensively analyse and dissect our own work as that tends to trivialize and limit its perception. It is strange that sometimes people put too much effort in trying to decipher what we personally intend with some aspect of the work, rather than experiencing and appreciating it on a personal level directly for themselves. Individuals are encouraged to approach it within their own context, and trust their own experiences and intuition. The concepts and themes of our work are not sometimes even in our hands. Usually, they start to emerge as the end of the current cycle draws near or after a *strong encounter*. However, we have never chosen the themes or concepts intentionally to match the current trends or fads; we prefer to follow our own instincts. It is true that Halo Manash is a celebration of life force and spirit, but the celebration can often be a consequence of truly harrowing and exhausting experience or *hunt*. Rather than a constant celebration, we see Halo Manash as a continuous pilgrimage and even if we are working as a group, we acknowledge that it is a journey everyone has to take alone. Finally, to answer your question; we think that the conceptual disparity is only superficial. We believe that people operating in the experimental and other underground music scenes are open-minded enough to understand and appreciate our work.

Halo Manash have played numerous live performances across the globe over the years. What are your most memorable locations/ places / countries you have played to date?

AIH: Our mini-tour in Russia in 2007 brings me good memories. It was our first time in Russia and we were totally amazed by the people and their attitude towards life and art and of the positive reception we got. Our tour in France back in 2009 was also something very special. Our two-week journey began in Haubourdin in the Gallery called *Vous êtes ici*, where we were to undertake a tree-fold invocation, in the form of an exhibition of photographs, a screening of films, and a series of three consecutive performances. After this we did several acoustic invocations at various sacred sites and places. Imagine an acoustic performance taking place in a barren small chapel (*Chapelle Saint Michel*), on the top of a misty mountain. Or another one taking place in the ancient abbey (*pointe Saint Mathieu*) where you could see a sky full of stars shining between the towering ruins. Our performances at Stella Natura, USA, have also been something very special; during the first time in 2009 we encountered *Fire*, returning there after couple of years in 2013 we encountered *Ice*. These memories, places and people we have met during our journeys are carved deep within me.

Likewise what is your approach to the live setting and to do play versions of released material, or is it new and improvised material? What is process for live performances and do you consider the performances as specific rituals and what is your expectation of the role of the audience? How have the audience reactions been to what you do?

AIH & OAK: For us the live performances are comparatively rare occurrences. They are based on the sonic and visual manifestations of the current cycle and carry the energy and spirit we have accumulated during the various preparation sessions. All of our live performances feature actions planned in advance, as well as actions arising in the very moment – and both are equally central to the performance. What comes to the musical instruments and other sound apparatuses, they are always manipulated and played live – we do not use backing tapes or samplers.

Knowledge and *transient improvisation* goes hand in hand, but of course, surprises also happen; sometimes the amplified sounds have been totally captured and transformed by *Outer Forces.*
For us, performing live can be a very intense and exhausting experience. Our current performances cannot be considered as rituals per se, but they are definitely more than mere shows. They offer a key to the receptive listener – you just have to figure out yourself where and how to use it. While performing we try to distance our egos to give space for the elemental manifestations and hope that audience would become part of the experience itself, rather than concentrate on the superficial aspects, such as persons on stage and so forth.
The response has been mainly positive, or maybe people have been too afraid to tell us the truth! Anyway, it has been a pleasure to perform in different countries and to experience people's reactions varying from serious contemplation to ecstatic frenzy.

Are your surprised by the current acceptance and seeming growing popularity of ritual oriented music?
AIH: I do not have any idea of the growing popularity towards ritual orientated music and from our perspective things seem to be going as before; we are not making spectacular record sales or world-wide tours. But I guess you right, compared to our early years interest seems to be growing.

Given that Halo Manash at its core appears to express an ancient yearning for spiritual connection and understanding, how do you reconcile this function with the modern age and the use of tools such as the internet to communicate and distribute global awareness of your artistic works?
AIH & OAK: We think there is no conflict between seeking the spiritual understanding by using modern technology. It is the content that counts not the medium in which it is presented. It is true that the full power of live performances cannot be attained from records, but on the other hand may lead to more personal interpretations. What comes to internet as a tool for communication and promotion, it is the necessary evil.

What are the future goals and what might currently on the horizon for Halo Manash?
AIH & OAK: We have already recorded the new full length album and are about to start the mixing and mastering work. We are also filming material for the forthcoming film, which will support and widen the overall experience of the underlying concept.
In addition to the recent *Caickuwi Cauwas Walkeus* re-release, more unreleased material have been discovered from the group's vault. A while ago we begin the process of converting the magnetism of the reels to digital numbers. A recording dating back to 29th of August 2008 is currently under work. It is the one of the very first calls that was performed and captured on tape in a private session just before we left to *Forest Music & Ocean Fire* tour to France in 2008. During that time only acoustic instrumentation was used. These sessions go under the name 'Tulimetsät'.
A couple of performances have been booked for the spring as well; in April we will perform in Tampere. In May we are going to perform in Stockholm and in June in Austrian Alps.

Any concluding comments?
All interested organizers, clubs, galleries and individuals are urged to contact us.

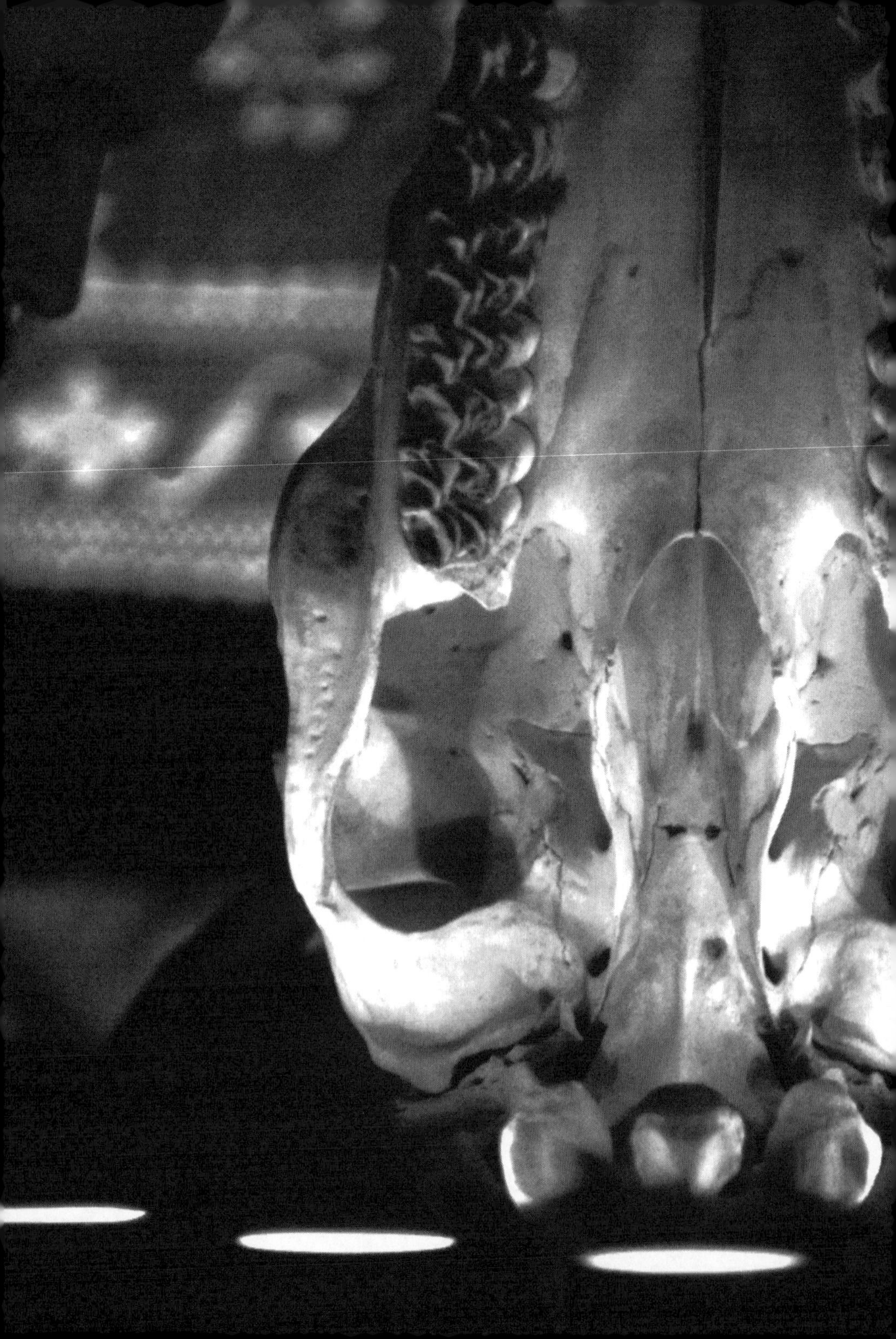

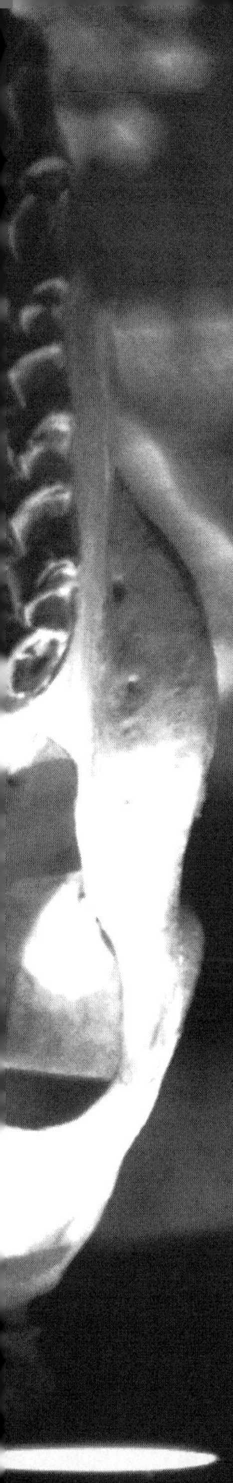

Aural Hypnox

Within the underground the Finnish label Aural Hypnox is clearly acknowledged as a leading light in dark ritual ambient oriented music. Equally with the artwork and packaging of releases being imbedded with a special aura due to their hand crafted nature, this has generated a cult like interest in the label's output. With the label being on hiatus from 2009, but recently reactivated in 2013 with a slew of new releases, it was opportune time to interview the two individuals behind the current version of the label, namely Antti Haapapuro (aka AIH) and J. Padatsu (aka OAK).

For the uninitiated, how would you describe Aural Hypnox, including its beginnings, its conceptual focus and whether you have a particular mission statement?

Antti Haapapuro aka AIH: Aural Hypnox came into being in the end of 2003, immediately after I quit working with the Blue Sector label, which I co-founded with Jaakko Vanhala in 2002. From the very beginning Aural Hypnox has concentrated only on releasing the output of the Helixes collective. Expanding out to support other interesting acts has been on the cards several times, but so far these groups Aeoga, Aural Holograms, Arktau Eos, Halo Manash and Zoät-Aon have been more than creative enough and demanding all the time and resources available.

The fundamental reasons for founding Aural Hypnox were numerous. The most important being the freedom concerning all decisions regarding production and aesthetics. In this era, when people and some labels forget their primal aims and go for easy profit, Aural Hypnox is able to provide all the Helixes collective members the exact milieu and framework which both the label and the artists, deem fit at a given time: both sides win.

In the recent silent-era of the label, between the 2009 and 2013, I was concentrating on finishing some personal matters and also gathering strength and funds for the future actions. At the beginning of summer 2013 I decided to ask my old time friend OAK, who had previously collaborated with Halo Manash & Zoät-Aon, to join in and run the label with me. So, from then on the label became a 'double-bladed knife' and as you might know these can be dangerous, but at the same time very effective. In other words, when two handicraft-orientated persons meet and start to plan and carry out things together, things tend to go wild!

For the unaware can you describe exactly what the Helixes collective, when this came into formation and its members originally came into contact?

AIH: One interpretation is that the Helixes collective is nothing but a group of friends with similar interests. There are other interpretations as well... The name for the collective was decided in May 2005 while I was driving with J. Vanhala (aka JKV) to Helsinki to meet our friends A. Litmanen (aka AIL) & A. Cederberg (aka Akiz or Adinath Puri), who we got acquainted with about a year or two before. From then on the name was used as a collective term for the activities of the involved persons. In addition to aforementioned gentlemen, the collective includes also A. Kukkohovi (aka IWO), J. Partanen, Mikko Pöyhönen (aka Riimu), J. Saivo and J. Padatsu (aka OAK). In addition, there are some people who have wished to work only in the shadows. Going through how people got in contact in the first place would be too complicated and impossible for me to write down. It would require the presence of all the involved persons.

How has the reception been to the label, be it today compared to its infancy? Did you set yourself particular goals and have these been met or have they altered over time?

AIH: The response has been pretty much positive most of the time. Of course in the beginning, no one really knew the label or the artist / groups, but little by little by hard work we got more attention among other labels and people in general. The goals that were set at the beginning were mainly artist-based and still are. In the very beginning I labelled Aural Hypnox as a non-profit label and it still is. So far, all of the money we have received has been directed straight to the production costs of new releases. I would not mind to get some salary from the work one day, but this is still something only time will tell.

In looking at the roster on the Aural Hypnox label, it would seem they form a relatively tight knit collective of artist. Is this perception correct and do you ever see this changing with an expanded label roster?

AIH & OAK: Aural Hypnox is not a traditional record label in a sense of releasing anything that we get our hands on and that sounds good. We value the personal perspective of the artists and for that we have to know them personally. So, the label roster might expand, but every addition is well thought to not compromise the integrity of the label.

The Helixes collective is a closed group of friends, who all know each other personally and with whom we both collaborate in mutual projects. It is likely that we will start releasing material of other projects at one point. As a matter of fact, we have been quite recently pondering and already made some initial planning about the possibilities to release material from Lingua Fungi and Pyhä Kuolema, as the personnel behind these projects have been part of our activities during many years.

Noting the use of a variety of handicraft techniques, this has become a central part of the Aural Hypnox aesthetic. Do you have any formal training or are these elements self taught artistic expression?

AIH & OAK: This is simply something directed against the mechanised consumer culture. Contrary to the mass-produced products, we found value in finishing even our regular editions with a personal touch. When we release limited deluxe editions, our aim is not to make collector's items – they are limited simply because they are totally hand-made and it would be impossible to make more of them.

We do not have formal training in handicraft techniques; we are self-taught through trial and error. The handicraft aspect of the label is mutual interest for both of us, and we enjoy experimenting with new techniques. We have a deep respect and interest towards artisanship and visual arts, but we also like to maintain the outsiders perspective to them. This enables us to use the techniques intuitively without putting too much weight on the tradition. That doesn't mean we take tradition lightly, for us the use of visual arts is a process of solve et coagula, we use one part here and another there to form the final whole.

You could say that the fundamental reason for this whole handicraft matter lie also deep in our personal history; we were both grown up in very small towns, where most of the activities and even material items had to be invented and made by yourself or together with a friend.

Given the variety of approaches you have used to date to present your releases, how do you approach the design process and selection of options for potential presentation of new releases?

AIH & OAK: In the design work we always try to reflect the pure vision and the concepts related to the album theme. The design is developed throughout the creation cycle and each and every component for the final release is chosen carefully to carry the intent and the theme of the album. Sometimes we have to give in to profane restrictions, but keeping most of the production in our own hands we are able to create a final presentation that would otherwise be impossible or at least extremely hard to accomplish.

Stamping and screen printing by hand is really labour intensive, but the personal touch is the key component. Starting from last year, every record and cassette cover, album booklets and inserts, t-shirts and long sleeves, back patches and incense covers have been cut and printed at the Aural Hypnox lodge and thus carries forth the seasonal currents of the label, the undertone of the label and the artists involved. It would be rather impossible for us to release something coming in a soulless, factory printed, jewel case. We could easily triple the amount of releases by doing so, but that would compromise the whole idea of the label.

What would be your personal favourite and proudest releases?

AIH & OAK: It's impossible to pick out a specific favourite from the catalogue. Design-wise we are improving release by release and currently we are totally impressed by the appearance of the new Aeoga deluxe box set. In that we used techniques that we had not tried out before and there is definitely some improvement seen compared to our previous deluxe releases. There is always something that could have been done better, but as humble seekers we try to learn and cultivate our techniques.

Likewise has there been a greater degree of interest in some artists or releases over others?

AIH & OAK: The degree of interest seems to vary from time to time according to our release schedule. The amount of live performances and overall activity seems to play a key role in this matter also; the groups who are performing or are working with new material are usually the ones people are eagerly following and supporting.

In greater sense, it seems that we have finally reached the state where the identity of the label is a promise for a well thought and presented release – and that is something we strive to hold on to.

In a global sense has there been any pattern in particular interest and engagement with the label, be it in purchasing music or organising gigs?

AIH & OAK: During the years, at festivals, clubs, galleries and events we have encountered different kinds of people with various views of the world. The interest towards our albums and performances seems to surpass the artificial sub-cultural genres. We have never really cared to over-categorize our music, therefore it has been great to see that wide range of people, experiencing music and art from different perspectives are attending our performances or buying records.

The people we have met on the road or are organizing gigs for us come from different backgrounds. They and the attending audience seem to follow their own paths or philosophical ideas. It has been a joy to discover how differently people worldwide interact and see things. For example in Russia people are often interested to hear the deepest meanings of our work and to have a discussion related to the art and philosophy. This is something that does not happen often in Finland. If you are after recurring patterns, one thing in common with most of the people worldwide is that they are tired to live according to the prevailing system that is based on competitive routines.

After our restart in 2013 we had to change our 'request-response' –based order system. Most of the music we sell nowadays is handled through our webshop. Unfortunately that does not leave much room for personal communication with the customers compared to the old days and that is why we can not make generalisations about the patterns of interests among the people who support the work of Aural Hypnox. Starting the new webshop was a conscious decision. We simply needed more time for the production work. On the other hand the means of communication have changed during the past years. Now most of the communication is handled through our Facebook page, which works as a platform for us to bring out in the open the actual work we do.

Given we live in a digital age, what is your view of the ease of access to all manor of weird underground music, without needing to commit the time to tracking down the actual release artefacts? Does this modern mode of music consumption have any relevance or negative impact to what you do with Aural Hypnox?

AIH & OAK: We sincerely believe that the ease for illegal download does not concern us as much as other and especially bigger record labels. We think that people are well aware that the physical manifestations are something crucial for an all-encompassing experience; in addition to the sonic formations they bring forth the inmost vision and Will of the artists or group in question.

What can be expected from Aural Hypnox in the coming months and/ or years?

AIH & OAK: Our plan is to start releasing, among new albums, the long since sold-out Blue Sector discography. The albums were originally released in very limited CD-r editions and deserve to be properly pressed. These long awaited releases include the very first Halo Manash album *Se Its En* and also an extensive collection of albums by I.corax, a duo formed in the late 1998.

Moreover, as an artist-run record label, we are constantly interested to discover and develop new and unusual ways. Quite recently we launched Aural Hypnox label series *Underworld Transmissions*, which is filmed and captured on tape in the private séances held in our subterranean lodge located in Oulu, Northern Ostrobothnia. The concept of the series is to invite artists from the Helixes collective, in different combinations, to join a séance and through sound and movement to establish an elemental communication. Each séance is guided by a unique automatic-portal-portrait reflecting the planetary and stellar distances seen at that particular time in the lodge altar mirror-receiver.

Noting your reference to seances above, as well as what appears to be the broader aim of the Helixes collective to seek spiritual and elemental communication through ritual music, what are your thoughts and expectations of how listeners should approach Aural Hypnox releases? Does it concern you if listeners approach the releases from a musical perspective only?

AIH & OAK: The people involved in the Helixes collective all have their own ways of addressing these matters and because of that we simply cannot speak for all of them. What comes to approaching Aural Hypnox releases, the use of symbolism is essential and important to us and the artists. In the groups we are personally involved we try to avoid too strict and limiting interpretations, rather the opposite. We encourage the people to find their own way to approach the essence be it in ritual contexts or as a listening experience.

Any passing comments or thoughts?

AIH & OAK: All active Aural Hypnox groups are interested of performing, so organizers, clubs, galleries and individuals are urged to contact us. You can support our work by visiting our shop at: www.auralhypnox-shop.com

reviews

by Richard Stevenson

Abandoned Asylum - *Derelicts Of Distant Hope* CD
Malignant Records 2013

Although apparently formed in 2004, *Derelicts Of Distant Hope* represents the formal debut album from this Polish project and yet another new addition to the Malignant roster. Upon cursory listens, this album (to my minds-eye at least), appeared to present Abandoned Asylum's version of the 'brooding menace of deep recesses, caverns and crypts' style of dark ambience. However this initial impression seemed to be rather at odds with the track titles, which are more indicative of galactic and deep space themes, evidenced through titles such as *Intersellar Transmissions* and *Shades Of Nebular Images*. Yet regardless of this potential misinterpretation of the sonic picture on my part, Abandoned Asylum delivers some excellent dark ambient material. Here some expertly construct soundscapes of interweaving / spiralling / drifting drones are to be found, intermixed with mechanised static and a sound production with a deep and echoed clarity. Likewise rather than being minimalist in tone, tracks follow an ebb and flow technique which builds to intense dark ambient crescendos.

The deep monolithic tone of *Drifting in Constant Eclipse* sets itself apart from other album tracks due to its prominent use of gregorian / choral styled chants, which works extremely well within context of the material, but also brings the inevitable comparison to raison d'etre. *Amongst Shapes Unknown To Man* sits at the core of the album and is slightly more animated than preceding material, based on a centrally prominent waiving element which cyclically rises to prominent heights, only to recede, repeat and increase in intensity with each rotation. *Echoes of Forgotten Origins* within its slightly heavier and grinding soundscape of deep sub-orchestral horn (and possibly buried choral vocals), features a great late track inclusion of a singular tone akin to a lone submarine depth sounder, which acts as a sonic beacon with the inky blackness. Alternately the cavernous windswept drones of *Storms In the Endless Void* builds to an intense climax and in the process sweeps the album to its conclusion.

Although not a long release at 43 minutes, *Derelicts of Distant Hope* is a focused and well executed album, which does not reinvent the wheel, so much as deliver the goods within the established parameters of the dark ambient genre.

Abre Ojos – *Gates* CD/DVD Secrets of Giza 2013

With a number of releases issued since 2009 (both self-released and on various micro labels), Abre Ojos have now been picked up by the new and emerging American label Secrets of Giza. This is the same label who have also recently released an album of another fellow Australian / Melbournian artist Illuminoscillate, so it is positive to see these (currently) obscure acts garnering some much warranted international attention. Also given that Abre Ojos is a multi-media project at its core, for this release Secrets of Giza have had the admirable idea of releasing *Gates* in both audio and visual form, meaning both facets of the project can be appreciated at the leisure and discretion of the listener / viewer.

From the commencement of the album it is immediately evident that *Gates* inhabits a slightly heavier sound, although still retaining a central focus on the droning partially harmonic dark ambient soundscapes. This is evidenced on the opening track *Falling Suns, Dying Stars*, which contains cacophonous almost death industrial rhythmic elements which intertwines with shimmering drones and abstract treated vocalisations. *Dirt Between Our Toes* continues this theme with its jagged metallic timbre and an abysmal percussive element, whilst *Light on Our Foreheads* delivers a piece of widescreen cosmic drones, deep tonal textures and whispered vocalisations. Of the 11 album tracks each play out as a variation on established sonics themes, however late album track *From Home, From Centre, From Self* rates a particular mention for its organic percussive tones generated by deep metallic chimes and booming Japanese war drums which are seamlessly blended into the modular synth collage.

Gates also displays an increased degree of focus which is reflected in the noticeably shorter length of tracks, which range from under four minutes to around six minutes in length (... whereas the tracks on *Häxan* were more sprawling by spanned between eight and 13 minutes each). Yet putting aside an analysis of focus verses sprawl, where Abre Ojos excel is through the display of restraint and the unhurried pacing of the soundscapes. Effectively the control displayed with the mixing and tonal separation of sonic elements is what makes this such a multifaceted experience - aka the ebb and flow of crystalline drones interweaving with heavier sections of grinding metallic resonance and catatonic bass heavy percussion.

For the visual side of things, the DVD contains the same musical content which is presented with moving imagery to compliment each composition. Again the visuals form a kaleidoscopic presentation of complex geometric patterns, amorphous organic shapes and swirling washes of colour which are constantly morphing and evolving in unison with the audio tracks. Occasionally some source video input video is detectable (...including imagery from 2001 A Space Odyssey amongst other random visuals), which are fed through a a variety of visual filters to the point of abstraction. With a passing comparison to *Häxan*, where it utilised a colourful palate for its visuals, on *Gates* the colour hues are generally more subdued, with a darker and more ominous overall mood.

With the release of *Gates* Abre Ojos have presented a consummate musical and visual statement that stands entirely on its own as a purely audio experience, but is also further enhanced with the presented DVD visuals. Although Abre Ojos clearly deserves a greater profile in the dark ambient underground than they currently have, hopefully *Gates* will be their own gateway release to wider recognition. Clearly a recommended release.

Aderlating - *Gospel of the Burning Idols* CD Black Plagve 2013

The rather prolific Aderlating return with their fourth official album since 2009, which forms part of an already extensive discography spanning 14 releases (including full lengths, splits, cassettes and digital only releases). Whilst Aderlating tend to inhabit a general black ambient/ black industrial type sphere, for *The Gospel of Burning Idols* it includes some more overt musically aspects which align with the black metal scene - albeit obliquely. Thus on this basis alone Aderlating are a project which should have quite a bit of crossover appeal for both underground metal and underground industrial types.
The crumbling walls of muted noise akin to the 'opening of the tomb' introduce the album and straight away brings to mind the classic *Great Death* era of Bighter Death Now. Yet from this leaping off point the sound quickly descend into a ritualised maelstrom of demonic drawled voices, sampled choir vocals, grinding mechanised noise, a bass heavy percussive thump and general cacophony of metallic percussive elements which collectively generate a rising sense of dread and unease. In simpler terms - a fantastic album opener. The ritualistic aura is also retained on the following piece *A Vulture's Tongue Disease* with its muted rumbling soundscape and droning choir vocals, yet it remains entirely chaotic due to the use of free-form black metal style drumming. Noting this track's merging of abstract ritual atmospheres and flailing black metal drumming, it sets the template for a number of the other album tracks which fall into a similar stylistic pattern - aka a maelstrom of industrial debris, sweeping echoed noise and a variety of vocal textures (muttered evocations / screeched curses / sampled choirs), as the kit drum percussion furiously flails somewhere off in the distance of a deep cavernous space. Late album track *Spewed On By Slaves Of Inhumanity* displays a slightly more focused death industrial sound, with its heavy bass thump and a rousing orchestral elements (heavy strings/ brass), yet as always there is still a sense that the track is on the verge of descending into a chaos at any moment.
A heavy ritualistic aura permeates the entire album which also imbues the dank and suffocating atmosphere of a cavernous tomb. But rather than being merely 'ambient' in texture, the overall feel is such that it has a prominently tense, chaotic and unhinged sound throughout. Likewise the driving free-form kit percussion edges the sound of Aderlating towards a live rehearsal/ lo-fi black metal band type sound, rather than a mere studio project, which also gives this album a certain tonal edge. Although the demonic and quasi satanic sounding aspects are in no way subtle, they are handled with such nightmarish intensity as to ensure it never enters 'cheesy' territory, which such material has been known to suffer from.
On the visual side of things the death and daemonic themed medieval paintings used as part of the cover provide a suitable visual counterpart to these unhinged black industrial musings. Although containing its own distinctive sound, *The Gospel of Burning Idols* will no doubt please fans of like minded groups such as MZ.412, some aspects early Brighter Death Now and Gnaw Their Tongues (which if not known is the main solo project of one of Aderlating's members), with its chaotic ritual cacophony.

Æva – ∞ LP Daudings Gjenklang 2013

In many ways the early 'Era 1' synthesiser works of Mortiis are a bit of a guilty pleasure for me, given I came across his self-described 'dark dungeon music' at a pivotal time during my burgeoning interest in underground music. So with Mortiis being an effective 'gateway' project at the time, this then quickly led my interest to Cold Meat Industry / Malignant Records/ Loki Foundation / Tesco Organisation / Cold Spring etc. thus resulting in my total emersion in underground dark ambient, industrial and power electronic music. But I digress....
Noting that Mortiis is considered by many as a bit of a joke project, nevertheless Mortiis effectively spawned his own dark ambient sub-genre of synthesiser derived 'dungeon synth' music, which has included numerous imitators over the years. Likewise with clear similarities to Mortiis, many of these 'dungeon synth' projects also have their roots and origins in the underground black metal scene rather than the industrial (and related) underground. Æva follow this same template by virtue of being an obscure side project of the excellent Norwegian black metal solo project Skuggeheim. If you are then familiar with any of Skuggeheim's releases, clearly having atmosphere derived from a distant, muffled and lo-fi sound takes precedence over 'clean' or 'professional' sounding recordings. With its inherent lo-fi atmosphere this is one of the key reasons why Skuggeheim hits the mark so flawlessly for me, and with the same sonic approach filtering through to Æva it perfectly fits the 'dungeon synth' genre parameters - i.e. the evocation of gloomy synth soundscapes.
Although Mortiis has been used as a contextual comparison, musically the sound of Æva is not typically medieval and even overtly orchestral in delivery. Here the music is more subdued and understated and has much more in common with the depressive sound of another of Mortiis' keyboard projects Vond, and the *Selvmord* album in particular – however Æva is even more abstract and lo-fi than this particular comparison. Thus of the three lengthy album tracks, each are centred around sparse synth textures, catatonic melodies (which occasionally resembles a synthesised piano or organ tone) and some deeper abstract droning elements, which each ebb and flow across intertwining musical segments. Given the sound is staunchly analogue and lo-fi in quality it could be said to be 'poorly' recorded, however the muffled and distant tone actually provides additional aura and atmosphere. Likewise rather than feeling like typical 'songs' the compositions are presented more as 'soundscapes' or 'movements'.
Whilst 'dungeon synth' music is certainly not a refined style of music, a typical trademark is that in the most part is it not expertly played or executed. Yet of much greater importance is the existence of certain 'attitude' and 'atmosphere', which incidentally Æva effortlessly achieves this special aura and elevates this album above being merely abstract synthesizer dirges.
Regarding its presentation the LP, it displays a number of interesting quirks, where the music has been pressed on a black label vinyl so as to play from the inside to outside edge, whilst Side B contains two separate pieces tracked in parallel/ side by side, which finishes with a locked groove. Lastly the packaging provides a feeling that this release is a special

obscurity, and whilst there is no actual cover a couple of fire singed insets are included within a plastic sleeve sealed with special sticker. Limited to 200 hand numbered copies, from the review you will clearly know if this particular 'dungeon synth' obscurity is for you.

Arktau Aon – *Ikuisuus Näkyy Luiden Läpi* CD Aural Hypnox 2013

With the revered and highly collectable cult label Aural Hypnox in self-imposed hibernation until recently (since 2009 to be exact), Arktau Aon is the first official release from the label since rising from its slumber. Here we are presented a 'lost' archival release from 2005, previously forgotten and recently discovered within the label's vaults. Arktau Aon constitutes the collaboration of two Finnish ritual / dark ambient projects (namely Arktau Eos and Zoat Aon), however in reality it is more a case of the merging of monikers than musical output.

Given the established and individually distinctive sounds of the two projects, it was initially assumed this album would sit within a ritualised dark ambient sphere (i.e. somewhere in the middle of the refined dark ambient sound of Zoat Aon and the composed ritual ambient style Arktau Eos). However in actuality this is far more organic in approach than this initially held expectation. This 'organic' assessment ultimately lies in the fact that this album does not use any synthetic sound sources, rather being entirely based on actual instruments including: gongs, chimes, disharmonic woodwinds, wailing horns, various percussive implements and chanted vocalisations etc. Accordingly with the album's total reliance on such real instrumentation it results in the mood being heavily imbedded with a traditional Asiatic and ritualistic styled atmosphere. Regarding the length of the release it sits slightly on the shorter side, being a mere 31 minutes and consisting of 13 short 'movements' (which range in length from just over one minute to the longest track at four minutes). Yet despite the short run time there is a high degree of variation between the 'movements', where some segments are relatively loose and abstract in style (hinting at an improving approach to playing), with other tracks being focused and composed in their rhythmic / percussive structures. Although the sound, atmosphere and overall direction differs somewhat from expectation, what it ultimately represents is ritual ambient music in the truest sense of the term, made all the more so with the apparent lack of any synthetic or electrified instrumentation.

For packaging the release comes housed in a special screen printed cardboard box, complete with two handmade photographic inserts, which continues the handmade handicraft aesthetic of earlier Aural Hypnox releases. Although this album may not achieve the pinnacle level of many of the other Aural Hypnox releases, it remains a strong and engaging ritual ambient excursion into the unknown.

Blitzkrieg Baby - *Porcus Norvegicus* CD Neuropa 2013

Blitzkrieg Baby is the twisted industrial music project of Kim Solve, who perhaps at this point in time is more recognised for his graphic design work for a range of underground labels, bands and associated music scenes. Nevertheless *Porcus Norvegicus* - being debut album for Blitzkrieg Baby - demonstrates Kim is extremely talented in creative fields beyond just graphic design and visual arts.

When relying on the term 'industrial' to describe Blitzkrieg Baby, it must be understood this is used in a relatively loose capacity, as the range of genre cues and influences presented on the CD are certainly diverse. Maybe making comparisons to aspects of Coil, Laibach, and NON will give an impression of the musical diversity on display here. There is also a dark cinematic quality to many of the compositions which play out as if being the soundtrack to an imaginary horror / suspense styled film. Album opener *First Movement, First Kill* has a certain apocalyptic tone which leans heavily on a tense cinematic orchestral sound, with its martial brass, booming timpani and shrill horror strings. Alternately *Pig Boy* is a superb militant industrial track, which is built on a heavy pounding beat / marching snare, disharmonic string / brass wails and aggressive screamed vocals. Although an extremely short piece, the fantastically titled *Disneyfied, delirious and HIV+* delivers a short ditty of a track constructed with up-tempo classical string samples to generate a weird carnivalesque vibe, which is total antithesis to the prior pieces. Alternately the following pair of tracks *Incinerator Symphony* and *Stalker* deliver further soundtrack worthy industrial / neo-classical compositions, with pounding percussion, twisted violins and horns of doom providing a suitably tense and anxiety inducing tone. *Fuck Me Like You Hate Me* differs quite significantly from the material which proceeds it, by virtue its monotonous grinding militant industrial beat and verse / chorus / verse yelled vocals, thus making it one of the more song oriented pieces. *Children In Uniform* is also another song oriented track, but here delivers a skewed industrial piece with layered marching snares, sporadic orchestral elements and vocals with a politically rally cry type quality. Another stand out track is the late album piece *Slasher*, that based on a solid dose of angular strings and pompous percussive backing draws a passing comparison to the musical works of fellow countryman WHEN and their brand of abstract experimental and orchestral weirdness (...which is obviously meant as a total compliment). Beyond the prevalent dark soundtrack type sound which is infused within most compositions, interestingly there is also a perverse and sly aspect of humour which underscores the album's atmosphere. This is something akin a knowing wink which highlights that Blitzkrieg Baby is not all ultra serious doom and gloom, which certainly gives the album an aesthetic sensibility not often found within such music. With reference to packing and presentation, as would be expected its design is impeccable, being presented as a mini gatefold card cover with 12 page booklet. Ultimately *Porcus Norvegicus* (translating to 'Norwegian Pig' perhaps?!) is a smart, sophisticated and expertly executed album, which certainly stands on its own within the current 'industrial' scene.

Blitzkrieg Baby – *Kids' World EP* MC Beläten 2014

Promptly following the 2013 debut, the twisted musical offspring of Kim Solve has returned with this cassette only EP (...also available digitally). But rather than constituting new music, this release features a collection of unreleased tracks and previously issued compilation appearances. Also interestingly this 'EP' has a total play time in the order of 40 minutes, which dwarfs the shorter length of the debut at 33 minutes. Confusion is the key it seems!

The first side of the tape collects together four previously unreleased compositions and opens with the title track, being a mid-paced militant industrial ditty, featuring a stoic mid-paced industrial beat, ominous horns and commanding spoken/ sung vocals delivering sarcastic lyrics describing lost innocence and violence desensitisation. *Loop* follows and sits more towards a dark ambient/ death industrial sound of grinding (you guessed it) loops, complete with a recorded diary entry articulating a bleak scene of subtle menace and paranoia. Up next *The Swine Supremacy* again morphs in style, being a plodding rhythmic industrial soundscape with the cleaver use of spoken vocals which recite random phrases in 'media newspeak' styled delivery. Noting the variety displayed on the first three tracks *Those They Could Not Fuck, They Killed* shifts yet again, being an instrumental track which is an excellent example of an ominous widescreen industrial soundscape, further accentuated by catatonic bass thuds.

For side B of the cassette it brings together four previously released compilation tracks and one previously unreleased track. The strange yet intriguing track *Half Pig Half Man* is up first, where shuddering, off kilter loops provides the basis and a degree of urgency for the sardonic vocal mutterings. *Broken Child* follows in subdued fashion and contains a morose atmosphere of wavering synths, rhythmic bass loops, upon which understated and fragile sung vocals are overlaid. *Incinerator Symphony No. I* is a standout offering, here evoking the best of the pummeling and shuddering bleakness of *The Slaughterhouse* era Brighter Death Now, where sparse harmonic notes (xylophone perhaps?) provides a nice sonic touch. *Children In Uniform MMXIII* (an alternate version to that featured on *Porcus Norvegicus*), returns to composed song based approach with militant rolling beats, shrill orchestral strings and yelled/ echoed vocals. This version is noted to differ from the original by the orchestral string being pushed to the background and a plodding bass brought to the fore. On the final track *Your Happy Place*, it is the track which deviates most significantly from the material which precedes it (...to the point of feeling almost tacked on), given it is a composition which flirts closely with dark industrial pop style. Here a plodding bass, two-step beat and programmed synth drive the piece forward, complete with spoken vocals and synth break flourishes (... whilst interesting, this style is something these ears are typically accustomed to).

Noting the *Kids' World EP* brings together earlier existing material, where this succeeds is with its further display of the wide variety of sonic approaches and playful nature that Blitzkrieg Baby employs under the 'industrial' banner. Likewise with its even greater deviance in sound and approach than was displayed on *Porcus Norvegicus*, it raises the question of exactly where Kim will take the project on the upcoming sophomore album?

Budrus - *Canine Visions IX* CD Freak Animal 2013

Budrus are an unusual and difficult to categorise project which covers some diverse sonic territory whilst managing to amass it into a coherent whole. Skin Area might be a good comparison in this regard, but not for a comparison to their sound, rather with respect of Skin Area's own diverse mixture of industrial and non-typical industrial elements. Given their diverse musical influences Budrus arrive at their own sound through a mixture of abstract pounding industrial, guitar based instrumental drone, (almost) martial atmospheres and power electronics attitude evidenced by the gruff, yelled vocals presented without distortion treatment (other than light echo).

In some ways the opening track *Canine Vision I* is the most straightforward, with its droning analogue synths and aggressive upfront vocals evoking an industrial/ power electronics tone, before the introduction of drums and synth layers which have a vague martial industrial sensibility. This martial sensibility is also evident with the pounding rhythm of *Greet Me*, which offsets the loose guitar drones, distorted noise layers and unhinged vocals. The excellent *Shores of Glass* delivers a spare melancholic drone tracks of sweeping tonal textures, sparse kit drums and slow clean guitars, with the mood being altered by the aggressive vocals appearing mid track. Likewise late album track *Wake up!* is an excellent example of the eclectic nature of the project: the vocals hint at power electronics aggression, the synth and percussion hint at martial / industrial genres, yet the the clean and distorted guitars pushes the composition into a sound realm all its own. Despite its varied musical expression ranging from sparse to focused and heavy, the overarching mood remains a melancholic one, either forming the main focus or remaining as the undercurrent to the more aggressive segments.

Beyond musicality comment is warranted regarding the visual presentation. Given that I consider the artwork of any release to be of central importance, to my aesthetic sensibilities the cover and logo do not do this album justice, and on face value it carries a visual feel more suited to a crust punk band or similar. As such I have pondered whether this album might have been better represented with something altogether different. Notwithstanding this aesthetic criticism, *Canine Visions IX* is a varied and ultimately difficult album to categorise, yet one which should confound expectations and reward those adventurous enough to check it out.

Contagious Orgasm / Kadaver - *A Tragedy Without A Border Line* CD Wrotycz Records 2011

Just so is stated up front, I will admit that I am not intimately familiar with the musical outputs of either of these contributing projects. However I am at least aware that the Israeli project Kadaver works within a broad power electronics and death industrial sound, whilst the long active Contagious Orgasm from Japan has traversed many sounds across experimental, noise, industrial and ambient spheres over the last 25 years.

For this collaborative album, three lengthy tracks are presented spanning between 17 and 21 minutes each. However in actuality the three tracks give the impression of being part of a singular and much larger album length piece, which spans aspects of experimental industrial, noise, and ambient. Given the sprawling nature of the tracks the relatively loose and freeform nature of the compositions is openly displayed, which flow and evolve through multiple segments, rather than adhering to a more focused and composed structure. As such some diverse sonic elements are utilised, ranging from flaying noise, micro-tonal field recordings, humming synth textures, spoken vocals samples, sampled and treated string quartet/ piano samples, pulsing distortion, hazy ambience and droning soundscapes etc. Likewise with the loose combination elements it achieves a hallucinogenic aspect to the bizarrely tinged atmospheres. Effectively the album's success is in its ability to evokes a dreamlike state, where tracks veer from the intensively nightmarish to the outright weird without being jarring or disjointed.

With my lack of familiarity with both projects I can't really say which aspects of this may lean towards each individual project, however this may be a moot point as this album has certainly been a surprising and unexpectedly challenging listen. Given the 'out there' aspects, clearly this would be an album suited for the more sonically adventurous, rather than for those wanting their fix of a particular genre.

Deathstench / Trepaneringsritualen - *Split* LP Malignant Records 2013

In the dying days of 2013 we have been blessed (cursed?) with a late coming highlight of the year, being released by the ever commendable Malignant Records. Pressed as a beautiful picture disc vinyl, this split pairs two of the current blackened and ritual infused, death ambient / industrial projects on Malignant Records / Black Plagve, namely: Deathstench and Trepaneringsritualen.

Starting with Deathstench, they present two tracks on their side. The caustic atmospheric noise of the first offering *Damnum Minatum* comes blasting from the speakers, containing a mine shaft depth styled echoed production, as screeched and distortion treated vocals shred the eardrums, along with layers of harsh industrial textures. Buried somewhere within the overblown production are cymbal crashes, blackened tremolo riffed guitars and moody synth lines, which provide a depressive and semi composed edge to the industrial noise chaos. For their second track *Temples of Dust* this features guest vocals of Alan Dubin, most notably recognised as the vocals of the excellent but defunct doom drone band Khanate. Displaying a greater degree of restraint by commencing with ringing ritual bowl hits and various other cavernous echoed textures, when Alan's vocals arrive they are agonised and delivered in his trademark screeched psychotic style, made all the more incisive by his proper enunciation of the lyrics. Over its nine minute span *Temples of Dust* would broadly slot under a death industrial / atmospheric noise tag thanks to the overblown wind-tunnel style of production, which also includes a range of metallic thuds, clangs and general metallic cacophony.

Flipping the picture disc over a 17 minute monster of a track is presented by Trepaneringsritualen and by featuring clearly defined segments this is akin to a number of tracks within larger framework. For the first seven minutes or so this is ritual ambient at its most gloomy, with catatonic tribal percussive thuds which cut through the inky muffled blackness of the production, along with distant echo treated slow chanted invocations which are almost Tibetan throat singing in style. Yet at around the seven minute mark, things really step into their own, with the rise of slow drawling demonic horns and mid paced percussive thumps. With a gradual upward trajectory further tribal / ritual percussion, militant rolling snare drums and grinding synths textures flesh out the rhythmic framework as a solid platform for the trademark garbled / croaked vocals, lastly complimented by a lachrymose synth line. Within this singular track this displays all the elements of what makes Trepaneringsritualen so great and contains their now trademark dank, oozing, ritual infused, death ambience / industrial sound. From music to presentation, this is an absolutely excellent pairing of acts which has hit all the right sonic and visual markers. With a limitation of a mere 250 copies and pressed on heavy vinyl with postcard, surely this won't be available for too long.

Folkstorm – *Folksongs* CD Old Europa Café 2011

Keeping up with the continual output of the hyper productive Henrik Nordvargr Björkk is a rather monumental task, meaning on occasion certain albums slip under the radar at the time of release. *Folkmusic* is one such album, which although a couple of years old deserves some belated praise and attention.

To slightly backtrack, Folkstorm was laid to rest in the early 2000's but did not stay dormant for long, with the 2005 album *Folkmusik* heralding the return of the reanimated Folkstorm corpse. *Folksongs* is the third post resurrection album which delivers some of the most focused and streamlined harsh industrial musings produced by the project to date. Notably the looser and (potentially) semi-improvised sound of earlier material has been overhauled here with 'song' based structures (...which evidently has been the result of experimenting with new musical equipment).

Over the 11 album tracks the refined 'song' based approach blends clinical industrial rhythms, militant drum machine beats, pulsing/ burrowing/ wavering noise, crumbling static, shredding

en
karte

distortion etc. However with reference to the structured elements it is necessary to point out that the beats and rhythms are very much of the mechanised factory type, and are clearly not of an industrial dance variety. Similarly with its hard and generally minimalistic programmed structures, complimented with vocals ranging from morbidly spoken through to roughly yelled (...all distortion treated mind you), it brings to mind comparisons to the early sound German stalwarts Haus Arafna (...a compliment no doubt).

Although the overall sound embodies an old school analogue type feel, the album has a brutally loud, crisp and sharp production which suits the harshness of the music perfectly. Likewise whilst *Folkmusic* retains a core sonic aesthetic of aggressive harsh industrial, there are a number of tracks where it forgoes aggression for slower ominous death industrial atmospheres, meaning there is a wide degree of sonic diversity across its relatively short 40 minute span.

Noting that Nordvargr has never opted to create 'easy' listening music, Folkstorm is clearly a project which sits at the harder end of what he produces. However even if you think you already know what Folkstorm is all about based on earlier output, you are likely to be rather surprised of how different *Folkmusic* actually is. Although the tracks are constructed with 'typical' harsh industrial elements of stilted rhythms, squelching noise, power drilling textures and an atmosphere of abrasive yet clinical morbidity, it is their focus and song structure which comes through so strongly and makes this an album with such immediate impact.

The Grey Wolves / Wertham / Survival Instinct – *Ramraiding Thee Abyss* LP Old Europa Café / Elettronica Radicale Edizioni 2013

Here is a new three-way split/ collaboration album which in many ways reflects the past, present and future of the contributing acts, whilst also remaining devoted to the underground scene from which they have been collectively spawned. Obviously the Grey Wolves and Wertham should already be well-known, however this LP also functions to introduce Survival Instinct who are noted to be: *'a splinter cell and an exit strategy, of and from, the Grey Wolves'.* Noting the potential ambiguity of this statement that seems to allude to a potential end to the Grey Wolves, this may or may not in fact be the case. Or perhaps it is just a solo project of either of the Grey Wolves members David Padbury or Trevor Ward? Not too sure on this point, so on with the review.

Noting the aggressive atmospheric noise meets power electronics tone of both the Grey Wolves and Wertham, in an overall sense this LP delivers exactly what is expected. Thus *Ramraiding Thee Abyss* opens with *No Good Deeds Will Be Left Unpunished*, which is appropriately a three-way collaboration, where the layered, mid-range fluctuating distortion and partially buried vocalisations combine into a heavy and urgent statement of intent. *Latin Day (Flashback - Ipswich Agro)* quickly follows and sees the Grey Wolves operating in the vein of their classic sound. That is to say it includes vague shuddering industrial rhythms which are caked in layers of noise filth, as antagonistic echoed vocals deliver an unintelligible sermon. *Shankill Butchers* sees Wertham functioning on their own, delivering intense cyclic, mid to low range rumbling distortion, with a heavily treated vocal attack. Straight forward and to the point with it scathing layered noise approach, TV reporter dialogue samples are also used to flesh out thematic context. *Rise Above the Flames* then follows and is the first solo offering of Survival Instinct and based on this track they are a very promising act. This piece takes a subdued and brooding approach which leans towards a death industrial sound. Here the production is less based on overloaded distortion, rather opting for composed and echoed treated tribal/ mechanical rhythms mixed with atmospheric noise. Certainly an excellent introduction to the project.

For the flip side of the vinyl Wertham in collusion with Survival Instinct deliver an instrumental track *Towards a Dark Horizon* which charts a course of composed industrial factory rhythms and an undercurrent of generally subdued sweeping and crumbling clamour. The Grey Wolves then appear again in solo guise on *Edging Ever Closer*, which is more atmospheric than typically grating, again with layered droning noise, scattered electronics and unhinged vocalisations. *Friday Night Boot Party* is another solo offering courtesy of Wertham, here looped conveyor belt sonics combine with atmospheric burrowing noise, which underscore the distortion infused vocals which are barked in delivery. The album is then concluded by another solo track from Survival Instinct, where moody synth textures of *New Phase Dawns* counterbalance mid paced jagged industrial loops and sporadic heavy bass tone blasts. Another great moment from this new project.

Without sounding like a patchwork of various projects, the three contributing acts manage to find common and complimentary ground on *Ramraiding Thee Abyss*, be it on solo standalone tracks or in otherwise collaborative guise. Likewise given the sheer number of years the Grey Wolves have been in existence as an active scene contributor (...28 years and counting), it is great to see that they have lost none of their urgency, antagonism and attitude. Pressed in pristine black vinyl (THE perfect format for this type of release), and with a slick gatefold sleeve adorned with suitable 'cultural terrorist manifesto' type statements and imagery, this album is everything it was hoped it could be, and in fact delivers more, given the strength and distinctive sounds of the Survival Instinct solo cuts.

Halo Manash - *Wesieni Wainajat* CD Aural Hypnox 2013

The return of Halo Manash with a new release on the recently reactivated Aural Hypnox label is welcomed news, particularly given the high rotation the last three albums received around these parts. Being the first release following the Forest Music 'treelogy' (trilogy) of *Language of Red Goats, Am Kha Astrie* and *Taiwaskivi, Wesieni Wainajat* is a 2012-2013 recording from the group. Interestingly this has also been issued on the new Aural Hypnox side label Underworld Editions, which includes a mission statement of: *'Underworld Editions presents rough and unusual glimpses to the hidden past and special manifestations of the present'.* Consisting of three lengthy tracks the overarching feel *Wesieni Wainajat* is one of a generally more composed sound, particularly when compared to the ritual ambient intent of the preceding trilogy. Yet this is not to say that this album is a huge departure from what precedes it, rather the overall feel of 'composition' seems to be mostly derived from the use of a droning pump organ as the key central instrument

on each of the pieces.
Kwlwsta opens the album, with a focused harmonic droning organ melody, where the soundscape is bolstered by sparse symbol percussion, distant disharmonic wailing horns and abstract sonic textures. There is a gradual upward trajectory to the track's building intensity, but this is done without jarring the droning ritual atmosphere. *Varjoista* is up next and sees Halo Manash deliver a track which may be the most composed and direct track they have released thus far in their career. Here the brooding organ again takes central prominence, being further underscored by sparse dulcimer hammered notes and a range of field recording textures (elements including: rustling leaves, splintering branches, or fracturing ice perhaps?). Yet this track elevates itself to an entirely higher level of consciousness through the introduction of mid-paced rhythmic percussion, courtesy of a bodhran drum (or similar). Thus with its swaying ritualised atmosphere, *Varjoista* is both the highlight and standout track of the album. For the final of the three compositions *Tulelle* delivers a lengthy somewhat abstract 18 minute composition, which aligns more consistently with the sparse ritual ambient music of earlier material. Although partly focused on a slow droning organ hum, this element is relegated to the background to allow a range of field recordings to take greater prominence, which seem to have captured diverse elements of: winds within the forest tree tops; a low cracking fire; distant bird calls; a babbling brook; mirco-tonal aquatic sounds and some unidentifiable sparse scratching type textures. With its extended length and low key vibe, this track is trance inducing and mediative in the best way possible.
It almost goes without saying that Aural Hypnox clearly understands that the physical manifestation of an album is just as important as the musical component. Being issued in a limited run of 350 CDs and 50 cassettes, the packaging is perfectly suited to the album's aura, consisting of screen printed raw cardboard box, with a range of hand printed and photographic inserts. With only three tracks and a play time of 39 minutes this may slightly feel more like an extended mini-album and by being released on the new sub-label (where it seems to qualify as a *'special manifestations of the present'*), it is unclear whether this is considered the main new album from the group or is more of an intermediate diversion. Either way, there are absolutely no complaints over its discographic status and short length, given this constitutes superb material from the group.

Halo Manash - *Caickuwi Cauwas Walkeus* CD Aural Hypnox 2014
Any new release from Halo Manash is welcomed news and whilst this is technically not a new recording this will constitute an unheard album for most listeners. Effectively this album is a re-release of the impossibly limited original version, issued in 2009 in a ridiculous edition of 29 copies. This current version comes in 444 standard copies and 49 special wooden box-set copies and has been issued on the new Stellar Mansion series, which has been established under the Aural Hypnox banner, with a mission statement of: *'...presenting past Helixes transmissions, sent back from distant stars...'*.
With the title translating to 'Afar Echoes the White Light', the album captures the trademark ritual ambient music of Halo Manash, which is also most comparable to the abstract stylistic slant of the Forest Music trilogy of *Language of Red Goats, Am Kha Astrie* and *Taiwaskivi.* Of the five interconnecting compositions (spanning 43 minutes), they flow forward at a catatonic pace, where each ritual ambient movement merges seamlessly with the next. Interestingly the promo blurb outlines that this album has been recorded using only acoustic instrumentation with no studio overdubs, which makes its droning ritual atmosphere all the more engaging.
To facilitate full immersion into the album's atmosphere, slow ritual chimes function to provide some melodic undertones and a vague sense of structure, whilst slow thumping ritual percussion provides a heartbeat like pulse to proceedings. Likewise a droning ritual undercurrent is created by the percussive notes of gongs and chimes which shimmer and ring out as echoed reverberations, whilst wood wind instruments and horns mournfully wail somewhere off in the distance. Ultimately this is extremely 'visual' ritual ambient music which articulates emanations from the spiritual either and gives rise to mind's eye visions of: a hazy twilight setting; forest branches spanning overhead forming a natural cathedral; tendrils of incense smoke rising from a makeshift altar etc.
Noting the limitation of the original edition, it is a certainly a welcome addition to Halo Manash's discography to have this album issued in a more generous number. Likewise it is worthwhile noting that the material herein is as strong as any Halo Manash have released to date and should allay any concern that this material might have been considered second-rate thus warranting its original limitation. As with all Aural Hypnox releases, this is issued in special handmade cardboard cover, here featuring archaic card stock and completed with screen printed images. Again Aural Hypnox deliver ritual ambient of the highest order and a feast for the eye and ear.

Human Larvae – *Womb Worship* CD L.White Records 2013
Human Larvae is one of the newer guard of German projects, being the solo project of Berlin native Daniel Burfoot. Choosing to operate at the edges of death industrial, power electronics and experimental noise, Human Larvae align comfortably with similar acts who function within the grey spaces between various abrasive underground 'industrial' related genres. Noting the solid debut album *Home Is Where The Hurt Is* was issued in 2008, Daniel issued a 2011 tape releases as part of the refining of his sound to a razor-sharp point for this sophomore album. *Perdition from the Virgins Mouth* opens the album in stunning fashion, where a gloomy, catatonically played piano note ring out against scratching junk metal tones, low bass thuds and agonisingly yelled/ distorted treated vocals. *The Truth I Failed To See* follows, yet operates in far more subdued territory, containing looped breathing sounds, understated wavering synth tones, distant conveyor belt rhythms and thematic dialogue sample. *Slave To Violence* steps up the tone in a more classic power electronics vein, relying on a bass loaded undercurrent, overblown metallic junk metal distortion and prominent screeched vocals, which in many ways reminds of the aggressive yet densely detailed sonic approach of recent Grunt material. In more direct terms - excellent. By pulling back on the throttle *Entwined In The Umbilical Noose* delivers a lengthy track with a cavernous wind tunnel aesthetic. Across

its span the piece shifts through various segments involving: a lone organ dirge; grating tonal textures; wheezing noise and droning three note melody. Located towards the centre of the album, *Methods of Possession* brings to mind the focused intensity of IRM, which is used as a positive comparison to highlight the quality found here. This particular track works on multiple levels by merging chaotic micro-tonal sonic detailing with organic sounding drones, over which the layered, distortion saturated vocals are delivered with desperate intensity.
Given that the use of abuse related dialogue samples is by now considered 'de rigueur' for this type of material, this can lead to the listener being somewhat desensitised to the intended impact. This is clearly not the case on *Wrapped In The Warm Sheets Of Mother Love*, being a track of driven distortion and burrowing noise, over which a sample referencing sexual abuse perpetrated by a mother (as recounted by the son) creates a strong and nauseating impact. This nauseous tone remains on *Obsession Intermezzo II* (despite containing a totally different sound to the preceding track), here featuring minutely amplified 'wet' textural sounds, low bass drone and menacing synth melody. The title track arrives as the concluding album composition, which expertly balances an atmosphere which is equally heavy as it is ominous. Here vaguely rhythmic drones, grinding textures, scattered junk metal noise and heavy echo distortion treated vocals are the order of the day, and whilst not necessarily covering new sonic territory for this style, Human Larvae nevertheless nails the sound perfectly.
Whilst *Womb Worship* is not a long album at 43 minutes, not a single minute of its play time is wasted on any second-rate filler. The mastering provided by James Plotkin is solid, hefty and suitably loud, yet also contains depth and tonal separation to allow the quieter tracks to breath with ample sonic space. With its tonal diversity and threateningly weighty atmosphere (even in its quieter moment), Human Larvae have succeeded in delivering a diverse and distinctive sound. By displaying an equal balance of aggression and restraint, *Womb Worship* is delivered with an absolutely convincing degree of focus and control. This album has already garnered extensive rotations around these quarters and is exactly the type of album to warrant many more repeat rotations in future.

I.Corax - *Cella Phantasma* CD Aural Hypnox 2013
Here is yet another new release on the reactivated Aural Hynox label and a further addition to the Underworld Editions sub-label series. This release also sees I.Corax being formally welcomed to the Aural Hypnox roster with *Cella Phantasma* constituting the very first recording session from the group (dating back to 1999), which has until now remained unreleased.
Without any elaboration the use of the terms 'dark ambient' and 'drone' can be rather vague descriptors, particularly given the wide reaching sounds and styles which are captured under this banner. Therefore to be a bit more creative the sound of I.Corax resides within a spectral netherworld, located on a plain somewhere between the real and spiritual realms. This description can be further put into context with a cross reference to label mate Halo Manash, whose use of real instrumentation is rooted in humanistic expression and attempted communion with the dream and spirit world. Alternately as I.Corax has fewer inherent sonic markers to indicate being the product of human hands, consequently their sound is more akin to emanations from a spectral realm.
Hunt is the first of four compositions being a track built on abstract sweeping tones, shimmering textures, a prominent (vaguely metallic) rhythmic pulse and a range of shadowy chanted vocals to provide a mysterious and ghostly atmosphere. Spanning an expansive 13 minutes it is a solid and engaging opening. Second offering *Kneeler* then opts for a slightly denser droning framework, complimented with metallic scrapping textures and echoed otherworldly insectoid rhythms which provides a highly distinctive sound quality. This chthonian atmosphere bleeds into *Naos*, again driven by eerie tribalesque rhythms and disembodied vocalisations, which all feel as if focused towards a direct ritualised intent. For the final of the four tracks *Nexion* it concludes the album on a slightly more subdued note. Here the composition constitutes a floating miasma of sound, evoked through layered field recordings, minimalist droning synth notes, ritual percussive implements and abstract metallic scraping textures.
Simmilar to the other releases in the Underworld Editions series, this has been issued in a limited run of 350 CDs and 50 cassettes, packaged in a screen printed raw cardboard box, with hand printed and photographic inserts. Although (again) on the shorter side at 36 minutes, the four presented tracks are absolutely worthy of detailed investigation. The release of this early recording of I.Corax is a welcomed one, noting also that all other earlier albums are due to be re-released on Aural Hypnox in the not too distant future.

Illuminoscillate - *Uniform Wall* CD Secrets of Giza 2013
The dark ambient genre is one particular music style that has expanded to such a point where it is simply impossible to hear everything which gets released year on year (...which in some ways is rather similar to the metal genre and its hundreds of sub-genres). Thus in this context the bigger known record labels are often viewed as the curators of the scene, making it then all the more difficult for more obscure acts (...and labels for that matter) to get noticed. Given Illuminoscillate are a relatively new Australian dark ambient styled project and Secrets of Giza are a new American label (...this being their second release), clearly both fall into the 'obscure' category. This however will hopefully change based on the quality of *Uniform Wall.*
Where Illuminoscillate particularly succeeds is through the presentation of an animated sound palate within a morphing dark ambient framework. A hazy enveloping miasma provides the overarching atmosphere, where the album's abstract and slightly mechanical oscillating drones are also underpinned by deep bass rhythmic elements that build to cascading intensity during select segments. Illuminoscillate's sound is also driven by the merging of the organic and synthetic, where it appears that field recording elements constitute a large portion of the base sonic input, which are then morphed and manipulated through a (modular?) synthesizer interface.
Two early album tracks *City Loop*, with its excellent low mechanized pulse, and the shimmering multi-layered drones of *Southern Obedience*, are both quite reminiscent of the molasses like drugged atmosphere of Hazard's unsung classic album *Lech* - yet when I posed this potential inspiration to Illuminoscillate member Matthew Casey he advised of no prior

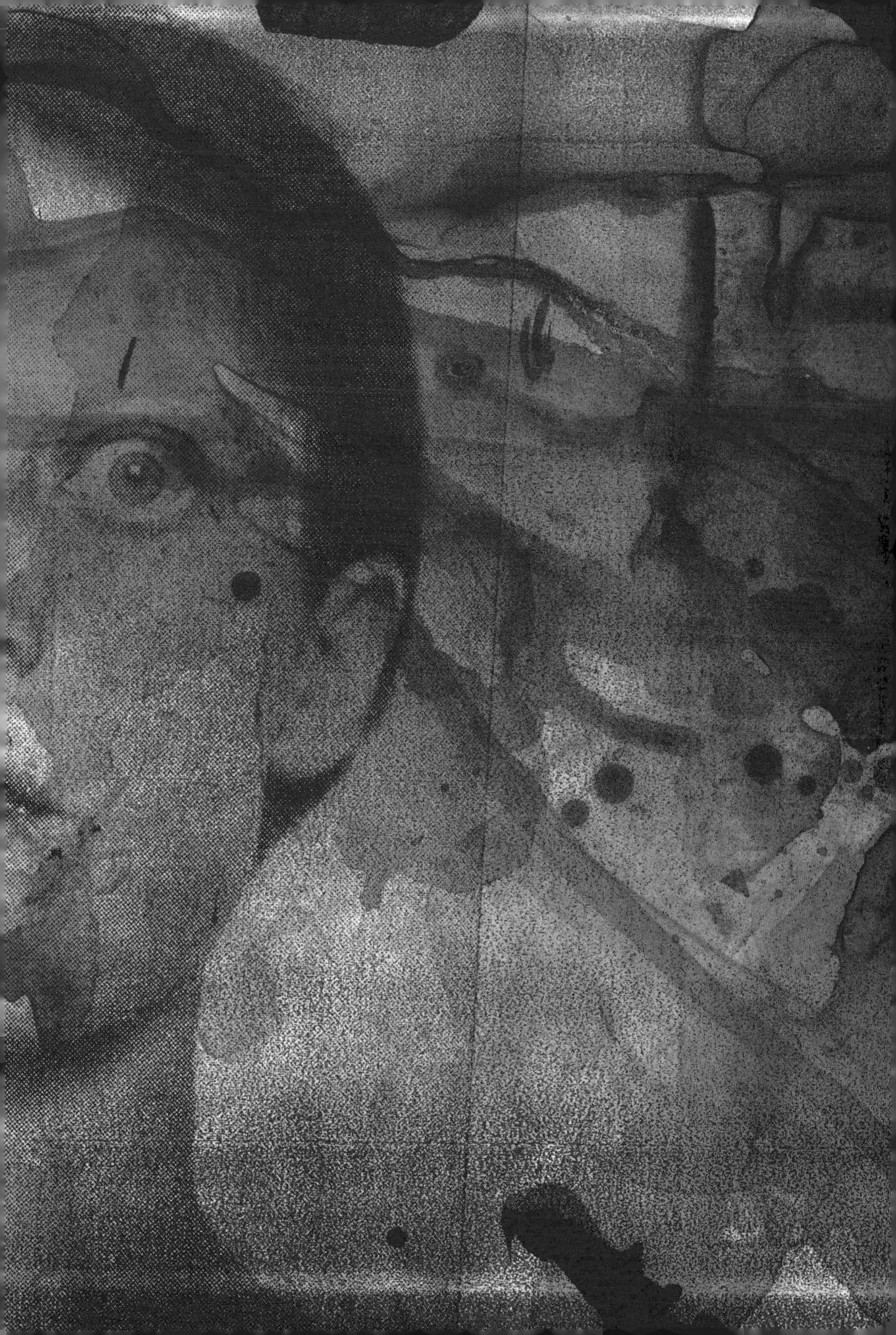

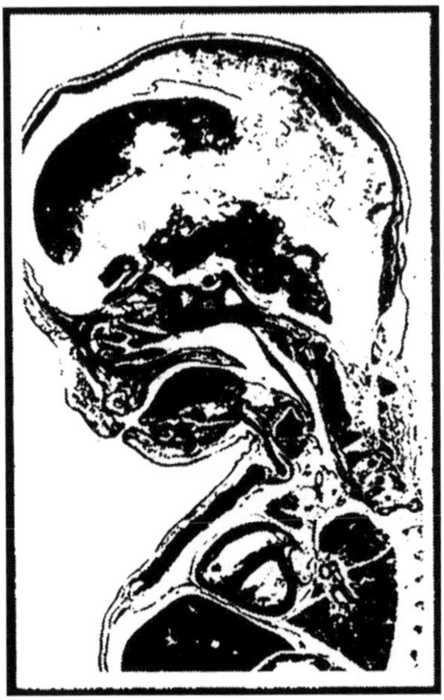

knowledge of *Lech* (...just a coincidence then). Mid album track *Widow of Fatigue* presents a more simplistic and subdued track which is built on a series of mechanized loops, while following track *Absent Teeth* pursues deeper abstract drone territory. Arriving towards the end of the album *Late November* provides a heavier sound, delivering a muted almost death industrial track due it its heavy bass pounding beat and animated electronics with a sharper tonal edge. This track bleeds into the concluding composition *Feeding Procedure* which erodes into sparse abstract soundscape of low grinding bass and other layers with shimmering tonality, which build to a intense crescendo before ushering the album to its conclusion.
With a slick six panel digi-pack presentation, coupled with the strong and focused soundscapes on display, surely *Uniform Wall* should gain some positive attention from wider dark ambient scene. Although project and label currently slot into the 'obscure' category, this is definitely worth taking a punt on.

Iron Fist of the Sun - *Who Will Help Me Wash My Right Hand* CD Cold Spring 2013
The rather prolific Iron Fist of the Sun (IFOTS) returns with a new album and continues with the now trademark Princess Diana themed artwork, yet it is not immediately evident whether this thematic material also extends to the lyrics and song titles. Putting questions regarding conceptual content aside, the album opens with the subdued track *For You I Will*, which utilises a repeated bass riff as the main focus, coupled with spoken vocals (...rendered indecipherable due to the distortion treatment), whilst a morse code 'bleep' delivers a coded message. *The Dog Has No Master* follows and is also relatively subdued with its deep bass pulse, scattered tonal noise and distortion warped vocals. Thus it takes until the third track *Be Forever Green* to really ramp up into a more 'standard' IFOTS power electronics sound, where all sound elements (i.e. queasy loops, pounding percussion and aggressive vocals) are tonally sharp and cleanly separated in the mix. The longest track on the album is the excellent 12 minute *Saltpurse,* which during its first half is clinical and morbid in atmosphere with multiple pulsing elements and low synth drones. Alternately the second half of the track is defined by excellent static riddled and melancholic synth layers over which aggressive vocals are delivered (...partly bringing to mind the sound of Nyodene D). The tile track then concludes the album, which is constructed with heavy and sharp multi-layered 'laser precision' digital distortion - again with the trademark distortion laced vocals. With only five tracks and a play time of 36 minutes, this is a relatively short release, yet with its meticulously constructed sound and sharp and clear production, it is another fine example of the varied approach IFOTS has taken to his particular style of industrial and power electronics.

John Murphy / Ben Taylor – *self titled* CD Cipher Productions 2014
Here we have a collaborative album featuring the combined inputs of the known John Murphy (of Knifeladder, Kraang, Shining Vril and MANY others), and the likely lesser known Ben Taylor (of Ebola Disco & Bordel Militaire). From the liner notes it also seems these recordings are already a number of years old (dating from 2004-2005), yet there is no indication of the reasons for its delayed release. Nevertheless this album can be filed under a broad experimental industrial style, which also feels as if it has roots in an analogue, tape culture oriented sound. Interestingly the conceptual content and focus of the release have been kept to a minimum (or purposefully excluded altogether), given the lack of project moniker, album title or even titles for individual tracks. Clearly this means the material on display needs to be appreciated on sonic quality alone. From the album's opening untitled cut, which offers up slow oscillating and shimmering drones, it sets a slow meditative pace which continues into the following composition, albeit upping the tension slightly with a range of more forceful 'industrialised' sonic layers and scattered percussive sounds. Track four then delivers an excellent example of a ritual ambient style, with a deeply cavernous sound production and low chanted vocal textures. Alternately track six represents the noisier end of the scale for the album, where it edges towards an overblown style of cacophonous industrial / atmospheric noise, although does maintain some harmonious textures which are partially buried within the texturally dense mix. Representing a particular album standout, track nine with its ambient / industrial tone, reminds of Anemone Tube's recent outputs. Here the complex multi-layered track featuring some heavily processed field recordings, looped vocalisations and micro-tonal textures. In the later third of the album. track 11 opts for a heavy ritual industrial sound based on catatonic bass thuds, shuddering electronics, ritual chimes and a series of garbled vocalisations. Likewise although late album track 14 does not deviate heavily from the preceding tracks, it delivers

an animated, droning industrial/ ambient piece, which bleeds into the final composition, being a shorter repetitive number based on slightly wonky and hallucinogenic toned loops.
From the liner notes the range of instruments used on the recording these include: ethnic instruments, pan-pipes, harmonica, theremin, tapes, processors, oscillators, pan-pipes, harmonica etc. However as these represent source inputs and sound processing tools, seeking to identify individual instruments within the mix is ultimately a pointless task. Yet in an overarching sense there is a ritual industrial quality to the album's atmosphere, however this is arrived at from the perspective of tonal range and sound, rather than specific ritualised intent (…for comparative purposes the Aural Hypnox collective could be referenced as an example of where ritual forms a key aspect of their approach). Also whilst some of the album's passages clearly display an improvisational stylistic slant, this never descends into messy or out of control sound experimentations, rather articulates an unhurried pacing and clear control to these experimental compositions.
Of the 15 untitled album tracks, each spans around three and seven minutes which results in an album which pushes the limit of the CD format (71 minutes in all), meaning a fair amount of sonic territory is covered under its chosen experimental industrial style. Thus without attitude, ego or pretence, Mr Murphy and Mr Taylor have issued an album which delivers a solid slab of darkly (and occasionally noisy), experimental/ industrial meditations.

K100 – *The Vault of Apparitions* CD Neuropa Records/ Unreality 2010

To introduce K100 to the unfamiliar, it is an obscure project operating within the field of dark ambience, although sole project member Kim Solve is likely to be better recognised for his other industrial act Blitzkrieg Baby. With K100 Kim has opted to focus on the more subtle and abstract side of musical expression, which nicely counterbalances the militant industrial bombast of Blitzkrieg Baby.
Although *The Vault of Apparitions* contains 12 compositions (spanning 51 minutes), as is often the case with this type of music it is best appreciated as a singular composition / body of work. Thus from the album's opening moments the atmosphere is hollow, distant and ominous, where low mechanised humming textures merge with sub orchestral drones. As the album progresses it becomes entirely apparent that this is also dark ambience of the deep shafts and subterranean caverns typology. Here the tonal reverberations of cavernous spaces mingle with other textures that sonically articulate the low distant rumble of far of thunder (…or perhaps some other far worse nameless entity lurking in the depths). But far from being all drone and drift, there are occasional vague metallic rhythmic tones intermixed with the yawning catacomb bass tones.
Likewise further sonic variety is achieved through other tonal elements such as ritual gongs / chimes and a Tibetan thigh bone horn, where the drawling horn note of the later instrument bleeds out into widescreen textural drones.
Broadly subtle in texture - like a dank fog which slowly creeps over the landscape – *The Vault of Apparitions* sits within stalking and suspenseful soundtrack territory. Also with the organic feel imbedded within the deep bass drones, the result has a partial affinity with the ritual drone works of the Aural Hypnox label collective. Given its abstract and subtle nuances *The Vault of Apparitions* is not an album of immediate impact. Rather it is an understated slow burner, where the key to unlocking its rewards are patience and detailed attention.

Kommando RJF - *Sweet Slow Suicide* LP Posh Isolation 2013

Leif Thuresson of the obscure 80's Swedish group RJF has finally returned, exactly 30 years on from the release of their debut album. Here RJF have been rebranded with the 'Kommando' tag and in place of missing original member Tryggve Persson, Leif has enlisted assistance from Tommy Carlsson and Kristian Olsson - both of whom should need no introduction due to their individual pedigree within the Scandinavian post-industrial scene.
To quickly back track, evidently RJF set a high water mark in the Swedish industrial underground by releasing a heralded album in 1983 (*Greater Success In Apprehension & Convictions*), before promptly disappearing. Supposedly a second album *Roped in Rubber* was recorded in 1984 only for the master tape to go missing, whilst attempts to record an earlier version of this album occurred as far back as 1991, but for various reasons were not completed. Whatever the actual facts are relating to missing master tapes and aborted recording attempts, time has marched incessantly on, resulting in the sophomore album being finally released three decades on from the debut. Better late then never as the saying goes.
From the first rotation is it evident that *Sweet Slow Suicide* is a punishing album in the best way possible, consisting of stripped back and staunchly analog power electronics. Given that in today's context the lo-fi experimental electronic minimalism of the debut RJF album is partly showing its age, this new incarnation opts for a different tactic by going for the jugular with a predominantly aggressive power electronics attack. Simple and straightforward in construction, the tracks are built on queasy oscillating electronics, aggressive noise, loose rhythmic bass tones and distortion scared vocals. Noting that the overall sound and attitude encapsulates a 'classic' power electronics sound, in actuality it is a sound which is is often attempted but rarely nailed as solidly as this. Likewise despite the general simplicity of the tracks, the wavering distortion, crescendos of noise and harsh vocals are delivered with both power and conviction for maximum sonic impact.
Although no details are provided as to who did what on this album, this is ultimately irrelevant when dealing with an album of this calibre. Plain text on two printed inserts rounds out the minimalist visual side of the album and its 300 edition mirrors the limitation of the debut album. A mandatory purchase.

Lamia Vox - *Sigillum Diaboli* CD Cyclic Law 2013

Although having not come across Lamia Vox before, they have recently joined the ranks of Cyclic Law (who have issued this their sophomore album), which will no doubt bring them into greater recognition. Being the solo project of Alina Antonova, Lamia Vox evokes a sound and aesthetic which is sits very much at home in the 'classic' early to mid 90's period of Cold Meat Industry (CMI). This is dark ambient music at its core, but approached from a more songlike perspective with the use of ritual, martial and neo-classical elements (...or more simply this is 'occult dark ambient' as coined by Alina).

Passing comparisons to the likes of In Slaughter Natives, Sephiroth, Desiderii Marginis etc will give an impression of stylistic linage, however this is not to say that Lamia Vox are merely retracing the well warn paths forged by others. Given the maturity of the compositions and the stylistic flair on display, it ensures that Lamia Vox have carved a niche of their own. However another possibly unavoidable comparison is Aghast, due to the use of Alina's vocals - ranging from ghostly whispers to choir like vocal textures - which are used sparingly throughout.

The heavy martial / tribal percussion of *Lapis Occultus* sets the ritualistic aura of the album early on and acts as a backdrop for whispered and sung twilight evocations. Likewise mid album track *Enemy of Heaven* arrives as a particularly rousing composition within a martial industrial construction. Here the militant snare drum provides focus, but offset against a deep piano melody, rousing orchestral textures and choir like vocals. Following track *Liberation* again approaches full martial/ neo-classical guise being a great example of a swelling orchestral and choir movement. Alternately the stalking sub-orchestral brass movement of *Evil Comes From the North* gradually builds with ominous tribal percussion and hypnotic synth textures, which in part gives rise to comparisons to the tribal flair of Sephiroth. Likewise the darkly foreboding classical style of the title track *Sigillum Diaboli* reaches ecstatic heights with its swelling orchestral brass and percussion, which also brings to mind the best parts of In Slaughter Natives' purgatorial bombast.

Although not wanting to denigrate Lamia Vox by a potential overuse of CMI related comparisons, conversely this should be viewed as a clear compliment. Given its shadowy tone and sophisticated execution, *Sigillium Diaboli* is proof enough of Lamia Vox's skills within the sonic dark arts.

Marrow Mandler - *Escapist Grounds* MC Beläten 2013 / German Army - *Burushaski* MC Beläten 2013 / Veil of Light - *Veil of Light* MC Beläten 2013

I have to admit that up until recently my interest in Beläten's releases had been targeted towards their ritual / industrial styled tapes, rather than those which more appropriately fit with the label's *'post avant garde pop for a pre-apolcalyptic world'* description. Nevertheless, here are the three new tapes which make up the latest batch releases from Beläten, which more faithfully align with the *'post avant garde pop'* tag line, despite sounding absolutely nothing alike.

On *Escapist Grounds* Marrow Mander deliver a sound which merges jittery programmed beats with cold minimalist synth style, maybe sounding something like the a bastard lovechild of Kraftwerk and Devo attempting a German industrial / synth pop album. In other words bizarrely excellent. The monotone commanding male vocals are also a highlight of Marrow Mandler's sound, which in some segments are morphed and slightly processed for good measure. *Bound Forward* is also a stand out track with the elephantine sway of its programmed beats and commanding half sung/ half spoken vocals.

German Army are up next (hailing from LA of all places despite what the name suggests), who deliver the most experimental of the latest batch of tapes being something like abstract post punk. The material on *Burushaski* ranges from programmed compositions to relatively abstract soundscapes, which are constructed with manipulated tape experiments, morphed radio samples, fractured tribal-esque beats, occasional wayward guitars (meandering bass and screaming solos), hallucinogenic vocals etc, which are wrapped up in hazy lo-fi analogue aesthetic. *Stone Walls* rates a mention, featuring some excellent mid paced clinical beats, vague melody and distant spoken/ sung vocals.

For the final of the tape batch Veil of Light deliver their debut EP, being a solo project hailing from Switzerland which aims at a 'classic' 1980's goth / post-punk sound of Joy Division, early Death in June and the Dead Can Dance debut for suitable reference. Across the six tracks Veil of Light blend stoic drum kit percussion, plodding bass lines, jangling and intertwining guitars, serpentine melancholic synths and commanding male vocals, which are presented as straightforward and catchy songs. For its apparent lack of originality, this is of little concern when the material presented is this strong, not to mention being absolutely faithful to the sound and era it emulates.

The slick presentation of the pro-print tapes and covers feature Beläten's now trademark graphic design template and aesthetic (including individual runic symbol for each release), which only adds to the sheer collectability of this emerging cult label. Whilst the tapes are work owning for their packaging and presentation alone, if you have any doubts about the music they contain, the complete Beläten catalogue is available for streaming on their website.

Negru Voda / Knös – *Face Without Face* CDr Malignant Records 2013

This new release from the Malignant Records stables constitutes a split album featuring two Swedish underground industrial projects, of which Negru Voda will be the more well-known given Peter Nyström's long establishment under the Negru Voda moniker (...as well as his previous involvement in the legendary Megaptera). Regarding Knös, whilst there is not much available information (other than being a solo project of one Fredrik Djurfeldt who issued a CDr back in 2008), their sound is at least entirely comparable and complimentary to that of Negru Voda.

For this split each act present five tracks each (first half to Negru Voda and the second half to Knös), which can be broadly categorised under an old school Swedish death industrial banner and a collective sound which emulates the gloomy analogue sound set down during the birth of the genre (aka early 1990's). Yet given how closely these two acts align in feel, there is not much to be gained by splitting hairs to differentiate

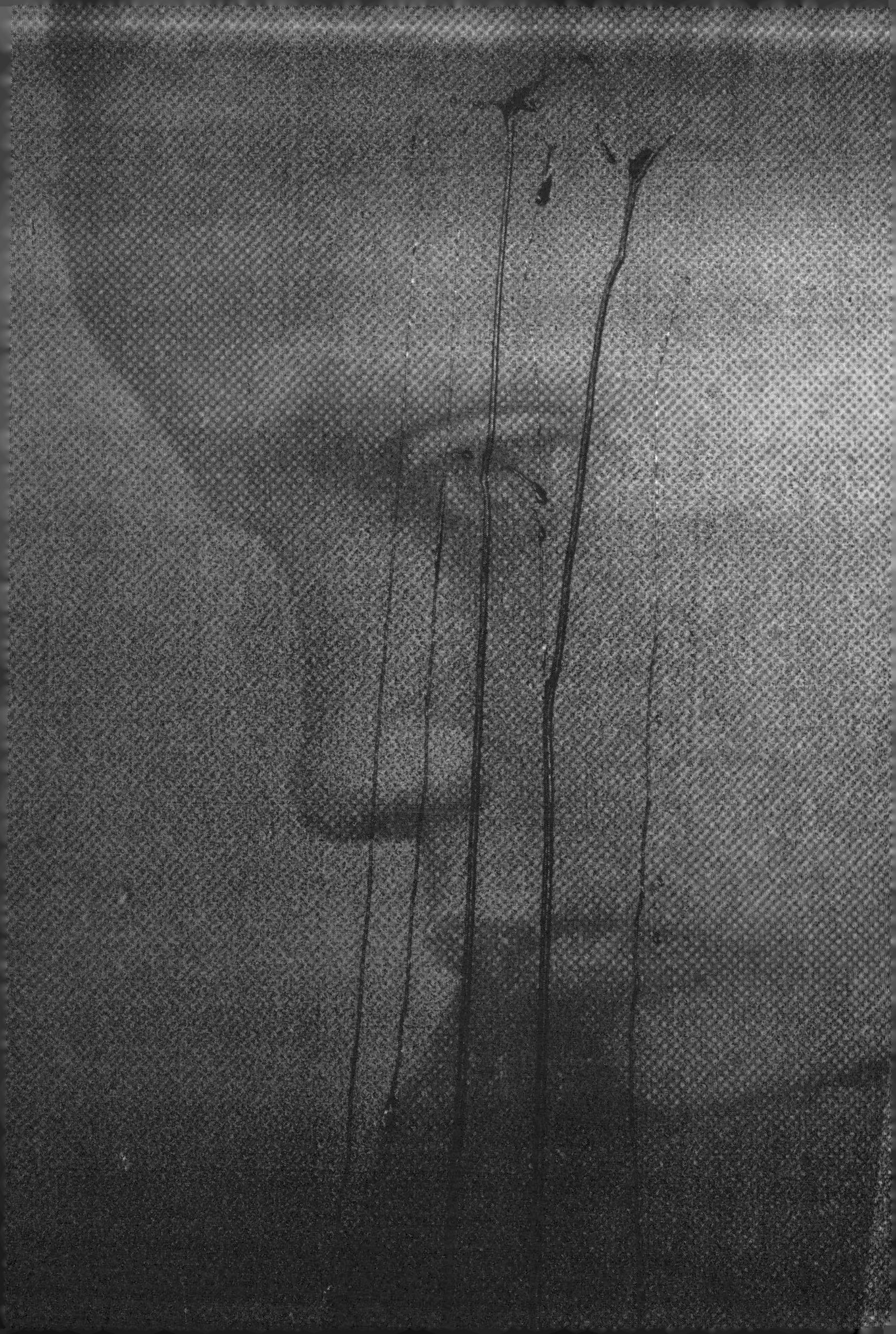

the sound between the two halves. Ultimately what we have here are two separate acts that are individually focused on delivering grim and pitch black, death industrial music. Being entirely driven by the ambience of idling engines and the clatter of mechanical factory processes, a heavy dose of random deep bass thuds, distorted radio chatter and smatterings of metallic clangs all add to the general meat grinding atmosphere. Whilst selected tracks are slow and murky in pace, alternately others step up a notch with heavy, pounding industrial beats in both rhythmic and arrhythmic patterns. However as is characteristic with this style, these never represent anything close to a dance floor beat. Spanning 52 minutes *Face Without Face* is utilitarian in approach and is exactly what should be expected from old school Swedish death industrial music. Clearly as neither act is looking to break conventions, this simply achieves a solid slab of caustic death industrial musings. Although a Cdr, this is pro-duplicated release in a limitation of a mere 150 copies.

Nyodene D - *Atop Masada* MC Nil By Mouth Recordings 2013

Nyodene D return following the well received *Edenfall* album of last year, and as with their other releases *Atop Masada* focuses on some interesting conceptual material. More specifically this tape deals with the Roman Siege of Masada in 73/74 AD resulting in the mass suicide of the Jewish Sicarii (aka *'dagger men')* population who has settled at the the fortress of Masada (located on an isolated mountain plateau in southern Israel). More generally the Sicarii were an extremist splinter group seeking to expel the ruling Romans from the Roman controlled provence of Judea through violent insurgency tactics including publicly attacking Romans and Roman sympathisers with concealed daggers. Beyond this micro history lesson the promo blurb more succinctly states: *'Thematically, this release examines the nature of honor, sacrifice and extremism framed in the historical context of the Roman siege of Masada'.*

Regarding its musical aspects the tape's 30 minutes are split into two lengthy tracks, featuring one per side of the cassette. *Grain To Ash* spans side A and focuses on the multi-layered looped power electronics side of Nyodene D, where queasy cascading loops and burrowing distortion roll relentlessly on once established in their groove. Vocals when they arrive hold a point of difference, as they are presented in a commanding half sung, half spoken drawl. The second track *Sicarii* differs somewhat, being slow and cavernous containing shrill ethnic tinged strings and catatonic and obliterating bass thump which coalesce as part of its expansive guise. Later in the track synth textures provide a greater cinematic flavour, which is offset against shuddering industrial noise and squalling junk metal abuse. As the track progresses it ramps up with increased intensity until the trademark heavy distorted and echo treated Nyodene D vocals make a welcome appearance. Excellent stuff.

Being dense and heavy in production, yet containing a certain clarity to the sonics both tracks works well within their long form expansive guise. Noting Nil By Mouth's special attention to packaging, here two double sided printed colour inserts are included with the pro printed tape which are all housed in a small burlap sack. Given its edition of a mere 130, this seems ludicrously limited for the quality of the material presented here. As such you know what to do.

Olle Oljud - *27/28* 7"EP Lamour Records 2014

Lamour Records is a relatively new Swedish label (lauched in 2012), which focuses on electronica, ambient and soundart. Although this is my first introduction to both this act and label, according to the promo sheet: *'Lamour records proudly presents composer and visual artist Olle Oljud, one of the most beloved artists in the Sweden's experimental music sphere'.*

I am not sure if this blurb is being slightly facetious, but this perception is partly due to having not heard of Mr Oljud before. That said, he may actually be extremely well regarded in the experimental circles he operates within - and I guess that is the nature of things when it comes to underground music and the potential reach of micro-scenes within a global context. But I digress. Here we have a two track 7"EP which seeks to showcase two differing sides to Olle's experimental sound works.

The first side presents *27 minimal* which does not take too much of a stretch of the imagination to discern that this particular track is minimalist in style, where here the composition aims towards a series electronic hums and drones. The track contains occasional 'cut up' stylistic textures which are also mixed with oscillating frequencies, which gradually build in intensity over its seven minute length. Overall *27 minimal* manages to be equally sharp yet subdued in tone, where it textural electronics creates a 'swarm of wasps' type sonic atmosphere. The track also balances a sound which feels partly controlled and partly improvised.

On the flipside *under 28* takes a more forceful route, with a stratum of mid ranged static and electronic distortion. Noting that this does not constitute harsh wall noise nor controlled power electronics styled distortion, this track achieves a sound which sits somewhere in-between. Mid track things slack off slightly to allow for some micro-tonal type experimentation and more broadly in amongst the waves of static there are some oscillating loops partially buried in the mix. These loops function to hint at some semblance of structure, thus avoiding the perception of being all out noise experimentation. Again the track manages to chart a course between the partly controlled and partly improvised.

For its presentation the two toned red haze coloured vinyl includes an individually hand painted abstract painting for each of the hand numbered 250 copies. With its varied focus this is an interesting 7"EP, particularly if your interests align towards the experimental sound art side of underground electronic music.

Phelios – *Gates of Atlantis* CD Malignant Records 2013

For long term fans of the dark ambient genre there can inevitably be a degree of presumption of what a new album will sound like, particularly given the parameters of the style have now been long established. So whilst Phelios broadly aligns within a dark ambient style, the project does manage to carve out a particular niche of their own with their animated and dynamic approach (…which is primarily achieved through the infusion of strong compositional structures).

On their previous offering (2010's *Astral Unity*) that album encompassed a brooding cosmic / sub-orchestral style, which included the occasional use of prominent percussive / rhythmic

structures. On *Gates of Atlantis* Phelios has continued within this established template, but this time around have increased the focus on the deep tribal/ percussive aspects. As such the opening title track is an excellent example of this approach with its moody sub-orchestral brass, mid paced tribal percussion and melodic song structures. From this launch point the album then moves through a wide variety of sounds and textures. Some passages display a degree of restraint, such as the deep sweeping cosmic radiance of *Temple of Yith*, whist *Spiritual Possession* storms out of the gloom with a pounding almost militant percussive streak set against doomy layered synth lines. Mid album track *Hibernation* arrives as another album highlight, delivering brooding widescreen drones which are underscored by rolling percussion which falls somewhere between a tribal and militant tonal aesthetic. On the concluding track *Ascension*, as the title might suggest it is lighter in tone with a hint of the serene and the ethereal, which sets it apart from the heavy sub-orchestral gloom of material which precedes it.
Given that much of *Gates of Atlantis* inhabits a strong compositional framework, its atmosphere is highly dynamic rather than benign or abstract, which is a pitfall dark ambient music can occasionally fall into. Likewise in recognition of the song based structures, interestingly these seem to ever so slightly hint at influences from other 'electronic' music genres, which in part explains the individuality of Phelios' sound.
For the cover imagery, this acts as a pertinent visual representation of the breadth and scope of the album (...a shadowy miniscule figure stands entirely diminutive against a massive imposing structure which extends out of frame...). What this image visually articulates can be easily applied to audial aspects of *Gates of Atlantis*. That is, Phelios composes music of such an imposing nature and colossal scale it all but dwarfs a mere human scale perspective. In a word – monumental.

Phragments - *New Kings and New Queens* CD Malignant Records 2013
Phragments finally return with new recorded material, some five years on from the last full length *Earth Shall Not Cover Their Blood*, also issued on Malignant Records. However interestingly the promo material indicates that rather than heralding a new direction for Phragments, this new album should be considered as a special and stand alone release. So from the first cursory listen it is evident that for this album at least Phragments have moved away from structured neo-classical (and occasionally martial infused) compositions, instead opting for more a more abstract dark ambient version of their sound. Likewise the six 'chapters' (as referred to on the cover) which make up *New Kings and New Queens*, have effectively been composed into a singular flowing 32 minute composition.
Noting its subdued tone and distant stormy atmosphere, the main focus is obviously not on any overt neo-classical elements, yet there are orchestral tonal elements buried in the mix giving the impression of a ghostly and muted neo-classical atmosphere. Here vast widescreen drones are underscored by a muffled orchestral tonality, which evokes a stoic and serious mood which evolves and unfolds at a catatonic pace. Yet the sustained solemn procession gives way to sacral atmospheres on both *When Memory Fails, We Disintegrate* and *New Queens*, given both utilise cathedral sized organs and quasi brass horn type drones.
Packaging wise, the CD is housed in a beautifully presented in a large odd sized eight panel fold out cardboard cover, the imagery of grey wintery mountain-scapes are a suitable visual representation. With deft compositional skill Phragments have delivered an commendable orchestral dark ambient album.

Profane Grace – *Nocturnal Omniscience* CD Ewers Tonkunst 2010
Profane Grace are a project I have known of for many, many years, but only previously having heard their 5th album *Epitaph Of Shattered Dreams* from 1999. Likewise up until now I had not delved into their biography to see exactly who was behind the project, although did have an impression they were linked to the underground metal scene. This perception was duly confirmed following a little bit of recent background investigation, where it seems Profane Grace have been around since 1992 and have direct linage to the American black metal band Demoncy. *Nocturnal Omniscience* is their seventh and latest album (...but already near a half decade old).
Stylistically Profane Grace evoke dark ambient music which very much fits in with the 'Cold Meat Industry' sound of the mid to late 90's, meaning gloomy, sub-orchestral soundscapes and horror soundtrack type atmospheres are the prevalent focus. Likewise with their connection to the black metal scene, Profane Grace could be slotted under either the 'black ambient' and / or 'dungeon synth' banners, noting other similar 'black ambient' / 'dungeon synth' projects include: Mortiis (era 1), Darkness Enshroud, Valefor, Aghast, Cernunnos Woods, Æva etc.
Of the nine albums tracks which span an hour's length, each composition is catatonic in pace and broadly embodies the atmosphere of a dank crypt, which evokes further visions of narrow passages and cavernous spaces lit only by light emitted from a lone flickering candle. Musically the sound is achieved predominantly with synthetic means, to generate abstract droning textures and deep mine shaft echoes, which are augmented by the droll tolling of funeral bells, occasional organ dirges, dragging chains, rasping unintelligible vocalisations, low monastic chants (unclear whether sampled or synth generated), scrapping metallic textures, sparse ritual chimes etc. Whilst many tracks are quite sparse and abstract, others such as *Trilogy of the Unangled Plain III* are structured around a central maudlin quasi-orchestral synth melody, or in the case of *Hymns to Selket* are driven by slow booming tympani percussion.
To its credit *Nocturnal Omniscience* achieves a depth and complexity much greater than *Epitaph Of Shattered Dreams*, which although played with a very similar sound palate, came across as more simplistic and one dimensional and a tad cheesy on some tracks as the synthetic means of music production simply did not match the pomp and majesty of the attempted medieval/ orchestral melodies. Although there is clearly nothing new or unique about what Profane Grace do that is not really the point, as *Nocturnal Omniscience* achieves a particular occult infused dark ambient sound with absolute ease. A cardboard slip sleeve with spot varnished images completes the packaging in simple and stylish means.

Propergol – *Paradise Land* CD Tesco Organisation 2012

After dropping off the map following their sixth album *Ground Proximity Warning System* way back in 2006, seemingly out of nowhere Propergol has made a rather welcome return. In order to provide some necessary context for this new offering, over the course of their 16 year career Propergol have always articulated a certain filmic and cinematic quality to their sound. However in the past this has been mainly due to the use of various movie dialogue samples scattered throughout their compositions. Also given the heaviness and harshness of the earlier material was rooted in the merging of heavy industrial and power electronics, this new album has instead opted to elevate its production to a level which feels more as the product of a professional sound studio. Thus this time around rather than just hinting at a cinematic sound through samples, *Paridise Land* comes across very much as the backing audio track to various scenes of a nameless motion picture. Here the production is deep and bass heavy, yet crystalline and clear, which adds a tonal heaviness to the sound which isn't as reliant on harshness as earlier material was.

After a brief introductory piece (*Running Scared*) the second track *911 Dispatcher* presents a moody orchestral strings type of dark ambience (complete with scattered radio chatter), which clearly articulates the differing approach taken on *Paradise Land.* Although the following track *Ymene* hints at the earlier approach of Propergol, here the sound is controlled with a tense and brooding heavy industrial sound, rather than being noisy and unhinged. *E.R.S* is a great example of the merging of the old and new elements of Propergol by using a well placed dialogue sample (lifted from a 'classic' Hollywood era movie), as synth layers and scattered industrial debris creates an atmosphere which balances on a knife edge between the etherial and the ominous. *Psycho Road* is the track which comes closest to the harshness of earlier material (freeform scattered noise and wavering distortion), yet the digital crispness of the production clearly positions this in context of the balance of the album. The following track *Escape From...* reverts to calmer territory given it evokes a sweeping dark ambient soundscape, but keeps things on edge with a stalking bass pulse and tone of brooding menace. Also worthy of a specific mention is late album track *Impossible Landing*, which is one of the most divergent tracks of the album, by virtue of being constructed with a programmed electronica beat, and moody synth textures which has far more in common with Atomine Elektrine than what Propergol would be typical recognised for. That said, there is no complaint from these quarters as this an excellent understated electronica track. The album concludes with the mammoth 16 minute *Bleu Nuit* which is the most experimental of the set, being a more abstract dark ambient/ electronica/ industrial cut up which moves through a number of somewhat disjointed segments and a myriad of dialogue samples. Whilst not a bad track at all, it however lack the focus of the material which proceeds it, meaning the album does not finish as strongly as it otherwise might have.

Spanning just on 70 minutes, there is a lot of sonic texture and detail to take in. Clearly some have lamented the lack of overt harshness here, which has in turn lead to accusations that Propergol have moved to an entirely dark ambient 'lite' version of their sound. Whilst this is certainly not the Propergol of yesteryears, it is great to see a project so confidently forging a new era of sound via unexplored sonic territories and a wider sonic palate.

raison d'etre - *enthralled by the winds of loneliness (redux)* CD Old Europa Café 2013

With the sheer number of years Peter Andersson has been musically active as raison d'etre obviously his project is extremely well recognised within the industrial / dark ambient underground. However for new listeners of dark ambient (and related) scenes, there may be a degree of unfamiliarity with raison d'etre's rather imposing back catalogue, particularly due to number of earlier albums being out of print for some time (...or maybe I am totally wrong on this point and newer listeners have already downloaded the entire back catalogue – who knows?!). Regardless, as this review blog celebrates the physical aspect of a release as an important and integral aspect, it is an opportune time to revisit this 'redux' version of raison d'etre's second album from 1994 (which incidentally has been issued one year prior to it being a 20 year anniversary edition).

For the 'redux' treatment, rather than merely being a remastered version it seems that Peter has used original sound sources (which have been re-sampled and restored) to re-record original programmed sequences, which have then been mixed and mastered to reflect the original album atmosphere. This has evidently been painstaking undertaken to provide a new multi channel recording, which has allowed a new stereo mix with greater dynamic range and professional upgrade to the sound (which is effectively the opposite of a level boosted and over-compressed remastering technique). So when comparing this 'redux' version to the original the sound quality is notably deeper and more expansive, where a multitude of previously hidden textural sound details are clearly audible and sit balanced within the mix. This is not to say that the original was one-dimensional however it does sound much flatter, muffled and less dynamic in comparison to this 'redux' version. In short the sound is impeccable, crystalline and breathes with both subtlety and intensity.

Likewise rather than approaching this review as if it were a brand new album, it is probably more appropriate to reflect on its historic context within the artist's discography. Accordingly one of the hallmarks of this earlier era of raison d'etre is the presence of an almost 'new age' tone to the music – albeit much bleaker and darker – due to the use of occasional flutes and woodwind instruments, wind chimes, ritual gongs, melancholic orchestral synth textures and the trademark religious choral vocals. *Enthralled by the winds of loneliness* also illustrates raison d'etre at a transitional point in the evolution of their sound. Whilst the album still sits squarely within a composed song structured realm, it displays a more confident, flowing and elongated compositional style, which differs quite drastically from the rigid and shorter track compositional style of the debut album from the year prior. This album also illustrates the emergence of abstract droning aspects, which would be elevated to take a much greater focus on later albums. Within this framework the overarching mood is one that embodies ominous, sacral and monastic atmospheres

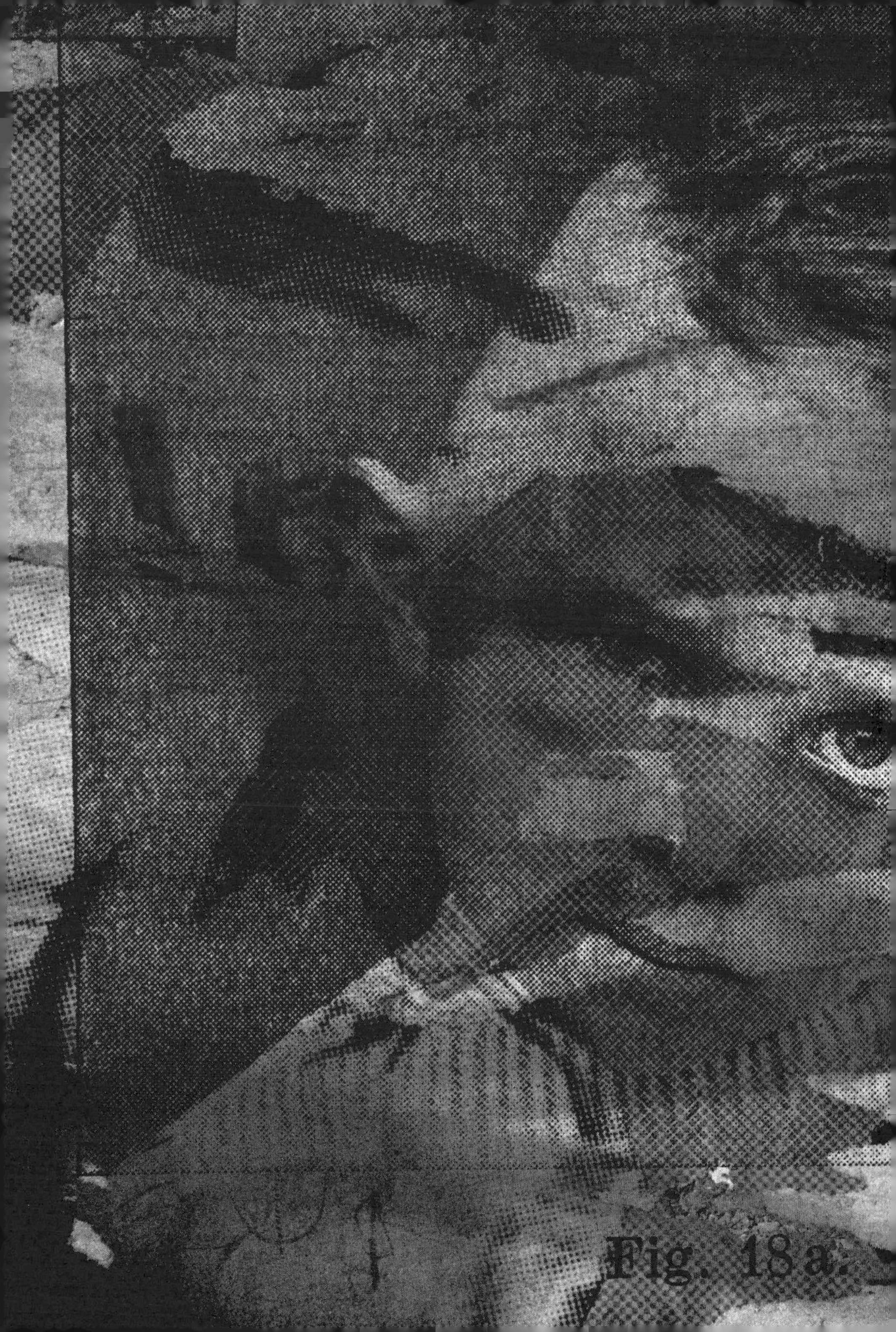

Fig. 18 a.

evoked through solemn percussion, Gregorian chants and string textures (which occasional rise to shrill intensity), whilst other segments plumb the depths of ominous drones, ritual gongs and devastatingly bleak solo choral vocals. Apart from the seven main album tracks, four bonus tracks are included here for good measure, including two from the *Conspectus* tape and two from other compilation appearances. Given these bonus tracks were recorded during the same era as the main album tracks, they at least sonically complement the remainder of the album and do not feel pointlessly tacked on – as is often the case with bonus material.
With its sleekly improved, professional and crystalline sound, the inclusion of four additional complimentary tracks and beautifully presented in a six panel digi-pack which has reworked elements of the original artwork, there is much discover/ rediscover here (as the case may be for either old or new fans). Effectively Peter has delivered a reinvigorated version of *enthralled by the winds of loneliness* which is a pleasure to be re-aquainted with.

raison d'etre – *In Sadness, Silence And Solitude* DCD :retortae: 2014
raison d'être – *The Stains Of The Embodied Sacrifice* DCD Ewers Tonkunst 2012
Noting raison d'etre have in recent years been facilitating a program of reissuing of earlier albums here are yet two more albums in this ongoing re-release agenda. However rather than these representing mere reprints, each of these new versions have been substantially expanded through the inclusion of a second disc of additional content.
In Sadness, Silence And Solitude represents the earlier of the two, being originally released way back in 1997 (...it may also be of interest that this album holds a rather special place for this reviewer, as it was one of albums critiqued in the first issue of Spectrum Magazine from 1998). To provide context within raison d'etre's own discography, *In Sadness, Silence And Solitude* presented a large stylistic leap away from composed song structures of earlier material. Effectively the sound shifted towards abstract droning territory by evoking barren windswept soundscapes, but maintaining links with the past through fleeting flourishes of Gregorian vocal chants, chimes, sparse ritualistic percussion, wailing horns, swelling quasi-orchestral synth melodies and morose piano notes. On the first disc it contains six original album tracks, which have been augmented by an additional two live tracks as well as a previously unreleased composition. For the second disc of this expanded edition, it contains 13 additional pieces, by bringing together nine previously issued compilation tracks and further four unreleased compositions. Noting that all of the material spread across the two discs derives from same time period (1996-97, with some being live versions of the main album tracks), they display a stylistic similarity which greatly assists in collective coherence of the listening experience. Additionally all tracks of this two disc expanded edition have been fully restored and remastered for optimal sonic impact.
Regarding *The Stains Of The Embodied Sacrifice* this constitutes an expanded edition of raison d'etre's most recent album from 2009 (excluding the two live album released in 2010 and 2012 respectively). On the first disc it contains the

original album tracks (without augmentation), which follow raison d'etre's established framework of abstract soundscapes and sparse monastic chants. However the sound is also slightly more animated and layered on *The Stains Of The Embodied Sacrifice*, with a greater focus on sonic elements which embody a jagged, scrapping and metallic tonality, as well as scant harmonic/ disharmonic piano notes and sparse angular orchestral strings and brass tones. Noting the intense and occasionally invasive sound quality, *The Stains Of The Embodied Sacrifice* very much manages to balance a duality of sound and approach. Thus the album is imbedded with an atmosphere which sways from being angelic and serene, to a feeling of being heavily oppressive (...something akin to the hellish torment of the damned). For the expanded edition, disc two contains six additional tracks (spanning 60 minutes) which constitute previously unreleased early versions of the original album tracks. Seemingly with these bonus tracks being constructed from the same sound sources as the main album tracks, they very much feel like alternate remixed versions. Both releases come housed in six panel fold out digi-card covers which faithfully recreates the original album artwork and provides a new physical platform in which raison d'etre can continue to be appreciated as one of dark ambient's exceptional and enduring artists. All to do now is wait for the imminent release of new album *Mise en Abyme* to see what it reveals.

Rapoon - *Calling The Rain* 7"EP Black Drone 2013

The relatively new Australian label Black Drone (which has been in operation since 2009), has recently issued a new 7"EP by the long active and very prolific Rapoon. Despite the self professed style of 'ethno-ambient', the two untitled tracks presented on each side of the vinyl differ quite significantly, which I guess is consistent with the general diversity found within Rapoon's works.

Side A of the vinyl delivers a quite 'song' focused composition, built on a loose rhythm, hymn like vocal textures and choppy trip hop beats. However due to the upfront mixing of the percussion they do not positively add to the track due to their stilted and simplistic programming, which also takes far too much focus away from the darker undercurrent (...basically to this ear the 'beats' sound rather dated).

However the flip side of the vinyl presents a much more pleasing composition. Here the sound is within an experimental dark ambient frame, which ever so slightly flirts with some heavier grinding sound elements. Accordingly various sweeping and low rumbling textures form vague loops which coalesce into a yawning mass of abstract sound. There is a noted ebb and flow in the way the various sound elements interact, but the composition is structured with a general upward trajectory over its seven minute length, including some unobtrusive and minimalist piano notes played towards the end which brings a melancholic tone to the overall mood.

The overall presentation is positive given Black Drone has pressed this on vinyl with decent thickness and heavy cardboard stock for the full colour cover. Whilst side A is not really to my liking, the side B track more than makes up for this.

Regosphere / The Vomit Arsonist - Split 7"EP Phange Tapes / Obfuscated Records 2013

One clearly positive aspect to split releases is that it provides opportunity to check out an act you might have otherwise missed. Whilst I am already well acquainted with The Vomit Arsonist, for this split Regosphere is the newbie act for me. The US project Regosphere step up to take the lead on the A side with their single track *Death, Like A Thief.* Here the composition is a multi layered affair with a prominent mid paced pounding beat / pulse upon which wavering noise, loosely rhythmic metallic clatter and distortion drenched vocals are overlaid. Focused and relatively straight forward, in some ways it resembles a more subdued and lurching version of Mental Destruction, which is more than positive introduction to the group. The group's self described style of 'anxiety electronics' is also pretty much on the mark.

Another rising US act, namely The Vomit Arsonist, take up the flip side with their track *Mind Turns Violent*, and deliver a composition within their trademark blending of death industrial and power electronics. The track is defined by a bass heavy, muffled and distortion overloaded production, where underneath this dank sonic mass an ominous droning synth and vague industrial rhythms can be detected, whilst the screeched vocals cut through with malice and spite. Great stuff as expected. The cover is a black and white doubled sided card fold out sleeve, including lyrics, which is a nice touch seeing as the vocal delivery and production on both tracks renders them indecipherable. With a limitation of 300 this is a straightforward 7"EP with commendable tracks from both projects.

The Rita / Caligula031 - *Self Shop* MC Nil By Mouth Recordings 2013

Nil By Mouth have again come up with some great item specific packaging where for this release the cassette and two colour printed inserts are housed inside a knee high stocking to tie in with the fetish concept of the release.

The Rita take up Side A with their lengthy single track *Mouths on Nylon, Hour Transaction* which at a most basic description contains scattered and blasting junk noise, offset against explicit voice recordings referencing the thematic material. The basic sound construction here has an extremely loose, overblown quality which is structured in segmented bursts as the female voices play out their fetish scenario, thus creating a certain sleazy noise aesthetic. Caligula031 feature on Side B and is actually my first introduction to this relatively new project of Marco Deplano. Here a lengthy power electronics track *Lady Vokovar* is presented, using mid ranged noise frequencies and wavering tonal layers which gradual build in intensity over its length. Alternately the hard and heavy barked vocals are rendered indecipherable due to their distortion treatment and being partly buried in the mix. Although relatively straightforward this track certainly hits the mark.

Given my personal tastes lean towards power electronics rather than junk noise type material for me Caligula031 is the pick of the day here. Either way *Self Shop* is highly collectable thanks to the packaging and made all the more so with its limitation of 180 copies.

RMEDL / K11 – *Chthonian Music* CD Cold Spring Records 2012

To provide an overview of the conceptual focus of this album, the promo blurb provides some succinct and useful insights: *'This multi-dimensional collaborative opera (audio installation and concept album) is a bridge between the conception of sound within the contemporary art scene, post-industrial culture and the avant-garde black metal musical scene. It focuses on creating a dialogic development between radical forms of concrete music, unorthodox sounds, conceptual arts and experimental recording practices of acoustic phenomena'*. To counterbalance this 'academic' explanation, 'Chthonian Music' is the result of a site specific sound installation project which was prepared and presented in an archaic underground vault (or according to the liner notes: *'ancient etrusian hypogeum sited in Cecina, Italy'*). If this later description is a tad confusing, a series of photos presented on the cover illustrates the archaeological space to be a series of long narrow tunnels connecting with a larger high ceiling vault.

With regard to the sound aspects of *Chthonian Music* the album has been created via the collaboration of an expansive list of contributors, including: Francisco Lopez, Christina Kubisch, Massimo Bartolini, Seth Cluett, Y.E.R.M.O., Seven Guitars, Luciano Maggiore, Gianluca Becuzzi, Andrea Marutti, Philippe Petit, Deadwood, Utarm, Burial Hex, Aderlating, Nordvargr and L'Acephale. However when considering the sheer number of contributing artists in context of the confined installation space, it is not clear from the liner notes whether contributing artists played live during the original performance, or whether source sound material was remotely submitted, which was in turn manipulated in real time during the installation by the project coordinators (Sandra Gronshi and Pietro Riparbelli). Despite such questions, where this album ultimately succeeds is that it transcends being merely an interesting idea and manages to connect the dots between multiple genres and emphasise their sonic overlap. It is also of interest to note that the album spans both 'low' (underground) and 'high' (academic experimental) art. As such *Chthonian Music* embodies musique concrete, experimental sounds, sweeping drones (abstract, harmonic and disharmonic), and the sonic dissonance of underground black metal (evoked through angular riffing and flailing drums). Such sounds also intertwine with other genres including segments of contemporary classical composition and ritual ambient soundscapes, which provides a diversity of sonic terrain yet still maintaining a coherent feel.

On the opening track *Mundvs*, natural woodland field recordings (insects, rain and distant thunder) mix with deep and rumbling bass drones before abstract distorted organ harmonics fleshes out the sound, resulting in a relatively gentle album introduction. Although the album consists of three tracks, the second composition *Katabasis* is split into five separate parts which play out as very much as individual tracks (rather than combining into a singular monster 55 minute composition). To provide a quick rundown of each segment:

- Part 1: ritual gongs/ chimes sit in the foreground, as experimental tones and layered ominous drones gradually build to moments of shrill intensity.
- Part 2: sub-bass drones mix with doomy acoustic guitars and croaked vocals, where the piece gradually elevates itself to ecstatic heights with its mechanised grinding loops, chanted vocals, dissonant black metal riffing and hammering metal kit drumming. This is black metal channelled in a very avant-garde manner and this is how I imagine current era SWANS would sound like if they ever tried their hand at black metal.
- Part 3: after the onslaught of the prior track, the next segment presents a melancholically beautiful piano piece, where the composition is loose, free flowing and heavily reverb treated, which is in turn underscored with a variety of other drone based elements. Mid track an organ takes over as the leading instrument to draw the track towards its conclusion.
- Part 4: is more tonally abstract, being constructed with field records/ musique concrete sounds and tense harmonic droning elements, before descending into a maelstrom of random metallic clatter, guitar reverb/ feedback and chaotic freeform kit drumming.
- Part 5: merges abstract musique concrete and ritual ambient elements with what sounds to be slow rumbling and reverberating doom drone guitar - however as a guitar is not listed instrument on the liner notes, this element may in fact be a heavily treated organ tone.

For the final album track *Nuktelia* it draws the album to a conclusion with a broad assemblage of the various sounds which precede it. Here the tone and atmosphere is one of an expansive cavernous space, where a lone violin plays out a maudlin melody against a backdrop of windswept drones. Later in the track, noise feedback, abstract riffed guitars, pummelling percussion and a moody piano tune each take turns in making an appearance.

For what is a rather academically focused concept album involving the contributions of a large list of artists, *Chthonian Music* hangs together extremely well as a varied yet coherent and immersive album. There is a lot to like here, whether it is channel the most abstract aspects of underground metal or flirting with more academic experimental sounds. As such the role of the project coordinators' in organising the original sound installation and this complimentary album to formally document the event should not be underestimated.

Rope Society – *One Word Definition* MC Cipher Productions 2013

This 35 minute cassette is the debut for Rope Society, being the analogue driven industrial / noise meets power electronics project of David Tonkin who would be better recognised for his main project Isomer. However as there is scant information regarding Rope Society, it is unclear whether it is intended to be continued side project, or if this is just a means to release harsher noise industrial material which would not fit comfortably under the Isomer banner. Either way seven untitled tracks are featured here on a pro-duplicated cassette and housed in special handmade packaging.

Track one starts with low rumbling noise before heavy scattered blasting noise tears out of the speakers, however it should be noted that this is not noise of the HNW variety. Shifting in a loose fashion the crumbling walls of analogue distortion build, collapse and then building again within amplified intensity. With

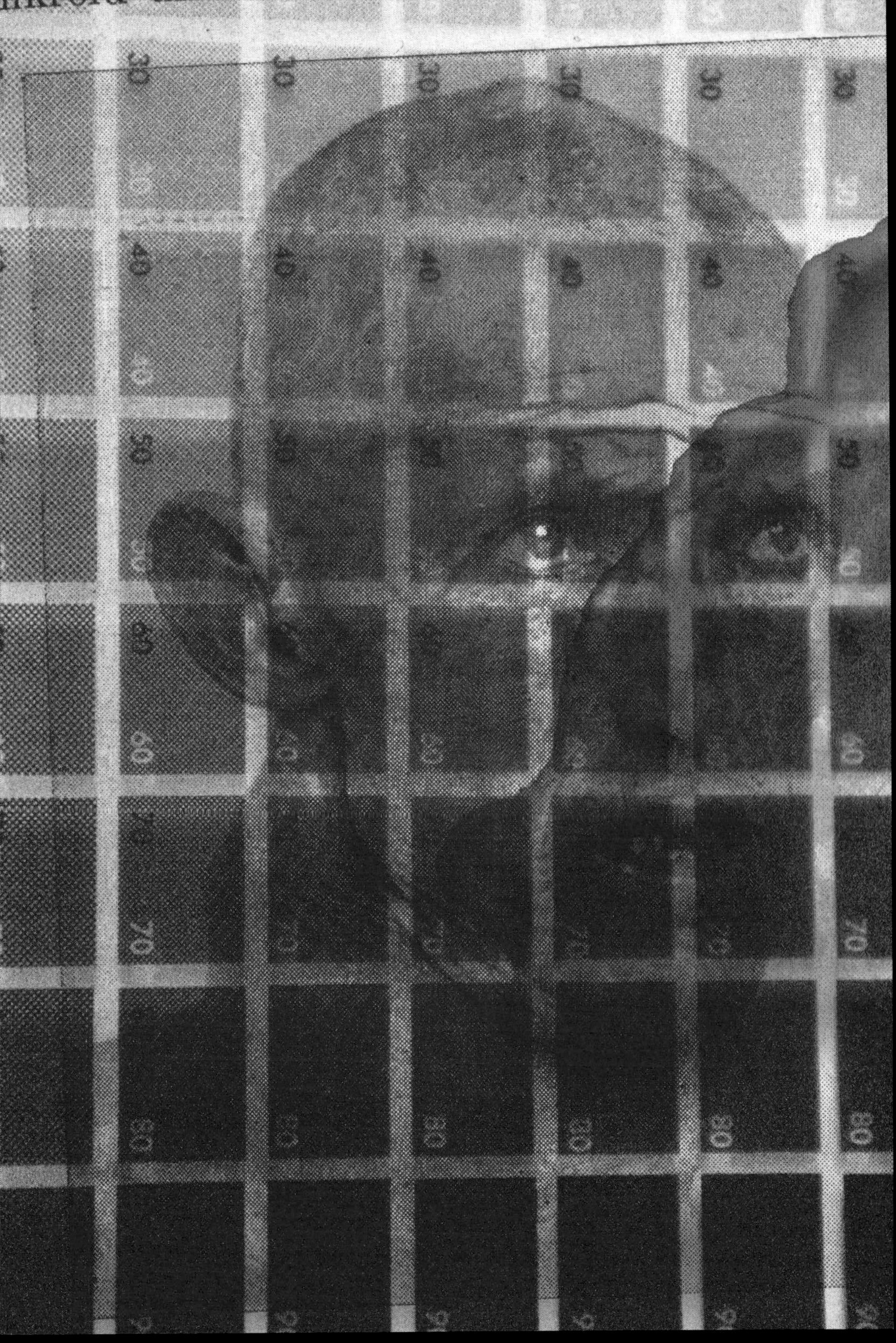

additional layered noise elements infused for further squalling and punishing effect, the sound is pushed to an extreme level by the end of its five minutes. Track two follows as a short track using a loose rumbling structure and partially buried vocals, noting also that the tonal quality of piece provides a nod towards a power electronics sound, albeit in a very loose and chaotic fashion. Track three establishes itself as the longest offering at seven minutes, being a piece of urgent, scattered and fractured noise that wavers from subdued to all out chaotic distortion blasts (complete with unintelligible radio dialogue sample). For these ears track four is a particular standout as it sits closest to a power electronics framework. Here shuddering machinery provides minimal queasy oscillating structure, with the further addition of grinding static and excellent heavily treated and barked vocals. This is the track which is closest in feel and sound of the last Isomer release, being the power electronics influenced *Nil By Mouth* MCD. Track five delivers a short and sharp piece of rumbling bass static and squalling mid to high range layered noise whilst track six opts for a heady dose of noise blasted cacophony as and static cutups swarm incessantly. The final of the seven tracks concludes the tape in more subdued fashion, containing a distant, echo infused textural experimental industrial sound manipulations, along with dialogue sample (referencing sound production and appreciation), as the layers of noise gradually follow an intensifying upward trajectory.

Whilst this tape feels like the material is seeking to balance structure and chaos, on *One Word Definition* sonic commotion us the ultimate victor. This mean the overall vibe of the release leans more heavily towards noise than power electronics, although the later does hold some influence over the sound. Although not breaking convention for this style of material, this is a solid tape which is more than improvised noise experiments. The special release specific packaging courtesy of Chris Groves of Cipher Productions is also noteworthy in both its simplicity and creativity.

Seirom – *Sparkle Night* MC Sulphurous Productions 2013

If you were to take Mories De Jong's main projects on face value (Gnaw Their Tongues, Aderlating etc), you would potentially have a skewed perception of an extremely disturbed mind at work. However given the capacity for individuals to hold differing and conflicting perspectives within their psyche (aka the duality and balance of darkness and light), Seirom is representative of beauty and fragility to counterbalance the harrowing chaos and seething darkness of Gnaw Their Tongues and Aderlating. In fact Seirom delivers such a blissful tonal quality that it was entirely unexpected from the same person behind Gnaw Their Tongues. Noting this alternate sonic perspective, interestingly Seirom was created to focus on lighter material espousing beauty and love, as apparently the unbridled negativity of Gnaw Their Tongues was causing negative psychological impact for Mories.

Although not Seirom's first release, *Sparkle Night* is a new two track 20 minute tape, featuring some beautiful cinematic quality, droning instrumental post-rock / shoegaze styled soundscapes. Noting that the compositions are structured using some typical band elements (guitar, bass, sparse drums etc) these are treated as washes of sound within the sonic palate, meaning this feels more like more likely a studio project than band. As such the title track displays droning synths, fireside field recordings, fuzzed out widescreen tremolo strummed guitars, sparse tinkling piano, warm enveloping electronics and a heavy dose of echo and reverb to provide a hazy and peaceful aura. Here the composition instead of building to a peaked crescendo, gradually elevates to an all-encompassing wall of warm enveloping sound, thus resulting in music of total emersion. The second of the two tracks *Only Miss You When It Snows* is slightly more animated, if only by virtue of the more focused percussive element, yet with its disappearance in the later third of the track it is back to blissed out territory, complete with quasi choir textures.

From the above it is clear that Seirom output is vastly different to that which might normally be expected from Mories. Essentially it a sound which has very much been turned on its head, akin to the same way his name has been inverted for this project's moniker. By way of a passing comparison, Seirom sits somewhere in-between the lighter ambient soundscape oriented tracks Justin Broderick has produced under the JESU moniker and the selected drone works of Aidan Baker/ Nadja. Being the first release on the new Sulphurous Productions and with a limitation is to a mere 50 copies which seems all too few for what is both an entirely surprising and rewarding listen.

Shift / HH – *Full Weight Of The Opposition* 10"EP Unsound Recordings 2013

Rather than constituting a split release this is a collaboration between these two UK based acts and features three tracks which traverse the border regions of power electronics, noise and industrial (to great result I might add).

Pigshit is a monolithic track which takes up the first side of the vinyl and features a sustained and crushing bass drone, upon which a loose mass of heavy metallic scraping sounds and looped junk noise are overlaid. Vocals then arrive as a fully separate sound layer (sitting high within the mix), being distorted and harsh, but also using sparingly throughout the track. On the vinyl's flip side *Truth Is Conflict* takes a similar sonic approach again utilising loosely constructed loops of metallic resonance and bass grinding intensity, again including the sporadic use of heavy power electronics vocals. The third and final track *Their Fall Will Be Harder Than Ours* differs slightly due to the heavy bass loops giving a sense of stilted rhythmic intensity over its extended length. Also setting this track apart are the vocals which are subdued and spoken in delivery, which works extremely well as a point of difference to a usual harder, aggressive and distorted power electronic vocal style.

Given all three tracks are expertly executed and have been recorded and mastered for sheer punishing effect, this 10"EP is an excellent and ferocious listen which is also testament to the high quality of the current crop of power electronics / noise / industrial acts operating out of the UK.

Shift - *Hatet / Misären* 7"EP Untergeschoss / Filth & Violence 2013

Evidently this 7"EP represents Shift's ode to Malmö - and this is not meant as a celebration, given the words of the artist: *"This is part one of my tribute to Malmö, the shithole I come from."* *Hatet-Misären (Kackerlackorna)* takes the lead and is straight forward and menacing in atmosphere with mid toned static drones, cavernous slow pounding beat, radio chatter (in Swedish?) and buried vocals which ramp up during various sections throughout (...random car horns and traffic noise leads the track to its conclusion). *Motstånd-Handling (Duscha Först, Gasa Sen)* takes up the flip side and starts with more radio samples (again Swedish?), but is heavier and more forceful than side A. Here the track is focused on a cascading/ crumbling layers of distortion, along with sporadically used harsh vocals. There is little to no variation in the track, just a great example of a forceful and barely composed power electronics style, underscored with harsh distortion charged vocals.

Short and sharp *Hatet / Misären* sees Shift in fine, if not slightly looser and regressive form (given the tracks appear less refined than other current material), but still delivering two harsh and no-frills power electronics tracks. The cover constitutes a photocopied sheet which suits this lo-fi and well executed 7"EP, issued in a limitation of 200 copies.

Shock Frontier – *Mancuerda Confessions* CD Malignant Records 2013

Shock Frontier are a relatively new US project which has arisen from the ashes of the defunct dark ambient project Psychomanteum, but has intentionally diverted direction towards the noisier and harsher sides of underground electronic music. To be more direct, Shock Frontier seeks to elicit through torturous means a corrosive blend of murky death industrial and atmospheric droning noise.

From the outset it is immediately apparent that *Mancuerda Confessions* facilities a sounds which edges towards the noisy and chaotic, but also imbeds enough structure to provide direction and focus. With its ragged frequencies, fried electrical drones and loose rhythmic structure, the opening track *Paroxysm* reveals a deep cut of corrosive ambience against which a dialogue sample implants a heavily misanthropic reality. *Angels Upon Iron Horses* then follows which amplifies its jagged industrialized textures, alarm siren pulse, grinding mechanised clatter and general tone of abstract industrial debris. Thus within the snapshot description of first two cuts, their collective approach is representative of a sound dragged along a knifes edge of structure and chaos, which plays out in variation across the album's whopping 72 minutes.

Over the course of the nine album cuts the densely layered compositions align scathing noise with swirling distortion, which are further augmented by jagged rhythmic segments and metallic mechanised pulsations. Yet to counterbalance these harsher aspects the compositions are underscored by corroded metallic drones and an overtly oppressive style of caustic ambience. Complimenting the album's general harrowing atmosphere, dialogue samples are scattered throughout which collectively function to hammer home a themes of societal decline and the debasement of humanity. As far as comparisons go the promo blurb nominates Megaptera as a suitable one, however this is slightly off the mark as Shock Frontier have far more in common with the harsh and scourging death industrial sound of the Swedish project Stratvm Terror.

Where this ultimately album excels is with its sonic representation of humanity at its absolute worst - akin to the peeling back of the layers of polite societal servitude. *Mancuerda Confessions* is very much rooted in a horrific reality of humanities potential for cruelty and domination - be it derived from political or religious extremism, or via societal isolation, narcissism and emotional detachment. Shock Frontier have expertly set such themes to sound in an extremely bleak and incisive way, which is certainly saying something as these ears are well attuned to similar material. Ultimately there is a narcissistic realism to this album which manages to claw its way under your skin and for this alone this album manages to push the envelope of unsettling underground electronic music.

Sickness / John Wiese - *Amnesia* 7"EP Freak Animal 2011

Although I am by no means an expert in noise appreciation, here we have a short and sharp studio collaboration 7"EP from two heavyweights in the noise genre. Cut at 45rpm, four tracks are presented (two per side) ranging in length from two to three minutes. This is supremely chaotic stuff, but not of a chaotic improvisational style, rather this is meticulously constructed and layered brutal noise, where the multiple layers and segmented cuts ups and individually audible within the sonic mass.

The first cut *Bright Region Xanadu* is crisp and tonally heavy, with its full spectrum dynamic harsh noise including intense cut ups and avalanches of scattergun noise. *Excise* follows and has slightly more breathing room with a pulsing bass undercurrent acting as a base for driven harsh noise and interjecting distortion. *Featherweight* is slightly more freeform with its heavy tonal squalls and wretched crescendos of distortion, which although dense is sonically clear with an abundance of minute tonal detail. Final track *Back to Xanadu* feels slightly more 'constructed' due to its use of broken loops, yet random cut ups and metallic overloaded distortion keep things suitably chaotic. Basically *Amnesia* is a short, heavy, intense, no-frills and absolutely to the point 7"EP, highlighting the focus and dynamics that can be achieved with harsh noise, as well as the control of two artists who have honed their skills to razor sharp intensity over multiple years and releases. In a word - brutal.

The Siamese Pearl – *Death-Darting Eye* MC Spine Scepter 2012

One of the joys of writing about underground music is that quite out of the blue you can made aware of obscure hidden gems. *Death-Darting Eye* from The Siamese Pearl is one such obscurity and whilst there is limited information on the project, here we have a super limited, deluxe packaged 30 minute cassette. With its dank and occult infused atmosphere, it is immediately evident that The Siamese Pearl channels an 80's lo-fi analogue industrial sound, which also contains selected rhythmic elements which hint at cold wave / post punk synth tone. Interesting this release is far more 'European' in style, appearance and flavour and by no means typical of what you might expect from an underground project hailing from

Miami, USA (of all places). To provide a sonic marker, some particular parallels for this would be the early ritual / ambient / experimental/ industrial based sounds of Coil or Current 93, and to a lesser degree the early works of Archon Satani. In other words The Siamese Pearl comfortably sits alongside some positive company.

On *Stretch of the Unkind* it opens the tape in fine form, being a brooding ritual industrial / dark ambient track, containing a variety of layered loops and drones. The following track *Hermetic Hermit* then steps things up a notch, being based on a pulsing coldwave synth line, mid range distortion and echo treated, monotone spoken vocals. A similar programmed synth, is also evident on *Night Specter*, but here follows the introductory segment containing abstract dark ambient, tape manipulations and distant horn like wails. *Chimera* then opts for a composition of loosely scattered noise and abstract grinding industrial soundscapes, prior to *Oedipus Of The Black Orifice* rounding out the first side of the tape with a short display of abstract tape loops, again featuring the nihilistic spoken vocals. *Attributable Decay* opens the flip side which again displays a relatively melodic piece, again with coldwave synth characteristics coupled with grinding manipulated loops. Interestingly on this track an additional vocal line is paralleled with the monotone spoken vocals, which are almost rap like in their delivery. Whilst this second vocal is rather perplexing at first, these are not as jarring as might be expected and in the end works well within the tracks sound. Up next is *Turnip Blood* which presents one of the tape's heaviest tracks, featuring looped grinding industrial factory clatter and again with the obligatory echo treated spoken vocals. *Axe* changes things up slightly with a ritual atmosphere being driven by synth drones and militant rhythms (which upon closer inspection are a looped breathing sample), constituting a solid basis for the stoic vocal invocations. *He's Not Kind To Other Wraiths* arrives as the final of the nine tracks, and concludes the tape with a lo-fi analogue windswept soundscape of Archon Satani-esque factory ambience. Excellent to say the least.

On the packaging side of things, the snake-skin printed cassette is housed in an oversized, screen printed cardboard box (adorned with with serpent motif no less), and includes a separate lyrics booklet. From its musical content, through to its packaging and associated occult themed visuals, *Death-Darting Eye* manages to hit all the right 'esoteric' markers.

Singular Cleansweep Operations – *Final Service* CD Teito Sound Company 2012

Rather than being a new underground project, Singular Cleansweep Operations are an obscure solo act which has direct linage to the equally mysterious German power electronics duo Operation Cleansweep. Yet apart from this limited information there appears is scant other details available – which is at least reflective of the parent projects modus operandi.

From the liner notes it nominates that the material on *Final Service* is derived from 1996 to 2010, yet it is unclear as to whether this means Operation Cleansweep is now a redundant project and this is the continuation of a solo member; or whether the album represents the final gasp and last remaining unreleased archival material (which is partially suggested by the title). Despite such questions, based on the underground status of Operation Cleansweep this offshoot release has at least raised some intrigue.

From cursory listens it quickly becomes apparent that whilst sitting within a general power electronics framework, the mood and tone is slightly more subdued than Operation Cleansweep. This in some ways this could be a potential pitfall, as having a direct link to the main project through its moniker, may give a false impression of what to expect. Yet as none of the material here constitutes second rate or throwaway material, it is really a matter of how the listener chooses to approach the album. Likewise to provide some context and to guide expectation, a good comparison would be the slightly more subdued and stalking approach Ex.Order take with their power electronics sound.

Across its 12 tracks (ranging in length from three to six minutes), each feature differing combinations of thick throbbing syths, well placed dialogue samples, slow pounding beats and hazy layers of sweeping noise. On a number of the tracks the oppressive atmospheres are amplified by morbid vocalisations, which are deadpan delivered and slightly distortion treated. Alternately some of the tracks articulate a cold military warfare type ambience based on abstract mechanised beats, radar blips and scattered radio chatter, whilst others utilise elements such as looped atonal piano notes, and disharmonic rhythmic elements. Mid album track *Verbrenne, Mensch!* pushes ever so slightly towards a full power electronics attack, with its ominous, oscillating textures and heavily flanged vocals - simple, straight forward and damn effective. Likewise *Revolutionary Suicide Council* is built on a potentially overused Jim Jones' last stand suicide sample, but works effectively here coupled with a prominent crackling / throbbing synth layer.

Rather than being overtly aggressive and brute force in sound, Singular Cleansweep Operations opt for queasy, uneasy and tonally threatening atmospheres. Whilst certainly not a classic of the genre, *Final Service* contains material of more than just elemental quality, meaning it is a solidly decent album overall.

Skull:Axis - *The Transparent Society* CD Peripheral Records / Death Continues Records 2013

This relatively obscure new release comes from the creative mind of Jason Bernard - aka Peripheral Records head honcho - who via this album demonstrates he has more than just a label boss's ear for quality and creative sounds.

From a cursory perusal of the album's cover the thematic focus of *The Transparent Society* is of central importance to the presented music, being summed up by the quote on the cover: *'surveillance induced morality: relics of cultural retardation'*. Although not knowing the context of this quote, it could however be easily be interpreted as a scathing comment on the British Government's well established obsession with attempting to monitor all pubic space through the installation of the ever expanding CCTV networks.

Regarding musical content the eight album tracks present a degree of continuity in sound and approach, meaning the album can be appreciated as a longer singular piece. Whilst there is also an abstract approach to the structure of the tracks the material is in no way improvised as the meticulous approach to the composition can be clearly heard. Accordingly the tone is

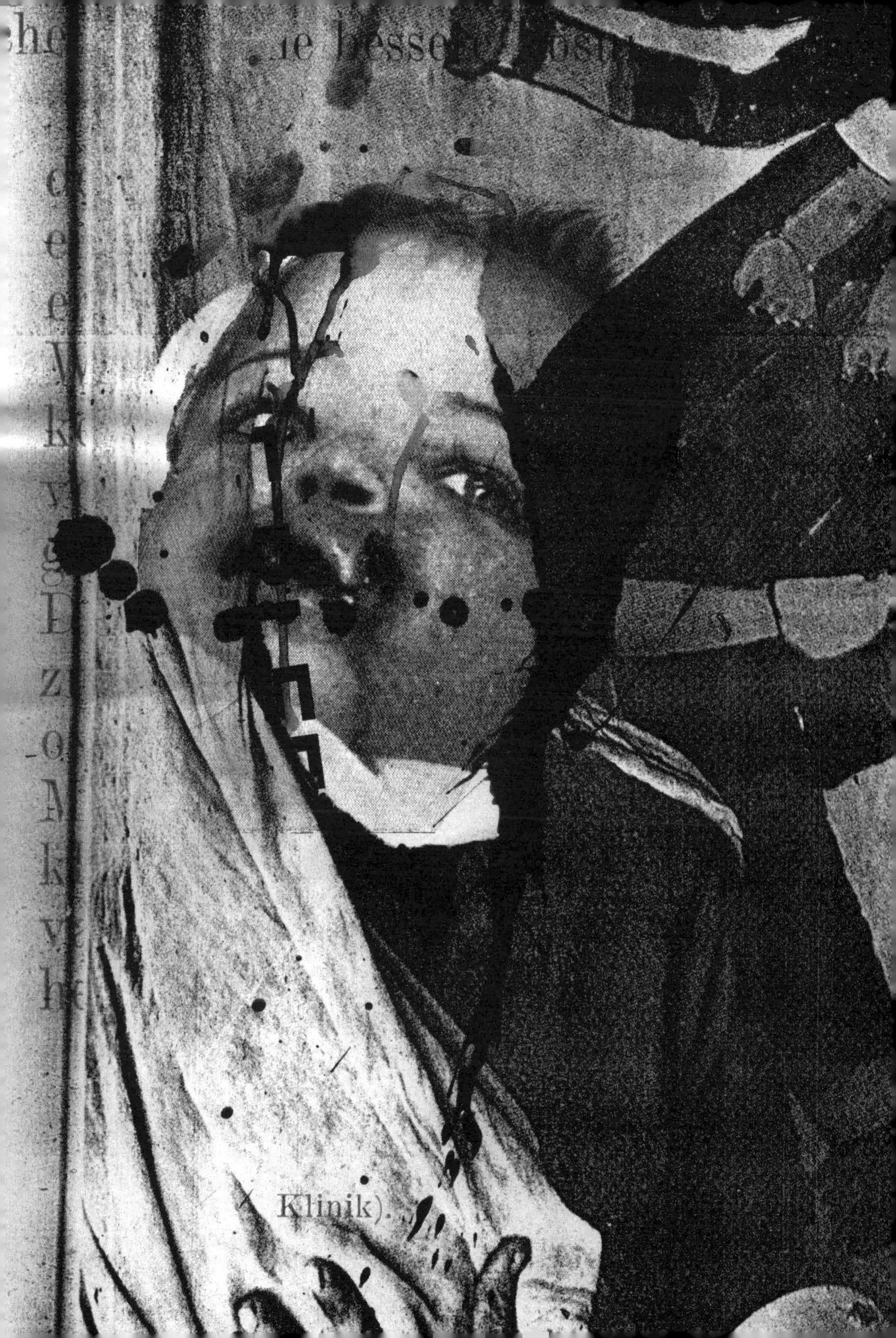
Klinik).

very much focused on washes of muffled distortion, repetitive radio chatter, mid to higher pitched analog synth layers, clinical transmission pulses, arrhythmic metallic 'clanks' and 'clangs' and droning factory ambiences. Ultimately *The Transparent Society* is very much rooted in a 'classic' German industrial vein but with a definite experimental bent. For a comparison maybe a less refined, abstract and vocal-less version of Anenzephalia would appropriately suit, whilst also highlighting the calibre of the presented material.

The visuals for the release also tie in nicely, where the xeroxed black and white imagery of outdated communications/ surveillance technology evokes a paranoid cold war type visual aesthetic. Given the bleak claustrophobia inherent in the sound these accompanying visuals perfectly tie in with the music and theme. With a ludicrously small pressing of 150 hopefully this album does not go unnoticed for it.

STAB Electronics - *The Non Alliant II* LP Unsound Recordings 2012

Although not knowing a great deal about this project, available online information indicates they are from the UK and supposedly commenced as a tribute to Marco Corbelli of Attrax Morgue following his death in 2007. In short STAB Electronics concern themselves with unpolished and scathing power electronics.

Noting that *The Non Alliant II* is the second in a pair of albums, this LP represented the opportunity for myself to get more formally aquatinted with the project, with my initial introduction being via the *We Gave Them the Future And They Wanted The Past* 2012 cassette compilation (on Unrest Productions). Based on the singular strength of the STAB Electronics featured compilation track *The Sins Of The Father*, this LP was immediately tracked down (particularly given that the T*he Non Alliant I* is long sold out).

Rough, heavy and loosely structured power electronics is STAB Electronics particular niche, being brutal, no frills and absolutely to the point. Each of the five album's tracks are built on a straightforward mixture of crumbling static, heavy distortion, throbbing bass, pulsing noise and loosely structured loops, which provides the platform for the shrilly intense vocals, which based on the ferocity of delivery is the singular element which takes this from good to great. In the most part the vocals are of the 'standard' power electronics style (ranging from hard sermon like delivery through to yelled and echo / distortion drenched), however it is their intensity of delivery which really takes it to the next level. Being generally heavy, visceral and unhinged, on a number of tracks the vocals are pushed to a point of absolute manic intensity. Likewise if the lyrics were not already blunt in their antagonism, some well placed dialogue samples lifted from *American Psycho* flesh out the intense levels of nihilism on display.

Packaging is simple and no-frills - black label LP and two printed inserts. Yet given its raw, visceral and oppressive atmosphere, having a limited press run of a mere 105 copies is FAR to few for an album of this calibre. Get it while you can (if you can).

Steel Hook Prothesis - *The Empirics Guild* Malignant Records 2013

Steel Hook Prothesis (SHP) are by now a well established name in the US scene and are certainly recognisable for their darkly sinister atmospheres created via a twisted mixture of dark ambient, death industrial and power electronics. *The Empirics Guild* represents their first proper album since *Atrocitizer* which was released in 2008.

Rendering Human Tallow opens the album with a horror soundtrack type vibe with a lone piano melody, but this is soon engulfed in a maelstrom of blasting distortion, which on closer attention is actually heavily processed vocals. Thus within the space of the first few minutes the oppressive tone of the album is clearly and forcefully established. Given SHP's demonstrated skill in creating broodingly sinister soundscapes, here the tracks are loosely contracted into 'movements' rather than typical songs. Likewise with their use of rasping and seething vocals which are heavily treated with scalpel sharp distortion, these have become are a particularly impressive trademark. *Debrided Necrotic Tissue* is noteworthy for its use of echo treated medical dialogue sample within a dark ambient guise, before shifting into sweeping distortion territory and completed with the trademark vocals. Likewise the following track *Gula* is impressive and pushes the tone up a notch with apocalyptic brass horn styled synth layers, metallic pounding rhythms, sweeping tonal noise and distortion flayed vocals. Alternately late albums track *Disease Incubator* allows slightly more breathing space with its lengthy excursion into sparse cavernous drone territory, whilst *The Blood Cough* is reminiscent of the noisiest aspects of another highly regarded death industrial project Stratvm Terror.

Clearly the overarching mood of the album is heavy and morbid thanks to the dark ambient and death industrial elements, whilst the power electronics aspects provide a sonic counterpoint by being sharp and focused, but never overbearing within the sonic template. Essentially *The Empirics Guild* is clearly recognisable as the work of SHP, who have within their established template delivered an impressive addition to both their own and Malignant catalogues.

Te/DIS – *Black Swan* 7"EP Galakthorrö 2013

Here we have the debut 7"EP from Te/DIS who seem to be a relatively new project, where incidentally the 'coded' moniker is shorthand for 'Tempted Dissident'. However other than this basic information there is not much else regarding the origins and heritage of this project. Nevertheless what is presented is hard rhythmic electronic / industrial musings which verge towards a coldwave / post-punk style, thus fits perfectly within the broad sound of the Galakthorrö roster.

The opening title track *Black Swan* sets the template by featuring icy cold, mid paced industrial percussion, wavering synth melodies and monotone partly spoken / sung vocals, which direct the sound towards a post-punk aesthetic. *OvID* then follows with a similar mid paced programmed post-punk style, but here features a more catchy combination of dour synth melody, rhythmic bass, mid paced pounding industrial programmed beat, again with the obligatory commanding sung / spoken vocals. *Tautology* opens the flip side of the vinyl with a more urgent and anxiety inducing tone, based on its faster paced electronic rhythm, pulsing static bursts, droning synth lines and aggressively delivered vocals. *Wait and See* is the final of the four tracks which reverts to a mid-paced rhythmic programmed beat which is mixed with a maudlin toned synth work out. With particular reference to the echo treated spoken/ sung male vocals, in many ways these reflect the more subdued output of later era Haus Arafna.

Despite being only a 7"EP release, Te/DIS manage to accomplish a highly varied sound and approach across its four tracks. Likewise with its stylistic minimalist design, pressing on slick black vinyl and issued in a limitation of 489 hand numbered copies, this is yet another collectable release from the Galakthorrö stables.

T.O.M.B. – *Third Wave Holocaust* CD Black Plagve 2013

Via this release T.O.M.B. (aka Total Occultic Mechanical Blasphemy) has been welcomed to the roster of Malignant Record's sub-label Black Plagve. Noting that the Black Plagve imprint caters for the harsher and less refined side of underground industrial related sounds, this should give a cursory indication of what to expect herein.

From the crude, filthy and overblown industrial noise aesthetic of the opening track *Antagonizing the Unknown*, this bleeds into the following piece *Electric Exorcism* and in the process establishes the tone for much of the album. Accordingly this wind tunnel style of echo blasted clamour is exemplified on these sweeping black industrial noise compositions (which span the album's 55 minutes). Yet by the time the third track *The Great Venerat Insult* arrives, the heavy intensity slackens off slightly to embody an expansive catacombal ambience, driven by slow ritualistic drums, rumbling bass and distant sweeping tones. *Na La Gore Na* then elevates the tone again where the morbid chanting and dank, echo treated atmosphere builds to overblown caustic proportions. Although the term 'respite' is entirely relative to an album such as this, *Disrupting Admin* is slightly less intense, where the catatonic bass guitar is distorted to the point of abstraction and combined with waves of crumbling static. *Vom Voodoo* mixes things up ever so slightly with the inclusion of (you guessed it) tribal hand percussion, yet the predominant overblown noise production remains as a constant. Interestingly the final of the ten tracks *Tribute to Hanhua*, sees the album concluded in subtle rather than seething guise, containing a cavernous aesthetic with far off choral chanting and what sound to be distorted gong tones.

With its freeform structure and noisy, echoed infused production, unfortunately *Third Wave Holocaust* suffers somewhat from a lack of variation between tracks which tend to blur into a singular and larger sonic mass. It is also a shame that on the visual side of things the album is let down in presentation given the rather ugly digital artwork, which is more akin to a bad B grade horror flick. To this ear this is the type of album that is amply adequate for a number of spins, but is unlikely to be elevated to an album that will warrant repeat visitations.

Trepaneringsritualen - *Konung Dómaldr Vid Upsala Hängd* MC Merzbild 2013

Konung Dómaldr Vid Upsala Hängd is a new limited edition MC from T × R × P which thematically relates to the norse legend of the Swedish King Domalde, whose ritual self sacrifice prevented an impending famine. This conceptual content is addressed within the cover image, which is a black and white excerpt of Carl Larsson's famous painting *Midvinterblot* ('Midwinter Sacrifice'), whilst the Swedish song titles roughly translate to: 'For The Benefit of the Swedes', 'Blood Rain' and 'The Corpse of the Fallen Dómaldr'.

Containing three tracks (repeated both sides of the MC), these essentially bleed into a singular 30 minute ritual death ambient composition. Although the first track leads off with some gritty textural static, the main focus is squarely the procession of slow deathly drums, swirling winds, wavering synth textures and croaked / echo distorted vocals, which combine to deliver an excellent track of slow brooding ritual menace. The second track is sparser in construction and encompasses an air of distant abstraction to its voluminous atmosphere. Here a lone cavernous bass thump provides focus in amongst various sweeping/ cavernous tonal elements and the call/ response of howling wolves. Third and final track continues the windswept sound in a slightly more forceful guise, building upon ominous drones, a slow percussive bass pulse and a melancholic synth line akin to the title track of Brighter Death Now's *Necrose Evangelicum* album - an excellent and harrowing conclusion to the MC.

If it wasn't already blatantly obvious, *Noise Receptor* is a big supporter of T × R × P, with *Konung Dómaldr Vid Upsala Hängd* being yet another excellent release within the project's expanding discography.

Trepaneringsritualen - *The Totality of Death* 2xCD Malignant Records / Silken Tofu 2013

With a decent number of limited and relatively obscure vinyls and cassettes issued since 2008, Trepaneringsritualen (T × R × P) have now stepped up to deliver their first CD release/s. Essentially forming a double compilation album - issued simultaneously in two parts on two separate labels - *The Totality of Death* features a hand picked selection of tracks lifted from T × R × P's rare and out of print back catalogue, along with a handful of previously unreleased pieces. Likewise with further reference to T × R × P's discography, interestingly *The Totality of Death* title was previously used for a 2011 private edition cassette compilation (but containing a different track list to here), before being conceptually recontextualised for these official releases.

Although at its core *The Totality of Death* is a compilation album, it has not been a case of merely reproducing used material in chronological order. Rather through careful selection and re-ordering of tracks it provides both albums' with an entirely focused coherence. Thus for the uninitiated *The Totality of Death* contains a superb blend of material spanning all aspects of T × R × P's occult and ritual infused death industrial sound - a sound which encompasses barren windswept soundscapes, queasy lurching rhythms, oozing ritual menace, croaked / distortion scarred vocals and tribal focused percussion, all delivered with a damp, musty and inky black production.

Opening *Programme A* (aka CD1 released via Malignant Records) *Death Reveler* is a fantastic statement of intent with its dank atmosphere of clanging ritualized rhythms and caustic garbled vocals. With a similar rhythmic bent *All Hail the Black Flame* is also a great example of T × R × P's lurching death industrial sound, which subsequently shifts towards more tense and ominous ceremonial soundscapes on the following a pair of tracks *Cherem* and *Lord of This World* (...the later of which rather symbolically has a run time of 3.33 minutes). The lengthy *Van Zeven Manieren Van Heilige Minne* appears to be one of the previously unreleased track, being is a collaborative piece with Hadewych. Over its 14 ritualized minutes the cavernous echoed soundscape relies on distant metallic clatter, sporadic ritual gong tones, disembodied vocals (in both spoken and choral guise), and some more formal instrumentation with the use of minimalist guitar and piano. With the sparse construction for much of the track it oozes forward at a sprawling pace, which shifts during the final third where heavy ritual percussion coalesces the track into a more focused and forceful guise. *Judas Goat* - which is effectively T × R × P's hit single - is a welcomed late album feature, which then leads into *C'Est Un Reve* (which is credited as a Death In June cover). Here the repeated vocal line is yelled here over a repetitive, lurching and relatively up tempo militant programmed backing and although virtually unrecognisable as a cover song, it is a forceful conclusion to *Programme A*.

Moving over to *Programme B* (aka CD2 released via Silken Tofu), it continues the journey through the shadowy underworld of T × R × P's sound. Early album track *Eurcarist of Shit & Piss* takes a stripped back and direct approach to it crude and distorted atonal pulsing beat and screeched vocals, whilst *Sacrament and Crucifixion* displays T × R × P in full death ambient / Brighter Death Now worship mode. Moving ever onwards through the combined two hours of material, there are yet a few more examples of compositions which align with the streamlined 'song' based approach T × R × P. These include the stilted clanging uptempo intensity of *Veil the World* with its croaked, distortion scarred vocals, which is equally applicable to the swaying voodoo tribal intensity of *Didymus Christ*. Used as the concluding piece for *Programme B*, the monolithic *Den Fallne Domaldrs Lik* opts for a slow grinding soundscape of catatonic drums and melancholic synth textures to evoke an atmosphere of brooding ritual menace.

Regarding presentation, both CD's feature almost identical graphics (save for minor variations in images and text), each being issued as six panel digi-packs to form complimentary companion releases. Likewise given T × R × P's penchant for hidden symbolism it is noted that track eight on both CD's features previously unreleased material, which perhaps symbolically represents the number '88', which itself can be interpreted in a number of ways (...intentional or coincidence I wonder?). Beyond such potential symbolic clues, if cult interest with T × R × P has not already been generated by their earlier releases, surely the *The Totality of Death* constitutes a pair of albums to serve this function for a much wider audience. However noting that *The Totality of Death* does not contain all material featured on earlier releases, these compilation

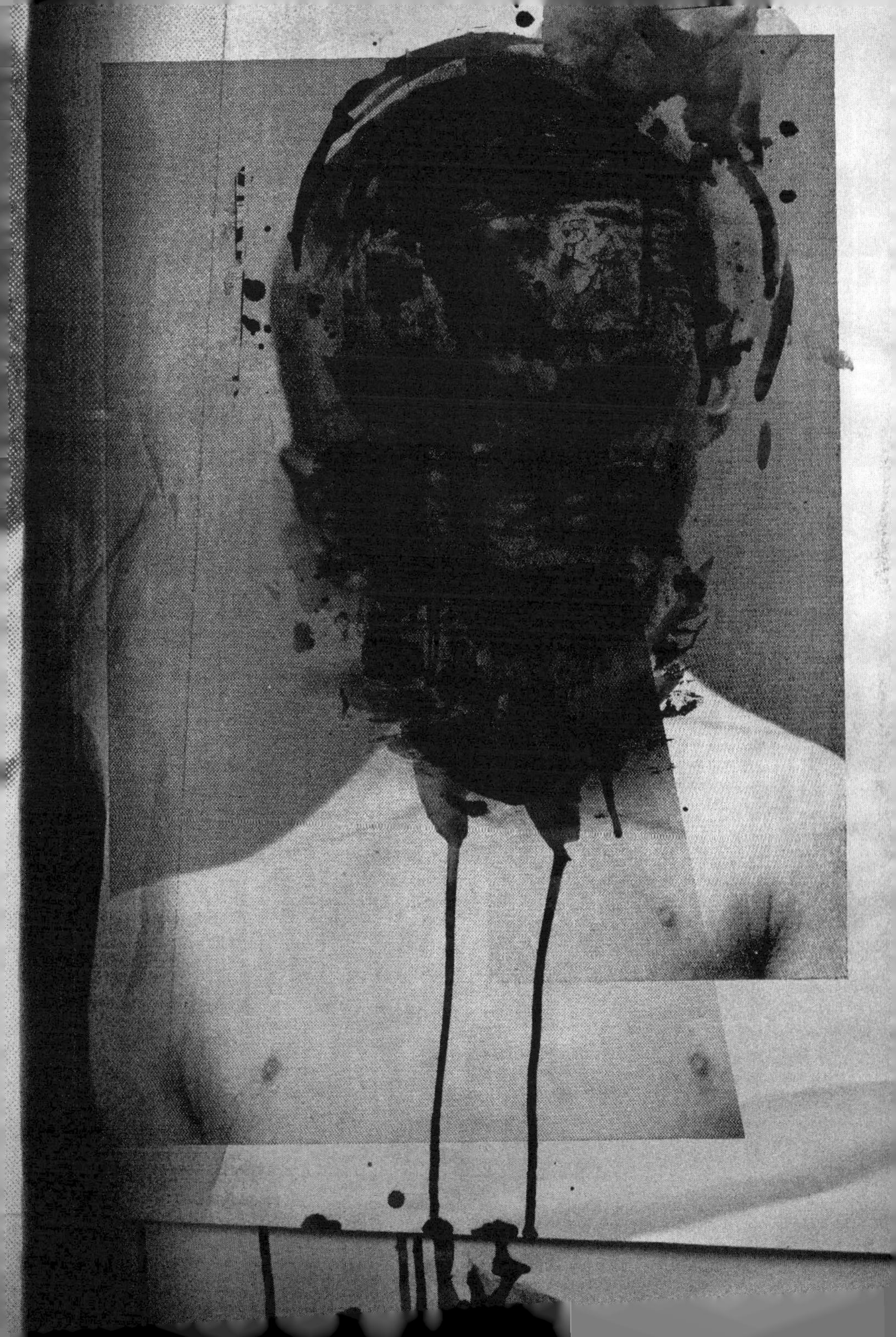

albums can be also considered as the likely generator of additional obsessive T × R × P complete-ists, who will be intent on tracking down all the original cassette and vinyl releases. Worthy, very worthy indeed.

Triangular Ascension - *The Chronos Anomaly* CD Cyclic Law 2013

Following *Noise Receptor's* glowing review of Triangular Ascension's debut album *Leviathan Device*, this sophomore album was awaited with anticipation and from the first cursory listen it is apparent the engaging and animated sonic template is again a central feature. However this time around the main dark ambient focus is complimented by selected tracks displaying a musicality which borders on the martial industrial and neo-classical genres. Another noted deviation is where *The Chronos Anomaly* appears to favour individual tracks within the album context, whereas *Leviathan Device* presented interlinking tracks as part of a bigger whole. So on face value at least the introduction of these aspects avoids a mere repetition of the debut.

On *The Chronos Anomaly* the attention to the recording's sonic clarity is again superb, containing a dense, heaving and bass heavy undercurrent, complimented with layered tonal drifts, washes of synth melodies and tasteful use of field recordings such as aquatic tonal elements, wind, chimes, insects, birds etc - but in no way sounding 'new age' despite what the later part of this description might imply. Surprisingly an acoustic guitar and maudlin flute make an appearance on *Sandstorm*, which provide a focal point against the sweeping dark ambient undercurrent. Likewise the use tribal percussion and sampled choir vocals of *Above The Remnants* are stunning, being another of the album's more musically focused pieces. On the final album track (the tellingly titled *Final Movement*), the melancholic neo-classical horns and orchestral strings drive the composition, whilst an almost flamenco styled acoustic guitar make a brief appearance. Given this tracks provides the concluding statement for the album, it clearly reinforces the differing composed elements which are to be found.

Regarding the conceptual focus of the album the promo states: *'The Chronos Anomaly is a representation of the struggle of man against the illusion of a past and a future and the subsequent degradation of our mind, body and soul. It invites the listener to open their eyes and consciousness to a state where time is but a memory, and memories are but products of the mind, where nothing is external'.* Noting this is quite philosophical content to encapsulate within an abstract musical form such as dark ambience, the masterful control of tone and atmosphere at least means such a description does not sound contrived. Given it appears that Triangular Ascension has sought to avoid merely retreading the same sonic template as the debut, *The Chronos Anomaly* has achieved a similarly strong album through slightly more musical and composed means.

Uncodified / Wertham - *Vindicta I* CD Old Europa Cafe 2013

On this new release Marco Deplano (aka Wertham), has teamed up with the relatively new Italian project Uncodified, which up until this point was an unknown quantity to these ears. Noting both artists work within a broad power electronics frame, here the two acts have sought to blend the sound of each individual project. Likewise for its thematic focus the promo material highlights that: *'Vindicta, is the first chapter of a trilogy focusing on grim/tragic aspects of Sardinian culture. 'Vindicta' tries to capture stills of a dying culture where family was sacred, the knife was considered a man's best friend, and blood called for blood'.*

On *Vindica I* it goes without saying that it displays a staunchly power electronics style. Yet here the focus is on meticulous constructed tracks which sit within seething, mid-toned sound range by combining multi-layered crumbling analog based distortion, metallic junk clatter, sweeping noise and the idling tones of rumbling factory machinery. Whilst the overarch sound is one that is brutally heavy, the album still delivers a churning atmospheric bent. What is also specifically evident is the firm control placed on the layered sound elements, which have a sharp focused tonality. As such the atmosphere is one of sustained sound elements which are delivered with burrowing and invasive intensity. On many tracks there is mid to high pitched piercing noise which takes on a centrally prominent focus and embodies a tinnitus like quality. In fact such noise sits within a sound range which pretty much reflect the tonal range of my own low grade tinnitus - something which I spend a lot of time simply trying to ignore, but which is effectively masked by this album when being played. Vocals when present are stylistically hard and yelled in delivery, being prominent in the mix and drenched in echo and distortion treatment - as are some dialogue sample which are scattered throughout various

tracks. The late album track *Il binario degli appesi* sets itself apart by using the tolling of a lone church bell (at the start and end of the track), whilst the spoken vocals are delivered as an almost religiously fevered mantra, although admittedly the message is lost on me given its delivery in Italian.
Clearly *Vindicta I* is not intent on reinventing what power electronics is and can be, rather it is the by product of skilled musicians working within the parameters of this style. To this end there is no clumsy handling of the noise compositions nor empty posturing to be found here. What can be found however is a hard hitting, meticulously composed and expertly controlled power electronics album which contains intelligently focused and conceptually interesting subject material. Recommended.

U-731 – *By All Means...* CD Black Plagve 2014

U-731 are a new American signing to the Black Plagve roster, being helmed by one Gordon Lazarus who has previously operated under the name Defiler, before taking up the current U-731 moniker. Yet noting this is U-731's debut album, rather strangely the promo blurb also highlights that *By All Means...* represents the swansong for the project. Incidentally Gordon intends to continue under the banner of United Front, however it is not at all clear whether United Front will continue with the sound and thematic content of this particular release.
Armed with this album U-731 clearly demonstrate they are an act that can stand on an equal footing with other US acts, and most particularly: Steel Hook Prosthesis, The Vomit Arsonist, Gnawed and Nyodene D. In fact such name-dropping goes beyond mere sonic comparisons, as five of the seven album tracks were produced in collaboration with John Stillings of Steel Hook Prosthesis (three tracks) and Andy Grant of The Vomit Arsonist (two tracks). Although this is oriented towards the scathing side of death industrial music, U-731 set themselves apart by weaving in a pessimistic dark ambient undercurrent, meaning they achieve a gloomier tone than their aforementioned peers. Speech and documentary dialogue samples also constitute a large part of U-731's sonic aesthetic, where these are intertwined seamlessly within the soundscapes to articulate a range of topics including: medical procedures, conspiracies, secret societies, covert government actions and WWII politics. Via this framework U-731 conjures seething atmospheres driven by caustic droning synths and mechanised industrial debris, which sporadically lets loose in a more focused death industrial style (and occasionally nearing power electronics intensity).
For the opening track *Forced Neurotic Displacement* it features an ominous undercurrent of heaving bass aggressiveness, minor key synths and corrosive outbursts, against which the trademark electric/ static hissed vocals of John Stilling are spewed forth. From this first introductory track it establishes a superb foundational offering. John Stilling again makes an appearance with his seething vocals on *The Mechanics of Embalming* which sit atop grinding mechanised industrial loops and a medical based dialogue sample addressing the track's title. Stepping away from a collaborative framework, mid album track *Freedom, Reaction-Resistance* sees Gordon Lazarus operating without external input. Here the track conveys a lo-fi, paranoid infused soundscape of drones, distant metallic clatter and speech samples addressing conspiracies and secret societies, before ramping up with looped distortion of crushing intensity. Being another collaborative offering, the following track *F.E.M.A Care* is the first of two tracks to feature the contributions of Andy Grant, who is in ultra-aggressive form where the anger of his vocal delivery has been ratcheted up few notches (...which is certainly saying something). This track commences in a subdued dark ambient fashion as a documentary sample articulates government conspiracies relating to covert martial law programs, before elevating to power electronics intensity with crushing distortion and static drenched/ emotion wracked vocals. In deviating from the material which proceeds it, *Sun Gan/ Last Rites* functions to conclude the album in brooding fashion, where relentless waves of static and morose synth textures usher in a radio broadcast (Winston Churchill?) announcing war had been declared on Germany as a consequence of their invasion of Poland in 1939. Later in the track the mood shifts through the use of choir vocal samples and the sound of exploding shells and gunfire which usher the album into oblivion.
Whilst the influence of Steel Hook Prosthesis and The Vomit Arsonist is undeniable on their collaborative tracks, rather than being a potential negative, their contributions are incorporated seamlessly into the album's overall concept and sound. Certainly *By All Means...* is a full realised, expertly executed and genre refined recording which is also one of the strongest debut albums issued in recent memory (noting that Shock Frontier's debut of 2013 holds a similar accolade). Recommended.

Various Artists - *Epicurean Escapism II* CD/ DVD / Catalogue The Epicurian / Silken Tofu / Peripheral Records 2013

Epicurean Escapism II forms the multi-media companion release to the festival of the same name (held in Berlin on 15th June, 2013). Noting this is the second festival release, when reflecting on the cassette / DVD / special packaging of the first compilation, this time around the format has been stepped up a notch to more comprehensively reflect the multi-media format of the festival. Here the release incorporates elements of all artistic aspects including: reproductions of a selection of exhibited artworks, a CD of material contributed by performing acts and a DVD that reproduces the screened short experimental films. These audio and visual elements have then been housed in an impeccably designed DVD sized fold out cardboard cover, highlighting that there have been no half measures when approaching this release.
To address the musical content first and noting the musical heritage of Ke/Hil, their heavily ominous and coldly nihilistic track is a great way to open the CD. *Dark Germany* amounts to an expertly crafted and dense layered composition of slow throbbing synths, swirling noise and distortion frayed vocals. Anemone Tube follow and deliver a pair a solid tracks (*Apocalyptic Fantasy* and *Accumulations*), which both adhere a general pattern of invasive cyclic noise, looped metallic clattered, managed/ barely recognisable field recordings and understated melancholic droning synth elements. Each of these tracks (again) displays the particular sound attributable to Anemone Tube, which as I have said before is testament to the mastery of his sonic craft. Moving on to *Leprous Driver*, Post Scriptum evoke more filmic composition imbedded

with an atmosphere brooding menace, here consisting of a slab of crystalline dark ambience (aka droning syths, spares piano notes, and unobtrusively layered background tones / noise). Following next is the mighty Trepaneringsritualen, who contribute two tracks on the shorter side (three to five minutes each). *Vanärat Är Ditt Namn* takes to a rhythmic song based approach of a repetitive throbbing beat and yelled verse / chorus / verse type vocals, while *End of Flesh* opts for slow ritual ambience, where a catatonic bass throb provides some sense of structure amongst the layers of swirling vocal invocations. To round out the compilation Dieter Müh issues forth the hefty 20 minute composition *Bethlehem*, which is a highlight amongst highlights. Here the track commences with a beautifully understated modern classical tone, with distant melancholic piano and abstract vocal sample cut ups. However this fragile segment ultimately acts as the intro passage for the main bulk of the tracks which features a mid paced, tribally infused dark ambience, which in some ways reminds of the early works of Morthound. To provide a final comment on the compilation, to my mind if the curation of such releases is not managed correctly they can either become frustratingly long due to the number of contributions and/ or suffer from submission of poor or second rate material. Thankfully no such complaints exist here, as with a (mere) seven excellent tracks by five artists, it is an easily digestible and most importantly an engaging and enjoyable listen throughout.
For the DVD segment of this release, this consists of six short films by Mike Dando of Con-Dom, issued under the collective title *We Who Were Living Are Now Dying*. Whilst not constituting new material from Con-Dom, the DVD sees the formal publication of six archival experimental films that Con-Dom produced between 1983 to 1994. Here these short films effectively act as the visual counterpart to a number of Con-Dom's heavy and harsh power electronics tracks, and whilst relatively crude and experimental in style, they consist of filmed footage and still images which are cut together as a sprawling visual collage. Conceptually there are a range of themes at play including: belief, religion, sin, spirituality, suffering, religious ecstasy, pornography, masturbation, sexual ecstasy, medical deformities, birth, death, race, racial hatred, family, honour, authority, war atrocities, crime etc. With its cut up collage technique the multiple utilised themes are presented for the viewer to analyse and pick apart in trying to stitch together the conceptual threads on display. Visually the films are quite dark and textured and which suits the material well, while there is also a faint black line flicker moving through the visuals. This later aspect could be due to the material being filmed on video, or otherwise as a result of the transfer to digital format from super 8 film - but either way this effect adds to the lo-fi grainy aesthetic of the films. As with Con-Dom's more recognised musical outputs, there is always a clear message at the core of Mike's work even if it gets somewhat muddied by the brute force approach. As such it is great to see that a similar approach is embodied within Con-Dom's experimental films, where it will take time to analyse presented content.
For the last part of this release it has sought to in part document the group art exhibition displayed as part of the festival (which incidentally was curated by African Paper Magazine). Contributing artists whose artworks were featured from Alex Tenningkeit, Andrew Liles, Carmen Burguess, Dennis Rudolph and Phillip Best, Rudolf Eb.er, and whilst each artist's outputs vary wildly in materials, style and aesthetic output they do generally hinge on a darker and/ or subversive tangents. Here a selection of the artists works are published in a 16 page full colour booklet, along with an essay by Uwe Schneider which outlines the concept of the festival and compilation and neatly ties together the various artist's inputs.
Although in the first instance this release is a memento of the festival it seeks to document, with its meticulous execution and sheer quality of its content, *Epicurean Escapism II* transcends this mere documentary role, to become an exceptionally focused multi-media release. Definitely worthy of detailed investigation and limited to a mere 350 copies.

Various Artists - *Philosophy of a Knife* CD Peripheral Records 2012

Being Peripheral Record's first compilation this is evidently the first in a series, and whilst not containing an iron clad conceptual statement, themes of blades, medical procedures, vivisections etc are evident on a number of the artist's compositions. So without and further fanfare, here follows a brief track by track review of the eleven contributions:

- White Walls are up first and present *Sacrificed* - a seething and ominous death industrial track complete with medical atrocity focused dialogue sample, which results in a sound not too dissimilar to Steel Hook Prosthesis. A great opening offering.
- Brighter Death Now's previously released *Kill Useless People* is up next, being a squelching noise and mid paced rhythmic power electronics assault, complete with the obligatory misanthropic ranted vocals. This is Brighter Death Now – no more, no less, no further comment.
- Staalkracht's *Human Vivisection* elects for an overblown, distortion driven and somewhat freeform industrial noise styled track, including wailing vocals being partially buried in the mix. In a word, chaotic.
- Contagious Orgasm alternately opts for an experimental soundscape, where *Evidence Destruction* is constructed with scraps of a melodious piano tune and voice samples, which then shifts into a pulsing electronic programmed segment. Certainly very different to the bulk of the other contributions.
- Bagman follow and appear to be very much of the new current crop of UK power electronics acts, where *The Hidden Blade* is constructed with layered pulsing sonics, burrowing noise and distorted shredded vocals. Hard and straightforward power electronics - and excellent for it.
- IRM yet again demonstrate why they are held in such high regard with the presentation of their live track *Order (Variation III)*. This excellent live rendition is faithful to the studio counterpart, but notably the vocals are more harrowing and urgent, being yelled / screamed over an anxiety including bed of oscillating electronic and layered noise. Fantastic as expected.
- Barrikad moves off into slightly more freeform territory with *Howls for Valerie Solanas: Confronting Misogynists*, which is a track of overblown junk metal abuse verging on a noise styled approach, with some minor elements of

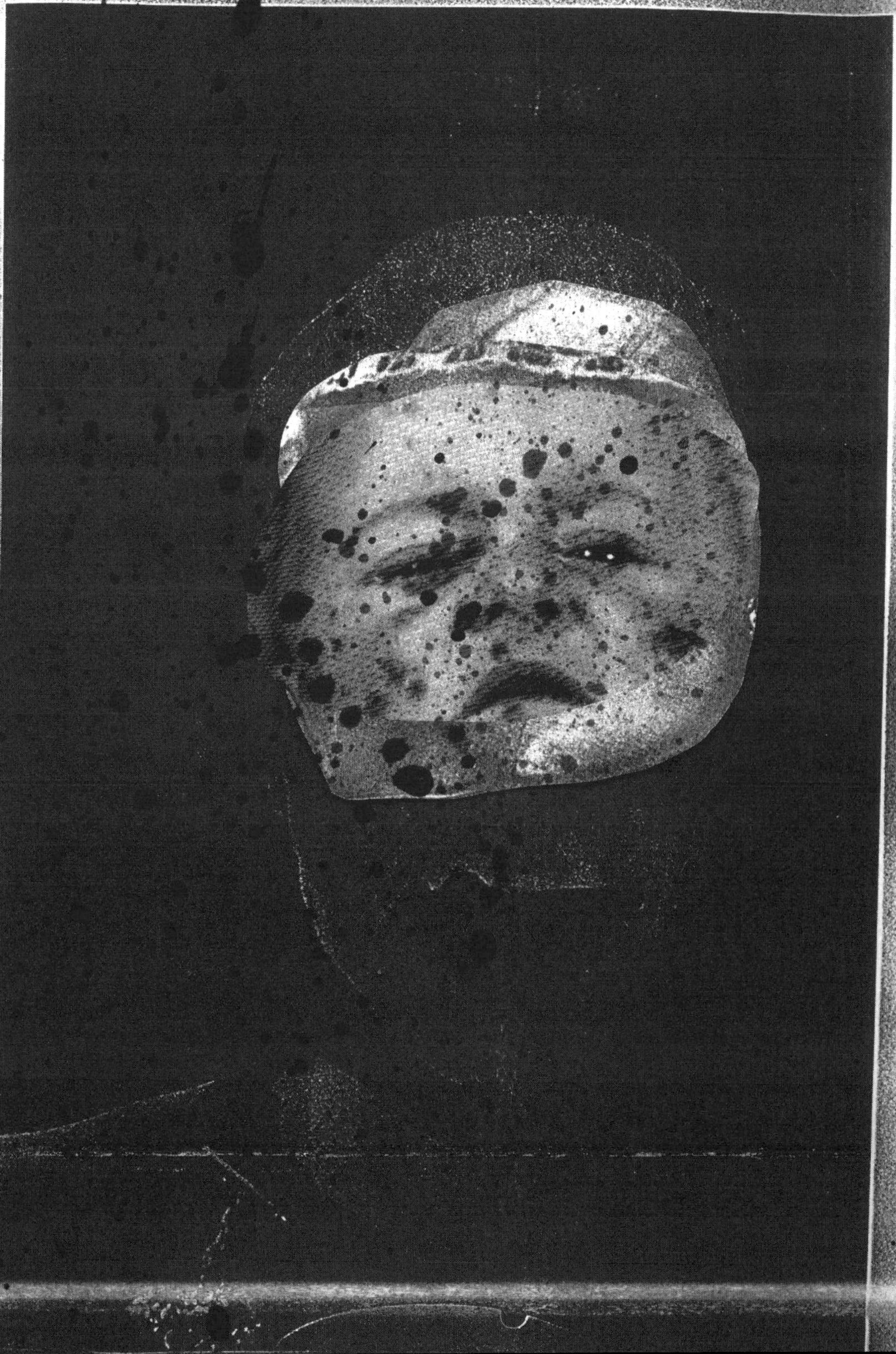

structure and vocals buried within the general cacophony. Solid, but not entirely my thing.

- Atrabilis Sunrise step up and stands out from preceding material on *The World is Full of Me*, which is evidently a live track. Here the sound is sharp dry and clinical, with a throbbing rhythmic undercurrent and yelled / flanged vocals which brings to mind the power electronics style of early Haus Arafna. Without doubt a standout composition.
- Dry Greed's offering comes in the form of *Nanking Safety Zone*, which is both noisy yet somehow hollow in tone and atmosphere, and with its overall grinding / sweeping timbre it reminds of the overblown mayhem of Propergol's early albums. In other words good.
- BrandKommando embraces an analogue industrial noise meets power electronics type style on their track *Unit 731*. The composition is relatively loose in construction, which contains further medical atrocity documentary samples and wailing vocalisations, which if a comparison was to be made it partly reminds of mid era Grunt. Translate this again as meaning a good track.
- Kristus Kut are the act to conclude the CD and delivers a weirdly experimental composition *The Call of the Mermaid*, which is based on cyclic drones (didgeridoo or sampled Tibetan throat singing?) and abstract micro-tonal scratching / scraping sounds etc, to create an unusual ritualised soundscape. Bizarre and almost slightly out of place of the CD.

Without labouring it, if you're not a fan of industrial noise, power electronics and related sounds this compilation will not alter your opinion of such genres - but this is not really the point. Clearly this compilation knows its target audience and delivers a solid collection of tracks from both recognised and more obscure acts. With a straight forward DVD styled packaging (limitation of 250 copies), obviously you will know if this is for you.

Various Artists – *phloq – compilation twelve* 2xLP phloq 2013

Sometimes it is good to check out totally unknown music scenes and associated projects as it means there are no pre-conceived notations of what to expect. This release fits the bill suitably as I have not previously come across the relatively young phloq label (launched in 2012), nor any of the featured artists. Whilst *phloq – compilation twelve* is obviously a compilation release from this Danish label, I am unsure whether it is representative of a particular Danish experimental/ ambient scene (…or even if all contributing artists are Danish for that matter). Nevertheless single tracks are presented by ten projects/ artists, which are spread across four sides of vinyl. Regarding the scope of acts and sounds presented, overall I would say the general focus of the label and contributing artists sits in the same tonal sphere as Touch Music, i.e. ambient, isolationist and experimental music which edges towards art / culture / academic fields. Obviously this is considered comparison and a compliment to the quality of the material found herein. In order to not to exclude any contributing artists here goes with a quick snapshot review for each:

- Dot: bleak yet animated isolationist ambience which evoke visions of desolate widescreen vistas.
- Isaktelefon: moody cinematic atmospheres generated through slow droning elements and layered sound textures.
- Flip Ja: abstract experimental sounds with microtonal detailing.
- Maulex: multi-layered abstract droning sounds with an liquidous sound quality.
- Phaedrus: droning slightly melodious ambient soundscapes edging towards a minimalist tangent.
- Malcolm Mahiti: muffled and heavy bass loaded isolationist ambience, with occasional injections of microtonal static.
- Krishve: abstract low grinding drone textures, infuse with a positive dose of timbral clips, pops etc.
- Mads Engell: abstract and experimental digital cut ups, with textural sound elements extending from low key to sharp and loud.
- Alex Morch: experimental/ contemporary classical consisting of looped conveyor belt type factory clatter, overlaid with layered melancholic cello.
- Jannick Schou: another experimental/ contemporary classical track consisting of minimalist angular orchestral strings and droning undercurrent, to create an intense cinematic atmosphere.

To my ear the standout tracks are from Dot, Isaktelefon, Malcolm Mahiti and Jannick Schou, but that said there are no poor or lacking contributions either, which says volumes for the high quality of the contributed material. Likewise due to the general 'soundscape' and 'ambient' nature of the compositions, they hang together positively as a coherent collection of tracks. Packaging consists of gatefold cover where the static infused abstract graphic art grades from white through to various shades of grey to black, which is a suitable visual representation for the abstract sound found within.

The Vomit Arsonist - *Reason* MC Nil By Mouth Recordings 2010

Given this tape obviously predates the excellent *Go Without* album from 2012, it illustrates sole project member Andrew Grant in slightly less refined form, but still resulting in an interesting and solid release.

Lifeless opens the tape with a grinding pulse and loosely constructed metallic factory clatter all wrapped up in a cavernous tonal aesthetic, upon which the aggressive, echoed distorted vocals are spewed forth. *Environment* plays with similar sound, but comes across as more aggressive in the vocal department (*"GIve me one reason. Give me one fucking reason")*, whilst also evoking a melancholic tone due to some some depressive synth lines. The highlight track of the tape is found in the form of *Existence*, which features layered ominous descending synth drones and distortion drenched vocals, which although simple in construction absolutely hits the mark. Alternately *Purpose* opts to deliver an aggressive and loosely looped power electronics piece, which makes way for the final track *Ten Suicides* which is a cover of a Bloodyminded song. Although less bleak than the original, it does manage to match the intensity within the frame of The Vomit Arsonists' sound.

Packaging is suitably DIY for the tape format, including black spray painted case and photocopied card inserts which are housed in a sealed mini 'garbage bag' style sleeve.

The Vomit Arsonist - *An Occasion For Death* CD Malignant Records 2013

If not counting the numerous cassettes and CDr's issued by The Vomit Arsonist since 2004, *An Occasion For Death* represents the third official album and the first issued by the leading underground label Malignant Records (which is certainly a welcomed pairing). As the last album *Go Without* was well received around here it also goes without saying that this new album was awaited with anticipation. Yet for those still not familiar with The Vomit Arsonist, this is the solo project of American artist Andrew Grant who typically excels at the blurring of death industrial and power electronics sounds. However from cursory listens to *An Occasion For Death*, it is immediately evident that this time around Andrew has focused less on a brutal power electronics edge and opted for a slightly more brooding death industrial tone. Thus being more harrowing than brutally heavy, this album is both bleak and nihilistic to its core.

The album opens with *Think God Out Of Existence* which has the feel of an extended introductory piece, being a desolately ominous death industrial soundscape of ebbing and flowing layered synth drones, which also contains a lengthy dialogue sample of atheism taken to a logical and heretical extreme. Yet it is the second track *At The Edge of Life, Everything Is An Occasion for Death* where there album really steps up a notch with slow looped bass pounding beat, sustained melancholic piano notes/ synth lines, a dose of unobtrusive static undercutting the composition and the distinctive distortion wracked vocals. In simpler terms this is The Vomit Arsonist's own sound done to absolute perfection. *Black Bile* represents another stand out composition, structured with an almost militant tinged mid paced percussive thump, grinding static, bleakly ominous synth lines, and the trademark distortion eviscerated vocals. Alternately *Torn Between Will and Desire* opts for a more forceful sound with a heavy combination of grinding static loops and mechanised idling factory noise, where the emotion wracked vocals again take a central focus (being distorted to the point of indecipherability). For the final of the seven album tracks, *Means To An End* mixes cavernous warehouse type ambience and rising synth drones to ratchet up the tension, before the introduction of a French dialogue sample and one final segment of grinding static and furnace blasted vocals.

Although less blunt force than earlier albums, here the reduced brutality has been replaced with an atmosphere of harrow bleakness elevated to central prominence. While only 43 minutes this is not an overly lengthy album, yet *An Occasion For Death* pack a heavy emotional punch within the available run time and in the process sees The Vomit Arsonist really coming into his own.

discretionary

terms for potential submission of material

Noise Receptor Journal is a personal endeavour where the majority of items reviewed have been sourced from my personal collection. Accordingly I don't have any sort of hidden agenda of using this as a means to getting as many free releases as possible. If nothing else, it constitutes a creative outlet where I can promote material I feel is worthy of support and added exposure. As such I am not interested in allowing unsolicited material to be submitted for review. I personally buy enough music to keep me very busy with music listening, and the last thing I need is to wade through bundles of material I don't have any passion or connection with. I am also not interested in fulfilling some sort of 'scene documenter' role, in trying to review every single new release which comes out. Quality over quantity I say!

Noting that I am not actively seeking submission of material to review, there may be circumstances where I accept some items, provided the following terms are agreeable:

- I will only review material that has been furnished with a physical release.
- The release must be current and have reasonable availability (i.e. not be limited to a stupidly low number).
- The genre of the music must be suitably aligned to the types of items reviewed herein.
- I will review CDs and vinyls (and perhaps tapes – depending on the release).
- If a release is produced on multiple formats, my preference is as follows: vinyls first, then CDs, followed lastly by tapes.
- I will generally not review CDr's (too often this is indicative of a hastily produced and / or derivative type release) .
- I do not review digital releases or accept MP3's, download links / files etc as a substitute for a copy of the actual release.
- If I do accept the submission of a release for review, a full and complete copy of the physical release must be provided. Any promo versions, or versions stamped 'promo', 'sample', or with corners cut off, holes punched in covers or other markings to indicate its 'promo' status, will not be reviewed.
- To reduce postage cost, sending CD's (including front / back covers) without the jewel cases is acceptable.
- Any items submitted will not be returned.
- I am not interested in reviewing hastily thrown together releases, with little care of quality, aesthetic and design.
- I am not interested in reviewing second rate and / or derivative releases – again quality over quantity. Before you seek to have an item reviewed, undertake a detailed assessment of your own work and make an honest judgement of how it stacks up against other 'pinnacle' works. If in your heart of hearts you feel that your material is second rate, or pales in compassion to comparative material – it is probably true – in which case I am not interested in reviewing it.

If the above terms are not agreeable that is quite fine by me. I will happily continue buying releases and reviewing the ones I feel are worthy, thank you very much! Life is too short to be burdened with listening to and writing about boring, bad, uninspired or derivative music. This is a passion – not a job! If you have got this far and are still interested in trying to submit an item for review, contact me with a proposal, including relevant details at: noisereceptor@hotmail.com

noise receptor
journal : issue no.3
sound with impact - analysing the abstract
aischrolatreia / alfarmania / fieldwork / genocide organ
kristian olsson / puce mary / survival unit / wertham

CENTRAL INDUSTRIAL AGENCY
SINCE 2001

noise receptor

journal : issue no.3

sound with impact - analysing the abstract **may 2015**

editorial

Welcome to the third instalment of *Noise Receptor Journal*, released one year on from the second issue and two years on from the first. At the time of the release of Issue No.1, the concept involved featuring a single long form interview and exclusive art to differentiate it from the already published web based reviews. Although Issue No.2 saw this concept evolve towards a format of multiple interviews, one critical element remains unchanged: being the goal to ensure all interviews are long form and in-depth and going well beyond cursory surface level questions to cover in detail the themes and concepts explored by featured artists. With this particular goal in mind, two of the interviews featured herein (namely the Wertham interview with Marco Deplano and the Alfarmania / Survival Unit interview with Kristian Olsson), are the longest featured in the magazine so far. As such I must extend my upmost thanks to all interviewed artists for taking their interviews so seriously and putting substantial thought into their detailed and thoroughly considered responses. For me, the music covered within the pages of *Noise Receptor Journal* amounts to something more than mere 'entertainment'; where there is both spirit within and intent behind such creative works. Undoubtedly each of the featured artists proves this perception to be correct. Noting the number and sheer length of featured interviews has increased the overall page count to double that of Issue No.2, I hope this amount to a fully immersive reading experience on your part. Special thanks to Kristian Olsson is also warranted for the submission of his strikingly grim artwork featured herein.

Regarding the overall response to *Noise Receptor Journal* thus far, it has been extremely positive and I am pleased there any many people across the globe who seem to appreciate the publication in physical form. However sometimes I do wonder if a large section of the newer 'internet' generation has simply missed gaining an appreciation of print media and underground 'zine culture. This observation is based on fact that the that the *Noise Receptor Journal* Facebook page has roughly double the number of 'likes' compared to the number of physical magazine which have been sold per issue to date. Noting that none of the featured interview content is available online, it seems that many are missing the best parts of this publication. Their loss really. Regardless, this magazine remains dedicated to all who value the permanence of print media and underground 'zine culture, so I extend my thanks to you for purchasing this publication. Read on, and I hope you enjoy what is contained herein as much as I enjoyed putting this publication together.

Richard Stevenson / *Noise Receptor Journal*

access

noisereceptor.wordpress.com
noisereceptor.bigcartel.com
noisereceptor@hotmail.com
follow noise receptor on facebook
spectrummagarchive.wordpress.com

credits

editor, interviewer, reviewer and layout designer: Richard Stevenson
cover and all review section artwork: Kristian Olsson
photo credits: Puce Mary: © Nikki Sneakers MMXIV. Wertham (in order of apperance): 1: Titti Gemin, 2: Ale Formenti, 3: Davide Maspero, 4: Davide Maspero, 5: unknown, 6: Aldo Volpe. Alfarmania / Survival Unit (in order of apperance): 1: Mikko Aspa, 2: uncredited, 3 & 4: Carolus Löfroos, 4: Carl Abrahamsson, 5: Mikko Aspa. Genocide Organ: photos unknown (provided courtesy of the artist). All remaining logos, symbols & artwork for Aischrolatreia / Fieldwork, Wertham, Alfarmania / Survival Unit by the artists.

contents

PUCE MARY

Since 2010 and particularly in the last couple of years Puce Mary (the solo industrial project of Frederikke Hoffmeier), has garnered a significant amount of underground interest and praise, noting this has resulted from the quality of her recorded output and force of live performances, rather than from any sort of calculated online promotion campaign. Although having given very few interviews to date, through her detailed responses below Frederikke demonstrates a strong and focused determination regarding her creative pursuits.

Would you care to introduce yourself - age, upbringing, education etc. and what are the circumstances which lead to awareness, interest and eventual involvement in underground industrial music?
My name is Frederikke Sophie Hoffmeier. I grew up in a coastal town just a short train ride north of Copenhagen. I was brought up, with an older brother, by my father and had little interest in anything worth mentioning up until I moved to Copenhagen as a 16 year old, where I met the people who introduced me to underground music and art. School was never particularly a strong suit for me, I tried a variety of things but dropped out of most. I feel well read and that I have a competent frame of reference for subjects that are important to me.

Puce Mary is an interesting choice of moniker, noting that 'Puce' is the French word for flea and / or colour of a bloodstain and that 'Mary' is clearly not your own name. Is there a particular meaning and story behind the choice of the project name?
A moniker is a name that adds to or stands in for something and that is what Puce Mary, as a name, is about. With a friend maybe this addition or substitute is affection, playful ridicule, or familiarity. For an artist, especially one working alone, it provides a degree of detachment from the popular idea that you are a fixed subject and that your art reflects that single person. I am not completely Puce Mary and Puce Mary is not completely me. Both of those words are the things you say but also carry several other meanings. The important thing is that they are not Frederikke or Hoffmeier. The ambiguity of the relationship between those two sets of words has been a boon for my music in a way so I will keep it that way.

With your musical output you employ a diverse range of sonic and stylistic approaches which draw from the broad industrial / power electronics / drone / noise styles, but combined in such a way as to achieve a individual stylistic bent. How much is this merging of styles and elements based on specific design, or the result of positive studio experimentation?
I would maybe argue that the specific design comes from prudent discrimination at the end of many hours of negative studio experimentation! I never set out to fulfill some specific design of genre combination though. The palate I use when recording, comes from as many musical influences and non-musical ones. I throw away and move on from hours and hours of recordings that function better as lessons in what I don't exactly want but might not understand so until I have seen those 'experiments' through. Some of the formal qualities of my work - sonic, structural or otherwise - come from the legacy of industrial music and noise and so on. I try to use the tropes from those music styles as guideposts though, not rules or goals, a common mistake in my view. It makes me cringe to think of my music described as 'fusion' or something. When precedent become imperative you lose the opportunity to create anything truly new or important. You just turn whatever you're making into an afterthought, secondary to a shitty combination of ideas or traditions that were perfectly fine on their own. There is no point to making (to say nothing of recording and releasing) something that merely proves a stupid string of hyphenated tag-lines describes something. I do have enormous respect for exceptional execution of simple forms though. It's a formula that has produced some of the best music ever made. I am doing something a little different though but very much in light of that respect I hold.

Listening to your albums gives the impression that you use old analogue synths and equipment to create your music, rather than digital or computer means. Is this in fact the case? If so is this an ideological stance against digital, or just the preferred method you employ? Do you have preferred equipment to build your material from, or is equipment used merely as a means to an end?
Well, over the years my set up and methods have changed. If you listen to material I released from five years ago, you will hear different gear. You will also hear music being made with a different answer to the question of whether what's being used is a compositional choice or a means to an end. At this point, while I still feel very sentimental for certain equipment but ultimately have a clear idea most of the time of how I want something to sound so don't particularly care how that sound is made. I have my preferences of course and I do think I could go on about the virtues of old analog gear but maybe that would be a rather generic rant.

The question relating to analogue and digital seems to also extend to the chosen mediums of your release, noting these to date have been limited to vinyl and tape with no CD or 'digital only' formats. Again is this a coincidence or by specific design? Have you had options to release your material on CD to date? What is your view on digital only releases? Ultimately what are your preferred mediums for the release of your material?
Again, I'm not too sure something particularly insightful is behind this choice. Tape and vinyl have distinct sounds. CDs have never really caught on for me since so much of the music I listen to is on tape or vinyl exclusively. I'm not fundamentally opposed to CDs. That they're not as cool as analog releases is a relatively uncontroversial opinion.

What artists, albums, literature, motion pictures etc. (if any) might you acknowledge as a critical inspiration sources for what you produce as Puce Mary?
There's a lot to list and it's a fine line between general interests, motivation and direct inspiration. I'll try and stick to the latter, but most important to me have been filmmakers: Ingmar Bergman, Kenneth Anger, Maya Deren, Pasolini, writers: Dostoyevsky, Bataille, Marquis De Sade, Yukio Mishima, recently E.M. Cioran, composers: Penderecki, Gyorgy Ligeti, Egisto Macchi and Carl Stone. I can't avoid claiming to be inspired by legends as Whitehouse, Vivenza, Etat Brut, TG and Genocide Organ. Friends and peers like Damien Dubrovnik, Vanessa Amara, Klaus Hansen, Swedish noise (Sewer Election, Alfarmania, Arv & Miljö and so on) and my accomplice J. Sanes.

In my review of your album *Persona* I made comments that you are at the forefront of a 'new generation' of acts, from your own perspective do you have an appreciation from where interest in your musical output is predominantly coming from, be it particularly countries or music scenes?
I am interested somewhat in where appreciation for my output comes from but it's a tepid appreciation and one I'm weary of over-concerning myself with. I'm not sure what that interest has to do, if anything, with my 'generation'. I think the most satisfying appreciation comes from people or places that you mutually respect and I've been lucky enough to have that with peers even from outside the insular world of extreme underground electronic music.

Age and gender are matters which bear consideration in the context of Puce Mary, mainly as the 'industrial underground' is a scene dominated by males and, perhaps somewhat simplistically, an overtly masculine perspective. Noting that first and foremost the focus should be on your music and artistic expressions, nevertheless do you have any personal insight to how you are perceived within the underground?
Being a woman seems to bear consideration in almost every context or occupation outside of home making. Male dominated perspective is hardly unique to underground industrial scenes. Female athletes perform in their own separate class for which an analogous sphere doesn't exist in extreme underground music (nor do I wish it did) but its absence is confusing or something to many people. My insight is this: being a young woman affords me certain differences when coming to the studio or stage. You're right in stating the focus should be my output. The focus on how an uncontrollable circumstance differs from the expected can be tedious. Dissecting that sort of banality isn't a concern to me and I pity those for whom it is. Bewilderment at womanhood is a mundane prison and seeing the simple minded rot in that cage is fine for a quick laugh but little more.

What have been your experiences with becoming involved with and building the profile of Puce Mary within the industrial underground? Have you had any particularly positive and / or negative experiences?
I would have to say that my involvement in 'profile building' has been almost completely forgone in favor of remaining involved as much as possible in building quality material. I do no PR type of shit or social media outreach or whatever falls into the category of profile building. I have great label support from Posh Isolation and try to make the best releases I can. It's a strategy that's served me well so far.

Noting you are Danish and that Denmark could be classified as a wealthy liberal Western country, do your personal surroundings, living arrangements etc. reflect this rather simplistic external perception of your home country? Likewise do the circumstances of your day to day life have a direct influence on your musical output?
I think the circumstances of day to day life are unavoidable influences on anything anyone does. Denmark is, yes, a wealthy, western country but there are other countries that fit that description that are nothing like Denmark and suffer a myriad of social problems that Denmark either avoids or partially avoids or does a phenomenal job of creating the illusion of avoiding. It's hard to say what, exactly, about being Danish has influenced what for me because obviously there are no controls to compare myself against. As I've travelled more to the States, however, and spent longer periods of time there, I have considered the effect certain aspects of my nationality and living most my life in a place with a measurably more socially conscious design and governance. It's a little bit difficult to navigate this discussion however just because it's often painted so black and white - as if Denmark is this culturally homogeneous, infinitely rich, social utopia while the US is a draconian police state marked by unconscionable levels of inequality teetering on the brink of collapse in endgame capitalism (well, maybe that isn't too far for the US). But I don't want to fall into that false portrayal of the situation. It really discounts an important, marginalized segment of Danish society who absolutely do not experience life in Denmark as vanilla paradise. So, is there an existential mark or freedom that comes with the types of security Danish society provides me? My gut reaction is no, that pain and privilege are relative. Rape, murder, lies and ruthlessness -

every element of the extreme limits of the human condition - are alive and well here in Denmark. But there's a bit of uncertainty in my answer. The visceral reaction I have had to walking through a place like Skid Row is something that struck a fierce blow to the more comfortable part of understanding the world I have somewhere.

Being a resident of Copenhagen what are your experiences / opinions of the Christiania commune as a social experiment to move away from a capitalistic market based economic model? In this context the mission statement of Christiania (co-authored by Jacob Ludvidvigsen) is relevant: *'The objective of Christiania is to create a self-governing society whereby each and every individual holds themselves responsible over the wellbeing of the entire community. Our society is to be economically self-sustaining and, as such, our aspiration is to be steadfast in our conviction that psychological and physical destitution can be averted'.*

Christiania on the other hand I give little thought to. I used to buy some weed there as a teenager I guess. Its lofty political ambitions stated like that sound admirable. Christiania's existence certainly contributes to the air of the city but I don't think it profoundly affect most people who aren't directly engaged with it.

From reading some of your available lyrics (and specifically from the *Persona* album), there appears to be a non-typical and perhaps personal psychological and self-analytical angle to your lyrical approach. Noting the first person style of the lyrics, are these written from your own perspective or perhaps more taking on particular characters and scenarios?

With regards to the first person perspective, I have always found it more effective to embody the voice being spoken with, regardless of whether or not that body is my own. Sometimes the ambiguity of whose body is speaking is the most powerful part. Embodying a listener or an external subject is a always a bit more like an easy way to settle the question of who is speaking by differing the question to who is being spoken to. People like easy answers but satisfaction is a quick study. Rereading this question the reader could wonder if it's the listener who is psychologically analyzing yourself to *Persona*, not me.

Noting that your lyrics are not included on the majority of your releases, is there is a broader thematic arc to how you approach your written material? Likewise noting that your vocals are generally distortion treated and somewhat unintelligible as a result, what is your view on the role of the voice being merely another instrument or sound layer? In this context does it diminish the importance, impact and message of the lyrics themselves?

I would say there is a certain thematic consistency to the releases if not some epic arc. The voice is, categorically, another layer of sound. It can also be a 'literal' instrument, as in layer in the song that you can take at face value to some extent. Words evoke more concrete meanings for people than abstract sounds. That doesn't mean they're more important though. The content of lyrics are affected by any way you deliver them. Degree of clarity is one pallets of meanings while, say, tone of voice is another. The meanings are merely different, not more or less important.

Within the cover art of *Persona* (as well as your blog) vintage glamour model images are featured where the eyes and mouths of the female models have been partially scratched out. Is this a direct comment on the modern construct of beauty, or something altogether different?
Far be it from me to tell someone else what they should take away from my art. I can say, though, that I didn't assemble those images with a specific manifesto or anything in mind having to do with beauty. There wasn't a direct comment on something altogether different either. That said they actually aren't glamour models but Danish porn models. One of them is a dead transvestite who was murdered in a hate-crime.

Some of your releases have also utilised the now somewhat standard industrial aesthetic of collage artwork of pornographic images. How do you view the use of such images in the context of the potential criticism of this being a 'cliché' (either in context of Puce Mary or the wider underground industrial scene), and what perspective do you bring to the use of such images?
The legacy of the music that those 'clichés' come from is a pretty important one with incredible artists in its canon. A significant part of what makes industrial and PE music, now in its fourth decade, effective is how those tropes are used. Can you create something interesting with the recognizable vocabulary of these kinds of music? Or are you just regurgitating clichés? I hope people find my perspective unique. I try to use the context of the history of extreme electronic music to express it the most effectively.

Furthermore noting the often repeated accusations of misogyny leveled by those outside of the industrial underground towards some aspects of the thematic preoccupation of industrial / power electronics / noise music, what is your view on this situation?
Haha, uh, yeah there are obviously really misogynistic themes in those music genres. I don't think that's a very controversial thing to say. It's not subtle. I think that lots of people love horror movies as well but understand that cutting someone's head off with an ax is wrong and would never do it.

Both of your albums *Success* and *Persona* do not feature any front cover artwork other than simple text. Is this perhaps a comment on the importance of the music over image?
It's not a comment on anything, I wanted the cover to be really simple because I thought that would look good and then I chose to do both of them that way to make it look like a series, since the two records compliment each other sonically.

I understand that you have quite close connections with the Posh Isolation label and associated groups and local scene. Would you care to talk a little about your involvement in the local sense the impact and influence it has had on you personally and what you do as Puce Mary?
I have been working with Posh Isolation since my first releases. They are my close friends, collaborators and there is relatively tight community about the label. The support I've had from a close collection of local peers, which includes many Posh Isolation artists, has been invaluable. Things like Posh Isolation and Mayhem gave me the space to incubate my music and establish the trajectory I am on now. I try and am expected to pull my weight in return. I think mutual support is the strongest way for artists to accumulate power, not by campaigning for themselves all over the place or by working narrowly within some kind of system or academy.
Mayhem is a venue in a former car mechanic shop, located in an industrial area in Copenhagen. It's run by a small community of artists focusing on experimental music. It holds rehearsal spaces for projects like Age Coin, Damien Dubrovnik, Iceage, Lower, Family underground, TOTO and myself. It's owned by the municipality and they have been trying to kick us out the last five years we've had it so they can build office spaces or some shit like that.

Playing live appears to be an integral part of your activities. What is your typical live setup and how do you see the live setting differ from what you do in the studio setting?
One large evolution in my music has been the way I play and record. From pure improvisation I began by writing minimal pieces which I would prepare and then play live. These pieces became tracks for releases each of which I would also record live. This basic approach to making a track is still fundamental to the way I arrange music. With the larger array of skills I have learned over the years, a larger spectrum of sound is available to me. I also have more options when it comes to recording. I still record live to tape , sometimes that's still the best way. But some of the work i do now is too complicated for what i can do with a 4-track recorder, so recording it digitally is the best way to get the exact sound i want.

It would seem that you have extensively toured both in the Europe and the US. How many shows have you played to date and typically how do these tours eventuate – by invitation or personal design? Are you happy with your live performances to date? What are memorable performances either for positive or negative reasons?
If I try and count the shows I come to about 40 since the fall of 2013. Most of the tours I have been on have been with other projects either by invitation or by cooperative design. I am grateful for all the incredible shows I've been able to play this last year, there's a little too many to mention them all. I was recently on great tour in Finland with Jaakko Vanhala and Mikko Aspa. I got a private Vapaudenristi show in Mikko's basement and played a very intense show at a tiny bar called the rooster pub in Lahti. The MAPS Fest in Queens, NY was a blast, set up by the Fieldwork guys. Dissonans fest at Fylkingen in Stockholm was a great night with IRM, Shift, Treriksröset and Arkhe. Touring and collaborating with Rodger Stella was definitely an experience worth remembering and I'm honored to have played with older act like Haters, Nurse with Wound, Dave Phillips, Consumer Electronics and collaborating with LR, Jesse Sanes and Sewer Election.

You have issued around 10 releases as Puce Mary since 2010 (and not including collaborations), in evaluating these today what are the releases you are most happy with compared to those in hindsight you may feel do not stack up today? Given your relatively fast rate of musical releases, what new material are you currently working on and how might it differ or build upon prior works?
I think that my rate of releases is pretty restrained. I work a lot and reject the vast majority of everything I record. Almost everything I do is pre-composed, rehearsed and honed and then carefully recorded. It takes a lot of time and there's no way to escape that. I spend a huge amount of time in the studio practicing, recording, mixing and editing and writing at home. I've gotten better and more efficient since 2010 as well. I guess I am pretty proud of my catalog so far. It's not all genius, no, however, I think by being rigorous and prudent and not over-reaching each step of the way I've managed to avoid putting out any real duds. What I am happiest with is that my releases have developed and continue to grow as opposed to having stagnated and begun to imitate themselves. I am currently working on an LP. That has been the main Puce Mary project for me for many months now. It will be different from and built upon previous releases.

Do you have other artistic pursuits outside of the industrial music you produce as Puce Mary?
I make music under my own name that is not Puce Mary, nor one specific thing in particular. I have other projects and collaborations that are of industrial and other styles of music. I also have been starting to score film and taking on other opportunities to make sound as one element in larger arrangements of work. I am currently scoring a feature length film that is under production in L.A., supposedly a modernized version of Lord of The Flies. Later this year, i get to be a part of a small team of artists that will make sound for a play about the Danish poet Michael Strunge, being played here in Copenhagen. I am exited to have gotten these opportunities to work with people who aren't from the same musical background as me and to be a part of bigger productions

where the sound isn't the main focus. It's both a relief to give up a certain amount of artistic freedom and a big challenge. Scoring films has been something I've wanted to do for a while.

The Pitchfork website is often labelled as an internet portal for all things (for want of a better term) 'hipster'. Noting that Puce Mary has had albums reviewed and general coverage provided via Pitchfork, what are your views on the role and influence of Pitchfork on promoting obscure underground music to a wider audience? Is it simply a case of their writers seeking to 'discover' the next obscure genre to hype before moving onto the next 'weird' or 'new' thing, or does their interest runs deeper and is ultimately sincere? Your thoughts and impressions?

Lame, empty entities who wait for artists to do all the hard work and then associate themselves with us, are just leeches masquerading as critics and curators. It's so transparent. The audience that really matters to me are people who find my music and take something special away from it. It doesn't matter to me where they find the music really. I don't give a fuck about people who enjoy feeling 'hip' that they are on to a 'new', 'weird' thing. I think the question that comes up more often is what my role, or the artists' role in general, 'should' be in engaging with more popular press or the commercial music industry. Mostly, I don't like to give them the satisfaction but in the long run I don't think that's what really matters. When I feel criticism embedded in the question of what I 'should' do, though, my reaction is really just *"fuck off."* Pathetic little, talentless trolls try and talk shit but I can do whatever the fuck I want and know better than anyone what's best for me. There are armies of corny, predatory parasites out there trying to syphon money or social gain out of the underground. That is the complete opposite of people who make all this happen for nothing but the satisfaction of making music, booking shows, what have you, and enjoying the fruits of their labor. Obviously the latter is the more valuable contribution yet, financially the former is rewarded more at large. It's extremely frustrating but not too different than the way the rest of the world works.

Any additional matters you would like to discuss which have not been raised?

No, just thank you for patience, interest and support.

All images © Nikki Sneakers MMXIV
Puce Mary at Nothing Changes 19 June, 2014

AISCHROLATREIA

Aischrolatreia (pronounced: 'ais-chro-la-treia') are a emerging project from the New York City underground. Having issued two tapes in 2013 on their own label Fieldwork, both releases demonstrate a strong intent and clear conviction through the presentation of a blend of filthy power electronics and rugged post-mortem soundscapes. From the strength of these two tapes I was convinced that Aischrolatreia had the right sort of approach and dedication to what they do, thus the perfect candidate for feature in *Noise Receptor Journal.* One half of the group P.K provided the responses to my line of questioning in early 2015 and confirmed my initial impression of their commitment.

Aischrolatreia seem to be a relatively new project, with two cassettes released during 2013. Would you care to introduce its members; the timeframe during the group was established; and the initial developmental phase up until the release of your debut tape *Sentient Prison?*

Aischrolatreia consists of two members: myself (P.K) and E.J. Aischrolatreia is the core unit of the label Fieldwork. Our first recordings were made during late 2011, and nothing published until autumn 2013. These sessions were initially developed through long distance exchange of tracks, until I relocated and we were able to rehearse on a regular basis. The material produced during this time developed very slowly, for two reasons: 1. we were still figuring out the direction we would take without setting an immediate stylistic limit, and 2. A physical release was inevitable, but shamelessly documenting our learning process was not an option. *Sentient Prison* is an accurate representation of this early period. The foundation was laid future works without restricting us stylistically, and its imperfections remain inspiring.

Is Aischrolatreia your first musical endeavour or do its members have a preceding history in other projects or bands? Likewise what is the background of individual members which led to interest and involvement in underground industrial / noise / power electronics?

Some time had been spent experimenting in private, but this is the first public project for either of us. Fanaticism towards extreme underground music and art has been a huge part of our lives for many years. We both reached the threshold where it was time to take action and create something that could stand on its own.

With the project name Aischrolatreia roughly translating to: *'the cult of the obscene; the worship of filth; a devotion to or worship of filth and obscenity'*, how did you come to choose this moniker? Noting that its meaning perfectly suits your sonic aesthetic, out of interest were other project name considered?

We threw around a bunch of names and ideas at first. Aischrolatreia appeared and it stuck. It's an obscure word, hard to pronounce for some people. This has somewhat alienated us, although that was not our intention. The name represents worship towards overt forms of obscenity and decay, as well as an altar to our deepest subconscious urges.

In my review of *Sentient Prison* I remarked that the sound of Aischrolatreia is one of loosely constructed power electronics aggression, but which also holds a clear affinity to a northern European 'post-mortem' style (aka a morbid industrial noise cassette culture sound). Would you agree with this assessment? Likewise what would be acknowledged as specific influences for Aischrolatreia; be it musical or any other artistic or cultural source?

This sound you mention is something we are intent on proliferating through Aischrolatreia as well as the Fieldwork label. Of course there is a drive to go beyond in terms of sophistication or technical abilities, but this is the foundation and the essence we aim to preserve. Our musical influences are primarily classic industrial and power electronics from Germany, Sweden, UK, and the essentials of American noise. Ritual music also is a huge source of inspiration, as much as it doesn't really manifest in our recordings.

Plenty of artistic and cultural sources have overt and subconscious influences on Aischrolatreia. Extremism and fanaticism of all degrees; whether religious or political has always been fascinating and is a regular topic of conversation. All forms of visual art, occult philosophy, and medical history. Some things play a bigger role in our 'real lives', which results in a stronger focus within the conceptual reaches of the band.

Where would you place Aischrolatreia within a genre linage and how do you feel the project may differ from contemporaries? Also from your own perspective are you seeking to create something particularly different, new or innovative, or are happy working within established genre parameters?

It is safe to say we fall under the umbrella of industrial music. More specifically, in reference to the previous question, this rugged postmortem sound and aesthetic,

We don't waste energy trying to convince people that we are making 'true' industrial, power electronics or whatever the fuck people need to keep labelling their work with, because what does that really amount to in 2015 anyway? Better chance of recognition if you swear you are the real thing? Our work will always belong to us, no matter what informed it. When no one is asking *"well, what is it?"*, and they are struck by the contents and presentation alone, then it's no longer an issue as far as we're concerned.

Regarding innovation and progression, there is definitely a fine balance of creating sound that as fanatics we would listen to ourselves without coming off as a shameless tribute act, and crossing into territory that others have not. There's always room to expand while still remaining true to the foundation. How is Aischrolatreia different from contemporaries? We keep our mouths shut until it is time to act. We only publish what we believe to be our highest quality work. You won't find Aischrolatreia on random splits, compilations, and collaborations on multiple labels. In general, I don't think we have much in common with what's happening in the US now. We don't follow what kinds of trends are 'in', nor go on about how special and different we are.

With the controlled pacing of your sound works coupled with track titles and artwork, it gives a distinct impression that there is a underpinning conceptual focus to what Aischrolatreia do, rather than being merely 'improvised' or 'noise for noise' sake. Is this a fair impression and would you care to elaborate on any conceptual approach employed or agenda you are seeking follow?

Your impression is correct. 'Noise for noise' sake does not appeal to us. Aischrolatreia is not strictly conceptual to the point where we refuse to make sound without a predetermined subject in place, or make work specifically regarding a time, location, or person. Often it is very abstract and the product of obsession with many different subjects at once. The first two tapes dealt with psychological issues, in varying states of severity as well as the aftermath of physical action that could potentially arise from them. *Sentient Prison* is focused on the struggle of flesh versus spirit, and lobotomization as a final escape from daily life. An audial portrait of madness, paranoia, intoxication, and dormant homicidal urges. We don't have a declared 'agenda' per se, if having an agenda means we are trying to convince anyone of anything. Aischrolatreia is our weapon against stagnation. If some people get the message, then so be it.

Do you utilise 'typical' equipment or sound sources employed in composition and how is the recording process approached? Do you employ any unusual recording equipment, techniques or locations?

We utilize an arsenal of stable, 'traditional' gear: monosynths, modular equipment, pedals, etc, as well as a reliable, professional setup for recording, mixing and mastering. Raw sounds are made with field recordings, destroyed tapes, metal objects, and more. One Aischrolatreia track may contain

recordings from several different locations or times. There's been plans to do some more site specific works too. We will see what time brings.

I also imagine your material is the product of a combination of a partly composed and partly improvised approach? Do members have specific responsibilities and are these roles equally shared?

Unpredictability and imperfection are sacred but we don't rely on that to carry the work. Everything is done within a parameter, as controlled as possible. Improvisation is not a dirty word in our eyes either. I think many people are too focused on creating precisely calculated and sequenced sound for the sake of it. Often you can light the fire and lock in to something without knowing exactly how it will turn out, and sort out the issues later. Still, there's always a constant in place that we have refined and determined to be a certain length and pace.

In the early days, the division was based on the type of sound being created. E.J would handle the drones and static, slow moving sounds, and I would be responsible for unpredictable and expressive noises. The tasks cross over much more frequently now. The remote exchange method that we started with hasn't fully gone away. Reference tracks are sent back and forth, rehearsed thoroughly, and eventually cursed to tape. 90% of the foundation stereo tracks are done studio-live with many takes until we are fully satisfied.

Is recording a slow laboured process or something which comes together easily? How much material do you produce compared to what you may use or discard? Have your working methods, processes and approaches evolved and been particularly refined over time?

Nothing has sped up, quite the opposite actually. We don't produce a ton of extra material, almost everything that is recorded gets used eventually. Not much time for jamming. Sounds are carefully prepared and then we assemble them live. Longer tracks can take months to fully refine.

We have improved our skills since the beginning, and there is room to develop further, be it learning new equipment, recording techniques, working in different environments, or under the command of bizarre circumstances. E.J is much more of a wizard in the gear department, an adept of synthesizers and recording technologies. I am better versed in using the maximum potential of a small selection of crude equipment. So far our work is an accurate representation of this meeting point.

Regarding track names, are the devised later to match sonic recordings, or vice versa where the sounds are guided by the intent implied by titles?

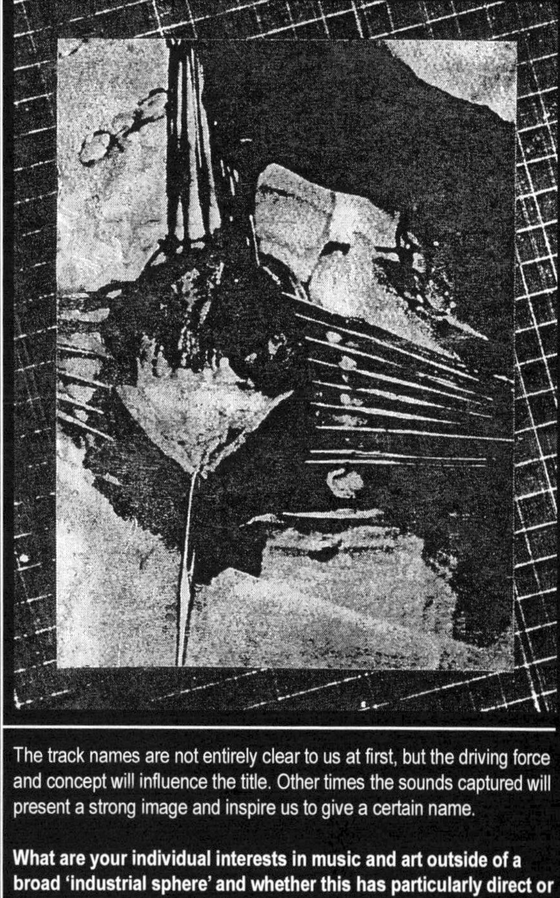

The track names are not entirely clear to us at first, but the driving force and concept will influence the title. Other times the sounds captured will present a strong image and inspire us to give a certain name.

What are your individual interests in music and art outside of a broad 'industrial sphere' and whether this has particularly direct or oblique influent over Aischrolatreia's material?

A majority of our interests fall within this sphere. We're interested in plenty of art and literature that probably doesn't fit the standard criteria as well. It's pretty laborious to split hairs about what is 'typical' and what isn't though. Everything makes some impression, even if it doesn't show its face in what you create.

Musically, we're both fanatics of black / death metal as well as plenty of Oi! and hardcore. Those don't have any direct influence on our material, even though they've been equally important as industrial / noise through the years.

What do you consider are the similarities and / or differences between what your produce collectively as Aischrolatreia and who you may be as individuals? Essentially do you view Aischrolatreia as an integral part of your 'self' or something which stands apart?

The ideas and concepts of Aischrolatreia are always dormant within us. If this was not the case, it would merely be an imagined projection, a game of dress-up. Aischrolatreia is a monument to our experience, without pressing on about boring 'personal' issues and events.

There is of course a dynamic with a two man project in which all of this comes together boils over and becomes something entirely deranged and unrealistic. Fantasy does have its place. At the end of the day if this was not in our blood, something we didn't feel was a direct part of us, then it would be just another faceless 'project'.

Vocals are a sporadically used element within Aischrolatreia's noise industrial soundscapes, but with these being heavily distorted and partially buried in the mix any message is completely lost. How important are the lyrics and what do you see is their role given their indecipherability? Would lyrics ever be printed on your future releases?
So far there is only one published track with vocals- the title track from *Sentient Prison*. These particular lyrics are not necessary to be known to anyone but us, although we may consider it for new works. The concept and atmosphere of Aischrolatreia is executed with instrumental tracks just fine; we don't pin vocals on top of tracks that are strong enough already. New material is being composed with a more dominant vocal section, as our ideas have only gotten stronger over time and must be dictated in this manner.

Aischrolatreia has performed live on a number of occasions. How many shows have you played and typically where? What are some of the best and worst performance experiences you have had? How do you view the live material of your material and how it differs from your formal recordings?
At the time of writing this, eight live actions have happened. We've performed in traditional 'clubs', DIY art spaces and home basements. We are ruthlessly critical of ourselves, regardless of what kind of reaction comes from the crowd. Our assessment of a performance is based primarily on how it felt to us. If conditions are right, performing feels like driving a tank towards a group of people. If something is not 100% like a weak PA system, or the rare occasion that we haven't been able to use projections, the feeling is passive. We don't play just any show for this reason. So far, we have not done the same set twice. Only two of our performances have been properly documented, and there remains six that nobody will ever see again. Our set usually consists of equal parts live created noise and prepared sound. This leads to a varying division of labor where duties are split for backing tracks, synths, amplified metal objects as well and vocals.
Brute force and direct aggression are a more significant aspect of playing live. Studio works possess more of a brooding atmosphere, when live we aim to punish the audience in a 20 minute time frame without foregoing the dexterity and layering of our recordings.

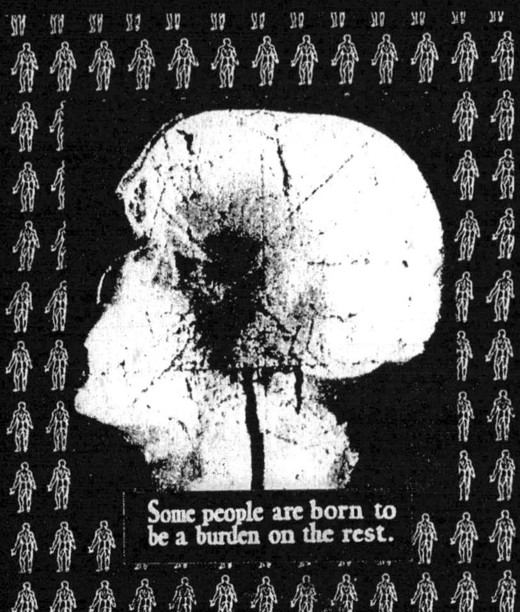

From a number of available YouTube videos of your live performances, I note that you employ a video projection backdrop of collage artworks. Is this use of material of critical importance to the presentation of Aischrolatreia in a live setting?
It is critical, and there's only been a couple times we weren't able to use it due to equipment malfunctions. It's important for the reason of taking people out of their usual party environment, and lifting the focus from us as people on a stage. Without this presentation, the feeling and atmosphere would be absent. It would just be another noise set. Nobody gets a chance to stand around and look at what gear we're using or what our hands are doing. The content of the video is closely tied to what we are working with at that time sonically, and is carefully sequenced with the sound being performed.

Within some of the projected visuals some subliminal messages are presented, where text is spliced in amongst the collage imagery and flashed on the screen for a micro-second. With the benefit of a video pause one of the discernible phrases is: *'Some people are born to be a burden on the rest'.* Would you care to explain the source, its subliminal presentation and its meaning within the conceptual context of Aischrolatreria?
This quote was found in the pages of a eugenics book and carried over into the early conceptual leanings of the band. We are not die hard believers in these ideas but this statement had a severe impact at the time, however taken out of context it may be in this case. It can be read as a firm belief in music and art as war, pushing beyond cheap entertainment. The ugly truth, always a thorn in your side.

I also note that during some of your live performances one of the members has utilised a balaclava and hood, but this is not the case for all shows. What is the role of these personality cloaking devices? Is this about presenting a strong stage presence, obscuring the individual or assisting with performance focus? Likewise how important is anonymity within context of Aischrolatria?

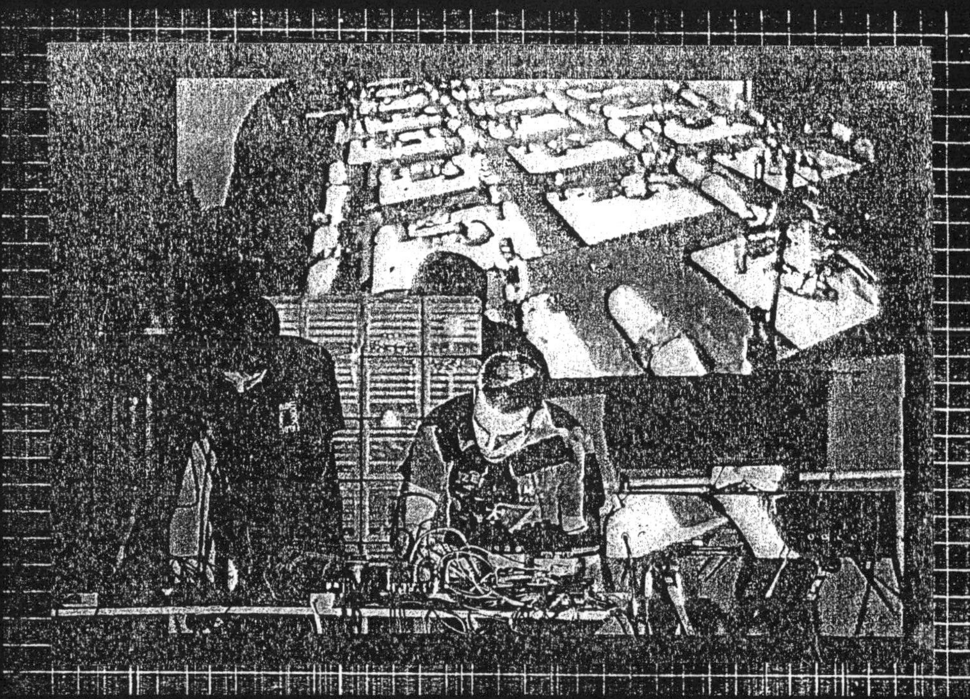

Strong stage presence is important, masked or not. We don't care if anyone knows it's us on stage, or behind the recordings either for that matter. We're not a hunched over knob twisting type of live band, nor do we jump around like apes and risk fucking up the performance. Nothing else to say about that.

True anonymity in this network is pretty much impossible as far as I'm concerned. I think the balance there lies with how much you are revealing in your actions. Like I said before: Keeping your mouth shut until it is time to act. Not giving absurd statements and provocations that you won't live up to, looking foolish by revealing all types of useless stories, photos, and details about your personal life. A mask can either reinforce this idea or degrade it.

From an insider's perspective what has been the level of scene interest in Aischrolatreia? Likewise is there any pattern to this interest, being it localised or potentially on a wider global level?

A handful of local fanatics picked up on our work after our first live performances and releases, but I'd say more interest has come from Europe and beyond. Some strong contacts in the U.S have been made as well for distribution and potential live performances. We are fine with not being in the spotlight here, as it leaves room for us to follow our own path, and not worry about pleasing the local crowds.

With only two limited cassettes releases having been issued to date, what new material can be expected in Aischrolatreria in future?

Aischrolatreia is currently recording full length material for the Fieldwork banner as well as some long established foreign imprints. Keep your eyes open but do not hold your breath.

Would you care to highlight any other musical projects you may be involved with, including solo activities?

I am responsible for H.C.O.D, and E.J does ARBITER as well. Both projects are radically different from what we do together as Aischrolatreia. H.C.O.D goes deeper into the ultra-primitive realms of power electronics and industrial noise. Raw, straight to tape recordings which still retain a certain amount of technical prowess. Conceptually it is much more focused on certain social / political / sexual ideas and events than Aischrolatreia. ARBITER is E.J's outlet for cold, mechanical industrial created with analog synthesizers, reel to reel tape, and field recordings. Live actions and releases for both projects are planned for 2015 and beyond.

Final comments?

Thank you Richard for the interview. Cheers to all we are in contact with.

FIELDWORK

Fieldwork are a new NYC based label launched in 2013, where their profile highlights they are a *"label for confrontational and unique sound work on analogue formats"*. With their releases broadly focusing on the filthy end of industrial, power electronics, noise and post-mortem sounds and coupled with a strong monochromatic visual presentation, Fieldwork are certainly a label to keep a keen eye on. P.K. - one half behind the label proffered some thoughts on what Fieldwork are seeking to achieve.

Fieldwork is a young 'micro' cassette label launched in 2013. Who is behind the label, what was the impetus for its establishment and do you have a clear agenda for its overall direction and growth?

Fieldwork is run by two individuals: P.K. (me) and E.J. of Aischrolatreia. The label was established as a means to publish ours and dedicated comrade's work with no restrictions. We grew out of nothing, out of a dead and jaded environment. The aim is to publish hard, uncompromising audio with severe commitment to [tactful, tasteful] packaging and design. We are rooted in 'tradition' but are very much thinking to the future and reacting to what is today.

I will make an effort here to distance Fieldwork from this term 'micro label'. That suggests we are operating with limitation as the driving force with no goal of expansion, which is far from true. We work within our means, and within the demand for this kind of sound and artwork. Our aspirations are big, but realistic. We're not shitting out noise-jams / splits /collabs on hopelessly limited short tapes with over the top packaging. Recording, designing, and physically producing these releases takes the breath out of us, and we present these works in only the most 'maximal' way possible. We're not making unsustainably large (or pointlessly small) editions, nor attempting to appeal to clueless mainstream or 'indie' markets for the sake of quick cash and cheap recognition. The same can also be said about the easy to navigate social media circuits of unconditional support so many people seem to be building careers from nowadays.

Given the word 'Fieldwork' refers to field research and collection of information outside of a laboratory; what led to choosing this as the label moniker and does your own definition of the work differ?

Fieldwork was an idea in action well before the label's establishment. We see a strong parallel in this concept of 'field research' with industrial, noise, and experimental sounds. The obsession with and deconstruction of subjects from the outside world, taken into the 'laboratory' and eventually re-presented.

Lately we are not too concerned with one dominant philosophy regarding the label. Just engaging in the work to the most fanatical extent is a fine M.O for us. That alone is an accurate and literal interpretation of the term. If anything, Fieldwork is a "neutral" platform through which the stronger conceptual leanings of individual units can be expressed.

Currently Fieldwork is cassette only, but the label profile is: *'NYC based label for confrontational and unique sound work on analogue formats'*. Does this mean vinyl releases in future are a possibility?

Yes. Producing vinyl is a massively expensive and potentially disastrous undertaking, but it is in the pipeline. In the meantime cassette suits what we are doing just fine, in terms of sound quality and aesthetics.

With the small roster of artists assembled under the Fieldwork banner are these projects perhaps focused on a collective of NYC based artists?

The only out of town acts that have been published are Swallowing Bile and Interracial Sex. Highlighting what is happening here in NYC in the realms of industrial filth has kept us busy enough. We've gathered a group of devoted individuals that we share a common vision and ideals with. This is well represented in the first Fieldwork compilation tape, *Rotten Contingent.*

Are all artists known to you personally before being asked to issue a release on Fieldwork? Also do you also have particular criteria for a project to be considered for a release on Fieldwork?

Every release thus far has been of someone that we know personally, given that all but one tape has been of NYC based artists. The city appears very small when dealing with this kind of thing. Often it's more of a mutual agreement to be released on Fieldwork rather than us directly asking, if that makes sense. We've all done gigs or worked together in some way prior. Operations up until this point have been quite insular, it's not like we have all these people asking us to release their stuff, nor are we regularly 'scouting' for new acts. Knowing that, please do not send unsolicited material to us. Our hands are full.

Criteria for a release is based on intent, concept, and of course, most importantly, quality of sound. There should not be any boring questions about what is being heard or seen.

intent is important, because there are a lot of acts out there hopping from label to label releasing 10 tapes a year, which to me appears only as a cheap grab for attention.

I note that the Fieldwork bandcamp page is used as a digital forum to sample your releases, but on most items you do not offer digital downloads, nor are provide digital download codes as part of the physical release. Do you have a particular view of the modern era of 'convenience' provided by digital downloads verses the permanence of physical releases?
You can download some out of print titles from this site. We just don't advertise it as a component of the label. It's really just a good marketing tool if done tastefully. I personally like being able to sample music before purchasing it, and I'm sure that has played a role in many people buying our releases. Is that 'convenient'? Most certainly, for us and the consumer. Is that a bad thing? No. Digital samples are a great way for the good stuff to be noticed, especially if it doesn't have a predetermined chance at success based on associations with other individuals, or chic, easy to digest concepts and aesthetics.

What are your views on the provision of digital downloads once the physical editions have sold out, or is the 'physicality' of the release an integral part of the experience which is lost if just dealing with digital files?
I don't see any problem with people being able to hear releases after they're sold out. Doing standalone 'digital' releases does not interest us, as manufacturing physical releases is half the battle. Without the tangible components, there would be no essence, no experience. As collectors ourselves, the ritual of listening to cassettes and LP's is very important to us. It's not this common 'analog vs digital' debate, but simply personal preference, to not use a simple promotional tool as the sole product.

Fieldwork as a label has a strong 'industrial' visual aesthetic with high contrast black and white text and collage artwork. Who is responsible for the design/ style and is this driven by formal graphic design education?
I am responsible for the execution, layout, and manufacturing of all artwork and packaging thus far. Of course individual acts provide source images they would like to use, but at the end, everything has gone through my hands. The visual component is equally as important as the sounds themselves, and takes just as much time and effort. I have a strong background in graphic design as well as other types of visual art and means of producing editions.

What other labels and/ or artists would you acknowledge as being a direct or indirect influence on what you are seeking to achieve with Fieldwork?
Fieldwork salutes the glorious days of Slaughter Productions, Broken Flag, MSNP and Zero Cabal, as well as strong contemporary labels like Lust Vessel, Styggelse, and Unrest Productions. Some of these imprints have much larger and extensive catalogs than we can see ourselves releasing, but overall the unmistakable cohesive vision is something we have much respect for and approach Fieldwork in the same regard.

Noting that Fieldwork is NYC based, what is the local scene like? Has it been difficult or easy to get attention and support?
It ranges from totally dead to relatively engaging. Usually it depends on if any shows are booked, and a lot of activity and attention swells around those. We've done two volumes of a festival titled M.A.P.S (Metropolitan Audio Pain Source), as well as hosted many tough U.S. acts in the interim.
A constant flow of support and attention on the local scale is not of importance. We don't provide any easily digestible personality or social scene for folks to latch on to, nor do we perform live more than once every few months. There is of course good noise and industrial happening here that is unaffiliated with us, and there was before we showed up.

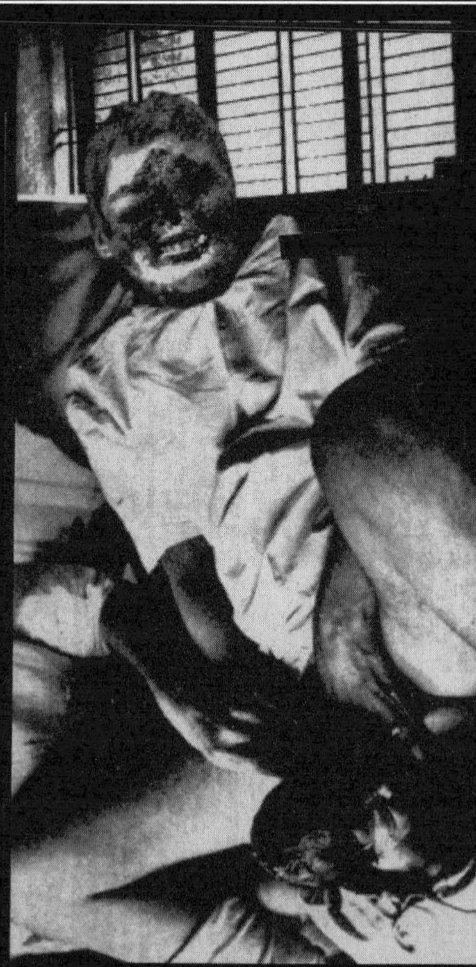

What is the typical edition size of releases you are issuing? Likewise are releases strictly limited or will you keep them in print as long a there is demand? Also is there any general pattern to the interest shown in the label thus far?
All but one tape has been less than 100 copies, which was the only one with a disclosed edition size due to being a special art edition. Like I said above, the goal is not to produce hopelessly limited releases for the sake of it. We work within the scope and reach that we feel is reasonable. We want to keep releases around for as long as people want them, or as long as that particular release is relevant to us. However, the time and money is often better spent on moving forward with new projects.

What would you acknowledge as your favourite label releases, and does this differ from what might have been the most successful* release to date? (* - I guess 'successful' is a relative term when dealing with an obscure underground scene and the small editions of Fieldwork's releases).
Each release has been important in the establishment and development of the label. I agree with your assessment that "success" is difficult to measure, so I won't attempt to here. My personal favorites in terms of sound, design, and contents are V/A *Rotten Contingent*, H.C.O.D *Coarse Defect*, and Aischrolatreia *Sentient Prison*. Each of those represents a milestone for the label.

What releases are in the pipeline for Fieldwork and will this extend to new projects?
More than I am able to disclose in detail at this time. Expect full length releases for all of the core units in the remainder of 2015. Some new blood will be likely be represented on the next Fieldwork compilation.

Final comments?
Hail to those who have given support, and a shrug to those who don't. Information can be found at fieldworklabel.blogspot.com. Thank you Richard for the interview.

WERTHAM

Although an introduction should really not be required, for those needing context Wertham are the Italian power-electronics project of Marco Deplano who has been operating under this moniker as far back as 1994. Over that time Marco has justified his position within the underground based on his sheer focus and determination in producing sonically harsh and thematically strong power electronics releases. Conducted in March, 2015 Marco talks at length on numerous topics relating to Wertham, other musical activities such as Caligula031, Foresta Di Ferro, as well as involvement with numerous underground scenes.

Wertham has been in operation for 21 years now; what were the circumstances which led to you starting the project and how did you originally become introduced to underground post-industrial music?

My very first acquaintance with industrial and power electronics happened in the mid 80's not too long after I started preferring music to toys. I befriended a bunch of kids at school who felt the same and we started exchanging information about our passions influencing each other. It was an everyday search of alien sounds, including metal, punk, hardcore and general weirdness. Somebody taped me an anonymous collection with the prime movers of the genre (SPK, Whitehouse, Ramleh, TG, Cabaret Voltaire, E. Neubaten, etc.), but I had to wait a few years before associating the correct names to the sounds when I accidentally got some fanzines on the subject through the notorious S.O.A. distro run by Mr Paolo Petralia. Also Mox from Monumentum (now Milano hardcore legend Incudine) taped me a few albums that led me to recognize the some of the culprits and at understanding where I had to investigate. Since my interests at the time and my craving for unconventional music fitted 100% with the aesthetic / cultural tastes, the rest came as a natural consequence. I started contacting people, getting into networking and to attend occasional gigs until I have found the right channels (one of which was Mr Alex Papa of Healter Skelter magazine / Ex Mondo Bizzarro gallery) and became actively involved.

The name Wertham obviously refers to Fredric Wertham, the infamous psychiatrist and author of *Seduction of the Innocent (1954)* which alleged that violent main stream media (including, film, TV, comic books etc.) was having negative and corrupting influence on the development of children. How did you originally come to be aware of this figure and what was the critical determinant in deciding to use the name?

Back in the 90's I was writing comics as a fulltime job. I was also teaching script writing in a school and I was very interested in the theory and history of sequential art, then, as you can imagine, it was impossible to not deal with Herr Wertham. I found amusing his kinky interpretations of non-sexual related contents. His morbid obsession on the subject and the consequent moral panic were enough to make me consider this name. I wanted a name that did not sound neither too English, nor Italian and, last but not least, if you pronounce Wertham in Italian (Vertam), it sounds quite aggressive, so it was fitting the purpose.

I also assume you entirely disagree with Fredric Wertham's theories and the use of the name is used as a sort of 'inverted' tribute? Do you see that the name still has specific meaning and currency today which has extended over the course of the development of the project?

Obviously, I disagree with most of his theories related to comics. People are both a product of environment (which is not a justification as many do-gooders like to think) and predisposition. Luckily, we are born different and we follow patterns in specific times of our lives to then deviate and explode, which makes things a bit more unsafe, yet exciting. If you are born a 'deviant', before turning into a killing machine, you can be influenced by everything, even factors that are not apparently dangerous. If you shoot heroin it is not necessarily your family's fault, it can be a simple reaction to peer-pressure, cultural trends and a misguided perception of pleasure and fun. It may be due to the frustration for a meaningless existence, too much love from your parents or something going wrong with your brain, or just superficiality. If something is damaged in you, no EC Comics can be blamed. I think Wertham was only partly responsible for what happened; the people around him who used his work as a handbook were the real threat. Political correctness is the biggest enemy of a society that claims to be free and can fly both conservative and progressive flags.

Frederick Wertham was not always a 'villain'. He wrote very interesting articles regarding young offenders that are still reasonable (and precious) after so many years, not to mention he was one of the very first specialists to work with serial murderers, bogeymen and super stars of the society of spectacle before the whole post September the 11th Islamic terror scare started. Incidentally, I think the first time his name occurred to me was in a biography about sexual predator and cannibal Albert Fish. So, I think the name still represent my work: misconceptions, taboos, true crime, and social-biology.

A large part of your lyrical approach and thematic content seems to be driven by your own personal experiences; meaning (without sounding twee) could be said that you are something of a 'social observer / commentator'. How do you see your approach to thematic material and is it always driven by first hand experiences, or do you sometimes take on 'personas' such as what Mike Dando has done with Con-Dom? What other material be it films, mass-media, literature etc. might you acknowledge as in influence for Wertham?

Indeed, most of my work is based on first / second hand experience. I like to take bits of myself, things I have heard from acquaintances, information I read and assemble possible landscapes that describe conflicts, be they street-related or intimate, never forgetting to include some sort of emotional level. Since 'the world outside' is my main interest this can lead to an uneducated and un-ideological social commentary, but I do not intend to criticize nor preach my views, although they might emerge every now and then.

I both use myself as the leading actor and, as you said, a different persona who better represents the situation. I do not pretend my writings to be 100% real, but I have the arrogance to think they are 100% realistic.

I blush for the comparison since I think Con-Dom's concept is one of the most complex and complete of the whole post-industrial culture. Mike works in a unique way, and *Colour Of A Man's Skin* is a perfect manifesto that should be studied at school when discussing both multiculturalism and racism.

I also deal with less persona subjects with a more historical / clinical approach; the recent Lombroso series, fits in this category and aim to be a rough audio-documentation of some of his theories yet often represented with contemporary examples. I really enjoy working on these releases as well since they bring less emotional burden.

Reality is the main influence, I am hooked on information and I love to spend hours digging in my own contradictions, being conscious that I might be wrong since too much news can become no-news and this is the backlash of 'social' information.

Regarding movies, you can see traces of William Friedkin's *Cruising*, which was crucial for many reasons: beside the obvious leather / BDSM aesthetic that was important in many visuals and live actions, I was struck by the analysis of duality and ambiguity in the repulsion / obsession of Pacino's character for something he did not conceive before finding himself stuck in a world so alien for him, yet so absorbing. The 'total environments' described in the leather clubs, the sense of urge, the predatory attitude, the claustrophobic atmosphere, all contributed it to make it classic. Not to mention the streets themselves, the same that made other flicks like *Taxi Driver, Hardcore, New York Ripper, China Blue and Midnight Cowboy* total classics, describing something that never existed in Italy. The work of directors like Gaspar Noe, Lodge Kerrigan, Alberto Cavallone, Augustin Villaronga, Ulrich Seidl, Wiktor Grodecki, Elio Petri, Shane Meadows, Aleksej Balabanov and the early movies by Nicolas Winding Refn and Lars Von Trier, all left a strong impression on me.

I also love British 'kitchen sink drama' and the new breed of ultra-realistic directors. Gary Oldman's *Nil by Mouth*, Tim Roth's *Warzone*, the *This is England* franchise (especially the TV episodes), they all describe pretty well situations I witnessed during my UK exile.

So-called Italian 'social' cinema from the 60's / 70's had a strong influence on my work as well (before it turned into minimalistic crap) although probably I am the only one to notice it, and of course the classic video nasties everybody watches in PE, plenty of German, Eastern European and Oriental Cinema, the new wave of French / Belgian cinema (Calvaire, Martyrs, Aute Tension, Innocence, etc.).

Two movies that really impressed me are from Greece: Dogtooth and Miss Violence (possibly the best movie I have seen in a decade).

Documentaries are as important as cinema and I like the fact they are finally getting the availability they deserve through YouTube and similar repositories. Literature was important as well at the beginning, but I read mostly non-fictional books. For what comes to novels Palahniuk, Houellebecq, Celine, Mishima, Junger, Lovecraft, have all been obsessions.

Last but not least, smut culture played a crucial role in all my projects. Directors like Rinse Dream, Lasse Braun, the Mitchell Bros, Riccardo Schicchi, the *Slave Sex* series, etc. illustrators like Picard, Frollo, etc. and different meat markets where the action goes.

One of your more recent themes deviates from the 'social observer / commentator' role is the recent *Vindicta* collaboration trilogy with fellow Italian industrial experimentalist Uncodifed, which focuses on *'grim / tragic aspects of Sardinian culture'*. Would you care to expand on this concept and what originally led you to your interest in this theme?

Well the interest runs in my blood since my family come from Sardinia, actually from two villages that represent interesting differences. Corrado Altieri (Uncodified, Candor Chasma, TH26, Monosonik, etc.) is from Cagliari as well, and we have been sharing the same interest on true crime, Sardinian tradition and power electronics, so it came natural to focus on some lesser known aspect of an island that is known internationally mostly as an expensive tourist resort with the misconception that most people are either shepherds or kidnappers. We felt the need to show the world there was much more than this, focusing of course on subjects that could go along with the sounds. In both records, Corrado assembled

most of the sounds in practically the final version, I added vocals, samples and did the final mix that was then mastered by Simon Balestrazzi (T.A.C, Candor Chasma, etc.), who I think, was as important as ourselves in the process since he boosted bass frequencies and balanced everything properly. *Vindicta* is a trilogy mostly based in the Barbagia of Seulo, a region of central-eastern Sardinia where my father's family comes from. Some of the happenings described are related to my own relatives, other are based on documented crimes, and then other information we gathered from different sources. We used a fictional protagonist to give hints of a culture that cannot be fully understood if you do not live it completely, where there existed different levels of law, where the behavioural rules the 'Barbaricino code' were stronger than those of the 'colonialist' order, made of 'special' laws that considered Sardinian different than other Italians, and had to be treated differently. The main character find himself involved in a blood feud for the wrong reasons and his brother get murdered and he immediately agrees with his family to call the blood of his family, to then live as a fugitive on the mountains, get caught by the cops and witnessing the notorious Sardinian jails. In the meantime we tried to include some side-stories related to different aspects of Sardinian culture and history, like the peculiar traditional euthanasia methods, or the waves of poverty-related suicides in my father's town Seui.
In the next volume, our nameless protagonist will be freed from the jail and will tell the difficulties of his new life as an emigrant in Belgian mines. We tried to avoid too in-depth social explanations and stick to the chronicle itself, without recriminating this or that injustice since reality speaks for itself. We have had an impressive feedback on both releases with extensive commentaries on the concept, so we are both very satisfied about it and we hope to not disappoint with the third chapter that will be released in 2016.

Are there typical processes involved with 'sowing the seeds of inspiration' for Wertham recordings? Also generally do you start with musical framework, or is there a requirement for thematic content to be bedded down first? Essentially what is your typical working approach and process?
Most of the time I record many sound sources on regular basis. I constantly collect samples, images and videos. Some time I select these sounds and create playlists according to atmosphere and place them in the same folder. Then I write lyrics and record vocals in the local rehearsal room Nerolidio (www.nerolidio.it) and, when the time comes I start long editing sessions, thus assembling in definitive tracks. I am very slow concerning Wertham recordings and this can take months. Vice versa it may happens that the concept comes first: I get obsessed with a subject write the lyrics and then imagine the sounds and try to get them as close as possible similar to what I have in mind. This can take ages and every now and then something gets lost in the process. Artwork and visuals are as important as sounds and text. Very often ideas erupt from an image and the rest follows, yet, as said reality is still the main inspiration.

In an overarching sense of you output over the past decade, I would say that whilst diversity is displayed there is also a singularity of tone and approach, which is clearly a characteristic of sound which can be attributed to Wertham. Do you agree with this assessment, what is the typical instrumentation employed in the current era? I also imagine your equipment and process has changed over time?
I am glad you sense this. I try to build different atmospheres, tending to keep vocals semi-recognisable without burying them under pile of effects, which may still happen from time to time, and I love boosting bass frequencies. Multi-layered structures are very important to me, which is something differing from my other project Caligula031. I try to use meaningful samples that are part of the narration.
I also include background field recordings taken in spaces that are somehow related to the subject. You may not feel them properly but it helps me to give sounds more wideness and maybe capture the essence of a real environment, so it makes me imagine the sound is not happening only inside a computer. Yes. Equipment has changed a lot. In the past few years I became an addicted to machines, and I have collected many during the years. Korg is still the main drive of backing tracks, but there are several new beasts that help me structuring the rest. I like especially self-built / artisan machines like Lumanoise, Leploop, Black Death / Yersinia Pestis, Bug Brand Weevil, Casper's Drone Lab and Nova Drone, Grendel Drone Studio… I am also in love with the latest Arturia Brute series.

Obviously Wertham sits within the established framework of power electronics, however what would you acknowledge as important external influences: either musical projects or specific albums which left an indelible mark on what you are seeking to do?
Well, essentially the roots of the genre on Come Organisation and Broken Flag, all projects released between the 80's and the 90's by A.W.B., Aquifer Sodality and many other Italian projects, Tesco, S.P.K., M.B., Ultra, NON, Krang, etc. I could go on for days. Anything released by these gentlemen left marks on me.
Picking up some records, Whitehouse *Thank Your Lucky Stars* since the title tracks was a classic example of structured PE. All early SPK due to their radical criticism and development of concept. Genocide Organ's *Save Our Slaves* box that taught me you can always push yourself further in term of aesthetic and taboos. Intrinsic Action *Sado Electronics*, because it was just perfect and fit with many of my obsessions. MB's *Symphony For A Genocide*, because it was just plain unachievable perfection, same as early NON's records.... there would be hundreds more.

Wertham is effectively your solo project, but you have enlisted external collaborators from time to time. How do you see the role of collaborators within the context of Wertham? Is it a free flow of creative ideas, or do you dictate the direction and scope of any collaborative input?
Both. Sometime I ask for specific sounds; other times, like it happens with Corrado Altieri (Uncodified), it comes from sharing ideas and sounds, other times somebody tells me *"hey look, I got this sounds that could fit Wertham"* and we proceed working on that.
When I used to play live, collaborators such as Trevor (Northgate) or John Murphy were totally free to follow the flow and add their mark. I remember gigs where backing tracks were completely covered by their extra sounds, turning the whole experience into something different and louder, which was great. It really depends on the mood.

21 years for any band or project is a long time: how do you maintain enthusiasm and drive to keep the project active and how may your motivations evolved with the passing of years?
Taking pauses every now and then, focusing on other projects and not releasing too much stuff. I already have an eight to five job, so I do not want to be put under pressure by music or I would hate it as it already happened with comics in the '90s. Passions must always be something you enjoy doing and not a burden. I do not think I will 'pull the plug' anytime soon, although there will never be an avalanche of Wertham releases. There is no need for that.

If you were to reflect on your upbringing and personal interests from childhood into youth which have in turn influenced who you have become as an adult, are the threads of interest which have always been there? Does who you have grown up into feel a fait acompli based on your earlier interests and obsessions, or could you have just as easily decided at some juncture to leave 'underground culture' behind?
I think many interests have always been there. I became who I am today in reaction to events, situations and experiences that I have either found satisfying, thus helping to build my tastes, or hurt / affected me, building my no-go areas and defining my enemies and filing my existential hit-list. Many people I met as a kid are still with me somehow and we crossed so much shit together that we developed the same sensitivity and view of the world. Others disappeared, stole money, died or self-obliterated themselves in the most entertaining ways.
Maybe I am less angry as I was until a few years ago. I am still keen to not take any shit from anyone and I do not intend to ever let anybody tell me what I have to think, listen, wear, eat and who I have to be, especially when pressures come by self-styled cultural vigilantes.
You never know what can happen in your life, so I cannot exclude anything, but considering I have started following underground culture when I was 11 (naturally first as a bystander, then as an 100% activist, now as an 'part timer') and am now 41, I don't see an end to my interest in 'underground culture' coming anytime soon. I do not believe the underground is an alternative per se since we all eat and shit like people who could not care less about radical aesthetic, but this is where most of my pleasures come from and I will stick to it until the day it will still have something to say.

With your reference above to not letting anyone tell you what to think, in 2011 the operators of *Who Makes the Nazi?* blog waged an online smear campaign against elements of underground industrial music, including Gaya Donadio and her *Hinoeuma The Malediction* London based events. To my mind the blog seems to be predominantly 'jumping at shadows', whilst also using underground music as a lightning rod to further their own political agenda / views. What are your thoughts on the tired arguments being thrown around by such blogs? Also in your thinking above "*to not take any shit from anyone*", is discussion and engagement with those throwing around such cheap accusations warranted, or should be simply ignored?
Every age had its own moral panic as every form of power had its professional witch hunters, secret services, snitches. Smear campaigns is still today the best way to diminish those who beg to differ. Communism had KGB, fascism had the Ovra, the church inquisition, Israel the Mossad, Iran the Guards of revolution, the USA the CIA, etc. you name it.... the aim of such organisations has always been to protect and serve the status quo. The digital age found its watchdog in bloggers, which may sound less romantic and exciting and

maybe can be compared more to virtual lynch mobs than actual policemen, yet this is the kind of conservative attitude they hide in the very depth of their heart. People playing watchdogs hidden in their rooms, under a fake name, wearing tinfoil hats while building conspiracy theories out of personal resentment – in case of musicians / artists - or, in case of journalist / researchers, economic gain or credibility at academic level. As the old saying goes *"No good deed will be left unpunished"*.
Politics is a fierce beautiful beast that cannot be tamed unless you are both fanatic and bright. I am none of these so, although I have quite precise way of how to organize my life, I will never try to convince you how you should live yours unless you don't enter my turf uninvited. In that case do not expect to receive roses from me.
The problem with this specific website is they got obsessed with a few characters using false claims to bake their theories and wage an all-out-war that resented pure stalking, mostly basing themselves on witnessing of dubious persons who, as said, evidently hold grudges with the victims who had nothing to do with politics, having gigs cancelled and other sort of nuisances. Similar freedom-fighters in the past were able to provoke attacks and damages to artists, I wonder what will happen the day somebody will present them the bill for this.
Regarding my previous answer I was not thinking about them, but several other kind of pressure you get from the environment / society around you. In comparison these liberal bloggers are just mosquitos. Anyway, debating with them is a loss of time and a way to feed their archive. You can only tease and joke about them, but I have better things to do. A few years back a similar site was harassing many people of the industrial / goth / whatever scene in Italy. Whenever you explained in detail any subject, your words were twisted and took out of context and used against you. On the other hand I am annoyed by people who attempt to provoke extreme reactions by using dangerous topics and then they complain about negative reactions. You cannot be enjoyed by everybody. There is no such thing like total freedom of speech.

Talking more broadly, I understand you have a background in other musical scenes, including punk / hardcore / Oi!. Did this involvement predate your involvement with the post-industrial subculture, and what is the extent of your involvement (if any) today?

Indeed, I played and collaborated with several punk / hardcore / Oi! bands, recording a few tunes with bands like Hideout, Erode and Outright, plus several collaborations (most recent with local fat-rock legends The Leeches, whose singer is currently my guitar teacher. I often hang out at Alta Fedeltà (refer to Alta Fedeltà's Facebook page), the local alternative vinyl shop run by Francesco of Erode / Hideout.
Many friends of yesterday are still around today, unfortunately others are no longer and still owe me money. I still buy many records and never dropped my passions, it is just something I do not feel like playing any longer. I am not reliable enough to attend rehearsals on a weekly basis, tour, etc., but those are my roots and I still enjoy a lot of great music coming from those ranks. Until a few years ago, I still helped organising gigs and events, doing artwork / contributions for fanzines, presenting gigs, being session musician / singer of bands, etc.
Hardcore, punk rock, street punk, Oi!, metal, etc. are things that never fails to entertain me and still represent a lot for me (also in purchases since I still buy a lot of records), but I am no longer interested in producing such sounds. Now I am too busy to be part of this, but I still hang around with the people. I am not somebody who drops interests, I usually accumulate them to say the least.

You also have ties to the early Norwegian black metal scene, noting you took the back cover background photo (the 'demongate') on Emperor's classic *In the Nightside Eclipse* album. How were you introduced to black metal and what was the extent of your involvement in the scene? Was there a localised black metal scene you were involved with at the time, or were you primarily involved through mail and tape trading? (the

later being predominantly my own experience residing in Australia at the time).

The first wave of Black Metal was an early discovery and probably my very first 'obsession'. As soon I discovered Venom they became my favourite band, then Celtic Frost, Sodom, etc… But when Bathory recorded *Under The Sign Of The Black Mark* things got serious, when I discovered the first wave of Scandinavian Death Metal I also discovered also the rougher Norwegian bands that were very influenced by Quorthon's work and I began writing to everybody who was starting to follow those atmospheres. My focus was Norway and Greece, yet there were great bands worldwide. I had many pen pals and tape traders I was in touch with and, although, I was hanging around and playing mostly in hardcore bands, my main interest have been that until my interest dropped when things started becoming too big and theatrical bands started coming from the UK. I got into black metal again when Carpathian Forest released *Black Shining Leather* (pure perfection), and in the past few years I have been listening may newer projects (Mgla, Clandestine Blaze, Deathspell Omega, Frangar, and hundreds of others). I am still in touch with some of the protagonists of that era I was lucky to witness at its peak. Tape and VHS trading were probably my main activity and I really miss those days when you had to hunt for things before getting them.

There is also an interesting story about where the 'demongate' photo originates from. Would you care to elaborate on this for benefit of readers?

The 'demongate' was part of the scenery of the acclaimed Dylan Dog Horror fest. A massive horror festival I worked for in Milan in the mid 90's, organized by comics publishing house Sergio Bonelli Editore, and dedicated to then Italy's most famous comic book. The 'demongate' was created by Sergio Stivaletti, famous Italian special effect designer, who worked with Dario Argento, Lamberto Bava, Michele Soavi, etc. The festival gathered approximately five to six thousand fans every night, entry was free and it hosted many directors and actors (Brian Yuzna, Lucio Fulci, Wes Craven, Robert Englund, etc.) who I gladly happened to interact with.

It was my first job and useless to say it was a dream.

I was corresponding with Samoth of Emperor and when I shared with him the pictures of the event he asked the permission to use it since he thought it fitted the purpose. Despite the fact Candlelight got my name wrong in the credits, it was a honour to have it associated with to such a classic record like *In The Nightside Eclipse*.

In recent years there has been a greater acknowledgement of crossover interest between underground black metal and post-industrial music scenes, which was not as apparent through the mid to late 90's (i.e. pre-internet to the emerging 'internet age') where genres and styles were more clearly separated. What do you see are the similarities between these scenes and how compatible are they, other than having a broad focus on 'extreme' ideas and concepts?

There is definitely a common will to research new sounds and extreme aesthetics with radical contents. There is a common criticism against the contemporary world and its symptoms. It is a fact that several people shifted from black metal to noise and I know many people who play industrial that also appreciate black metal, but I see them as quite separate things, although I like to enjoy both. There have been some interesting attempts to cross styles every now and then, and I myself collaborated from time to time with black metal bands. Research in sound (as in many other expressions) should never stop.

I understand your professional work is as a marketing manager of an IT company, where you live in Italy but work in Switzerland. Do your work colleagues have an appreciation of your interests and activities outside of work, or do you prefer to keep these spheres of your life entirely separated?

I share thoughts on the subject only with a couple of colleagues who are interested in electronic devices but that is about it. There is not much time to discuss such things since we have quite a hectic working schedule. I never have problems to say what I do and what I think when asked, but my job life is separate from my sound related activities.

Do you consider that there may be differences or potential contradictions between your 'power electronics persona' evoked through the presentation of your musical works and who are in day to day life?

I live with the same mind-set 24 hours / seven days a week, this is who I am and I like it. Naturally, I channel the natural aggression resulting from the reactions to the environment into destructive forms of creativity instead of going around on the prowl and getting into trouble, but my outlook on life never changes. I am very satisfied about my current life with all its contradictions and daily problems. I only wish I had more spare time to spend with my girlfriend and do my own things, but work is work after all and during this period of economic crisis I am not complaining to have a job that keeps me over-busy on a daily basis. Unemployment is my biggest nightmare, I have been through it and I hope I will never have to face it again, so I am glad to accept this compromise.

What constitutes 'extremism' or 'taboos' for you personally? Does your interest in 'difficult' material focus primarily on it only within the context of underground music, or does your interest extend further?

Many of the subjects I deal with are the effects of real obsessions. Others are more theoretical and historical which, obviously, I cannot really experience. We all have limits and boundaries. I tried to stretch mine and understand how far I could go before collapsing. I defeated many irrational fears yet probably others were born while aging. I deal with subjects that obsess me trying to drag a line in between myself and the situations I find fascinating yet not fully representing my tastes. This research occupies most of my waking thoughts.

Taboos are made to be broken when they slow down your path to self-realisation and they are often based on irrational reactions to social / moral / religious dogmas. But sometime they are indicators of endless pits that you should not attempt to cross. Nobody forces you to try anything, just find what is done for you, live for it and crush whoever tries to silence you.

There are subjects, situations and people I don't want to deal with it. It is not a matter of fears and taboos, but after bad experiences or just different tastes in matters of fun and outlook on life. My interests are simply somewhere else and I have chosen to not interact with these people in order to avoid mutual annihilation.
Extremism means taking your choices to their fullest purposes, no matter what external factors try to stop you and this is not necessarily a negative thing, unless you just do this to follow blindly a herd or a leader to fill an existential void within yourself.
Extremists very often see the truth in abandoning themselves to a cause, but every now and then, the cause loses its meaning and leaves space for paranoia leading you to obliteration. Live your life to the fullest, but do not blame on the others when you destroy yourself in the process, or don't bother me with the consequences. Don't ask me for money. I am just not interested in you.

I understand you have been suffering quite severely from tinnitus in recent years and assume this is entirely the result of abuse of your hearing from loud volume? What has been the evolution of this affliction and the current steps you are you having to take to manage it? Is it negatively impacting on what you do musically?
Yes. I had a very difficult moment a few years back. I already had some symptoms, obviously due to an unsafe life at loud volume, but the shit hit the fan after being submitted to unnecessary unwanted noise of train wheels at Como railway station. I dealt with it for a while but then it became annoying and had to stop playing live and being more careful when recording. It took me a couple of years to understand that I was not disabled but just having an issue I had to deal with by forming a different attitude and, although I am still not 100% fine, things go better.
An essential step was to change earplugs and understand my limits. As a very smart German musician who had the same problem once said, you should not lock yourself at home completely as I was trying to do, but play on the safe side. I changed my line of work and this somehow helped me understanding better the nature of sound itself. I only wish I had some moments of real silence in my head but seems it is not possible due to the constant background harsh noise. It could have been worse.

You have been generally active since the projects inception, but it was not until 2008 that the first full length album was released. I assume this was not part of the greater plan, but what prevented you being able to release a debut full length sooner?
There was a CD planned for 1998 / 99, but I lost most of it in a computer crash due to my own stupidity. Only a few backing tracks survived. After that, there was no reason to release just another lousy record with cheap sounds and undefined concept, which was what exactly the CD would have sounded like before I had the time to focus on the release properly, recording it with decent gear and have the text defined. I didn't feel comfortable with most tracks recorded until then and I wanted to be at least 90% satisfied of the CD. I don't think it is a ground-breaking masterpiece, but I am at least happy of how it turned out and fully represented what I wanted to express. And this was also thanks to Lou Chano and the guys at Quadraro Studio helped me with the mastering.

In recent years there seems to be a wealth of activity in the Wertham camp, noting there appeared to be a break in activity between 2010 to 2013. Is this in fact the case or was this a matter of delays in releases being issued?
I stopped performing and attending gigs, I have reduced my presence on social network and focused more on recording in studio, better understanding electronics, testing new gear and focusing on Caligula031, which has been my main focus in the past few years. I had no need / wish to release new records and I was not happy about the recording of the second full length *Bodies*

Under Siege that will be completed hopefully this year. In the meantime, I worked on the Lombroso trilogy and the *Vindicta* collaboration with Uncodified that really took a long time for mostly documentation since Corrado did an excellent work with sounds.

Would you care to talk about your experiences playing live with Wertham, be they positive or negative? What have been your most recent performances and are any planning in the near future?

Well playing live have been most of the time very positive. Every time I have learnt something new, met amazing people and written very entertaining pages that still make me laugh today. It was essential to build the network of friends and collaborators but at the moment I have lost interest in this form of expression. Last gigs I spent more time travelling and recovering in the hotel then actually on stage and having fun with friends, plus I was unable to evolve from what I had been doing for over three to four years. Last but not least, the constant arguing with organisers that could not keep up their words and that considered DJs more important than the performing projects, moaning about being unable to pay expenses while the venue was full, especially in the pub area. Nothing against DJs and dancehalls (some are great and I witnessed sets that were as exciting as gigs all around Europe), just not my cup of tea.

Best gigs were for sure every time I performed at Hinoeuma, the Consumer Electronics festival in Berlin, the two Finnish gigs and a devastating experience at Monza's squat 'Boccaccio', where Trevor and I reached insane volumes, the sound engineer at the mixer was a real third member. I also have fond memories of whenever I played in Holland and, as Foresta Di Ferro, Wien. Another gig I am very fond of was the Triumvirat fest in Yverdon were I shared stage with Die Weisse Rose (risking lighting the stage on fire) and with Michael and Annabel.

Then tinnitus came and it was a good excuse to step out from this. I decided that there were enough projects around to play live and I should have focused in recording new material. No future gigs planned for at least another year or two. But if I'll come back on stage it really should be a completely different form of act… Less karaoke for sure.

When did you move to the UK and where and what were the factors which led to your relocation? Noting your disgust and disdain for contemporary UK society is palpable on *Memories From The Pigsty, what were your impressions of what to expect before mo*ving there, and how may have these differed from the realities you were confronted with? What would you say are the best / worst experiences of you time living in the UK?

I moved at the end of 1999. My previous two years had been quite difficult to say the least, partly due to the complications of a quick yet serious life-threatening disease, nothing that could not be solved by intense ingestion of antibiotics, but that took a long recovery period due to several complications I won't bore the precious readers of *Noise Receptor* with. I lost most things I had and a big part of myself in the process and it was natural to take a bit of fresh air and relocating somewhere else. UK was obvious choice since my then-girlfriend was living there. Not everything was as bad as I described on the CD released by the gentlemen at Tesco, but for a big part of my stay I have been wondering how the hell I ended up being there. I think big part of the problem was not the place itself or Britain in general, but the fact I was the wrong person in the wrong place at the wrong time. A non-drinking, non–meat-eating, non-football obsessed bloody wop in the heart of Chavland. The social structure was also very different from where I came from. I have always been hanging around in different kinds of tribes, real wolf packs where each member was standing shoulder to shoulder with the others. Every community I have been part of I always had somebody to rely on as I was always ready to stand for my friends (and I do not mean necessarily 'dangerous' situations…) and finding myself surrounded by people whose habits were very different from mine was quite a shock. What really horrified me was the low level of literacy, social skills and general perspective in life of people living in council flats. Yob / Chav culture, armies of teen-moms, so called Yardies, young offenders…you name them. Any stereotype became real. Everything was fascinating from a scientific point of view, but sharing the same vital space became a nightmare. Worst situations have been of course the constant state of tension whenever I had to deal with some hostile locals. Life was extremely expensive, which was quite frustrating to say the least since I was unable to save any money. I arrived with nothing and left with nothing. All the fun seemed to be in London and the first period it was difficult to reach due to economic problems. The last year things changed a little bit and I spent more time around with my friends in the capital making those months memorable and the whole experience worth living. I loved cruising around UK and Scotland. Impressive places with intact historical value. Many of these really left me speechless. Oxford, Bath, Glastonbury, Hadrian's Wall, the Ipswich town centre itself was superb, they all had unique atmospheres and I long visiting them again one day with a different mind. Too bad these real-life postcards were ruined by scumbags that not did not appreciate the place they were living as much as I did…

The text in the cover of *Memories from the Pigsty* refers to Seven Sisters Road and Finsbury Park, where I assume these descriptions are in reference to your attendance at Gaya Donadio's Hinoeuma The Malediction industrial nights held at the Red Rose Club (incidentally being where we first became acquainted in person). What are you recollections of these events, either as an audience member or performer?

Well, Hinoeuma was the best place to leave Ipswich's working class reality and feel at home. Great festivals at loud volume, a friendly staff and a series of events that were always left something everlasting in my memory. I have seen some amazing gigs, learned how to perform on stage and got to know many of my then-idols-now-friends. Gaya and her collaborators were always very friendly and supporting and it's

great to think that a single Italian did all this. We had some peculiar experiences there, and it was funny to meet every now and then friends from Germany and Italy.
Best memories for sure the festival with Death Pact International, Genocide Organ, Death Squad, etc. and the massive gig that included Foresta Di Ferro, Ostara, Andrew King and so on. All Whitehouse gigs were absolutely the best things I have seen for what concerns power electronics, with bottles flying, very loud volumes, etc., as every power electronic gig should be. I had the occasion to learn a lot of how to work properly on stage with gear and met many people who became friends. There were also other great events in other locations (Slimelight, Underworld, etc.), but Hinoeuma sounded as if it was born for this reason.

Many years ago when I was publishing Spectrum Magazine and in contact with Douglas Pearce of Death in June, upon hearing I was moving to the UK gave some sage advice of something like: *"don't let the old country wear you down"*. I didn't really understand this at the time as I was off on an 'adventure' but these words came to hold more meaning as the years went by and the sheen of 'living in London' wore away (...but ultimately is was visa issues which was the catalyst for me leaving the UK). What were the events / factors, which led to your own departure from the UK?
Well, I didn't like living in Suffolk. Despite the fantastic landscape and the brilliant people I was working with, I felt a bit like being in confinement. As said, the cost of living was too high for my revenue, everything worth to live for was going on in London, I missed my family and friends and I felt I could not grow at all in the job I was doing. So as soon I saw that things didn't go as expected and things seemed to be moving faster in Italy than in UK, I decided to return back. And so I did.
I didn't have much time to live it as an adventure since I was working in an underpaid 9-5 factory job, which helped me in many extents, but definitely was not what I wanted to do. With a better job and in a least white-trash ridden area, with more connections I would have probably enjoyed myself a lot more, but I really couldn't live freely while being concerned with paying all my bills and spend money to reach London where all my friends were. As said, I was the wrong person at the wrong place. But I would do it again since it opened many doors both workwise and related to music.

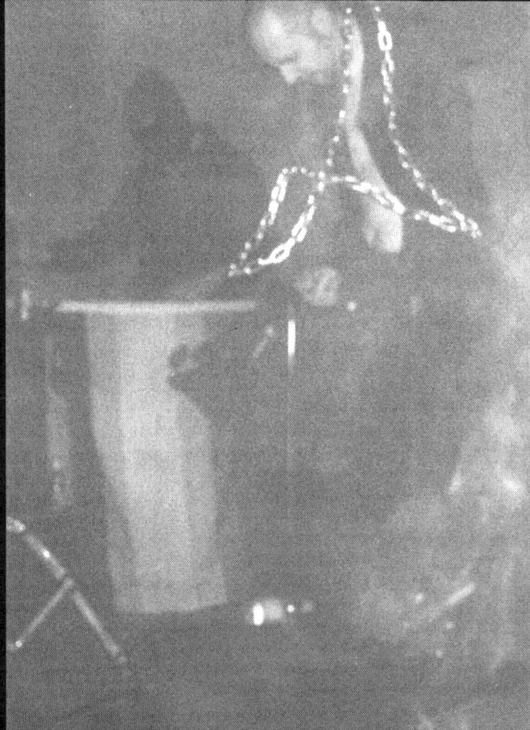

How does you time in London compare to your current surroundings? Despite your apparent disdain for many elements of modern UK life, are there aspects you miss?
Definitely. It was not a completely negative experience. I felt unsafe most of the time when alone which is something I never did even when around in the slums of Milan, Como, etc. Yobs and Yardies, white trash streets kids, there was an aggressive atmosphere that probably was amplified in my head, but was definitely very different from where I was coming from where you knew who your enemies were and you just tried to avoid them. Yet I am missing many aspects of UK. The people I got along with (even outside the music scene) were very down to earth persons that really shown appreciation for my company. Their politeness and sense of humour (did I already mentioned that stereotypes are always based on truth?) is something completely alien to where I come from. I will sound dumb but I miss BBC and Channel 4 programs, laughing at tabloid's titles, spreading marmite on Hovis bread, old women calling you "luv" in shops, old geezer in pubs treating you like they've been knowing you for a life (not that I hung around in pubs that often, but it happened a few time). I loved the nights in London where found myself different scenarios even three four times per night, starting with traditional folk singer's night, to then move to the Slimelight packed with every kind of night creature you can imagine and ending at birthday parties with goths and hooligans under the same roof. But more than anything I am missing the friends who were a joy to be with and very helpful when I could not do anything else than banging my head against the wall.

During my own time in London for a short while I resided in what was effectively a long standing community housing squat in Bonnington Square, Vauxhall. Evidently Brendan Perry of Dead Can Dance had also lived in the Square during his initial time in London in the early 1980's and the piano in the house I was living in has been used to compose some of their songs. I must say that I found this to be a rather striking coincidence given the sheer number of places I could have potentially ended up living in London couple with the facts that I am a rather big Dead Can Dance fan. Have you had any similar weird coincidences in your own life?

Well yes. These sort of weird things occurred to me every now and then. The weirdest coincidence that ever happened to me was a last-minute choice to go to the cinema to attend a debate regarding horror movies and becoming so annoyingly enthusiastic during the discussion that the poor lad hosting the event, who incidentally worked for the aforementioned comics publishing houses, asked me to collaborate with him. That was a life-changing adventure that lasted six years until I moved to Suffolk.

Another weird coincidence has been getting hooked - mostly on the theory - of interactive kit controller Arduino and discover that one of its creator Massimo Banzi either lived or had an office in the same building were my girlfriend Titti lived. Then after a few months I discover that he started teaching at SUPSI, a Swiss University whose labs were in the same block of the company I work for. We recently moved offices and we are now inside the same building of the SUPSI headquarters but I still haven't managed to meet him despite my intelligence effort. For us geeks this guy is like Einstein and although my interest is mostly theoretical, I definitely want to meet him.

Through a number of recording projects including the Death Pact International release and the recent *Ramraiding the Abyss* collaboration LP you have an ongoing working relationship with the Grey Wolves. Did this association this result from your time in the UK or something prior?

Not exactly. DAP was one of the very first persons I got in touch with when I started with my friend RH- (aka cook / painter Massimiliano Pini) the Soffitta Macabra tape label. The Grey Wolves participated in our *Fuck Off We Murder* compilation and I passed them some videos for the joint performance with Con-Dom at Deadly Action in Lille. We had already performed as Death Pact International in Esterhofen around 1998 with Grey Wolves, Ain Soph and Nocturnal Emissions and then at Hinoeuma. We also met at several shows.

It comes natural to work with people you share tastes and a good laugh or two, and I definitely did with them. I hope we'll do more in future since I am very fond of how the *Ramraiding the Abyss* thing turned out. It took several years but the result fits what we had in mind… same goes for the Death Pact International *Siege* boxset, it was great fun assembling it.

Since 2010 you have also operated under the Caligula031 moniker which works broadly within a similar sonic palate to Wertham. What do you see are the main similarities and difference as you see them?
Caligula031 is a conceptual work focusing mostly – but not exclusively - on the subject human trafficking and the slow decay of Insubria, a once rich area between northern Italy and southern Switzerland, which is slowly collapsing, turning into a swamp due to economic crisis and, let's say, a very bad management of human resources. The current work deals mostly with slave-trade from Eastern European countries to Lombardy and Tessin (the southern part of Switzerland, where prostitution is tolerated yet is supplied by the same people who throw girls on the streets in other part of Europe).
Sound-wise, the idea behind Caligula031 has always been to have a more direct and in your face project that could stick to what I started with Wertham's *Sleaze* tape, which is more basic and unedited than the rest of the current material. This is not meant to be a repository for left-overs but a project with a life of its own with a limited use of digital editing, more focus on high / mid frequencies, less protagonist vocals and, somehow, a more experimental approach in the choice of instruments and sound sources. Most sampled material is directly recorded on-site, documenting things happening on trains, etc. Similarities might be the sound of the voice and the use of pulsing background tracks.

Noting the name Caligula031, this could potentially refer to the year 31AD when Caligula at the time was an adolescent and effectively a prisoner of Tiberius, whom Caligula evidently planned to kill but did not go through with his intention. Does the name 'Caligula031' perhaps mean something to the effect 'harbouring vengeful intent', or something completely different?
Well, your idea is actually brilliant and I might consider adding it to my official bio! In fact the 031 tag is Como's phone area number. The project started focusing with things happening in Como / Tessin region, so it somehow marked my turf. But them it moved abroad. Caligula is both the Roman Emperor you referred to, known for both his enormous sexual appetite and his despise for representatives of the bureaucracy and one of the, apparently, worst brothels in Berlin. When I saw this I thought it had to be used somehow. Considering I played for a few months with street-punk band Erode (King Herod), you can definitely say I have a thing for emperors / kings' names.

Foresta Di Ferro is your post-industrial / neo-folk hybrid collaborative project between John Murphy, Richard Leviathan and yourself. Noting that the group was active in the early 2000's (coinciding with your time in London) and has release only the single album this far, is the project abandoned or simply on extended hiatus due to the three members living in different countries?
The project was on hold but never formally disbanded. We did several gigs with different guests and all the time (apart from Madrid that was just awful) it has been a great party. Now, we have less occasions to meet but we are working on the new record entitled *Might be never, may be forever* which we hope to complete by the end of 2015. Our friends at "Trips und Traume" from Rome recently re-released on vinyl *Bury Me Standing* and it is going pretty well, so I supposed we have to work hard now to keep up expectations.

In 2013 you launched the Elettronica Radicale Edizioni label, which appears to function as a collaboration with, or sub-label to Old Europa Café. Would you care to describe what led you to decide to launch a 'physical' release focused label in the current 'digital' climate? Also what is the underpinning agenda and future aims of the label and what might be in the pipeline for future?
A project's worth must be rewarded and supported by funding them. This is not asking too much considering how much passion, time and money they put in what they do. This is why I still buy many records, more than those I actually listen, sadly, due to time limitations. Digital formats are good only to test new purchases. Furthermore, a release is something I can listen, look, read, touch. Something that I cannot hold in my hand does not exist unless it is something specific like the excellent work of net label Radical Matters, which goes far beyond simple download. I have Bandcamp pages, they sell every now and then, but I prefer to use them as a window for our releases. But without this immersive dimension I have no interest whatsoever in this.
ERE was born to release my own material and the one of my closest friends in which I am involved every now and then (Uncodified, Grey Wolves, The Rita, Iugula-Thor, etc.). It is an independent label yet I accept to co-release some records in order to have enough copies to give all my friends and contacts that often have problems to get them, especially in presence of limited releases. The idea is to release records every four to six months, a few CDs and a series of conceptual box sets covering different subjects. Tapes and CDs are the favourite formats at the moment, yet I am looking for a decent vinyl alternative. I can't print much because I have limited storage space and no time to ensure proper distribution so I am not accepting submissions. But I am planning new releases from Iugula-thor, The Rita, the third chapter of *Vindicta* and a series of box sets names *Encyclopedia Of Radical Electronics* focusing on specific aspects of sound, they will include exhaustive booklets and information. It is taking longer than expected (one year at the moment), but I hope it will be worth the wait, as the old saying goes, Rome was not built in one day…

To conclude the interview on a more socio-political note, in our private communications we have briefly touched on the economic upheavals which have struck many European counties in recent years. Noting that Euro currency was established to facilitate and streamline European trade and having been in operation for well over a decade now, what is your impression of the functional operation of the European Union, economically, culturally and politically? Likewise how do see the European political and cultural landscape changing over coming decades?

I think I am not the right person to discuss economics. I earn money working, I pay taxes, I spend (mostly for food, comics and gear), and I try to not give too much money to banks. The European Union as it was built is just the effect and the product of banks interests. There was not one single attempt to create a real European consciousness as all those who hold dear our history hoped for. The Euro itself was a wasted occasion from the very beginning and its movements and power are limited and is moved by those who pull the strings of the economy: banks, multinationals, etc. The usual friends. I see no advantages in this. I am too ignorant to tell you if we could gain some benefits by exiting the EU at the moment as different movements (both from left and right) are suggesting, but it looks to me that it is a failed experiment.
Politically speaking, there is no EU. We live in the shadow of what the States chose for us, it has always been like this and will be like this until governments will really focus on what people need and not what is more convenient and does not disturb our real leaders overseas, participating in wars of interest with the excuse of bringing peace in the name of anti-terrorism, removing presumed dictators from third-world countries when they stop being useful as watchdogs to oil plants, waging useless wars in the name of this or that cause, and so on. I don't see any change at the horizon, so I focus on other things hoping that the company I work for won't be crushed by the crisis.
In the future decades I see that these Euro-sceptical movements getting stronger, with Germany and France keeping the lead of the economy. New restrictive laws on communication and more suspects on those who dare to criticize this situation, but nothing changes. History has ended and we are fucked, so let's hope to not hurt ourselves too much. Furthermore, I am curious to see how the new Isis terror scare will be handled…

Final comments / thoughts?
Many thanks to you for taking the time to ask about my work. 2015 will be a very busy year and I hope nobody will be disappointed.
Build your own some gear, form your own project, make a zine, make your own noise and don't waste time with those who want to silence you.
Many thanks for the extensive interview. For updates regarding my projects please make sure to visit: wertham.wordpress.com and soundcloud/wertham

Photo credits (in order of appearance): 1: Titti Gemin, 2: Ale Formenti, 3: Davide Maspero, 4: Davide Maspero, 5: unknown, 5: Aldo Volpe.

HOSPITAL PRODUCTIONS
NEW YORK CITY
HOSPITAL PRODUCTIONS
UPCOMING 2015
AKITSA LP/PIC LP/CD/CASSETTE
SKIN CRIME BOX
FLUTTER
CLAY RENDERING
V/A A BIRD'S EYE VIEW INTO A MACHIAVELLIAN WORLD OF SECRECY CASSETTE BOX

ALFARMANIA SURVIVAL UNIT

When I was previously publishing *Spectrum Magazine* back in the late 1990's and early 2000's Kristian Olsson was just starting to make his presence known within the industrial underground through the ritual dark ambient collective Heid and his solo power electronics project Survival Unit. Now some 15 years later Kristian has evolved into a long term scene devotee and proven his commitment to a staunchly underground ethos. Having conducted few interviews over the years, it seemed to be an opportune time to subject Kristian to a detailed interrogation regarding all of his activities including: Survival Unit, Alfarmania, solo and collaborative musical projects, live performances, visual arts and his label Styggelse. This detailed and rather long form interview was conducted via email in April, 2015.

Although Alfarmania is you current project, this clearly needs to be considered in context of your prior project Survival Unit; which is a reasonably well known and recognised name. Noting that I understand that Alfarmania started before Survival Unit officially ceased, in reflection what are your impressions of the transitional shift between the two projects?

Obsessed with early post-mortem culture and shaped by the consequences of an outlaw life, it was simply a necessity to deal with it. At the time I had worked intensely with Survival Unit for some years and it restricted my creative output. I needed to work with something else. In retrospect this commitment was one of the things that kept me from falling down into the pits of chemical hell and some very bad situations caused by living this life.

First document was *From Fix to Fix* – the result of a long period of isolation in a basement with limited gear. I had no interest in spreading the material. In those days Death was constantly present – a companion and part of my life... I sent archive copies of everything I recorded to Proiekt Hat, in case something would happen. He immediately offered me to release it through his cassette label Hatband.

This was in one of the darker periods of my life and my musical work was the only thing that separated me from being consumed by worms. It was the beginning of the end for Survival Unit.

My impression of the arc of Survival Unit's development was that at its commencement you were very much influenced by the politically antagonistic industrial noise/ power electronics of The Grey Wolves, but the sound of the project evolving towards something more personal over time, which then let into the fully fledged 'post-mortem' sound of Alfarmania. What are your impressions of the evolution of your style and the similarities and differences between Survival Unit and Alfarmania?

There is no point in denying that I drew inspiration from the works of the European power electronics scene in the early days of SU, in particular that of The Grey Wolves. Eventually my perspectives widened and there was a need for me to do something else, to fully explore a path of my own.

In the initial phases, Alfarmania differed from Survival Unit in sound and vision. Nowadays there are perhaps more similarities. The underlying basis of all my work remains the same throughout the years. Regardless of what kind of cultural expression I use, it has always been a way for me to explore the abyss within and that which lies beyond. Underneath all of these social and political constructions, there is a sinister current running through all my work and that will always be the foundation of what I do.

What would you acknowledge as the critical influences for your chosen style as well as your general approach to music/ sound production?

For as long as I can remember I've messed around with tape decks and creating disturbing sounds. I learned the basics of sound production as a young teenager when I and a friend shoplifted a Fostex 4-track recorder. From there on it was used for many recordings, both noise and black metal projects. We borrowed and stole whatever we could find to make these sounds. It was a great deal of experimentation in those early days as I could hardly even afford a distortion pedal.

Through various sources I started to explore the industrial underground and bands like SPK, Grey Wolves, Genocide Organ and BDN. At some point I got to borrow a whole

box of tapes from Proiekt Hat. Most of them came from the distribution service that Harri operated in the 80s. Stuff from Nekrophile Rekords, Aquilifer Sodality, Broken Flag, Iphar and so on. Hearing this opened up a chthonic pathway and widened my perspectives in approach to sound. Proiekt Hat has served as a teacher and friend for many years, from whom I've learned a great deal. Most influential in terms of sound production though, even if I have learned most of it on my own.
Another source of inspiration has been musique concrete / electro acoustic composers and movie soundtracks.

From my perspective Survival Unit could be deemed the 'political' given its overall thematic focus, whilst Alfarmania is more 'social' (for want of a more appropriate term) in its focus, and by 'social' I mean the preoccupation with aspects of the squalid underbelly of society. What is your perspective on the similarities and differences in thematic focus between Survival Unit and Alfarmania?
Survival Unit was an ideological project, as much a spiritual quest. Fuelled by youthful nihilism and burning hatred with the diseased modern world. Once I fully opened my eyes, I realized this was no time to portray the beauty of the past or living in some irrational pipe-dream. Humanity is doomed to drowning in its own materialistic vomit. Ignorant masses happy in their bulletproof sofa bunkers. Safe in their illusion of living in a golden age. Instead of swimming like retarded ducks in the pond of ideological debris, the intention was to grab the sword with both hands and ram it into the heart of this diseased civilization. Survival Unit was an iconoclasm tearing down the utopian façade. The cataclysm of the paradigm shift which would break humanity's bonds and return him to the world from which he hides in fear of his conscience. When the faith in existing political and social institutions is lost, when the constructions of the intellect lead nowhere… Man breaking free from humanity, from the shackles of slave morality.
The new man, forged in the fires of dissolution, finding his life-essence and strength among the ruins. In retrospect I see very little hope for any collective awakening, things will have to get so much worse before people open their eyes. Let the sickness pervade. There is no cure. It is too late.
Alfarmania still moves in a similar conceptual field, though in other areas than political. Tactics and techniques change and evolve with time.

It is apparent that Survival Unit formally ceased activities following the landmark *Fentanyl Martyrs* DCD in 2007, however since this time you have played live as Survival Unit on at least two occasions in recent years, including Nordic Audio Modern Festival (Lithuania 2012) and War & Hate III (Sweden 2013). What is the actual status of Survival Unit these days?
When "Fentanyl Martyrs" came out I felt there was little left to be said and done with Survival Unit. After that the project was put to rest, but it is not dead. Both live shows in 2012 & 2013 was a temporary resurrection since Alfarmania was partially on ice after Tony had dropped out and I had no live lineup. The performance at War & Hate was a memorable event. David / Blade couldn't make it so instead Set Teitan (Watain / Dissection) and Hugo (Khmer Noir) joined me on stage. Audience was on fire, half of them being local criminals and the rest people from black metal & noise underground. There had been weird rumors circulating before the festival so very few actually dared to visit the event. During our show a huge black metal skinhead took a carpet cutter and carved up his whole chest, then smeared people with his blood, like in an ecstatic trance. A young girl was walking around without her pants urinating on the ground. There were random acts of violence in the audience. Set kicked someone in the face with his boots so even more blood covered the stage. The whole festival was in this spirit – the kind of things you don't write about.
Concert in Vilnius was mostly because Lashisha / Autarkeia invited us. The outcome of Survival Unit would have looked very differently if it hadn't been for his help. A man willing to make great sacrifices for what he believes in!
To answer the question… Survival Unit may return when you least expect it!

Clearly you are the founder, core member and main driving force behind Survival Unit and Alfarmania, however both projects have included the involvement and collaboration of other members over the years. What do you see as the functional role and influence of collaborating members and what did you see as the main elements they brought to each project? Likewise what is the current status of the membership of Alfarmania?
Founding father and scapegoat. Both projects are my creations and continue to be so, even as collaborators and members changes with the times. Structure of Survival Unit was more open and I maybe didn't think so many times about whom I worked with. The only important thing was to move onwards.
To mention a few of the people who were influential collaborators in Survival Unit in one way or the other over the years: David "Blade" Berglund, Otto Trupp, Grey Wolves, Marco Deplano, Troy Southgate, Thomas Ekelund (long before Trepaneringsritualen) and Martin (Green Army Fraction).
As stated before, Alfarmania is not as outward directed as Survival Unit and I have a rather clear vision of the sounds I want to achieve. There are a few persons that I continue working with year after year. In these situations we know exactly what there is that needs to be done, no need for words or instructions. The times I've been recording with Proiekt Hat has been like this, almost telepathic. Some personnel are recruited for their artistic / technical skills – some for their contributions in other ways.
In early days of Alfarmania, David Berglund helped me out live (also in Survival Unit). Tony Hallén assisted me with additional synthesizer sounds between 2007-2010. He was mostly around during gigs but dropped out of the whole industrial scene some years ago due to personal issues.

For a year now I have performed live with the assistance of my old friend Viktor Ferner (Baymon / Striktlickers). We have known each other for a long time and he knows what I'm after. In the past we did some collaborative recordings with Alfarmania and his now defunct d-beat / hardcore band Striktlickers. I asked him to join me when playing at Röset festival last year and after that we made the decision for him to join the live setting of Alfarmania (also occasional studio sessions). We share many views and beliefs that are way beyond the limitations of culture and music. I've grown to realize the importance of a spiritual bond with those I work with, rather than selecting people for their long subcultural C.V. Not all people are cut out for this kind of commitment as I put hard pressure on their achievements at times. It isn't strange that some people drop off along the way.

What is the meaning underpinning your chosen moniker Alfarmania? Noting that you previously used a slightly differing spelling of Alpharmania is the name perhaps a comment on the masculine dominated aspects of underground industrial and power electronics scene?
The name was suggested to me by a local friend long time ago (now dead and buried). Honestly not the best name but it was fitting to the music. A wordplay on pharmaceutical company 'Alpharma' and mania. The state of intoxication when you are a beyond the edge of depravity and drifting towards death. Alfar is a rootword for the Allfather – the primordial and the wild. 'Farma' is also Baltic slang for bad drugs that you get sick or die from.

Noting the apparent focus of Alfarmania on trash culture, drug lifestyle, junky themes and societal decline, does this focus and interest of material in any way reflect your personal lifestyle and/ or surroundings?
While the Swedish people are busy complaining in social media about their insignificant materialist lives and the latest trends in offensiveness, there is a lot going on underneath the smokescreen laid out to deceive the masses that everything is in order. Tear apart this thin membrane and its true nature will be revealed – a desperate and diseased civilization struggling to uphold its' final grasp on humanity before sinking down into endless perdition.

Honestly I have a very hard time to see any happy outcome for the future of Europe or Western civilization as a whole. We have all helped dig this grave and there isn't much to be done about it. I have since long abandoned idealism. The world, all of its great wisdom and science is now drained and hollow.
The great emptiness remains to be predestined in the human constitution as a final goal for its movement of throughout history. The road leads only to its doom. For thousands of years, man has been in the centre of its projects of science and wisdom. Nowadays this has been replaced by social relations and tendencies. Mankind reduced to resonance body for commercial and political slogans, dog-like crawling under power structures.
Alfarmania deals with no actual agenda. In some ways it deals with experiences from my own life, my surrounding environment and that of others. I've drawn much inspiration from the outlaw side of society that is pushed away as non-existent or used as scapegoat for the real problems.
My surroundings these days have little to do with degenerate lifestyle, rather the opposite. Still it continues to inspire. Like a wanderer through the inferno of the lower castes and regions of society.

Given the underground's predominant interest in the presentation of negatively focused themes, I was interested to read an interview with Mories De Jong of Gnaw Their Tounges, who discussed the fact that he started the ethereal ambient project Seiorm as a means to purge the wallowing negatively of much of his other musical output (which was

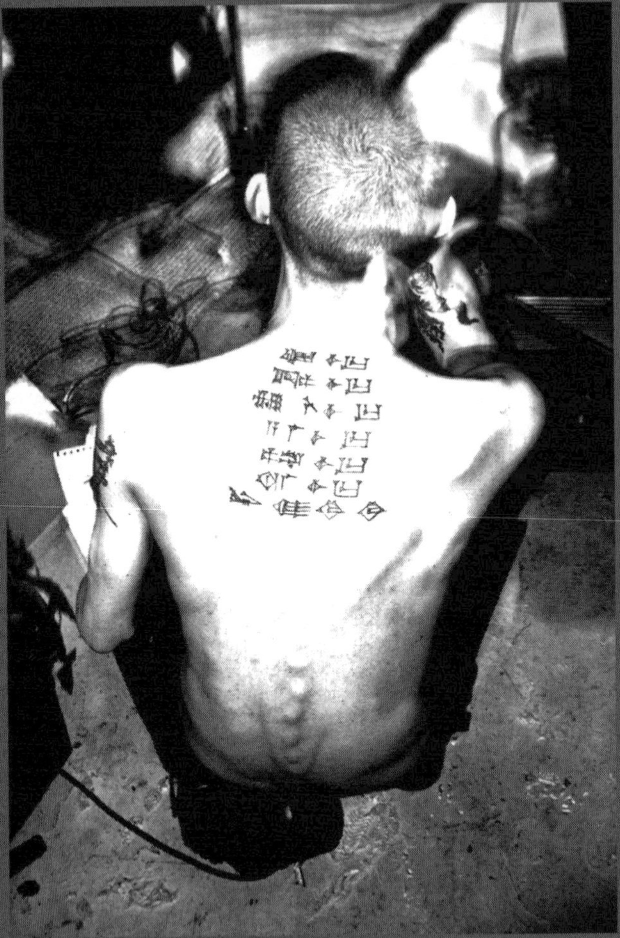

Taking a step back, Survival Unit started when you of a relatively young age. What was the musical pathway which led you to underground industrial/ power electronics music and was Survival Unit your first musical project?
After being involved in the black metal underground scene, I found this to be rather shallow and drifted towards darker territories, pushing the extremes further. At a young age I started experimenting with tape recorders and feedback through some cheap synth and other devices I could find. Through mail-order catalogues of Cold Meat Industry and Laughing Eskimo a whole new world opened. Most of my time was spent sending letters with well-concealed cash across the world.
I joined forces with a local psycho that was also into industrial music and the occult, and we formed FDH (that some years later became Survival Unit). This was around second half of the 1990s. We experimented a lot with mind alterations and occultism, breaking down boundaries of all sorts. In 2005 the death of my friend with whom everything started with, marked the beginning of a new era – a new course in my life and lifework.
Around the same time I collaborated with some people from Stockholm in a dark ambient project called Heid. We did some recordings together that were released by Malignant Records and Cold Meat Industry. Our final recordings took place in 1999… after that it we all went in completely different directions and the group was terminated. Some lessons learned. From there on I focused solely on industrial / power electronics, with a few exceptions.

As with Survival Unit, Alfarmania is a project to which you have played live on numerous occasions. Within the context of Alfarmania's live performances I note that on occasion you have choose to wear a distinctive white mask. Is the mask intended to assist performance focus, obscure personality or something different?
I got it as a gift from a friend who came to my show after returning from a long visit in Libya, where he was hanging out with an artist doing only portraits of Gaddafi. The mask was used during performances

evidently having an negative impact on his personal psyche at the time). What are your impressions of focus on negativity as it applies generally to underground music as well as you as you individually?
Modern culture is negativity in its literal form. Materialistic profanity and exalted stupidity, derived of all kind of deeper purpose and meaning. We live in the age of degeneration and corruption where spiritual development is nothing. Humanity in this age will never realize the fact that it is its own worst enemy, its own executioner. Therefore it will continue to wade in the cultural sewage of our times until everything is drowned. Acceptance and understanding of these things is necessity.
These days I wouldn't regard myself a negative person really. For as long as I can remember I've had a different outlook on life, but that doesn't stop me from seeing positive things and having a lot of love for my nearest & dearest. No reason to waste it on astral lice or emotional parasites. With the risk of using an old clichéd answer – working with this kind of art and music is a form of catharsis. Yet at the same time I do embrace the enormous potential and destructive power that comes from these abysmal depths.

where he poured alcohol over his suit and then set himself on fire while running into the crowds of fancy bars in Stockholm. My reasons for using mask were to make performances detached from human emotions. To hide the face, liberate the demons of the mind. That particular hood is no longer in use for Alfarmania but we have some custom made for future performances.

To date you have released a large number of cassettes, with far fewer on CD and vinyl, meaning you obviously you have clear affinity to an underground cassette culture. Do you care to expand on this interest in cassette related culture (both currently and historically)? Is this your general preferred format and what area your views on other formats such as vinyl, CD and digital?
Cassette was the format I started working with. It was cheap and easy to do. I had a background from the tape-trading and demo cassette underground, so this was the way I knew how to spread music. There were some years when CDR was the way you spread noise and it left such a horrible aftertaste. Reviving the cassette format was one of the best things that could happen to industrial music underground. With that not merely as pointless nostalgia but using something that actually worked in the past to spread new material and ideas. Undeniably I have put out more tapes than any other format, but I have no problems with releasing works also on CD and vinyl. You can make both cheap and classy releases regardless what format. People should be more selective with what they release.
Tape has also been a vital part when I've been making music. It has enormous potential when it comes to shaping and molding sounds, working with different speed, multiple channels, looping and so on.

When commencing on a new recording project, how do you approach the production of your material? Is this thematic / content led or potential driven by a process of experimentation and gradual refinement? Do you have a process of established approach to music production?
Most common is to begin around a conceptual foundation, an idea. It can be weeks of preparations with gathering raw sounds, finding locations for field recordings, making backing tapes / loops, writing lyrics etc.
Then I enter my studio where I record live session based on this material. Mostly with several recording devices (lined to tape deck, different microphones, handheld recorder, reel-to-reel, 4-track recorder etc). Depending on situation I can be alone or have other musicians helping me out.
At this point I can get totally caught up in the process and enter a trance-like state that can last for hours where the music creates itself with me as the instrument. For the past years I've had the privilege to have a studio in a bunker-like underground basement. Entirely isolated from the outside world. My equipment is always rigged up and plugged in so whenever I feel the urge I can make it happen. Experimentation and improvisation with sound has become much easier. In the past I was dragging around my equipment to abandoned places and shady places just to record... Often with lowlife scum hanging over my gear, like a flock of vultures.
Anyway, final stage is that I select what I feel is relevant to use. Maybe add some layer of sounds and cut it down if necessary. When all this is done and I've mixed it down, I make a master tape and later transfer to computer at home (there is a total absence of computers in the studio).
For field recordings I often go to abandoned factory location with tons of scrap metal and a huge hall with amazing natural reverb.

Beyond your own current musical activities, you have been instrumental in assisting the revival of two of cult Swedish underground industrial/ power electronics projects, namely Blood ov Thee Christ and RJF (now operating as Kommando RJF). Were the individuals behind these projects still directly involved in the underground scene or did you play a part in reinvigorating their interest? How was such contact initially made, and how did the collaborations come about? Likewise is your involvement and activity in both an ongoing one?
When I first heard the *Master Control* tape from Blood Ov Thee Christ, I was stunned by the fact that something this sick and evil had been recorded in my own backyard, decades before I was active. The more I looked, I realized the dirty fingerprints of Harri Honkaniemi was everywhere in the Swedish underground. Harri had been hiding in the woods for some years, living a life far away from his past. I had heard many weird anecdotes about him, in particular in his years as an acid shaman. Learning about his involvement in the post-mortem scene made it necessary to track him down. About 14 years ago I attempted to release *Theory and Practice of Hell* – live recordings from Slave State in Belgium. Harri had attended this gig during one of his visits to Club Moral and had taken some photos.
He was a bit reserved talking about his past, as if trying to hide from himself. His old sins were behind him, much like he is these days (a born again Christian). This all changed once relocated to Sundsvall some years later. This town was his base of operations in the 80s and returning to the crime scene did awaken something in him (unfortunately also his bad habits).
Around this time Tommy Carlsson was very keen on releasing *Master Control* on his label Segerhuva. He was the one who first dubbed it for me and I considered this a holy grail of Swedish power electronics. Naturally I aided him in convincing Harri to do this and his return was a fact. I had a lengthy talk with Harri, interviewing him for the first issue of my magazine Shocktilt. After this we started to hang out on a regular basis and agreed to make a live performance for the release party of *Master Control*.
I was organizing a festival called Brytbröt in an abandoned church in Sundsvall. Performing acts included Karmanjakan Intonarumori (nowadays called Bestializer), Alfarmania, Proiekt Hat, Sewer Election & Treriksröset. It was also the

first live aktion from Blood Ov Thee Christ since 1988 so we had to make it special somehow. We found an old coffin that we forced Harri into and dragged him up from the basement to the stage. In this chaos I managed to knock out a tooth of a reporter from Vice Magazine that was reviewing the event. I also remember having my first fight with Honkaniemi on stage… It was a sick and violent night that really set the standard for what was to come. After resurrecting Blood Ov Thee Christ the nucleus of the group consisted of Harri and me, involving few session members such as Proiekt Hat and Mazza (both of them had been involved in past incarnations of the group). We made a number of recordings and shows for some years, but around the time he was going to prison again I was so fed up with him that we put the project to rest. Each time we would get together something really fucked up and bad would happen. I was the one doing all the work, so I decided it was time for me to focus on my own projects instead. This old man drained the energy out of me. Parting ways with Honkaniemi was perhaps one of the better decisions I've made with my musical career. It has now been almost five years since we went different paths but we have made peace and I might be open to some recordings in the years to come.

The RJF story… I was asked by Segerhuva to write an essay on the history of the group for the CD reissue of *Greater Success in Apprehension & Convictions*. Leif Thuresson is another weird character from the industrial scene. He dropped out of everything in mid 80s but has remained true to this lifestyle ever since. We talked a lot when I interviewed him for the first issue of Shocktilt. We stayed in touch after this. For nearly a decade he has been making late-night phone calls on a regular basis, having lengthy and often intoxicated discussions about art, life, death and authors such as Celine, Cioran, Artaud and Nietzsche. Some years ago he started talking about making recordings for *Sweet Slow Suicide* – the second album of RJF. Originally planned to come out in the late 1980s, but never happened. Leif wanted me and Tommy Carlsson to make it reality, being the only ones fully initiated into the nucleus of RJF and also as representatives of three generations of Swedish industrial music. Posh Isolation did an excellent job releasing the LP and I'm very proud of our achievements with the music. Before making the recordings we agreed there will be no more work as Kommando RJF and that remains carved in stone.

From an outsiders perspective it seems that Sweden is rather a hotbed of activity for underground industrial/ dark ambient/ power electronics type music. Why do think that Sweden (and Nordic countries in general), have been such a focus for this type of music? What is the acceptance or even awareness of such 'difficult' music within the broader musical and artistic circles?

Sweden has a long history of experimental music but I don't really think we have a big scene. Without a few devoted souls carrying the heavy burden and keeping the threads together, it would be nothing. Same goes for Finland and Denmark I guess. Maybe outsiders see it differently. Sweden had a very promising scene at several occasions but I think most people got lazy and more interested in doing more commercially accessible things. What you label as difficult music has partly moved away from the obscure underground circles into a more 'accepted' scene. Nordic people may have an open mind for such things due to cultural diversity, but in another sense we are most restricted. I don't care if people want to make fashion shows out of industrial music, there will always be a core of fanatics doing it the way it should be done.

Given you appear to be continually hyper-productive with a variety of projects being active at any one time (be they solo under your own name or as collaborations with other artists), what currently active projects are you working on?

Actually I have slowed down the pace over the past years for the sake my own well-being. Certain changes in my lifestyle also provided me better focus and motivation. Lack of time for working with these things is a constant problem however.

I have been doing solo recordings under my own name since 2001. The sound work is more ritualistic and experimental. Rooted in industrial music traditions. Dark and back to basics, but not as confrontational as Alfarmania or Survival Unit. Working under my own name makes it easier to focus on sound for the sake of sound, without a conceptual burden. Later this year Freak Animal will release a CD called *Ligranorex*. Most of the material is taken from a private cassette I issued in 2012 and extra material from recording sessions I did for Irkallian Oracle's *Grave Ekstasis* album.

I have also done some recordings together with one of the members of Reverorum Ib Malacht that I will continue with when time allows. This summer I also hope to deal with a project I've been working on with Stephen Bessac (Kickback).

Ghoulbog is a ritual music group I'm involved in together with people from the black metal act Nidsang. We made some recordings few years ago that came out as cassettes *Fjälldesperadon* and *Den Andra*. We are all busy with our other projects but when the time is right we will get together to record a new album.

No idea when (2021?), but there will also be more recordings with Proiekt Hat. Following what we did with *Furyfication* LP (2007) and *Astral Slaktmask* (2014).

Noting your comments above above recording with a member of Reverorum ib Malacht, they are a particular group who have courted a degree of controversy in black metal circles due to conversion of members to Roman Catholicism. Given that you also have an affiliation with members of Watain who are professed 'orthodox satanists', what is your view on Reverorum ib Malacht's conversion and the associated controversy?

I have worked with both orthodox catholics and devilworshippers over the years. Even back when I did Survival Unit, I had Bo Cavefors, a known catholic, provide spoken word parts for some songs. Roman Catholicism is hardly the religion that we should be concerned about these days… Judeo-Christianity is like an animal without teeth.

Naturally I'm not a follower of this faith myself but many times I prefer the company of such people compared to profane scene apes. Everyone searching for transcendence have to find their own path. Many are mistaken and think it is a question of academic studies and rational thought, they are in a surface illusion…
I have little interest to interact with the black metal scene nowadays. Once I was drawn to the spiritual and transcendental side of this music, but soon came to realize this was an illusion with a few rare exceptions.
Watain are serious and devoted people that I've known for many years. Erik used to be involved with WMJ Organisation together with the people from Iron Justice. Before joining Dissection, Set and I played together in a band called Bloodline and also recorded some work with Survival Unit. They asked me to provide an intro for their live rituals and it was an honor doing so…
Reverorum Ib Malacht have a unique vision when it comes to their music. Unlike many other bands they actually have managed to take this music a step further.

Reverorum ib Malacht via their recordings demonstrate an extremely dark and mysterious atmosphere which is rather unique in their bridging of black metal, dark ambient and ritualised atmospheres. What is the sound and direction of the recordings that your made to date?
Since my girlfriend lives in the city of Uppsala, I've spent a lot of time there the past years. It is also where their studio is located. The Malacht studio is a modular temple, with Hieronymous Lundin as the high priest. We have been recording mainly with his Serge and Buchla synthesizers (actually covered in real pergament). There is absolutely no elements of metal music in what we've done. Ritualistic industrial, close to my solo recordings I would say. I am not sure in what context the sounds will be used.

What is currently in the works for Alfarmania and what themes, concepts and sounds are to be explored on current and upcoming material?
Right now the finalizing phase of recordings for a full length LP on Tesco. It has been in the workings for some years now. It should be out before the Heavy Electronics III festival in Mannheim this summer.
There is an unreleased LP called *Farsot* that we recorded in 2007 for Dogma Chase (Japan). Maybe this will also come out this year on some other format. Ukrainian label Old Captain recently reissued *From Fix to Fix* cassette on CD, soon followed by a CD version of *At Ulleråker*.
The conceptual / thematic nature of Alfarmania has changed over the years and is perhaps less focused on social issues and more on the abysmal labyrinths of the mind.

Over a number of years you have established yourself as a recognisable and prominent collage artist, where your style builds upon an early DIY industrial culture cut and paste aesthetic but has elevated it to a more refined and individual style. Can you explain process and development of artistic and stylistic form?
For as long as I can remember I've had an obsession for the dark and morbid in art. In my early teens I was editing fanzines dealing with black metal and industrial / noise. I learned how to hotwire the xerox copy machine at the library so I could use it without paying and spent countless hours exploring the alchemical potential of glue and scissors. I guess with time you evolve your artistic skills and it was not interesting for me to continue doing the same thing year after year. I am a traditionalist in many ways but have never liked stagnation. Even if the ideas have been there I have lacked time and motivation to work with art the past years.

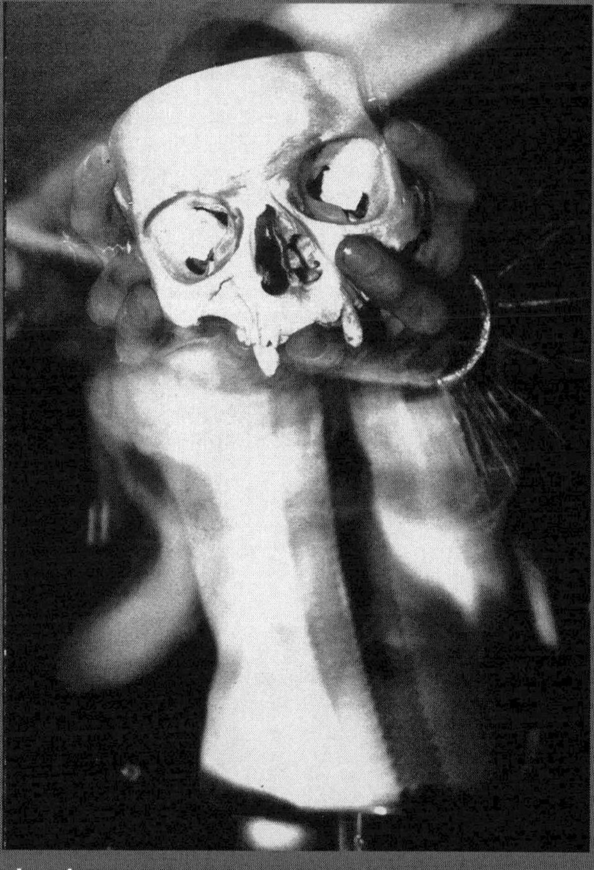

What artists (be it visually or thematically), would you acknowledge as having a direct influence on the artworks you produce? Does this differ from a range of other artists you might hold in high regards?
My earliest influences were seeing artworks in death / black metal artworks and zine. Later in industrial / noise. Biggest inspirations was Grey Wolves, Coup De Grace and SPK. For as long as I can remember I have been absorbing inspiration from classic art, religion, horror movies, occult traditions, anatomic sketches, comic books, political propaganda, literature, record covers, photography, non-art etc. Everything that have been characterized by a certain atmosphere... the biggest muse has always been Death in her many shapes.

Do you work exclusively with found source images, or do you take photos for collage use? What is your approach to developing artwork collages, both in style and theme? Do you work to a particular end intent or let the pieces evolve of their own accord? Is there any central/ core theme underpinning your work and do you have a particular defined agenda which guides your work?
The process is in many ways similar to when I create music. I begin with a conceptual theme, gather source material that I think will be useful and then let it grow forth through my subconscious. An almost unwritten rule for me when it comes to artwork is that I always try to find exclusive source material. Often through old magazines or books, or I make my own photographic arrangements. I spent many years building my visual archives and they are still most useful. Many times I use the Xerox machine as tool but also the textures of old paper is important to create certain impression. Apart from using ink and glue, I often use ingredients as blood, semen, nicotine and ashes. It gives life to the creation. Personalizes and charges the art. Many times when I work I get into a state of mind that reminds what I've read about in works of artists as Austin Osman Spare and Rosaleen Norton, related to automatic drawing. The art creates itself from my inner depths, disconnected from my conscious brain. The hand of the devil guides all my work, in one way or the other.

Do you produce artworks in differing mediums away from the recognised collage style? From my impression of your collage work, it thematically and stylistically spans a divide between 'high' and 'low' forms of art. Do you agree with this assessment and what do you see as the roles and influences of both?
In some of my exhibitions I have worked with installations with human remains and other artifacts. Object collage. I have also been doing drawings, silkscreen and photography, but I lack the skills that I wished I had. I am just a self-taught artist and many times it feels strange to even talk about what I do in terms of art, especially when comparing it to the works of true masters.
Some of these other techniques were included in the *Ghoulson* book. I guess they can be seen somewhere in the future.
As I stated in earlier answer, my inspiration is drawn from many different sources and I would have felt stagnated in my artistic expressions if I worked with the same dirty xerox aesthetics year after year.

I understand you have exhibited your artworks as part of industrial type festivals, however have you exhibited your work in galleries outside of the immediate underground industrial and related scenes? What has the response been in context of differing forums?
Conventional art spaces and galleries aren't the optimal place to exhibit art of this kind. Despite this fact, I have had a couple of 'real' exhibitions over the years. In Sweden, Norway and Balticum. The response has been good, with exception of a few upset visitors. The art establishment is something I don't want to be a part of more than necessary. I have no urge to attract new people with what I do, especially not pretentious artfags. No to new support.

A book publishing an extensive collection of your artwork *Ghoulson* has been slated for release for some time now. What is its current status and likely release?
The *Ghoulson* book was completed from my end in first months of 2012. Autarkeia was supposed to have published it shortly after but they ran into some other problems and it was postponed. I worked intensely with its completion to meet the deadline we had set. Naturally my interest in it faded after it had been delayed for several years.

I still regard the material solid enough to be published, but I consider it a bit outdated and I'd rather work with new ideas. Some of the artworks have been used in other publications, for example in this issue of *Noise Receptor*. Independent publishing these days is extremely easy, so it is possible I will make a private edition of the *Ghoulson* book once I've raised some funds.
Other long delayed book plans included *Swedish Brutes* – with text and visual material from me, Stefan Danielsson and Martin Bladh. Unfortunately I think this will never be realized either.

Beyond your underground activities, as your day to day employment I understand that you split your time between running and managing a gallery space, in addition to managing a studio complex and administrating musical activities for a cultural education institution. Noting these roles would seem to quite closely align with your personal artistic and music pursuits, however in reality are these personal activities and employment entirely separated? What is a 'typical' day or week for you?
I'd rather not bore the readers by discussing in-depth details of my employment, but let's say that I'm very satisfied with the possibilities of my current job. I have access to both xerox machines and a huge underground basement where I have my studio. Now and then I have the opportunity to curate interesting art shows at Galleri Granen, but most of the times it is same old routine. The border between personal activities and employment is very blurred but there is an important task to provide some alternatives to the flood of degenerate cultural waste.

Since 2005 you have been operating the cassette only label Styggelse, which to date has issued some 50 odd releases. Given the label seems intent on fostering support for cassette culture (and particularly did so during the early 2000's where tapes were not the 'cult' item they have become today), what is your personal view on the role of label and has its focus altered over time and have your achieved what you aimed to do?
The label was founded 10 years ago from the ashes of Krimljud, another label I had been running with some local people. One of the reasons for starting Styggelse was to spread power electronics & industrial music on cassette format. Back in those days the cassette culture was an uprising force in Sweden. Many great labels such as Abisko, Gothenburg Blood Cult, Hatband, Harsh Head Rituals, UGP, Vemod & Vigilante Tapes. I can't speak for Styggelse alone but the Swedish tape culture made a big impact on the international noise scene and set the standards for years to come. Nothing lasts forever... Obviously countries like Finland and Denmark are more active on this front nowadays. Eventually it will be revived here again.

Noting the general limitation of your releases, where have these been predominantly distributed? Is this typically Swedish focused or has there been interest from abroad? What have are the typical editions you have been working with and how has the response been overall? Has the label achieved the level of recognition you hoped/ planned for?
There has always been a rather big demand for Styggelse releases, both in Sweden and from abroad. I wish that in the past I would have operated the label in a more professional way and worked harder finding proper distribution outlets.
In early days it was almost exclusive distribution by Segerhuva (Sweden) and Molehill (Japan). Since both of them disappeared I have dealt with distribution myself, of course with help from some mail orders and stores.
Editions are usually somewhere between 50-300 copies. If they're not limited editions I duplicate them as long as there is demand. Many of the titles from the Styggelse catalogue are therefore still available for those asking.
The work I've done with the label has been most satisfying, with a few exceptions. I have always done things in my own pace and never had intention of releasing things for the sake of gaining recognition or fame. Looking back in retrospect I am proud of what I've done. There are some exceptionally good releases there and some that are not so good.
Ironically I have gained more attention for the work I did with the sub-label Bolvärk that I started some years after Styggelse. The intention was to work in similar way but with black metal and other non-electronic music. Most successful of the releases was Irkallian Oracle and No Future that sold better than any of the Styggelse releases.

Back in 2005 two Survival Unit bootleg releases were falsely issued under the Styggelse name, namely the *Honest, Reliable, Trustworthy / Nazi Boy'* 7"EP and the *Asshole* CD (with the later not even including a Survival Unit sound work). What is the actual story behind these bootlegs as it seems both odd and nonsensical to bootleg an obscure underground project with an even more obscure label? Was this someone's idea of a practical joke or personal attack?
It is old story but I think worth revealing some details about. It was a response from Ron Lessard since I was slow sending him stuff from a trade that we did ages ago. The tape label hadn't even started up back then so he was fast to help me establish the name in underground, hehe… I certainly deserved this lesson since I was a lazy fuck back then. I cared about little or nothing in those years. Of course I wish I would have done some things different but some lessons you simply need learn the hard way. Worth pointing out is that I have never been a nazi and I've always tried to stand by my word and agreements (even if it has taken time in the past)… I felt sorry for the people he ripped off selling this crap to. Shortly after this came out, I responded with doing a Survival Unit tape – *Trade Your RRRecords for a Coffin*. It could only be obtained by sending in your RRRecords releases and they would be broken into pieces and then assembled into the cover art. I was surprised with how many people ordered it and it felt horrible to destroy all the rarities that I was sent, but still I couldn't care less.

What are the current and future plans for the label?
Styggelse has been inactive for a couple of years, with the exception of *Slutstationen* compilation that I released last year and a few private editions. There will be a couple of new tapes this year to celebrate the 10 year anniversary of the label. Among them can be mentioned Aischrolatreia, a most promising American unit. There will also be a retrospective tape collecting the recorded material of Hollow Men (a post-mortem project operated by Petter Marklund / Memorandum in the mid-80s), a new tape from Alfarmania and a reissue of Kommando RJF cassette (joint release with Chefsideologens Bolag).

Final comments or additional topics you wish to address?
Thanks for your patience and interest.

Photo credits (in order of appearance): 1: Mikko Aspa, 2: uncredited, 3 & 4: Carolus Löfroos, 4: Carl Abrahamsson, 5: Mikko Aspa.

KE/HIL
Music for the Prekariat
ZONE 0 CD / LP
www.tesco-germany.com

:REMEMBERING: GENOCIDE ORGAN

: 2006 PROFILE :

In existence for two decades now, the Mannheim, Germany based Genocide Organ have slowly but surely risen to a cult level within the heavy industrial / power electronics scene. Such a status has in part been achieved through their production of an extremely physical sound approach, however its combination with delux packaging must not be underestimated, given the collector fetishism that surrounds their limited recording output. Yet for all their notoriety within the post-industrial scene, Genocide Organ remains relatively obscured and somewhat shrouded in mystery. This is in part caused by the group refraining from including member photos on releases, yet more specifically is due to refusing to conduct interviews. Personally I am only aware of one interview, published in 1999 via the fifth issue of the cult underground publication *Descent Magazine*. Interestingly the introductory blurb stated that after the interview was conducted the group requested it not to proceed to print (such a request went unheeded of course). Despite the obscure identities of the individuals behind Genocide Organ, the fact remains that the group contains four key members: Wilhelm Herich, R. Freisler, D.A.X & Doc M Riot (presumably all assumed identities), with R.Freisler later leaving to be replaced by B.Moloch (of Anenzephalia infamy).

As a collective it is evident that each of the four members has specific roles within Genocide Organ, relating to studio composition, live mixing, video arts & stage performance. With reference to live actions, a direct physical approach of noisescapes with confrontational vocals is employed, along with the symbolic use of religious and political iconography via video projections and performance art. Selected examples of such visual installations have previously involved: the Mannheim / Genocide Organ symbol being cut from a sheet of steel with a blow torch, the burning of a wooden / chainmesh cross, & the display and later destruction of crosses plastered with images of political leaders. Although live performances are few and far between within Europe, or even in their native Germany, the collective have still garnered an international underground following, having been invited to give select live actions across the globe, with countries including England, Russia, America and Japan.

In order to analyze and critique Genocide Organ's recorded output, it is evident from their lyrics, texts, images and dialogue samples that there is a clear focus on matters relating to war, the Ku Klux Klan, conspiracy theories, American imperialism, terrorism, the Third Reich, fetishism etc. Furthermore their releases come armed with titles such as: *Klan Kountry, Mind Control* and *The Truth Will Make You Free*. Additionally packaging utilises images that appear to embody loaded connotations, or otherwise seem to evoke esoteric symbolism. To put it in another context, a quote is taken from Lina Baby Doll of Deutsch Nepal whom has been a long standing fan and more recent comrade of the group: *"Genocide Organ, the heroes of German electronic chock-treatment are one of the most physical appearances within industrial culture. Every piece of sound they've released, and all live performances I ever experienced have been 100% "ultra" in all directions possible. Just to feel the weight of the heavy vinyl, study the sleeves and almost cut your hands open by the scalpels attached, among the dried bloodstains on the unpolished surface is an experience worth the long and hard search for the items. For me it's not the extreme approach of the group that make them interesting, it's the ability to withhold the possibility to go way to far out in the wasteland of cheap fetish commercialism, which for me is a sign of both intelligence and style. These are people who have got more to show than a poor tattoo and some piercings, this group shows you the truth whatever it might be. And the truth will make us free!"*

Essentially the convergence of elements (visuals, titles, text, dialogue samples, set to extreme electronic sound and overlaid with shouted/ distorted vocal delivery), creates a sensory overload ensuring that ambivalence towards their releases is almost impossible. And within such a context Genocide Organ HAVE provoked reactions from listeners: be those individuals who perceive the group have certain sympathies that align with their own, or vocal detractors labeling the group extremists, or more crudely: hate mongers. Yet of the negative responses generated, it should be said that if an individual is unwilling to look beyond the face value of ideas presented, their ability to fully appreciate or truly understand certain kinds of musical and artistic expression is immeasurably hampered. Additionally, if art (of any form) is deemed to be the pinnacle of emotional expression, each individual should interpret each emotion intrinsically stimulated: be that positive or negative. Therefore when the

extreme sound / visual art of Genocide Organ acts as the point of stimuli, any such emotive knee jerk reactions should in no way negate the validity of the art form itself. Thus for those listeners intelligent enough, or otherwise uninterested in forming simplistic & polarized views of Genocide Organ, the fascination lies in the extremity of approach provoking a myriad of intellectual questions.

But what do Genocide Organ actually stand for and represent? Do they stand for something, or nothing at all? Are they a group simply taking a mirror to modern society, reflecting the squalled depths of hatred and violence that humanity is capable of sinking to? Or do they truly embrace a nihilistic worldview and only stand to accelerate the modern world's decline? Alternately are they politically/ philosophically/ religiously inspired and seek to impose their brand of ideological indoctrination, or are they merely apolitical controversy seekers? Or are they simply purveyors of 'ultra' dry humor and irony pushed to an absolute extreme? Put any of these assertions to the groups however, none will be forthcoming with affirming or denying such theories and/ or allegations: the virtues of silence perhaps?

Equally, are the questions raised in the listener's mind significantly more important than any answer that the group could ever provide? Therefore with reference to modern society, are there any political or philosophical ideas that can be viewed in a simplistic black and white context? Consequently could it be said that Genocide Organ embrace the infinitesimal shades of interpretative grey in the way they choose to operate? Quoting from the aforementioned Descent interview it might just give some insight into the mindset of the group (or failing that, simply adding to the confusion): *"We never say what we think, and we never believe what we say, and if we tell the truth by accident, we hide it under so many lies that it is difficult to find out"* & *"Everything is as it is and nothing is as it should be"*. (*Descent Volume 5#: The Death Issue* June 1999).

Yet with time marching incessantly on, 2004 marked the release of the album *In-Konflikts*, likewise highlighting the five year gap between it and the prior *The Truth Will Make Your Free* LP. In an apparent change of tactic it would seem that the group have come the closest to revealing their core intent via the press statement accompanying the release: *"Genocide Organ don't reflect a concrete event of whatever nature, this is an abstract questioning of everything with anything, a call to action, which ends in a waste of energy ...a call for a movement which is a waste of time...a nihilistic pessimistic worldview which leads somewhere.....we all fill just space and are part of IN-KONFLIKTS"*. However, should this statement accepted merely on face value, or specifically questioned due to Genocide Organ's subterfuge and deceptive double speak of years past? Particularly could this statement be just another ideological illusion, another psychological sleight of hand and yet another philosophical 'house of smoke and mirrors'? To specifically justify such assertions a further statement included within the album's sleeve provides ample vindication: *"If you ask what this is all for, none can tell you. Never ask where this will end, you already know it anyway. What will be left behind is just a note in a history book. You might have the possibility to see but you will never know. As long as we not (sic) cross the final border all efforts will be meaningless. Don't be amused, entertained or educated ... that is not the intention"*.

To conclude it is clear that there is no single or for that matter simple interpretation that can be said to holistically represent Genocide Organ. Therefore it is useless for anyone but the group themselves to pontificate about knowing the exact answer. Thus without providing any sort of iron clad theory, could the question be posed: is confusion the real key to Genocide Organ's intent? The final interpretation is up to you.....

Richard Stevenson, January, 2006.

Article Chronology

2001/ 2002: At the time pre-planning for issue 6# of Spectrum Magazine was being undertaken and whilst I wanted to feature an interview with Genocide Organ I already knew this was highly unlikely given the group had a long established aversion to interviews, which effectively remains today. However not to be deterred from featuring some sort of content relating Genocide Organ, it was decided to write an analysis article focusing on the themes and motivations underpinning the project. The preparation of the article was also a means to document and order my own thoughts and interpretations of the meaning and intent behind the project particularly given then was little concrete information coming from the group themselves.

2002/ 2003: Towards the middle of 2002 for various reasons the decision was taken to cancel the publication of Spectrum Magazine issue 6#. Given the Genocide Organ article has been written, rather than the article going to waste it was eventually published in Degenerate Magazine (Finland) Issue 3# in 2003.

2004/ 2005: With is formal publication of the article in a respected underground magazine the article has served its purpose, yet late 2004, I was approached by the group themselves to see if I would be interested in having the article translated and published in the German *Zinnober Magazine* at some point during 2005. I of course jumped at the chance and chose to slightly expand the article as at the *In-Konflikt* has just been released. However once the article rewrite was completed and duly translated in German, disappointingly it was not published as intended given *Zinnober Magazine* folded operations before publication.

2006/ 2007: Following the setback caused by the folding of *Zinnober Magazine*, in 2006 the group asked whether I would be interested in having the article published as part of the planned ten year anniversary *:REMEMBER:* reissue. I was extremely honoured by this request and took it upon to myself to further refine and update the article, however in the end a decision was taken to only publish a short excerpt of the article as part of the *:REMEMBER:* 10 year anniversary re-release issued in 2007.

2015: Seeing that the full 2006 version of the article has to date remained unpublished in a print magazine, it is being published here for current interest and archival posterity. Hopefully the article will be of interest to readers of *Noise Receptor Journal* and more importantly raise questions in your own minds about how you interpret the meaning and intent behind Genocide Organ.

Photos: year / location / members

Photo 1: 1990 / Lever (after performance) / Riot, Herich, D.A.X
Photo 2: 1993 / Heavy Electronics Festival, Ubstadt-Weiher / Herich
Photo 3: 2000 Lille / Riot
Photo 4: 2000 / Lille / Herich, Moloch
Photo 5: 1993 / Heavy Electronics Festival Ubstadt-Weiher / Freisler, Herich, D.A.X., Riot
Photo 6: 2000 / Lille / Herich, Moloch, Riot
Photo 7: 1994 / Lille / D.A.X, Riot, Freisler, Herich
Photo 8: 1996 / Hannover / Herich, Freisler, D.A.X, Riot

reviews

by Richard Stevenson

Abre Ojos / Illuminoscillate – *A Place Of Quiet / Circle Of Spit* 7"EP Secrets of Giza 2013

Two of Australia's purveyors of modular synth driven dark ambience have teamed up for this short and sharp double A side vinyl 7"EP. Given the relative stylistic synergies between the two, hopefully this split will serve to further raise the profile of both projects.

Although the title of Abre Ojos' piece *A Place of Quiet* might be slightly misleading, it is anything but quiet. Presenting a piece of partly ritualised, multi-layered dark ambience, it includes shimmering mid ranged pulsar harmonics, sporadic gong tones, crumbling bass thumps and sub-orchestral power drones, all infused with a slight static edge. Whilst this is not significantly far from the established sound of the project, is slightly set apart due to its increased degree of drive and urgency. *Circle of Spit* is Illuminoscillate's offering and dives head long into a track of grinding black hole ambience which is partially mechanised in tone. Here a subdued percussive pulse is soon engulfed by forceful cyclic waves of sound which multiply in intensity. There is a clear and forceful tonal strength to these galactic synth drones which radiate an inherent power, before the track collapses into oblivion.

With the length limitations imposed by the format, both project manage to articulate a slightly more urgent sound than the abstract and long form works of their album counterparts. And whilst functioning within a similar sonic palette, each project clearly articulates an individual take on the experimental droning dark ambient sound. With a limitation of 100 copies is both an interesting and worthy release.

Aeoga – *Temple Treye* CD Aural Hypnox CD 2014

Temple Treye is Aeoga's third album since 2004 and evidently was recorded in 2006 but remained unreleased in the archives until now. To provide some contextual comparison the first two Aeoga albums balanced a sound between ritual soundscapes and dark ambience in a sprawling 'widescreen' style, with this general structure being retained on *Temple Treye*. Yet this pairing of ritual and dark ambient soundscapes has been augmented with a direct compositional focus to provide a clear sense of direction and drive which differs from the sparser droning framework of earlier albums.

On the opening piece *Feast of the Stance*, a prominent single wavering note (horn or perhaps organ?) forms a key focus as low drone and chimes provide a more abstract undercurrent. *Between the Crescent Hooks* follows and establishes a framework of more forceful drones and mid paced rhythms (loosely abstract guitars and rolling hand drum percussion), which gradual elevate in intensity in an upwardly ascending trajectory over its eight minute expanse. Pulling back to more abstract territory *Telemorphic Cuts* features prominent but lower register sustaining organ drones, with shimmer ritual chimes, with field recordings placed within the background (creaking wood etc. and distant wailing tones etc.). *Temple Treye* then ups the ante again and constitutes the stunning centre piece of the album. Here the title track features a composition of doom laden grinding drones, heaving bass textures, disembodied and echoed chanted vocalisations and sparse chimes, before mid-paced ritual percussion drive the tone forward to its conclusion. *Transparallel Mist* delivers a long form meditative layered drone work with micro-tonal textures, spare ritual percussive sounds, shrill and dissonant bowed strings and an undercurrent of sustained deep bass whines. Then in a type of cyclic synergy, the opening track is reprised on *Feast of the Trance*, where a similar soundscape and the same wailing sound texture bring the album full circle.

Whilst Aeoga do inhabit a sonic palate which is clearly comparable to other Aural Hypnox acts, on *Temple Treye* they exemplify a sound which is quite a bit more composed, dynamic and forceful than other label acts. Issued in two versions, including 444 standard editions (screen printed, folded cardboard sleeve with booklet insert), it also comes issued in an edition of 49 deluxe hand-made box sets (pictured), which includes a silk-screen printed canvas pouch, three large collage artwork inserts and a wooden handcrafted, fire seared, screen printed, leather hinged 'altar' styled cover (aka the *Tricuspid Treye-skladen*). Certainly this represents a striking artisan's handicraft compliment for the ritualised music found within. Despite the limited box set being already sold out, the standard edition should be readily available.

Aischrolatreia – *Sentient Prison* MC Fieldwork 2013

This is the debut tape for the American project Aischrolatreia and associated label Fieldwork where it seems the same two individuals are behind both entities. Noting Fieldwork's mission statement that they are a: *'NYC based label for confrontational and unique sound work on analogue formats'*, this professional duplicated tape and cover fits the bill perfectly, given the presentation is slick and visually grim in equal measures. As for the sonics, the tape presents an album's worth of grinding noise and industrial debris strewn soundscapes (four lengthy tracks spanning 40 minutes). The overall tone is one that verges on loosely constructed power electronics aggression, but also holds a clear affinity in style and sound to the Swedish 'post-mortem' project Alfarmania and associated morbid industrial noise cassette culture. Essentially a dank claustrophobia permeates all aspects of the sound, where fractured, churning factory machine rhythms and grinding industrial filth proliferate. Although 'noise' is used as a descriptor, this however does not verge anywhere near HNW territory, rather there is tonal separation of noise layers to allow a breadth of sound with room to breathe (yet to further qualify this, the atmosphere of *Sentient Prison* is akin to breathing a tainted atmosphere of choking smoke and ash). As such this is obscure analogue worship of shuddering distortion and squalling noise, which are presented as loosely constructed arhythmic industrial soundscapes. Sporadic incursions of anguished vocals are also evident yet relegated to another layer in the oppressive sonic mass, thus with an unhurried and calculated approach it generates an atmosphere of slow brooding menace despise its outwardly jagged tonality.

With the name 'Aischrolatreia' roughly translating to: *'the cult of the obscene; the worship of filth; a devotion to or worship of filth and obscenity'*, the chosen moniker could not have been better suited to the project. Thus in a no-frills capacity *Sentient Prison* is a solid, gritty and oppressive tape, and one which highlights both Aischrolatreia as a project and Fieldwork as a label to keep an interested eye on.

Alfarmania / Proiekt Hat – *Astral Slaktmask* MC Chefsideologens Bolag 2014

Although being familiar with the individual output of both projects, their two prior collaborations passed me by (being the *Sundsvalls Elit* MC from 2006 and the *Furyfication* LP from 2007), therefore I am not quite sure how this compares. Yet from sampling this cassette it would seem that Proiekt Hat's involvement has tempered the longer form compositions typical of Alfarmania (as this tape is very much a collection of individual tracks), whilst also injecting a greater degree of stilted, mechanised structure. Also interestingly it seems that apart from the three listed collaborations with Alfarmania, Proiekt Hat have been otherwise inactive, noting the last solo release was the *Make Sense* MC from 2006.

Given that both acts are imbedded within a lo-fi analogue Swedish industrial noise / power electronics cassette culture (aka – 'post-mortem' sound), the sound of each project compliments the other rather well. As such this tape is very much concerned with the presentation of reverb drenched analogue atmospheres and stilted caustic industrial rhythms (akin to malfunctioning conveyor belts and the like). Tracks are built upon a filthy bed of shuddering industrial debris, queasy wavering textures, random radio chatter, and general abandoned factory ambience, which is further cut through with wailing emergency sirens, drawling fog horns and other sonic clutter to generate a cold war 'radiation fallout' type ambience. The title track *Astral Slaktmask* rates a mention, being a tense track of meat grinding mid-range frequencies, sweeping drones and sporadic industrial bass thump, which stretches out over an extended length. *Full Tank* also elevates the mood through a more forceful composition of idling factory rhythms, crumbling noise and burrowing mid-range textures, and a blast furnace aesthetic typical of Alfarmania. Moving through a range of reverb drenched warehouse type atmospheres, post-apocalyptic soundscapes and passages of dark brooding death ambient intensity, the tape closes out with *Cut Felling II*, containing a queasy oscillating tone and distant machine gun blasting type distortion. Excellent stuff. Given the apparent desire for both projects to remain obscured within the underground cassette culture (or failing that, total apathy on their part for underground 'popularity'), *Austral Slaktmask* function as another audio monument to the apparent ease with which Alfarmania and Proiekt Hat evoke rugged analogue industrial noise soundscapes which are heavily imbedded with sense of dread and unease.

Alfarmania – *From Fix to Fix* CD Old Captain 2015

Originally issued on Proiekt Hat's tape label Hatband in 2004, *From Fix to Fix* was Kristian Olsson's first official foray under the guise of his new (at the time) musical project Alfarmania. Although containing some rough analogue qualities similar to Survival Unit, rather than the aggressive and antagonistic approach of that project, *From Fix to Fix* demonstrated Alfarmania's intent to deliver a more subdued post-mortem sound infused with foreboding angst. Alfarmania also differentiated itself by focusing on junkie and drug cultural, rather than the political focus of Survival Unit.

The title track leads off the album as an industrial noise meets post-mortem sound (at its murkiest), including drudging and lurching loops, queasy oscillations, shrill fire alarm bells and sporadic drug referencing samples; thus with its miasmic swirling quality it represents a solid and focused introduction. The lengthy piece *The Pale Horse Riders* is another excellent track of muffled churning industrial tonality, oscillating analogue drones and layered sustained distortion. The incorporation of a morbid death industrial pounding structure late in the piece provides some warranted focus, whilst extend drug use / user related samples again hammer down the chosen theme. Moving back towards more chaotic sonorities, *Lossa Stasen* features scattered metallic scrapping junk metal and fluttering higher toned noise and slow thudding drums of doom set within cavernous echoed tonal atmosphere. The pair of short tracks *Immune to Boredom* and *Down and Dirty* both feature clanging / swirling / chaotic industrial noise soundscapes, before the album launches headlong into the extended depths of depravity of *Sanatorium Alfarmania* – a 25 minute audial representation of the decent into drug induced psychosis. Here mechanized factory loops and buzz saw tones sit within a cavernous rumbling tonal mass, which draws the listener deep into the long form composition. Being sprawling and freeform, over its extended length additional sounds are added for harder effect (chaotic distortion, scattered siren noise, semi-buried agonized vocalizations etc.), it generates a psychedelically nightmarish effect in the process.

In reflecting of where this album sits within Alfarmania's creative arc, it is noted to contain tracks which are relatively focused and structured, thus differentiating it from later output from the project which featured a slightly looser, abstract and psychedelic post-mortem sound. The cover collage artwork of courtesy of Kristian is an excellent visual representation of the feel and mood, although the quality / thickness of the cardboard stock of the digi-pack could clearly have been improved. Having missed the original tape, it is great to finally be able to hear this album, being the focused initial strike of the now lauded Alfarmania.

Am Not - *Unpunished* CD Unrest Productions 2015
Up until recently I had only been peripherally aware of the unusually named Am Not, but this totally changed upon the release of the promo track / video for *Dark Heart Katanga* in late 2014. The video coupled with the music functioned as a singular and direct demonstration of one the strongest newcomers to the UK industrial / power electronics scene, and apart from the music being absolutely on point the accompanying video demonstrated an extremely focused thematic approach. Based on this track alone *Unpunished* was a release I was very much looking forward to and after hearing it following its recent release it does not disappoint.
The Unpunished opens the album with a solid blending of programmed elements, mixed with a heavy dose of junk metal sounds and swirling distortion. Vocals are then presented in a direct spoken style, being mixed up front for clarity and impact, with this piece squarely demonstrating Am Not being able to cultivate an individual sound within a broader power electronics / industrial / heavy electronics framework. *Beware The Black Peril* follows and sits more squarely within anthem style of pounding pulsing structure and focused flanged vocals and also nails this sound perfectly. Revving drones and overblown metallic distortion infuse for ferocious impact on the instrumental *Archangel Drone,* which is followed by the exceptional *Dark Heart Katanga* - a track driven by fast paced heavy artillery rhythms (of fist pumping proportions), further underscored with sustained organ dirge drones and slightly treated but completely audible spoken vocals to create seven minutes of structured PE anthemic perfection. The rougher distortion mangled vocals and static charged metallic pounding rhythmic approach on *The Hate That Dare Not Speak its Name* also function to highlight the sonic diversity of Am Not's approach. After the short and direct choppy distortion squall of *Extremophilia* the album concludes with *Folie A Deux;* another track of direct pounding intensity and rough yelled and flange treated vocals (which reminds somewhat of the short lived Swedish project Iron Justice).
Rather than being vague or ambiguous in intent, all lyrics are published on the six panel, cleanly designed digi-pack, and illustrate an interesting 'colonial' thematic angle which has been taken to common themes of political and societal control. With the expert blending of clean and clinical programmed elements with rougher and more chaotic sound sources, *Unpunished* is infused with a direct and focused approach. Far from being a mere copyist project with their debut album Am Not have built upon the foundations of power electronics and industrial and have twisted them into a sound of their own. Recommended.

Arbiter – *Negatively-Existent Cell* MC Fieldwork 2014
With scant information available on this apparently new project this cassette appears to be Arbiter's debut release. Although I am uncertain of the country of origin, if I were to hazard a guess I might suggest that Arbiter are an American project but which is heavily influenced by a Northern European 'industrial noise' and an analogue experimental 'tape manipulation' sound. Noting that the cassette format does the grit and intensity of this material suitable justice, with its short length (approximately 15 minutes) this could have equally been suited to another analogue medium – the 7" vinyl (...but with that said Fieldwork have to date been staunchly focused on cassette only releases).
Although *Negatively-Existent Cell* does contain sound elements which push towards nosier realms the overarching tone is one of stalking & controlled industrial noise abstraction. Thus calling this experimental industrial or even 'post-mortem' is relevant with each descriptor doing this adequate justice. Also not that I like to generally quote slabs of press releases, I do feel the succinct two sentence promo statement is exactly on the mark, and I quote: *'Two tracks of freezing paranoiac industrial. Rich layers of analogue synthesis and mechanical decreptitude'.*
The first track *Lead Laden Assemblage* by fact of its title already begins to paint a 'mind's eye' picture of the sound on display. Here analogue muted industrial to droning noise characterises the opening passage to generate a thick tone and laborious atmosphere. Things then get more complex with some understated microscopic metallic 'contact microphone' recorded textures (i.e. think a large metal canister being slowly warped and crushed), whilst the wavering / oscillating abstract factory clamour becomes slightly more forceful and rabid. The second piece *Shattered Abstractions* is slightly more loose in construction, having a more distant and cavernous atmosphere, but gradually elevates itself into more overblown and cacophonous territory consisting of shuddering blocks of sound, where morose oscillating drones are then used to tie together the overall atmosphere to achieve a broodingly excellent track.
Fieldwork may not be the biggest or the most prolific of labels, but they are doing an excellent job in building an underground industrial noise focused micro cassette label with a striking visual aesthetic. Arbiter are an excellent addition to the roster, where this is a strong and convincing debut recording.

Arktau Eos – *Scorpion Milk* CD Aural Hypnox 2014
Not constituting a new album from Arktau Eos, rather this is a re-release of an earlier limited CDr version from 2006 which formed a formed a companion to the main *Mirrorion* album issued at the same time. For this new version the packaging has been redesigned (noting the original edition constituted 222 copies with special hand painted cover). This new edition of 500 copies is housing in a beautifully designed, gold screen printed, deep metallic maroon cardboard fold out cover, with additional eight page booklet and screen printed insert.
Forming a singular meditative composition, *Scorpion Milk* covers the well-established ritual dark ambient sound of the Helixes Collective (aka the general Aural Hypnox label roster), but its structure has been further re-contextualized into a singular long form and album length drone work. Across the minimalism of its 48 minute span Arktau Eos display a single minded determination which ensures it remains fully engaging despite the catatonic pace and evolution of the composition. Here string instruments are played in a sparse manner, where strings are played / struck / bowed, with the resulting singular reverberating notes left to ring and radiate out and shimmer off into the distant catacomb depths. In select passages barely present ritualistic chimes and sparse higher ranged atonal played piano notes sit off in the distant, whist wavering chants and whispered evocations rise from the ether. Although in no way constituting 'doom drone' in scope, this is perhaps how the doom drone experimentalists Sunn 0))) might sound if they were to choose play with entirely acoustic

instrumentation (food for thought).
To conclude a minimalist review for a minimalist album, *Scorpion Milk* is every part as strong as other albums from Arktau Eos and more broadly the Aural Hypnox label. Sublime.

Armour Group – *Live Assault* MC Trapdoor Tapes 2014
German Army – *German Army* MC Trapdoor Tapes 2014
Word of Life Church SS – *Death Pig* MC Trapdoor Tapes / Magik Crowbar 2013

By way of a brief label introduction, Trapdoor Tapes are a micro-tape label from Australia that has issued around 80 releases in relative obscurity since 2005. Releasing material from both local projects and known international acts, the general focus is on the murky end of underground noise and industrial they have carved out their own particular niche, issuing limited editions with a lo-fi sound and rough DIY photocopied visual aesthetic. Following below is a short rundown of a recent batch of releases from the label.
Amour Group is up first and a rather mysterious project. From the limited available information Armour Group is an Australian act involving Harriet Kate Morgan & Luke Holland. *Live Assault* seems to be debut release and as is suggested by the title is a 16 minute tape of two short live recordings (or perhaps are excerpts of longer live sets?). Here the sound is concerned with ominous shuddering industrial noise with a rough, grinding, reverb drenched tone. Mangled vocals are then spewed forth over this analogue base, whipping in their distorted intensity. Being rather loose and chaotic but also maintaining a vague sense of structure, the predominant lower end rumble occasionally breaks out into a high pitched noise squall. Likewise with the recording being somewhat muffled in tone, it only tends to amplify the audio grit. Essentially the static fried frequencies, cascading noise, war zone samples and muffled industrialised rumble generates fierce and oppressive battlefield ambience. In a no-frills capacity Armour Group deliver a grime and chaos infused atmosphere which builds to overblown intensity. Solid and aggressive stuff.
Up next is a new tape from hyper productive German Army (in excess of 20 releases since 2011) which delivers another eclectic offering. Possibly to be described as a bizarre version of post-punk mixed with tribal post-industrial, this description still does not quite do this justice. To provide another marker there is something similar to the quirky playfulness of Deutsch Nepal, but which German Army entirely make their own. Being less post-punk and slightly weirder in scope than other German Army material I have heard, there is a psychedelic 'stream of consciousness' style to the material. Spanning 12 tracks and 32 minutes the material is mostly instrumental where there is an overarching hazy lo-fi aesthetic at play. Here the compositions rely on quirky groupings of elements which include: layered tribal-esque rhythms and beats, ritualistic gongs / chimes, meandering bass, casio keyboards and programmed beats, weird synth soundscapes, samples choral vocals, overblown drone riffs etc. Where vocals are infrequently used they feature in a strangely twisted spoken disembodied style, and to add to the twisted and disorientating nature of the tracks they occasionally sound like multiple songs are being played over one another. The final album track *Pagan Fruit* rates a mention for its beach sunset Americana vibe where layered bluesy but uplifting guitars shine. On this tape German Army retains a consistent quality of output, despite the hyper speed of new releases.
For the final of the tapes Word of Life Church SS is not all like what the project name might suggest, meaning this is neither martial industrial nor power electronics. Rather the group's sound delivers lo-fi analogue industrial noise soundscapes. For sake of context this Australian project appears to consist of a loose collective of contributors which have included the inputs of Ben Taylor, Harriet Kate Morgan, Luke Holland and Tom Miller depending on the release (…noting that Ben Taylor is not featured on this particular recording). Two lengthy untitled tracks make up this 30 minute tape, where the lo-fi, muddied post-industrial sprawling filth is loose and semi-improvised in feel. Likewise its subdued and muffled analogue rumble begs a comparison to a European 'post-mortem' cassette culture sound. With a hollow, muffled and distant echoed tone the atmosphere is one of slow grinding and general elevating menace. The flip side features a similar tone, where some stilted quasi militant percussion provides a muted semblance of structure which gradually gets buried under layered sonic grit. Being rather more subdued than my initial expectation, on face value this tape sounds more like a solo project than the product of a collective approach. An oppressive analogue electronic tape nonetheless.
To wrap up the mini-label showcase, from sound to DIY visual aesthetic Trapdoor Tapes have a focused and well-rounded understanding of what they are seeking to achieve, and will surely please listeners who seek out industrial, noise and general weird underground musical obscurities.

Atrium Carceri & Eldar - *Sacrosanct* CD 2012 Infinite Fog Productions

This is a bit of an older album which I have recently checked out, and whilst I am well aware of both projects, I have not necessarily listened to a great deal of their rather large discographies (each with 10 or so albums each to date). Likewise the projects should be recognized for their former association with the cult but now defunct Cold Meat Industry label.
So to establish where the sound of this collaboration might fall, generally speaking Atrium Carceri delve into a cinematic dark ambient sound, whilst Eldar have been more varied in the musical expression under a general 'industrial' banner, covering elements dark ambient, martial industrial and neo-classical etc. Despite the differences in sound for each project, for this collaboration the sound palate has opted to largely stick to animated dark ambient realms. Early album track *Tomorrow's Dust* is of the sweeping cinematic style with a darker undercurrent weaving throughout, whilst the programmed pulse provides an aspect of force to the compositions structure. *Freeman* is a touch divergent with its minimalist programed beat (more akin to a rhythmic heart beat thump), mixed with sweeping yet solemn orchestral layers. Similar programming in the form of rolling tribal and electronics tinged percussion reappears on mid album track *Betrayal,* while occasional flourishes of musicality are also apparent, such as minimalist piano which features *So They Speak, SOL* and *Burial.* Ultimately what is delivered on *Sacrosanct* is an album which sits staunchly within a dark ambient realm - a realm of dusky twilight and desolate streets filled with crumbling and abandoned buildings; and if you look closely at the mostly black cover, a darkened silhouette of a city skyline is featured which is a rather apt visual representation of the album's mood. This a solemn and enjoyably immersive listen and although I would not put this is a 'classic' or even 'astounding' category, rather this is a strong and very enjoyable dark ambient album - nothing more, nothing less.

Aural Hypnox – *Underworld Transmissions I* MC Aural Hypnox 2014
Aural Hypnox – *Underworld Transmissions II* MC Aural Hypnox 2014

Through the newly launched *Underworld Transmissions* series the Aural Hypnox label has been turned into an 'artist / project' of sorts through the use of an intriguingly conceptual device. Thus in words of the label: *'Underworld Transmissions is Aural Hypnox label series, filmed and captured on tape in the private séances held in our subterranean lodge located in Oulu, Northern Ostrobothnia. The concept is to invite artists from the Helixes collective, in different combinations, to join a séance and through sound and movement to establish an elemental communication. In greater sense, apart from personal goals, the séances aim to bring forth the seasonal currents of the lodge; the undertone of the Aural Hypnox label and the artists involved'.* Due to its apparent improvisational nature, the musical output of both cassette's sits more at the abstract end of label's discography and in sonic terms this is possibly most comparable to the minimalist style of Aural Holograms (a lone album was released by Aural Hypnox back in 2007).

On *Underworld Transmission I*, the first side of the tape features *Séance I / 2013 (November 2013)* and is a composition of deep subterranean atmospheres, slow sustained drones generated by sparse bowed and blown instruments. Additionally some distant chants appear to mark the path, and assist in evoking a minimalist meditative aura. *Séance I / 2014 (January 2014)* takes up the second side, and although still minimalist in style is slightly more animated, with a mid-pointed tonal range and wavering notes looping in a non-melodious patterns. Of these two séance offerings (and specifically when considered as an audio document) this is somewhat less engaging.

Moving onto *Underworld Transmission II*, *Séance II / 2014 (March 2014)* is captured on the first side of the tape. The track takes a short moment to get going but quickly elevates into a heavily cinematic, ritual ambient soundscape. Although drones form the compositional backbone, tense and urgent abstract sounds sweep and pan through the speakers, coupled with sustained atonal horn and string notes which rise to elevated crescendos of almost modern classical proportions (Penderecki certainly comes to mind in the later more animated sections of the piece). *Séance III / 2014 (April, 2014)* is then found on the second side, evoking a dank catacomb atmosphere with slow pounding ritualised thump, buried chants and abstract scraping / creaking textural sounds, which at its sonic peak is not too far from a death industrial style. Great in other words.

With each release being limited to a mere 50 copies, the professional duplicated tapes are packaged is in a small fold out cardboard box, with a 10 panel booklet of sigils and séance associated images. Whilst musically these are at the slightly more abstract end for the Aural Hypnox Collective, nevertheless these releases clearly constitute special collectible obscurities which are destined to be highly sought after by label fanatics. However for those not interested in the physical aspect of these releases, each séance has been published with an accompanying ritualised video which can be viewed via on Aural Hypnox's website.

Brighter Death Now – *With Promises of Death* CD Familjegraven 2014

Brighter Death Now (BDN) aka Roger Karmanik has finally returned to reclaim his position in the death industrial / power electronic underground. Whilst Roger's general absence in the past few years was widely noted it was not a case that he had officially quit, rather was on self-imposed hiatus based on some major personal upheavals (what doesn't kill you makes you stronger as the saying goes). Likewise with the paralleled demise of the Cold Meat Industry label, *With Promises of Death* also marks the launch of Roger's new label Familjegraven which is dedicated to releasing all things related to BDN (like a phoenix from the ashes as the saying goes).

To place *With Promises of Death* within BDN's back catalogue it needs to be considered in context of the overall arc of the project, where BDN's legacy is built upon a clearly unequalled run of classic albums which includes: *Great Death (I, II & III), Necrose Evangelicum, Innerwar* and *May All Be Dead.* However on the following albums *Obsessis* and *Kamikaze Kabaret* (issued during the early to mid 2000's period) there was a definite feeling of diminishing returns and perhaps a lack of conviction or Roger merely going through the motions. Likewise despite having numerous releases since 2005's *Kamikaze Kabaret*, these are mostly live albums or compilations*, which means that *With Promises of Death* is the first proper full length in nine long years. Noting that the BDN's sound and visual aesthetic has been long established, you should by now have at least a cursory appreciation of what to expect. So although this new album picks up within what will be a recognised vein, at the same time Roger has not sounded this vital and invigorated in years. Thus rather than reinventing the BDN sound, this album 'cherry picks'

elements and approaches from early albums which in turn makes for a varied sounding release. The title track leads off the album and includes an excellent introductory ranting religious speech sample (which can also be re-contextualised to have parallel meaning to Roger's own circumstances), and when the track itself kicks in it is a barely restrained wall of sweeping industrial noise, crushing bass tones, semi-buried rhythmic pulses and yelled distortion echoed vocals which mirrors the most aggressive moments of *Innerwar.* The following piece *Hate is for Beginners* then takes up mantle of the throbbing mid paced rhythmic approach of *May All Be Dead*, whist the production of *Tempting Murder* has a certain tone and aggressiveness again lifted from *Innerwar.* Alternatively the squelching tone and idling rhythms *The Cover Up* is not particularly typical of any former album, whereas *Incomprehensible Evil* marks the album's gradual descent into the murky death industrial depths found on *Necrose Evangelicum.* The following *To Die Lullabye* forms is another piece lifted entirely from the *Necrose Evangelicum* mold and with is grim industrial drones, and meat grinding ambience perhaps even arcs back further to the focused sound of *The Slaughterhouse*. Excellent in other words. *In the Shadow of Death* in some ways is the most divergent piece of the album with its rolling / pounding rhythmic drive and clearly audible half sung / half chanted vocals placed prominently in the mix is absolutely superb and perhaps marks a future direction for Roger within the established BDN template. The final track *End of the 80's* is an almost throwaway ditty, consisting of a sampled cabaret / jazz song overlaid with sparse and sporadic clanging metallic industrial textures and sampled vocal passage, but the meaning is lost on me as it is not in English**.
Having been a long term devotee of BDN (the personal impact which the *Great Death* box set had on my appreciation of 'music' 20 years ago now cannot be underestimated), I was obviously intrigued but equally apprehensive of what Roger would deliver on this new album. Having let this album settle into my psyche over the course of a couple of months, it is an album which will demand an equal position well up the ranks of BDN's discography and although it may not topple the recognised classics, it instead delivers a strong, faithful and most importantly a vital sounding edition to the BDN canon. Certainly a welcomed return.

---

* - The two issued LP's in the *1890* series are part of a separate and specific concept, thus stand apart within BDN's discography.
** - This track could also been seen as in keeping with the bleak / black humour which has often characterised Roger's work, but which is often undetected or unacknowledged.

Cold Life – *Cold Life* MC Trapdoor Tapes 2014
Military Position – *Anti-Human* MC Trapdoor Tapes 2015
Here is another batch of releases from Trapdoor Tapes which function to collectively illustrate the diversity of 'industrial' material being issued by the label.
For the Cold Life tape this would appear to be their debut tape, which is focused on analogue, synth driven, minimal industrial to post-punk music (which I must admit seems to be relatively in vogue in recent years). five short-ish tracks feature here (being repeating both sides of the tape), where the material is structured around simplistic programed mid-paced to up-tempo beats, over which the straight-forward synth melodies generally follow. Vocals are then overlaid in a partly spoken / sung style, which are also partially treated with a flange or vocoder effect depending on the track. There is also a rough 'under-produced' and noise infused feel to the production which gives it a degree of sonic grit and texture, which obviously works well with the analogue tape format. The mid tape track *Safe* slightly deviates from the general approach described above, by featuring a darker edge to its soundscape, built around a minor keys synth line and more subdued programming. As demonstrated on this tape Cold Life nails its chosen analog electronic post-punk style with flair and a certain 'no-frills' directness. Although not necessarily bringing anything new to the table this will obviously be of clear interest for those into this style.
Military Position on the other hand is the solo project of Harriet Kate Morgan which focuses on crude analogue industrial expression mixed with elements of a muted power electronics tone. This 22 minute tape features four tracks (two each side) with the visual presentation opting to skew the typically expected colours and visual themes.
We Rot commences the tape with a relatively simplistic heavy and ominous toned analogue industrial loop (being gradually morphed over its length), and slightly flanged spoken vocals brings to mind the delivery of vocals of Puce Mary - which no doubt is based on the fact that both projects being female fronted and inhabiting a similar sonic style. *Destruction and Abuse* follows, being constructed with 'idling machine' sounding loops, where the spoken vocals are mostly buried under the sonic mass (a section consisting of a 'whipping' loop is tacked onto the end before it cuts out as the side finishes). *The Personal is the Political* opens the second side of the tape, although is listed on the cover as the final of the four tracks. With its apathy inflected and mild echo and distortion addled spoken vocals, it again bringing to mind the vocals of Puce Mary, which here are combined with rumbling bass tone and minimalist death industrial pulse. This is the standout of track of the tape by nailing a convincing analogue death industrial sound. The final track *Privileged and Weak* contains a couple of segments, including a short interlude of heavy mid-paced pounding industrial beat and flanged vocals (great!) which cuts out somewhat abruptly before the main section arrives with slow and queasy oscillations (proceeding through a few sectional rotations before cutting out due to tape length).
Overall *Anti-Human* is a solid offering insofar as it demonstrates some strong ideas from a project finding its feet. This is not faultless tape, noting that added volume for sonic punch and more layering of elements for extra complexity and diversity would steps things up a notch. But such quibbles aside, more importantly it displays all the hallmarks of having the right sound, direction and ideas: where the approach of Military Position will no doubt be further refined with future releases.

Concrete Mascara – *Relic Of Vanity* 7"EP Filth & Violence / Untergeschoss 2012
Sick Seed – *Helsingin Synagogat* 7"EP Filth & Violence / Untergeschoss 2013
Graustich – *Werwolf Integrity* 7"EP Filth & Violence / Untergeschoss 2014

Here is a handful of 7"EP's which have been co-released via the two underground Finnish labels Filth & Violence and Untergeschross. Although each release can be broadly slotted under the power electronics / industrial genres, they also differ drastically in sound and approach, thus demonstrating the diversity which can be achieved under such genre classifications. Diverse vehement malice if you will.

Up first is Concrete Mascara (with this being my first introduction to the project), who incidentally hail from the US. From this release they clearly operate at the brutal and nasty end of power electronics and industrial noise. *Vapour Slave* opens the 7"EP and works on almost on two separate levels, where this forms an amalgam of mid to high range squalling and punishing noise, which floats over a crushing bass rumble and anguished vocal attack. Weighty to say the least. *Pylons of Skin* is found on the flip side, and here maintains a similar dual layered approach, balancing ear shredding high-pitched noise and a wall of crushing bass and chaotic oscillating textures.

Up next is Sick Seed with their *Helsingin Synagogat* 7"EP, where they embody a rather different approach for what the project might be recognized for. The opening title track is pretty much a direct industrial 'song', being built around crude cave man styled bass playing, squelching feedback loop and screeched / yelled vocals, with a later segment getting even more loose with a chaotically riffed electric slide guitar (?!?). Strange, strange indeed. Side B brings a more 'standard' Sick Seed approach on the blink and you will miss it *Teeth Pt.2* (only one minute 22 seconds in length), which brings junk metal rumble, random power tool generated sounds and yelled vocals (for interest's sake *Teeth Pt.1* was of similar style / length and issued on the split release with Shift). The final of three tracks *Angel Smith* then reverts back to the weird. Here sparse and distant junk metal clatter are accompanied by loose twangy acoustic guitar and spoken vocals to create an 'industrial folk' version of Finnish noise (?!?). Noting that this track is dedicated to the 'outsider' folk / blues musician Jandek, this is at least an explanation for the deviation of sound.

Up last are Graustich, who are yet another previously unknown project, but based on this 7"EP are a very promising act. On the first track *Es Geht Wieter* it is introduced with a WWII radio sample, which bleeds into an undercurrent of oscillating textures, complimented with a pounding militant industrial beat, swooping aircraft bomber samples, and flanged partially buried vocals to create a simplistic yet entirely effective industrial / power electronics sound. *The Roots of Evil* follows with a heavier oscillating bass rumble and thundering catatonic beat, before a crushing wall of distortion seeps into the mix. On side B *Werwolf* is more animated with thick mid-range burrowing pulse and squelching noise, German language samples, queasy descending atonal notes, and loose militant styled percussion. Although Graustich embody a relatively straight forward (semi-subdued) power electronics approach, all sonic elements are handled with skill for maximum effect.

In a general sense none of these 7"EP's would qualify as 'gateway' releases for those uninitiated to the power electronics genre, but that is far from the point. Obviously both Filth & Violence and Untergeschoss are both intent on releasing the nastiest examples of power electronics / industrial noise for the educated underground connoisseur, with each of these 7"EP's being clear examples of this modus operandi.

Consumer Electronics – *Estuary English* 2xLP Dirter Promotions 2014

Following William Bennett's disbandment of Whitehouse in 2008, Phillip Best obviously threw his attention into his own Consumer Electronics project, which since its reactivation in 2007 has gone through a couple of collaborative line-ups. Most recently it has solidified around Phillip Best (obviously), Russell Haswell as producer / electronics and Sarah Froelich (now Sarah Best) also on electronics and occasional vocals. Yet in the months before this album was released a minor 'internet controversy' erupted in response to a number of recent live shows, raising question of what could potential be expected from the new album. Topics of contention focused on the supposed digital sound of new material, the use of (gasp!) 'techno beats', and not least Sarah's vocals. Such controversy was further stoked when it was announced the new album was a mere 22 minutes long, but being pressed at 45rpm on 2xLP.

Given that I personally do not care for the digital vs analogue debate; I am more interested in the overall feel and impact of a recording. So yes, *Estuary English* does feature a digital, crisp, clean and most importantly loud production, but this works given the tonal variety across its six main tracks and the sheer force of its sonics. But this is also a Consumer Electronics album; where a huge degree of focus will be on the vocals and lyrics. Thankfully *Estuary English* features some of Phillip's most focused and densely constructed lyrics to date, which are all the more powerful given the force of their delivery and most importantly the quality of their recording. Effectively each spat word drips with disgust and sheer disdain, being an eviscerating 'naughty word' laden examination of contemporary UK society and cutting individual focused psychoanalysis. In fact, regardless of its sonic backing it is the lyrics, the spiteful means of their delivery and their clarity which makes them THE standout element of the album.

Teknon opens proceedings, with a clear focus on the vocals which can hardly be ignored given they are sharply focused and mixed upfront - the only musical elements being a 'barely there' fractured squelching tone. *Affirmation* follows and is structured around an queasy oscillating drone and scattered sound elements, with the ranting vocals again being pushed to the front of the mix. *Sex Offender Boyfriend* is easily the album standout; an absolute revelation of a track, featuring muted muffled semi rhythmic beat and droning sweeping layers which pan left and right through the speakers, whilst the brilliantly dense and manic vocals are pushed to over the top, self-choking intensity. This album is worth it for this piece alone in all its four minute glory. *Come Clean* follows, constituting a fierce reworking of *Cockpit* from the *Crowd Pleaser* LP from 2009, here being a two minute blasting wall of piercing tones and shuddering, overdriven noise mayhem; the vocals processed with a sharp digital edge and semi-buried within the mangled sonic mass. Another album highlight. However *Co-opted* is the weakest track on offer (and longest at five minutes), but not so much for the musical

framework of grinding semi-muted 4/4 techno structures and pulsing sweeping digital noise (….although the 'music' does sound somewhat pedestrian and uninspired). Rather this track is the weakest for its absolute lack of lyrics, where only the single phrase *"Co-opted by Cunts"* is repeated over and over, consequently becoming flaccid in its potential impact. But then again maybe I am missing the point and each listener is meant to critically self-evaluable whether they are in fact one of the 'cunts' co-opting the underground power electronics scene? Interestingly this is the only piece where Sarah gets to display her vocals but which are relegated to a mere couple of wailing backing vocal lines late in the track. Critically speaking Sarah's vocals pail in compassion to the rock hardened spite of Phillip's, so it remains to be seen whether Sarah's vocals will become a lead feature on future albums. After this somewhat filler of a piece, the title track redeems proceedings with blasting digital mayhem and the sharply invasive lyrical tirade. Finishing with a rather poetic 30 second spoken word piece *Air Lock, Estuary English* feels FAR longer than its mere 22 minutes play time, which only exemplifies the extent of ideas crammed into this album over such a short span.

Noting I did not come to this album with any of expectations of what I wanted it to be, rather I aimed to listen with an open ears to the potential alternative directions Phillip might be pushing the project. Regardless of the back and forth arguments over the short run time, its digital sound, the chosen format of two x 45rpm LP's for such a short release etc., this has been for me at least one of the most listened to and appreciated albums of recent times. It is an album I have returned to regularly, and despite its outwardly spiteful negatively, when it hits its mark there is an aspect of unbridled ecstasy when listening to this. The apparent outward chaos on initial listens also falls away over repeated listens, to revealed the degree of meticulous detail of the album's construction. Although Consumer Electronics have often been passed off as a mere a side note to Whitehouse, *Estuary English* demonstrates they remain an individual force to be reckoned with.

Deaf Machine – *Transistor* CD Raubbau 2008
Deaf Machine – *Found Sounds* CD Raubbau 2008

The label Rabbau seems to be similar to myself, in that they have a soft spot if not all out obsession for early 1990's Swedish industrial obscurities. Deaf Machine is one such project whom were a short lived project of Mikael Svensson who was also a founding member of Megaptera before his departure leaving Peter Nyström to carry on. Deaf Machine also have a loose connection with the early era of the Cold Meat Industry label, noting that two of their tracks where included on *In the Butcher's Backyard* compilation from 1993. In order to prevent Deaf Machine from languishing in total obscurity, Raubbau have taken the initiative to release the complete recordings of Deaf Machine (spanning two separate CD's).

Transistor was the first recording from the project and given the original tape was issued in 1992 in only 10 copies it gives an indication of exactly how obscure the project was and no doubt this re-release will be the means for many to hear this music for the first time. Looking back at the context of when this material was released, this was during a time when the Swedish death industrial sound was in its infancy and its key hallmarks were still being bedded down. Likewise given its obscure muffled sound, and occasional scattered micro-tonal elements, there is partial a degree of affinity here with a 'post-mortem' style. Thus *Transistor* inhabits a loose analog sound, primarily built on fuzzed out radio static, cavernous bass addled tones, morbid tonal pulsations and slow thumping industrial rhythms, whilst on occasion radio songs and news reports randomly bleed into the mix. Given the newly designed cover imagery features ice covered plants and frozen landscapes, it is a suitable representation of the cold industrial soundscapes found within. The cover also features liner notes include text provided by scene notables Jason Mantis, Kyle Wright and Bauke van der Wal (among others) which provides context to the early impact of the group.

The second CD *Found Noises* functions to collect together all remaining recordings from the group, which includes: five tracks from a 1992 split tape with Instant Cold Commando (two of these tracks were also featured on the Cold Meat Industry *In The Butcher's Backyard* compilation); one track from 1995 on Harmonie's Le Cénacle cassette compilation; one track from 1994 on Slaughter Productions Death Odors CD compilation; and one unreleased track (year unlisted). For the sound of *Found Noises* it follows the established stylistic template, however has been slightly honed in focus and execution to inhabit a darker and more forceful hue (whereas *Transistor* was slightly more experimental in guise). Radio chatter is still sporadically used, but the darker sound is augmented with garbled, chanted vocals and slow thrummed bass to bulk out the lower end of the sound. *Reaction* is a particular stand-out, with it muffled echoed soundscape and semi-buried maudlin synth line, while the movie dialogue samples and grinding death industrial sounds of *At The*

End and *Silent Intruder* also draws parallels to the early works of Megaptera. *Injection* is the most divergent piece on offer with its focused electronic programming, while the final album track (and seemingly the final recording for the project) comes in the form of *Final Destination*, which was originally featured on the now classic *Death Odors* compilation. Here the extended track is a great example of a mechanically driven, rhythmic death industrial soundscape, with floating layered synths etc. and showed much promise from a project which for whatever reason simply did not continue further (the cover includes a short interview with Mikael Svensson which covers the reason why).
With both CD's representing a history lesson on one of the obscurest projects of the Swedish death industrial sound, Raubbau should be commended for resurrecting these recordings and issuing these albums for both posterity's sake and general listening pleasure.

Death Pact International - *Australian Units* CD L.White Records 2014
Here is another instalment in the Death Pact International (DPI) conceptual 'cultural terrorist manifesto' experiment, where the following statement provides important context: *'A moniker devised in 1985 by members of what are now The Grey Wolves. Anyone may use the DPI name to release music, publish printed material, or perform at live events. Such material has no copyright and is the property of everyone. It may be reused or reprinted by any person in any manner, provided that the DPI name is retained'.*
This time around DPI constitutes a loose collective of Australian artists which should have already been self-evident from the album's title. Although identifying individual contributions to this album is really missing the point, nevertheless *Australian Units* has been developed with the inputs of both recognized and obscured projects, including: Bonsai Kitten, Burden of Administration, Chrysalis, Die Like A God, Ebola Disco, Isomer, Michael J Ellingford, Screwtape and Streicher. Sitting at the more scuzzy end of industrial and combined with unrefined power electronics, some pieces also veer towards a dark ambient and / or noise vein, which collectively span a whopping 75 minutes. Yet without attempting to match tracks to contributors, some impressions and highlights of the 16 tracks are outlined below. *Intro* leads off the album being a relatively subdued and short piece of industrial noise built with shuddering tape loops, junk metal abuse and looped sample, before the second *untitled* track launches into a full power electronics barrage of loosely layered and distortion blizzard focused angst, including partially buried barked vocals. Both pieces are crude, aggressive and certainly hit the mark. On the other hand the fourth track *Void* is focused on chaotic distortion blasts and choppy noise cut ups where its intensity is emphasized due the sporadic gaps of almost silence. The fifth piece *Degenerated Blood* then features a militant orchestral underpinning (mangled samples perhaps?) counterpointing its rough industrial noise, building to cascading intensity over its length. *Sins of Memory* stands out from the bulk of material by virtue of being more industrial tinged dark ambience with its maudlin sub-orchestral synth textures and looped Australian accent inflected sample, as an agonised voice screams somewhere off in the depths of some cavernous space. The ninth *untitled* track then marks its approach with shuddering industrial noise and semi-buried vocals, with an underpinning sustained quasi-orchestral drone for solid effect. The twelth (again) *untitled* piece provides some respite from the sonic chaos of preceding pieces, where it is built around cavernous factory basement drones (…as machines slowly grind on the levels above…), with the whispered vocalisations providing an unnerving element. Late album cut *You* is a short track embodying an atmosphere of urgency, driven by harsh cyclic distortion, squalling noise and unintelligible treated vocalisations, being focused and absolutely to the point. *Wall of Spiders* then forms the last official track (a sixteenth unlisted is featured), being chaotic and barely structured tempest of mid toned noise.
Intriguingly the final unlisted track features a prominent sample of an aggressive and psychologically unhinged phone conversation with a call centre operator (which itself is echo treated and mixed with a sweeping industrial noise backing). Thus this sample along with a number of other excellent samples scattered throughout the album functions to collectively illustrate the harshness of the Australian accent, as well the psyche of certain aggressive and antagonistic character types, and provides a positive degree of local flavour to this particular DPI unit. In an overarching sense *Australian Units* is sprawling in feel which clearly can be put down to the multiple sources of sonic input. Yet at the same time a general degree of coherence is provided by the generally unrefined, brutal and loose approach to its mix of power electronics and industrial, meaning the album does not feel like a collection of disparate tracks on an unfocused compilation. For its presentation a slick 'slim line' DVD case with printed DPI manifesto completes the well rounded package.

Decondition – *Sukellan Tuntemattomiin Syvyyksiin* CD Nuit Et Brouillard 2014
Decondition are a Finnish project previously unknown to these ears, although a prior cassette *The Universal Nothingness* was released by Freak Animal back in 2006. Evidently the 13 tracks featured here were recorded during various sessions both prior to and after *The Universal Nothingness* sessions, and with the title translating to *I Dive into Unknown Depths* it appears a hefty dose of nihilism is the conceptual underpinning of the album. To provide a quick overview of their approach, Decondition inhabit a sonic realm which is an amalgam of overblown distortion, off kilter factory clatter, clanging junk metal arrhythmia and occasional segments of respite.
From the opening passages of the album the crumbling waves of distortion and squalling static articulate the sonic timbre of harsh noise, yet there is a semblance of structure due to cyclic loops, imbedded samples and occasional barrage of unintelligible aggressive vocals which provides an industrial verging on power electronics angle to the sound. The third track functions to prove this point; when *Dark Clouds Over My Inner Landscape* arrives it demonstrates a focused, loosely rhythmic and pulsing power electronics offering. Despite it clattering intensity mid album piece *Disease Within* manages a partially meditative quality, which is mostly due to its grinding cement mixer rhythmic loops (as agonised vocals yell a sermon of angst and inner turmoil). *Wheel of Change / Passage of Time* is another standout due to it pulling back on the heady distortion of preceding material, instead utilising a rhythmic militant industrial approach. Late album track *Aistiharhojen Luoma Todellisuus [Sukellan Tuntemattomiin Syvyyksiin]* is another example of restraint (and one of the longer album tracks at just six and a half minutes), with a

subdued soundscape of cavernous industrial drones and slowly manipulating textures. This paring back of intensity bleeds into to the final album track *Deep Sleep In My Dreams*, but on this piece accommodates a more suitably drugged and hazy atmosphere to match its title.

On a cursory level this album appears rather punishing and admittedly Decondition do deliver a strong set of industrial / noise / power electronics for the underground genre fanatic (which is further complimented with suitable decaying factory images). Yet there is also clear variation to be discovered within its general harsh abrasiveness. In effect this is a solid, hour's length album of noisy, distorted, arrhythmic to rhythmic industrial noise abuse, mixed with elements of power electronics aggression and offset by moments of restraint.

Dissecting Table / Sektor 304 – *Utopia / Decay* LP Malignant Records 2014

Dissecting Table and Sektor 304 have teamed up for this split release which is the second paring of these two industrial projects. On the earlier split CD from 2012 it featured each act remixing the others source material, whereas this split features new individual material from both.

Dissecting Table lead off on the first side where Ichiro Tsuji delivers a slab of his trademark pummeling, manic and chaotic rhythmic industrial. *Ideal Market* features digital squalling noise placed over a base of fast paced tribal / rhythmic metallic percussion including mirroring bass guitar playing (in amongst the general chaos the track does fall into occasional moments of respite). *Cover Pressure Rank* follows and matches the commotion of first track, but here the drumming approach is more of a standard kit style than tribal driven (in fact segments of this track are even more squalling and chaotic than anything preceding it). Although the last of three tracks *Blind Despair and Hope* does not significantly deviate in style, it does evoke an atmosphere akin to a 'chase' scene from a 1980's styled horror movie. Being stylistically quirky in tone the final segment pulls back to a short section of calm Asiatic ritual chimes before one final chaotic rhythmic run to the final vinyl groove. Essentially your appreciation of the first side of the vinyl will be very much guided by your feelings for prior Dissecting Table material as this is pretty much solid and typical fare for the project (aka overblown rhythmic industrial chaos).

Moving onto Sektor 304's side, it presents a singular sound work spanning four interconnecting tracks. *Motion Through Pressure* leads off with a lurching militant industrial throb, which is less of the industrial percussive style the band is known for (and effectively acts as the introductory segment). Leading directly into *Vertical Structure Control,* the second segment is more stereotypical of Sektor 304, meaning excellent classic sounding 'oil barrel' industrial with a heavy percussive structure. Here Martin Bladh is featured as a guest vocalist, where his slightly treated spoken vocals make an appearance (seemingly reciting technical related information), as a second heavier vocal line urgently yells in the background (is this also Martin? Not quite sure). *Aftermath Data Analysis* falls into a more minimalist camp with a metallic throb / clinical pulse and sparse industrial scraping textures, again featuring the layered spoken vocals of Martin. The final segment *Power Through Strength* arrives to reprise the slow lurching militant industrial rhythm of the opening passage, but drawing this out over an extended length. Here the piece expertly builds tension through the gradual introduction of heavier percussive / metallic elements, in addition to a misanthropic dialogue sample. As displayed on their side of the vinyl Sektor 304 continue to expand the scope of their now recognized 'old school' (but forward thinking) industrial approach, by pushing their sound into more diverse sonic territories, with simply excellent results.

Given the chosen format it is great to see that Malignant Records are embracing the vinyl medium which also includes the recent Jarl / Skin Area collaboration split LP. However with a limitation of only 200 copies, this is unlikely to be around for long.

Downfall of Nur - *Umbras E Forestas* CDep Ksenza Records / Infinite Fog Productions 2015

Ordinarily I would not review black metal releases despite having followed the arc and evolution of the genre since the early 1990's. Downfall of Nur are something a bit different; an Argentinian one man band who plays furiously epic folk tinged black metal which is seamlessly blended with passages of ritual dark ambience. Although considered an 'EP', the four tracks here span 38 minutes, thus being longer than many 'classic' full length black metal albums.

Featuring a staunchly organic tone and the seamless weaving of forest based field recordings into the mix, the sound has a very earthy feel (and to expand this description further, it is a tone of dank moss strewn undergrowth; devoid of light, deep under a forest canopy). In some way could draw parallels with the Cascadian Black Metal band Fauna, while other sections remind very much of the Portuguese neo-folk / dark ambient hybrid group Karnnos. Vocals when present not a prominent element, featuring a throaty rasp which in some moments resembles the vocals of post-prison Varg (which isn't actually a negative comment as the comparison might suggest).

Album opener *Sa Aurora De Sos Asatros* sprawls out over an 11 minute expanse and through a number of segments of epically riffed to tremolo played guitars. The drums are pleasingly 'live' sounding in their playing with an organic edge to their production and thankfully avoiding the dreaded overproduced 'click track' sound. Mid track some synth use appears but is understated as a singular melody line which interweaves with and counterpoints the guitars. The second offering *Su Canticu de Sol Montes* is a piece purely focused on ritual ambient spheres, where the dour echoed woodwind playing, ritual drums and 'distant storm' field recordings begs a particular Karnnos comparison. *Lunas Anthigas* then launches headlong into a raw, furious and flailing black metal drumming storm, which maintains an epic folk edge to its riffs (mid track it recedes into a storm addled soundscape before launching back into a black metal guise). The final self-titled track includes a slight change in mood, where although the drums are still flailing in intensity, the riffs have a slightly less aggressive edge being forlornly epic in tone, whilst the second half of the track contains elements akin to a post-black metal style (surely that description will have some black metal 'purists' running for the hills).

With *Umbras E Forestas* Downfall of Nur have produced a recording which displays conviction and passion and which effortlessly shifts its mood from black metal to ritual dark ambience. Not being a mere traditionalist / copyist type band, they are managing to do something interesting within a black metal style, which to a greater degree has lost power through sheer repetition of the sound over the last decade/s.

Ebola Disco / Rope Society - *Flies for Friends* 12"EP Tesco Organisation 2015

Here is a new split EP which functions to provide some welcomed international attention and focus on two projects from Australian industrial underground, namely Ebola Disco and Rope Society. Noting Ebola Disco are probably known to very few outside of the Australian underground, they have also been a relatively obscured project within Australia due to their sporadic releases and live performances over the years. In fact they are a group I have been aware of for many years, but only managed to listen to selected material more recently. By way of backstory, Ebola Disco were formed in around 1997 and features Matt Casey on vocals and Ben Taylor on noise equipment, having primarily played numerous live shows and managing only a mere few formal releases in the process. Ebola Disco lead off side A with the title track *Flies for Friends* which is a long form track from 2008 and was recorded live in studio, which goes someway to explain the loose approach to its industrial soundscape meets power electronics abuse and differs substantially from the shorter, direct and all out aggressive chaotic noise attack of other Ebola Disco tracks. Spanning around 17 minutes *Flies for Friends* is aggressive and unhinged, but also displaying a controlled approach to its 'caveman' styled power electronics. Starting off on a minimalist guise of scattered, buzzing frequencies (with the scarred vocals barely breaking through the static), the mood and tone is gradually elevated with throbbing pulsing analog synth manipulations. Later squelching 'buzz saw' frequencies, fluttering noise and processed spitting vocalisations gain prominence to elevate the track further. Yet in its final third it steps up again with an overblown mass of rumbling bass, swopping 'helicopter blade' distortion and choppy interjections of static; being an excellent build up and ending. All in all *Flies for Friends* is the pinnacle recording I have heard from the group and certainly justifies a formal LP pressing.

On side B, David Tonkin (aka Isomer) further flexes his industrial noise / power electronics muscle as Rope Society, which has seen a handful of releases under this new project name in recent years. Two tracks are featured here and have a much greater focus on junk metal sound sources. *Rudimentary* is the first track, with a solid dose of deep echoed metallic clatter and grinding atonal synth drones, which with a gradual upward trajectory and elevating force builds to chaotic bass rumblings. Distortion scarred vocalisations are also discernible but only as another sonic element, noting the track uses a gradual build up / breakdown which is repeated a couple of times over the duration. Although *Rudimentary* is a solid piece, *Traitor* is the better of the two featuring queasy oscillating synths, controlled squalling feedback and apathetic spoken vocals with a slight distortion treatment. Sprawling out with a singular grinding focus, the atmosphere is a weighty one, which elevates to more crushing intensity in its later section, including the vocals increasing to a distorted roar.

The pairing of Ebola Disco and Rope Society for this release is a positive one given it represents a collective demonstration the often crude and loose yet clearly aggressive approach of the industrial projects operating on these shores. For the cover the packaging is slick and clean in its graphic design presentation, including selective spot varnishing, to round out an excellent feature on the Australian industrial noise / power electronics underground.

En Nihil / Procession of the Black Sloth - *Mask of the Predator, Flesh of the Prey* MC Whispering Eye Recordings 2013

This split cassette features En Nihil - whom with I am already familiar with - and introduces the interestingly monikered Procession of the Black Sloth. But rather than just being a basic split, here each act have focused their material around the following concept: *'The reality you know could change at any moment. What you once knew will never come back beyond this point. In the blink of an eye an existence of serenity and normality can change into a horrific, living nightmare. You are now just prey at the mercy of a predator'.* So clearly no happiness and sunshine to be found herein then.

En Nihil lead of the first side of the tape where is quickly becomes apparent for this release the project have forgone the recent brooding dark ambient template and opted for a death industrial to industrial noise style. With a generally loose and rugged approach En Nihil's side spans both the harsh and subdued. The first two tracks (*The Death Collector* and *Bone Trophies*) follow a general pattern of loosely structured noise to evoke a stalking and seething death industrial tone. *And Time Will Crumble With Their Bodies* then functions to elevates the mood, consisting of layers crumbling static, loosely looped bass rumble and stabbing shards of noise, where these elements are structured to achieve a gradually elevating intensity. For En Nihil's final track it steps into an all-out static noise squall with sporadic harsh and chaotic noise cut ups and despite this description it is not of a HWN style given the track ebbs and flows in intensity, building to noise crescendos and falling away again.

Moving onto the flip side the relatively young project Procession of the Black Sloth (PotBS) are a both a surprise and a revelation with their strong 'cinematic' death industrial offerings. The first track *Unexpected Demise* features a clanging metallic structure which brings to mind early Megaptera. In other words it off to a great start. When the vocals appear they are rather unique for the death industrial genre, having an aggressive guttural yell to unhinged shrieking style, which is more akin to underground metal spheres than typically of industrial or power electronics. Across PotBS's side the vocal delivery and sonic treatment is highly varied (echoed, delayed, flanged etc.) which makes the vocals a standout element of the project's style and sound. Following the opening cut the next offering *Take the Power* pulls back on the aggression and contains a deep reverb drenched death ambient atmosphere, complete with distant wailing vocals and rattling chains (the track then morphs into caustic death industrial in the latter half of the piece). The remaining tracks (*Under the Floor, The Only Way* and *Discarded.... Forgotten*) variously contain combinations of junk metal clatter, loose creaking noise, sweeping synth drones, distant echoed layers, scattered dialogue samples and diverse vocals which facilitate a general death ambient to death industrial tone. Likewise across PotBS's side of the tape there is a general suspense / horror soundtrack vibe, which is evoked by snippets of movie dialogue or the vocal approach used to achieve same effect. Thus in some ways the project's approach brings to mind the heavy dialogue sample approach of Propergol, even if the end result of PotBS sounds rather different from this comparison. This is a commendable split tape where both projects have approached the same conceptual theme but which has resulted in vastly different sonic results. From my perspective each project turn in solid offerings, but if comparing the two it is a situation where the newcomer wins out in style and interest due to the 'new project surprise' factor.

Femeheim – *Grenzniederkunft* CD Death Continues Records 2013
Stadingers – *Deadly Silent Impuse* CD Death Continues Records 2013

Death Continues Records are a relatively new Belgian label and despite having issued a mere five releases since 2012, they have established a clearly defined aesthetic and sonic approach. As such the initial impression is that Death Continues Records are seeking to draw a direct lineage to the aesthetic and sound of Slaughter Productions, which can be further translated to mean lo-fi, old school, death industrial of a late 1980's early 1990's vein. To date album packaging has been rather rudimentary (utilising standard jewel cases), and with the graphic presentation being straight forward in style it again reflects the general Slaughter Productions approach.

Femeheim is up first and delivers a sonic expression which encompasses lo-fi analogue death industrial musings. Tracks are mostly between two and four minutes in length, meaning they quickly set down a mood rather than stretching out over an extended length. Containing a mix of elements, here buzzing / burrowing lo-fi analogue frequencies, stilted percussive thumps and grinding frequencies form slow loose rhythmic patterns, while partially mangled samples (choir vocals, marching tunes etc.) add to the sordid death industrial tone. Vocals are also an occasional feature, which range from spoken to screeched, but usually flanged or distortion drenched. Although sporadic tracks use mid paced pulsing structures to increase atmospheric urgency (almost power electronics in tone on late album track), a sullen tonality remains a constant. So without necessarily being ground-breaking, all in all Femeheim deliver a solid example of morbidly minimalistic death industrial music, which sits somewhere between the minimalist psychological tension of Atrax Morgue and the heaving / pounding tone of Brighter Death Now's *Great Death* era.

Stadingers is up next and differs slightly due to its dank droning sound, which sits between a dark ambient and death industrial tone (but leaning more towards the later). The title track opens the album with atonal droning textures which are possibly generated via a guitar, but any real resemblance to a guitar riff has been abstracted to the point of unrecognizability. As the album progresses, the crude analogue sound provides a soot and grime infused atmosphere, which also articulates a sonic aesthetic of a cavernous industrial space (far off tarnished vocalisations make an occasional appearance, but always garbled and unintelligible). *Putiphar* stands out with its use of a prominent dialogue sample over a throbbing / thumping mechanised industrial base (yet the looped sample actually looses a bit of potential impact through overuse). A dank, oppressive and muffled analogue feel is present throughout, which when coupled with the crude looseness to the compositional approach (evidenced by the occasional atonal warbling synths), all tends to amplify a lo-fi late 80's early 90's vibe of dark experimental / ambient music.

As suggested by the label name Death Continues Records appear intent on raising a recognisable banner under which death industrial obscurities can be issued to a wider audience. In more specific terms this is about fostering a 'classic' death industrial sound independent of genre fads or trends. Both album's from Femeheim and Stadingers achieve this aim, where each will suit those whose listening habits yearn for the early era of the death industrial genre. As a final comment, if these two albums were to be ranked, for these ears at least Femeheim wins out for its slightly more focused (yet subdued) morbidly morose atmospheres.

Femeheim – *Dominium Terrae* CD Death Continues Records 2014

Femeheim have returned with their second album, following the debut from only a year prior (reviewed above) and whilst it was staunchly a lo-fi death industrial affair, the sonic focus of *Dominium Terrae* has been expanded to combine direct power electronics tracks within a slightly more focused death industrial framework.

Pleasingly Femeheim has maintained a direct approach to classic genre traits where album opener *Camera Silens* features a stilted mechanical thrum with a filth infused analogue tone, before bleeding into the caustically ominous throbbing industrial drone of *Ewiger Suhnetod.* The third piece *Voluntas... Infamia* then features a direct and excellent throbbing and squelching analogue tone and garbled / flanged vocals, noting that if this track were played in isolation without me being told who it is, I would swear it is from the earlier brute force era of Genocide Organ (as a rather direct compliment this track comes across something like an alternate slightly more laidback version of Genocide Organ's *White Power Forces*). For good measure the following piece *Absolute Umkehrung* opts to channel the pummeling mechanical rhythms of Megaptera, before settling down into a tryptic of slightly more subdued death industrial territory, with lone analogue modulations, throbbing / wavering frequencies etc. Late album track *Oppertunistsche Infektion* pushes back towards power electronics territory with the flanged vocal presentation and singular burrowing mid-toned frequency. The title track then concludes the album which is structured around heaving mid toned cyclic throb, spoken to yelled vocals and slightly mangled choral singing.

Dominium Terrae is an album that again demonstrates Femeheim clearly understand the classic base elements of the death industrial and power electronics genre and consequently can deliver a strong, genre specific album, where this album has taken a step up from the debut given its more focused and direct approach. Straightforward graphic presentation rounds out the release, which reflects a simplistic yet stylised visual aesthetic reminiscent of Slaughter Productions.

Fieberflug - *über Calais* CDr Les Forges Alliées 2014
Fieberflug - *Schande* MC Les Forges Alliées 2014

These releases represent my first introduction to Fieberflug, however for some reason I had the impression that the project was much older than 2009 (being the year when their debut release was issued - perhaps I am confusing them with another project of which I now can't recall?). Regardless, Fieberflug is a German industrial project of one Daniel Simon whom also operates under the more possibly well know monikers of Flutwacht (power electronics) and Amputation Desire (ambient industrial). With Fieberflug Daniel is concerned with a classic German industrial sound, which also draws from northern European expressions of death ambient and death industrial.

Here we have two recent releases which have been issued on the small DIY French label Les Forges Alliées.
Up first is the *über Calais* CDr, this features four tracks: three apparently studio works and the fourth being recorded live during a concert in Calais on 17 January, 2014. Here the sound is generally death industrial in approach, utilizing a heavy dose of metallic focused, echo and reverb toned factory clatter. The cavernous opener *Inkubationsphase1* features an industrial soundscape of sustained windswept drones, before bleeding into the heavy metallic clanging tone of *Inkubationsphase2*, where metal on metal sounds generate a slow pounding industrial rhythm. The third piece *Neberwachter* functions more as a subdued cyclic industrial drone, where sparse looped metallic elements and stoic quasi militant percussion provide structure and focus over its extended length. The fourth and final piece is the live recording (and longest at 25 minutes), which seeks to merge distant muted industrial drones with more focused metallic 'factory ambience' orientated loops, and sporadic metallic bangs and clangs. The sound is slightly more muffled than the preceding studio pieces and has a slow burn approach as the track gradually morphs into more overblown scope, but stopping short of full power electronics territory. Mid to late track pulling back to calmer realms of sustained industrial drones combined with semi-rhythmic loops, prior to the final push back into distorted and overblown spheres and although a solid piece, to this ear the studio tracks come across as more convincingly overall. Packaging is slightly divergent to the norm by including a plain unbranded CDr and a series of four transparent card, which are housed in a zip lock bag.
Moving onto the more recent *Schande* tape, it contains four tracks: the first three on side A and a lengthy forth piece on the side B. This tape is mostly concerned with lo-fi mechanical death ambient musings. The material is minimalistic focused, staunchly analogue and suitably dank and cavernous in its tone. Rough, slow and sporadic metallic clangs and ringing notes (sounding like industrial sized Tibetan singing bowls), give some semblance of structure, as the underpinning factory ambience drones bleed off into the inky blackness. Slow paced metallic loops, distant factory clatter and random bumps, thuds and clangs are gradually added and subtracted as the material progresses, where a prominent wheezing sound element is perhaps some heavily treated vocals. The lengthier tape side final piece *Schande* sits in more minimalist windswept plains, with semi-buried throbbing elements, cyclic cavernous loops, distant clangs and echo treated vocal moans. With the later section of the track the morphs from a death ambient to death industrial sound through the introduction of more forceful loops and metallic elements. Overall the mood of *Schande* is one which edges towards the early sound of Brighter Death Now or Archon Satani (which is rather large praise from these quarters), albeit slightly less 'evil' sounding. Packaging consists of a clear tape with labels and two x transparent inserts housed in a zip lock bag.
Regardless of the fact that Fieberflug are not really bringing anything new to the table, I am still a sucker for this sort of dankly atmospheric analogue industrial music. With Fieberflug's material being focused yet unhurried in pace it brings to mind the sound of the early 90's underground coming from the pre CMI tape label Sound Source or perhaps Slaughter Productions; where this description alone will be a indicator of if this is something for you. I also appreciate Fieberflug's music more than what I have previously heard from Flutwacht and Amputation Desire, meaning for me at least this is more than a 'mere' side-project. Lastly if you were to start with either of these releases the *Schande* tape would be the pick for its minimalist old school death industrial sound.

Funerary Call / Crown Of Bone - *Funerary Call / Crown Of Bone* MC Fall of Nature 2015
Trauma - *After Visiting Hours* MC Fall of Nature 2015
Although Fall of Nature was effectively silent during 2014, 2015 is off to a strong start with a swag of new releases; two of which are reviewed below. The first cassette is a split between the ritual dark ambient Funerary Call and the harsh noise Crown of Bone, whilst the second tape is a re-release from an obscure UK death industrial project Trauma. Both releases are slickly presented, including professionally pressed and printed cassettes and J cards, which is noteworthy given the small editions of each.
On the split cassette Funerary Call lead off by featuring two lengthy tracks of sparse yet intense dark ambience, and whilst building upon their recognized ritualised aesthetic the tracks sit at the longer, free form and abstract end of what the project do. The first track *Idols Of Perdition* is more animated and heavingly heavy than usual and works on two broad levels, including yawning cavernous black depths and focused micro tonal 'scratching' elements. Grinding synths (emulating hellish horns of death) and creaking metallic elements also substantially augment the mood, and when vocals are also present which amount to a hoarse whisper bleeding into the overall sonic mass. The second piece *Silent Prayers Of Execration* commences in sparse ritual chimes and sustained wailing elements, before a prominent cyclic bass drone gradually sweeps the track to its conclusion. All in all a solid two track offering from Funerary Call.
Noting that straight forward harsh noise has never quite been my favorite of styles, Crown of Bone's side was always going to compare with difficultly to Funerary Call's side. Nevertheless Crown of Bone deliver two lengthy tracks of grim static and blasting back noise which effectively combine to form a single cassette side track. As such a sustained mid-range distortion is coupled with lower bass rumble, whilst vocals of a grim black metal rasp can be detected semi-buried within the mix. Likewise underneath the wall of static there are detectable dynamics, constituting a gradual shift and flow to various the layers of distortion, where on occasion the mid-range elements fall away to reveal the underpinning / grinding bass tone structures, which are themselves gradually elevated in bulk and force. Mid-way through their side of the tape the blasting wall of mid-range static sheds back into the mix, again with the grim static shredded vocalizations.
Noting my own personal listening tastes, Funerary Call's side was always likely to be preferred side (and has been proven in the detailed listening), however Crown of Bone do a commendable grimly focused black noise approach, which compliments the occult thematic stance of the tape, as evidenced by its visuals.
For the second reviewed release Fall of Nature have dug up a rather obscure UK project to reissue their 2008 CDr *After Visiting Hours* on tape. Self-described as *'Slow Growing Surgical Death Noise'*, this is good descriptor of what to expect. As such the material is sparsely constructed, where there is definite room to breathe between sonic elements, including loose looped mechanical rhythms, clinical toned drones, throbbing textures

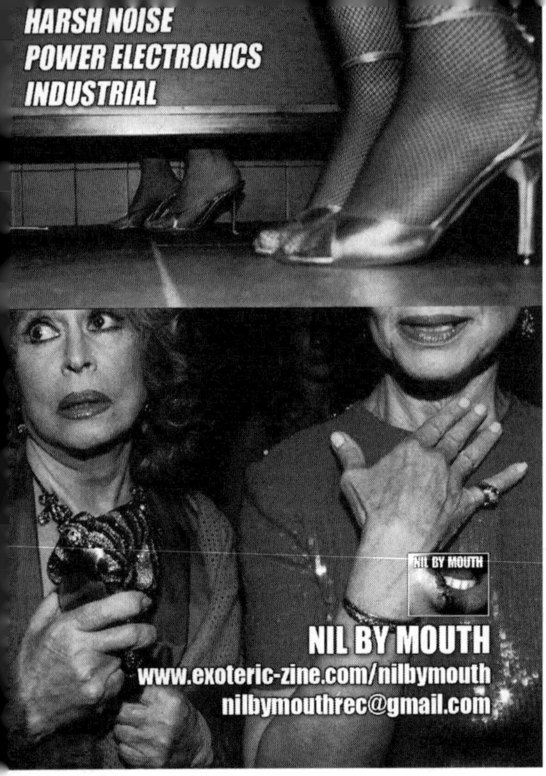

etc. A slow and controlled pacing across the eight tracks is also a clear hallmark, where each piece averages a length between five to six minutes. Occasional dialogue samples are utilized to compliment the basic medical themes, whilst there is also definite affinity with the sound and visual aesthetic of early Slaughter Productions releases. Noting its mid-90's minimalist style it is impregnated with a certain clinical morbidity and although Trauma's tape will not change perceptions of this type of material, this has an unrefined and obscured charm all the same. Clearly Fall of Nature should be commended for excavating this from the underground to give the project some greater spotlight and evidently new material from Trauma will be released on Fall of Nature will be issued in future, so something to look out for.

Genocide Organ – *Archive IV* 10"EP Tesco Organisation 2014
Genocide Organ return with a welcomed forth release in the 10"EP achieve series. As with the other prior archive releases the group continue to demonstrate they have been sitting on a wealth of unreleased material which far from being second rate actually equals the output of their most recognised and lauded releases. For this 10"EP it features approximately 24 minutes of previously unreleased material from 1992 and 1996. five of the six of the track here were recorded in 1992 evidently shortly after *Save Our Slaves* and are unified under the title of *The Lesson*. Evidently these mostly instrumental tracks were intended to be released on a 10"EP which obviously never eventuated. For the sixth track this is derived from 1996, being recorded soon after the *Mind Control* album. So potentially classic era stuff then? Well yes - absolutely in fact.

Noting the early to mid-1990's era of these tracks they accordingly align more closely with the prototype unpolished and aggressive power electronics sound of the group, before a more refined and controlled sound was to take prominence on later output. Thus here the main approach is the presentation of an amalgam of grinding and burrowing loops, sustained noise, and static fried tones which are structured in a myriad of mid paced semi-rhythmic structures, whilst smatterings of dialogue samples to flesh out thematic content – here relating to various aspects American imperialism and societal oppression. Likewise the fifth and final track from *The Lesson* series differs from the rest of the instrumental tracks in that it contains aggressive yet drawling and lamenting vocals. *Nix-on* the sixth and final track on the 10"EP features as a slightly more subdued soundscape track of semi-rhythmic pulses and layered swirling battlefield textures, which includes dialogue samples of (you guessed it) President Nixon. Without putting too much of a point on it Genocide Organ has long been recognised purveyors of scathing power electronics and this is clearly with good reason. Any 'new' material from the group – including previously unreleased material in the archive series – is clearly welcomed, with this release yet again demonstrating their early dominance of such a style and approach. Noting the collectability and fetishisation of Genocide Organ's output the physical edition was sold out on pre-order, however for those who missed it the tracks can be obtained digitally.

Gnawed – *Feign and Cloak* CD Malignant Records 2014
2012 was the year the formal debut Gnawed album *Terminal Epoch* was issued, which incidentally was a highly lauded release around these parts. So with a bit of background investigation it seems that a further five to six tapes (including splits releases) have been issued since then, where *Feign and Cloak* forms the second album and first for Malignant Records. Noting that *Terminal Epoch* was described by this reviewer as: *'a heavy, no frills, and straight to the point power electronics / death industrial album'*, much the same descriptor could be employed here. Yet in doing so this would ignore some of its subtle difference. More specifically what sets this new album apart is the fact that it is slightly more subdued, where a restrained brooding intensity has been elevated to the fore, meaning this album perhaps leans more towards death industrial than typically aggressive power electronics.
Eight tracks spanning 44 minutes forms the context of *Feign and Cloak*, where a rough and guttural tone is instilled at the core the album - a tone which gradually seeps out of the speakers as rust stained filth. Whilst the opener *Time Undone* includes some background metallic clatter, it is as if the scrap metal abuse is occurring somewhere far off in a subterranean basement rather than being front and centre in the mix. Yet as the metallic rumble cyclically builds to increased prominence, it is as if you the listener is slowly creeping forward to catch a glimpse of what is creating the metallic cacophony. So in this context if the opening could be considered as somewhat subdued, the second track *Burning the Hive* is a direct kick to the chest with its heavy rumbling industrial loop and sustained organ dirge blast. Likewise when the static infused ripping vocals arrive, this is an example of where Gnawed absolutely excel in their chosen sound and one of the album's tracks which verges on a power electronics tone. The title track (located towards the middle of the album), is another

excellent offering, featuring mangled militant rolling snare, waves of rolling inky black distortion, as the sparse spoken to hoarse yelled vocals bleed out of the speakers as an unintelligible sonic mass. *Pestilence Beholden* follows based on a backbone of heavy rhythmic death industrial, formed by a pulsing analogue tone and metallic infused loop, again with the searing distorted vocal attack. The late album track *The Drowning Fire* articulates a shuddering, creaking metallic avalanche of sound which is both crushing and brooding in its atmosphere, while the final album track *Torch to Ceder* round out the album with a blend of sustained drones and crumbling static which coalesces into semi-structure via its multi-layered approach.

Clearly with *Feign and Cloak* Gnawed are not deviating from their chosen direction, rather are seeking the further refinement of their sound to absolute honed intensity. Noting that only Gnawed's two main albums have been heard around these parts - and both being excellent albums from the US death industrial / power electronics scene - maybe it is time to track down some of the more obscure cassette releases.

The Grey Wolves - *Blood and Sand* LP 2014 Cold Spring Records

Not constituting a new album, this represents a welcomed reissue of this classic yet subdued album from The Grey Wolves on the most important of physical formats - vinyl! So for those late to the party, *Blood and Sand* originally constituted half of a split cassette release from 1990 on Old Europa Cafe (Shock City was the other obscure project featured on the other half). In hindsight what is rather special about The Grey Wolves side is that it showcased an atmospheric industrial noise style, rather than the politically charged, heavy power electronics sound the project are most recognised. This vinyl version is the second edition issued via Cold Spring Records who originally reissued the tape on CD in 2002. For this latest edition the artwork has been slightly reinterpreted and the sound further boosted via further remastering.

As for the music, two lengthy track are presented (one each side of the vinyl), which spans an album of nearly an hour's play time. For the first title track *Desert Storm* is a slow moving and tensely brooding piece containing sweeping sounds, throbbing rhythms and indecipherable radio voices which flits between semi-structure and a free form flow. This amalgam of disparate elements are then layered in such way to generate a tense yet muted modern technological warfare styled atmosphere. The second piece *Gulf Breeze* takes a similar tactic of wielding a tensile and caustic tone, yet does introduce (late in the piece) a heavily processed guitar / kit drums based element within the noise layers.

With its suffocating battlefield ambience mixed with its atmospheric noise inclinations, one of the greatest aspects of this album is a threatening undercurrent of aggression, with a sense it is ready to burst forth from the speakers in full sonic warfare at any moment. Whilst this aural obliteration never entirely eventuates, *Blood and Sand* is no less of a release without it and highlights the tensile atmosphere which has been expertly created. As such *Blood and Sand* functions as a prefect example of the lesser know atmospheric noise side of The Grey Wolves.

The Grey Wolves / Genocide Organ – *Absolute Truth* 12"LP Tesco Organisation 2014

Whist the impatient wait for new full length albums from both The Grey Wolves and Genocide Organ continues, *Absolute Truth* comes as a welcomed stop-gap release. This mini LP presents the classic Grey Wolves cut *Beyond Hypocrisy* in its original form (lifted from their 1996 album *Catholic Priests Fuck Children*), along with a further three different versions.

On the first side of the vinyl it has been cut at 45rpm for maximum sonic impact, where the original version of The Grey Wolves classic is presented first in all its powerful and chaotic glory. With a base of churning noise and throbbing industrialised rhythms, the heavily treated vocals contain a particularly distinctive tone of English antagonism in their delivery. What also elevates the impact of this track is when the throbbing bass sporadically drops out, to then absolutely hit hard when dropped back into the mix. Being weighty and with an enveloping urgency *Beyond Hypocrisy* is English power electronics at its finest, being entirely worthy of its classic status. The second version presented is taken from Genocide Organ's 2012 live performance in their hometown of Mannheim, where during this performance Dave Padbury joined the group on stage to deliver this punishing version of The Grey Wolves classic. Essentially this is a faithful live presentation of the studio version, where the flanged vocals sit slightly higher in the mix. Whilst the live recording clearly hints at the heaviness of the live performance, it however cannot match the sonic weight of the studio mix which immediately precedes it.

On the flip side two further versions of *Beyond Hypocrisy* are presented, effectively being lengthier soundscape mixes of the original (with this side of the vinyl cut at 33rpm as a result). *Absolute Hypocrisy* is up first and has a subdued yet tense atmosphere and without any detail of who contributed to this track, this very much comes across as modern day Genocide Organ cover version, given the tone and sonic approach is quite similar to the sound of *Under Kontrakt*. The lengthy introduction section is constructed with layered burrowing noise, media samples and maudlin antagonistic vocals, before the recognisable throbbing industrialised rhythms of original version kick in. From here it includes the addition of what sounds like new layers of crumbling noise, radio chatter and vocals which sound very much like they are courtesy of Wilhelm Herrich of Genocide Organ. The final version is *Absolute Hypocrisy (Nietzche Mix)*, which is a remix of source material take from the original version. Here the sound is more 'soundscape' in presentation, where then original vocals are elevated to the forefront of the mix, the heavier chaotic noise and throbbing rhythmic elements set to the background, and droning sub-orchestral layers added to provide a dark cinematic quality.

Given that The Grey Wolves and Genocide Organ are often lauded as definitive groups of the power electronics genre, this release is testament to exactly why this has been and continues to be the case. Each version of *Absolute Hypocrisy* which is presented on *Absolute Truth* contains elements faithful to the original, yet also containing defined and distinct qualities to allow them to each stand on their own. Clearly *Absolute Truth* is destined to become another sought after vinyl from The Grey Wolves and Genocide Organ. Recommended.

Grunt – *Myth of Blood* LP Freak Animal 2015

Three years have already passed since the release of the exceptional *World Draped In A Camouflage* album, where this new full length follows a similar approach bedded down on the last, i.e. by featuring a collection of individual and uncompromising tracks; each displaying a clear diversity of approach within a general industrial / noise / power electronics framework.

The opening cut *Black Flag* commences the album in unhinged fashion with swirling / grinding layered noise, sporadic junk metal sounds and harsher static elements as the screeched / distorted vocals yell the track's title (sampled operatic vocals are also used but barely discernible and only becoming apparent after a number of listens). This is followed by the early album standout *Ghosts of Old Europe*, being based on a basic structure of sustaining buzzing tone and background lurching loops, further augmented with a heady dose of metallic clangs and distant wailed vocals. Additionally semi-buried droning abstract strings add a melancholic tone, as Mikko's prominent trademark gruff yelled and slightly treated vocals provide a level of raw aggression. *Interrogation Paranoia* then shifts the mood toward more noisier realms, based on its spitting and sustained frequencies (mid to higher piecing tonal range), whilst the vocals are more antagonistically accusing in their delivery. *Linkola Legacy* arrives as the most divergent track of the album, based around a fractured and partly rhythmic tone, sounding like a switch being flicked between different noise generator settings. Wet and squelching sounding static infused loops feature as the backing for *Unmarked Graves*, which is then pushed into noisy chaotic realms with further layers of distortion and rough barked vocals. *Ordeal of Water* is based around a core of junk metal abuse and as a consequence is loose and chaotic, where the vocals relegated to gurgled and pain inflected screams which do not seem to be articulating any actual words. The title track is another clear standout, with sustained mid toned distortion and revving noise loops, as an underpinning accordion drone provides a dour edge to the track's mood. A low cyclic noise drone commences *Saws Are Waiting*, but evolves in the latter half to contains a rather fist pumping and anthemic PE quality, due to its strong militant rhythmic loop and (again) trademark wailed vocals of Mikko (junk metal clatter also makes a late track appearance). Focused and forceful, each of the 10 tracks are perfectly controlled, again being an absolute demonstration of Mikko's mastery of his honed sound. This stands as a testament to his ability to construct varied and distinct PE compositions which never forsakes a gritty industrial and noise infused underground aesthetic. Given its individual track based approach this quite feels like the brother / companion album to *World Draped In A Camouflage*, although it does not achieve the same level of immediate impact, rather is more of a slow burner in revealing it true character. Regardless, *Myth of Blood* is another extremely strong addition to Grunt's catalogue.

Halo Manash - *Se Its En* CD Aural Hypnox 2014

This CD is not a new album for Halo Manash, rather is the release of their super limited debut album from 2003 which was issued in an edition of only 100 copies. Accordingly the liner notes associated with the original version provides useful context: *'Se Its En is an album dedicated to seven specific dreams I saw between November 2002 and February 2003. Basically every track is an individual separate part, but when they are listened in a given order they form entirety - A guide to transformation, to dynamic wholeness. Se Its En perfects the whole'.*

Noting the central focus of later Halo Manash albums is a reliance on played instruments and ritual percussive implements, this debut differs in that organic instrumentation is coupled with a far more prominent droning synthetic base. As such the sound and atmosphere is drive and underpinned by melodious and sustained analogue synthesiser generated notes, where combinations of sparse percussion provides a general sense of structure within selected tracks. Additionally low whispered to garble chanted vocalisations add to the spiritual and ritualised atmosphere.

The format of the album follows a reasonably focused and strict format of seven tracks at exactly seven minutes each; yet with the tracks morphing and interlinking into each other, as with most of Aural Hypnox's releases they form singular enveloping album length meditative journeys. Halo Manash have always operated in the regions between dark ambient and ritual ambient, overall *Se Its En* typically leans towards a dark ambient framework, with some ritual ambient elements incorporated for good measure. Yet interestingly it is the fifth composition *Ulterior* with its prominent tribalised percussive drive partially reflects a sound and style of Halo Manash's latest album *Wesieni Wainajat*.

Although that the personal preference of this reviewer leans more heavily towards Halo Manash's organic ritual ambient style found later albums, *Se Its En* is still a fine debut and demonstration of where the project began and where they have evolved over the course of subsequent albums. Packaging reflects the current Aural Hypnox format of cardboard fold out sleeve, and printed screen printed booklet and inserts.

Herz Jühning – *Paradise* 7"EP Galakthorrö 2014

Herz Jühning is an existing member of the Galakthorrö roster but has only issued three releases since 2007 (consisting of two 7"EP's and a full length album). This is his third and latest release containing four tracks spread across 15 minutes of wax. Whilst drawing broadly from an German industrial and power electronics sound it is also driven by a more song focused sensibility to be the epitome of the 'angst pop' style which defines segments of the Galakthorrö roster. The sound of *Paradise* is also noted to slightly differ from the more direct industrial / power electronics approach of Herz Jühning's earlier material.

My Confession is the first track and is based on a clinical and jittery beat and squelching rhythm. Likewise with the inclusion of understated female lead vocals it definitely spans a German 'industrial' style (in terms of sound and production) and 'song' approach (in terms of succinct catchy structure), hence justifying the aforementioned 'angst pop' tag. *To The Stars* follows and for this reviewer is the absolute stand out track of the EP, featuring a throbbing rhythmic groove and energetic mid paced 'pulsing' programmed drum machine structure. Additionally the monotone heavily accented German vocals (half sung / spoken in English) perfectly suits this melancholic yet head nodding tone of the track.

Road To Paradise opens the flip side and is more of a minimalist industrial composition consisting of clinical programming, minimalist synths, meandering bass and understated semi-chanted / spoken vocals. For the final of the four tracks *Im Totraum* is the most understated and 'industrial soundscape' track on offer, where maudlin spoken vocals, vague industrial rhythmic clatter and shuddering bass toned synths characterise proceedings.
On *Paradise* (and with particular reference to side A), Herz Jühning has certainly nailed the 'angst pop' sound within his general approach. Whilst this release won't alter anyone's established perceptions of 'angst pop' influenced German industrial, this is of little consequence as the physical format of 659 copies is long sold out from Galakthorrö, obviously snapped up by fans and aficionado of Herz Jühning.

I.Corax - *The Cadaver Pulse I: Sealed in a Radiant Larval Maelstrom* CD Aural Hypnox, 2014
I.Corax - *The Cadaver Pulse II: Mothelix Liquescent* CD Aural Hypnox 2014
With I.Corax having been inducted into the Aural Hypnox fold via 2013's *Cella Phantasma* album, the label is now taking the opportunity to reissue their first two albums (via the Stellar Mansion series). With both albums in their original form being released in 2003, for this reissue the packaging has been updated and redesigned in line with the established Aural Hypnox aesthetic, featuring stunningly designed card fold out covers and a range of printed card inserts. Likewise noting the *I* and *II* title designation; effectively these two separate albums can be considered as companion halves.
Whereas the sound of many of the Aural Hypnox's roster tend to be rooted in organic instrumentation, I.Corax's sound differs slightly as their music sounds to be the result of sonic studio processing. Likewise with the use of analogue synthesizers and samplers, in addition to sound sources of more organic origin (such as field recordings, ritual instrumentation), the heavily processed yet highly detailed tone brings to mind the sound of label mate Zoat Aon. But rather than being a loose comparison, this impression is specifically explained by the fact that sole Zoat Aon member Jaako Vanhala is also one half of I.Corax. Stylistically both albums follow a similar template by featuring a series of tracks which interlink into a greater whole, thus given the transitions from one track to the next effectively go unnoticed, this allows each album to sprawl out and gradually unfurl. This interlinking structure also reflective of the fact that there are no individual track titles, rather just a series of 'states' (differentiated only with individual roman numerals).
On *The Cadaver Pulse I: Sealed in a Radiant Larval Maelstrom* its characteristic feature is being a darkly brooding and intensely enveloping recording. The multidimensional sound is in part imbedded in a drone framework, but at the same time also highly animated, where the swirling sonic textural mass is extremely dense in its multi-layered approach. This works particularly well when the 'ghosts' of original sound sources (organic instrumentation, field recordings etc.) can be subtly detected within the mix. At the album's core there is an intense grinding momentum, and although abstract there is a real sense of movement and animation, but equally controlled to stop short of being chaotic. Occasional fragments of ritualised chimes and shrill atonal woodwind type instruments feature, whilst alternate segments use looped sound elements (metallic sounds, scraping textures etc.) to provide a semblance of vague rhythmic structure. As a counterpoint to the heavy molasses like tone of *Part I, The Cadaver Pulse II: Mothelix Liquescent* is moderately lighter in atmosphere and offers some respite with its shimmering more ambiental form of sonic expression. Here wavering drones and bending synth chords are mixed with processed natural environment field recordings and sporadic Asiatic chimes. Likewise a swelling ebb and flow style characterise proceedings here, where the hallucinogenic swirling tone and warm synth reverberations generates an overarching atmosphere somewhere between ritual ambient and abstract 70's moog space synth experimentation.
With its focused roster of projects and generally infrequent release schedule Aural Hypnox has maintained an exceptionally high standard of release, where I.Corax is a project perfectly suits the label's sound and aesthetic. With the issue of these two companion albums they represent sonically detailed and animated recordings which transcend being mere background music and warrant a detailed and engaged attention.

I.Corax – *From Goldem Flesh to Silverb One* Aural Hypnox CD 2014
I.Corax – *Kuilu* CD Aural Hypnox 2014
After recently inducting I.Corax into the Aural Hypnox fold, the release campaign of the project's back catalogue continues. Here we have two additional reissues of earlier I.Corax albums dating from 2003 and 2004 respectively, both of which were released on the short lived Finnish record label Blue Sector.
Up first is *From Goldem Flesh to Silverb One* which is credited as a live studio rehearsal which was recorded in preparation for a live performance in September, 2003. This album spans 46 minutes with eight interlinking untitled tracks, thus unfurls as a singular long form compositions. Embedded within the core of the album is a hazy disorienting tone within a constantly morphing and enveloping aura. As such the album broadly covers an animated atmosphere of layered looped elements, including wailing ritual horns, with other passages spanning serene widescreen ritual / dark ambient soundscapes which to a degree reminds of the atmosphere of label mate Zoat Aon. Other passages seek tensile droning ritual ambient atmospheres underscored with prominently layers of natural / nature based field recordings, throbbing bass undercurrents, sparse ritualised chimes and twisted unintelligible vocalisations.
The next album *Kuilu* was issued in 2004 its original form, however the recording itself dates from March 2002, being a live recording of I.Corax's first live performance. As such four tracks spanning 40 minutes (six to 13 minutes each) evoke sweeping and darkly brooding atmospheres which is a touch less animated and slowly paced when compared to *From Goldem Flesh to Silverb One. The Face of the Sun* opens proceedings with subdued but shimmering looped structure, where additionally sound elements and disorienting vocalizations are gradually added to greater swirling miasmic effect. This piece bleeds directly into the next tracks *Menhir* which follows a similar sonic template of loose loops and scattered sonic elements but introducing a slow thumping ritual beat to provide a greater degree of focus. Alternately with its sparse swilling structure, distant widescreen drones and low sporadic bass thumps *Tephra* follows a more straight forward dark ambient sound, whilst the

final of the four pieces *Animus Desertis* concludes the album in a style and sound reminiscent of 1970's space synth music, complete with darkly brooding galactic toned echoed / droning / sweeping synth lines and microtonal / scratching sound elements etc.

Noting that the more recent studio recorded material of I.Corax incorporates a greater degree of synthetic elements and encompasses an overarching swirling, chaotic and at times disorientating atmosphere, these two earlier recordings are somewhat more controlled and seem to be underscored a greater reliance on actual played instrumentation. As such this would seem to be the sonic by-product of these recordings being derived from a live setting, rather than the more complex studio recordings from the project. As per the established visual aesthetic for Aural Hypnox, the packaging for both constitutes beautifully designed screen printed cardboard covers, with a range of printed inserts and booklets. Both albums are available separately or otherwise housed together in a hand-made silkscreened cloth pouch in a limited edition of 77 copies.

IRM – *Closure* CD Malignant Records 2014

With an underpinning shrill drone it takes a mere 19 seconds and four ultra-slow, echoed floor tom strikes for the new IRM album to explode in full force of what the project are recognised: i.e. layered noise / drones of Eric Jarl, thick atonal bass guitar playing of Mikael Oretoft and the agonised dual vocals of Martin Bladh. Yet by equal measures by the time the album concludes its 50 minute span, a diverse array of soundscapes and moods have been explored, thus illustrating the expanding niche IRM have carved out in the experimental post-industrial underground. Although at the outset of their career IRM were an adherent to a direct power electronics sound, over the course of four main albums they have evolved into something altogether different and now encompass a far more abstract, experimental and artistic take on the core abrasive elements. *Closure* is the fifth formal album from the group and features nine untitled tracks (or could be considered as nine parts of a single work), and is evidently the third and final part of a trilogy which commenced with 2008's *Indications of Nigredo* EP and continued with 2010's *Order4* album.

After becoming familiar with the structure and flow of *Closure* two elements clearly come to the fore. Firstly the album functions as a focused collection of individual tracks and secondly it includes the use of prominent instrumentation such as floor tom / tympani percussion (by Ulrik Nilsson), atonal cello strings (by Jo Quail) and even sections with recognisable bass melodies (…whereas previously the bass guitar has been predominantly used as a weighty abstract layer to bulk up the lower end of sound). Also intriguingly a couple of album passages evoke a 'high art' theatre styled atmosphere through the narrative based spoken vocals. The most prominent example of this is third track consisting of shimmering metallic textures, ticking clock, theatre audience noise and moody twilight bass melody, as Martin narrates a surreal dreamlike theatre scene which appears to deal with the murder or execution of the self (possibly relating to an attempt at the expulsion of elements of the ego). This psychological soundscape and surreal narrative is akin to a form of stream of consciousness (perhaps like that which derived from an immersive hypnotism session), where this dreamlike / nightmare narrative clearly begs a comparison to the current lyrical approach of Scott Walker. Yet to have it said Martin's vocal style substantially differs from the Mr Walker's crooning, where Martin brings his own unique, urgent and visceral approach. Interestingly a similar theatre narrative and surreal stream of consciousness approach to lyrical passages was utilized on the last album *Order4*. Yet that album was equally immersive as it was impenetrable due to the strict rules imposed (four tracks of exactly 15 minutes each), which resulted in a singular piece spanning four interconnecting soundscapes / movements. As such the flow of the new album is much more conducive as a collection of individual tracks, which can be experienced either individually or as part of the greater whole. Likewise with full lyrics being printed within the booklet a complex web of thematic inspiration is hinted at within the text*, noting these range from short collections of words, abstract sentences and passages of dense narrative. Despite the lyrics being included in the 20 page booklet, deciphering a clear meaning is a complex one, given the often abstract and surreal context of their presentation. Yet it is exactly this complexity of thematic approach which makes IRM such an engaging project, where the lyrical intricacy functions as sort a puzzle to be solved.

Putting thematic preoccupations aside, the fourth track of *Closure* standouts due its employment of a differing and more varied vocal approach, where the clipped pronunciation and partly yelled vocals follow the stilted percussive structure, as rattled steel chains resonate in the background. Apart from its noted differences, many of the compositions do feature IRM's modern era sound (which sits somewhere between industrial drone to power-electronics soundscapes), featuring tense drones, slow atonal bass guitar strums and vocals alternating between spoken passages to agonised dual vocal lines. Likewise others pieces function as a form of psychological analysis, where two differing vocal lines call and respond to a list of abstract words over a minimalist industrial drone. Additionally with the sporadic inclusion of unusual sound elements such as a child's wind-up toy, queasy laughing and lone crying / sobbing, these aspects elevate the album's surreal edge.

With IRM continuing to forge headlong into more 'artistic' realms, this will perhaps alienate some fans merely interested in the visceral and more direct side of the project. Yet equally IRM could not be accused of pandering to anyone's expectations other than staunchly following their own creative muse, which in turn is further expanding the sound and focus of the project. Bearing witness to the gradual evolution of IRM from their infancy has been an engaging and rewarding experience, being yet another step in the process of expanding outer limits of a recognisable sound IRM, where *Closure* is a striking achievement on the part of the group.

---

* - The lyrics make reference to *Onan*, who was a minor biblical character in the Book of Genesis: the second son of Judah, and who was killed by Yahweh (God). Interestingly religious scholars have interpreted that the execution resulted from Onan 'spilling seed' (i.e. sexual acts associated with non-procreation), and retribution for being unwilling to father a child by his widowed sister-in-law. Yet despite the passing reference to Onan (which seems perfect for the scope of Martin's lyrical obsessions), the balance of the lyrics do not provide any further hint at the myth and metaphor surrounding this religious figure.

In Slaughter Natives – *Cannula Coma Legio* CD Cyclic Law 2014

Clearly not being a project to rush their releases, the long-standing and cult revered In Slaughter Natives has resurfaced after a 10 year break from the last formal album *Resurrection*, which in turn was preceded by an eight year gap between it and 1996's *Purgate My Stain*. Despite these long passages of silence it is great to see that In Slaughter Natives is still active after all these years, considering that the debut release was issued way back in 1989.

Regardless of the slow pace of releases unquestionably In Slaughter Natives were hugely influential in establishing the 'Cold Meat Industry' sound and more broadly the northern European industrial underground. Likewise in hindsight it can be acknowledged that In Slaughter Natives were a precursor the 'martial industrial' genre, although their trademark orchestral industrial doom has stood out from and has not been replicated by the majority of projects of a 'martial industrial' style (which are predominantly influenced by early to mid-20th century history and era). Thus In Slaughter Natives stand apart with their distinctive and recognisable neo-classical compositions, which articulate a hellish atmosphere of religious laments and amounts to a sonic representation of purgatorial damnation.

With this necessary background out-of-the-way, evidently *Cannula Coma Legio* is technically not the new album from the group, rather is billed a stop-gap release prior to the release of the actual new album in 2015. So for this release it contains three new tracks which are set alongside a series of reworked and upgraded versions of earlier material. Yet interestingly all of the material which has been brought together for this release works perfectly as a coherent whole. This has been achieved by the fact that new versions substantially differ from the originals versions to the point of being almost unrecognisable, and in a number of instances the original melodies and structural elements of known compositions only reveal themselves after multiple detailed listens. This is most evident for the updated versions of the earliest reworked material, where in some instances the programmed sound of the original versions have not held up fully with the passage of time. Yet the reason why the new versions work so well here, is that they have ben elevated to full bombastic orchestral intensity.

With *Cannula Coma Legio* seamlessly merging brooding and understated neo-classical passages with sections of booming orchestral bombast, the greatest reference point is with respect of *Purgate My Stain* (THE classic in In Slaughter Natives discography), an album with a slow building intensity which explodes into passages of orchestral doom at appropriate moments. Given this new album manages a similar sound and approach to *Purgate My Stain*, is clearly an indication of how *Cannula Coma Legio* is appreciated around these parts.

Do not let the fact that this album is promoted as a teaser for the new album give any sort of impression that this material is second-rate. *Cannula Coma Legio* is as strong as *Purgate My Stain* thus demonstrating In Slaughter Natives are still an underground heavyweight. It is also fantastic to see the project releasing some of their strongest material some 25 years since the debut. Bring on the next release!

Isolator – *Culture & Principle of Anti-Human Exaltation* CD Black Plagve 2014

Teeth Engraved With the Names of the Dead – *Starving the Fires (Pt.1)* CD Malignant Records 2014

Malignant Records and the associated sub-label Black Plagve have recently added two new artists to their rather substantial roster and in the process issued the formal debut albums from each. Having been issued at the same time and noting the general degree of affinity both projects have with their chosen musical approach, this is a logical enough reason for these albums to be reviewed together.

Isolator are up first and slot within a rather bleak black industrial / black noise / black ambient framework. Noting the potential overuse of the 'black' descriptor this based on the impression this underground death industrial / ambient / noise which has links with and takes inspiration from black metal spheres (a cursory review of the album title and track names clearly attests to this). As such Isolator delivers grim black hole grinding ambience mixed with dissonant abstract guitar riffing, where the guitar elements are wielded as droning layers rather than a typical 'band' element. Likewise when vocalisations are present, they are semi-buried within the mix and range from chanted to a black metal rasp.

Cast Into Blood opens proceedings with potent molten atmospheres, where deep organ dirge drones, caustic reverb riff distortion and whispered vocalisations set the scene for the album. *Mankind Shall Reap The Mistakes God Hath Sown* follows where a guitar tone rises more prominently with abstract riff distortion, coupled with the lamenting orchestral synths and choirs semi buried within heavily echoed mix. Y*our Heaven Will Writhe Within The Chaos Of My Hell* is lengthy in both name and run time, which descends into a discordant downward spiralling and bass heaving mass, complete with buried synths and deathly croaked vocalisations. Perhaps some vague similarity to Sunn 0)))'s ode to black metal on *Black One* could be used as a passing reference due to the heavy, slow riffed guitars. For final of the five tracks *In the Blood of Our Kingdom* pares back on the bass crushing heaviness to more subtle Angelo Badalamenti styled moody synth drone soundscape. Yet even with this respite it gradually evolves into a doom riddled riff-fest, with sporadic incursions of deathly drawled vocals and flailing kit drumming being played somewhere off in the catacomb depths.

Hellish in its black noise intensity and whilst loose and abstract to a point, Isolator display a clear degree of control sophistication to the construction of their overall sound and atmosphere. In a word – harrowing.

Up next are the project with the rather lengthy moniker of Teeth Engraved With the Names of the Dead (Teeth Engraved for short), where they adhere to a more strict death industrial sound. Whilst less dense in tonality and more murky and muffled in tone, Teeth Engraved's sound encapsulates a widescreen soundscape format. Ultimately this is music of droning and grinding ambience, mixed with soot infused soundscapes, reverb drones and general inky sonic blackness. On occasion the material also steers towards a black noise / ambient style as evidenced through the inclusion of dissonant riffed guitars.

Radians sets the scene with a muffled yet sweeping soundscape which is padded out with micro tonal elements of general metallic and industrial rubble. *Vital Remains* then conforms to a well-worn death industrial markers of maudlin minor keyed synths,

grinding noise and partially mangled medical based dialogue samples. *Shredded Sky, Hung in Tatters* offers up a rather heady piece, sounding as if the product of field recordings made of an industrial incinerator (i.e. gusting heat waves and strewn ash exhaust), as oscillating grinding textures rise and fall, with atonal synths and croaked vocals relegated to another layer in the chaotic mass. *Lacerate* then builds on a base of grinding waves of morbid distortion, which are further augmented by dissonant tremolo strummed guitar, echoed feedback, maudlin sub-orchestral synths. Alternately the glass gargling and croaked vocals of *Broken From Inside* are elevated to the absolute foreground of a blasted atonal oscillating death industrial soundscape, where the vocals resemble another crushing echoed layer than anything remotely human. For the final track *When Storms Come* this arrives as a monolithic 25 minute offering, where mid paced cyclical waves grind incessantly on and feeding back distortion rides the knife-edge of becoming a high pitch squall. Dour minor keyed synth undercurrent and general creaking metallic wreckage only adds the shuddering ambience. Through a slow evolving, unhurried and controlled approach, Teeth Engraved achieve a strong 'soundscape' take on various classic elements of death industrial genre to create a very robust and refined debut album.

Whilst displaying their own individual flair, both albums from Isolator and Teeth Engraved are very strong in their grim blackened death industrial / ambient approach and display exactly what so many current American projects are doing so well with variations on a central death industrial theme. Both albums also function to again demonstrate the knack of Malignant Records to maintain an extremely high quality level within their ever expanding discography.

Jarl / Envenomist – *Tunguska Event* CD Zoharum 2014

For this album the Swedish Jarl (aka Erik Jarl of IRM) has teamed up with Envenomist; an American project helmed by David Reed whom I incidentally have not come across before. Thematically this album refers to the *Tunguska Event* which occurred in Siberia in 1908, where there was a massive unexplained explosion (estimates ranged from three to 30 megatons) caused possibly by an asteroid or comet exploding in the upper atmosphere, whilst other theories have included: an explosion of underground gas; a crashed UFO; or black hole passing through the earth. So although this event and potential explanations make perfect thematic fodder for this type of release, rather than the music taking a literal interpretation of the theme; sonically the album engenders a 'mysterious' and 'covert scientific research' type of tonal aesthetic.

Five tracks spanning 43 minutes makes up the album and with the title of each track being relegated to being referenced as Part I to V, is it is a partial acknowledgement that each part covers a tonally similar sound by playing out variations on the clinically edged and animated dark ambient sound. Here a tensile sonic aesthetic prevails; one where mid-ranged tonal shards of sound and surgical pulses swirl and entwine, but also never reaching harsh noise oriented realms. Being multi-layered in construction, the tracks are often built on a base of a low level rhythmic mechanical churn, over which radar buzzing sounds, subdued siren tones and sweeping drone textures interweave. Noting that much of Jarl's output inhabits a more minimalist realm, a fair amount of morphing and twisting territory is traversed here and

having not heard Envenomist's material before I can't say how it directly compares, but it would seem logical that his input has provided the more dynamic edge to material.
Packaging consists of a six panel fold out eco-wallet, design courtesy of Karolina Urbaniak, and features what appears to be aerial satellite photography of the region to match the album's theme. Although *Tunguska Event* is a dark ambient album at its core, it also skews the typical cavernous / deep space sonic aesthetic of much of the genre by its sound being heavily rooted in clinical industrialized tones within a fluid and flowing structure, making an interesting album in the process.

Ke/Hil – *Zone O* LP Tesco Organisation 2015

When approaching this review I quickly revisited the debut *Hellstation* album from 2010 which I remembered to be a strong if not relatively straightforward album, but something more of a side note to the members' Brigant Moloch & Wilhelm Herich main activities in Genocide Organ. This re-listening confirmed my impressions of it, but also functioned to highlight the forward leap demonstrated on *Zone O* which has substantial honed the bleak and oppressive, vaguely industrial atmospheres found on *Hellstation*. Essentially there feels to be a greater depth and complexity at play on *Zone O* which sits more within a 'heavy electronics' vein given the tonal structures never pushes into harsher industrial or power electronics realms. Intriguingly the artwork of *Zone O* with its reference to *Hellstation* on the map based artwork seems to be building a particular concept, perhaps based of the failings of contemporary based social engineering. The opening track *Work* hits hard with its complex layering (artillery fire pulse and throbbing synths), where the spoken vocals are of a emotionless authoritarian style. *Church* opts for a shuddering / wavering tonal soundscape of muted synths and non-invasive distortion, as sampled solo choir vocals bleed into the mix to give a maudlin edge. *Poverty* is a touch more rhythmic, with a muted pounding tone, wavering synths and slightly treated spoken vocals, whilst *Passages* opts for a more subtle subterranean styled atmosphere of dour synth drones and subtle static shifts. This is followed by the shuffling and lurching synth textures, interweaving muted static and of *Bridges* makes for an excellent ending to the first side of the LP.
Side B opens with the rather forceful *Infirmary Anthem*; a track of pulsing tones and queasy oscillating synths, with cyclic incursions of mid-range distortion, and when this structure is considered alongside its echoed tinged spoken vocals it is the closest that Ke/Hil have come to date of sounding like Anenzephalia. A structured rhythmic approach returns on *Ghosts of a Common Past,* including a central mid-paced pounding programmed beats, swirling industrial tinged soundscape, whilst *Children of the Devolution* steps off in another direction, featuring tensile soundscape of sub-orchestral sonic elements and distant aggressive crowd noise; with the vocals providing an apathetic proclamation of intent.
Where *Zone O* excels is in its articulation a heavy and oppressive atmosphere; one with a feel of covert surveillance and a sense of deep-seated paranoia of industrialized 'Kafkaesque' proportions. Noting that both members of Ke/Hil have previously functioned under the Anenzephalia banner but with that project currently on ice, perhaps this is the reason for the create step up displayed on *Zone O*. Regardless of the reasons of 'why', if you perhaps like me were not totally blown away by the debut *Hellstation*, this second albums is an entirely different proposition. If it wasn't already apparent from the above - this is a great album.

Kranivm – *Insanatorivm* LP Urashima 2014
Kranivm – *The Brighter Edge of Death* LP Urashima 2014
Kranivm – *I – The Blood* LP Urashima 2014

As much knowledge as one can amass regarding underground musical obscurities (20+ years and counting on my part), there can still be projects which slip by unnoticed. Thus it was not until Urashima recently reissued Kranivm's entire back-catalogue across three separate LP's that I became aware of the project and more importantly that it was a side project of the late Marco Corbelli aka Atrax Morgue. Noting that Kranivm was evidently Marco's response to his personal obsession with Brighter Death Now, it makes it even more odd that Kranivm simply passed me by for all these years (...better late than never as the saying goes). So to quickly recap on context, Kranivm was a short lived project operated for a mere two years between 1993 and 1995 with three x cassette's issued on his own Slaughter Productions label. Each of these tapes has now been pressed on its own separate LP as part of this re-issue.
Regarding Kranivm's general sonic direction it effectively pushed the death ambient sound of Brighter Death Now into more obscure, lo-fi and unrefined realms, where the atmosphere is dank, morose and morbid in the absolute best way possible. There is also a definitive aura of the early to mid-1990's which reflects the era of when this material was produced. However one element which sets this apart from pure BDN plagiarism is the occasional use of sampled Gregorian chants, which for obvious reasons begs a passing comparison to raison d'etre, particularly with regarding to their more abstract and noisy industrial / ambient soundscapes.
Insanatorivm was the first statement from the project and features oozing analogue, inky black, bass addled darkness, where the Gregorian chants of the opener *Rex Profanae* work particularly well against the layered bass rumble. *Words of Death* then features a 'barely there' death ambient structure of bass layers and random semi rhythmic knockings, whilst *Cryptic Regions* is pretty much spot on as the title may suggest - a dank, distant and echoed subterranean soundscape of the highest caliber. Side B of the LP features two lengthy pieces *Insanatorivm pt.I* and *Insanatorivm pt.II* which are more subdued and grim in tone, with low shuddering bass tones and a general barren windswept ambience, further complimented with ranting dialogue samples on part I and distant Gregorian chants on part II.
The Brighter Edge of Death was the second Kranivm release and displays a particular homage to Brighter Death Now via its title. Again the music is very much in a distant death ambient style, complete with metallic echo infused soundscapes, dour muted synths, sporadic low bass thuds, whilst the first track features religious laments in the form of sampled Gregorian chants. There is also a type of continuation of the material found on the preceding *Insanatorivm* LP particularly as *Insanatorivm pt.III* and *Insanatorivm pt.IV* are included as the first and last tracks on this LP.
I - Blood comes as the final release and deviates slightly into more 'active' realms by featuring eight shorter tracks. Opening piece *La Noche de Terror Ciego* creates a classic horror soundtrack vibe with sporadic industrial noise and plodding piano (Sampled? Not sure). Broadly speaking the death ambient tone

of the first two LP's remains here, but the layered semi-melodious synths and semi-buried sampled classical music give this a slightly differing edge. Overall the material on *I - Blood* is also a touch more active in its layering and on occasions reminds of what Brighter Death Now achieved on their early work *The Slaughterhouse*.
Although issued as three separate LP's they are best appreciated in the complete totality of Kranivm's recordings, rather than being separated into individual LP's. Although Kranivm's work does not deviate from a relatively simplistic death ambient / industrial template, this is done with the particular bleak minimalism which is characteristic of Marco's work and in this context is done so with absolute finesse to nail a sound of analogue gloom perfectly. With Urashima's ongoing limitation of 99 copies, you best know what to do.

Krank / The Grimsel Path – *Verdant Hum* MC The Epicurean 2014
This split tape features two of John Murphy's current musical outlets and contextually functions as a sort of unofficial addendum to the recent Last Dominion Lost *Towers of Silence* LP, particularly as the two releases were issued at the same time and via the same label. By way of background Krank is John Murphy's long running solo project which has a legacy spanning back to 1981 (under the original Krang Music name), but is assisted here by Till Brüggemann, who incidentally also guested on Last Dominion Lost's recent album. Alternately The Grimsel Path features the two main Last Dominion Lost members John Murphy and Jon Evans, noting also that the moniker The Grimsel Path has contextual links back to Last Dominion Lost, with this project name being a track title off the first Last Dominion Lost album. With background context out of the way Krank lead off the tape with the single 20 minute composition *NAOS Number 1*. The piece is an 80's sounding ritual industrial soundscape, consisting of grinding synth textures, scattered wavering tones, fragmented sonic oscillations and occasional percussive elements such as bells and singing bowls etc. The composition is quite loosely structured with not real driving rhythm or beat, rather is built around blown out abstract synth chords, with a very analogue tone and associated sonic warmth. Also featured are liquidous sounding 'micro' tones and contact mic-ed clanging metal on metal arrhythmia. Whilst there is an element of freeform improvisational playfulness its sound, the track is also carefully controlled and paced to generate its grimly dissonant atmosphere.
For The Grimsel Path's six tracks, these are live recordings from 2012 when the group performed at the Foetus Frolics Festival in Berlin and inhabits quite a similar tonal sphere to Krank's side. In fact if you were to not closely listen to the material you might be of the impression that both sides of the tape are from the same project. Nevertheless where The Grimsel Path's side differs is that it is slightly more focused due to the format of shorter stand alone tracks and includes sporadic vocalisations which are wholly absent from Krank's side. The sound could also be described a slightly less refined version of the experimental / industrial / ritual soundscapes found on the recent Last Dominion Lost offering. Unhinged clanging electronics, misfiring machinery and general industrial debris mark the opening piece *Deviation*, whilst *Scorched Earth* features humming suspenseful horror synths (aka Angelo Badalamenti style), otherworldly vocalisations and a production of cavernous echoed depths. *Run Please Master* then ups the ante somewhat with a stilted rhythmic drive and cinematic synths late in the track, whilst *Sideshow of the Soul* features a low bass throb, over which a mostly subdued but sometimes chaotic scattered industrial noise soundscape is positioned.
For the visual side of things the collage artwork courtesy of Kristian Olsson is suitably grim and 'industrial' in tone, with the music featured on a pro-duplicated tape. Where *Verdant Hum* succeeds is in the fact that it is another fine example of a release featuring the best elements of an early industrial ritual sound without sounding purposefully 'retro' or 'old school'. A worthy release warranting more than the limitation of 100 copies which were pressed, and perhaps demands a vinyl repress at some point.

Kristoffer Oustad – *Filth Haven* CD Malignant Records 2015
Kristoffer Oustad of the duo based projects Kristoffer Nyströms Orkester and V:28 has recently moved into solo territory with *Filth Haven*, although I am only familiar with Kristoffer Nyströms Orkester's album *Overlook Hotel* as a comparative benchmark (given I am aware of V:28 by name only).
Regardless, the opening album piece *Elberton 1979* is a strong composition using booming brass horns (of hell) to evoke a martial industrial tinged dark ambient tone. This is quickly backed up with *Anti-clockwise Rotation*; a hallucinationary tinged, subdued rhythmic industrial meets dark ambient piece and within the context of these first two tracks it demonstrates Kristoffer to be skilled in writing dark musical compositions within the general 'CMI sound'. The third offering then comes in the form of the amazing nine minute *Row Me Over*, being part soundscape and part dark ambience. With a backing of outdoor field recordings (forest sounds, creaking oars, croaking crows etc.), these blend with desolate and melancholic sub-orchestral synth drones and low level microtonal cracking metallic textures for excellent tonal impact. This piece represents a 'sonic tapestry' of the highest order and specifically reminds of the desolate bleakness of raison d'etre's classic album *within the depths of silence and phormations*. *Liquidator* features as another industrial tinged dark ambient track, with rumbling echoed elements, noninvasive sweeping textures and muted semi-orchestral drones to create a track with a general soundscape sprawl. Late album track *The Sun Maker* is slightly more forceful with its blend of various creaking and rhythmic tones with octave shifting dour sub-orchestral elements and violin synth pads to evoke an melancholic edge, and then steps up again on the final track *The Arch* with a looped and churning sub-militant industrial structure, which is heavily process with bass reverb and undercurrent of creaking metallic elements.
Seemingly stepping out of the shadows of his other collaborative projects, Kristoffer Oustad will no doubt establish his solo prominence through this excellent industrial / dark ambient album. Likewise with *Filth Haven* being quintessentially 'nordic' and bleak in feel, it is a more than suitable continuation of the legacy set down by the CMI (and related) troop.

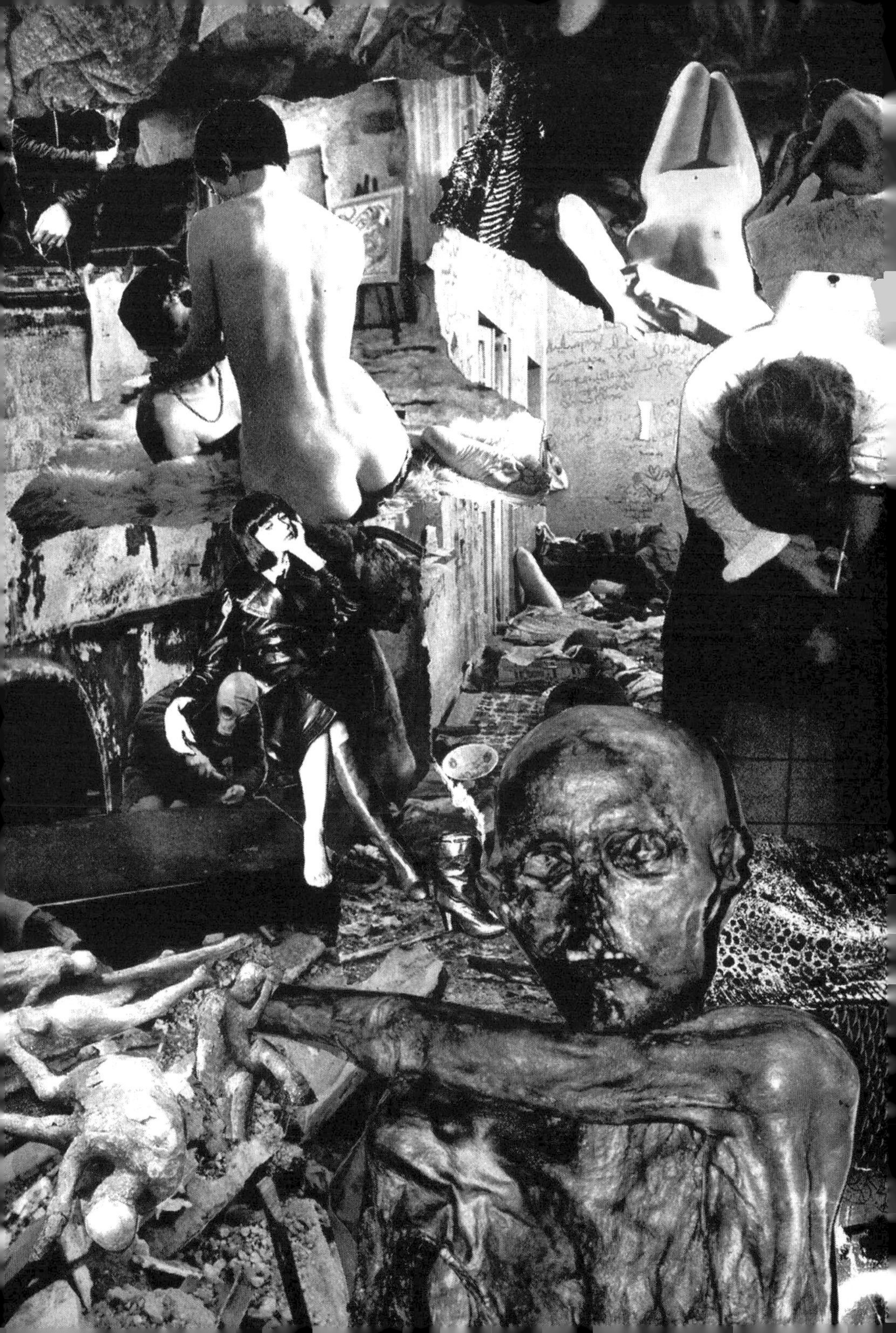

Last Dominion Lost – *Towers of Silence* LP Silken Tofu / The Epicurean 2014

Although a semi-obscured project Last Dominion Lost do have a certain aura surrounding them which is particularly derived from the legacy of its various members. Thus in their original early 90's incarnation the project included two former SPK members - Dominik Guerin and John Murphy - who teamed up with John Evans to complete the trio. Yet the material recorded during this initial formative period remained unreleased until 2004, when at the time Tesco Organisation issued *The Tyranny of Distance* album as a historic archive of the group's earliest recordings. To then fast forward another decade, the sophomore album has now been issued which includes recent recordings made between 2012 and 2014. Noting that Dominik Guerin has departed the group, for this album John Murphy and John Evans remain as the core members, who have enlisted the input of Julian Percy alongside guest contributions of Ash Wednesday, Till Brüggemann, Annie Stubbs, David Barrett, and Ricky Garrett. What is revealed on initial listens is that *Towers of Silence* is very much a direct continuation of the early industrial era - aka the pivotal 1970-80's period during which the genre base elements were being set down. Likewise given the pedigree of core members a direct lineage can be drawn to the tribal infused, percussive industrial sound of early pioneers SPK. Certain tracks also draw linage with early industrial experimental soundscape works of Current 93, where incidentally John Murphy was involved with their seminal classic *Dog's Blood Rising* album. However it is not like Last Dominion Lost have purposefully aimed to sound 'retro' or 'old school', rather this is simply the project going about creating their brand of industrial music which reflects the both legacy of members and length of time being involved in the industrial and related underground music scenes. Also what sets the sound *Towers of Silence* apart from being merely being regressively focused is the James Plotkin's mastering which has provided the album a sharp, loud, forceful and modern tenor. Covering a wide myriad of tonal territory across its 10 compositions the range of sonic elements include: shuddering / wavering analogue synths, clanging metallic rhythms, maudlin vocals (spoken, chanted and disembodied evocations), wailing horns, stoic martial kit percussion, disorientating tonal pulses, warbling sound layers, etc. Yet despite the diversity of sound on display one constant characteristic is an unnerving aura which weaves through *Towers of Silence* regardless of whether the tracks encompass subdued soundscapes or embody industrial percussive clamour.

The first cut *Stagma* represents a strong opening statement of clanging metallic textures, revving atonal synths, sporadic heavy percussion and aggressive vocal treatments - yet this piece hardly characterises the balance of the album. The following *Sektor F* then seeks to balance brooding analogue synths and gradually elevating metallic industrial outbursts (which becomes rather chaotic towards track's end), complete with cyborg vocals which replicate those of the Daleks in their sonic treatment and which completely works despite what this description implies. On *S.E.A.T.O* the group merges an industrial soundscape with tribalised percussion, where the lamenting vocal line of John Murphy informs us to: *"Leave us. We don't Want You. You're not relevant anymore. You have nothing that we need"* etc. Here the vocals are drawled over subdued soundscape and rolling tribal / militant percussion, which in their playing style are also clearly that of Mr Murphy - being forceful but equally understated. *Caesium Sunrise* then features as an excellent queasy atmospheric soundscape of wavering droning synths, garbled vocals and ritualised industrial clamour. *Kavam* potentially represents the most typical genre type track of the album, being a minimalist and loose experimental industrial soundscape which acts as a base for interview dialogue sample of a woman talking through a disturbing imprisonment ordeal. Whilst not a bad track is a little lacklustre compared to the balance of the album (...and somewhat tellingly this piece is relegated to the end of the first side of the vinyl).

Moving back into a strongly focused tribal / militant / industrial style side B opens with *Hexatom* - a track of sparse percussion, wailing horns and dominant half sung vocals. Although the track *Chlorpromazine* would seem to be making a direct reference to a pharmaceutical drug used to treat schizophrenia, here the composition's hazy and anxiety infused atmosphere is clearly more akin to as internal soundscape of a mentally unhinged mind. *Chöd Ritual* then arrives as another album standout and spanning yet more deviating terrain where percussive hand drumming, warbling vocalisations and sustained eastern tinged horns generate a track of sweepingly hazy tribal industrial. For the final two album cuts *Minol* spans a loose industrial / noise soundscape with creaking metallic debris, whilst the final title track follows a similar path but is augmented with militant percussive thrum and wailing ethnic tinged textures. Given that any new material from Last Dominion Lost was not an expected proposition, this has allowed the project used the element of surprise to deliver a categorically authoritative and quintessentially industrial album - where the descriptor of 'industrial' is used in widest context of the term. The artwork and presentation of the album is also perfectly suited, being slick and understated and incorporating visual representations of the 'towers of silence' and the religious practice of using such structures for sky burials. Whereas the debut was very much a historical document and testament to the past and early phase of the project, *Towers of Silence* is very much a distinct marker for the rather promising future of Last Dominion Lost. However let's hope it is not another decade before the next album surfaces.

Leila Abdul-Rauf - *Insomnia* CD Malignant Antibody 2015
From the initial moment of the opening track *Midnight* where disembodied echoed female vocalisations float forth from the speakers in combination with a musty soundscape and distant chimes, it inevitably draws comparisons to the sound of classic female fronted CMI act Aghast and stands as a very strong and positive introduction to the album. Yet this initial comparison is quickly shattered as the album continues and moves through a number of hazy night-time atmospheres to present an overall musicality to eclipse the initial comparative impression.
Although *Insomnia* is steeped in elements of dark ambience, it is also imbedded with a level musicality and evocative atmospheres which make it much more 'filmic' and soundtrack styled. Likewise the use of a floating and hazy trumpet throughout a number of the tracks, coupled with the clean sung haunting female vocals and understated piano provides a dusky and darkly hued night-time atmosphere. *He Sits in His Room* deviates slightly with its more focused musical frame of plucked to sweeping synth notes and prominent ethereal female vocals (the late track sweeping trumpet solo again evokes a twilight feel).
The overarching mood of *Insomnia* is one a bleak cinematic film-noir style, where the hazy solo trumpet gives a haunting late night cabaret vibe; akin to something from a David Lynch film where a vaguely nightmarishly edge lurks at the periphery of perception. In some ways the filmic musicality on *Insomnia* feels rather alien to the larger focus and output of Malignant Records, but also illustrates that darkness can also be exquisitely beautiful. Divergently recommended.

Lingua Fungi – *Melankhton* CD Aural Hypnox 2014
Via this release Aural Hypnox has expanded their label roster to include the Finnish comrade Lingua Fungi, whom incidentally this reviewer has not come across before. However for contextual sake this addition makes complete sense as the individual behind the project (Jaakko Padatsu aka OAK) is an integral part of the Aural Hypnox label. With a bit of background research it is noted that Lingua Fungi has issued some seven releases since 2006 (including tapes and collaborations), and although *Melankhton* was issued in 2014 the album was recorded, mixed and mastered in 2006. Noting this is the first album heard by Lingua Fungi and that this material dates from the earliest days of the project, it is unclear of how this fits within the scope of other albums.
On face value this album fits within the broader ritual ambient oeuvre of the Aural Hypnox label, however what sets it apart is that it is also most musical, evidenced through the use of prominent use of acoustic guitars. Thus the sound of Lingua Fungi is one where a backing of field recordings and abstract drones are coupled with focused melodic musical passages. Also with the project self-describe themselves as *'acoustic drone and ambient'*, this is quite on the mark. As such compositions are structured around a bed of nature based field recordings (crackling fire, babbling brook etc.), over which the droning textures and more prominent musical elements are laid. The use of clean / acoustic guitars is also subject to studio treatments where on the opening track *Wavy Guests* the acoustic guitar and percussion has been sampled and played backwards for twisted effect. The later section then ramps up into full musical guise with mid paced prominent bass guitar and driving percussion and again coupled with looped backwards musical elements to achieve a wonky disorientating tone. Of the melodic musical passages some segments prominent acoustic guitars and hand percussion of middle-eastern melody structures are utilised, with the second track *Departures* being a particularly strong example. The title track also builds on this general format but includes woodwind instruments for added musical effect. Yet that said not all musical passages are middle-eastern tinged, give the track *Detached* has a floating, forlorn and melancholic tone to the melodic acoustic guitar.
Of the five album compositions all are between 10 to 12 minutes each, thus allowing a general sparseness for the overarching atmosphere to slowly evolve, noting also that each piece moves through a number of distinct drone focused and musical structured segments. Although squarely of the tribal and ritual ambient sound of Aural Hypnox, Lingua Fungi elevate it into far greater musical realms with excellent result. A recommended surprise.

Melanchoholics – *Solar Café* CD Eibon Records 2014
The Melanchoholics are a project whom I was previously aware of by name alone; but had never heard their music until now. *Solar Cafe* is their third and final album, given the group has disbanded due to the untimely passing of a group member. Noting that the project moniker obviously hints at darker realms of the human psyche, what we have here is abstract guitar driven dark ambient soundscapes. As such a floating, hazy and maudlin ambience marks the bulk of proceedings, where the predominantly abstracted guitars intermingle with drones and tonal washes of sound.
Essentially cinematic in scope, the soundscapes of *Solar Café* are constructed with treated synths drones and shimmering guitars, where ringing bass notes and scattered unobtrusive industrial debris flesh out the sound. Treated spoken / sampled vocals on occasion flit in and out of the mix, coupled with what sound like looped field recordings to provide further textural depth. Clearly the sparse clean guitars resplendent with radiating reverb provide a melodic underpinning to various segments, where the understated playing also adds to the emotional impact. Interestingly there is also slight 'post-rock' quality to the melodic scale of the guitars, although this is far from 'riffed' driving musical songs; being more akin to an sparser version of Neil Young's extremely sparse guitar work on the *Dead Man* soundtrack (but here with a reduction of the particular Americana twang which characterized Neil's guitar playing). To pick out a particularly track from the nine compositions (46 minutes), *The End Belongs To This World* it contains a somewhat out of place and jarring interludes, where what can only be described as lo-fi basement black metal sporadically interject; being almost as if the result of crossed radio frequency. Although an interesting sonic

effect, it however has the negative impact of distracting from the overarching mood which both precedes and follows it.
Perhaps boarder compassions could be drawn to the occasionally guitar driven album *The Goddess Who Could Make the Ugly World Beautiful* by Morthound; or the recent ambient / post-rock tinged Sigma Octantis album *Dissipations.* But specific comparisons aside, *Solar Cafe* evokes an effortlessly bleak and melancholic yet occasionally beautiful atmosphere, which will clearly appeal to listeners of cinematic scoped dark ambient and abstract guitar based music.

Mshing – *Exterminate* 3"CDr L.White Records 2014
Mshing constitutes an Australian project (helmed by Luke Holland), whom have not cropped up on this radar before but incidentally have been around since 2005. Noting that Mshing already have 20+ releases to their name, evidently earlier material was more of a harsh noise variety, whereas on this release the project has gravitated towards a death industrial / power electronics style and sound. Given that the harsh noise does not amount to much of this reviewer's listening habits whereas obviously a lot of death industrial / power electronics does, it seems an opportune time to check out the project.
The short two minute track *Cleanse* opens proceedings with festering analogue death industrial piece, where a vague element of structure provided by a slow thumping rhythm (distorted bass or drum machine – not sure?). *Exterminate* is up next with a more loosely constructed rumbling mass of bass heavy sonics and seething, semi-buried, distortion and echo treated vocals which are spoken in delivery rather than the typical aggressive shouted / yelled delivery. The instrumental *Defile* continues with a similar sonic sphere, but contains a slightly greater sense of structure with its throbbing and cascading mid paced rhythmic loops. Certainly a solid offering. For the final track *Weaken* it elevates towards a more direct yet loose power electronics squall, with sharp mid-toned shuddering distortion and unintelligible aggressive treated vocalisations.
Overall this mini-release is both heavy and seething, but at the same time somewhat subdued compared to typical overtly aggressive elements of genre, meaning aural violence is implied rather than executed through an all-out sonic assault. Given that on this short 21 minute release Mshing display strong abilities with a bleak death industrial / power electronics sound, it will be interesting to see where the project heads on future offerings.

Morthound – *Mortology 1990-1996* 5xCD Raubbau 2014
This special box set is a lavishly presented 5xCD archival release of the classic Swedish act Morthound, whom somewhat confusingly was also known as Morthond (depending on the release). Here the box set functions to re-release and re-package: the debut cassette (for the first time on CD); the main trilogy of albums released on the lauded Swedish Cold Meat Industry (CMI) label; and a further CD of scattered compositional remains. In taking an initial overview of the varied styles and sounds encapsulated within Morthound's complete discography, with the passage of time it is abundantly clear that solo project member BJ Nilsen was a significant contributor to the development of the now recognised CMI sound. Likewise despite the extremely varied musical approach displayed between albums, the constant thread is an atmosphere of filmic and soundscape oriented compositions.
Death Time is up first, which originally was the debut cassette released on the CMI cassette side label Sound Source, and demonstrates the tentative steps of an artist finding his way. Here loose tape manipulations and smatterings of radio / movie samples intermingle with slow ominous throbbing synths and deathly pounding industrial rhythms, being very characteristic of the emerging 'CMI' style and sound of the time. Likewise *Anœsthetic* and *Entertainment in the Desert* with their tribal percussive thump provide vague hints at a later direction and sound of the project.
Noting the initial steps taken on *Death Time*, a further step forward is evident on the formal debut album *This Crying Age*. By specifically building upon the early template, the debut album pushed Morthond's sound into a far more refined experimental soundscape / dark ambient style. Features four tracks and spanning 54 minutes *This Crying Age* articulates a sonic mood of cold arctic wastelands and ominous dreamlike to nightmarish soundscapes, which are punctuated with ticking clocks, disembodied voices, programmed synths, smatterings of loose industrialised rhythms and the emergence of spare ethnic percussion and woodwind instruments. Thus with its barren arctic ambience *This Crying Age* displays sparse abstract filmic styled soundscapes and at the time of its release clearly helped bed down the nordic CMI dark ambient sound.
Following only a year later in 1992, *Spindrift* represented a significant evolution and resulted in their tour de force album (noting that at this stage the moniker had also evolved slightly to that of Morthound). Merging experimental dark ambient soundscapes with structures that on occasion veer towards on pop-songs, *Spindrift* still manages to maintain a dark undercurrent throughout. Also with the emergence of prominent world music relates influences, the album created a style which could be referred to as 'ethno-ambient'. Here the compositions are awash with moody synth melodies / piano movements, percussive industrial / tribalised rhythms, female sung lead vocals (on *Herb of Grace*), and again with smatterings of movie dialogue samples. *Riverine* represents the pinnacle of Morthound's ethno ambient sound, being an amazing piece of mid paced Asiatic rhythmic chimes and percussion, booming tympani percussion and piano accompaniment which settles into a looped meditative groove which gradually evolves over a 17 minute expanse. In a word this track is marvelous, although somewhat oddly the track has been reordered from being the album's opening track to that of its centrepiece. As a bonus *Shrivatsa* has been added to this re-release (originally from the *Karmanik Collection* compilation CD), and is another absolutely transcendent ethno ambient composition of floating ritual ambience (hurdy gurdy drones, chimes, tabla and soaring flute accompaniment).
With a span of a further two years 1994 saw the release of the third and final official album *The Goddess Who Could Make the Ugly World Beautiful*, again displaying a major stylistic shift. At the time of its release fans of *Spindrift's* ethno-ambient style were shocked by the heavy use of industrial tinged guitars, where repetitive pummeling Godflesh styled guitars and thumping program drum machines sit atop a base of dark ambient to industrial soundscapes. Whilst the guitar oriented sound of project has never been a favourite of Morthound's around these parts, there are enough filmic dark ambient tracks on the album to make it not totally guitar dominated and in fact with guitars

featured on only three of the seven album tracks, referring to this as the 'guitar' album is slightly misleading. Of the non-guitar pieces, the hazy yet brooding dark ambient atmospheres of *Hibernation* (complete with vague disembodied voices floating in and out of the mix), in part mirrors where BJ Nilsen would take his sound post Morthound and as displayed on the debut album *Lech* issued under the Hazard moniker. *Syyzygy* also sees the 'ethno ambient' be reprised in full guise, here with full Indian flavour evoked through tabla percussion and sampled ethic female vocals. Yet for all its outward display of stylistic diversity, the crowning achievement of this album is the concluding track *World End*. Being an amazing soundscape of doomy droning layers and multitude of abstract yet cinematic sound textures (unintelligible vocal snippets adding to the nightmarish edge), the track breaks out into a final segment of dark industrial tribalism with mid paced ritual drumming and wailing female vocals. Fantastic.
The final of the five discs is titled *Unleashed 1990-1996*, which collects together an additional nine previously unreleased Morthound compositions. *Woodstock Mayhem* is noted to engender a freeform structure and almost industrial noise style to its distortion squall, which is clearly a differing sound for the project despite the wide variety of styles already covered. Likewise *Down the Hall* provides a solid example of ominous 'unknown lurking fear' type of dark ambience. For the latter half of this CD are a collection of long-form sprawling, minimalist / abstract dark ambient compositions, some with tinges of ethno influences (ritual gong, woodwinds etc.), others with a slight mechanised approach, which equally arcs back to the cold minimalism of *This Crying Age* as much as it also mirrors several elements of the hazy swirling atmospheres of Hazard's debut album *Lech*. Although this disc is slightly less focused than other albums in this set (obviously down to the multiple original sources), this is still a solid complimentary disc to bring together the remaining loose threads of the project.
Where *Morthology* excels is that it is far beyond being just an archival 'completest' release. This is an expansive and expertly realised document of all Morthound recorded output and functions as the perfect mechanism to revisit the complete back catalogue in reinvigorated packaging and sound. Listening to this set in its totality is a pleasure and is illustrative of the ripples of influence which have radiated out from the early to mid 1990's when these albums were originally released. For old or new fans alike, your Morthound history lesson awaits.

Murderous Vision – *Ghosts of the Soul Long Lost: Volume Three* 3xCD Live Bait Recording Foundation 2014

Here we have a triple album which functions to archive various limited and out of print recordings from the group. Being the third in the archive series, it also marks a celebration of the 20th anniversary of Murderous Vision and contains recordings from number of different eras of the project.
In reissuing an album from 2000, *Suffocate…The Final Breath* takes up the first disc, where its title is very fitting for the overall atmosphere and mood. Here the material forms stalking yet subdued soundscapes which drift between dark ambience and death industrial. As such slow thumping beats, tribal-esque rhythms and churning factory sounds are offset against the disorienting ebb and flow of a sweeping undercurrent. Other album pieces occupy a freeform style with a general tonal abstractness, where an electronic fog evokes a trancelike ambience. Whilst this album certainly has it excellent moments, some tracks are slightly ambling and directionless at times and with a length of 74 minutes, dropping a few of the less engaging pieces might have made this a far more focused album. Also one notable aspect of the sound is its general sonic 'crispness', which is slightly more clinical in tone than European counterparts of the equivalent time.
Salvation on Sand Mountain takes up the second disc and jumps forward a decade in the creative arc of the project. Originally forming a cassette album from 2010 released on Danvers State Recordings, the stylistic shift is clearly evident given this album straddles a death industrial to power electronics sound. The release also functions to showcase seven guest vocalists, with project lead Stephen Petrus featuring on a further two tracks. Fierce and focused in tone, the second disc mirrors all the best elements of the current American death industrial / power electronics scene with caustic, slightly rhythmic driving tracks. Likewise the divergent approach that each of vocalists take provides a clear degree of variation between each composition, demonstrating that individuality is still a clear possibility in the 'yelled distortion drenched vocal' style. Of the vocal led tracks *Lies of the Beast?* differs given it is more subdued in tone and includes female spoken vocals. With the bulk of the album constituting a rather punishing collection of tracks, the concluding piece is rounded out with a longer form, pounding and distortion fried industrial offering. Accordingly the instrumental framework serves as a base for religious based sermon samples relating to the track's title and its thematic focus (i.e. a fringe Alabama religious sect which involves the handling of deadly snakes as a demonstration of faith).
For the third and final disc it compiles two prior separate releases, including a four track live studio recording *Echosphore* from 2010, in addition to three tracks originally issued in 2011 on the *Corpse Abuse* split with Skin Graft. Up first is the *Echosphore* material which interestingly achieves a kind of mid-point between the first two discs. Here the material is more soundscape oriented and less 'song' focused than the second disc, but far more direct, rough and loud than the first disc. As such the sound sprawls as a swirling distorted mass, punctuated with looped rhythmic elements, scattered improvised noise squalls and quasi-chanted / moaned vocal textures. The tone also has a sharp, harsh and overblown aesthetic with hints at the live studio creation. Alternatively the *Corpse Abuse* tracks function as much shorter and more focused compositions. By providing slightly more breathing space and rhythmic undercurrent, these tracks are more controlled in a throbbing / oscillating death industrial style, complete with suitable thematic dialogue samples and aggressive vocalisations.
As a complete package this is a strong document of the varied approach of the project, which as displayed here extends from sprawling, occasionally ritualised dark ambient / industrial soundscapes, and on to focused aggressive and focused death industrial to power electronics compositions. As an archive this is also a testament to the long-standing and ongoing dedication of Stephen Petrus to the post-industrial underground.

Nekrofellatio – Pesadilla En Una Noche Sin Estrellas CD Death Continues Records 2014

This rather mysterious Italian project (helmed by Leonardo Carballo Canto), returns with their second album and again on the same label who released their debut. As with the first album it seems Nekrofellatio is intent on channelling the morbid minimalism of the fellow Italian project Atrax Morgue, but still manages to do this with enough individual flair so as to be just a 'mere' copyist project. Yet, whereas the debut displayed a loose crudeness to the death industrial musings, on this new album there is a much greater degree or control and restraint on display. Essentially tracks are constructed with minimal fuss – usually a central oscillating analogue tone – around which other muted occasionally rhythmic layers are added for atmospheric effect. Echo and reverb also play a strong part in the foggy atmospheres created.

Sex Electronic Poison opens the album is suitable fashion with cold and slow evolving minimalist drones, smattering of dialogue samples, 80's horror synths and muted grinding static. Things then kick in in an impressive fashion on *Unidos Por La Sangre* with warbling atonal synths, choral vocals and rolling industrial / tribal rhythms and garbled demonic vocalisations. *Muneco De Carne* then opts for the heavy use of multi-layered and intertwining dialogue samples (religion, death and abuse seem key topics here), which are set against a loose yet stifling analogue distortion base which ramps up in intensity over the track's span. *Disgusted By Humans* also pushes into more urgent territory, with forceful rhythmic loops and waves of echo infused distortion. *Demoni* functions as a touch more unhinged and chaotic, including field recordings of random crowd noise, screamed violence and a grinding upsurge of static. Late album track *Reanimated Flesh* opts for slightly more mechanised rhythmic structure with mid paced factory-esque loops.

All in all this is not an outwardly aggressive album, rather it is one which embodies a slow, tense and stalking atmosphere which has been honed to razor sharpness through the mastering undertaken by John Stillings (aka Steel Hook Prosthesis). With ten tracks at just short of hour's playtime, this is a far more focused and accomplishes album than the debut, and should more than please any fan of Atrax Morgue's morbid analogue minimalism.

Night Science - *Issue V* Cipher Productions 2014

Here we have the fifth instalment of Chris Groves' *Night Science* magazine, some long four years since the last and although the release of new instalments does not happen at a rapid rate, each issue is absolutely worth the wait. Issue V is the biggest issue yet spanning a massive 158 pages; eight detailed and lengthy interviews; a monumental 92 pages of live show and album reviews; and topped off with a CD of tracks from interviewed projects. Artists featured in this issue include: Alberich, Niellerade Fallibilisthorstar, Hal Hutchinson, Anemone Tube, Mlehst, Skin Graft, Kazuma Kubota and Fragment Factory.

Although Issue V follows a similar visual and stylistic template, there has been a subtle refinement of design, where everything is slightly more clean and defined in presentation. The print quality has also stepped up a notch too, which is slick clean and very professional. Regarding the interviews, these are all detailed and long-form, being written specifically for each artist and generally speaking demands at least a cursory level of knowledge of the underground music being covered to get the most from the questions and responses. As a specific example the Hal Hutchison interview introduction makes reference to an earlier interview in *Special Interests Magazine*, thus using that as a 'springboard' for a continuing series of questions. Having read all interviews in detail, personally the one from Alberich, Niellerade Fallibilisthorstar, Hal Hutchinson and Anemone Tube made for most immersive reading (based on my listening preferences). Regarding the reviews these are uniformly excellent as Chris is a strong and descriptive writer, where his writing style is sharp and focused, intelligent and insightful and covering a wide variety of known and obscured releases in a broad industrial / death industrial, noise power electronics and experimental spheres. He also clearly holds strong opinions on what in his estimation are less focused elements of a particular release and is willing to state his view. For those items which I have reviewed myself, on occasion I noted some divergent opinions that Chris and I have, which made for interesting comparisons of opinion and re-evaluation of said releases.

Moving onto the CD, to my mind this really functions mostly as a 'taster' for interviewed acts if readers are not familiar with their work, thus I have chosen not to review it as if were a typical compilation album. However I will say that in this day and age when most music is available to sample at the click of a mouse, it is commendable that Chris has continued to issue the sampler CD as part of the magazine.

For me personally, the strongest element of *Night Science* is the fact that Chris' listening preferences contains only a partial crossover with mine, given a large portion of his listening is firmly entrench in the noise and related fields. This then means *Night Science* contains lots of lesser known projects and reviewed releases, making for very informative and immersive reading and listening (rather than simply me reading interviews and reviews of artists / albums I might have covered myself). Without question *Night Science* is absolutely one of the strongest underground industrial / noise / power electronics print magazines out there and is mandatory reading, regardless if you initially recognize interviewed artists or not.

Nyodene D - *Mouths That Reap The Harvest* LP Urashima 2014

Following the excellent full length *Edenfall* on Malignant Records (from 2012) and the *Atop Masada* MC on Nil By Mouth Recordings (from 2013), Nyodene D return with a new album on the cult Urashima label. However with this release containing three lengthy tracks spanning around 28 minutes of music, this feels more like an extended EP than a proper full length.

To place the sound of this LP it needs to be considered within context of the focused power electronics sound of *Edenfall*, as well as the more expansive and experimental sound of *Atop Masada*. Thus where *Mouths That Reap The Harvest* stands is that it continues the template of the later MC by encapsulating longer form and slowly evolving tracks. Side A is taken up with the single extended track *Ansuz Ascending* where its structure follows a long drawn out build-up, consisting of a central pounding beat, grinding drones and cyclically elevating noise. The track's upward movement is slow and ominous where the distortion is mid-range and skirts the edge of a higher pitched and sonically invasive tone. It is then only towards the latter half of the track that the aggressive yet slow drawled and flanged vocalizations kick in with morose intensity.

For side B *Jera In Merkstave (Black Harvest)* opens with a militant thrum which is soon coupled with slow looped static and antagonistic vocals which radiate off into the distance due to the slow echoed treatment. With its oscillating structure and wavering drone undercurrent this piece provides a more direct power electronics feel. *The Thunder Comes* is the third and final track and is slightly more morose overall. Here it uses an atonally wailing trumpet to excellent effect, coupled with a relatively minimalist drone-scape and subdued but heavily flange treated vocals. Within the later section the grinding looped noise subtly builds, as the warbling and wailing trumpet also increases in playing intensity. Noting the use of a non-typical instrument, the trumpet on the piece begs a comparison to mind IRM due to their similar use of similar brass instrumentation on their *Four Studies For Crucifixion* 10"EP.
Overall there is a rougher and slightly noisier edge to the sound of the LP, being less 'polished' than the shaper sound found on *Edenfall,* which also probably has a lot to do with the analogue format of the vinyl. As such *Mouths That Reap The Harvest* is another excellent addition to Nyodene D's quickly expanding discography and pretty much with all Urashima's outputs 99 copies simply feels too few, so move quick before this disappears for good.

Post Scriptvm – *Benommenheit* CD Tesco Organisation 2014
Whilst Post Scriptvm have been a familiar name for many years this is actually their fifth album and third release for Tesco Organisation. Yet with *Benommenheit* being the first album heard around these parts, it has played the role of providing formal introduction to Post Scriptvm's sonic world (obviously this is symptomatic of the case that some artist's miss out on warranted attention due to the sheer volume of material out there). Nevertheless on first impressions *Benommenheit* slots nicely within a broad post-industrial soundscape style, but approached with a distinctive and highly refined sound. Clearly Post Scriptvm are a project which rely on meticulously composed structures and where there are elements 'studio trickery' at play, which begs a more than passing reference to the current era and 'soundscape' oriented material of Propergol (this impression seems to be further solidified by that fact that Post Scriptvm's second album was released on Proergol's own label Hermetique). Across its nine track and 55 minute span *Benommenheit* delves into loosely composed post-industrial structures consisting of: stilted rhythms, wonky sound textures, hallucinogenic sonic treatments, vague disembodied voices, random radio chatter and the occasionally foray into composed segments with orchestral instrumentation. Of the more composed style *Faces Like Masks* is one such example, with its tense soundtrack styled sub-orchestral mood. Likewise *Eerie Cargo* is imbued with a mood specifically suggested by the title, being one of tense, sparely layered soundscape textures and sporadic percussive and piano flourishes. Late album track *Clinging On Like Grim Death* moves into a differing sonic environment and is heavier than anything which precedes it, being a metallic percussive industrial number of loose clanging rhythms and sampled operatic styled vocals. *Mal De Debarquement* then rounds the album out in maudlin electronics soundscape guise, of layered sweeping orchestral synth textures, sparse industrial grinding / clanging tones and scattered indecipherable vocoder drenched vocalisations. Despite its sonic variation, there is a an overarching atmosphere of paranoia throughout, which gives an impression of hidden surveillance and unseen watchers which could be described as rather *'Kafkaesque'* (...for non-Kafka readers this can be defined as *'marked by a senseless, disorienting, often menacing complexity'* or *'surreal distortion and sense of impending danger').* As such *Benommenheit* is a varied and darkly experimental album, which also does not shy away from pushing into abstract, surreal and hallucinogenic territory at times (again dovetailing nicely with the often absurdist tone of Kafka's described bureaucratic oppression). Clearly this is the work of careful compositional structuring and refinement, which has a depth of sonic texture and detail, whilst most importantly maintaining a focused and engaging atmosphere throughout (and an album which highlights the error of not checking out the group sooner). A recommended release.

Praetorian Guard - *Ever Bloom Those Flowers of Rome* MC Trapdoor Tapes 2015
Praetorian Guard are a group focusing on militant tinged industrial soundscapes, being the collaborative result of Matt Casey and Ben Taylor of Ebola Disco and Andrew McIntosh of Screwtape (but also not sounding nothing like these projects). I have no idea if this is a one off recording collaboration or something more permanent, but *Ever Bloom Those Flowers of Rome* appears to be their only available recording.
With the stormy industrial soundscapes on display, there is a miasmic swirl to the layering of sonic elements and general analog roughness to the sound, thus providing a muted windswept quality. Sustained synth textures and rumbling bass addled distortion provide the backbone, where a semi-buried militant orchestral feel is also apparat, but it is not really a case of there being prominent orchestral elements rather just a general feel of this and on sporadic occasion partially buried violins and trumpets (samples or synths? Not sure). In other segments a militant percussive thump gives a greater degree of movement, coupled with sampled choir vocals. Vocals are also featured throughout, taking a variety of guises, including: spoken style but blended low within the mix; pitch shift morphed beyond easy recognition; or agonisingly yelled to match the passages pushes towards slightly more chaotic and overblown territory.
Although the militant industrial atmospheres created do in part hit their intended mark, with the material spanning two hours and containing no individual tracks (elongated soundscapes span the entirety of each side of the tape), the overall release is in part ambling and aimless, thus ending up being a bit of a slog to maintain interest and focus for the entire duration. So although this tape suits its purpose in short doses, it is also something I have not listened to in its entirety of a single listening session. Regardless of whether Praetorian Guard are intending to continue as a project, some greater focus and shorter length would no doubt strengthen the end result.

The instrumental track *Pigs* opens the second side of the album, with a layered militant thrum and hissing distortion textures, and whilst threatens at breaking out into all out sonic chaos, never actually eventuates. *Impure Fantasy* is next and an another cinematic industrial soundscape styled track of sustained organ drones, abstract echoed layers, muted percussive textures and vocals which sit somewhere between spoken word and sampled movie dialogue. The title track concludes the album and is the most minimalist track on offer. Built with a basic and loose structure of slow menacing echoed bass layers, the track gradually coalesces into a vague structure as the screech distorted vocals are acerbically delivered.

With three tracks per side, interestingly the album seems follows an almost template approach, where a focused industrial / power electronics track is followed by a cinematic soundscape and rounded out by another loose industrial composition. Plan or coincidence? Not quite sure. Noting the myriad of sonic expressions on display, *Persona* is a diverse and varied album which is 'industrial' to its core given all its aspects are captured under this broad stylistic banner. It is also a clear demonstration that Frederikke is not afraid to experiment with her chosen sound and direction for Puce Mary. Recommended.

Puce Mary - *Persona* LP Posh Isolation 2014

Puce Mary is the industrial / power electronics project of Frederikke Hoffmeier who since 2010 has been steadily raising her profile via a series of releases, each of which are displayed a gradual improvement in sound, focus and direction. *Persona* forms the third official album.

The Course opens the album in fine fashion, featuring a strong distinctive throbbing industrial rhythm, fluttering higher pitched tones, metallic clanging structure and vocalisations delivered in a relatively subdued, distortion filtered style. This a blood boiling, fist pumping track and clear standout, where Frederikke demonstrates her skill of how to nail with clinical precision a structured industrial / power electronics track. Although potentially referencing Pharmakon in relation to this this track may on face value seem entirely lazy (given both projects are part of a new generation of female fronted underground industrial / power electronics acts), this comparison has far more to do with the clinically sharp sound and rhythmic construction of this opening piece, than any perceived similarity in vocal delivery or the fact that both projects are helmed by women. Following this extremely strong and focused opening cut, the sound takes a drastic left turn the following track *The Viewer* is a lengthy and tensile cinematic styled soundscape with a muted undercurrent of rumbling bass, slow militant percussive beats, creaking metallic debris, shimmering atonal synths etc. *Gestures* then arcs back towards a more focused style, where basic throbbing rhythms, atonal warbling synths and slow drawled vocals articulates a lethargic drugged out haze.

raison d'etre - *Collected Works* CD Infinite Fog Productions 2013

The long standing and highly revered raison d'être can be classified as one of the pinnacle acts and pillars of the second wave of the dark ambient scene, noting the first wave was pioneered by the dark ambient genre founder - Lustmord. But whereas Lustmord over the years has plumbed the dark depths and uninhabited cavernous recesses of the earth; then later turning focus on deep space themes; raison d'être has instead maintained a constant focus on an inward looking spiritual approach, evoked through sacral ambient soundscapes. By now raison d'être have carved their own dark ambient niche which can cut to the core of the inner psyche. Essentially the feeling of religious laments bleeds through all aspects of Peter's music and one which draws on the spiritual capacity of the human condition. This for me is where Peter excels with his musical works.

So what we have here should be self-evident from the title - a collection of tracks, drawn together under the banner of a compilation album. However given the consistent thematic threads that runs through Peter's works, this album does not feel like a compilation of disparate compositions. This is assisted by the fact that the majority of the compositions come from the later era / current sound of the project, where the majority of tracks date from between 2001 to 2010 (with one track from as far back as 1999). As such the album's style is based on long form soundscapes compositions of subterranean drones, sampled and slightly treated sacral chanted vocals, distant ritual chimes, scraping metallic textures, sparse piano (on selected tracks) and the ever present quasi-orchestral synth pads.

If you are already well acquainted with a large proportion of Peter's work there are no surprises to be found here, but this for me is simply not an issue give the pinnacle level in which he operates. Artwork also comes courtesy of Martin Bladh, who has painted a series of 'death mask' pictures of Peter Anderson at various stages of his life (thus far) and presented across the four panel digi-pack. Recommended - as is pretty much the case with all of raison d'être's output.

raison d'etre – *Mise en Abyme* CD Transgredient Records 2014

Raision d'etre return with a new album some five years since the last official full length, and whilst not necessarily deviating greatly from their recognised sound, solo member Peter Anderson is still producing interesting variations on well established themes. This album also sees raison d'etre shifting to a new label following the unfortunate demise of Cold Meat Industry, with Transgredient Records being a side label to the respected Drone Records.

Noting that 2009's *The Stains of Embodied Sacrifice* articulated a sonic environment of sacral dark ambience, including selected passages which veered towards a jarring post-classical sound, a similar sonic aesthetic has been explored on *Mise en Abyme* (translating to *'placed into the abyss'*), but here condensed into four lengthy compositions (12 to 17 minutes each). *Abyssos* opens the album and could thematically represent the decent into the abyss of one's own psyche. Dour sub-orchestral synths, windswept drones and metallic scraping textures mark the path and while the mood commences as serene, over its expanse it gradually builds to an intensely peaked crescendo. The following track *Infernous* clearly implies a heavier visage, which does in fact deviate heavily from anything previously found in raison d'etre's discography. Towards the middle of this piece micro-tonal grating metallic textures and heavy clanging scrap metal cacophony mark a large portion of the sound (… these sonic elements appear to have been sourced from scrap metal recording sessions, which have in turn been sonically manipulated into vaguely rhythmic effect). Whilst *Infernous* has the potential to jar listeners who are more familiar with the ambient and sacral side of raison detre's sound, this track clearly seems to be a sonic representation of self-flagellation. Yet with the underscoring elements of wailing quasi-brass horns and sub-orchestral drones, Peter positions these heavier metallic elements squarely within the framework of raison d'etre. *Katharos* then arcs back to more familiar territory of a floating melancholic atmosphere (perhaps acting as a means of catharsis to the heavier grating elements of the *Infernos* which preceded it), here utilising sampled Greek Orthodox chants, swelling sub-orchestral waves, sparse ritual chimes and subtle metallic scraping textures. The final album track *Agraphos* rounds out the album in calmer fashion by gradually building in an upward sweeping trajectory, as if seeking to elevate above the depths and heaviness of earlier album passages. Despite its slightly lighter tonal guise, it is still a track heavily infused with a dark and gloomy mood, again constructed with the Gregorian chants and sweeping soundscapes, sparse chimes / tolling church bells and a general sonic palate infused with a thumping echoed depth.

Whilst *Mise en Abyme* does not necessarily turn the tables on what has come before, rather it represents yet another step in the continual refinement of raison d'etre's style. As such Peter (again) effortlessly demonstrates his skill in evoking a sacral dark ambient sound, which very much suits solo appreciation and contemplation and introspection on the part of the listener.

Rope Society – *Dissolve* MC Trapdoor Tapes 2015

David Tonkin (aka Isomer) has returned with his second release under the Rope Society moniker, noting this is his side project focusing on a mix of rough analog focused industrial noise and power electronics abuse. In an overarching sense the approach of Rope Society which could be described as David's personal and current take on 'classic' hallmarks of early industrial / power electronics cassette culture but also sidestepping any sort of cynical attempt to emulate an obvious 'old-school' sound.

Head Above Water commences the tape is relatively subdued fashion, with a low shuddering oscillation and semi-buried barked vocals before things really kick in with *Behavioural Interventions* – a track of skuzzy, squalling and choppy industrialised noise with spoken vocals are positioned low in the mix and semi-mangled with echo treatment. A particular highlight of the tape comes in the form of the final track for side A, where *Hate Campaign* features a buzzing power electronic drone at its core which has a burrowing and corrosive sonic quality, as some more sporadic and deeply echoed metallic elements are gradually infused to building effect. A focused and effective sound.

Side B features a further three tracks, where *Answered In The Negative* is the first and being quite 'post-mortem' in sound – i.e. deep, muffled and distant sounding industrial noise clamour, with a great degree of echo and metallic heft, again with a gradually elevating intensity. *Eyes Shut Tight* then function to amplify the tone again by featuring a straightforward singularity; incorporating a bass rumbling / squealing toned sonic mass with sporadic incursions of rough barked vocals. *Bestial* is the final of six tracks, and concludes the tape on relatively subdued industrial noise terms, with an excellent breadth and tonal separation to its layers. As such the echoed vocals sit well off in the distance; the rumbling bass textures hover ominously overhead; with clattering metallic elements separated within the mid tonal spectrum. An excellent concluding piece.

Overall *Dissolve* is a strong release and to this ear is more focused than the debut 'One Word Definition', however this impression is also driven by my own personal sonic preferences, where this tape sits towards dank, bass intoned industrial noise, rather than harsh noise elements which were more prominently displayed on the first tape. Also noting that a few more upcoming recordings from Rope Society are already in the pipeline (including releases on Tesco Organisation and Untergeschoss), meaning the project's profile should continue to positively increase.

Sewer Goddess – *Painlust* CD Black Plagve 2015

Since 2006 the Boston native Sewer Goddess (helmed by Kirsten Rose) has been delivering her particular brand of death industrial muck which on occasion verges on power electronics aggression. *Painlust* is the new opus (and second album if not counting the live album *Disciples Of Shit: Live Waste* from 2001), and a surprising one at that given it demonstrates a substantial evolution in sound. Essentially there has been a intentional streamlining and refinement of the project into a formal band structure (now including bass, drums and guitars), but not forsaking the grit and grime of the tone of earlier material. *Plague Axis* open the album with a crushing death industrial sound; one of creaking metal, sustained minor key drones, pounding beat and screeched vocals to set the tone with grim intent. The following piece *My Grave* the arrives as the first demonstration of the shift towards a structured 'band' focus, where the death industrial sound is augmented with slow pummelling Godflesh styled industrial styled guitars (albeit of a darker doom metal heaviness), here with Kristian's vocals being in a distinctive drawled spoken style. *Flog* follows a similar template of a mid-paced churn of guitar / drums / bass but here the drawled vocals are force-fed through a distortion treatment, with this track being a fantastic display of the evolved band driven approach. *Black Meat And Bones* is a song of a more forceful ilk, with a driving / pounding percussive backbone, spitting machinery, screeched vocals and austere but shrill guitars, while the slow rhythmic drag and pull of the bass / drums / guitar of *Get the Rope* achieves a very death industrial feel, despite its more typical band formation. Representing a grand conclusion *Melena's Mask* pushes back towards a mid-paced industrial guitar throb, heaving driving percussion and rhythmic machine backing, here Kristen's vocals being multi-tracked to included drawled passages and screeched screams.

With six tracks at around 28 minutes, this is by no means a long album, but has compressed a massive sound into this short timeframe. The album artwork by André Coelho Sektor 304 is suitably grim and mechanical in style, although to my mind some of other images within the booklet would have made for a more striking cover. Noting I have appreciated what Sewer Goddess were about on earlier releases, *Painlust* is a quantum leap forward in style and sound with the honed band focused sound a real revelation to behold.

Sigma Octantis – *Dissipations* CD Malignant Antibody / OPN 2014

In collaboration with the French label OPN, Malignant Records have used their sub-label Malignant Antibody to issue the fourth album and apparently the final release from Sigma Octantis. Although having not heard of Sigma Octantis before, from the introduction provided by *Dissipations* they deliver an interesting amalgam of stylistic elements cherry picked from a number of genres (including: animated dark ambient, 1990's era tribal-industrial and post-rock), where these disparate elements are blended in such a way as to not sound derivative of any of the genres in particular. Noting also that the defunct cult Swedish project Morthound is used a reference point within the promo blurb, this is actually quite a spot on reference point, given a similar musicality, diversity and playfulness is demonstrated here (and particularly reference Morthound's albums *Spindrift* and *The Goddess Who Could Make the Ugly World Beautiful*).

Album opener *Vieil ocean, aux vagues de cristal* starts proceedings with a typical dark ambient drone melody but it is not long before rousing tribal rhythms kick in over which a solo piano melody provides a dour, down tuned mood, yet the tone morphs again with the later introduction of a twanging guitar line providing a post-rock sensibility. On *Errance Definitive* the tribal-industrial rhythms sound as if almost an outtake of Deutsch Nepal's classic album *Deflagration of Hell,* but the later section soars off into territory all its own through the use of shimmering synths and quasi-orchestral textures (late track again morphing towards a post-rock tone). Likewise with its slightly middle eastern tinged melodies, *Des astres tranquilles* encompasses a sonic atmosphere somewhat reminiscent of the most mellow and musical passages found on ISIS's final album *Wavering Radiant* (which is a complimentary comparison to make). The final track *Farewell* is also an absolute album standout, being a moody melancholic track of swelling cinematic orchestral melodies and driving tribal industrial hand percussion. Throughout its course it drops away into quiet segments of post-rock tremolo guitars and rock kit drums before building to the final crescendo to rival the build ups of Mono or Explosions in the Sky and generating an absolutely stunning and sublime song in the process.

Eight tracks in all cover just short of an hours play time and although my personal listening habits extend to a wide range of music outside the main focus of *Noise Receptor Journal,* Sigma Octantis are not a project which have ever cropped up on my radar before. Therefore recognition should be afforded to Malignant Records for issuing this album which is slightly off tangent the main bulk of their musical output, particularly as it is a great album which may have otherwise passed by unnoticed.

Shift – *Altamont Rising* LP Unrest Productions / CD Cold Spring Records 2014

The solo helmed Shift have been steadily building their profile for a decade now and whilst the previous full length album *Bulk* from 2009 received a fair degree of critical praise, *Altamont Rising* further elevates Shift's sound to a level which represents their magnum opus to date. As with earlier material Shift has carved out a niche sound which inhabits the border regions between noise and power electronics, yet the sonic aggression and density on display here is monolithic even by Shift's standards.

Utilising layered industrial noise filth and scathing junk metal clatter to produce a heavily drudging atmosphere, Shift's approach is too structured nor chaotic enough to quality as pure noise, yet equally is more freeform and 'soundscape' oriented that than a typical power electronics 'song' approach. Effectively Shift construct their compositions by bedding down layer upon layer of industrial clamour, where each layer also embodies a vague looped rhythmic structure. Thus with the sonic layers complementing and competing for supremacy in equal measures, it provides a loose sense of structure to what otherwise could be a chaotic mass of sound. Also with each composition effectively bleeding into the next, it only adds to atmosphere of enveloping moroseness, as the oppressive caustic distortion, buried samples, garbled radio chatter and sporadic anger infused vocals combine to gradually grind and crush the listeners psyche.

Circling Raptor opens the album with thick, heavy and laborious waves of distortion, which combine into a crushing mass of sound. This track then flows directly into the slightly more structured *They Don't Suffer Enough,* which is characterised by crumbling layers of loosely rhythmic, low to mid-range industrial noise muck, prior to the introduction of the album's first vocals which are distortion saturated and barked in full power electronics guise. One of the album's most direct tracks is *Shelter* which opens the second side of the LP with driving mid-paced distortion loops, sampled background crowd noise and fiercely oppressive and borderline unhinged vocal attack. This mood is pushed to even further extremes on *Rising* with it's the pulsing distortion, squealing noise and heavily flanged vocals. Yet notwithstanding the totality of its oppressiveness, the final album track *The Greatest Ecstasy* finishes on a slightly differing tangent, mostly due to the vocals, which take the form of an intense whisper (with elongated method of lyrical pronunciation), as the multi-layered slab of cyclic rumbling industrial noise grinds incessantly to the

JAGUAR
SUN
THE JETS
BASEL
BASEL
BLACKY
JAGUAR

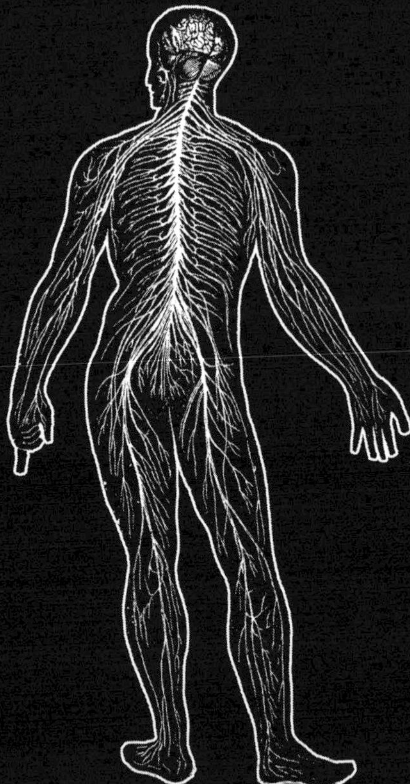

album's final vinyl groove.
The LP version of *Altamont Rising* is limited to a mere 100 copies, issued on heavy weight vinyl and housed within a screen printed rough card stock cover with a couple of printed inserts, with a less limited CD version issued via Cold Spring Records. Through *Altamont Rising*, Shift have ascended to their full potential which was previously hinted at and achieved to varying degrees on prior releases. In shorter terms this impression could be expressed as: *Altamont Rising* equals an absolute demonstration of Shift's ascendancy.

Skin Area / Jarl – *La Petite Mort* LP Malignant Records 2014
La Petite Mort is a collaborative album between Skin Area (aka Martin Bladh and Magnus Lindh) and Jarl (aka Erik Jarl) – noting that Erik and Martin also form two thirds of the revered power electronics project IRM. Whereas Skin Area's previous albums inhabited a wildly diverse experimental post-industrial sound (bordering on being almost disjointed at times), the involvement of Jarl (who is known for his own solo experimental dark ambient material), seems to have tempered the direction of *La Petite Mort* into focused drone ambient territory. Also given that Martin utilises his distinctive voice within Skin Area (and coupled with the involvement of Erik Jarl), this album begs a passing comparison to IRM. Although this is acknowledged as a partially lazy descriptor, nevertheless the sound of *La Petite Mort* could be considered as an ambient drone take on IRM's far more forceful and visceral sound works.
Tantalus opens with LP with a spare soundscape of animated organic shimmering textures and quasi-drone like tones, as the monotone spoken vocals of Martin's Bladh articulate a psychological perspective on masturbation representing a safe surrogate for self-annihilation. This theme obviously has some sort of conceptual link to the track's title, noting Tantalus is a Greek mythological figure subjected to eternal punishment for sacrificing his son and serving his corpse at a banquet of the Gods. The composition also reveals some partially hidden disharmonic piano tones and string instruments within the soundscape, which shifts the mood into a tense passage of building and densely layered sounds and abstract vocalisations (coughs, croaks and garbled voices). *Charybdis* arrives next and functions in slightly more animated guise with its clinical rhythmic pulse, whilst shrill disharmonic orchestral strings provide a degree of tenseness. The track is further complimented by Martin's morose spoken vocals addressing abstract thematic content (*"placenta nest of whiskers"*?).
Scylla opens the second side with micro-tonal examinations of scrapped / manipulated strings, as tense bowed instruments are gradually overlaid. Think of a more abstract styled Penderecki and you are part way there. The later half of the track then shifts mode with morose muted harmonic drones, rhythmic pulses and (strange) field recordings of the barking of neighbourhood dogs (interestingly the atmosphere here accommodates a hazy dreamlike aura which verges towards an 'unknown fear' type of nightmare). *Pelops* is the last of four compositions and despite its abstract frame is the most 'composed' with muted strumming of some sort of stringed instrument, alongside more intensely shrill droning sounds and minimalist abstract bass guitar and garbled vocalisations, which give rise to a spoken passage of Martin's even more downtrodden vocals which return to the thematic context of the first track (a further conceptual link is provided by the fact that in Greek Mythology*, Pelops was the sacrificed son of Tantalus).
Despite its overall ambient drone like quality, this music is far from being minimalist and abstract, rather is heavily engaging and strikingly animated due to its detailed attention and layering of the individual sonic textures. On the packaging front there is the stark minimalist artwork courtesy of Martin Bladh, which is included on the cover and a series of thirteen single sided A4 printed inserts.
La Petite Mort represents the most honed material heard from Skin Area to date (possibly due to the involvement of Jarl), and consequently delivers experimental ambient drone works of the highest calibre, which whilst clearly born of the underground absolutely elevates itself into a non-derivative niche all its own. With a limitation of 220 copies, this seem far too few.

* – The conceptual influence of Greek mythology is also present on tracks *Charybdis* and *Scylla* – both being mythical sea monsters. Further context of the potential conceptual meaning is expressed by the Greek Mythological idiom *'between Scylla and Charybdis'* which effective means *'having to choose between two evils'.*

Skorneg – *Foehn* CD Malignant Records 2014
Skorneg are a new signing to the rapidly expanding Malignant roster, with the project being a collaboration between Frédéric Arbour (Visions member and Cylic Law label boss) and Christian Corvellec (of another Canadian project Skinwall whom are unknown to these ears). Regarding their particular style Skorneg articulate a 'barren galactic landscapes' to 'vast deep space' type of dark ambience, here featuring four tracks which sprawl over an expanse of 43 minutes.
Whilst the initial impression of the tonal scope is one of a gargantuan universal scale, evidently the album's inspiration is far more earthbound based on its thematic context of: *'the northern elements of Glaciers, Winds and the exploration of such rugged territories, both physically, intellectually and spiritually'.*
Regardless of any 'mind's eye' visual impressions evoked, *Fohen* skilfully conveys animated and multilayered textural dark ambience, where each of the four tracks are constructed with deep, drifting and swelling sub-orchestral drones which are propelled forwards with churning and driving undercurrent. They also follow a similar compositional approached by setting down a minimalist structure and then gradually build and morph their sound over their expanse.
In order to articulate the overarching feel of *Foehn*, this could be creatively described by quoting the title of one of Inade's tracks, being: *The Engine of Space*, given the use of subtle, almost mechanised rhythms. This reference also functions as a further descriptive link given the material on this album begs a passing comparison to the less composed and more flowing and abstract style of Inade. Interesting the second track *Serac* quite clearly stands out from other album tracks, where the piece builds upon a cyclic swirling structure, before elevating significantly at around the three minute with slow booming galactic horns and muted driving and rhythmic electronic programming.
Without dwelling on the point *Foehn* will be a solid and satisfying release for dark ambient music devotees, but then again this is almost expected given the pedigree of those involved – i.e. the Cyclic Law label boss and released on Malignant Records.

S.T.A.B. Electronics – *Instruments for Operating on Mutant Women* LP Urashima 2014

Here is third vinyl only LP from the formidable S.T.A.B. Electronics – a project which has been steadily elevating their profile with each new release. So in comparison to earlier albums, where *Instruments for Operating on Mutant Women* particularly excels is that it somehow manages to hone the aggressive sound of the last LP *The Non Alliant II* into even more focused form. As with other S.T.A.B. Electronics releases their approach is marked with generally minimalist song structures, based on few layers of looped analogue rhythms and processed droning noise, where the unhinged vocals are again an absolute standout. Likewise the range of sonic treatments applied to the vocals (flanged, distorted, delayed etc.), ensures the aggressive vocal approach is far from being one dimensional.

Although having a solid analogue quality, the recording is at the same time crisp and loud to really drive home the honed aggression. As such rough and overblown atonal synth layers are arranged in loose rhythmic patterns and further processed to the point of a fracturing noise deluge. Although the seething flanged vocals take a prominent and forthright position in the mix, these are also offset with well sourced dialogue samples to flesh out some of the thematic content. The UK derived dialogue sample on the track *Aggressors* (not sure where this is sampled from) is such an example which works perfectly with the blend of mid paced squelching / pulsing / burrowing layers, as the unhinged vocals ramp up the mood to greater aggressive heights. Alternately the mid to higher end chaotic squall of *A Little Transgression* brings to mind later era hyper rhythmic Whitehouse such as that found on *Racket,* although the vocals here retain the strong and identifiable stamp of S.T.A.B. Electronics. Whilst *Ex Fat (For S.G.O.)* encompasses a relatively passive, throbbing bass track, the subdued tone only services to amplify the seething anger of the vocal barrage. For the track *Defaced (Burnt with Acid)* it contains snippets of an interview relating to the track's theme (sampled from 'current affairs' type interview). This dialogue is then countered by the first person lyrics (written from the perspective of the attacker) which are spat with insidious aggression over a queasy and stilted loop: being an example of conceptually strong and expertly executed. For the final track *Nothing More I Can Give (Marco's Lament),* this is obviously a specific tribute to Marco Corbelli, and in honour of his memory seeks an Atrax Morgue style route of looped power electronics minimalism, complete a lamenting synth line partially buried in the mix.

Noting this has been released on the cult label Urashima label, this contextually makes sense given Urashima are reissuing much of Atrax Morgue's back catalogue on vinyl, as well as the fact that S.T.A.B. Electronics originally started as a tribute to the untimely passing of Marco Corbelli of Atrax Morgue. However with a limitation of a mere 99 copies (the same with most of Urashima's releases) this seems far too few for an album of this calibre. An obviously recommend release and really deserving of a larger print run.

Streicher CD - *Annihilism* CD Old Captain 2015
Kulmhof - *Morality's Simulacra* MC Major Carew 2015

Over the last few years the influence and dare I say it cult of Streicher seems to have been perceptibly rising, thanks in part to the re-release campaign spearheaded by the Freak Animal side label Industrial Recollections, but most importantly due to the distinctive sound that Ulex Xane cultivated as part of his power electronics aka 'Oi! Noise' project. Although Industrial Recollections previously issued a compilation CD in 2009 with all of the *Annihilism* tracks (in addition to other rare pieces), here Old Captain has re-issued *Annihilism* as a 20th anniversary edition, with revised and updated artwork courtesy of Marco Deplano. The music itself comes from the early recording period (1989 to 1991 but not released until 1995), with the philosophy of the project neatly wrapped up in the *Annihilism* title. Yet if the implied meaning of the album title was somehow missed, the opening spoken word piece leaves no opportunity for confusion about what the group stands for (and surely the heavily accented spoken female voice only adds to the strange allure of Streicher for non-Australians). It is then of interest that Streicher's ongoing legacy and influence can be distinctly heard on tracks such as: *Rectify or Cease, Mutilation Victim, Decomposed Whore* and *Destroy You Motherfuckers.* Noting that time and age have not wearied the force of these pieces, direct linage can be drawn from muffled mechanical churn, chaotic distortion and general industrial unease of these tracks to the likes of Alfarmania and similar ilk. Equally tracks such as *Nothing Has Any Meaning* and *I Don't Give a Fuck* function to deliver a hammer blow of Streicher's crude power electronics complete with the harsh and growled vocal barrage of Ulex, although comparatively speaking these pieces do not stand up as well today and perhaps now lack the direct impact they may have had some decades ago. *Nullify/ Obit* stands out substantially from the rest, given it is a spoken word passage read over a classical music backing, whilst the album concludes with the short but excellent *Parade Fascisti;* a sullen track of stoic rolling martial drums which fade into silence before one last vocal barrage attack.

Given that it is great to have *Annihilism* more widely available again, it is a shame that the label has chosen to press the digi-pack in rather flimsy cardboard stock which is prone to easy denting and marking. Although a minor gripe this re-release deserved better.

Not to be one to rest on legacy alone, Ulex Xane over the years has issued a large volume of material under a variety of guises. Kulmhof appears to be the latest adopted moniker which functions in general Streicher territory, albeit featuring a slightly updated, louder and less muffled sound. With this being the debut release, although uncredited to an actual label it has been released by Major Carew – a pseudonym of a UK underground artist.

Sterilization of Species is the first piece: an instrumental track of granulated distortion, buzzing tonality and vaguely agitated mechanised loops / rhythms, with a sound that is rough and suitably loud. Sitting squarely on the power electronics / industrial rather than harsh noise side of the fence and with little to no variation or evolution, this track is caustic and invasive in the best way possible. *Mémoires Retards* on side B is a differing affair, based on a subdued, slightly fractured pulsing / rhythmic loop where added layers push into churning distorted territory over its length, yet still remain subdued compared to side A.

With a total run time of nearly 20 minutes, Kulmhof is a clear display of the fact that time has not cowed Ulex from producing harsh and direct power electronics / industrial material. The pro-duplicated tape and colour cover appear to be intentionally lurid in design (fluro green tape) with quote on the cover from Jean Baudrillard giving a hint at thematic preoccupations (perception of reality and its 'reproduction'), despite being entirely instrumental. An obscurity worth tracking down, with further details for ordering available via: majorcarew@hotmail.com

Stuzha - *Butugichag* CD Ksenza Records / Infinite Fog Productions 2015

Having not come across this Russian dark ambient project before, this is their second album since 2011 and as the name translates to 'Severe Cold' this along with the cover image gives a hint at the sonic preoccupations of this album. The liner note further highlight that the album is dedicated to prisoners of Kolyma Labour Camps, with the visuals also reflecting this theme within its six panel digi-pack. four lengthy tracks make up this album (average of 10 minutes a piece), which each containing their own version of a desolate icy pitched tone. Ultimately Stuzha deliver the aural presentation of glacial barren vistas, which at times approaches an isolationist ambient tone, although there is generally more underlying movement and sonic elements (such as sparse piano) to make this more animated than the pure isolationist ambient works of someone like Thomas Koner. Also on more than one occasion Northaunt comes to mind as an appropriate benchmark of the style and feel of this music, as does a number of other Cyclic Law related releases in a similar sound.

The opening piece *A Night By The Foot of the Mountain* comes positively roaring out the of the speaking, with think walls of bass intoned drones and field recordings to match the title context (crackling fire, footfalls in snow covered ground, clanging gates, barking dogs etc.), thus generating a widescreen 'mind's eye' picture in the process. *Uranian Mines* follows and apart from its sweeping to rumbling drones, has a large portion of its sound based on slow scraping metallic textures, but is a rather laid back in overall mood. *Raging Blizzard* is much as the title suggests, but this is the sound of it experienced indoors, as the muffled sounds of the storm and its whipping winds rage unabated outside (... late piece the tone elevates to the point where it sounds like the roof is going to be ripped off). The final album track *Lilac Polar Darkness* is the most musical piece on offer and presents a slightly more serene tone of interweaving semi-orchestral drones and treated washes of sparse guitars which follow a broad ebb and flow style, as a mediative means to conclude the album.

In a general underground scene context and over the arc of the last decade (or more), Russia has been gradually elevating its status in underground ambient and industrial spheres, where this Siberian project released on a Russian label stands as a strong testament to the calibre of material coming from such quarters.

Te/DIS – *Comatic Drift* LP Galakthorrö 2014

Following the debut 7"EP *Black Swan* from 2013 (also released on Galakthorrö) Te/DIS - aka Tempted Dissident – have quickly followed up with their debut full length album to further hone their chosen 80's tinged post-punk / cold wave / angst-pop amalgam. While the tone of Te/DIS's style is one which is influenced by 'industrial' music, the actual music is not harsh, nor in any way abrasive. Being very much in a bleak, cold and clinical analogue programmed guise, the straightforward and direct songs are mostly driven by mid based beats which intermingle with icy synths and rhythmic stabs. Likewise the vocals remain as a distinctive and trademark element where, where the clear male vocals are delivered in a commanding monotone style. Given the cold feel of the music is very 'German' in style, the vocals (albeit exclusively sung in English) suit the music very well; however I could imagine that these would be a 'love' or 'hate' element for some listeners. *Close Range* begs a particular mention, with low slung bass driven groove and interweaving synth lines, which differentiates it from the stilted electronic patterns of earlier tracks. *Shootout with a Stranger* is another particular album standout given its slight sonic deviation of doom addled minor tuned synths, throbbing bass and some animated mid paced drum machine / high hat percussive elements, again completed with the commanding semi-sung vocal presentation.

If any criticism were to be leveled at *Comatic Drift*, it would be that there is a general 'sameness' to the overarching style and sound of the twelve songs and which is perhaps not as diverse as that demonstrated on the debut 7"EP. But aside from this very minor gripe Te/DIS's formal debut album fits perfectly within Galakthorrö's roster.

Terra Sancta – *Exile* CD Malignant Records 2014

The long-standing yet semi-obscured (and perhaps rather underrated) Australian dark ambient project has finally returned with a new album. This is their third, following a long six year break since 2008's full length *Aeon* (…although 2011 saw the release of the *Sunken | Buried | Forgotten* EP, this rather short 21 minute 'between albums' release simply did not achieve the pinnacle heights of the early full lengths). So with regard to *Exile*, Terra Sancta is still concerned the sonic representations of windswept desert landscapes, yet on this new release there is a sense of an even greater clarity and expansive tonal breath, as in comparison earlier material was slightly more murky, echoed and 'deep mineshaft' in tone. With its minimalist ambience, there is also an additional undercurrent of minor keyed drone chords and buried melodies which provide a sense of vague harmonic structure and is what really makes this material shine.

Empires of Ashes and *Kingdom of Dust* combine to introduce the album over a span of 15 minute which is monolithic in scope. Here the barren and windswept desert drones are offset with ambient sub-orchestral harmonics, which include synth layers which function to replicate the mood of deep resounding horns, maudlin strings and choir like vocals with truly sublime results. *Celestial Extinction* arrives as the album's collaborative composition and features the inputs of fellow label mate Rasalhague. As such the track differs with (ever so slightly) more movement and animation to its ebb and flow and by being a touch heavier and more bass driven brooding composition. *Desolate Land* is then positioned at the centre of the album, where the title is very much evoked through the use of 'whipping storms' field recordings coupled with minimalistic atonal drones. Alternately the later sections of *Vanishing Point* sees the introduction of some heavy scrapping metallic textures, but these are partially blunted in tone so as not to be obtrusive alongside the heavy maudlin synth drones (which partly resemble orchestral motions and choir like layered textures). Being the shortest track at less than four minutes, *End Path* concludes the album again reflecting the sound of the buried orchestral drone chords which are found throughout the album.

By now with dark ambient being a rather bloated genre, Terra Sancta handle their sound with class and style and sidestep becoming clichéd, or worse forgettable background music. Whilst Terra Sancta do not seek to break the mould of the genre there are really a sense of something MORE within this album – the sound of a project which has been refined and elevated above even the high standards of earlier albums. With its illustration of barren, desolate and abandoned landscapes, the imagery of the six panel digi-sleeve suitably rounds out the visuals of the album.

Theologian & STROM.ec – *Hubrizine* CD Malignant Records 2014

On *Hubrizine* Theologian have teamed up STROM.ec however rather than a typical 50/50 collaboration it seems that Strom.ec provided the base source material which Theologian has then shaped and sculpting it into its final form. Evidently this release also functions to celebrate the two project's shared appreciation of Philip K. Dick, which is partially reflected and evidenced though what could be described as 'sci-fi' slant to the album's general tone and atmosphere.

With regard to potential expectations this was always going to be clearly coloured by the fact that Theologian inhabit death industrial to power drone territory, whilst Strom.ec deliver sharp and clinical power electronics. But rather unexpectedly *Hubrizine* does not sound at all like as a collaboration of these two might suggest. Whilst tonal influence from death industrial and power electronics is evident (and sporadically make their presence felt on selected tracks), these in the most part are sidelined rather than forming core album elements. Thus the sound here is focused towards an experimental industrial and dark ambient slant, which combines celestial synth drones, twisted studio elements and generally subdued (yet sporadically abrasive) industrial rhythms.

Up first *Involuntary Dilation* forms a rather lengthy ambiental introduction, which is essentially a wavering experimental soundscape, featuring a low clinical drone / hum and skittish maudlin piano tune which is fractured and twisted through skillful studio trickery. This piece is most certainly is a subdued surprise and sets the album off a fantastic start. The next piece *EM19* encapsulates schizophrenic tendencies, where on the one level it is ambient and serene, yet on another it contains a clanging metallic industrial approach, complete with aggressive vocalisations. A similar duality to compositional approach is also prevalent on *Ubik* although the industrial / power electronics elements are slightly more muted, refined and less chaotic. With the title track located at the core of the album, it is a monster at 18 minutes long and encompassing sprawling dark ambient drone and subdued industrial noise which in the final minutes ramp up into a proper aggressive power electronics mode. Alternately *World War Terminus* is a cinematically scoped dark ambient piece, with unfurls with subdued emotional intent. This is a sublime composition and certainly not the type of maudlin emotive track I would have ever expected from either act.

Noting that *Hubrizine* originally formed a 2013 digital release (which was also given a physical release on cassette in a mere limitation of a mere 12 copies), this material is far too strong to fall into obscurity, hence clearly the reason for Malignant Records giving it a proper rerelease treatment. The album particularly demonstrates the skillful approach Theologian has employed with using Strom.ec's source material, where compositionally countering and divergent elements are blended and interwoven, to perfectly balance elements of aggression and serenity. Although *Hubrizine* is a surprising album given its sound and direction is vastly divergent from initial expectations, but more importantly and to the point is a superb and mature release.

Theologian – *Pain of the Saints* DCD Malignant Records 2015

Since the disbandment of his Navicon Torture Technologies (NTT) project in around 2010, Lee Bartow (aka Theologian Prime) has spent the last few years building the profile of his new project Theologian. So, to quickly reflect on NTT's legacy, Lee demonstrated a hyper productivity to his output by issuing 60 NTT releases in the years between 1997 and 2010. This work ethic has then translated over into Theologian where he has outdone himself even by his own standards; having issued a massive 45 releases since 2010. With many of these releases being collaborations or live material, *Pain of the Saints* is the latest 'official' album, where the presented material spans two discs and in excess of two and a half hours of music. Interestingly on the thematic front Lee has moved away from internalised topics of personal anguish and catharsis, towards an externalised analysis of the hypocrisy of the church, including matters relating to martyrdom and later sainthood.

By now Lee has undoubtedly established a recognisable approach which draws from death industrial, dark ambient, (industrialised) noise and doom drone spheres; where these elements are combined with a particular 'sonically overloaded' and weighty approach, meaning from the opening moments this feels and sounds very much like Theologian. As such massive slow pounding rhythmic loops often provide the structural backbone, whilst multiple synth drones and layered sub-orchestral elements are then bedded down over an extended length (the longest track sits at excess of 13 minutes). Vocals also range from an anguished wail to partially sung, but are rendered indecipherable with shredding distortion or elongated drone treatment which coagulate within the sonic mass.

CD1 (subtitled *piss*) contains a wide range of sonic styles where the opening cut *Savages* acts as a sort of microcosm of this layered multi-directional approach. Here the cyclic layered shimmering drones, sweeping sub-orchestral layers and rolling militant percussion set the scene, before looped mechanized elements take hold and settles into a lengthy 10 minute industrialised groove. *Infection* then presents sustained drones and thundering militant rhythmic chaos and although the following *Serpentine Angels* commences in rather serene fashion soon enough the stoic industrial pounded beat and shredded vocals reappear. Ultimately some respite is found in the shimmering laid back spectral sub-orchestral sound of *Gravity* which is a revelation and standout of a track based on its moody cinematic ebb and flow. For the later half of the first CD it continues the established pattern of looped and rhythmically / percussively

driven offerings, where vague melodic elements are buried within the vast wide-screen structures. For the final track of CD1, *Sainthood is Suffering* comes across as a rather divergent piece due to its throbbing, almost dancefloor oriented industrial beats. Although an interesting track it however feels slightly out of place and more like a 'tacked on' remix than a proper album track. CD2 (subtitled *jism*) continues the journey by showcasing more monolithic tonal blocks of sound, where aside from the vast rhythmic / percussive structures of the opener (*The Lies Of The Past Become The Prayers Of The Future*), the tracks are generally more subdued and cinematic, including an elongated compositional style for hypnotic effect. *Suppuration* is a piece which works particularly well in blending the moody synth drones, scarred vocalisations and more abrasive rhythmic elements. However being the inverse of many other compositions the heavier elements gradually drop away to reveal the serene drones. *Their Gelded and Rapacious Hearts* follows a similar path where its maudlin synth driven tone remains the focus throughout its 10 minute expanse, whilst *Blessed Prey* also stands out due to its prominent violin motif within the sweeping ambient drone framework. *Redemption Is An Impossibility* presents a slight deviation with its use of thrummed bass guitar and rolling drum kit percussion that edges the piece towards more chaotic realms. Much like CD1, the second disc is concluded with a rather sonically divergent track; here *Self-Flagellation as Faith* is a dark synth driven rock song (complete with kit drumming) and comes across very much like that of Jarboe era SWANS due to the crooning female vocals (...an excellent concluding moment). *Pain of the Saints* clearly succeeds in its presentation of a strong and varied collection of tracks which demonstrates the focused and high calibre output of Theologian. Despite its extended length the album is not bogged down by superfluous content, although with the sheer volume of material here it is a takes a certain focused resolve to listen to this album in full given it warrants full emersion and not sporadic 'cherry-picked' listening. Rounding out the release is an oversized eight panel digi-pack with beautiful cover painting and slick graphic design care of Lee himself. If you haven't kept up with the hyper-productive output of recent years, this would be a perfect place recommence your appreciation of Theologian's cinematically rendered yet resolutely industrialised sonic world.

Trepaneringsritualen – *Perfection & Permanence* LP Cold Spring Records 2014

Since 2008 Trepaneringsritualen (T × R × P) have issued 18 releases across numerous formats, which have collectively functioned to display a varied approach to a death industrial / ritual ambient sound. Likewise for anyone who has followed the project's creative arc over this time, it has involved a gradual shift toward more 'song' focused compositions, where the culmination of this process was the *Judas Goat* 7"EP of 2013, that at the time of its release felt like T × R × P 'hit' single. For this new album T × R × P has opted for its creative core to be built around this honed song based approach, whilst thematically the album addresses the principle of duality from a number of differing angles, including that found within varied religious iconography, as well as the dualism of the ego and the self.

For the album's opening track *Venerated and Despised* it is very much of the stalking and slow ritual ambient style, which at under three minutes feels like an introductory piece of sorts. *A Black Egg* then marks the first focused track of the album, containing a brooding bass line and flourishes of tribal percussion, as the prominent hoarse croaked vocals (in a verse chorus verse format), retain a central prominence and really hammer home the rhythmic song based approach. *Castrate Christ* then elevates the urgent atmosphere further, with heavy pounding and mid paced tribal death industrial format, as multi-layered vocal lines add variation. *Alone/A/Cross/Abyss* is another great example of the use of multiple vocals lines (in both sonic treatment and lyrical delivery), along with a swaying rhythmic bass line leading the tribal death industrial sound.

An album standout track come in the form of *The Seventh Man* – an anthemic pounding death industrial track at its most potent, built with grinding bass lines, caustic synths and fractured drum machine programming. Clearly this is the death industrial tone of mid era Brighter Death Now, but sped up to urgent tribal proportions and further augmented with ritualised intent, where the album's title forms a chant within the song's framework.

This catchy song format continues with the swaying / pounding rhythms and clanging metallic percussion of *Konung Kront I Blod*, yet still imbedded with an ample dark death industrial tone. Yet not all album tracks are of a focused rhythmic type, where the piece *Thirty-Nine Lashes* is very much a religious lament of the forsaken damned, whilst *Liken Ingen Jord Vill Svälja* and *A Ceaseless Howling* are abstract ritualised death ambient soundscapes. *He Who Is My Mirror* rounds out the relatively short album (approximately 40 minutes) with another focused tribal percussive track, with booming war drums and grinding synths and the now trademark hoarse vocals.

Clearly the album's overarching atmosphere is one of cathartic rhythmic death industrial - something akin to salvation through punishment and oppression. Whilst a diverse range of ritual atmospheres and soundscapes have been explored on earlier material, as highlighted there has also been an evolution towards a more structured song based style. *Perfection & Permanence* is effectively the culmination of this direction and is the most focused and song structured release from T × R × P yet. So on one hand this album displays a definite level of 'accessibility' for those listeners not as accustomed to obscure underground music genres. Yet at the same time T × R × P have not forgone or lost the murky ritualised elements which make their music so visceral and engaging. Accordingly *Perfection & Permanence* represents another step in the continued evolution and rise of T × R × P. Available on either 500 black or 500 white vinyls (obviously being another reference to the 'duality' concept), as well as unlimited CD.

Trepaneringsritualen – *Papist Pretender* 2x7"EP La Esencia 2014

Here is yet another item to add to the Trepaneringsritualen (T × R × P) collection which is special edition vinyl issued to commemorate a May, 2014 live performance in Barcelona, Spain. Being released in two versions the first is the 'standard' single 7"EP in an edition of 350 copies and a more 'limited' double 7"EP version in an edition of 169 copies. The packaging is beautifully presented which features a large fold out poster cover, multiple inserts and postcards and one x black and one x white 7" EP. Also to provide context for the release's theme, the cover includes a cryptic alphabetical analysis of the phrase *Vicarius Filii Dei* (which refers to Saint Peter, generally regarded as the first Pope by the Catholic Church), effectively equaling its numerical value to 666 (aka 'the number of the beast' as nominated within the Book of Revelations).

The title track leads off the release where *Papist Pretender* adheres to T × R × P's recent song based focus, yet still retaining a dark ritualised death industrial sound (...of note the title's initials mirrors the initials of the recent full length *Perfection & Permanence*. Coincidence or by design?). Here the lyrics and the hoarse distorted drawl of the vocal delivery follow a verse / chorus / verse format, which closely follow the heavy militant percussive thrum. Side B brings the track *Feral Me* and although adheres to a song based style, it opts for a tribalised death industrial sound complete with swaying rhythm and sporadic breaks of rolling tribal drums, where the layered vocals are a particular standout.

For the second 7"EP, Side C features a cover version of a classic track from The Moon Lay Hidden Beneath a Cloud (for those unaware were a pre Der Blutharsch project). Whereas the original untitled version (from the album *Were You Of Silver, Were You Of Gold?*), had a folky and slightly up-tempo marching medieval melody, here cover version is faithful to a point, noting that T × R × P has slowed the speed slightly to remove the up-tempo mood and to create a much heavier and darker atmosphere. Here the main melody prominently remains, but the militant rhythm also feels more of a solemn march to war, where T × R × P clearly places a strong and individual stamp on the song, particularly due to the thumping rhythmic structure and trademark garbled and rasping vocalisations. The final of the four tracks is *Castrate Christ (The Sixth Hour)*, which is an alternate version of *Castrate Christ* which is featured on the recent full length *Perfection & Permanence*. This version has slowed the song to an extremely slowed crawling pace, which clearly differs from the urgent rhythmic pummelling of the original. In fact on first listen this sounded if it was a 45rpm song being played at 33rpm speed, but once accustomed to the catatonic pace, the accompaniment of a slow soundscape drone only adds to the brooding atmosphere. With the myriad of T × R × P releases issued in recent years and without necessarily repeating themselves the project manages to morph and twist their sound into interesting directions, whilst still keeping a foot firmly in a northern European ritual death industrial style. Another special release in T × R × P's canon.

Trepaneringsritualen - *Ritualer, Blot & Botgöring* CD Infinite Fog Productions 2014
Trepaneringsritualen - *Veil The World* CD Cold Spring Records 2015

Noting the limited and obscure nature of much of Trepaneringsritualen's (T × R × P) earliest output, coupled with increasing interest in the project in recent years, there has been obvious label interest in re-releasing this material. Hence Infinite Fog Productions and Cold Spring Records have been good enough to give the first two releases from T × R × P a repress in a less limited CD format.

Although the debut tape *Ritualer, Blot & Botgöring* from 2008 had already been repressed on vinyl in 2012 (in an edition of 275 copies), Infinite Fog Productions has issued this new edition on CD with the inclusion of two bonus tracks. Given I have already reviewed the LP version previously (reviewed in Issue No.2), I will focus this review on the additional tracks. *Death Is Your Friend* is the first bonus offering and originally featured on an obscure 2008 compilation cassette *White Nights*. This piece is rather straight forward in structure, which means it deviates from the main bulk of sprawling death industrial soundscapes. Here rough and forceful grinding loops blend with overblown distortion, while garbled vocals and voice snippets are wrapped up into a dank muffled production. The second bonus track is *Seeing What I Suffer*, which delves into a militant occult sound, featuring ritualistic drones and heavy militaristic drumming, all the while the vocals pushing it into the song oriented approach of recent material. This particular track is of epic proportions (even by T × R × P's standards), and whilst *Death Is Your Friend* is a relatively stock standard offering, *Seeing What I Suffer* is a fantastic bonus and conclusion to the expanded album. The packaging for *Ritualer, Blot & Botgöring* is rounded out with slick four panel digi-pack with new inner panel imagery of trepanning to match that of the cover.

In its original form *Veil the World* was issued in 2011 in an edition of 40 tapes and housed in an embossed and varnished box including art prints and rusty nails, and so as to keep some visual continuity with this re-release, images of nails feature prominently on the six panel digi-pack. In reflecting today on the music featured on *Veil the World*, on selected tracks it demonstrates the gradual move of T × R × P towards more structure focused realms. Also although six of the nine original tracks of *Veil the World* were featured on the two compilation CD's titled *The Totality of Death*, it is nevertheless great to have the original collection of tracks together under the proper release banner (but to add an element of confusion, the original 7th track *Field of Blood* has been replaced with another track *Akeldama* and the order of the last two tracks switched).

Cherem opens *Veil the World* as a ominous ceremonial soundscape which paves the way for the title track, and when it comes roaring from the speakers it is in the guise of pounding tribal militancy, resplendent with the now trademark croaked vocalisations. Alternately *Lightbringer* has a more a slow burning feel, with droning beat and vocals sitting amongst swirling layered noise, while *Drunk with Blood* is another focused rhythmically swaying offering (here the rhythm is based on looped mid-range distortion and shuddering sonic textures). This focused piece is followed by a triptych of tensile death industrial soundscapes (*Nekyia, Akeldama* and *Invocation*), each featuring disembodied vocalisations or invocation focused dialogue samples for good measure. The final of the nine album tracks is *C'est Un Reve*, which is technically a Death in June cover song, where the chanted vocal line is yelled here over a repetitive, lurching and relatively up tempo militant death industrial backing. In truth this is virtually unrecognisable as a cover song, meaning T × R × P have absolutely made it their own and in the process providing a forceful conclusion to the album.

Given the limited nature of original versions both of these re-releases are worthy editions to T × R × P's discography, and functions to showcase the early evolution of sound and differing approaches the project has taken within a Swedish death industrial framework.

Troum – *Mare Morphosis* CD Transgredient Records 2013

Expectations relating to any project's artistic output can be an interesting thing. On one hand you might think you have a handle on what a project is about and what a new album may encompass, yet there are also those who manage to transcend such expectations which is clearly to their credit. So enter Troum, an act I have listened to sporadically over the years, without necessarily checking out every new release. Yet if asked to categorise their sound, I would have said with some degree of certainty that they produce ethereal ambient drone music with a focus on hypnotic trance like soundscapes. So then enter *Mare Morphosis*, Troum's new album, which functions to completely shatter this perception. Whilst base elements adhere to a transcendent ambient drone framework, these however have been substantially augmented with composed sub-orchestral elements and even a strong influence from post-rock music (throughout certain album passages).

The single album length composition commences with a structure of ethereal drones (mid paced minor keyed loops, interlinking in various patterns), which then sees the introduction of a lone maudlin violin melody. Yet the biggest surprise is when without warning the track breaks out with full post rock rhythm section (drumming and bass guitar), as the transcendent mood swells in cyclic fashion with the accompanying drones and rousing violin phrase. From here and with a structure of slow metamorphosis, the track gradually moves through a number of subdued droning passages (which reduce to a minimalistic structure), before building and elevating again, repeating over a number of cycles. Through one of these mid album segments the use of kit drumming returns, but here it is in more of a free-form and loose failing style, offset with a loose almost Middle Eastern style harmony. Likewise the end passage is a stunning example of transcendent swelling harmonic drone ambient which still maintains a partial post-rock sensibility in tone, despite not being driven by any drum / bass backing (think Eluvium for suitable reference).

In terms of the overall arc of the album its builds to a number of crescendos through the early and mid-phases of the album, before gradually cycling down towards the end over an overall 51 minute expanse. Given the single track format *Mare Morphosis* presents a bit of an 'all or nothing' proposition, by requiring the album to be appreciated in a single span, which could potentially be frustrating if wanting to forward to a particular segment of the album. Yet minor formatting issues aside, by sidestepping all preconceptions *Mare Morphosis* delivers a complex, animated and fully engaging drone work, one which is far more than incidental background music. Given this album demands focus and attention, it also sees Troum seamlessly incorporating musical influences from outside the regular frame of reference for this type of material. A rewarding listen.

Uncodifed / Wertham – *Vindicta II* CD Old Europa Café / Elettronica Radicale Edizioni 2014
Uncodifed – *Hardcore Methodology* CD Old Europa Café / Elettronica Radicale Edizioni 2014

As should be clearly apparent from the title, this is the second instalment in the *Vindicta* series and again focuses on aspects of Sardinian criminal history and culture. For this instalment: *'The concept slightly moves from the blood-feud / knife obsessive themes of the first work, toward the aftermath of the war between families that lead the protagonist of our tale to turn into a feral life style on impenetrable mountains, 'living like boars and sleeping like foxes', until his capture and subsequent confinement in the notorious Boncammino's jail. The solitude of the forced mountain life meets the despair of 30 years of life in a cage of the notorious legal larger.'*

As with the first collaboration the individual sound and direction of both Uncodified and Wertham are clearly complimentary and again deliver a strong and focused amalgam of their styles. Essentially *Vindicta II* encompasses a collection of tracks where the bulk of proceedings are marked by various combinations burrowing atonal synth lines, shuddering industrial clamor, static fried frequencies and echo treated spoken / shouted vocals. As such the album is one which expertly combines grinding industrial noise and shuddering yet muted power electronic structures. The sound of the album also differs from *Vindicta I* in that it is far less sonically invasive in tone, where *Vindicta II* also achieves a controlled and restrained feel to its outwardly aggressive elements. With the sound frequencies generally sitting at the mid to lower range, this is also a clear differentiating point from the first instalment which contained many tracks with prominent elements of mid to high pitched tinnitus inducing noise. Also whilst being clearly aggressive the production of *Vindicta II* is one which is also low key and sweepingly atmospheric. Noting its sonorous consistency, this is an album best appreciated in its totality; as an overarching block of sound, rather than singling out specific pieces; where a tone of general noise squalor and an atmosphere of tense oppression and confinement prevail, thus suitably reflecting the album's thematic focus. Yet given the strong coherence of the bulk of the album the final track deviates quite markedly from the balance of the album as it encompasses the later era of Haus Arafna styled piece of subdued atonal rhythmic power-electronics.

Essentially the second instalment in the *Vindicta* series is faithful to the sound and concept of the first, yet also achieves a differing tonal approach which sets it apart. With a third CD in the trilogy planned to round out the concept, which based on the strength of the first two is a release on the horizon to look out for.

Released at the same time as *Vindicta II, Hardcore Methodology* is the new album from Uncodifed and whilst technically a solo outing, eight of the tracks feature collaborations with other artists, including: Gianlica Favaron, Bologna Violenta, Caligula 031, Sshe Retina Stimulants and Simon Balestrazzi. Tonally *Hardcore Methodology* presents a varied recording which spans many aspects of harsher underground experimental sounds and encapsulates fractures synth textures, sparse loose rhythmic elements, atonal synth drones, grinding bass tonality etc. The album displays a sharp and loud production with a certain sonic crispness to the tone and as stated by the promo sheet the album encompasses *'abrasive post-industrial experimentation'*.
Generally more abstract and varied in tone and approach that *Vindicta II*, the overarching feel of the album is as a collection of sonic experimentations rather than being structured around a strong central theme. Evidently the album's title does make some conceptual reference to the obsessive methodologies employed by directors of Hardcore movies, however exactly what such methodologies are and how they relate to this album is not clear (perhaps the album is abstract homage to 'obsessiveness', but here focused on experimental industrial sounds?).
Although there are many strong brooding segments (such as *(L) Hotel*) and other tracks with excellent tonal qualities (such as the sonically invasive *Collection of Clothes*) which are spread throughout the album, I can't shake the feeling that the album plays out as a collection of sporadic tracks which lacks an element of coherence due to the track's being on the shorter side (between 16 seconds at the shortest and the longest at four minutes). A clear misstep is also evident on *Anterooms* where the sullen mood is jarringly interrupted by the inclusion of a pre-set rhythm from a cheap casio keyboard (?). But countering this, late album tracks *Cotton Pads* and *Methodology 3 (end of report)* each contain a fierce higher range tonal spectrum which would not be out of place on the *Vindicta I* album, sans the aggressive vocalisations.
Although *Hardcore Methodology* constitutes an interesting listen with some excellent sonic moments, to this ear it also suffers from a bit of a scattergun approach and lack of thematic focus. Whilst this presents somewhat of an issue for this reviewer, for others not who prefer straight sonic experiments for their own sake, this could fit the bill perfectly. But when placing *Hardcore Methodology* in direct comparison with *Vindicta II*, the later wins out in style, focus and finesse.

Various Artists - *Epicurean Escapism I* CD / DVD Silken Tofu / The Epicurian 2014

In August 2014 the third instalment of the *Epicurean Escapism Festival* was held in Berlin, when concurrently this *Epicurean Escapism I* compilation was released to commemorate the first instalment of the festival from 2012. So whilst such a post festival release would not ordinarily cause too much confusion, this ignores the fact that a compilation tape and accompanying DVD was already issued in 2012 in association with the first Epicurean Escapism festival, and intriguingly the majority of content on the original version is not featured on this set. For this updated version it includes new and additional material from the majority of the same acts whom were featured on the original tape compilation. Likewise the packaging here differs from the original in that it mirrors the style and formant of the *Epicurean Escapism II* compilation (released in 2013), where the CD and DVD were housed in a catalogue booklet to provide a visual document of participating artists. Does all this amount to unnecessary confusion? Possibly, yet it is ultimately the quality and interest of this compilations content which is of far greater importance.
For the musical parts, Krank leads off the CD (the rebranded Kraang project of the John Murphy), but now featuring the inputs of Annie Stubbs and Till Brüggemann. Here the project delivers a hazy and disorientating industrial soundscape of sporadic horns, loose loops, swirling industrial fragments and ritualised sonic clutter. However the surprise comes with the edition of late night lounge / jazz vocals courtesy of Annie Stubbs, where these 'song' focused vocals are clearly an interesting and divergent addition to counter the generally non-musical focus of the post-industrial soundscape.
IRM follow next and whereas a live track was featured on the original tape compilation, here they step up with an exclusive contribution in the form of a lengthy track *Triptych*. This 17 minute track effectively amounts to 'medley' composition which remixes material lifted from the conceptual triptych formed by 2008's *Indications of Nigredo* MLP, 2010's *Order4* and the recently issued 2014 album *Closure*. Moving through three main segments, this track covers the majority of known and lauded elements of IRM. Agonised physiological focused vocals, tense droning soundscapes, thrummed atonal bass, and crunching metallic noise mark the path, and whilst recognised elements of original tracks remains, these have been recontextualised into new and engaging forms to compete a strong and focused track.
For the third track Human Larvae and Anemone Tube have collaborated on an extended piece, noting that both previously featured separate tracks on the original tape. With both acts having quite distinctive sounds, they have certainly achieved a pleasing amalgam here. Effectively containing two halves, the first part is an excellent slower burner of cyclic layered loops to generate droning power electronics soundscape, with the sharp distortion and delay treated vocals of Human Larvae sitting perfectly within the mix. For the latter half the piece moves toward more serene quasi-orchestral drone to dark ambient territory, where I assume that Human Larvae's aesthetic has driven the first half, whilst Anemone Tube the later. All in all it is a great pairing of the divergent sound of these two projects.
Jarl - being the solo project of Erik Jarl of IRM – should be a relatively well-recognised project by now, whom presents the fourth and final track of the CD compilation. Here Jarl deliver a monolithic 25 minute track *A Case Of Inbreeding: A Homage To My Doppelganger*, where Jarl does what he does rather well. Essentially a subtle drone and low pulse mark the introduction, where there track forges a gradually droning evolution as additional looped layers and added at a glacially pace. The atmosphere of the track balances the ominous with the serene and spans its length with ease and general fits the recognised Jarl sound.
Moving onto the DVD Martin Bladh presents a collection of his experimental short films under the rather self explanatory title of *Video Works*. Following full immersion with these collected film works the overarching impression is that it is very much like being plunged rather voyeuristically into the personal mindset of Martin's obsessions, which might have otherwise been conducted in private beyond prying eyes if not for the existence of these films. Across the complete series of films the camera captures

various obsessive scenes playing out, where the camera itself is occasionally visible in a strategically placed mirror, which functions to blurs the line between participant, observer and voyeur. Essentially experimental filmmaking in its styling, the short video juxtaposes visual cuts ups of various scenes - some somewhat disturbing - being acted out, complimented with a soundtrack ranging from interview / dialogue to industrial noise soundscapes. The scenes across the five short films involve numerous cut up scenes which visualise different versions of physco-sexual themes which have been reflected across the bulk of his artistic output to date. Some of the various elements on display include the exploration of the self / ego, sexual obsessions, death, murder, self-mutilation and self-castration. Some obvious influences from Francis Bacon and Hermann Nitsch and the Viennese Actionist movement are clearly evident (and have been acknowledged by Martin himself), yet the central placement of his own obsessions at the core of his work, without flinching from any ramifications concerning how he may be perceived, clearly elevates his work to a point where it is wholly his own. Brief context and associated impressions of each of the short film follows below:

- *DES* forms part of his artistic study of Martin's fascination with the UK serial killer Dennis Nilsen, where this video is the counterpart of the book of the same name and obviously exploring the same thematic material. Of particular interest is that some of the more poetic spoken lyrics of this piece were also utilised on IRM's latest album *Closure*, which illustrates Martin's cross pollination of themes and ideas across multiple artistic platforms. The film cuts between various staged scenes which also reflects the book's content, and also uses extensive dialogue samples from both interviews with Dennis as well as audio sampled from an audiobook for Brian Master's biography on Dennis entitled *Killing For Company: Case of Dennis Nilsen.*
- *Cycle* functionally operates as a visually comparative work, which appears to contrast a young and happy child (old home footage of who appears to be a young smiling Martin), counterpointed with visuals potentially relating to the person he has evolved into through the explorations of his obsessions, which is set to interview dialogue and sporadically harsh but generally subdued experimental industrial noise backing.
- *Pig and Tomboy* (the only film featured on the original compilation version), involves a naked seated figure and a standing aggressor in a pig mask who manipulates his compliant and possibly drugged subject. This main scene (amongst others) progresses seemingly in response to an audio collage of interview dialogue (which has been collated and contributed by Peter Sotos), which deals with a girl's decent into drug use, prostitution and subsequent death by unknown means.
- *Hole* is the shortest film work on offer, which with its visual cutup of close up shots of teeth, lips and the inside of the mouth set to an anxiety inducing and skittish soundscape, is mostly abstract in its delivery and potential interpretation.
- The title of the final film *Matt 5:29 – 30* obviously refers to the biblical passage which states: *'If your right eye causes you to stumble, gouge it out and throw it away. It is better for you to lose one part of your body than for your whole body to be thrown into hell. And if your right hand causes you to stumble, cut it off and throw it away. It is better for you to lose one part of your body than for your whole body to go into hell'*. However here this passage has been reinterpreted in context of Martin's own obsessive preoccupations. Thus within the film it shows two small mirrors placed at right angles in front of a short stool, where the naked figure of Martin (back to the camera) performs what is clearly meant to represent self-castration. Noting this has been a constant theme of Martin's work (and particularly as this was a central theme of the IRM album *Order4*), the film's low droning soundscape and thematic preoccupations could be considered as a visual addendum to *Order4*.

Given that the content and concepts explored are obviously deeply personal to Martin, his film works are a bold display of his personal obsessions and perhaps internalised perceptions of himself. Whilst some may view the visual material as 'shocking', this is far from amounting to any sort of clumsy attempt at shock value. Although these video works may not clearly be of interest to all, but for anyone intrigued by Martin's lyrical and conceptual preoccupations, these films provide further visual exploration.
Moving onto the visual presentation of the compilation set, within the oversized cardboard booklet 'catalogue' cover, Martin Bladh provides further art and writing under the title of *Victim and Executioner.* Across 24 pages it provides artwork and a range of writings providing additional information on Martin's inspirations and obsessions. This includes quotes from third parties, personal impressions and background information framing the context of his own film works, in addition to a conceptual written piece *Off-Stage Slideshow,* as well as structural details for a theatre piece *Death of Narcissus II.* This additional visual and written material certainly makes for complimentary and interesting reading and functions to both confirm and refute some of the above impressions of Martin's film works (particularly given the above review of the short films were written prior to reading this information).
Over the three years that the Epicurean Escapism festival has been operating it has quickly elevated itself to being at the forefront of multi-angled festival which seeks to bring together music, film, visual art. For those not able to attend in person, these releases are excellent documents of each of the events, to ensure there is a legacy beyond the merely the memory of those in attendance. This is also another fine example of how a well a compilation as a format can work when a focused and nonstandard approach is employed. Recommended.

COLD SPRING
CELEBRATING 25 YEARS IN 2015
SUTCLIFFE JUGEND
Offal 2LP / CD Power Electronics
非常階段
HIJOKAIDAN · EMERGENCY STAIRWAY TO HEAVEN
HIJOKAIDAN
Emergency Stairway... LP/CD Japanoise
IFOTS
WE CAN YIELD OUR OWN FOOTSTEPS
IRON FIST OF THE SUN
Yield... LP/CD Power Electronics
MZ. 412
Hekatomb
MZ.412
Hekatomb CD Black Industrial
SKULLFLOWER
Draconis 2CD Industrial/Noise
VEIL THE WORLD
TREPANERINGSRITUALEN
Veil The World CD Death Industrial
MOLOCH
Die Isolation CD Black Metal/Ambient
TUNNELS OF ĀH
THUS AVICI
TUNNELS OF AH
Thus Avici CD Esoteric/Industrial
khost
copper
lock hell
KHOST
Copper Lock Hell CD Doom/Noise
SOL (feat. DIE WEISSE ROSE)
Where Suns Come To Die CD Esoteric
SUTEKH HEXEN
Become CD Ritual / Noise / BM
PERFECTION
PERMANENCE
TREPANERINGSRITUALEN
TREPANERINGSRITUALEN
Perfection & Permanence CD/LP
KEROVNIAN
KEROVNIAN
Far Beyond... CD Black Ambient
Treatment Of The Dead
TREATMENT OF THE DEAD
Cold Spring Sampler
A nice-price CD sampler of our current / forthcoming releases. Sealed card slip. Features: Coil / Nine Inch Nails, Merzbow, Trepaneringsritualen, Troum, Skullflower, Z'EV, Burial Hex, Sol, Iron Fist Of The Sun, Khost, Tunnels Of Ah, Shift, Mesektet, and Sutekh Hexen.
£4 or FREE with any order over £20 from our webstore.
WWW.COLDSPRING.CO.UK
STORE.COLDSPRING.CO.UK (FREE UK P&P) | FACEBOOK/TWITTER: COLDSPRINGHQ

Various Artists – *No Good Deed Goes Unpunished* DCDr Malignant Antibody 2014

Personal tragedy struck Stephen Petrus on the 8th January, 2014, when fire destroyed his home and all his possessions. And who exactly is Stephen Petrus you ask? Well, if you even have to ask that question, clearly you have missed his long standing commitment and contribution to the underground (15+ years) through Murderous Vision, In Death Throes, Umbra (amongst many other projects), in addition to being label boss of Live Bait Recording Foundation and director of the 2010 *City / Ruins: Art in the Face of Industrial Decay* documentary (which focused on the underground industrial / noise scene of Cleaveland, Ohio). This DCDr is a benefit release kindly coordinated by Malignant Records, with all proceeds being donated to Stephen to assist in him with the re-establishment process.

Clearly this is a great initiative and a positive cause to support by buying a copy of this release. But apart from the provision of financial assistence to a fellow underground member, as a bonus you just so happen to get a two CDr stellar compilation of tracks from underground artists (both leading and emerging), including: Phragments, Inade, Kristoffer Nystroms Orkester, The Vomit Arsonist, Æther & Trepaneringsritualen, Shock Frontier, The Scapegoat Mechanism, Theologian, Bereft, Megaptera, United Front & Shock Frontier, Sewer Goddess, Sektor 304, Steel Hook Prostheses, Blitzkrieg Baby, Dreaded, Fire In the Head, Swollen Organs, and Naxal Protocol.

As all musical contributions are of a quality ranging from good, to great, to excellent, there is absolutely no excuse to hem and haw about whether to pick this up. Likewise the quality of the artwork and pro-CDr pressing elevates it above a 'mere' CDr release, which evidently was done so to keep this in print as long as there is demand. To conclude with a question: exactly what are you waiting for?

Various Artists – *Slutstationen* MC Styggelse 2014

This mammoth 90 minute compilation tape has been curated by the relatively obscure, staunchly underground and analogue focused Swedish label Styggelse which is helmed by Kristian Olsson of Survival Unit / Alfarmania infamy. *Slutstationen* functions as a varied and comprehensive collection of Nordic based sonic experimenters, who can broadly be filled under industrial noise and power electronics styles as general unifying descriptors. Featuring a total of 16 artists, this includes known artists, rising acts and other more obscure projects (to these ears at least). Likewise noting that *Slutstationen* translates to 'The Endstation', this is evidently the third and final compilation in a series and based on the quality and focus displayed here it is unfortunate that the first and second tapes in the series passed me by.

Side A features the largest number of contributions from recognised / established projects (which can tends to increase the expectation somewhat), so on with the brief rundown of each.

- Vit Fana – *Antoniuseld:* opens the tape where a mellow maudlin synth line (horror soundtrack style) give way to slightly metallic radio signal styled loops, where later on a pounding beat and sustained drone ratchets up the tension. A solid introduction to both the project and the compilation.
- Puce Mary – *The Course*: delivers high pitched sustained tones which mix with an ominous mid-paced death industrial type beat, where added layers gradually build intensity (mostly loose loops and field type recordings). Late track vocals are presented in a heavy, commanding / distorted yelled style, to complete a strong and solid offering (which also fosters Puce Mary's rising profile).
- Brighter Death Now – *Enough*: represents the long awaited return of Roger Karmanik who delivers a track which interestingly is neither of the all-encompassing darkness type or all out aggression style of what the project is known. This is something altogether different, with a fast paced pulsing rhythmic structure, mirroring plodding bass and squelching industrial noise. Probably it is only the subdued spoken vocals are a partially recognisable element. Good but certainly different to what might be expected.
- Alfarmania – *Nåldyna:* is a hallucinogenic and caustic post-mortem offering, where sparse noise, dialogue samples and piano loops give way to muddied wall or of layered industrial noise filth. Solid stuff and on par with Alfarmania's prior output.
- Shift – *Wipe Them Out:* demonstrates the sheer excellence of Shift's approach. Here the crushing wall of multi-layered industrial noise / power electronics squall mirrors and matches the weight, heaviness, density and aggression of Shift's latest full length album *Altamont Rising*. In other words this is simply crushing.
- Händer Som Vårdar – *Jag Blev Stolt:* seeks a sonic route based on (what sounds like) abstract tape loop manipulations and scattered dialogue snippets, which gradually evolves within a loose structure (yet remaining minimalist and abstract throughout).
- Theta – *Scopaesthesia:* features a cavernous industrial 'wind tunnel' aesthetic, where some shaper distortion manages to rise to the surface of the churning sonic mass. Overall the piece manages to stay on the industrial noise rather than HNW side.
- Arv & Miljö – *Johnny*: rounds out the first side of the tape through micro-tonal exploration of metallic tones which gradually coalesce into a loosely composed structure and is completed with Swedish dialogue samples.

Flipping over to side B it is noted to collect together a more obscure range of acts and whilst some are familiar by name, all are unknown within a sonic capacity.

- Ochu – *Sopa:* opens the second side with slowly evolving ambient ritual drones, which are built up in layering to become far more forceful and animated, verging on death industrial towards the end.
- Negative Climax – *Kaa Anta Ilahama:* opts for more post-industrial spheres, utilised layered heavily distorted drones, where chanted vocals and wooden flute providing a slight ritual edge.
- Treriksröset – *Tillägnad Gubb (Vila I Frid):* function in a capacity of a squalling, loose and chaotic noise approach. Here a rumbling undercurrent drives the lower end with high pitched noise sitting within the foreground.
- Maniac Cop – *Fires Blanks:* delivers a relatively basic rugged industrial noise aesthetic, combining filth infused rumbling bass and shuddering mid ranged textures.
- Teufelsdröckh – *Namnlös Och Odödlig:* with lethargic drones, factory styled field recordings and windswept

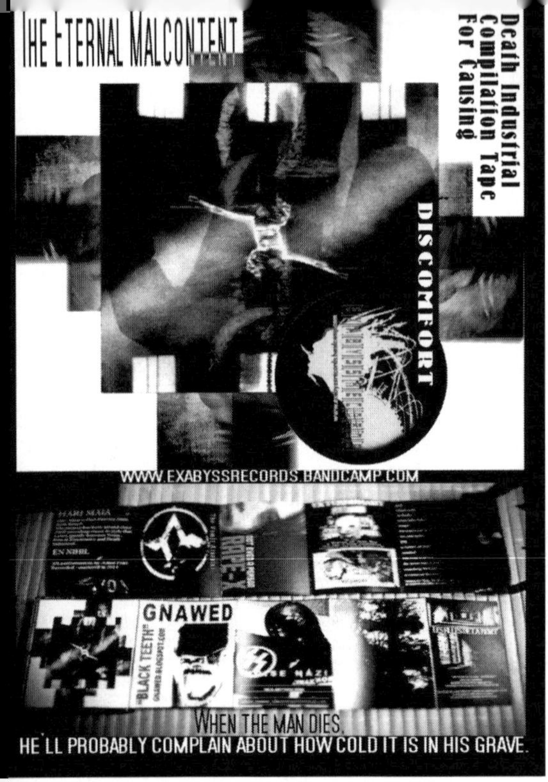

ambience, creates a solid example of an experimental / industrial 'post-mortem' type sound exploration.

- Vårtgård – *Slåss:* delivers a more forceful industrial noise track, featuring a jagged, crumbling wall of distortion, offset with an scattered chaotic noise and aggressive vocals rendered indecipherable in distortion treatment.
- Arkhe – *Vrakloge:* move back into subdued territory by presenting an excellent post-industrial soundscape, where a low distant rumble and oscillating textures – akin to the rotors of an approach helicopter – generate a slow building atmosphere. In effect the muffled and distant ambience and low toned rumble creates an engaging meditative aura.
- A Feast For Vultures – *The Prodigal Returns*: constitutes the final compilation contribution, which is a loosely constructed and 80's 'old-school' sounding industrial track. Contained a plodding rhythmic thump, scattered crackling noise and mid-toned atonal drones, it spans a partly composed and partly improvised style. However the track abruptly ends mid-way and seemingly not by choice but due to the limit of the tape's length. A bit of a shame really.

My own personal barometer for assessing how well conceived a compilation is comes down to whether you get 'lost' along the way between various tracks, and clearly this can be more prone to happen with tapes due to the lack of track numbers to follow. Therefore to its credit *Slutstationen* mostly avoids this pitfall, where I only became 'lost' at one point during this tape, which then had more to do with the lack of adequate space between the end of one song and the start of the next (between Treriksröset and Maniac Cop if it must be known). Overall I would say the first side is stronger than the second, but this is not to say that any of the contributions on side B are sub-par. With a limitation of 250 copies and even a more limited distribution, this tape justifies the effort in tracking down a copy.

Various Artists – *Stein: Interpretationen Eines Geologischen Materials Und Seiner Symbolik* 2xLP, 7"EP Verlautbarung 2013

Compilations can be approached in a couple of ways. On one hand they might be 'just' a collection of tracks and on the other they may be structured around a strongly defined theme or concept. This compilation is definitely of the later where 'stone' forms the thematic focus. 15 predominantly northern European artists have provided contributions (although at least three acts are from the UK), who have made a wide variety of interpretations in sonically approaching this theme and in the process created a diverse and comprehensive listen. Although collectively the artists' have an general experimental bent, this is not of a clinical academic type, rather all artists' have a solid footing in the darker genres spanning: experimental, noise, industrial, field recording, ritual ambient etc. As such this is not a compilation of stuffy academic experimental sounds, rather it is the dirty and caustic sounds of the underground. So, on with a track by track run down:

- Irgun Z'wai Leumi – *Landslide Floorfiller*: This somewhat obscure side project of Proiekt Hat bring a piece of filth infested, heavy burrowing distortion and mid paced mechanised tape loops. Having a thick, weighty, yet warm analogue sound (where overlapping layered loops build in intensity), it is an excellent introduction.
- Amph – *After Nature:* opts for a queasy pulse and micro tonal layered sounds which are fine granted and detailed. The track is minimalist in structure but highly animated and rather forceful by tracks end and a great example of tape experimentations with a darker undercurrent.
- Hal Hutchinson – *Dead Weight:* delivers an example of his recognised raw junk metal abuse which has lots of tonal space and depth. Not being overlay chaotic, this is noise from a 'breathing' experimental angle, where it sounds to be have been constructed with multiple junk metal recording sessions. With an atmosphere of cascading metallic clatter, it very much sounds like a washing machine being thrown down a stairwell.
- Enklav – Skiffer – *Förbannad Jord:* sits within a 1980's 'clanging' analogue industrial sound, which combines loose thumping rhythms with micro tonal textures sitting well in the background. Death industrial meets tape experimentations perhaps?
- Vårtgård – *Grufvan*: delivers forceful electronics waves as an example of solid old school death industrial grinding structures, burrowing textures etc. Being of a monotonous structure there is only gradual evolution throughout.
- Clew Of Theseus – *Stronghold*: forms a track of meditative drones which is quasi-ritual in tone. The mood in one where a deep, hollow and distant drone merges with metallic synth elements which contain a buried harmonic quality.
- Kristian Olsson – *Stenlunga:* is loose and less chaotic and oppressive than Kristian's main work as Alfarmania. Sparse tape manipulations build with a muffled sound and distant squall – like being inside a tornado bunker as the storm

rages outside. What sounds like a lone organ drone lament is buried within the mix which a nice touch.

- Niellerade Fallibilisthorstar – *Kilhacka:* delivers a distant, muffled and hollow drone which cyclically builds with more fine grained 'crunching' textures. Metallic gong like tones, dense rumbles and random textural sounds add sonic diversity.
- MNEM – *Troktopillar*: forms a track of heavy industrial noise loop manipulations, where stilted conveyor belt type loops form the main basis as more forceful looped layers are added and subtracted from the composition.
- Jeph Jerman – *Lithiary Redux:* focuses on experimental, micro-tonal sound textures which are somewhat 'wet' in tone and sounding like field recordings made in the hull of a ship. Here is the track has a great detailed atmosphere built on blend of scratching, tapping, scraping sound elements.
- Doroga – *Kiviteline*: constitutes an excellent ritual ambient track which is sparse in composition, featuring gongs, chimes and slow thudding ritualistic beat, with the overarching atmosphere being of an echoed depths of catacomb. With skin, metal and bones listed as sound sources / instruments this provides an idea of the ominous tone.
- Dieter Müh – *Fältspat:* delivers an experimental ambient soundscape which is located somewhere between the borders of dark ambient to post-industrial music. Vague rhythmic structures, stone scraping sounds and distant, minimal drones mix to generate a mysterious sonic aura.
- Ochu – *Ren Marmor (För George Mallory)*: Here loose ritual percussive elements mix with minimal tape loops etc. Sparse and echoed, with a gradual layering of micro-sounds textures (contact microphone in a bowl of rocks?) and occasional gong hits provides a solid and engaging atmosphere.
- Contrastate – *Haunted:* Sounding only as Contrastate can, their offering is distant, forlorn, mysterious, tragic in equal measures. Here warm layered organ type drones, occasional rhythmic loops and slow drawling poetic vocals give a distinct Contrastate flavour. 'Beauty in darkness' seems a complimentary description for this dark midnight and film noir type atmosphere.
- Feine Trinkers Bei Pinkels Daheim – *Notschrei:* Last album track reverts to the experimental where sound clutter and sweeping atonal textures function in an ebb and flow style. The track also moves into animated 'wind tunnel' drone territory as well as sacral drone ambient with orchestral elements and sampled choirs.

Stein is an example of a compilation which absolutely works in terms of both sonic variety and conceptual focus. It features a strong, varied and intelligent set of experimental underground compositions, made all the more engaging due to the presence of a solid conceptual basis. Pressed on heavy weight vinyl, housed in a thick card stock cover and complimented with additional booklet containing individual artwork and text for each project's offering rounds out the presentation. A rock solid compilation (if such an obvious metaphor is not in poor taste).

Wilt – *From Depths Profound And Inconceivable* CD Fall of Nature 2015

Wilt – *A Daemonic Alteration* MC Fall of Nature 2015

Wilt are a project I was vaguely aware of in the early 2000's but dropped off my radar for whatever reason, but if remembering correctly the project focused on experimental dark ambient with a slightly noisier slant. From a quick look at their Discogs listing Wilt have remained continually active since 1999 and over the last 15 years have been extremely active in fact, with in excess of 70 releases to their name. Here are two new releases from the project, issued at the same time, but on differing formats. On the aesthetic front, it appears the group have evolved towards a more occult focus as evidenced by both by titles and the darker, yawning, black noise tinged dark ambient sound.

From Depths Profound And Inconceivable features 14 tracks (between three and seven minutes each), with nearly 70 minutes of music. Although all generally dark and brooding in sonic texture, there is a myriad of musical angles on display; some being staunchly dark ambient, whilst others having a doom drone frame of reference due to the use of guitars (both distorted and clean depending on the track). A crumbling, distorted rumble which underpins many pieces indicates a rougher edge to proceedings; yet depth and space is also evident within the drone framework, thus providing a broadly expansive and enveloping tone. Regarding particular tracks, *Buried Temples of Belial* starts the album strongly with sampled Tibetan throat chanting, before the introduction of a heavy and prominent (slow plucked) atonally distorted guitar. Although the introductory programmed synths on *Into the Sightless Vortex of the Unimaginable* are rather uninspired and stock-standard; later the sound morphs positively to include a multitude of caustic and distorted layers (abstract guitars and overblown ritual singing bowl playing?). *Shadowed Souls Around A Blazing Alter* represents a particularly doom drone focused piece, of rising / falling static riddled cyclic guitar waves while *An Ancient Circle of Monoliths* is a great example of the 'yawning abyss' style of echoed abstract synth derived dark ambience (including mid-range static coursing through the centre of the composition). After a series of both noisy and subdued droning styled pieces, the final album track *Desolate Mountains* provides a nice deviation with its dour interweaving acoustic guitars and distant rumbling backing.

Moving on to *A Daemonic Alteration*, it forms another complete album with nine tracks in all, but with each being on the shorter side the overall play time is far less than the companion CD. The title track which opens the tape includes buried mechanised rhythms which intermingle with crumbling sub-orchestral drones, whereas organ dirge tones and treated abstract guitars are added to *Fallen* as a slight deviation to the ambient drone framework. The short piece *Some Nameless Thing* is then cut from a darker hue, with its layers and heavier toned bedrock distortion which cyclically push towards a death industrial tone. Side B opens with *A Shadowed Portal* which is far weightier and crushing than preceding material (blast furnace walls of industrial distortion and doom drone feedback), before the sustained and elongated quasi-orchestral drones of *An Abyss Of Seething Chaos And Cerulean Splendor* take over. The final track *Winter Solstice Procession* has a maudlin mood of slow manipulated choir like textures, sparse clanging elements and minimalist undercurrent plays out like a raison d'etre cast off (from the early days of the project), which although hardly original, nails this sound and tone with flair.

To directly compare the two releases, the cassette comes across as the more focused work whereas the CD plays out as a sprawling collection of individual pieces, yet each demonstrates interesting ideas through their blending of elements drawn from black ambient / dark ambient spheres as well as smatterings of a doom drone sound, without necessarily being slavish to either of these genres.

Yen Pox – *Between the Horizon and the Abyss* CD Malignant Records 2015

Although I was not expectantly waiting for a new Yen Pox release, the announcement that 2015 would herald a new album did catch me by surprise. I guess this is symptomatic of the glacial pace of new releases, making the fact that there is a new album from the duo all the more impressive, given it has been a LONG 15 years since the last full length *New Dark Age* and some 13 years from the collaboration album *Mnemonic Induction* with Troum (..with those sorts of timeframes, surely some newer fans to dark ambient music would not appreciate the impact that earlier albums had). Whilst 2011 did see the release of a 10"EP *Universal Emptiness*, to my mind this was a bit of a between albums 'stop gap' release, as Yen Pox's sprawling compositions are much better suited to the full length album format.
From the opening moments of *Between the Horizon and the Abyss* it does not disappoint, with *The Awakening* revealing a track of engulfing and downward spiralling sub-orchestral drones. Here its sonic tapestry is multi-faceted and all encompassing, where layer upon layer of dense drones fold in on themselves; combining, fracturing and radiating out again with renewed strength. But before falling into a recognisable pattern, the next piece *White of the Eye* opts to feature a main driving tone derived from a mangled only vaguely recognisable guitar, which presents a divergent tone for the group within a heavy and swirling sub-orchestral drone framework . *Cold Summer Sun* continues the expanded sonic palate with a multitude of sparse clanging metallic textures to generate a more 'industrialised' version of Yen Pox's typical dark ambient sound. Likewise further sonic variants include: the layered ghostly vocals (male and female) on *In Silent Fields* (which although all separated provide a broad choir like texture); and the middle-eastern hue of the wailing horn and sparse flute playing of *Ashen Shroud.* Given the vast variation in tonal quality and instrumentation used; far from being passive listening, this demands full engagement and presents a massive constantly churning mass of sound. Towards album's end the pair of tracks *Tomorrow in Ruin* and *The Procession* revert to a cataclysmic sub-orchestral dark ambient frame; which is a sound Yen Pox appear to be able to evoke with ease.
With the monolithic sound of Yen Pox's dark ambient soundscapes, they effortlessly articulate a vast cosmic sonic scale which overshadows a human scale perspective, which is perfectly reflected in the artwork. Noting that the artwork of *New Dark Age* was lacklustre at best (and downright cheesy at worst), it did not go anywhere near doing the music of that particular album the justice it deserved. That failing has been rectified here, where the artwork is superb in evoking a sense of monolithic scale and awe through complex geometric patterns and a stand of ominous monoliths. On this new offering Yen Pox hit all of their old hallmarks, whilst expanding the sound anew with a varied sonic palate and source instrumentation. *Between the Horizon and the Abyss* is no less than a revelation and welcomed return of a pinnacle act.

discretionary

terms for potential submission of material

Noise Receptor Journal is a personal endeavour where the majority of items reviewed have been sourced from my personal collection. Accordingly I don't have any sort of hidden agenda of using this as a means to getting as many free releases as possible. If nothing else, it constitutes a creative outlet where I can promote material I feel is worthy of support and added exposure. As such I am not interested in allowing unsolicited material to be submitted for review. I personally buy enough music to keep me very busy with music listening, and the last thing I need is to wade through bundles of material I don't have any passion or connection with. I am also not interested in fulfilling some sort of 'scene documenter' role, in trying to review every single new release which comes out. Quality over quantity I say!
Noting that I am not actively seeking submission of material to review, there may be circumstances where I accept some items, provided the following terms are agreeable:

- I will only review material that has been furnished with a physical release.
- The release must be current and have reasonable availability (i.e. not be limited to a stupidly low number).
- The genre of the music must be suitably aligned to the types of items reviewed herein.
- I will review CDs and vinyls (and perhaps tapes – depending on the release).
- If a release is produced on multiple formats, my preference is as follows: vinyls first, then CDs, followed lastly by tapes.
- I will generally not review CDr's (too often this is indicative of a hastily produced and / or derivative type release) .
- I do not review digital releases or accept MP3's, download links / files etc as a substitute for a copy of the actual release.
- If I do accept the submission of a release for review, a full and complete copy of the physical release must be provided. Any promo versions, or versions stamped 'promo', 'sample', or with corners cut off, holes punched in covers or other markings to indicate its 'promo' status, will not be reviewed.
- To reduce postage cost, sending CD's (including front / back covers) without the jewel cases is acceptable.
- Any items submitted will not be returned.
- I am not interested in reviewing hastily thrown together releases, with little care of quality, aesthetic and design.
- I am not interested in reviewing second rate and / or derivative releases – again quality over quantity. Before you seek to have an item reviewed, undertake a detailed assessment of your own work and make an honest judgement of how it stacks up against other 'pinnacle' works. If in your heart of hearts you feel that your material is second rate, or pales in compassion to comparative material – it is probably true – in which case I am not interested in reviewing it.

If the above terms are not agreeable that is quite fine by me. I will happily continue buying releases and reviewing the ones I feel are worthy, thank you very much! Life is too short to be burdened with listening to and writing about boring, bad, uninspired or derivative music. This is a passion – not a job! If you have got this far and are still interested in trying to submit an item for review, contact me with a proposal, including relevant details at: noisereceptor@hotmail.com

Laplaquenoire.com French E-shop/Mailorder for Extreme Metal,Industrial,Electro
Wide range of yinyls,cd
Contact:**laplaquenoire@gmail.com**

noise receptor
bonus material

T REPANE RINGSRIT UALE N

...an industry of ritual and death...

In mid-2016 I was contacted by another publication about potentially reprinting my interview withTrepaneringsritualen from *Noise Receptor Journal Issue No.1.* The offer was accepted and the opportunity was taken to both expand and update the introduction, as well as ask a series of additional questions. However, the updated interview never made it into print. For the sake of posterity the additional material dating from early 2017 is published below. It should be read as an addendum to the original interview that featured in *Noise Receptor Journal Issue No.1.*

The first murmurings from the underground cult Trepaneringsritualen (aka T × R × P) came in the form of the 2008 cassette, *Ritualer, Blot Och Botgöring*, but given its limitation to 75 copies it barely made a ripple at the time. The project then fell into silence for 3 years, upon which, in 2011, two further obscure cassettes were issued, including the *Veil the World* (in an edition of a mere 40 copies) and *Martyrium* (136 copies). 2012 marked far greater interest in the project, a result of the exceptional *Deathward, To The Womb* 10" ep. This was in part due to its larger run, greater availability and online promo videos. But the most important factor was the quality of the ritual death industrial music, exactly the point at which my own intrigue with the project was generated.

Behind the unusual moniker of T × R × P is Thomas Ekelund, a Swedish musician whose history in producing and releasing music extends back to 2000, when his primary project was the melancholic industrial/drone pop, Dead Letters Spells Out Dead Words. He was also behind the now defunct labels Fukk God Lets Create and When Skies Are Grey, and the current label edifice Belaten [note: also defunct as of 2018].

Being from Sweden, T × R × P draws inspiration from the classic 'CMI' type sound, but this is not mere homage, given that Thomas has direct links back to Cold Meat Industry scene through an obscure collaborative project, Swollen SS with Lina Baby Doll of Deutsch Nepal, and has previously been enlisted by Roger Karmanik (aka label boss of Cold Meat Industry) as a sessional live bass player for Brighter Death Now.

T × R × P are a project with an approach and sound delivered with intelligence and conviction, and have garnered high praise in a short space of time. Melding occult and heretical religious themes and a heavy ritualistic aura with hallmark aspects of Scandinavian death industrial, T × R × P produce a sound that acknowledges its heritage and at the same time achieves a trademark of its own.

2012 appeared to be a watershed year, in that there was a huge amount of activity from the project, including a substantial number of releases, coupled with extensive touring worldwide. This certainly raised the presence and profile of the music. Also around the time there was a definite refinement in sound and approach, where the ritual death industrial soundscapes morphed into heavily rhythmic and song-focused pieces, complete with prominent and grimly delivered vocals in a verse/chorus/verse style, which in part suited the live performance format. The zenith of this song based approach was 2014's *Perfection & Permanence* album (on Cold Spring Records), and with this being the last full length album it remains to be seen if T x R x P's sound will continue or deviate from this more refined template [note: 2017's *Kainskult* followed this template]. But before we have an answer to that particular question, and to further explore the ideas and motivations behind T × R × P, Thomas Ekelund has provided a lengthy and insightful analysis of his work.

To speak of Dead Letters Spells Out Dead Words (DLSODW), in 2016 Cloister Recordings reissued an earlier tape on LP. Was this a one off or do you envisage or desire a larger released campaign from DLSODW back catalogue?

I haven't had any particular interest in getting the back catalog reissued, but I am beginning to re-evaluate that position a bit. I have quite a complicated relationship with DLSODW, it's a very destructive spectre, and I have worked very hard to limit its powers. But even destructive forces may have a positive impact on one's existence Should the opportunity arise at some point to do further reissues, I would gladly consider it, but it's not something I am actively pursuing.

With reference to ritual and enlightenment, what do you see is the role of ritual in the current largely secular atheistic modern world, and do you consider that your music or live 'rituals' can create an element of spiritual transcendence for an audience member who may hold no personal spiritual belief? Is a listener's or audience's reaction of interest to you at all or is T × R × P a purely personal pursuit?

It seems to me that capital-R ritual has been exorcised from our world entirely. The so-called rituals we see these days are either fancy-dress play-acting or a euphemism for materialistic obsessions. I used to think that the spiritual decline was a symptom of the modern world. But perhaps it's the other way around; our times are the end-times, Kali Yuga, Fimbulvetr, whatever you want to call it. The gods have all but left us in preparation for the coming renovation of creation?

Your guess is as good as mine when it comes to what a spiritually void person gets out of T × R × P. I would imagine that it's merely a spectacle, a bit of entertainment to escape a barren existence, if only for a moment. T × R × P is doubtlessly a personal pursuit, and a large part of it is conducted away from prying eyes. But the public workings serve their purpose. As I've said many times before, there is still a lot about T × R × P that I don't fully comprehend, but I find that a public ritual — in the right circumstances, with the right people in attendance — is an enormously powerful tool with which to come closer to that gnosis. That being said, any journey across the abyss is essentially a solitary one.

Since our original interview in early 2013 there has been an explosion in both the number of releases as well as broader underground interest in T × R × P, which has culminated in a quite busy live performance schedule over recent years. How have you personally perceived this increased interest and awareness in what you do? In turn has this interest in any way influenced what you want to achieve with the project?

The T × R × P curse has spread far wider than I could've ever imagined. It has put me in places I didn't know I needed to be, and it has forged friendships that has proven to be immensely influential in reaching understanding of why this is happening. Mass-appeal isn't a factor, I do the work that needs to be done and that may prove popular, or it might not.

From available online footage it would appear your live setup involves a 'playback' backing track, live vocals and perhaps some live electronics. This setup certainly allows you the opportunity to achieve a confrontational approach with the audience. However, do you see your live set evolving towards a fully live electronic base? Would additional live members ever be considered an option?

A full live band is in the stars, and the only reason it has yet to materialize are purely mundane issues of economy and logistics. It will happen. In the interim, I will continue with the basic setup I have utilized so far — your assessment of which is correct — and focus my energy on the Ritual, rather than twisting knobs.

Of your official albums, *Perfection & Permanence* from 2014 was the last, and displayed a very streamlined and direct song-based approach which had been toyed with on early releases, such as the *Judas Goat* and *Papist Pretender* 7"eps. Where does this direct sound of *Perfection & Permanence* sit within material you may be currently working on or planning?

I have never questioned where I am led in these matters. The material takes the form it's supposed to have. Since *Perfection & Permanence*, and *Papist Pretender* were completed, this has meant more abstract, collaged works — the bonus material on the recent *Deathward, To The Womb* reissue being a prime example — and experiments with trance state drumming, but there are also more of typically song structured material in various stages of completion that will see publication at one point or another.

Credits & details:

Photo 1 by Nicky Hellemans
Photo 2 by Kim Solve

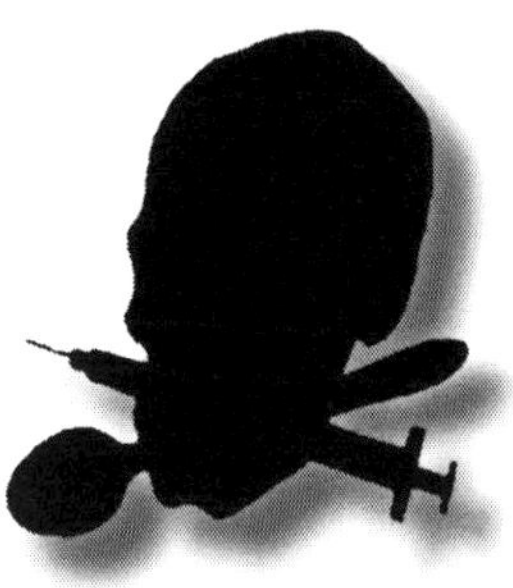

ALFARMANIA SURVIVAL UNIT

In mid-2016 I was contacted by another publication about potentially reprinting my interview with Alfarmania/Survival Unit from *Noise Receptor Journal* Issue No.3. The offer was accepted, and the opportunity was taken to both expand and update the introduction, as well as ask a series of additional questions. However, the updated interview never proceeded to print. For the sake of posterity the additional material dating from early 2017 is published below. It should be read as an addendum to the original interview in *Noise Receptor Journal* Issue No.3.

Kristian Olsson of Sundsvall, Sweden, once a young upstart, has through sheer perseverance and dedication become a stalwart advocate of true underground post-industrial music. Through long-term and ongoing involvement he has proven himself beyond all doubt to be a dedicated supporter of all aspects of the underground, both past and present.

My own awareness extends back to the late 1990s (at a time when I was publishing *Spectrum Magazine*), when Kristian was starting to make his presence known within the underground through the ritual dark ambient collective Heid and his solo power electronics project Survival Unit. Never one to settle on a single project or creative pursuit, over the years Kristian has issued a wealth of artistic material, be it musical focused or visually based. This extends to art exhibitions, running his own label *Styggelse* (over 60 releases since 2005) and *Shocktilt Magazine* of which two issues have been released to date, a decade apart, in 2006 and 2016 respectively.

Given that a large part of underground post-industrial music is concerned with, if not all out obsessed with the seedy underbelly of society, Kristian has taken such interests to their logical conclusion through full immersion. Not one to be satisfied with dealing with such themes on a cursory level, Kristian has followed his creative muse into numerous dark recesses of the human condition. As alluded to in the interview, this has led him down some personally destructive paths. Some two decades later, Kristian is still dedicated to the cause and has evolved into a long-term scene devotee and proven his commitment to a staunchly underground ethos. Beyond his own music and legacy, he has been instrumental in shining a torch in the darkest corners of the late 70s and early 80s industrial underground through his *Shocktilt Magazine*, in addition to hailing the current leading lights (no matter how obscure).

More recently, Kristian has been instrumental in resurrecting two classic Swedish power electronics projects, namely RJF and Blood Ov Thee Christ, and during their brief periods of reactivation he contributed as a guest member. To this end RJF was resurrected in 2013 as Kommando RJF for one final album *Sweet Slow Suicide*, while Blood Ov Thee Christ became active again in 2007 with a flurry of releases before chaotically imploded a number of years later.

Despite his extensive and ongoing involvement in the underground, Kristin has conducted few interviews over the years, therefore it seemed an opportune time to subject Kristian to a detailed interrogation regarding all of his activities, past and present, covering predominantly Survival Unit and Alfarmania, but also extending to his solo and collaborative musical projects, live performances, visual arts and his label Styggelse.

You hint at some personal and philosophical positions that act as a sort of constant underpinning of your conceptual artistic outputs. Would you care to elaborate?

In many ways I would claim my life and artistic trajectory has been a Faustian or Promethean quest. Throughout my life something has been speaking to and through me, an ever-present calling that I've heard since my earliest years. The Black Flame or the inner spark. Emanations of the acausal.

My works are perhaps mostly known for portraying a nihilistic and misanthropic conception of an exoteric reality, but underneath this there is also the esoteric. Working with these subject matters is purgative. Transforming the social and spiritual disease into a cure. The modern world is so detached from spirituality and purpose that it will drown in its own materialistic vomit. Like in the viparita karani where the life-current is reversed and eventually even death ceases to be.

In the process of Death and Rebirth of the initiate in various hidden societies, one returns from the burial granted the sight of the afterlife. Descending into the underworld and taking part of the wisdom hidden therein. Crossing the abyss and overcoming the human condition. Merging with the shadow side, the beast within, instead of letting it consume you. Once you have crossed the threshold there is no turning back. It is an individual journey towards this awakening. No prefixed systems, shortcuts or easy solutions. Many paths may lead there, but few are willing to sacrifice their Self…

Firstly one must plunge the sacrificial dagger into the burden of morality or it will drag you down with it to its depths.

The apologetic and explanatory approach so many artists today have towards their output sickens me. No place for self-censorship nor self-righteous fools. Not everything should be analyzed or explained. It's already laid out there in the art and music, as indicators for those with the eyes to see it. What we do must constantly aim to be lawless and infinite — it is a path that will never be safe unless you settle for subjugated mediocrity. Civilizational decline is not a new occurrence. For each ending cycle there has always been the prophetic artists and poets portraying this process. The flames of enlightenment is in a constant struggle with the darkness of ignorance. The huge totalitarian machinery designed only to enslave and crush mankind, to feed its gargantuan hunger.

You appear to be constantly seeking out personal contact with fringe dwellers and free thinkers, who function far away from the mainstream or 'acceptable' modern thought. Is there any pattern to how you become interested in such individuals and how you initiate contact? Who are the notable individuals you have met that have influenced you, your thoughts and approach to life?

Networking has always come naturally for me. It's like setting the pyres alight, leading the way for myself and for others. My artistic achievements as a mirror reflecting my inmost self, at the same time as it evokes transformative states within those who approach it, pushing them to cross the line.

At one point, when experimenting with vāmācāra tantric techniques, I was granted visions confirming that there exists a collective unconscious after all. I have of course studied this in the past, but this was a deeper form of understanding. It became clear to me that there is a purpose with what I am doing, making threads and manifesting the sinister numinous.

I do not consider myself a social person really. More introspective and solitary, but bound by necessity to interact with other people. Only in recent years I have come to really apprehend the concept of love and that the entire world isn't my enemy. Learning humility is an extremely important lesson that sharpens the knives rather than dulling them.

The fringe dwellers and free thinkers that you refer to are often connected through some irrational magnetic force to a greater whole. Pathways crossing because of necessity or synchronicity. The webs of wyrd, often linking together those most different from each other. Academics, anarchs, criminals, magicians, mercenaries, outsiders, sexual deviants… whatever it may be. I could list so many that has inspired me but the Individual is rarely what I value the most. The fire baptism the truly visionary needs to go through. Endurance through the barbed wire and muddy waters. Obstacles and hardships of the road. Sacrificing the Self strengthens the vision towards becoming something greater.

Video backdrops appear to be an integral part of your Alfarmania live performances, albeit these are more of an abstract artistic type. Do you care to talk about your approach to live performance and how much the potential audience is a consideration in what you do? What have been your most memorable shows to date?

There is really little new about what I do, but why reinvent the wheel when you can still push the wagon forwards to new grounds. Being a kid of the VHS-generation, I have nearly magical memories of seeing NON perform on Swedish television as a young boy. Third generation copies of *SPK Despair*, *Come Org Ultra* and *True Gore*. In times before the internet this was cracking my skull open and filling it with subversive inspiration. It made me realize the magnitude of combining this medium with my own soundwork. Plant and cultivate seeds in the shadowside of the mind. The many layers through which the conscious and subconscious projections can flow.

Later I became very interested in arthouse cinema and actionist films. Some attempts have been made at this, but it almost became too successful so it remains in the vaults for now. Performing live is a loathsome, yet necessary evil. Paradoxically in some regards most rewarding, in others a form of flagellation whipping me to carry on doing this. I've lost count of the number of live shows since I began in the mid-90s. Although I get more routine, it is as challenging for my nerves. The interaction with the audience, those who really listen, makes it all worthwhile. It transcends all subcultural boundaries and justifies the weeks of preparations before each set. The actual emancipation is ritualistic. Once standing there it makes me nothing but a vessel, opening up something truly demonic. Each time I try to have complete control — instead it ends with the total loss of it. The most memorable shows are those I remember the least from. When done in the right way, live performances can be the ultimate way to experience this music and serve as an extension of my other workings. A purifying discharge of energies — within and without.

There's been numerous incidents of violence and confrontations at our gigs, but I'd have that any day before pretentious scene-apes standing with crossed arms in the back of the venue. We both come from a background of black metal and d-beat punk — where at least some of this energy can be found.

In 2015 and 2016, Alfarmania played quite a number of shown in Europe and the US (specifically the Metropolitan Audio Pain Source: Volume 3 Festival in New York City). What are your memories of these shows, and are they positive or negative? What are your impressions of America itself, on a personal or ideological level?

Our transatlantic travels in the past years has led to the solidification of Alfarmania as a unit. Working with Ferner has been rewarding in many aspects. Since he joined we've kept a low profile but still performed in Berlin, Helsinki, London, Mannheim, New York, Stockholm etc. As a typical European I must admit having certain prejudices towards America and Americans, but it proved to be one of the best trips I've done. Many thanks to the crew around the Fieldwork label & M.A.P.S. festival and Sean Ragon. It was great to go on a longer trip with my old friend Tommy of Treriksröset. We ended up doing a short and very intense live set as Kommando RJF on the second night of the festival... the show took place in a small basement, much like a darkroom in *Cruising* or something. Me and TC wore black and hoods. Leif was present through amplified long-distance telephone call. I mounted a contact microphone to a rusty machete to sing through. The venue was being torn to pieces by an extremely agitated audience. I nearly slashed open the face of one guy with the blade. Lucky for him he got no permanent reminder of RJF in NYC. This summer I'm returning to the US but to make a solo performance in San Francisco.

My impressions of New York — an extremely nihilistic city. Asphyxiating in its own selfish materialism. Maybe one of the reasons why I enjoyed staying there for a while, knowing I can retreat to the northern stillness. If I'd live there it wouldn't take long until I had perished in my own degeneracy…

Swedish people are so programmed by centuries of Lutheran brainwash that we almost don't know what to do with so many options — so much of the Coca-Cola-freedom. Deep forests and high mountains surrounding us here. Majestic nature with all it can offer. But most Swedish people prefer to stay inside their houses because they are habitual creatures safe in their dissatisfaction and mediocrity. Living in this part of the country makes it easy to retreat to the feral and absorb the archaic wisdom therein. In the downward rush of history, the forest is a fortress and temple. Here we can live and wait for the turning of the tides. Here at the crossroads you can find devils and spirits that have been around since long before we settled here. Western civilization is like a flock of wanderers on a frozen lake that is dissolving into huge floes. The surface of conceptions is frangible and the depth of the elements, that has been there forever, shimmers through the cracks and joints.

America is a standard example of this age of dissolution. The collective hysteria of the political piggies on both sides of the fences. Choirs of endless complaint. Cries of the easily offended are so loud that they drown out the warning signals that usually alarms us that the people are being pegged into submission by those in power. I'm afraid it doesn't matter how much they demonize their scapegoats. It won't break the chains. The era of constant conflict is here. A low-trust serf society with ever-growing surveillance and police state measures replacing individual freedom and autonomous movement. Ultra-totalitarianism rising in the shadow of the western democracies. Economic and population growth just for the sake of it, much like the cancerous cell.

No doubt we're living in the endtimes, but we'll endure longer than people think. Much like animals caught in quicksand, we are fighting more to get out of the materialistic abyss but only sink deeper the more we fight unless we seek deeper meaning in things.

Credits & details: Photo by Oliver Frank/Infinite Beat of Kristian Olsson performing as Alfarmania at the Tesco Organisation 30th Anniversary show, 27 October, 2017, Mannheim, Germany.

BLITZKRIEG BABY

With various releases issued since the debut album in 2013, Blitzkrieg Baby have functioned as a studio-based project. But it was in 2019 as part of the Cloister Recordings 5th Anniversary festival, Dominion's of Flesh (Stockholm 1st & 2nd November, 2019), that main member Kim Solve made the decision to take the project into the live arena.
Having attended the festival and witnessed firsthand the group's debut show, the short and sharp set constituted a strong and polished performance. Familiar tracks were played, including Cannibal Commando and War Gods, alongside new tracks Violence and One by One, which sounded excellent on first listen. Crowd response between tracks was extremely enthusiastic, and it was great to see how well Blitzkrieg Baby songs translate to the live arena.
With the Blitzkrieg Baby interview from Issue No.2 reissued in this book, it seemed an opportune time to ask some supplementary questions to explore Kim's decision to perform live and how he found the debut show. The addendum interview below was conducted via email in December 2019.

You have been a predominantly studio band to date. In November 2019 you played your debut performance at the Cloister Recordings 5th Anniversary show Dominion of Flesh. I assume that this may have resulted from a request from label boss Marcus LaBonte? If that is indeed the case, did it take much convincing to take Blitzkrieg Baby's music onto the stage?

I've wanted to perform live with Blitzkrieg Baby for some time now. Marcus LaBonte presented us with not only the opportunity, but was adamant that we perform live. If not for him, we wouldn't have even started to adapt Blitzkrieg Baby for the live setting.

How did you approach the show and determine how you would present the material live, i.e. how did you decide who to ask to assist you in the performance, as well your own own approach to the live situation?

When figuring out how to play Blitzkrieg Baby's music live, it was paramount for me that I perform on an instrument where I could connect with the music in real-time. Playing pre-recorded material while standing in front of the audience was not an option. Since the beginning, and on many Blitzkrieg Baby recordings, bass has been a key instrument, therefore, playing bass was a natural place for me within the sound and gave me the possibility of an immediate physical connection with the music.

Although a Blitzkrieg Baby performance could include any material that I want and any type of presentation I want it to be, I was attracted to the possibility of playing the more song-based material, which was only made possible thanks to the considerable talents of Per Åhlund and Anders B., both of whom invested their time and talent performing vocals, synthesisers, effects and percussion. Without them, this gig would not have happened.

From my own perspective in the audience, it was clear that your set was extremely well received. How did you personally find the crowd reaction and from your perspective how did you feel the show went overall?

The setting for Blitzkrieg Baby's debut performance could not have been better. The venue was an old slaughterhouse, intact with tiled walls and plastic sheets covering the doorways. The audience was enthusiastic and appreciative, and some people had travelled from afar just to see us. The sound and lighting far exceeded expectations and it was a solid event all around. Regarding the performance itself, it went according to plan.

In some of our post-show discussions, I was surprised to hear that the debut performance of Blitzkrieg Baby was also your first live performance ever as part of a band, particularly given how confident you appeared. Was there any point in the

past where playing live may have happened, but for whatever reason did not?

After the release of the *Cannibal Commando* EP on Beläten in 2015, two years or so after our last *Noise Receptor* interview, there were some requests to perform in London and Berlin. However, I was focused on finishing ongoing recordings and hadn't prepared for live performances, so there was no way I could go through with them at the time. Therefore, the Stockholm gig was the first real opportunity.

You commented that you were not sure if you would like performing live. Now, given the post-show context, what are your impressions of performing live and potentially continuing the live format? Do you see the format of members and instrumentation of the live group remaining the same or potentially being altered in any way?

Personally, I found the experience rewarding. I trust Per and Anders both want to do this again and make further Blitzkrieg Baby performances possible. The format might change somewhat if needed, or perhaps, more likely, expand. In which way would only be speculation at this point.

The audience for your debut performance were well suited to what you do, and focused on the underground post-industrial scene you operate within. If you are to perform again, do you see perhaps select special shows, or more of a typical tour format?

I suspect that we will be into doing select shows for now, where we are ensured that we have what we need to perform in the manner we wish.

You have described your music as 'Norwegian dystopian electronic music' and 'ultra negative industrial pop'. While I am aware that you are a huge Coil fan, what are you a fan of in the pop scene, whether or not it is an influence on what you create with Blitzkrieg Baby?

I enjoy pop music from all eras, but my heart certainly lies in the 80s pop music. The 80s was the golden era of pop for so many reasons. If I start listing specific groups, I won't be able to know where to stop — there are too many to mention.

Since the first interview conducted in 2013, you have had a slew of releases, including the *Kid's World* EP (2014), the *Cannibal Commando* tape (2015) *War Gods* tape (2018), as well as the second album *Homo Sapiens Parasitus* (2019). Additionally a third album *Genocidal Sextasy* is slated for release in 2020. Does this amount to all of the material you have recorded to date under the Blitzkrieg Baby banner, or is there still more music lurking in the vaults?

War Gods had been delayed two years when it came out in 2018, as Beläten took a well-deserved break from doing releases. Also, when we spoke back in 2013, the album I was referring to — although unnamed at the time — was *Homo Sapiens Parasitus*, which didn't come out until August 2019. In other words, after years of delay. In the meantime, we have continued to create material. The third full-length, *Genocidal Sextasy* on Cloister Recordings, was 'pre-released' in a limited test press edition in connection with our performance at Dominion of Flesh. The regular edition will, as you mentioned, be out in 2020, along with the vinyl reissue of our debut album, *Porcus Norvegicus.*

The track, Violence, that you saw us perform in Stockholm, will be released on a flexi single through Mustard Relics. Aufnahme + Wiedergabe from Berlin will release a 12" with Blitzkrieg Baby tracks remixed by Ancient Methods, Luciano Lamanna, Antoni Maiovvi and Espen T Hangård.

For several years now, I have been working on a long-term Blitzkrieg Baby series called *The International Blitzkrieg Coalition*, where I create tracks with artist friends from around the world. *The International Blitzkrieg Coalition Document I* is a tape made together with Corrugator Supercillii back in 2013 and 2014. *The International Blitzkrieg Coalition Document II*, called *Nurture Nothing, Destroy Everything*, is a CD release featuring tracks made together with Armour Group, Theologian, Arkhe, M77, Vær Hos Meg Naar Mitt Timeglass Utrinder, Of Earth And Sun, Pestorgel, Thomas Ekelund of Trepaneringsritualen, Anders B., and Zweizz. Both of these releases will be out through Malignant Records, hopefully also in 2020.

Blitzkrieg Baby's fourth full length album is in the final stages of recording and is scheduled for a yet to be disclosed label sometime later in 2020. I am currently working on material intended for several EPs and the fifth and sixth full length albums, most of which I aim to release in 2021 or later. Besides that, I will spend much of 2020 working on material for my other project, Swarms, some of which is scheduled for release through Cyclic Law.

Photo: credits & details: Photos by Peo Bengtsson at *Dominion of Flesh,* Cloister Recordings 5th Anniversary festival, 1st November, 2019, Stockholm, Sweden. Photo 1 of Kim Solve. Photo 2 of Per Åhlund.

SPECTRUM COMPENDIUM

noise receptor journal

Richard Stevenson is the man behind *Noise Receptor Journal*, an Australian fanzine dedicated to industrial music. A fervent advocate of those who value the permanence of underground publications, he produced his first fanzine *Spectrum Magazine* two decades ago.

Republished in the form of a book in February 2019, *Spectrum Compendium* reprints all five issues along with interviews and reviews originally intended for the planned, but ultimately abandoned, sixth issue of *Spectrum Magazine*. It also includes insightful bonus archive material, like live photos covering industrial performances from that period and personal correspondence with artists. With more than 50 interviews and 600 detailed reviews spanning the various industrial sub-genres, in addition to the archival documents, *Spectrum Compendium* is a critical publication highlighting the post-industrial underground as well as celebrating key artists and labels of the late 1990s and early 2000s. With Richard's more traditional role as 'the interviewer', it was time to turn the tables and to question him about the book itself, *Spectrum Magazine's* history, and his current endeavour *Noise Receptor Journal*, as well as to broach different aspects related to industrial music culture.

—Cyril Adam

How was the *Spectrum Compendium* project initiated and how do you feel, overall, about the final product? The book reproduces scanned pages of all five issues plus content for the unpublished sixth issue and a wealth of bonus archival material (live pictures, personal correspondence, an interview with you, etc.). Was it defined from the beginning that these archives would be included or was it a specific demand of the publisher, or something that evolved over time? More generally, what kind of personal impressions did you experience in going back over your own history during the book's creation?

Well, the concept for the book had been kicking around in the back of my mind for many years, but mostly as a vague thought of: *'it be great to have the issues of Spectrum Magazine released as a book'*. It was only after seeing how well *METALION: The Slayer Mag Diaries* (by Jon "Metalion" Kristiansen, published in 2011) was received in the underground metal scene that I really thought more seriously about making *Spectrum Compendium* a reality as a sort of equivalent publication for the post-industrial underground.

So in around 2012–13 I contacted various publishers to pitch the idea of the book, but was met with resounding silence from all the publishing houses I contacted. Incidentally, Headpress was not one of them as I was not at that point aware of their activities. It was only later in 2015 that I became aware of Headpress, which coincided with when I was first introduced to Jennifer Wallis, editor of the book *Fight Your Own War: Power Electronics and Noise Culture*. Following my contribution of a couple of chapters to that book and after seeing the quality of the production, it reinvigorated me to see if I could make *Spectrum Compendium* a reality. It was then in early 2017 that, with the encouragement of Jennifer, I pitched the idea to Headpress and within a matter of months a contract had been signed, which was much faster than I ever anticipated given I did not expect Headpress to be interested enough to take the book on. But with the benefit of hindsight, I suspect that the success of *Fight Your Own War* influenced the decision of Headpress given both books cover the same sort of niche underground spheres.

As for matters of content, during the initial discussions with Headpress it was mainly about just republishing the five issues of the magazine, along with the various remaining threads intended for the cancelled sixth issue. However, the more I got into pulling together all the relevant parts, it dawned on me that I had a wealth of related archival material from the 1998–2002 period the book covers that would make for excellent additional content. In a quite freeform approach the inclusion of additional material was discussed and agreed with Headpress during the process of collating everything. I have to mention David Kerekes, the 'head' of Headpress, as he was great to deal with during the entire process; particularly during the desktop design phase, I was given far more leeway with design-related matters than I had anticipated. In the final phase I was even allowed to take over the files to address micro finicky design tweaks that perhaps only I would notice. But I figured I wanted to get it perfect and not leave any small design element which would annoy me later.

As for the finished book, in many ways it has exceeded my wildest expectations, particularly with the hardback special edition which has a solidness and sturdiness which suits the material perfectly. I was even quite surprised to see how well the issues hung together visually when published in the single volume. However, I guess that is due in part to the careful cropping and alignment of reprinted pages which allowed me to clean up the page edges, which on occasion in the original print magazines looked slightly messy due to the offset printing and uneven border trimming. While *Spectrum Compendium* certainly has a role in giving the original magazines longevity and greater exposure, I have to admit it was also quite a selfish endeavour to have it published for inclusion on my own bookshelves. So, from that perspective, I am still amazed that everything came together in the way it has and I could not be happier.

In terms of going back over my own history, I never really stopped following or turned my back on the underground, so I never felt like I was revisiting a closed chapter. The era that is covered in *Spectrum Compendium* was so influential in my initial appreciation and understanding of the underground that I feel it is constantly with me, not some long forgotten phase in the past to be dug up and reminisced about. The fact that I am still publishing in print via *Noise Receptor Journal* also allowed me to view *Spectrum Magazine* in the context of continuity, rather than a more cynical case of backwards-looking nostalgia. I guess I also view it in the context of a constant thread of interest (perhaps more correctly described as an all-out obsession) which directly connects my younger days in my late teens and early 20s to the person I am now. Perhaps the era of *Spectrum Magazine* feels more like it was 10 years ago, but certainly not 20 years.

However, to consider the broader context, perhaps what I was most surprised about was the impressions of others who contributed forewords to the book and the importance they placed upon *Spectrum Magazine.* When publishing *Spectrum Magazine* I was certainly not within an active scene in the physical sense, so I just did what I did given the imposed isolation of Australia and got the issues out there; I didn't expect major players to actually care about and be so engaged with what I was doing. I therefore was beyond surprised to hear that Nordvargr used *Spectrum Magazine* to discover new music. I was equally blown away at the Cold Meat Industry 30th Anniversary show in Stockholm, Sweden (November 2017) when label head honcho Roger Karmanik thanked me for all I have done for the underground. That was another completely unexpected and very humbling compliment.

At the beginning of the book, there are a number of forewords and reflections by artists and label managers which contextualise *Spectrum Magazine* and describe how the underground was functioning at the time of its production. Some of these texts also underline *Spectrum Magazine*'s place within a particularly active, yet changing, period in the industrial underground. The shift brought about by the internet is mentioned as well as the fact that, in retrospect, it was a rising time for many bands and labels. You also approach this aspect in your own introduction to the book and I would like to come back to that: what are your views on this transitional period for the industrial movement at the time when *Spectrum Magazine* was operating?

During the late 1990s/early 2000s, when *Spectrum Magazine* was operating, I guess there was a real sense of global interconnectedness between labels, artists and fans. Stephen Petrus talks extensively about this in his foreword for *Spectrum Compendium*, which highlighted a golden era when international postal was cheap, and the internet functioned as a promotional platform, but people were still interested in all forms of physical media.

Regarding where we have got to today, there has been a gradual decline in physical connection and focus which is inversely related to the increase in online connection and the volume of social media information being circulated globally. As alluded to nearly four decades ago by SPK's album title *Information Overload Unit,* clearly the underground is suffering from too much information which distracts and fragments the focused attention which was previously present within the scene. Perhaps there is an equal amount of activity globally, but it is hidden in smaller and more insular localized scenes, where waning interest in physical media and the exorbitant manufacturing and postage costs means far less opportunity to get your material out there. Also, there appears to have been a marked rise in the number of releases being issued, and I am often left scratching my head when I am asked to check out a new project who have issued a huge number of releases in a relatively short space of time. Projects are free to do whatever they want, but surely there is some lack of quality control in choosing to issue so many releases? I even remember one artist who said something to the effect that they did not know which releases their best were, or even if they were good, as it was up to the fans to decide. Clearly, I feel this sort of attitude is to the overall detriment of the underground as it only further diverts attention away from discovering the pinnacle releases, and adds to the 'information overload' scenario.

I also remember that back in the 1990s/2000s there was a huge hunger for relevant and interesting material, but now it is the inverse where people have to wade through the barrage of useless information which often hides or clouds what is truly interesting and important. This is where I see the role of underground publications: to cut through this 'noise of information' and provide some clarity away from clickbait articles and constant online bickering. Social media has its purpose, function, and role, but on a whole it has become tedious beyond measure.

You always emphasise the curatorial role of the printed media in underground culture: the fact that fanzines can be revisited over the years tends towards a more in-depth reading compared to the ephemerality of web publications. So, not from an author's point of view but from a reader's one, did you experience some unexpected enjoyment in rereading some of these interviews and reviews? Did you rediscover artists you might have put aside since that time, or others you were surprised to realise had disappeared from the scene?

My main aim with *Spectrum Magazine* and later with *Noise Receptor Journal* was to issue publications that I would want to read (and reread) myself. This has meant that at sporadic points over the years when I leaf through my own archive of zines I ended up revisiting *Spectrum Magazine* as part of the process. Equally the contents of *Spectrum Magazine* are indelibly imprinted in my mind, so I would not say there is any interview content which was forgotten, and therefore to be rediscovered, but certainly I have used it as springboard to decide what older albums I might want to give another spin. Likewise, in rereading interviews there are often little titbits of information I had forgotten, but mostly I remember the broader lines of questioning and the responses.

I guess with people disappearing from the underground, that is just a case of the constant churn of people that become involved and lose interest at some point. That is completely fine as there is no point remaining involved if there is lack or interest or the dreaded cynicism has seeped in. For whatever reason, I have maintained a positive interest for close to 25 years now, so I will stay involved as long as the passion and interest is there. Clearly there are others like myself who have been around just as long as I have, and in fact a lot longer in many cases.

The cover design of the book is a photo by Warren Mead. It seems that this artwork particularly resonates with you as you own the original piece too. What is the history of this picture and how was it chosen for the book against other design options? The cover of the fourth issue of *Spectrum Magazine* is also a cropped version of a photo by Warren Mead, as is the cover of the first issue of *Noise Receptor Journal*. These artworks from the same artist that punctuate your three printed endeavours appear to make a connection between them. Was it perhaps the only logical decision to use a Warren Mead photo for *Spectrum Compendium*?

Actually, choosing to use the Warren Mead photo for the main cover image was a completely last-minute decision. Originally, I didn't have any concept at all for the cover (other than to use the original font for general branding and visual continuity), given Headpress said that their graphic designer would come up with something appropriate. However, when I received the first draft of the cover, to my mind it was not appropriate and didn't have a strong visual impact to represent the book overall. But at the time Headpress were on a tight deadline to get the book cover released to the market for pre-release promotion so the pressure was on to find a better option — and quickly. That led to a 'lightbulb' moment for me when I realised Warren Mead's 'church silhouette' photo would be perfect for the cover. So I immediately mocked up a draft version, and upon seeing it David at Headpress agreed it was the cover image we should use. I don't know exactly why I did not think of using that image sooner, but as soon as the decision was made, it felt completely right, and even more so that the original framed image has been hanging on my wall in Australia since I purchased it from Warren in 2000, and that an interview with Warren (and the full image) was included in an interview in *Spectrum Magazine* Issue No.4. As for the image, it was the main photo in Warren Mead's *Dark Poland* photographic exhibition in Melbourne, Australia in 2000; it is a twilight silhouette of a church and surrounding forest somewhere in the depths of Poland.

I had never heard of or met Warren before attending the

exhibition, which was a series of photos he had taken in Poland, all with a darkly gothic and medieval flavour. Given the visuals were so striking and similar to the aesthetic of *Spectrum Magazine* I got talking to Warren at the exhibition and discovered he was broadly aware of dark ambient music, which then led me to conduct and feature an interview with him in Issue No.4. In the months following the release of the issue I kept in contact with Warren, and he offered to sell me the original framed image from the *Dark Poland* exhibition at a reasonable price, which I immediately accepted. I lost contact with Warren when I moved over to the UK in 2001, and despite searching extensively for him online prior to the publication of *Spectrum Compendium*, I have not been able to locate him at all and he seems to have disappeared completely, or at least is not maintaining any social media presence or working as a photographer these days.

When I interviewed Warren back in 2000 he sent me three high resolution images for use. One was used for the cover of *Spectrum Magazine* Issue No.4 (i.e. 'soldiers'), one has now been used for the cover of *Spectrum Compendium* (i.e. 'church silhouette') and the third was used for the cover of *Noise Receptor Journal* Issue No.1 (i.e. 'gothic church'). As *Noise Receptor Journal* ultimately came off the back of the process of me launching the *Spectrum Magazine Archive* blog in 2012, it was when digging through my archives from the *Spectrum Magazine* era that I discovered Warren Mead's images. As 'gothic church' image had not been used for a magazine cover at that point, it seemed a logical choice to use what I had to hand and provided continuity between the older *Spectrum Magazine* era and the newly emerging *Noise Receptor Journal* era. I also like the fact that pretty much all the important writing and visuals I have had at my disposal over the years have been put to good use through my publications.

As regards the visual aspect of your various publications, how would you describe your evolution from using various artists' images for the different covers of *Spectrum Magazine* issues to a more consistent visual creation with *Noise Receptor Journal*, which uses artwork from a specific artist throughout the entire issue? Each fanzine reflects the individual drive of its creator in its aesthetic choices so what are yours, from *Spectrum Magazine* to *Noise Receptor Journal?*

There are actually a number of differences in the design 'rules' which I established to specifically differentiate *Spectrum Magazine* from *Noise Receptor Journal.* These strict design 'rules' are more applicable to *Noise Receptor Journal*, where it allows new issues to be prepared in a consistent and uniform manner, which has a perhaps more timeless style.

Back when I started *Spectrum Magazine* I did not have such design 'rules' and it was more a process of the design, look and feel evolving over time. However, as I ended up using band logos and promo shots in *Spectrum Magazine* it meant that each interview ended up with its own specific design and look; while the designs became more refined and elaborate as the issues progressed, it also introduced a degree of pressure to continually come up with a different look and feel for each interview layout. With *Noise Receptor Journal* I wanted to get away from that and have a more simplistic and consistent design aesthetic which allowed the interview text to be the main focus — which is the most important part of what I am wanting to do with *Noise Receptor Journal* anyway. That is where I came up with the design 'rules', where each interview would be laid out in a similar manner, with key images used as either insets or full pages as appropriate. Equally, for the keen eye, other design rules include: always using black or grey background for interviews, always having reviews printed as black text on white, and always using contributed artwork on the right-hand panel of every second spread to break up the review section text. There were then a range of design and style choices made for *Noise Receptor Journal* which were the effective opposite of that for *Spectrum Magazine.* For example, the chosen 'logo' for *Noise Receptor Journal* is uncapitalized lower case, as this was the complete opposite to the block capitals of *Spectrum Magazine*. Whereas *Spectrum Magazine* was A4, *Noise Receptor Journal* is half that size at A5. While *Spectrum Magazine* was printed as a folded and stapled magazine, *Noise Receptor Journal* is a perfectbound booklet. So, although *Noise Receptor Journal* is clearly a continuation of what started with *Spectrum Magazine*, equally there were a range of specific decisions taken to make sure it would look and feel like something new and different.

As for the idea to have one artist contribute artwork for both the cover and review sections, this was in direct acknowledgment of the fact that many musicians are also visual artists, and this would be a way to celebrate that. Equally, choosing to have a colour cover for Issues No.3 and No.4 of *Noise Receptor Journal* was in response to the chosen artworks for the covers essentially demanding to be printed in colour in order to do them justice. Also, clearly my 'talent' (if you want to call it that) leans more towards writing and desktop publishing, so by inviting an artist to contribute artwork it means I can focus on those strengths in getting issues of *Noise Receptor Journal* completed and released. But like everything, there is time to change tactics and evolve. Personally, I had previously worked with visual arts back in my late teens, but after receiving Dominik Fernow's collage artwork for Issue No.6 I was inspired to get back to creating collage artwork myself. That process has led to a series of collages I am rather happy with which are featured in Issue No.7 of *Noise Receptor Journal* (August 2019) and on the cover of this book.

In the introduction to *Spectrum Compendium,* you clearly explain your initial motivations in creating *Spectrum Magazine* and the different steps that led you to achieve it. The turning point was when the fanzine *Audio Drudge* stopped, meaning there were too few magazines produced that covered the subgenres of industrial music you wanted to read about. So, was your personal drive to publish *Noise Receptor Journal* a slightly different urge than *Spectrum Magazine*?

Actually, the motivation to start *Noise Receptor Journal* was completely different to *Spectrum Magazine* and happened slowly and organically. During 2012 I went through the process of setting up and launching the *Spectrum Magazine Archive* blog, which previously included download links to PDF versions of *Spectrum Magazine*, but which have now been removed with the release of *Spectrum Compendium.* That process invigorated me enough to consider launching a review blog, and I was also inspired by a close friend, Scott Van Dort, who had started a music review blog of his own. I figured I could do the same and get back to writing about underground music in a forum which would be easily manageable online (in my introduction to *Spectrum Compendium* I also highlight Scott's role in originally inspiring me to create *Spectrum Magazine*). However, the potential of turning the *Noise Receptor* blog into a printed 'journal' was not even a thought at the time, and I was happy enough to write sporadic reviews on material I was inspired by. But around the same time I remember reading an online discussion with Mikko Aspa where he said something along the lines of: *'things which are not important remain unfinished, but what is truly important gets done.'* I remember being quite inspired by its simplicity in describing motivation, and it set in motion a chain of thoughts which led to the later launch of *Noise Receptor Journal*. Around the time of reading the Aspa comment, I think I had been publishing online reviews for around six months, but I began to feel there was something missing as regarded tangibility. Initially I was resistant to the thought of launching another magazine as I knew the amount of work it would entail, and I had no idea how a new print endeavour would be received. So, I came up with the idea of publishing a 'journal' and one which was based around the premise of featuring a single long-form interview, associated artwork and various reviews. In my mind it would allow the print version of *Noise Receptor Journal* to be a short and focused document without the headaches of publishing a longer publication, waiting for multiple interviews, chasing up advertisers etc., as well as attempting to keep postage costs down with a smaller publication. So really the first issue of *Noise Receptor Journal* was very much 'testing the water' and anyone who has followed the publication since will note that it has substantially evolved in terms of the overall length and content of each issue since.

But in getting back to how the first issue of *Noise Receptor Journal* came about, I remember deciding on a Friday evening that I would ask Thomas Ekelund of Trepaneringsritualen for a long-form interview and artwork, and if he said 'yes' I would proceed with publishing Issue No.1. I duly sent Thomas an email on the same night and when I woke up the next morning he had already replied with a positive response. Around the same time I was made redundant from my job, so with the resulting increase in spare time I spent my time relearning InDesign and around four to five weeks later the first issue was released. In hindsight it was a very easy and organic way in which it all came together. Equally the expansion and growth of *Noise Receptor Journal* over the following seven years has felt similarly organic, without any significant hassle or pressure.

When you started *Spectrum Magazine* the internet was in its early stages and the printed medium was still a natural option compared to web-based magazines. Between the time *Spectrum Magazine* was created and as *Noise Receptor Journal* continues to evolve in the present day, what are your impressions on the evolution of the fanzine's ethos as well as the concrete aspects of it: the distribution network, the computer layout progress, and the costs for the producer? The last two issues of *Spectrum Magazine* were limited to 500 copies while you have published an equal amount since the third issue of *Noise Receptor Journal*. Does that mean that the audience for this type of printed underground publication is wider than it was 20 years ago?

I think the fanzine ethos is still there, albeit at a reduced level. To make a personal observation on this, I remember when at a local Melbourne show I had zines for sale and someone commented *'why bother printing when you could just do an online blog?'* I guess that is a common perception regarding the convenience and reach of an online portal, but then a website simply does not achieve that tangible aspect of having a physical magazine for in-depth and repeated reading. With *Noise Receptor Journal*, none of the interviews featured in print have been republished online to date and there is no intention to do so in future. Obviously, this will limit the overall 'reach' of the interviews, but then in the post-industrial underground is this even needed? With this music featured in *Noise Receptor Journal* being of such a sub/micro-genre, those 'in the know' will either know about the publication already or will come across it at some point in time. Also, given the way the post-industrial scene operates thematically, now more than ever, the underground does not need interlopers coming across it and misunderstanding what it is all about (...not to say that there is a singular motivation or meaning to the entire scene — which clearly there is not...*). Noise Receptor Journal* exists in the DIY spirit of *'by fanatics for fanatics'*, so the publication finds its audience accordingly.

It is primarily a passion project and not driven by profit, but it is also nice to realise that *Noise Receptor Journal* exists in a space where it does not lose money: when some small profit is made I can reinvest it into buying rare items I would not otherwise be able to spend 'real' money on (which closes the loop of why it exists in the first place).

But of the overall audience, I think that it has diminished rather than grown since the days of *Spectrum Magazine* — but this comment is made from a position of isolation away from the main hubs of activity in Europe and America. I have come to this conclusion mainly from the fact that the number of copies of releases being pressed by most labels (including 'cult' labels) has reduced significantly over the past decade. Take just one example: Genocide Organ's *The Truth Will Make You Free* LP was issued in 1999 in an edition of 1,760 copies, which was around the time the post-industrial scene had reached an apex of sorts with global interest and activity. But fast forward to today, Genocide Organ's main albums are issued in editions of around 500 copies. While some might argue this is purposefully limiting copies to manipulate demand, there can be no argument that most other labels have reduced edition sizes significantly, from CD runs which used to number in the thousands, but which have now shrunk to a few hundred. This also cannot be merely explained by people streaming or downloading music, as post-industrial music has always had the fetishistic collector mind-set heavily embedded within it, and I can't imagine the majority of fans have moved over to digital downloads only.

When I attended post-industrial shows in Europe in 2015, 2016 and 2017, after an absence of 10 years, I was struck by the noticeable lack of a younger audience; with me being already around 40 it was rather odd that I felt like one of the younger ones there. If my impressions are representative of what is happening across the board, it means large parts of the post-industrial underground are not attracting a new and younger audience, which can only spell further declines in interest as older people gradually move away from the scene. I do acknowledge that there are newer labels and projects from younger generations which appear to be creating and building their own networks and scenes. But it remains to be seen if they have the stamina and longevity to continue operating over the coming decades and not just in the short term.

So, to come back to the question at hand, perhaps I feel that 500 copies of the last issues of *Spectrum Magazine* was too few for the level of activity at the time, but now given the quite narrow focus of *Noise Receptor Journal* I feel that 500–600 copies is about right.

Usually around 80% of the print run is sold or distro-ed in the first months, and the remaining copies gradually sell down over the following years. Likewise, there is always the potential to have sold-out issues reissued in a collated book at some point if demand warrants it.

With distribution networks, on a whole they are mostly the same today as they were when *Spectrum Magazine* was operating. Most of the major players are still active and interested in stocking a print publication focused on what they release, while many of the smaller labels that have folded have been replaced with new labels to carry the torch forward.

As a final comment on the print run of *Noise Receptor Journal*, all issues have now been issued in 450–600 copies each. With various reprints, Issue No.1 has been issued in 500 copies, No.2 in 450 copies, Issue Nos 3, 4 and 5 in 500, and No.6, No.7 and No.8 in 600 copies.

After the publication of the fifth and last issue of *Spectrum Magazine* in 2001, you said that the amount of time you were dedicating to it was almost out of control and that you wanted to reduce your workload; but this never happened and *Spectrum Magazine* ceased to exist. In the book, you explain that different factors led you to lose the drive to keep *Spectrum Magazine* up but also that the termination of the fanzine was related to your move to London. This seems surprising as, located in Europe, contact with the artists as well as the actual diffusion of the fanzine would certainly have been easier than when based in Australia? Did you ever suffer from some form of regret about how this adventure ended? And, during the years after, did you not feel like restarting another physical publication before *Noise Receptor Journal*?

There is actually a bit more to the story than was included in my introduction to *Spectrum Compendium,* which perhaps warrants some retelling here. After I moved to London in mid-2001 my original intention was to be away for around a year before returning to Australia. By late 2001 it was clear in my mind that I would be away for much longer than that, but I had various loose ends to tie up in Australia first. Given all of my computer equipment was back in Australia, I figured I could head home in mid-2002, wrap up the various loose ends, finish up *Spectrum Magazine* Issue No.6 (and the associated compilation CD) and release it before heading back overseas. That was the concrete plan set in place in late 2001 and all potential interview and song contributors were advised of the deadline that I would need their completed work submitted by. But, when I got back to Australia six months later, less than half of the required submissions had been provided, so I was really left with no option but to cancel the issue.

Essentially the reasons for not continuing *Spectrum Magazine* when living in London were mostly economic. A couple of years before moving to London I had spent a few thousand dollars on a decent desktop computer and — due to the massive size of computers at the time — it was simply not feasible to take it with me overseas, and I did not have the financial means to buy another computer in the UK with all the necessary technical specifications and programmes. I had chosen London as a base to travel and see as much of Europe as possible, so all of my spare money was redirected into travel. When living in a place like London, where there is always something going on, it was refreshing for me to simply get out and about and enjoy life, rather than constantly being seated at a desk writing about music.

At the time of folding *Spectrum Magazine*, rather than feeling regret I actually felt annoyed and frustrated that I was putting all this effort into promoting artists and the underground, yet many could not be bothered to meet arranged deadlines when I had provided in excess of eight months for interviews to be completed. But then again *Spectrum Magazine* had a great run in its time, with the five issues released, and clearly my head was focused elsewhere on travel and life when Issue No.6 was due out anyway. So, I guess it was a natural and appropriate decision to quit it.

In the years following quitting *Spectrum Magazine* I don't remember any strong desire to start another print magazine; as I mention, the later launch of *Noise Receptor Journal* happened quite organically. But sometime during the late 2000s I obtained a couple of issues of an underground black metal zine, *Oakenthrone*, and I remember thinking how refined in artwork and design it was, how I could never compete with it on the same level, and that underground zines had certainly evolved. This is not to say that producing a zine is in any way a competition but it was a case of seeing where standards were with similar underground publications. Perhaps I felt that anything I would produce would not be at the same level — or so I thought at the time.

You did *Spectrum Magazine* from 1998 to 2001, then between 2002 and 2011 you continued to review records or write articles for various fanzines and websites, and the *Noise Receptor* blog was launched in 2012. That means, for more than two decades, and even without your own medium, you never stopped reviewing music. Analysing output from the industrial scene seems to be a major personal drive and a regular commitment. Where does that need to document the industrial underground come from? Is it sometimes difficult to maintain enthusiasm for this continuing task? Nowadays, how do you manage your work for *Noise Receptor Journal* on a daily basis?

Well that is not actually the case — but perhaps the review page on the *Noise Receptor* blog denoting '2005–2011 reviews' would lead you to that conclusion: that designation is more related to the year reviewed albums were released, not when those reviews were necessarily written.

Anyway, when I moved back to Australia in 2006 my writing and reviewing had all but stopped. I was still actively listening to underground music, but not as much as in the past and felt I needed some 'distance' from writing about such music. That period of writing inactivity extended for longer than planned, for around six years, before I decided I wanted to become more active and was fully reinvigorated to start writing about underground music again.

But, my need to document the post-industrial scene has always been driven by the perception that there is inadequate coverage to do these forms of music justice. Also, I certainly enjoy the process of writing as it is part of coming to terms with and contextualising my own thoughts on a particular release; the fact that others appreciate the reviews and find them useful is a sort of added bonus. I guess by sheer virtue of the years I have been doing this, I have established a personal routine which has continued for large blocks of time. I have consequently amassed quite a volume of written work which I have mostly self-published in physical form; this makes it seem more substantial than having hundreds of reviews and dozens of interviews scattered across multiple websites and blogs.

But of waning enthusiasm: during the days of *Spectrum Magazine* I had a PO Box listed and consequently got flooded with second rate releases, which I then felt some sort of weird obligation to write about as the effort had been made to send me a copy. There is nothing that will kill your enjoyment of writing about music more quickly than having to slog through releases you don't really like as part of the review process. I promised myself I would not let that happen with *Noise Receptor Journal*, and consequently I don't have a postal address listed nor do I actively encourage promos. This means that what I do choose to review, I like, which makes the review process enjoyable; the majority of reviews featured are of releases I have purchased myself. Also, my current review regime with *Noise Receptor Journal* is to publish one review a week, and one print issue a year, which makes everything less stressful and more manageable in a way that *Spectrum Magazine* was not. In the days of *Spectrum Magazine* and particularly around the time of Issues No.4 and No.5 I was writing something like 150 reviews in a six-month period, which is completely insane. In that sort of situation there is simply no time available to just enjoy listening to music, and when music is playing you are constantly thinking about what to say about it.

Nowadays I make sure the great majority of my listening time is for enjoyment so as to avoid potential review burnout. My job also affords me lots of time where I can use headphones and listen to a large volume of music throughout the working week. This means that when it comes to writing a review, usually I will have already listened to the release multiple times and will be broadly aware of what I want to say, so the reviews usually come together quite quickly. Similarly, interview questions are prepared in spare moments before and after work and then sent off to the artist to work on for a number of months. Once the interviews start coming in, I work on each as they come through and then there is the final push to publication over a six- to eight-week period as adverts are booked and all layouts are finalised. The process for getting a new issue of *Noise Receptor Journal* released is pretty well established now, and the fact that the reviews have progressively come together over the preceding year means there is less of a rush to the deadline. With *Noise Receptor Journal* I feel I have struck the right balance of its demands on my time and I can keep it going without it getting unnecessarily pressured or stressful, which would diminish enjoyment of the whole endeavour.

In some of your *Spectrum Magazine* editorials you clearly referred to potential protestors, which suggests that you expected to get some negative reactions to the coverage of certain bands or the use of certain visuals. As the offensive and controversial acts in *Noise Receptor Journal* are much more consistently included than in *Spectrum Magazine,* what are your thoughts on that aspect? These days, does the printed underground fanzine have more freedom of speech in comparison to a website when it comes to covering potentially misleading or anti-social material?

Those editorial comments in *Spectrum Magazine* to which you are referring were made from a perception that someone 'might' try and create trouble, as I had noted some early trolling and shit-stirring occurring on select music-related subscriber emails lists. But in actuality that ever eventuated — either with *Spectrum Magazine* or now with *Noise Receptor Journal*. Clearly there is a decided lack of any sort of underlying agenda on my part (other than promoting post-industrial music and exploring artists' motivations through interviews), and I guess that comes out strongly enough in my writing, so consequently there is nothing to grasp onto or interpret as being 'problematic'.

I do agree that I have covered more artists in *Noise Receptor Journal* who at face value could be deemed 'controversial', but equally they are also projects/artists who have a lot more to say in terms of explaining their chosen themes and artistic motivations. These are the projects/artists I gravitate towards as they spark interesting questions for further exploration. Granted, there are plenty of acts that deal with base-level hatred, aggression and all manner of perversions, and usually they fall into two camps: the first being those who use such material merely to be offensive and/or because it is an established trope of the underground, or the second, those who are genuinely interested in and obsessed with such material. But in both instances, because the motivation appears direct and to the point, this places some limitations on an interview being able to explore intent. While I am not at all discounting the role of such supposed 'controversial' or 'offensive' material and the valid role it can have musically and thematically within the post-industrial underground, it also does not make for very interesting interview fodder, as there is less nuance and ambiguity to explore. For those particular types of artists and releases, they retain their power to shock, offend, confuse or engage (whatever the artist's intent may be) by employing a methodology of NOT explaining motivation and meaning.

From my perspective the concept of freedom of speech should be an unquestionable premise; censoring concepts, ideas or even thoughts is a thoroughly pointless exercise, as it will always be a question of what is deemed to be 'offensive' and by whom, and that will change significantly from group to group, and person to person. I agree that *Noise Receptor Journal*'s content is somewhat hidden as the interviews are only published in print. But for all the alleged antisocial tendencies of the projects and artists covered, you would be very hard pressed to find anything controversial in the responses provided. Likewise, for anyone intent on judging or categorizing a project/artist on a narrow face value interpretation, they would probably be sorely disappointed given that the responses illustrate far more thought and nuance at play.

You have stated that your concern for some industrial subgenres like neo-folk has faded away in the past decade while your interest in more extreme music has grown, especially power electronics. How has this progression developed over the years? More generally, how has your musical taste evolved since you began discovering experimental music? Even though power electronics was initially connected to industrial music, it must be agreed that over the last 30 years, it has become more related to noise music. What is your own perception of the connections and differences between noise and power electronics?

My waning interest in neo-folk was pretty much inevitable due to the fact that the whole scene and sound became so watered down to become a parody of itself. The legacy of Death In June looms large in this, where few people can equal or better the template set by Douglas P many years ago. On that front, when I caught up with Douglas earlier in the year I was intrigued to hear him say he wanted to side-step his own 'neo-folk' shadow — hence why *ESSENCE!* is quite divergent from what might have been expected by many fans. To my ear the only project who have managed to carry the 'neo-folk' genre forwards is Of The Wand And The Moon, whose *The Lone Descent* album is an absolute modern classic. Perhaps I am missing something, but of all the newer names mentioned, I have not found anything of interest. If a truly ground-breaking neo-folk act exists, I will hear about them at some point or another. I am not hating on neo-folk, though, it's just that I have not heard anything in the last decade or so which is doing something more convincingly, differently or more evolved than others have already done.

In terms of the broader evolution of my interest in underground post-industrial music, dark ambient was my first love and I expanded from there into death industrial, heavy electronics, power electronics and included side-steps into neo-folk and martial industrial and the like. But even with wildly different sounds, these scenes are often tied together by similar themes and visual aesthetics, so I don't see them as being totally separate at all. That said, my listening preferences have evolved towards harsher and noisier material over the last 10 years or more. Since launching *Noise Receptor Journal* I have also chosen to be quite a bit narrower in focus, but it still revolves mostly around the death industrial, power electronics and heavy electronics axis, with the only neo-folk feature being the interview with Death In June in Issue No.6 and the review of *ESSENCE!* in the same issue. Given that my listening preferences have been honed towards harder and heavier material, thematic content should also not be discounted as a critical component. Essentially a strong idea or theme functions to stimulate the mind where, apart from the musical side of things, there is a potential meaning and message to interpret and understand. This is also why there is less of a focus on reviewing dark ambient material, as there is usually not a complex theme at play, and there are clear limits on using catch-all descriptors like 'atmospheric' or 'cavernous' (but both of which I still use more than I would like).

With power electronics' relationship to noise, to my mind there actually appears to be a couple of camps at play. There are those with a clear lineage to European-based industrial, and on this front the recognised German power electronics/heavy electronics sound stands centre stage. The Finnish scene perhaps has a sound more heavily rooted in or influenced by the noise tradition, but even then the majority are still decidedly very 'European' in sound and approach. It would then seem that the noise-oriented power electronics is more prevalent in North America; early Prurient could be categorised as a major proponent of that sound. While I have listened to my fair share of noise music over the years, equally it is not a sound which has captured my obsessive listening and collecting tendencies. This means that consequently I am not fully across the noise scene and its ongoing development; however, what is often billed as straight power electronics to my ear sometimes seems to be more straight noise/HNW with vocals.

To speak specifically regarding noise, to my mind it is a valid form of sonic expression and primarily an outlet for aggression, so by its very nature it attracts the reckless abandon of youth. But for the very same reason it seems to be a genre or style which churns through projects at a rapid pace: as quickly as a young project emerges and issues a slew of releases, they just as quickly disappear when their interest and perhaps rebellious and youthful aggression wanes. In the past I have referred to this as the 'Wolf Eyes effect', which is a comment on how massive the noise scene was during the heyday of Wolf Eyes in the mid-2000s. But where are the majority of those projects and fans now? On the whole interest has dissipated, leaving the long-standing noise stalwarts to continue, who were already active well before that hyped-up era. But from a personal perspective, I have always been attracted to a degree of sophistication and artistry in power electronics, no matter how aggressive, atonal or chaotic the end result is. The likes of Grunt, Genocide Organ and Am Not are masters of their craft, and while using noise as a critical sonic element, it is used as a compositional element in their widely differing approaches. For my own personal preferences, harsh noise with vocals which is billed as power electronics just does not really do it for me.

In the eighties, industrial and metal music were completely separate and the audience not connected at all. You have said that you have an extreme metal musical background and that it was this musical environment, in the mid-nineties, that led you to discover dark ambient, which then opened the doors to the whole of the industrial underground. What are your recollections from these days and are you still a listener of extreme metal? Today, it is not unusual that black metal and power electronics be handled by the same distributors because these two subcultures have some common audiences. With regard to their concerns for extreme sound and intent, what is your view of the similarities and contradictions between black metal and power electronics?

Although I came from a metal background, I never felt like a true 'metalhead'. My early interest in pretty standard metal music was more about teenage testosterone, but later my attraction evolved to embrace the misanthropic, nihilistic and philosophical aspects of black metal, which provided a springboard into the same sort of thematic elements in post-industrial music. Being a teenager in the mid-90s when I was deep into black metal it was a bit of a case of situational isolation in Australia. None of my immediate friends were into underground metal (nor wanted to hear a bar of it for that matter), it was a case of me just letter-writing and connecting with the global network of bands and labels. That process resulted in me meeting Scott Van Dort who resided in the same city, and through our shared musical interests and mutual desire for something more we sort of gradually evolved out of the metal underground. Around the same time the main distributor of obscure underground metal (Modern Invasion Music) started distributing Cold Meat Industry material, which was a major gateway into the post-industrial underground, as was getting in touch with Darrin Verhagen of Shinjuku Thief/Dorobo Records who also resided in the same city as I did. But my interest in black metal, as well as post-industrial music later, was very much a fascination from afar: you would read about all the goings-on in Northern Europe in fanzines which made it all seem quite exotic given I was effectively living at the bottom of the planet. I guess this self-imposed isolation remains a factor today, as very few people I am in regular contact with locally have any real understanding of the music I listen to and write about. This is completely fine as it has always been a personal obsession where I have never felt the need for any form of validation from immediate peers to continue this interest. Obviously, I then connected with the global network through social media and get to infrequently catch up with those contacts in person when I manage to get to an international festival.

I do in fact still listen to black metal on occasion, but I mostly find that I revert to the second era classics rather than releases in the decades since. I did go through a period in the early 2010s of picking up tons of newer black metal releases, but the majority of those purchases have since been sold off again as I found that they did not have the longevity to capture my interest beyond those initial listens. I have also had the opportunity to see a number of second wave black metal bands tour Australia in recent years and while initially I was excited to see them live, in the end it was mostly a let-down as they did not live up to expectations. Perhaps I should have known better.

I am then very picky about what newer black metal bands I listen to, and it is usually those bands who understand that the impact of an underground black metal band can be infinitesimally increased by remaining obscure and purposefully not providing information about the group, and who avoid divulging mundane information about members in their ordinary lives. The second wave of black metal was ultimately so powerful as an art-form due to information being limited and filtering out gradually through 'zines, with this process functioning to amplify the overall aura and musical/thematic impact. Today much of the mystery and aura of black metal is completely destroyed through the internet, social media and even in some scenarios choosing to play live. This is perhaps a pointlessly purist point of view, but even so it seems to factor heavily into whether I find a newer black metal band to be of interest — or not. The likes of Bekëth Nexëhmü, Reverorum ib Malacht and Deathspell Omega seem to completely understand and appreciate that purposeful obscurity adds to the overall aesthetic and appreciation of what they are doing musically and thematically. But more generally, in a way black metal has become the equivalent of punk music, where standard 'genre' albums are issued in their hundreds each year, but these mostly do nothing except further dilute the original essence of the genre, given the majority seem to be happy with aping what has come before. But, then again, the same accusations get levelled at the various post-industrial genres all the time, so what the fuck do I know? Each to their own I guess.

I do agree that many metal listeners have crossed over into post-industrial spheres, and I don't see any contradiction in this, particularly in the current era. Apart from the internet having a central role in breaking down barriers between scenes and genres, I also think that black metal introduced a degree of seriousness and a conceptual and philosophical framework that was mostly missing from underground metal previously. With those sorts of thematic preoccupations also at play within the post-industrial underground it is only natural that it will generate crossover interest. This is exactly the pathway and process by which I became introduced to the post-industrial underground. I would say that the actual number of metal listeners crossing over to post-industrial music remains extremely small, given that the post-industrial underground is still an extremely niche scene compared to underground metal.

However, one amusing contradiction is that the majority of metal fans simply do not understand post-industrial music at all. Anyone who actively listens to extreme metal has trained their ear to appreciate that style of music, but then they seem unable to do so with power electronics and related music. It seems a very closed-minded way to approach similarly underground music genres, given both are resoundingly shunned and ignored by the mainstream.

The tape format was a very familiar medium when we began discovering underground music in the old days but it progressively disappeared throughout the nineties. Consequently, there were very few tape reviews in *Spectrum Magazine*, but because this medium has risen from the ashes there is now a substantial amount of such reviews in *Noise Receptor Journal*. What are your thoughts on the tape resurrection and what do you think it has brought to industrial underground culture?

Tapes have always held a key place in the underground and are a perfect format for the feel and presentation of the more obscure offshoots of post-industrial music. Thus, where vinyl is not a feasible option, cassettes cannot be beaten for that certain underground effect, but equally tapes can also be chosen as the only physical edition of a release — as in the heyday of the format in the 1980s and early 1990s. Thankfully tapes have never completely disappeared from the post-industrial underground, and while less were produced through the early 2000s they have found favour again in more recent years.

However, I must admit that given my background in collecting lofi demos and obtaining badly dubbed tapes through tape trading, for quite a number of years I considered cassettes to be a second-tier format for actual music appreciation, but I had to completely re-evaluate that view a few years ago when I finally joined the 'cult' of the Nakamichi tape deck after buying a second-hand CR-3 model from 1989 in excellent working order. Even though it is far from the top model in the Nackamichi range, it has an amazing sound which I was completely stunned by upon first listen. Having a Nakamichi tape deck has without doubt made me completely re-evaluate the cassette as a sonic format and has consequently reinvigorated my love of collecting tapes.

As a format, cassettes are also a far better choice to replace the curse of shitty home burnt CD-r which was a 'thing' for far too long through the late 1990s and 2000s. But with all that said, the tape seems to be a bit too hyped at the moment, particularly when a tape can cost as much as the CD or even LP in some instances. But whatever, if people love tapes now, fine. I am sure the current interest will drop off, but it will remain as a valid format option for post-industrial music with nods to both tradition and nostalgia in equal measure.

The 'Spectrum' name was chosen in order to indicate that the fanzine would cover a wide spectrum of sounds ranging across the various post-industrial subgenres. The 'Noise Receptor' name seems to restrain this idea in warning the future reader of more extreme material that has been covered, which is actually the case. How did you come to choose the name 'Noise Receptor' for your latest publication, and why a 'Journal'? Besides, how do you see the evolution of *Noise Receptor Journal* in the future?

Yes, you are correct about the reasons for choosing the name 'Spectrum', as at the time I wanted something clean, simple and non-descript, rather than perhaps something a bit more typical of underground post-industrial culture. However, in choosing the name 'Noise Receptor', I have always enjoyed playing with words and having double or triple meanings, even if it is mostly subtle and mainly for my own amusement. I first came across the term 'noise receptor' in a technical report relating to noise and vibration from industrial-scale mining activity. In that context a 'noise receptor' is an abstracted and depersonalised term for a human who can hear mining-related noise. In choosing this term as a title, it means I am the 'noise receptor' and, according to the magazine tagline, I am listening to 'sound with impact' and 'analysing (the) abstract' types of music. The second meaning is a play on words as most 'normal' people who are not aware of post-industrial music generally consider it to be 'noise', while the third meaning is an inside joke on the fact that I personally do not actively listen to or write about pure 'noise'-related music. This multi-layered meaning of the name works perfectly with the abstracted and ambiguous way that much of the post-industrial music chooses to operate.

As for the 'journal' bit, it implies more of an academic or in-depth publication, which is essentially what I am seeking to do in exploring the themes and motivations of artists in detail. This differs from a 'magazine' which is often more concerned with basic articles and standard media promotion of new releases. Perhaps this is being overly pedantic, but by embedding these concepts in the publication title, along with the other 'rules' established around design, it means the end product can be very sharply honed, which to my mind is far better than a publication not being sure of its focus and aim.

With regard to the potential evolution of *Noise Receptor Journal*, I see that from here it is really just micro-level adjustments to design and layout within the parameters of the established format. I guess it is then more of a case of seeing how long the passion remains to keep releasing new issues, which is mostly driven by there being a range of artists and projects I am interested enough in interviewing. Time will tell I guess, but I only really take things as they come from issue to issue. As usual, as soon as a new issue is completed and released, my mind automatically turns to the next one and who may be appropriate to feature next.

On a more personal level, what attracts you to and keeps you engaged with post-industrial/power electronics and related music after all these years?

To use an analogy, normal mainstream music and underground post-industrial music have the same relationship that graphic design has to fine art. In both scenarios one has a commercially-focused purpose to sell something, while the other exists only due to the artistic drive and desire of the creator, regardless of audience or fame. Clearly no-one involved in post-industrial music is doing so to become famous, get rich or obtain the accolades of the masses. Therefore, it has an imbedded artistic integrity far beyond that of a 'professional musician' attempting to write a hit song and sell as many copies as possible. Likewise, the complexity, ambiguity and intentional confusion appeals strongly to me too: learning the sonic complexity of a release is only one part of the attraction, but also the mental engagement and stimulation where the 'theme' or 'idea' being presented can be a sort of puzzle to be interpreted and better understood. It is also a musical form which cuts though typical mainstream platitudes and hypocrisy and explores material which would be commercial suicide in any other form of 'entertainment'. The concept of 'entertainment' plays no substantial role as a driving force, rather it is the mode of the individual's expression, whatever that may be for the artist in question. Above all it is the fact that, as an underground scene taken as a whole, it is purposefully complex, difficult, controversial, vague and ambiguous in its meaning and message, and therefore demands a lot from its audience which makes for a continually changing and highly engaging form of expression.

On a whole, post-industrial music is not concerned with some hackneyed attempt at making the world a better place (whatever that means to the individual), but rather is intent on exploring the world in all its complexity, apathy, deviancy and cruelty with an unflinching gaze. I personally do not see my interest in this sort of music as a perverse or gleeful voyeur's view of the world slowly going up in flames, but equally that interpretation or point of view in not invalid. I have always had a fair degree of morbid curiosity which underpins my psychological frame of mind, including a clear attraction to the darker characteristics and duality of the human condition, which I guess is all tied to an aspect of existential yearning to understand who and what we are. Perhaps even in my younger years my mind-set could have been characterised as aligning more strongly with the Freudian identified 'death-drive' (*Todestrieb*), yet I guess once you have developed a taste for strong subject matter you are then locked into a pattern of actively seeking it out. But this sort of mind-set is hardly new or unique to the human condition, given the history of such preoccupations in art and theatre: the medieval *danse macabre*, *memento mori* and *vanitas* paintings, Artaud's theatre of cruelty, and Viennese Actionism to name just a few.

Clearly not everything within the underground appeals to my artistic sensibility. *Noise Receptor Journal* (and previously *Spectrum Magazine*) is simply a window onto what I personally find most engaging, but equally I am only one person with one perspective on post-industrial/power electronics-related music. If anyone feels my coverage is too narrow (or too wide for that matter), I would implore people to start their own publications to cover exactly what they want to read about and document their own opinions. I for one would certainly want to hear more of such publications.

Regarding the responses toward *Spectrum Magazine* at the time it was operating, you noticed that the feedback came more from record labels than people. Is it the same thing today with *Noise Receptor Journal* or do you receive direct feedback from individuals? On the other hand, do you have a clear overview of the people who bought *Spectrum Magazine* at the time and the ones who purchase *Noise Receptor Journal* now?

You are right that I continue to get good feedback from labels on new issues. This is much the same today as it was in the days of *Spectrum Magazine*, which I guess is part of the process of ongoing communication, sorting out wholesale orders and trades etc. Strangely, I rarely get direct comments or feedback, maybe a handful at most for a new issue. But when I do, it is certainly appreciated that folk seem to get exactly what I am seeking to do with my publications.

I perhaps have never had a clear appreciation of the people who purchase either *Spectrum Magazine* or *Noise Receptor Journal*, but you would have to assume it is the same quite diverse range of people who are attracted to post-industrial music. Sometimes when I release a new issue it feels a bit like it drops like a stone as it seems to disappear with little comment. But what I do is obviously appreciated as issues have always sold well and quite quickly, so clearly there is an established readership. Also, with the rise of social media, even if I have not received direct comments from readers, I have noticed that many people have put up social media posts about receiving a new issue, so clearly they appreciate it enough to warrant a personal status update. Regardless of all that, I will simply continue to do what I do and release new issues as long as the passion remains, and hope readers enjoy both *Noise Receptor Journal* and the *Spectrum Compendium* book.

As a conclusion, if you have any additional matters or final comments to share, please feel free.

No, I think everything has been more than adequately covered. Thank you, Cyril, for your interest in my publications, and it has been interesting to be the interviewee for once after so many years as the interviewer.

Interview conducted by: Cyril Adam.

Thank you: to Jennifer Wallis for proofreading and editorial suggestions.

Photo: credits & details: Photo by Melenie Stevenson. Portrait taken at Ron Mueck's *Mass* sculpture (2017), National Gallery of Victoria, Melbourne, Australia.

A HEADPRESS BOOK
First published by Headpress in 2020
headoffice@headpress.com

NOISE RECEPTOR JOURNAL: VOLUME 1
sound with impact – analysing the abstract

Cover collage and book design : RICHARD STEVENSON

10 9 8 7 6 5 4 3 2 1

A CIP catalogue record for this book is available from the British Library

ISBN 978-1-909394-72-8 (paperback)
NO-ISBN (hardback)

HEADPRESS. POP AND UNPOP CULTURE.